Little Women

Little Women

LOUISA MAY ALCOTT

Illustrated by Louis Jambor

Illustrated Junior Library

GROSSET & DUNLAP, PUBLISHERS

NEW YORK

Preface

GO THEN, MY LITTLE BOOK, AND SHOW TO ALL

THAT ENTERTAIN AND BID THEE WELCOME SHALL,

WHAT THOU DOST KEEP CLOSE SHUT UP IN THY BREAST;

AND WISH WHAT THOU DOST SHOW THEM MAY BE BLEST

TO THEM FOR GOOD, MAY MAKE THEM CHOOSE TO BE

PILGRIMS BETTER, BY FAR, THAN THEE OR ME.

TELL THEM OF MERCY; SHE IS ONE

WHO EARLY HATH HER PILGRIMAGE BEGUN.

YEA, LET YOUNG DAMSELS LEARN OF HER TO PRIZE

THE WORLD WHICH IS TO COME, AND SO BE WISE;

FOR LITTLE TRIPPING MAIDS MAY FOLLOW GOD

ALONG THE WAYS WHICH SAINTLY FEET HAVE TROD.

Adapted from John Bunyan

Contents

PART FIRST

Contents PART SECOND

Little Women

PART FIRST

CHAPTER ONE

Playing Pilgrims

"CHRISTMAS won't be Christmas without any presents," grumbled Jo, lying on the rug.

"It's so dreadful to be poor!" sighed Meg, looking down at her old dress.

"I don't think it's fair for some girls to have plenty of pretty things, and other girls nothing at all," added little Amy, with an injured sniff.

"We've got father and mother and each other," said Beth contentedly, from her corner.

The four young faces on which the firelight shone brightened at the cheerful words, but darkened again as Jo said sadly:

"We haven't got father, and shall not have him for a long

time." She didn't say "perhaps never," but each silently added it, thinking of father far away, where the fighting was.

Nobody spoke for a minute; then Meg said in an altered tone:

"You know the reason mother proposed not having any presents this Christmas was because it is going to be a hard winter for everyone; and she thinks we ought not to spend money for pleasure, when our men are suffering so in the army. We can't do much, but we can make our little sacrifices, and ought to do it gladly. But I am afraid I don't"; and Meg shook her head as she thought regretfully of all the pretty things she wanted.

"But I don't think the little we should spend would do any good. We've each got a dollar, and the army wouldn't be much helped by our giving that. I agree not to expect anything from mother or you, but I do want to buy 'Undine and Sintram' for myself; I've wanted it *so* long," said Jo, who was a bookworm.

"I have planned to spend mine in new music," said Beth, with a little sigh, which no one heard but the hearth brush and kettle holder.

"I shall get a nice box of Faber's drawing pencils; I really need them," said Amy decidedly.

"Mother didn't say anything about our money, and she won't wish us to give up everything. Let's each buy what we want, and have a little fun; I'm sure we work hard enough to earn it," cried Jo, examining the heels of her shoes in a gentlemanly manner.

"I know *I* do—teaching those tiresome children nearly all day, when I'm longing to enjoy myself at home," began Meg, in the complaining tone again.

"You don't have half such a hard time as I do," said Jo. "How would you like to be shut up for hours with a nervous, fussy old lady, who keeps you trotting, is never satisfied, and worries you till you're ready to fly out of the window or cry?"

"It's naughty to fret; but I do think washing dishes and keeping things tidy is the worst work in the world. It makes me cross; and my hands get so stiff, I can't practice well at all"; and Beth looked at her rough hands with a sigh that anyone could hear that time.

"I don't believe any of you suffer as I do," cried Amy; "for

you don't have to go to school with impertinent girls, who
plague you if you don't know your lessons, and laugh at your
dresses, and label your father if he isn't rich, and insult you
when your nose isn't nice."

"If you mean *libel*, I'd say so, and not talk about *labels*, as if
papa was a pickle bottle," advised Jo, laughing.

"I know what I mean, and you needn't be *statirical* about it.
It's proper to use good words, and improve your *vocabilary*,"
returned Amy, with dignity.

"Don't peck at one another, children. Don't you wish we had
the money papa lost when we were little, Jo? Dear me, how
happy and good we'd be, if we had no worries!" said Meg, who
could remember better times.

"You said, the other day, you thought we were a deal happier
than the King children, for they were fighting and fretting all
the time, in spite of their money."

"So I did, Beth. Well, I think we are; for, although we do
have to work, we make fun for ourselves, and are a pretty jolly
set, as Jo would say."

"Jo does use such slang words!" observed Amy, with a re-
proving look at the long figure stretched on the rug. Jo immediately sat up, put her hands in her pockets, and began to
whistle.

"Don't, Jo; it's so boyish!"

"That's why I do it."

"I detest rude, unladylike girls!"

"I hate affected, niminy-piminy chits!"

"'Birds in their little nests agree,'" sang Beth, the peace-
maker, with such a funny face that both sharp voices softened
to a laugh, and the "pecking" ended for that time.

"Really, girls, you are both to be blamed," said Meg, beginning to lecture in her elder-sisterly fashion. "You are old
enough to leave off boyish tricks, and to behave better, Josephine. It didn't matter so much when you were a little girl;
but now you are so tall, and turn up your hair, you should
remember that you are a young lady."

"I'm not! And if turning up my hair makes me one, I'll wear
it in two tails till I'm twenty," cried Jo, pulling off her net, and
shaking down a chestnut mane. "I hate to think I've got to grow

up, and be Miss March, and wear long gowns, and look as prim
as a China aster! It's bad enough to be a girl, anyway, when I
like boys' games and work and manners! I can't get over my
disappointment in not being a boy; and it's worse than ever
now, for I'm dying to go and fight with papa, and I can only
stay at home and knit, like a poky old woman!" And Jo shook
the blue army sock till the needles rattled like castanets, and
her ball bounded across the room.

"Poor Jo! It's too bad, but it can't be helped; so you must try
to be contented with making your name boyish, and playing
brother to us girls," said Beth, stroking the rough head at her
knee with a hand that all the dishwashing and dusting in the
world could not make ungentle in its touch.

"As for you, Amy," continued Meg, "you are altogether too
particular and prim. Your airs are funny now; but you'll grow
up an affected little goose, if you don't take care. I like your
nice manners and refined ways of speaking, when you don't
try to be elegant; but your absurd words are as bad as Jo's
slang."

"If Jo is a tomboy and Amy a goose, what am I, please?"
asked Beth, ready to share the lecture.

"You're a dear, and nothing else," answered Meg warmly;
and no one contradicted her, for the "Mouse" was the pet of
the family.

As young readers like to know "how people look," we will
take this moment to give them a little sketch of the four sisters,
who sat knitting away in the twilight, while the December
snow fell quietly without, and the fire crackled cheerfully
within. It was a comfortable old room, though the carpet was
faded and the furniture very plain; for a good picture or two
hung on the walls, books filled the recesses, chrysanthemums
and Christmas roses bloomed in the windows, and a pleasant
atmosphere of home peace pervaded it.

Margaret, the eldest of the four, was sixteen, and very
pretty, being plump and fair, with large eyes, plenty of soft,
brown hair, a sweet mouth, and white hands, of which she was
rather vain. Fifteen-year-old Jo was very tall, thin, and brown,
and reminded one of a colt; for she never seemed to know what
to do with her long limbs, which were very much in her way.

She had a decided mouth, a comical nose, and sharp, gray eyes, which appeared to see everything, and were by turns fierce, funny, or thoughtful. Her long, thick hair was her one beauty; but it was usually bundled into a net, to be out of her way. Round shoulders had Jo, big hands and feet, a flyaway look to her clothes, and the uncomfortable appearance of a girl who was rapidly shooting up into a woman, and didn't like it. Elizabeth—or Beth, as everyone called her—was a rosy, smooth-haired, bright-eyed girl of thirteen, with a shy manner, a timid voice, and a peaceful expression, which was seldom disturbed. Her father called her "Little Tranquillity," and the name suited her excellently; for she seemed to live in a happy world of her own, only venturing out to meet the few whom she trusted and loved. Amy, though the youngest, was a most important person —in her own opinion at least. A regular snow-maiden, with blue eyes, and yellow hair curling on her shoulders, pale and slender, and always carrying herself like a young lady mindful of her manners. What the characters of the four sisters were we will leave to be found out.

The clock struck six; and, having swept up the hearth, Beth put a pair of slippers down to warm. Somehow the sight of the old shoes had a good effect upon the girls; for mother was coming, and everyone brightened to welcome her. Meg stopped lecturing, and lighted the lamp, Amy got out of the easy chair without being asked, and Jo forgot how tired she was as she sat up to hold the slippers nearer to the blaze.

"They are quite worn out; Marmee must have a new pair."

"I thought I'd get her some with my dollar," said Beth.

"No, I shall!" cried Amy.

"I'm the oldest," began Meg, but Jo cut in with a decided—

"I'm the man of the family now papa is away, and *I* shall provide the slippers, for he told me to take special care of mother while he was gone."

"I'll tell you what we'll do," said Beth; "let's each get her something for Christmas, and not get anything for ourselves."

"That's like you, dear! What will we get?" exclaimed Jo.

Everyone thought soberly for a minute; then Meg announced, as if the idea was suggested by the sight of her own pretty hands, "I shall give her a nice pair of gloves."

"Army shoes, best to be had," cried Jo.

"Some handkerchiefs, all hemmed," said Beth.

"I'll get a little bottle of cologne; she likes it, and it won't cost much, so I'll have some left to buy my pencils," added Amy.

"How will we give the things?" asked Meg.

"Put them on the table, and bring her in and see her open the bundles. Don't you remember how we used to do on our birthdays?" answered Jo.

"I used to be *so* frightened when it was my turn to sit in the big chair with the crown on, and see you all come marching round to give the presents, with a kiss. I liked the things and the kisses, but it was dreaful to have you sit looking at me while I opened the bundles," said Beth, who was toasting her face and the bread for tea, at the same time.

"Let Marmee think we are getting things for ourselves, and then surprise her. We must go shopping tomorrow afternoon, Meg; there is so much to do about the play for Christmas night," said Jo, marching up and down, with her hands behind her back and her nose in the air.

"I don't mean to act any more after this time; I'm getting too old for such things," observed Meg, who was as much a child as ever about "dressing-up" frolics.

"You won't stop, I know, as long as you can trail round in a white gown with your hair down, and wear gold-paper jewelry. You are the best actress we've got, and there'll be an end of everything if you quit the boards," said Jo. "We ought to rehearse tonight. Come here, Amy, and do the fainting scene, for you are as stiff as a poker in that."

"I can't help it; I never saw anyone faint, and I don't choose to make myself all black and blue, tumbling flat as you do. If I can go down easily, I'll drop; if I can't, I shall fall into a chair and be graceful; I don't care if Hugo does come at me with a pistol," returned Amy, who was not gifted with dramatic power, but was chosen because she was small enough to be borne out shrieking by the villain of the piece.

"Do it this way; clasp your hands so, and stagger across the room, crying frantically, 'Roderigo! save me! save me!'" and away went Jo with a melodramatic scream which was truly thrilling.

Amy followed, but she poked her hands out stiffly before her, and jerked herself along as if she went by machinery; and her "Ow!" was more suggestive of pins being run into her than of fear and anguish. Jo gave a despairing groan, and Meg laughed outright, while Beth let her bread burn as she watched the fun, with interest.

"It's no use! Do the best you can when the time comes, and if the audience laugh, don't blame me. Come on, Meg."

Then things went smoothly, for Don Pedro defied the world in a speech of two pages without a single break; Hagar, the witch, chanted an awful incantation over her kettleful of sim- mering toads, with weird effect; Roderigo rent his chains asun- der manfully, and Hugo died in agonies of remorse and arsenic, with a wild "Ha! ha!"

"It's the best we've had yet," said Meg, as the dead villain sat up and rubbed his elbows.

"I don't see how you can write and act such splendid things, Jo. You're a regular Shakespeare!" exclaimed Beth, who firmly believed that her sisters were gifted with wonderful genius in all things.

"Not quite," replied Jo modestly. "I do think 'The Witch's Curse, an Operatic Tragedy,' is rather a nice thing; but I'd like to try Macbeth, if we only had a trap door for Banquo. I al- ways wanted to do the killing part. 'Is that a dagger that I see before me?'" muttered Jo, rolling her eyes and clutching at the air, as she had seen a famous tragedian do.

"No, it's the toasting fork, with mother's shoe on it instead of the bread. Beth's stage-struck!" cried Meg, and the rehearsal ended in a general burst of laughter.

"Glad to find you so merry, my girls," said a cheery voice at the door, and actors and audience turned to welcome a tall, motherly lady, with a "can-I-help-you" look about her which was truly delightful. She was not elegantly dressed, but a noble-looking woman, and the girls thought the gray cloak and unfashionable bonnet covered the most splendid mother in the world.

"Well, dearies, how have you got on today? There was so much to do, getting the boxes ready to go tomorrow that I didn't come home to dinner. Has anyone called, Beth? How is your cold, Meg? Jo, you look tired to death. Come and kiss me, baby."

While making these maternal inquiries Mrs. March got her wet things off, her warm slippers on, and sitting down in the easy chair, drew Amy to her lap, preparing to enjoy the happiest hour of her busy day. The girls flew about, trying to make things comfortable, each in her own way. Meg arranged the tea table; Jo brought wood and set chairs, dropping, overturning, and clattering everything she touched; Beth trotted to and fro between parlor and kitchen, quiet and busy; while Amy gave directions to everyone, as she sat with her hands folded.

As they gathered about the table, Mrs. March said, with a particularly happy face, "I've got a treat for you after supper."

A quick, bright smile went round like a streak of sunshine. Beth clapped her hands, regardless of the biscuit she held, and Jo tossed up her napkin, crying, "A letter! a letter! Three cheers for father!"

"Yes, a nice long letter. He is well, and thinks he shall get through the cold season better than we feared. He sends all sorts of loving wishes for Christmas, and an especial message to you girls," said Mrs. March, patting her pocket as if she had got a treasure there.

"Hurry and get done! Don't stop to quirk your little finger,

and simper over your plate, Amy," cried Jo, choking in her tea, and dropping her bread, butter side down, on the carpet, in her haste to get at the treat.

Beth ate no more, but crept away, to sit in her shadowy corner and brood over the delight to come, till the others were ready.

"I think it was so splendid in father to go as a chaplain when he was too old to be drafted, and not strong enough for a soldier," said Meg warmly.

"Don't I wish I could go as a drummer, a *vivan*—what's its name?—or a nurse, so I could be near him and help him," exclaimed Jo, with a groan.

"It must be very disagreeable to sleep in a tent, and eat all sorts of bad-tasting things, and drink out of a tin mug," sighed Amy.

"When will he come home, Marmee?" asked Beth, with a little quiver in her voice.

"Not for many months, dear, unless he is sick. He will stay and do his work faithfully as long as he can, and we won't ask for him back a minute sooner than he can be spared. Now come and hear the letter."

They all drew to the fire, mother in the big chair with Beth at her feet, Meg and Amy perched on either arm of the chair, and Jo leaning on the back, where no one would see any sign of emotion if the letter should happen to be touching. Very few letters were written in those hard times that were not touching, especially those which fathers sent home. In this one little was said of the hardships endured, the dangers faced, or the homesickness conquered; it was a cheerful, hopeful letter, full of lively descriptions of camp life, marches, and military news; and only at the end did the writer's heart overflow with fatherly love and longing for the little girls at home.

"Give them all my dear love and a kiss. Tell them I think of them by day, pray for them by night, and find my best comfort in their affection at all times. A year seems very long to wait before I see them, but remind them that while we wait we may all work, so that these hard days need not be wasted. I know they will remember all I said to them, that they will be loving children to you, will do their duty faithfully, fight their bosom enemies bravely, and conquer themselves so beautifully that when I come back to them I may be fonder and prouder than ever of my little women."

Everybody sniffed when they came to that part; Jo wasn't ashamed of the great tear that dropped off the end of her nose, and Amy never minded the rumpling of her curls as she hid her face on her mother's shoulder and sobbed out. "I *am* a selfish girl! but I'll truly try to be better, so he mayn't be disappointed in me by and by."

"We all will!" cried Meg. "I think too much of my looks, and hate to work, but won't any more, if I can help it."

"I'll try and be what he loves to call me, a 'little woman,' and not be rough and wild; but do my duty here instead of wanting to be somewhere else," said Jo, thinking that keeping her temper at home was a much harder task than facing a rebel or two down South.

Beth said nothing, but wiped away her tears with the blue army sock, and began to knit with all her might, losing no time in doing the duty that lay nearest her, while she resolved in her quiet little soul to be all that father hoped to find her when the year brought round the happy coming home.

Mrs. March broke the silence that followed Jo's words, by saying in her cheery voice, "Do you remember how you used to play Pilgrim's Progress when you were little things? Nothing delighted you more than to have me tie my piece bags on your backs for burdens, give you hats and sticks and rolls of paper, and let you travel through the house from the cellar, which was the City of Destruction, up, up, to the housetop, where you had all the lovely things you could collect to make a Celestial City."

"What fun it was, especially going by the lions, fighting Apollyon, and passing through the Valley where the hobgoblins were!" said Jo.

"I liked the place where the bundles fell off and tumbled downstairs," said Meg.

"My favorite part was when we came out on the flat roof where our flowers and arbors and pretty things were, and all stood and sung for joy up there in the sunshine," said Beth, smiling, as if that pleasant moment had come back to her.

"I don't remember much about it, except that I was afraid of the cellar and the dark entry, and always liked the cake and milk we had up at the top. If I wasn't too old for such things, I'd rather like to play it over again," said Amy, who began to talk of renouncing childish things at the mature age of twelve.

"We never are too old for this, my dear, because it is a play we are playing all the time in one way or another. Our burdens are here, our road is before us, and the longing for goodness and happiness is the guide that leads us through many troubles and mistakes to the peace which is a true Celestial City. Now, my little pilgrims, suppose you begin again, not in play, but in earnest, and see how far on you can get before father comes home."

"Really, mother? Where are our bundles?" asked Amy, who was a very literal young lady.

"Each of you told what your burden was just now, except Beth; I rather think she hasn't got any," said her mother.

"Yes, I have; mine is dishes and dusters, and envying girls with nice pianos, and being afraid of people."

Beth's bundle was such a funny one that everybody wanted to laugh; but nobody did, for it would have hurt her feelings very much.

"Let us do it," said Meg thoughtfully. "It is only another name for trying to be good, and the story may help us; for though we do want to be good, it's hard work, and we forget, and don't do our best."

"We were in the Slough of Despond tonight, and mother came and pulled us out as Help did in the book. We ought to have our roll of directions, like Christian. What shall we do about that?" asked Jo, delighted with the fancy which lent a little romance to the very dull task of doing her duty.

"Look under your pillows, Christmas morning, and you will find your guidebook," replied Mrs. March.

They talked over the new plan while old Hannah cleared the table; then out came the four little workbaskets, and the needles flew as the girls made sheets for Aunt March. It was uninteresting sewing, but tonight no one grumbled. They adopted Jo's plan of dividing the long seams into four parts, and calling the quarters Europe, Asia, Africa, and America, and in that way got on capitally, especially when they talked about the different countries as they stitched their way through them.

At nine they stopped work, and sung, as usual, before they went to bed. No one but Beth could get much music out of the old piano; but she had a way of softly touching the yellow keys, and making a pleasant accompaniment to the simple songs they sung. Meg had a voice like a flute, and she and her mother led the little choir. Amy chirped like a cricket, and Jo wandered through the airs at her own sweet will, always coming out at the wrong place with a croak or a quaver that spoilt the most pensive tune. They had always done this from the time they could lisp

"Crinkle, crinkle, 'ittle 'tar,"

and it had become a household custom, for the mother was a born singer. The first sound in the morning was her voice, as she went about the house singing like a lark; and the last sound at night was the same cheery sound, for the girls never grew too old for that familiar lullaby.

CHAPTER TWO

A Merry Christmas

JO was the first to wake in the gray dawn of Christmas morning. No stockings hung at the fireplace, and for a moment she felt as much disappointed as she did long ago, when her little sock fell down because it was so crammed with goodies. Then she remembered her mother's promise, and slipping her hand under her pillow, drew out a little crimson-covered book. She knew it very well, for it was that beautiful old story of the best life ever lived, and Jo felt that it was a true guide-book for any pilgrim going the long journey. She woke Meg with a "Merry Christmas," and bade her see what was under her pillow. A green-covered book appeared, with the same picture inside, and a few words written by their mother, which made their one present very precious in their eyes. Presently

The girls never grew too old for that lullaby

[SEE PAGE 15]

Beth and Amy woke, to rummage and find their little books also—one dove-colored, the other blue; and all sat looking at and talking about them, while the east grew rosy with the coming day.

In spite of her small vanities, Margaret had a sweet and pious nature, which unconsciously influenced her sisters, especially Jo, who loved her very tenderly, and obeyed her because her advice was so gently given.

"Girls," said Meg seriously, looking from the tumbled head beside her to the two little nightcapped ones in the room beyond, "mother wants us to read and love and mind these books, and we must begin at once. We used to be faithful about it; but since father went away, and all this war trouble unsettled us, we have neglected many things. You can do as you please; but I shall keep my book on the table here, and read a little every morning as soon as I wake, for I know it will do me good, and help me through the day."

Then she opened her new book and began to read. Jo put her arm around her, and, leaning cheek to cheek, read also, with the quiet expression so seldom seen on her restless face.

"How good Meg is! Come, Amy, let's do as they do. I'll help you with the hard words, and they'll explain things if we don't understand," whispered Beth, very much impressed by the pretty books and her sisters' example.

"I'm glad mine is blue," said Amy; and then the rooms were very still while the pages were softly turned, and the winter sunshine crept in to touch the bright heads and serious faces with a Christmas greeting.

"Where is mother?" asked Meg, as she and Jo ran down to thank her for their gifts, half an hour later.

"Goodness only knows. Some poor creeter come a-beggin', and your ma went straight off to see what was needed. There never *was* such a woman for givin' away vittles and drink, clothes and firin'," replied Hannah, who had lived with the family since Meg was born, and was considered by them all more as a friend than a servant.

"She will be back soon, I think; so fry your cakes, and have everything ready," said Meg, looking over the presents which were collected in a basket and kept under the sofa, ready to be produced at the proper time. "Why, where is Amy's bottle of cologne?" she added, as the little flask did not appear.

"She took it out a minute ago, and went off with it to put a ribbon on it, or some such notion," replied Jo, dancing about the room to take the first stiffness off the new army slippers.

"How nice my handkerchiefs look, don't they? Hannah washed and ironed them for me, and I marked them all myself," said Beth, looking proudly at the somewhat uneven letters which had cost her such labor.

"Bless the child! She's gone and put 'Mother' on them instead of 'M. March.' How funny!" cried Jo, taking up one.

"Isn't it right? I thought it was better to do it so, because Meg's initials are 'M. M.,' and I don't want anyone to use these but Marmee," said Beth, looking troubled.

"It's all right, dear, and a very pretty idea—quite sensible, too, for no one can ever mistake now. It will please her very much, I know," said Meg, with a frown for Jo and a smile for Beth.

"There's mother. Hide the basket, quick!" cried Jo, as a door slammed, and steps sounded in the hall.

Amy came in hastily, and looked rather abashed when she saw her sisters all waiting for her.

"Where have you been, and what are you hiding behind you?" asked Meg, surprised to see, by her hood and cloak, that lazy Amy had been out so early.

"Don't laugh at me, Jo! I didn't mean anyone should know till the time came. I only meant to change the little bottle for a big one, and I gave *all* my money to get it, and I'm truly trying not to be selfish any more."

As she spoke, Amy showed the handsome flask which replaced the cheap one; and looked so earnest and humble in her little effort to forget herself that Meg hugged her on the spot, and Jo pronounced her "a trump," while Beth ran to the window, and picked her finest rose to ornament the stately bottle.

"You see I felt ashamed of my present, after reading and talking about being good this morning, so I ran round the corner and changed it the minute I was up; and I'm *so* glad, for mine is the handsomest now."

Another bang of the street door sent the basket under the sofa, and the girls to the table, eager for breakfast.

"Merry Christmas, Marmee! Many of them! Thank you for our books; we read some, and mean to every day," they cried, in chorus.

"Merry Christmas, little daughters! I'm glad you began at once, and hope you will keep on. But I want to say one word before we sit down. Not far away from here lies a poor woman with a little newborn baby. Six children are huddled into one bed to keep from freezing, for they have no fire. There is nothing to eat over there; and the oldest boy came to tell me they were suffering hunger and cold. My girls, will you give them your breakfast as a Christmas present?"

They were all unusually hungry, having waited nearly an hour, and for a minute no one spoke; only a minute, for Jo exclaimed impetuously:

"I'm so glad you came before we began!"

"May I go and help carry the things to the poor little children?" asked Beth eagerly.

"*I* shall take the cream and the muffins," added Amy, heroically giving up the articles she most liked.

Meg was already covering the buckwheats, and piling the bread into one big plate.

"I thought you'd do it," said Mrs. March, smiling as if satisfied. "You shall all go and help me, and when we come back we will have bread and milk for breakfast, and make it up at dinnertime."

They were soon ready, and the procession set out. Fortunately it was early, and they went through back streets, so few people saw them, and no one laughed at the queer party.

A poor, bare, miserable room it was, with broken windows, no fire, ragged bedclothes, a sick mother, wailing baby, and a group of pale, hungry children cuddled under one old quilt, trying to keep warm.

How the big eyes stared and the blue lips smiled as the girls went in!

"Ach, mein Gott! It is good angels come to us!" said the poor woman, crying for joy.

"Funny angels in hoods and mittens," said Jo, and set them laughing.

In a few minutes it really did seem as if kind spirits had been at work there. Hannah, who had carried wood, made a fire, and stopped up the broken panes with old hats and her own cloak. Mrs. March gave the mother tea and gruel, and comforted her with promises of help, while she dressed the little baby as tenderly as if it had been her own. The girls, meantime, spread the table, set the children round the fire, and fed them like so many hungry birds—laughing, talking, and trying to understand the funny broken English.

"Das ist gut!" "Die Engel-kinder!" cried the poor things, as they ate, and warmed their purple hands at the comfortable blaze.

The girls had never been called angel children before, and thought it very agreeable, especially Jo, who had been considered a "Sancho" ever since she was born. That was a very happy breakfast, though they didn't get any of it; and when they went away, leaving comfort behind, I think there were not in all the city four merrier people than the hungry little girls who gave away their breakfasts and contented themselves with bread and milk on Christmas morning.

"That's loving our neighbor better than ourselves, and I like it," said Meg, as they set out their presents, while their mother was upstairs collecting clothes for the poor Hummels.

Not a very splended show, but there was a great deal of love done up in the few little bundles; and the tall vase of red roses, white chrysanthemums, and trailing vines, which stood in the middle, gave quite an elegant air to the table.

"She's coming! Strike up, Beth! Open the door, Amy! Three cheers for Marmee!" cried Jo, prancing about, while Meg went to conduct mother to the seat of honor.

Beth played her gayest march, Amy threw open the door, and Meg enacted escort with great dignity. Mrs. March was both surprised and touched; and smiled with her eyes full as she examined her presents, and read the little notes which accompanied them. The slippers went on at once, a new handkerchief was slipped into her pocket, well scented with Amy's cologne, the rose was fastened in her bosom, and the nice gloves were pronounced a "perfect fit."

There was a good deal of laughing and kissing and explaining, in the simple, loving fashion which makes these home festivals so pleasant at the time, so sweet to remember long afterward, and then all fell to work.

The morning charities and ceremonies took so much time that the rest of the day was devoted to preparations for the evening festivities. Being still too young to go often to the theater, and not rich enough to afford any great outlay for private performances, the girls put their wits to work, and— necessity being the mother of invention—made whatever they needed. Very clever were some of their productions—pasteboard guitars, antique lamps made of old-fashioned butter boats covered with silver paper, gorgeous robes of old cotton, glittering with tin spangles from a pickle factory, and armor covered with the same useful diamond-shaped bits, left in sheets when the lids of tin preserve pots were cut out. The furniture was used to being turned topsy-turvy, and the big chamber was the scene of many innocent revels.

No gentlemen were admitted; so Jo played male parts to her heart's content, and took immense satisfaction in a pair of russet-leather boots given her by a friend, who knew a lady who knew an actor. These boots, an old foil, and a slashed doublet once used by an artist for some picture, were Jo's chief treasures, and appeared on all occasions. The smallness of the company made it necessary for the two principal actors to take several parts apiece; and they certainly deserved some credit for the hard work they did in learning three or four different parts, whisking in and out of various costumes, and managing the stage besides. It was excellent drill for their memories, a harmless amusement, and employed many hours which otherwise would have been idle, lonely, or spent in less profitable society.

On Christmas night, a dozen girls piled onto the bed which was the dress circle, and sat before the blue and yellow chintz curtains in a most flattering state of expectancy. There was a good deal of rustling and whispering behind the curtain, a trifle of lamp smoke, and an occasional giggle from Amy, who was apt to get hysterical in the excitement of the moment. Presently a bell sounded, the curtains flew apart, and the Operatic Tragedy began.

"A gloomy wood," according to the one playbill, was represented by a few shrubs in pots, green baize on the floor, and a cave in the distance. This cave was made with a clotheshorse for a roof, bureaus for walls; and in it was a small furnace in full blast, with a black pot on it, and an old witch bending over it. The stage was dark, and the glow of the furnace had a fine effect, especially as real steam issued from the kettle when the witch took off the cover. A moment was allowed for the first thrill to subside; then Hugo, the villain, stalked in with a clanking sword at his side, a slouched hat, black beard, mysterious cloak, and the boots. After pacing to and fro in much agitation, he struck his forehead, and burst out in a wild strain, singing of his hatred to Roderigo, his love for Zara, and his pleasing resolution to kill the one and win the other. The gruff tones of Hugo's voice, with an occasional shout when his feelings overcame him, were very impressive, and the audience applauded the moment he paused for breath. Bowing with the air of one accustomed to public praise, he stole to the cavern, and ordered Hagar to come forth with a commanding "What ho, minion! I need thee!"

Out came Meg, with gray horsehair hanging about her face, a red and black robe, a staff, and cabalistic signs upon her cloak. Hugo demanded a potion to make Zara adore him, and one to destroy Roderigo. Hagar, in a fine dramatic melody, promised both, and proceeded to call up the spirit who would bring the love philter:

> "Hither, hither, from thy home,
> Airy sprite, I bid thee come!
> Born of roses, fed on dew,
> Charms and potions canst thou brew?
> Bring me here, with elfin speed,
> The fragrant philter which I need;
> Make it sweet and swift and strong,
> Spirit, answer now my song!"

A soft strain of music sounded, and then at the back of the cave appeared a little figure in cloudy white, with glittering wings, golden hair, and a garland of roses on its head. Waving a wand, it sang:

> "Hither I come,
> From my airy home,
> Afar in the silver moon.
> Take the magic spell,
> And use it well,
> Or its power will vanish soon!"

And, dropping a small, gilded bottle at the witch's feet, the spirit vanished. Another chant from Hagar produced another apparition—not a lovely one; for, with a bang, an ugly black imp appeared, and having croaked a reply, tossed a dark bottle at Hugo, and disappeared with a mocking laugh. Having warbled his thanks and put the potions in his boots, Hugo departed; and Hagar informed the audience that, as he had killed a few of her friends in times past, she has cursed him, and intends to thwart his plans, and be revenged on him. Then the curtain fell, and the audience reposed and ate candy while discussing the merits of the play.

A good deal of hammering went on before the curtain rose again; but when it became evident what a masterpiece of stage carpentering had been got up, no one murmured at the delay. It was truly superb! A tower rose to the ceiling; halfway up appeared a window, with a lamp burning at it, and behind the white curtain appeared Zara in a lovely blue and silver dress, waiting for Roderigo. He came in gorgeous array, with plumed cap, red cloak, chestnut lovelocks, a guitar, and the boots, of course. Kneeling at the foot of the tower, he sang a serenade in melting tones. Zara replied, and, after a musical dialogue, consented to fly. Then came the grand effect of the play. Roderigo produced a rope ladder, with five steps to it, threw up one end, and invited Zara to descend. Timidly she crept from her lattice, put her hand on Rodigero's shoulder, and was about to leap gracefully down, when, "Alas! alas for Zara!" she forgot her train—it caught in the window; the tower tottered, leaned forward, fell with a crash, and buried the unhappy lovers in the ruins!

A universal shriek arose as the russet boots waived wildly from the wreck, and a golden head emerged, exclaiming, "I told you so! I told you so!" With wonderful presence of mind, Don Pedro, the cruel sire, rushed in, dragged out his daughter, with a hasty aside:

"Don't laugh! Act as if it was all right!"—and, ordering Roderigo up, banished him from the kingdom with wrath and scorn. Though decidedly shaken by the fall of the tower upon him, Roderigo defied the old gentleman, and refused to stir. This dauntless example fired Zara: she also defied her sire, and he ordered them both to the deepest dungeons of the castle. A stout little retainer came in with chains, and led them away,

looking very much frightened, and evidently forgetting the
speech he ought to have made.

Act third was the castle hall; and here Hagar appeared,
having come to free the lovers and finish Hugo. She hears him
coming, and hides; sees him put the potions into two cups of
wine, and bid the timid little servant "Bear them to the cap-
tives in their cells, and tell them I shall come anon." The
servant takes Hugo aside to tell him something, and Hagar
changes the cups for two others which are harmless. Ferdi-
nando, the "minion," carries them away, and Hagar puts back
the cup which holds the poison meant for Roderigo. Hugo,
getting thirsty after a long warble, drinks it, loses his wits, and,
after a good deal of clutching and stamping, falls flat and dies;
while Hagar informs him what she has done in a song of exquisite power and melody.

This was a truly thrilling scene, though some persons might
have thought that the sudden tumbling down of a quantity of
long hair rather marred the effect of the villain's death. He was
called before the curtain, and with great propriety appeared,
leading Hagar, whose singing was considered more wonderful
than all the rest of the performance put together.

Act fourth displayed the despairing Roderigo on the point
of stabbing himself, because he has been told that Zara has
deserted him. Just as the dagger is at his heart, a lovely song
is sung under his window, informing him that Zara is true, but
in danger, and he can save her, if he will. A key is thrown in,
which unlocks the door, and in a spasm of rapture he tears off
his chains, and rushes away to find and rescue his ladylove.

Act fifth opened with a stormy scene between Zara and
Don Pedro. He wishes her to go into a convent, but she won't
hear of it; and, after a touching appeal, is about to faint, when
Roderigo dashes in and demands her hand. Don Pedro refuses,
because he is not rich. They shout and gesticulate tremendously, but cannot agree, and Roderigo is about to bear away
the exhausted Zara when the timid servant enters with a letter
and a bag from Hagar, who has mysteriously disappeared. The
letter informs the party that she bequeaths untold wealth to
the young pair, and an awful doom to Don Pedro, if he doesn't

make them happy. The bag is opened, and several quarts of tin money shower down upon the stage, till it is quite glorified with the glitter. This entirely softens the "stern sire": he consents without a murmur, all join in a joyful chorus, and the curtain falls upon the lovers kneeling to receive Don Pedro's blessing in attitudes of the most romantic grace.

Tumultuous applause followed, but received an unexpected check; for the cot bed, on which the "dress circle" was built, suddenly shut up, and extinguished the enthusiastic audience. Roderigo and Don Pedro flew to the rescue, and all were taken out unhurt, though many were speechless with laughter. The excitement had hardly subsided when Hannah appeared, with "Mrs. March's compliments, and would the ladies walk down to supper."

This was a surprise, even to the actors; and, when they saw the table, they looked at one another in rapturous amazement. It was like Marmee to get up a little treat for them; but anything so fine as this was unheard of since the departed days of plenty. There was ice cream—actually two dishes of it, pink and white—and cake and fruit and distracting French bonbons, and, in the middle of the table, four great bouquets of hothouse flowers!

It quite took their breath away; and they stared first at the table and then at their mother, who looked as if she enjoyed it immensely.

"Is it fairies?" asked Amy.

"It's Santa Claus," said Beth.

"Mother did it"; and Meg smiled her sweetest, in spite of her gray beard and white eyebrows.

"Aunt March had a good fit, and sent the supper," cried Jo, with a sudden inspiration.

"All wrong. Old Mr. Laurence sent it," replied Mrs. March.

"The Laurence boy's grandfather! What in the world put such a thing into his head? We don't know him!" exclaimed Meg.

"Hannah told one of his servants about your breakfast party. He is an odd old gentleman, but that pleased him. He knew my father, years ago; and he sent me a polite note this afternoon, saying he hoped I would allow him to express his friendly feel-

ing toward my children by sending them a few trifles in honor of the day. I could not refuse; and so you have a little feast at night to make up for the bread-and-milk breakfast."

"That boy put it into his head, I know he did! He's a capital fellow, and I wish we could get acquainted. He looks as if he'd like to know us; but he's bashful, and Meg is so prim she won't let me speak to him when we pass," said Jo, as the plates went round, and the ice began to melt out of sight, with "Ohs!" and "Ahs!" of satisfaction.

"You mean the people who live in the big house next door, don't you?" asked one of the girls. "My mother knows old Mr. Laurence but says he's very proud, and doesn't like to mix with his neighbors. He keeps his grandson shut up, when he isn't riding or walking with his tutor, and makes him study very hard. We invited him to our party, but he didn't come. Mother says he's very nice, though he never speaks to us girls."

"Our cat ran away once, and he brought her back, and we talked over the fence, and were getting on capitally—all about cricket, and so on—when he saw Meg coming, and walked off. I mean to know him someday; for he needs fun, I'm sure he does," said Jo decidedly.

"I like his manners, and he looks like a little gentleman; so I've no objection to your knowing him, if a proper opportunity comes. He brought the flowers himself; and I should have asked him in, if I had been sure what was going on upstairs. He looked so wistful as he went away, hearing the frolic, and evidently having none of his own."

"It's a mercy you didn't, mother!" laughed Jo, looking at her boots. "But we'll have another play, sometime, that he *can* see. Perhaps he'll help act; wouldn't that be jolly?"

"I never had such a fine bouquet before! How pretty it is!" And Meg examined her flowers with great interest.

"They *are* lovely! But Beth's roses are sweeter to me," said Mrs. March, smelling the half-dead posy in her belt.

Beth nestled up to her, and whispered softly, "I wish I could send my bunch to father. I'm afraid he isn't having such a merry Christmas as we are."

CHAPTER THREE

The Laurence Boy

"JO! Jo, where are you?" cried Meg, at the foot of the garret stairs.

"Here!" answered a husky voice from above; and, running up, Meg found her sister eating apples and crying over the "Heir of Redclyffe," wrapped up in a comforter on an old three-legged sofa by the sunny window. This was Jo's favorite refuge; and here she loved to retire with half a dozen russets and a nice book, to enjoy the quiet and the society of a pet rat who lived near by, and didn't mind her a particle. As Meg appeared, Scrabble whisked into his hole. Jo shook the tears off her cheeks, and waited to hear the news.

"Such fun! only see! A regular note of invitation from Mrs. Gardiner for tomorrow night!" cried Meg, waving the precious

paper, and then proceeding to read it, with girlish delight.
"'Mrs. Gardiner would be happy to see Miss March and
Miss Josephine at a little dance on New Year's Eve.' Marmee
is willing we should go; now what *shall* we wear?"

"What's the use of asking that, when you know we shall
wear our poplins, because we haven't got anything else?" answered Jo, with her mouth full.

"If I only had a silk!" sighed Meg. "Mother says I may when
I'm eighteen, perhaps; but two years is an everlasting time to
wait."

"I'm sure our pops look like silk, and they are nice enough
for us. Yours is as good as new, but I forgot the burn and the
tear in mine. Whatever shall I do? The burn shows badly, and
I can't take any out."

"You must sit still all you can, and keep your back out of
sight; the front is all right. I shall have a new ribbon for my
hair, and Marmee will lend me her little pearl pin, and my new
slippers are lovely, and my gloves will do, though they aren't
as nice as I'd like."

"Mine are spoilt with lemonade, and I can't get any new
ones, so I shall have to go without," said Jo, who never troubled herself much about dress.

"You *must* have gloves, or I won't go," cried Meg decidedly.
"Gloves are more important than anything else; you can't
dance without them, and if you don't I should be *so* mortified."

"Then I'll stay still. I don't care much for company dancing;
it's no fun to go sailing round; I like to fly about and cut
capers."

"You can't ask mother for new ones, they are so expensive,
and you are so careless. She said, when you spoilt the others,
that she shouldn't get you any more this winter. Can't you
make them do?" asked Meg anxiously.

"I can hold them crumpled up in my hand, so no one will
know how stained they are; that's all I can do. No! I'll tell you
how we can manage—each wear one good one and carry a bad
one; don't you see?"

"Your hands are bigger than mine, and you will stretch my
glove dreadfully," began Meg, whose gloves were a tender
point with her.

"Then I'll go without. I don't care what people say!" cried
Jo, taking up her book.

"You may have it, you may! Only don't stain it, and do behave nicely. Don't put your hands behind you, or stare, or say
'Christopher Columbus!' will you?"

"Don't worry about me; I'll be as prim as I can, and not get
into any scrapes, if I can help it. Now go and answer your note,
and let me finish this splendid story."

So Meg went away to "accept with thanks," look over her
dress, and sing blithely as she did up her one real lace frill;
while Jo finished her story, her four apples, and had a game of
romps with Scrabble.

On New Year's Eve the parlor was deserted, for the two
younger girls played dressing maids, and the two elder were
absorbed in the all-important business of "getting ready for
the party." Simple as the toilettes were, there was a great deal
of running up and down, laughing and talking, and at one
time a strong smell of burnt hair pervaded the house. Meg
wanted a few curls about her face, and Jo undertook to pinch
the papered locks with a pair of hot tongs.

"Ought they to smoke like that?" asked Beth, from her perch
on the bed.

"It's the dampness drying," replied Jo.

"What a queer smell! It's like burnt feathers," observed Amy,
smoothing her own pretty curls with a superior air.

"There, now I'll take off the papers and you'll see a cloud of
little ringlets," said Jo, putting down the tongs.

She did take off the papers, but no cloud of ringlets appeared, for the hair came with the papers, and the horrified
hairdresser laid a row of little scorched bundles on the bureau
before her victim.

"Oh, oh, oh! What *have* you done? I'm spoilt! I can't go! My
hair, oh, my hair!" wailed Meg, looking with despair at the uneven frizzle on her forehead.

"Just my luck! You shouldn't have asked me to do it; I always spoil everything. I'm so sorry, but the tongs were too hot,
and so I've made a mess," groaned poor Jo, regarding the black
pancakes with tears of regret.

"It isn't spoilt; just frizzle it, and tie your ribbon so the ends come on your forehead a bit, and it will look like the last fashion. I've seen many girls do it so," said Amy consolingly.

"Serves me right for trying to be fine. I wish I'd let my hair alone," cried Meg petulantly.

"So do I, it was so smooth and pretty. But it will soon grow out again," said Beth, coming to kiss and comfort the shorn sheep.

After various lesser mishaps, Meg was finished at last, and by the united exertions of the family Jo's hair was got up and her dress on. They looked very well in their simple suits— Meg in silvery drab, with a blue velvet snood, lace frills, and the pearl pin; Jo in maroon, with a stiff, gentlemanly linen collar, and a white chrysanthemum or two for her only ornament. Each put on one nice light glove, and carried one soiled one, and all pronounced the effect "quite easy and fine." Meg's high-heeled slippers were very tight, and hurt her, though she would not own it, and Jo's nineteen hairpins all seemed stuck straight into her head, which was not exactly comfortable; but, dear me, let us be elegant or die!

"Have a good time, dearies!" said Mrs. March, as the sisters went daintily down the walk. "Don't eat much supper, and come away at eleven, when I send Hannah for you." As the gate clashed behind them, a voice cried from a window:

"Girls, girls! *Have* you both got nice pocket handkerchiefs?"

"Yes, yes, spandy nice, and Meg has cologne on hers," cried Jo, adding, with a laugh, as they went on, "I do believe Marmee would ask that if we were all running away from an earthquake."

"It is one of her aristocratic tastes, and quite proper, for a real lady is always known by neat boots, gloves, and handkerchief," replied Meg, who had a good many little "aristocratic tastes" of her own.

"Now don't forget to keep the bad breadth out of sight, Jo. Is my sash right? And does my hair look *very* bad?" said Meg, as she turned from the glass in Mrs. Gardiner's dressing room, after a prolonged prink.

"I know I shall forget. If you see me doing anything wrong, just remind me by a wink, will you?" returned Jo, giving her collar a twitch and her head a hasty brush.

"No, winking isn't ladylike; I'll lift my eyebrows if anything is wrong, and nod if you are all right. Now hold your shoulders straight, and take short steps, and don't shake hands if you are introduced to anyone: it isn't the thing."

"How *do* you learn all the proper ways? I never can. Isn't that music gay?"

Down they went, feeling a trifle timid, for they seldom went to parties, and, informal as this little gathering was, it was an event to them. Mrs. Gardiner, a stately old lady, greeted them kindly, and handed them over to the eldest of her six daughters. Meg knew Sallie, and was at her ease very soon; but Jo, who didn't care much for girls or girlish gossip, stood about with her back carefully against the wall, and felt as much out of place as a colt in a flower garden. Half a dozen jovial lads were talking about skates in another part of the room, and she longed to go and join them, for skating was one of the joys of her life. She telegraphed her wish to Meg, but the eyebrows went up so alarmingly that she dared not stir. No one came to talk to her, and one by one the group near her dwindled away, till she was left alone. She could not roam about and amuse herself, for the burnt breadth would show, so she stared at people rather forlornly till the dancing began. Meg was asked at once, and the tight slippers tripped about so briskly that none would have guessed the pain their wearer suffered smilingly. Jo saw a big redheaded youth approaching her corner, and fearing he meant to engage her, she slipped into a curtained recess, intending to peep and enjoy herself in peace. Unfortunately, another bashful person had chosen the same refuge; for, as the curtain fell behind her, she found herself face to face with the "Laurence boy."

"Dear me, I didn't know anyone was here!" stammered Jo, preparing to back out as speedily as she had bounced in.

But the boy laughed, and said pleasantly, though he looked a little startled:

"Don't mind me; stay, if you like."

"Shan't I disturb you?"

"Not a bit; I only came here because I don't know many people, and felt rather strange at first, you know."

"So did I. Don't go away, please, unless you'd rather."

The boy sat down again and looked at his pumps, till Jo said, trying to be polite and easy:

"I think I've had the pleasure of seeing you before; you live near us, don't you?"

"Next door"; and he looked up and laughed outright, for

Jo's prim manner was rather funny when he remembered how they had chatted about cricket when he brought the cat home.

That put Jo at her ease; and she laughed too, as she said, in her heartiest way:

"We did have such a good time over your nice Christmas present."

"Grandpa sent it."

"But you put it into his head, didn't you, now?"

"How is your cat, Miss March?" asked the boy, trying to look sober, while his black eyes shone with fun.

"Nicely, thank you, Mr. Laurence; but I am not Miss March, I'm only Jo," returned the young lady.

"I'm not Mr. Laurence, I'm only Laurie."

"Laurie Laurence—what an odd name!"

"My first name is Theodore, but I don't like it, for the fellows called me Dora, so I made them say Laurie instead."

"I hate my name, too—so sentimental! I wish everyone would say Jo, instead of Josephine. How did you make the boys stop calling you Dora?"

"I thrashed 'em."

"I can't thrash Aunt March, so I suppose I shall have to bear it"; and Jo resigned herself with a sigh.

"Don't you like to dance, Miss Jo?" asked Laurie, looking as if he thought the name suited her.

"I like it well enough if there is plenty of room, and everyone is lively. In a place like this I'm sure to upset something, tread on people's toes, or do something dreadful, so I keep out of mischief, and let Meg sail about. Don't you dance?"

"Sometimes; you see I've been abroad a good many years, and haven't been into company enough yet to know how you do things here."

"Abroad!" cried Jo. "Oh, tell me about it! I love dearly to hear people describe their travels."

Laurie didn't seem to know where to begin; but Jo's eager questions soon set him going, and he told her how he had been at school in Vevay, where the boys never wore hats, and had a fleet of boats on the lake, and for holiday fun went walking trips about Switzerland with their teachers.

"Don't I wish I'd been there!" cried Jo. "Did you go to Paris?"

"We spent last winter there."

"Can you talk French?"

"We were not allowed to speak anything else at Vevay."

"Do say some! I can read it, but can't pronounce."

"Quel nom a cette jeune demoiselle en les pantoufles jolis?" said Laurie good-naturedly.

"How nicely you do it! Let me see—you said, 'Who is the young lady in the pretty slippers,' didn't you?"

"Oui, mademoiselle."

"It's my sister Margaret, and you knew it was! Do you think she is pretty?"

"Yes; she makes me think of the German girls, she looks so fresh and quiet, and dances like a lady."

Jo quite glowed with pleasure at this boyish praise of her sister, and stored it up to repeat to Meg. Both peeped and criticized and chatted, till they felt like old acquaintances. Laurie's bashfulness soon wore off, for Jo's gentlemanly demeanor amused and set him at his ease, and Jo was her merry self again, because her dress was forgotten, and nobody lifted their eyebrows at her. She liked the "Laurence boy" better than ever, and took several good looks at him, so that she might describe him to the girls; for they had no brothers, very few male cousins, and boys were almost unknown creatures to them.

"Curly black hair; brown skin; big black eyes; handsome nose; fine teeth; small hands and feet; taller than I am; very polite, for a boy, and altogether jolly. Wonder how old he is?"

It was on the tip of Jo's tongue to ask; but she checked herself in time, and, with unusual tact, tried to find out in a roundabout way.

"I suppose you are going to college soon? I see you pegging away at your books—no, I mean studying hard"; and Jo blushed at the dreadful "pegging" which had escaped her.

Laurie smiled, but didn't seem shocked, and answered, with a shrug:

"Not for a year or two; I won't go before seventeen, anyway."

"Aren't you but fifteen?" asked Jo, looking at the tall lad, whom she had imagined seventeen already.

"Sixteen, next month.

"How I wish I was going to college! You don't look as if you liked it."

"I hate it! Nothing but grinding or skylarking. And I don't like the way fellows do either, in this country."

"What do you like?"

"To live in Italy, and to enjoy myself in my own way."

Jo wanted very much to ask what his own way was; but his black brows looked rather threatening as he knit them; so she changed the subject by saying, as her foot kept time, "That's a splendid polka! Why don't you go and try it?"

"If you will come too," he answered, with a gallant little bow.

"I can't; for I told Meg I wouldn't, because—" There Jo stopped, and looked undecided whether to tell or to laugh.

"Because what?" asked Laurie curiously.

"You won't tell?"

"Never!"

"Well, I have a bad trick of standing before the fire, and so I burn my frocks, and I scorched this one; and, though it's nicely mended, it shows, and Meg told me to keep still, so no one would see it. You may laugh, if you want to; it is funny, I know."

But Laurie didn't laugh; he only looked down a minute, and the expression of his face puzzled Jo, when he said very gently:

"Never mind that; I'll tell you how we can manage: there's a long hall out there, and we can dance grandly, and no one will see us. Please come?"

Jo thanked him, and gladly went, wishing she had two neat gloves, when she saw the nice, pearl-colored ones her partner wore. The hall was empty, and they had a grand polka; for Laurie danced well, and taught her the German step, which delighted Jo, being full of swing and spring. When the music stopped, they sat down on the stairs to get their breath; and Laurie was in the midst of an account of a students' festival at Heidelberg, when Meg appeared in search of her sister. She beckoned, and Jo reluctantly followed her into a side room, where she found her on a sofa, holding her foot, and looking pale.

"I've sprained my ankle. That stupid high heel turned and gave me a sad wrench. It aches so I can hardly stand, and I don't know how I'm ever going to get home," she said, rocking to and fro in pain.

"I knew you'd hurt your feet with those silly shoes. I'm sorry. But I don't see what you can do, except get a carriage, or stay here all night," answered Jo, softly rubbing the poor ankle as she spoke.

"I can't have a carriage, without its costing ever so much. I dare say I can't get one at all; for most people come in their own, and it's a long way to the stable, and no one to send."

"I'll go."

"No, indeed! It's past nine, and dark as Egypt. I can't stop here, for the house is full. Sallie has some girls staying with her. I'll rest till Hannah comes, and then do the best I can."

"I'll ask Laurie; he will go," said Jo, looking relieved as the idea occurred to her.

"Mercy, no! Don't ask or tell anyone. Get me my rubbers, and put these slippers with our things. I can't dance any more; but as soon as supper is over, watch for Hannah, and tell me the minute she comes."

"They are going out to supper now. I'll stay with you; I'd rather."

"No, dear, run along, and bring me some coffee. I'm so tired, I can't stir!"

So Meg reclined with rubbers well hidden, and Jo went blundering away to the dining room, which she found after going into a china closet, and opening the door of a room where old Mr. Gardiner was taking a little private refreshment. Making a dart at the table, she secured the coffee, which she immediately spilt, thereby making the front of her dress as bad as the back.

"Oh, dear, what a blunderbuss I am!" exclaimed Jo, finishing Meg's glove by scrubbing her gown with it.

"Can I help you?" said a friendly voice; and there was Laurie, with a full cup in one hand and a plate of ice in the other.

"I was trying to get something for Meg, who is very tired, and someone shook me; and here I am, in a nice state," answered Jo, glancing dismally from the stained skirt to the coffee-colored glove.

"Too bad! I was looking for someone to give this to. May I take it to your sister?"

"Oh, thank you! I'll show you where she is. I don't offer to take it myself, for I should only get into another scrape if I did."

Jo led the way; and, as if used to waiting on ladies, Laurie drew up a little table, brought a second installment of coffee and ice for Jo, and was so obliging that even particular Meg pronounced him a "nice boy." They had a merry time over the bonbons and mottoes, and were in the midst of a quiet game of "Buzz," with two or three other young people who had strayed in, when Hannah appeared. Meg forgot her foot, and rose so quickly that she was forced to catch hold of Jo, with an exclamation of pain.

"Hush! Don't say anything," she whispered, adding aloud, "It's nothing. I turned my foot a little, that's all," and limped upstairs to put her things on.

Hannah scolded, Meg cried, and Jo was at her wits' end, till she decided to take things into her own hands. Slipping out, she ran down, and, finding a servant, asked if he could get her a carriage. It happened to be a hired waiter, who knew nothing about the neighborhood; and Jo was looking round for help, when Laurie, who had heard what she said, came up, and offered his grandfather's carriage, which had just come for him, he said.

"It's so early! You can't mean to go yet?" began Jo, looking relieved, but hesitating to accept the offer.

"I always go early—I do, truly! Please let me take you home. It's all on my way, you know, and it rains, they say."

That settled it; and, telling him of Meg's mishap, Jo gratefully accepted, and rushed up to bring down the rest of the party. Hannah hated rain as much as a cat does; so she made no trouble, and they rolled away in the luxurious closed carriage, feeling very festive and elegant. Laurie went on the box; so Meg could keep her foot up, and the girls talked over their party in freedom.

"I had a capital time. Did you?" asked Jo, rumpling up her hair. and making herself comfortable.

"Yes, till I hurt myself. Sallie's friend, Annie Moffat, took a fancy to me, and asked me to come and spend a week with her, when Sallie does. She is going in the spring, when the opera comes; and it will be perfectly splendid, if mother only lets me go," answered Meg, cheering up at the thought.

"I saw you dancing with the redheaded man I ran away from. Was he nice?"

"Oh, very! His hair is auburn, not red; and he was very polite, and I had a delicious redowa with him."

"He looked like a grasshopper in a fit, when he did the new step. Laurie and I couldn't help laughing. Did you hear us?"

"No; but it was very rude. What *were* you about all that time, hidden away there?"

Jo told her adventures, and, by the time she had finished, they were at home. With many thanks, they said "Good night," and crept in, hoping to disturb no one; but the instant their door creaked, two little nightcaps bobbed up, and two sleepy but eager voices cried out:

"Tell about the party! Tell about the party!"

With what Meg called "a great want of manners" Jo had saved some bonbons for the little girls; and they soon subsided, after hearing the most thrilling events of the evening.

"I declare, it really seems like being a fine young lady, to come home from the party in a carriage, and sit in my dressing gown, with a maid to wait on me," said Meg, as Jo bound up her foot with arnica, and brushed her hair.

"I don't believe fine young ladies enjoy themselves a bit more than we do, in spite of our burnt hair, old gowns, one glove apiece, and tight slippers that sprain our ankles when we are really silly enough to wear them." And I think Jo was quite right.

CHAPTER FOUR

Burdens

"OH, dear, how hard it does seem to take up our packs and go on," sighed Meg, the morning after the party; for, now the holidays were over, the week of merrymaking did not fit her for going on easily with the tasks she never liked.

"I wish it was Christmas or New Year all the time; wouldn't it be fun?" answered Jo, yawning dismally.

"We shouldn't enjoy ourselves half so much as we do now. But it does seem so nice to have little suppers and bouquets, and go to parties, and drive home, and read and rest, and not work. It's like other people, you know, and I always envy girls who do such things; I'm so fond of luxury," said Meg, trying to decide which of two shabby gowns was the least shabby.

"Well, we can't have it, so don't let us grumble, but shoulder our bundles and trudge along as cheerfully as Marmee does. I'm sure Aunt March is a regular Old Man of the Sea to me, but I suppose when I've learned to carry her without complaining, she will tumble off, or get so light that I shan't mind her."

This idea tickled Jo's fancy, and put her in good spirits; but Meg didn't brighten, for her burden, consisting of four spoilt children, seemed heavier than ever. She hadn't heart enough even to make herself pretty, as usual, by putting on a blue neck ribbon, and dressing her hair in the most becoming way.

"Where's the use of looking nice, when no one sees me but those cross midgets, and no one cares whether I'm pretty or not?" she muttered, shutting her drawer with a jerk. "I shall have to toil and moil all my days, with only little bits of fun now and then, and get old and ugly and sour, because I'm poor, and can't enjoy my life as other girls do. It's a shame!"

So Meg went down, wearing an injured look, and wasn't at all agreeable at breakfast time. Everyone seemed rather out of sorts, and inclined to croak. Beth had a headache, and lay on the sofa, trying to comfort herself with the cat and three kittens; Amy was fretting because her lessons were not learned, and she couldn't find her rubbers; Jo *would* whistle and make a great racket getting ready; Mrs. March was very busy trying to finish a letter, which must go at once; and Hannah had the grumps, for being up late didn't suit her.

"There never *was* such a cross family!" cried Jo, losing her temper when she had upset an inkstand, broken both boot lacings, and sat down upon her hat.

"You're the crossest person in it!" returned Amy, washing out the sum, that was all wrong, with the tears that had fallen on her slate.

"Beth, if you don't keep these horrid cats down cellar I'll have them drowned," exclaimed Meg angrily, as she tried to get rid of the kitten, which had scrambled up her back, and stuck like a burr just out of reach.

Jo laughed, Meg scolded, Beth implored, and Amy wailed, because she couldn't remember how much nine times twelve was.

"Girls, girls, do be quiet one minute! I *must* get this off by the early mail, and you drive me distracted with your worry," cried Mrs. March, crossing out the third spoilt sentence in her letter.

There was a momentary lull, broken by Hannah, who stalked in, laid two hot turnovers on the table, and stalked out again. These turnovers were an institution; and the girls called them "muffs," for they had no others, and found the hot pies very comforting to their hands on cold mornings. Hannah never forgot to make them, no matter how busy or grumpy she might be, for the walk was long and bleak; the poor things got no other lunch, and were seldom home before two.

"Cuddle your cats, and get over your headache, Bethy. Good-by, Marmee; we are a set of rascals this morning, but we'll come home regular angels. Now then, Meg!" and Jo tramped away, feeling that the pilgrims were not setting out as they ought to do.

They always looked back before turning the corner, for their mother was always at the window, to nod and smile, and wave her hand to them. Somehow it seemed as if they couldn't have gone through the day without that; for, whatever their mood might be, the last glimpse of that motherly face was sure to affect them like sunshine.

"If Marmee shook her fist instead of kissing her hand to us, it would serve us right, for more ungrateful wretches than we are were never seen," cried Jo, taking a remorseful satisfaction in the snowy walk and bitter wind.

"Don't use such dreadful expressions," said Meg, from the depths of the veil in which she had shrouded herself like a nun sick of the world.

"I like good strong words that mean something," replied Jo, catching her hat as it took a leap off her head, preparatory to flying away altogether.

"Call yourself any names you like; but *I* am neither a rascal nor a wretch, and I don't choose to be called so."

"You're a blighted being, and decidedly cross today because you can't sit in the lap of luxury all the time. Poor dear, just wait till I make my fortune, and you shall revel in carriages and ice cream and high-heeled slippers and posies and red-headed boys to dance with."

"How ridiculous you are, Jo!" but Meg laughed at the nonsense, and felt better in spite of herself.

"Lucky for you I am; for if I put on crushed airs, and tried to be dismal, as you do, we should be in a nice state. Thank goodness, I can always find something funny to keep me up. Don't croak any more, but come home jolly, there's a dear."

Jo gave her sister an encouraging pat on the shoulder as they parted for the day, each going a different way, each hugging her little warm turnover, and each trying to be cheerful in spite of wintry weather, hard work, and the unsatisfied desires of pleasure-loving youth.

When Mr March lost his property in trying to help an unfortunate friend, the two oldest girls begged to be allowed to do something toward their own support, at least. Believing that they could not begin too early to cultivate energy, industry, and independence, their parents consented, and both fell to work, with the hearty good will which in spite of all obstacles is sure to succeed at last. Margaret found a place as nursery governess, and felt rich with her small salary. As she said, she *was* "fond of luxury," and her chief trouble was poverty. She found it harder to bear than the others, because she could remember a time when home was beautiful, life full of ease and pleasure, and want of any kind unknown. She tried

not to be envious or discontented, but it was very natural that
the young girl should long for pretty things, gay friends, accomplishments, and a happy life. At the Kings' she daily saw
all she wanted, for the children's older sisters were just out,
and Meg caught frequent glimpses of dainty ball dresses and
bouquets, heard lively gossip about theaters, concerts, sleigh-
ing parties, and merrymakings of all kinds, and saw money
lavished on trifles which would have been so precious to her.
Poor Meg seldom complained, but a sense of injustice made
her feel bitter toward everyone sometimes, for she had not yet
learned to know how rich she was in the blessings which alone
can make life happy.

Jo happened to suit Aunt March, who was lame, and
needed an active person to wait upon her. The childless old
lady had offered to adopt one of the girls when the troubles
came, and was much offended because her offer was declined.
Other friends told the Marches that they had lost all chance of
being remembered in the rich old lady's will; but the un-
worldly Marches only said:

"We can't give up our girls for a dozen fortunes. Rich or
poor, we will keep together and be happy in one another."

The old lady wouldn't speak to them for a time, but happening to meet Jo at a friend's, something in her comical face
and blunt manners struck the old lady's fancy, and she proposed to take her for a companion. This did not suit Jo at all;
but she accepted the place since nothing better appeared, and,
to everyone's surprise, got on remarkably well with her irascible relative. There was an occasional tempest, and once Jo
had marched home, declaring she couldn't bear it any longer;
but Aunt March always cleared up quickly, and sent for her
back again with such urgency that she could not refuse, for in
her heart she rather liked the peppery old lady.

I suspect that the real attraction was a large library of fine
books, which was left to dust and spiders since Uncle March
died. Jo remembered the kind old gentleman, who used to let
her build railroads and bridges with his big dictionaries, tell
her stories about the queer pictures in his Latin books, and
buy her cards of gingerbread whenever he met her in the
street. The dim, dusty room, with the busts staring down from

the tall bookcases, the cozy chairs, the globes, and, best of all, the wilderness of books, in which she could wander where she liked, made the library a region of bliss to her. The moment Aunt March took her nap, or was busy with company, Jo hurried to this quiet place, and curling herself up in the easy chair, devoured poetry, romance, history, travels, and pictures, like a regular bookworm. But, like all happiness, it did not last long; for as sure as she had just reached the heart of the story, the sweetest verse of the song, or the most perilous adventure of her traveler, a shrill voice called, "Josy-phine! Josy-phine!" and she had to leave her paradise to wind yarn, wash the poodle, or read Belsham's Essays by the hour together.

Jo's ambition was to do something very splendid; what it was she had no idea, as yet, but left it for time to tell her; and, meanwhile, found her greatest affliction in the fact that she couldn't read, run, and ride as much as she liked. A quick temper, sharp tongue, and restless spirit were always getting her into scrapes, and her life was a series of ups and downs, which were both comic and pathetic. But the training she received at Aunt March's was just what she needed; and the thought that she was doing something to support herself made her happy, in spite of the perpetual "Josy-phine!"

Beth was too bashful to go to school; it had been tried, but she suffered so much that it was given up, and she did her lessons at home with her father. Even when he went away, and her mother was called to devote her skill and energy to Soldiers' Aid Societies, Beth went faithfully on by herself, and did the best she could. She was a housewifely little creature, and helped Hannah keep home neat and comfortable for the workers, never thinking of any reward but to be loved. Long, quiet days she spent, not lonely nor idle, for her little world was peopled with imaginary friends, and she was by nature a busy bee. There were six dolls to be taken up and dressed every morning, for Beth was a child still, and loved her pets as well as ever. Not one whole or handsome one among them; all were outcasts till Beth took them in; for, when her sisters outgrew these idols, they passed to her, because Amy would have nothing old or ugly. Beth cherished them all the more tenderly for that very reason, and set up a hospital for infirm dolls. No pins

were ever stuck into their cotton vitals; no harsh words or
blows were ever given them; no neglect ever saddened the
heart of the most repulsive: but all were fed and clothed,
nursed and caressed, with an affection which never failed. One
forlorn fragment of *dollanity* had belonged to Jo; and, having
led a tempestuous life, was left a wreck in the rag bag, from
which dreary poorhouse it was rescued by Beth, and taken to
her refuge. Having no top to its head, she tied on a neat little
cap, and, as both arms and legs were gone, she hid these deficiencies by folding it in a blanket, and devoting her best bed
to this chronic invalid. If anyone had known the care lavished
on that dolly, I think it would have touched their hearts, even
while they laughed. She brought it bits of bouquets; she read
to it; took it out to breathe the air, hidden under her coat; she
sung it lullabies, and never went to bed without kissing its
dirty face, and whispering tenderly, "I hope you'll have a good
night, my poor dear."

Beth had her troubles as well as the others; and not being
an angel, but a very human little girl, she often "wept a little
weep," as Jo said, because she couldn't take music lessons and
have a fine piano. She loved music so dearly, tried so hard to
learn, and practiced away so patiently at the jingling old instrument, that it did seem as if someone (not to hint Aunt
March) ought to help her. Nobody did, however, and nobody
saw Beth wipe the tears off the yellow keys, that wouldn't keep
in tune, when she was all alone. She sang like a little lark about
her work, never was too tired to play for Marmee and the girls,
and day after day said hopefully to herself, "I know I'll get my
music sometime, if I'm good."

There are many Beths in the world, shy and quiet, sitting
in corners till needed, and living for others so cheerfully that
no one sees the sacrifices till the little cricket on the hearth
stops chirping, and the sweet, sunshiny presence vanishes,
leaving silence and shadow behind.

If anybody had asked Amy what the greatest trial of her
life was, she would have answered at once, "My nose." When
she was a baby, Jo had accidentally dropped her into the coal
hod, and Amy insisted that the fall had ruined her nose for-

ever. It was not big, nor red, like poor "Petrea's"; it was only rather flat, and all the pinching in the world could not give it an aristocratic point. No one minded it but herself, and it was doing its best to grow, but Amy felt deeply the want of a Grecian nose, and drew whole sheets of handsome ones to console herself.

"Little Raphael," as her sisters called her, had a decided talent for drawing, and was never so happy as when copying flowers, designing fairies, or illustrating stories with queer specimens of art. Her teachers complained that instead of doing her sums, she covered her slate with animals; the blank pages of her atlas were used to copy maps on; and caricatures of the most ludicrous description came fluttering out of all her books at unlucky moments. She got through her lessons as well as she could, and managed to escape reprimands by being a model of deportment. She was a great favorite with her mates, being good-tempered, and possessing the happy art of pleasing without effort. Her little airs and graces were much admired, so were her accomplishments; for besides her drawing, she could play twelve tunes, crochet, and read French without mispronouncing more than two-thirds of the words. She had a plaintive way of saying, "When papa was rich we did so-and-so," which was very touching; and her long words were considered "perfectly elegant" by the girls.

Amy was in a fair way to be spoilt; for everyone petted her, and her small vanities and selfishnesses were growing nicely. One thing, however, rather quenched the vanities: she had to wear her cousin's clothes. Now Florence's mamma hadn't a particle of taste and Amy suffered deeply at having to wear a red instead of a blue bonnet, unbecoming gowns, and fussy aprons that did not fit. Everything was good, well made, and little worn; but Amy's artistic eyes were much afflicted, especially this winter, when her school dress was a dull purple, with yellow dots, and no trimming.

"My only comfort," she said to Meg, with tears in her eyes, "is that mother don't take tucks in my dresses whenever I'm naughty, as Maria Parks' mother does. My dear, it's really dreadful; for sometimes she is so bad, her frock is up to her knees, and she can't come to school. When I think of this *deggerredation,* I feel that I can bear even my flat nose and purple gown, with yellow skyrockets on it."

Meg was Amy's confidante and monitor, and, by some strange attraction of opposites, Jo was gentle Beth's. To Jo alone did the shy child tell her thoughts; and over her big harum-scarum sister, Beth unconsciously exercised more influence than anyone in the family. The two older girls were a great deal to one another, but each took one of the younger into her keeping, and watched over her in her own way; "playing mother," they called it, and put their sisters in the places of discarded dolls, with the maternal instinct of little women.

"Has anybody got anything to tell? It's been such a dismal day I'm really dying for some amusement," said Meg, as they sat sewing together that evening.

"I had a queer time with aunt today, and, as I got the best of it, I'll tell you about it," began Jo, who dearly loved to tell stories. "I was reading that everlasting Belsham, and droning away as I always do, for aunt soon drops off, and then I take out some nice book, and read like fury till she wakes up. I actually made myself sleepy; and, before she began to nod, I gave such a gape that she asked me what I meant by opening my mouth wide enough to take the whole book in at once.

"'I wish I could, and be done with it,' said I, trying not to be saucy.

"Then she gave me a long lecture on my sins, and told me to sit and think them over while she just 'lost' herself for a moment. She never finds herself very soon; so the minute her cap began to bob, like a top-heavy dahlia, I whipped the 'Vicar of Wakefield' out of my pocket, and read away, with one eye on him, and one on aunt. I'd just got to where they all tumbled into the water, when I forgot, and laughed out loud. Aunt woke up; and, being more good-natured after her nap, told me to read a bit, and show what frivolous work I preferred to the worthy and instructive Belsham. I did my very best, and she liked it, though she only said:

"'I don't understand what it's all about. Go back and begin it, child.'

"Back I went, and made the Primroses as interesting as ever I could. Once I was wicked enough to stop in a thrilling place, and say meekly, 'I'm afraid it tires you, ma'am; shan't I stop now?'

"She caught up her knitting, which she had dropped out of her hands, gave me a sharp look through her specs, and said, in her short way:

"'Finish the chapter, and don't be impertinent, miss.'"

"Did she own she liked it?" asked Meg.

"Oh, bless you, no, but she let old Belsham rest; and, when I ran back after my gloves this afternoon, there she was, so hard at the Vicar that she didn't hear me laugh as I danced a jig in the hall, because of the good time coming. What a pleasant life she might have, if she only chose. I don't envy her much, in spite of her money, for after all rich people have about as many worries as poor ones, I think," added Jo.

"That reminds me," said Meg, "that I've got something to tell. It isn't funny, like Jo's story, but I thought about it a good deal as I came home. At the Kings' today I found everybody in a flurry, and one of the children said that her oldest brother had done something dreadful, and papa had sent him away. I heard Mrs. King crying and Mr. King talking very loud, and Grace and Ellen turned away their faces when they passed me, so I shouldn't see how red their eyes were. I didn't ask any questions, of course; but I felt so sorry for them, and was rather glad I hadn't any wild brothers to do wicked things and disgrace the family."

"I think being disgraced in school is a great deal try*inger* than anything bad boys can do," said Amy, shaking her head, as if her experience of life had been a deep one. "Susie Perkins came to school today with a lovely red carnelian ring; I wanted it dreadfully, and wished I was her with all my might. Well, she drew a picture of Mr. Davis, with a monstrous nose and a hump, and the words, 'Young ladies, my eye is upon you!' coming out of his mouth in a balloon thing. We were laughing over it, when all of a sudden his eye *was* on us, and he ordered Susie to bring up her slate. She was *parry*lized with fright, but she went, and oh, what *do* you think he did? He took her by

the ear—the ear, just fancy how horrid!—and led her to the
recitation platform, and made her stand there half an hour,
holding that slate so everyone could see."

"Didn't the girls laugh at the picture?" asked Jo, who rel-
ished the scrape.

"Laugh? Not one! They sat as still as mice; and Susie cried
quarts, I know she did. I didn't envy her then; for I felt that
millions of carnelian rings wouldn't have made me happy,
after that. I never, never should have got over such a agoniz-
ing mortification." And Amy went on with her work, in the
proud consciousness of virtue, and the successful utterance of
two long words in a breath.

"I saw something that I liked this morning, and I meant to
tell it at dinner, but I forgot," said Beth, putting Jo's topsy-
turvy basket in order as she talked. "When I went to get some
oysters for Hannah, Mr. Laurence was in the fish shop; but he
didn't see me, for I kept behind a barrel, and he was busy with
Mr. Cutter, the fishman. A poor woman came in, with a pail
and a mop, and asked Mr. Cutter if he would let her do some
scrubbing for a bit of fish, because she hadn't any dinner for
her children, and had been disappointed of a day's work. Mr.
Cutter was in a hurry, and said 'No,' rather crossly; so she was
going away, looking hungry and sorry, when Mr. Laurence
hooked up a big fish with the crooked end of his cane, and held
it out to her. She was so glad and surprised, she took it right
in her arms, and thanked him over and over. He told her to
'go along and cook it,' and she hurried off, so happy! Wasn't it
good of him? Oh, she did look so funny, hugging the big, slippery fish, and hoping Mr. Laurence's bed in heaven would be
'aisy.'"

When they had laughed at Beth's story, they asked their
mother for one; and, after a moment's thought, she said soberly:

"As I sat cutting out blue flannel jackets today, at the rooms,
I felt very anxious about father, and thought how lonely and
helpless we should be if anything happened to him. It was not
a wise thing to do; but I kept on worrying, till an old man
came in, with an order for some clothes. He sat down near me,

and I began to talk to him, for he looked poor and tired and anxious.

" 'Have you sons in the army?' I asked, for the note he brought was not to me.

" 'Yes, ma'am. I had four, but two were killed, one is a prisoner, and I'm going to the other who is very sick in a Washington hospital,' he answered quietly.

" 'You have done a great deal for your country, sir,' I said, feeling respect now, instead of pity.

" 'Not a mite more than I ought, ma'am. I'd go myself, if I was any use; as I ain't, I give my boys, and give 'em free.'

"He spoke so cheerfully, looked so sincere, and seemed so glad to give his all that I was ashamed of myself. I'd given one man, and thought it too much, while he gave four, without grudging them. I had all my girls to comfort me at home; and his last son was waiting, miles away, to say good-by to him, perhaps! I felt so rich, so happy, thinking of my blessings, that I made him a nice bundle, gave him some money, and thanked him heartily for the lesson he had taught me."

"Tell another story, mother—one with a moral to it, like this. I like to think about them afterwards, if they are real and not too preachy," said Jo, after a minute's silence.

Mrs. March smiled, and began at once; for she had told stories to this little audience for many years, and knew how to please thém.

"Once upon a time, there were four girls, who had enough to eat and drink and wear, a good many comforts and pleasures, kind friends and parents, who loved them dearly, and yet they were not contented." (Here the listeners stole shy looks at one another, and began to sew diligently.) "These girls were anxious to be good, and made many excellent resolutions; but they did not keep them very well, and were constantly saying, 'If we only had this,' or 'If we could only do that,' quite forgetting how much they already had, and how many pleasant things they actually could do. So they asked an old woman what spell they could use to make them happy, and she said, 'When you feel discontented, think over your blessings, and be grateful.' " (Here Jo looked up quickly, as if about to speak, but changed her mind, seeing that the story was not done yet.)

"Being sensible girls, they decided to try her advice, and soon were surprised to see how well off they were. One discovered that money couldn't keep shame and sorrow out of rich people's houses; another that, though she was poor, she was a great deal happier, with her youth, health, and good spirits, than a certain fretful, feeble old lady, who couldn't enjoy her comforts; a third that, disagreeable as it was to help get dinner, it was harder still to have to go begging for it; and the fourth, that even carnelian rings were not so valuable as good behavior. So they agreed to stop complaining, to enjoy the blessings already possessed, and try to deserve them, lest they should be taken away entirely, instead of increased; and I believe they were never disappointed, or sorry that they took the old woman's advice."

"Now, Marmee, that is very cunning of you to turn our own stories against us, and give us a sermon instead of a romance!" cried Meg.

. "I like that kind of sermon. It's the sort father used to tell us," said Beth thoughtfully, putting the needles straight on Jo's cushion.

"I don't complain near as much as the others do, and I shall be more careful than ever now, for I've had warning from Susie's downfall," said Amy morally.

"We needed that lesson, and we won't forget it. If we do, you just say to us, as old Chloe did in 'Uncle Tom,' 'Tink ob yer marcies, chillen! Tink ob yer marcies!'" added Jo, who could not, for the life of her, help getting a morsel of fun out of the little sermon, though she took it to heart as much as any of them.

CHAPTER FIVE

Being Neighborly

"WHAT in the world are you going to do now, Jo?"
asked Meg, one snowy afternoon, as her sister came tramping
through the hall, in rubber boots, old sack and hood, with a
broom in one hand and a shovel in the other.

"Going out for exercise," answered Jo, with a mischievous
twinkle in her eyes.

"I should think two long walks this morning would have
been enough! It's cold and dull out; and I advise you to stay,
warm and dry, by the fire, as I do," said Meg, with a shiver.

"Never take advice! Can't keep still all day, and not being
a pussycat I don't like to doze by the fire. I like adventures,
and I'm going to find some."

Meg went back to toast her feet and read "Ivanhoe"; and Jo began to dig paths with great energy. The snow was light, and with her broom she soon swept a path all round the garden, for Beth to walk in when the sun came out; and the invalid dolls needed air. Now, the garden separated the Marches' house from that of Mr. Laurence. Both stood in a suburb of the city, which was still countrylike, with groves and lawns, large gardens, and quiet streets. A low hedge parted the two estates. On one side was an old, brown house, looking rather bare and shabby, robbed of the vines that in summer covered its walls, and the flowers which then surrounded it. On the other side was a stately stone mansion, plainly betokening every sort of comfort and luxury, from the big coach house and well-kept grounds to the conservatory and the glimpses of lovely things one caught between the rich curtains. Yet it seemed a lonely, lifeless sort of house; for no children frolicked on the lawn, no motherly face ever smiled at the windows, and few people went in and out, except the old gentleman and his grandson.

To Jo's lively fancy, this fine house seemed a kind of enchanted palace, full of splendors and delights, which no one enjoyed. She had long wanted to behold these hidden glories, and to know the "Laurence boy," who looked as if he would like to be known, if he only knew how to begin. Since the party, she had been more eager than ever, and had planned many ways of making friends with him; but he had not been seen lately, and Jo began to think he had gone away, when she one day spied a brown face at the upper window, looking wistfully down into their garden, where Beth and Amy were snowballing one another.

"That boy is suffering for society and fun," she said to herself. "His grandpa does not know what's good for him, and keeps him shut up all alone. He needs a party of jolly boys to play with, or somebody young and lively. I've a great mind to go over and tell the old gentleman so!"

The idea amused Jo, who liked to do daring things, and was always scandalizing Meg by her queer performances. The plan of "going over" was not forgotten; and when the snowy afternoon came, Jo resolved to try what could be done. She saw

Mr. Laurence drive off, and then sallied out to dig her way
down to the hedge, where she paused, and took a survey. All
quiet—curtains down at the lower windows; servants out of
sight, and nothing human visible but a curly black head leaning on a thin hand at the upper window.

"There he is," thought Jo, "poor boy! All alone and sick this
dismal day. It's a shame! I'll toss up a snowball and make him
look out, and then say a kind word to him."

Up went a handful of soft snow, and the head turned at
once, showing a face which lost its listless look in a minute, as
the big eyes brightened and the mouth began to smile. Jo nodded and laughed, and flourished her broom as she called out:

"How do you do? Are you sick?"

Laurie opened the window, and croaked out as hoarsely as
a raven:

"Better, thank you. I've had a bad cold, and been shut up a
week."

"I'm sorry. What do you amuse yourself with?"

"Nothing; it's as dull as tombs up here."

"Don't you read?"

"Not much; they won't let me."

"Can't somebody read to you?"

"Grandpa does, sometimes; but my books don't interest him,
and I hate to ask Brooke all the time."

"Have someone come and see you then."

"There isn't anyone I'd like to see. Boys make such a row,
and my head is weak."

"Isn't there some nice girl who'd read and amuse you? Girls
are quiet, and like to play nurse."

"Don't know any."

"You know us," began Jo, then laughed, and stopped.

"So I do! Will you come, please?" cried Laurie.

"I'm not quiet and nice; but I'll come, if mother will let me.
I'll go ask her. Shut that window, like a good boy, and wait
till I come."

With that Jo shouldered her broom and marched into the
house, wondering what they would all say to her. Laurie was
in a flutter of excitement at the idea of having company, and
flew about to get ready; for, as Mrs. March said, he was "a lit-

tle gentleman," and did honor to the coming guest by brushing
his curly pate, putting on a fresh collar, and trying to tidy up
the room, which, in spite of half a dozen servants, was anything but neat. Presently there came a loud ring, then a decided voice, asking for "Mr. Laurie," and a surprised-looking
servant came running up to announce a young lady.

"All right, show her up, it's Miss Jo," said Laurie, going to
the door of his little parlor to meet Jo, who appeared, looking
rosy and kind and quite at her ease, with a covered dish in one
hand and Beth's three kittens in the other.

"Here I am, bag and baggage," she said briskly. "Mother
sent her love, and was glad if I could do anything for you.
Meg wanted me to bring some of her blancmange; she makes
it very nicely, and Beth thought her cats would be comforting.
I knew you'd laugh at them, but I couldn't refuse, she was so
anxious to do something."

It so happened that Beth's funny loan was just the thing;
for, in laughing over the kits, Laurie forgot his bashfulness,
and grew sociable at once.

"That looks too pretty to eat," he said, smiling with pleasure,
as Jo uncovered the dish, and showed the blancmange, surrounded by a garland of green leaves, and the scarlet flowers of
Amy's pet geranium.

"It isn't anything, only they all felt kindly, and wanted to
show it. Tell the girl to put it away for your tea: it's so simple,
you can eat it; and, being soft, it will slip down without hurting your sore throat. What a cozy room this is!"

"It might be if it was kept nice; but the maids are lazy, and
I don't know how to make them mind. It worries me, though."

"I'll right it up in two minutes; for it only needs to have the
hearth brushed, so—and the things made straight on the mantelpiece, so—and the books put here, and the bottles there, and
your sofa turned from the light, and the pillows plumped up
a bit. Now, then, you're fixed."

And so he was; for, as she laughed and talked, Jo had
whisked things into place, and given quite a different air to
the room. Laurie watched her in respectful silence and when
she beckoned him to his sofa, he sat down with a sigh of satisfaction, saying gratefully:

"How kind you are! Yes, that's what it wanted. Now please take the big chair, and let me do something to amuse my company."

"No; I came to amuse you. Shall I read aloud?" and Jo looked affectionately toward some inviting books near by.

"Thank you; I've read all those, and if you don't mind, I'd rather talk," answered Laurie.

"Not a bit; I'll talk all day if you'll only set me going. Beth says I never know when to stop."

"Is Beth the rosy one, who stays at home a good deal, and sometimes goes out with a little basket?" asked Laurie, with interest.

"Yes, that's Beth; she's my girl, and a regular good one she is, too."

"The pretty one is Meg, and the curly-haired one is Amy, I believe?"

"How did you find that out?"

Laurie colored up, but answered frankly, "Why, you see, I often hear you calling to one another, and when I'm alone up here, I can't help looking over at your house, you always seem to be having such good times. I beg your pardon for being so rude, but sometimes you forget to put down the curtain at the window where the flowers are; and when the lamps are lighted, it's like looking at a picture to see the fire, and you all round the table with your mother; her face is right opposite, and it looks so sweet behind the flowers, I can't help watching it. I haven't got any mother, you know"; and Laurie poked the fire to hide a little twitching of the lips that he could not control.

The solitary, hungry look in his eyes went straight to Jo's warm heart. She had been so simply taught that there was no nonsense in her head, and at fifteen she was as innocent and frank as any child. Laurie was sick and lonely; and, feeling how rich she was in home love and happiness, she gladly tried to share it with him. Her face was very friendly and her sharp voice unusually gentle as she said:

"We'll never draw that curtain any more, and I give you leave to look as much as you like. I just wish, though, instead of peeping, you'd come over and see us. Mother is so splendid, she'd do you heaps of good, and Beth would sing to you if *I*

begged her to, and Amy would dance; Meg and I would make
you laugh over our funny stage properties, and we'd have jolly
times. Wouldn't your grandpa let you?"

"I think he would, if your mother asked him. He's very kind,
though he does not look so; and he lets me do what I like,
pretty much, only he's afraid I might be a bother to strangers,"
began Laurie, brightening more and more.

"We are not strangers, we are neighbors, and you needn't
think you'd be a bother. We *want* to know you, and I've been
trying to do this ever so long. We haven't been here a great
while, you know, but we have got acquainted with all our
neighbors but you."

"You see, grandpa lives among his books, and doesn't mind
much what happens outside. Mr. Brooke, my tutor, doesn't
stay here, you know, and I have no one to go about with me
so I just stop at home and get on as I can."

"That's bad. You ought to make an effort, and go visiting
everywhere you are asked; then you'll have plenty of friends,
and pleasant places to go to. Never mind being bashful; it
won't last long if you keep going."

Laurie turned red again, but wasn't offended at being accused of bashfulness; for there was so much good will in Jo,
it was impossible not to take her blunt speeches as kindly as
they were meant.

"Do you like your school?" asked the boy, changing the subject, after a little pause, during which he stared at the fire, and
Jo looked about her, well pleased.

"Don't go to school; I'm a businessman—girl, I mean. I go
to wait on my great-aunt, and a dear, cross old soul she is, too,"
answered Jo.

Laurie opened his mouth to ask another question; but remembering just in time that it wasn't manners to make too
many inquiries into people's affairs, he shut it again, and
looked uncomfortable. Jo liked his good breeding, and didn't
mind having a laugh at Aunt March, so she gave him a lively
description of the fidgety old lady, her fat poodle, the parrot
that talked Spanish, and the library where she reveled. Laurie
enjoyed that immensely; and when she told about the prim
old gentleman who came once to woo Aunt March and, in the

"He isn't as handsome as my grandfather..."

[SEE PAGE 60]

middle of a fine speech, how Poll had tweaked his wig off to his great dismay, the boy lay back and laughed till the tears ran down his cheeks, and a maid popped her head in to see what was the matter.

"Oh! That does me no end of good. Tell on, please," he said, taking his face out of the sofa cushion, red and shining with merriment.

Much elated with her success, Jo did "tell on," all about their plays and plans, their hopes and fears for father, and the most interesting events of the little world in which the sisters lived. Then they got to talking about books; and to Jo's delight, she found that Laurie loved them as well as she did, and had read even more than herself.

"If you like them so much, come down and see ours. Grandpa is out, so you needn't be afraid," said Laurie, getting up.

"I'm not afraid of anything," returned Jo, with a toss of the head.

"I don't believe you are!" exclaimed the boy, looking at her with much admiration, though he privately thought she would have good reason to be a trifle afraid of the old gentleman, if she met him in some of his moods.

The atmosphere of the whole house being summerlike, Laurie led the way from room to room, letting Jo stop to examine whatever struck her fancy; and so at last they came to the library, where she clapped her hands, and pranced, as she always did when especially delighted. It was lined with books, and there were pictures and statues, and distracting little cabinets full of coins and curiosities, and sleepy-hollow chairs, and queer tables, and bronzes; and, best of all, a great open fireplace, with quaint tiles all round it.

"What richness!" sighed Jo, sinking into the depth of a velvet chair, and gazing about her with an air of intense satisfaction. "Theodore Laurence, you ought to be the happiest boy in the world," she added impressively.

"A fellow can't live on books," said Laurie, shaking his head, as he perched on a table opposite.

Before he could say more, a bell rung, and Jo flew up, exclaiming with alarm, "Mercy me, it's your grandpa!"

"Well, what if it is? You are not afraid of anything, you know," returned the boy, looking wicked.

"I think I am a little bit afraid of him, but I don't know why I should be. Marmee said I might come, and I don't think you're any the worse for it," said Jo, composing herself, though she kept her eyes on the door.

"I'm a great deal better for it, and ever so much obliged. I'm only afraid you are very tired talking to me; it was *so* pleasant, I couldn't bear to stop," said Laurie gratefully.

"The doctor to see you, sir," and the maid beckoned as she spoke.

"Would you mind if I left you for a minute? I suppose I must see him," said Laurie.

"Don't mind me. I'm as happy as a cricket here," answered Jo.

Laurie went away, and his guest amused herself in her own way. She was standing before a fine portrait of the old gentleman, when the door opened again, and, without turning, she said decidedly, "I'm sure now that I shouldn't be afraid of him, for he's got kind eyes, though his mouth is grim, and he looks as if he had a tremendous will of his own. He isn't as handsome as *my* grandfather, but I like him."

"Thank you, ma'am," said a gruff voice behind her; and there, to her great dismay, stood old Mr. Laurence.

Poor Jo blushed till she couldn't blush any redder, and her heart began to beat uncomfortably fast as she thought what she had said. For a minute a wild desire to run away possessed her; but that was cowardly, and the girls would laugh at her; so she resolved to stay, and get out of the scrape as she could. A second look showed her that the living eyes, under the bushy gray eyebrows, were kinder even than the painted ones; and there was a sly twinkle in them, which lessened her fear a good deal. The gruff voice was gruffer than ever, as the old gentleman said abruptly, after that dreadful pause, "So you're not afraid of me, hey?"

"Not much, sir."

"And you don't think me as handsome as your grandfather?"

"Not quite, sir."

"And I've got a tremendous will, have I?"

"I only said I thought so."

"But you like me, in spite of it?"

"Yes, I do, sir."

That answer pleased the old gentleman; he gave a short laugh, shook hands with her, and, putting his finger under her chin, turned up her face, examined it gravely, and let it go, saying, with a nod, "You've got your grandfather's spirit, if you haven't his face. He *was* a fine man, my dear; but, what is better, he was a brave and an honest one, and I was proud to be his friend."

"Thank you, sir," and Jo was quite comfortable after that, for it suited her exactly.

"What have you been doing to this boy of mine, hey?" was the next question, sharply put.

"Only trying to be neighborly, sir," and Jo told how her visit came about.

"You think he needs cheering up a bit, do you?"

"Yes, sir; he seems a little lonely, and young folks would do him good perhaps. We are only girls, but we should be glad to help if we could, for we don't forget the splendid Christmas present you sent us," said Jo eagerly.

"Tut, tut, tut! That was the boy's affair. How is the poor woman?"

"Doing nicely, sir," and off went Jo, talking very fast, as she told all about the Hummels, in whom her mother had interested richer friends than they were.

"Just her father's way of doing good. I shall come and see your mother some fine day. Tell her so. There's the tea bell; we have it early, on the boy's account. Come down, and go on being neighborly."

"If you'd like to have me, sir."

"Shouldn't ask you, if I didn't," and Mr. Laurence offered her his arm with old-fashioned courtesy.

"What *would* Meg say to this?" thought Jo, as she was marched away, while her eyes danced with fun as she imagined herself telling the story at home.

"Hey! Why, what the dickens has come to the fellow?" said

the old gentleman, as Laurie came running downstairs, and brought up with a start of surprise at the astonishing sight of Jo arm in arm with his redoubtable grandfather.

"I didn't know you'd come, sir," he began, as Jo gave him a triumphant little glance.

"That's evident, by the way you racket downstairs. Come to your tea, sir, and behave like a gentleman," and having pulled the boy's hair by way of a caress, Mr. Laurence walked on, while Laurie went through a series of comic evolutions behind their backs, which nearly produced an explosion of laughter from Jo.

The old gentleman did not say much as he drank his four cups of tea, but he watched the young people, who soon chatted away like old friends, and the change in his grandson did not escape him. There was color, light, and life in the boy's face now, vivacity in his manner, and genuine merriment in his laugh.

"She's right; the lad *is* lonely. I'll see what these little girls can do for him," thought Mr. Laurence, as he looked and listened. He liked Jo, for her odd, blunt ways suited him; and she seemed to understand the boy almost as well as if she had been one herself.

If the Laurences had been what Jo called "prim and poky," she would not have got on at all, for such people always made her shy and awkward; but finding them free and easy, she was so herself, and made a good impression. When they rose she proposed to go, but Laurie said he had something more to show her, and took her away to the conservatory, which had been lighted for her benefit. It seemed quite fairylike to Jo, as she went up and down the walks, enjoying the blooming walls on either side, the soft light, the damp sweet air, and the wonderful vines and trees that hung above her—while her new friend cut the finest flowers till his hands were full; then he tied them up, saying, with the happy look Jo liked to see, "Please give these to your mother, and tell her I like the medicine she sent me very much."

They found Mr. Laurence standing before the fire in the great drawing room, but Jo's attention was entirely absorbed by a grand piano, which stood open.

"Do you play?" she asked, turning to Laurie with a respectful expression.

"Sometimes," he answered modestly.

"Please do now. I want to hear it, so I can tell Beth."

"Won't you first?"

"Don't know how; too stupid to learn, but I love music dearly."

So Laurie played, and Jo listened, with her nose luxuriously buried in heliotrope and tea roses. Her respect and regard for the "Laurence boy" increased very much, for he played remarkably well, and didn't put on any airs. She wished Beth could hear him, but she did not say so; only praised him till he was quite abashed, and his grandfather came to the rescue. "That will do, that will do, young lady. Too many sugar plums are not good for him. His music isn't bad, but I hope he will do as well in more important things. Going? Well, I'm much obliged to you, and I hope you'll come again. My respects to your mother. Good night, Doctor Jo."

He shook hands kindly, but looked as if something did not please him. When they got into the hall, Jo asked Laurie if she had said anything amiss. He shook his head.

"No, it was me; he doesn't like to hear me play."

"Why not?"

"I'll tell you someday. John is going home with you, as I can't."

"No need of that; I am not a young lady, and it's only a step. Take care of yourself, won't you?"

"Yes; but you will come again, I hope?"

"If you promise to come and see us after you are well."

"I will."

"Good night, Laurie!"

"Good night, Jo, good night!"

When all the afternoon's adventures had been told, the family felt inclined to go visiting in a body, for each found something very attractive in the big house on the other side of the hedge. Mrs. March wanted to talk of her father with the old man who had not forgotten him; Meg longed to walk in the conservatory; Beth sighed for the grand piano; and Amy was eager to see the fine pictures and statues.

"Mother, why didn't Mr. Laurence like to have Laurie play?" asked Jo, who was of an inquiring disposition.

"I am not sure, but I think it was because his son, Laurie's father, married an Italian lady, a musician, which displeased the old man, who is very proud. The lady was good and lovely and accomplished, but he did not like her, and never saw his son after he married. They both died when Laurie was a little child, and then his grandfather took him home. I fancy the boy, who was born in Italy, is not very strong, and the old man is afraid of losing him, which makes him so careful. Laurie comes naturally by his love of music, for he is like his mother, and I dare say his grandfather fears that he may want to be a musician; at any rate, his skill reminds him of the woman he did not like, and so he 'glowered,' as Jo said."

"Dear me, how romantic!" exclaimed Meg.

"How silly!" said Jo. "Let him be a musician, if he wants to, and not plague his life out sending him to college, when he hates to go."

"That's why he has such handsome black eyes and pretty manners, I suppose. Italians are always nice," said Meg, who was a little sentimental.

"What do you know about his eyes and his manners? You never spoke to him, hardly," cried Jo, who was *not* sentimental.

"I saw him at the party, and what you tell shows that he knows how to behave. That was a nice little speech about the medicine mother sent him."

"He meant the blancmange, I suppose."

"How stupid you are, child! He meant you, of course."

"Did he?" and Jo opened her eyes as if it had never occurred to her before.

"I never saw such a girl! You don't know a compliment when you get it," said Meg, with the air of a young lady who knew all about the matter.

"I think they are great nonsense, and I'll thank you not to be silly, and spoil my fun. Laurie's a nice boy, and I like him, and I won't have any sentimental stuff about compliments and such rubbish. We'll all be good to him, because he hasn't got any mother, and he *may* come over and see us, mayn't he, Marmee?"

"Yes, Jo, your little friend is very welcome, and I hope Meg will remember that children should be children as long as they can."

"I don't call myself a child, and I'm not in my teens yet," observed Amy. "What do you say, Beth?"

"I was thinking about our Pilgrim's Progress," answered Beth, who had not heard a word. "How we got out of the Slough and through the Wicket Gate by resolving to be good, and up the steep hill by trying; and that maybe the house over there, full of splendid things, is going to be our Palace Beautiful."

"We have got to get by the lions first," said Jo, as if she rather liked the prospect.

CHAPTER SIX

Beth Finds the Palace Beautiful

THE big house did prove a Palace Beautiful, though it took some time for all to get in, and Beth found it very hard to pass the lions. Old Mr. Laurence was the biggest one; but after he had called, said something funny or kind to each one of the girls, and talked over old times with their mother, nobody felt much afraid of him, except timid Beth. The other lion was the fact that they were poor and Laurie rich; for this made them shy of accepting favors which they could not return. But, after a while, they found that he considered them the benefactors, and could not do enough to show how grateful he was for Mrs. March's motherly welcome, their cheerful society, and the comfort he took in that humble home of theirs

So they soon forgot their pride, and interchanged kindnesses without stopping to think which was the greater.

All sorts of pleasant things happened about that time, for the new friendship flourished like grass in spring. Everyone liked Laurie, and he privately informed his tutor that the Marches were "regularly splendid girls." With the delightful enthusiasm of youth, they took the solitary boy into their midst, and made much of him, and he found something very charming in the innocent companionship of these simple-hearted girls. Never having known mother or sisters, he was quick to feel the influences they brought about him; and their busy, lively ways made him ashamed of the indolent life he led. He was tired of books, and found people so interesting now that Mr. Brooke was obliged to make very unsatisfactory reports; for Laurie was always playing truant, and running over to the Marches'.

"Never mind; let him take a holiday, and make it up afterwards," said the old gentleman. "The good lady next door says he is studying too hard, and needs young society, amusement, and exercise. I suspect she is right, and that I've been coddling the fellow as if I'd been his grandmother. Let him do what he likes, so long as he is happy. He can't get into mischief in that little nunnery over there; and Mrs. March is doing more for him than we can."

What good times they had, to be sure! Such plays and tableaux, such sleigh rides and skating frolics, such pleasant evenings in the old parlor, and now and then such gay little parties at the great house. Meg could walk in the conservatory whenever she liked, and revel in bouquets; Jo browsed over the new library voraciously, and convulsed the old gentleman with her criticisms; Amy copied pictures, and enjoyed beauty to her heart's content; and Laurie played "lord of the manor" in the most delightful style.

But Beth, though yearning for the grand piano, could not pluck up courage to go to the "Mansion of Bliss," as Meg called it. She went once with Jo; but the old gentleman, not being aware of her infirmity, stared at her so hard from under his heavy eyebrows, and said "Hey!" so loud, that he frightened her so much her "feet chattered on the floor," she told her mother; and she ran away, declaring she would never go there any more, not even for the dear piano. No persuasions or enticements could overcome her fear, till, the fact coming to Mr. Laurence's ears in some mysterious way, he set about mending matters. During one of the brief calls he made, he artfully led the conversation to music, and talked away about great singers whom he had seen, fine organs he had heard, and told such charming anecdotes that Beth found it impossible to stay in her distant corner, but crept nearer and nearer, as if fascinated. At the back of his chair she stopped, and stood listening, with her great eyes wide open, and her cheeks red with the excitement of this unusual performance. Taking no more notice of her than if she had been a fly, Mr. Laurence talked on about Laurie's lessons and teachers; and presently, as if the idea had just occurred to him, he said to Mrs. March:

"The boy neglects his music now, and I'm glad of it, for he was getting too fond of it. But the piano suffers for want of use. Wouldn't some of your girls like to run over, and practice on it now and then, just to keep it in tune, you know, ma'am?"

Beth took a step forward, and pressed her hands tightly together to keep from clapping them, for this was an irresistible temptation; and the thought of practicing on that splendid instrument quite took her breath away. Before Mrs. March could reply, Mr. Laurence went on with an odd little nod and smile:

"They needn't see or speak to anyone, but run in at any time; for I'm shut up in my study at the other end of the house, Laurie is out a great deal, and the servants are never near the drawing room after nine o'clock."

Here he rose, as if going, and Beth made up her mind to speak, for that last arrangement left nothing to be desired. "Please tell the young ladies what I say; and if they don't care to come, why, never mind." Here a little hand slipped into his, and Beth looked up at him with a face full of gratitude, as she said, in her earnest yet timid way:

"Oh, sir, they do care, very, very much!"

"Are you the musical girl?" he asked, without any startling "Hey!" as he looked down at her kindly.

"I'm Beth. I love it dearly, and I'll come, if you are quite sure nobody will hear me—and be disturbed," she added, fearing to be rude, and trembling at her own boldness as she spoke.

"Not a soul, my dear. The house is empty half the day; so come, and drum away as much as you like, and I shall be obliged to you."

"How kind you are, sir!"

Beth blushed like a rose under the friendly look he wore; but she was not frightened now, and gave the big hand a grateful squeeze, because she had no words to thank him for the precious gift he had given her. The old gentleman softly stroked the hair off her forehead, and, stooping down, he kissed her, saying, in a tone few people ever heard:

"I had a little girl once, with eyes like these. God bless you, my dear! Good day, madam," and away he went, in a great hurry.

Beth had a rapture with her mother, and then rushed up to impart the glorious news to her family of invalids, as the girls were not at home. How blithely she sung that evening, and how they all laughed at her, because she woke Amy in the night by playing the piano on her face in her sleep. Next day, having seen both the old and young gentleman out of the house, Beth, after two or three retreats, fairly got in at the side door, and made her way, as noiselessly as any mouse, to the drawing room, where her idol stood. Quite by accident, of course, some pretty, easy music lay on the piano; and, with trembling fingers, and frequent stops to listen and look about, Beth at last touched the great instrument, and straightway forgot her fear, herself, and everything else but the unspeakable delight which the music gave her, for it was like the voice of a beloved friend.

She stayed till Hannah came to take her home to dinner; but she had no appetite, and could only sit and smile upon everyone in a general state of beatitude.

After that, the little brown hood slipped through the hedge nearly every day, and the great drawing room was haunted by a tuneful spirit that came and went unseen. She never knew that Mr. Laurence often opened his study door to hear the old-fashioned airs he liked; she never saw Laurie mount guard in the hall to warn the servants away; she never sus-

pected that the exercise books and new songs which she found
in the rack were put there for her especial benefit; and when
he talked to her about music at home, she only thought how
kind he was to tell things that helped her so much. So she enjoyed herself heartily, and found, what isn't always the case,
that her granted wish was all she had hoped. Perhaps it was
because she was so grateful for this blessing that a greater
was given her; at any rate, she deserved both.

"Mother, I'm going to work Mr. Laurence a pair of slippers.
He is so kind to me, I must thank him, and I don't know any
other way. Can I do it?" asked Beth, a few weeks after that
eventful call of his.

"Yes, dear. It will please him very much, and be a nice way
of thanking him. The girls will help you about them, and I
will pay for the making up," replied Mrs. March, who took
peculiar pleasure in granting Beth's requests, because she so
seldom asked anything for herself.

After many serious discussions with Meg and Jo, the pattern was chosen, the materials bought, and the slippers begun.
A cluster of grave yet cheerful pansies, on a deeper purple
ground, was pronounced very appropriate and pretty; and
Beth worked away early and late, with occasional lifts over
hard parts. She was a nimble little needlewoman, and they
were finished before anyone got tired of them. Then she wrote
a very short, simple note, and, with Laurie's help, got them
smuggled onto the study table one morning before the old
gentleman was up.

When this excitement was over, Beth waited to see what
would happen. All that day passed, and a part of the next, before any acknowledgment arrived, and she was beginning to
fear she had offended her crochety friend. On the afternoon of
the second day, she went out to do an errand, and give poor
Joanna, the invalid doll, her daily exercise. As she came up the
street, on her return, she saw three, yes, four, heads popping
in and out of the parlor windows, and the moment they saw
her, several hands were waved, and several joyful voices
screamed:

"Here's a letter from the old gentleman! Come quick, and
read it!"

"Oh, Beth, he's sent you—" began Amy, gesticulating with unseemly energy; but she got no further, for Jo quenched her by slamming down the window.

Beth hurried on in a flutter of suspense. At the door, her sisters seized and bore her to the parlor in a triumphal procession, all pointing, and all saying at once, "Look there! look there!" Beth did look, and turned pale with delight and surprise; for there stood a little cabinet piano, with a letter lying on the glossy lid, directed, like a signboard, to "Miss Elizabeth March."

"For me?" gasped Beth, holding on to Jo, and feeling as if she should tumble down, it was such an overwhelming thing altogether.

"Yes; all for you, my precious! Isn't it splendid of him? Don't you think he's the dearest old man in the world? Here's the key in the letter. We didn't open it, but we are dying to know what he says," cried Jo, hugging her sister, and offering the note.

"You read it! I can't, I feel so queer! Oh, it is too lovely!" and Beth hid her face in Jo's apron, quite upset by her present.

Jo opened the paper, and began to laugh, for the first words she saw were:

MISS MARCH:

 Dear Madam—

"How nice it sounds! I wish someone would write to me so!" said Amy, who thought the old-fashioned address very elegant.

"I have had many pairs of slippers in my life, but I never had any that suited me so well as yours," continued Jo. "Heart's-ease is my favorite flower, and these will always remind me of the gentle giver. I like to pay my debts; so I know you will allow 'the old gentleman' to send you something which once belonged to the little granddaughter he lost. With hearty thanks and best wishes, I remain

 "Your grateful friend and humble servant,

 "JAMES LAURENCE.

"There, Beth, that's an honor to be proud of, I'm sure!

Laurie told me how fond Mr. Laurence used to be of the child who died, and how he kept her little things carefully. Just think, he's given you her piano. That comes of having big blue eyes, and loving music," said Jo, trying to soothe Beth, who trembled and looked more excited than she had ever been before.

"See the cunning brackets to hold candles, and the nice green silk, puckered up, with a gold rose in the middle, and the pretty rack and stool, all complete," added Meg, opening the instrument and displaying its beauties.

" 'Your humble servant, James Laurence'; only think of his writing that to you. I'll tell the girls. They'll think it's splendid," said Amy, much impressed by the note.

"Try it, honey. Let's hear the sound of the baby pianny," said Hannah, who always took a share in the family joys and sorrows.

So Beth tried it; and everyone pronounced it the most remarkable piano ever heard. It had evidently been newly tuned and put in apple-pie order; but, perfect as it was, I think the real charm of it lay in the happiest of all happy faces which leaned over it, as Beth lovingly touched the beautiful black and white keys and pressed the bright pedals.

"You'll have to go and thank him," said Jo, by way of a joke; for the idea of the child's really going never entered her head.

"Yes, I mean to. I guess I'll go now, before I get frightened thinking about it." And, to the utter amazement of the assembled family, Beth walked deliberately down the garden, through the hedge, and in at the Laurences' door.

"Well, I wish I may die if it ain't the queerest thing I ever see! The pianny has turned her head! She'd never have gone in her right mind," cried Hannah, staring after her, while the girls were rendered quite speechless by the miracle.

They would have been still more amazed if they had seen what Beth did afterward. If you will believe me, she went and knocked at the study door before she gave herself time to think; and when a gruff voice called out. "Come in!" she did go in, right up to Mr. Laurence, who looked quite taken aback, and held out her hand, saying, with only a small quaver in her voice, "I came to thank you, sir, for—" But she didn't finish; for he looked so friendly that she forgot her speech, and, only remembering that he had lost the little girl he loved, she put both her arms round his neck, and kissed him.

If the roof of the house had suddenly flown off, the old gentleman wouldn't have been more astonished; but he liked it—oh, dear, yes, he liked it amazingly!—and was so touched and pleased by that confiding little kiss that all his crustiness vanished; and he just set her on his knee, and laid his wrinkled cheek against her rosy one, feeling as if he had got his own little granddaughter back again. Beth ceased to fear him from that moment, and sat there talking to him as cozily as if she had known him all her life; for love casts out fear, and gratitude can conquer pride. When she went home, he walked with her to her own gate, shook hands cordially, and touched his hat as he marched back again, looking very stately and erect, like a handsome, soldierly old gentleman, as he was.

When the girls saw that performance, Jo began to dance a jig, by way of expressing her satisfaction; Amy nearly fell out of the window in her surprise; and Meg exclaimed, with up-lifted hands, "Well, I do believe the world is coming to an end!"

CHAPTER SEVEN

Amy's Valley of Humiliation

"THAT boy is a perfect Cyclops, isn't he?" said Amy, one day, as Laurie clattered by on horseback, with a flourish of his whip as he passed.

"How dare you say so, when he's got both his eyes? And very handsome ones they are, too," cried Jo, who resented any slighting remarks about her friend.

"I didn't say anything about his eyes, and I don't see why you need fire up when I admire his riding."

"Oh, my goodness, that little goose means a centaur, and she called him a Cyclops," exclaimed Jo, with a burst of laughter.

"You needn't be so rude; it's only a 'lapse of lingy,' as Mr. Davis says," retorted Amy, finishing Jo with her Latin. "I just

wish I had a little of the money Laurie spends on that horse,"
she added, as if to herself, yet hoping her sisters would hear.

"Why?" asked Meg kindly, for Jo had gone off in another
laugh at Amy's second blunder.

"I need it so much; I'm dreadfully in debt, and it won't be
my turn to have the rag money for a month."

"In debt, Amy? What do you mean?" and Meg looked sober.

"Why, I owe at least a dozen pickled limes, and I can't pay
them, you know, till I have money, for Marmee forbade my
having anything charged at the shop."

"Tell me all about it. Are limes the fashion now? It used to
be pricking bits of rubber to make balls," and Meg tried to
keep her countenance, Amy looked so grave and important.

"Why, you see, the girls are always buying them, and unless
you want to be thought mean, you must do it, too. It's nothing but limes now, for everyone is sucking them in their desks
in schooltime, and trading them off for pencils, bead rings,
paper dolls, or something else, at recess. If one girl likes another, she gives her a lime; if she's mad with her, she eats one
before her face, and don't offer even a suck. They treat by
turns; and I've had ever so many, but haven't returned them;
and I ought, for they are debts of honor, you know."

"How much will pay them off, and restore your credit?"
asked Meg, taking out her purse.

"A quarter would more than do it, and leave a few cents
over for a treat for you. Don't you like limes?"

"Not much; you may have my share. Here's the money.
Make it last as long as you can, for it isn't very plenty, you
know."

"Oh, thank you! It must be so nice to have pocket money!
I'll have a grand feast, for I haven't tasted a lime this week. I
felt delicate about taking any, as I couldn't return them, and
I'm actually suffering for one."

Next day Amy was rather late at school; but could not
resist the temptation of displaying, with pardonable pride, a
moist brown-paper parcel, before she consigned it to the in-
most recesses of her desk. During the next few minutes the
rumor that Amy March had got twenty-four delicious limes
(she ate one on the way), and was going to treat, circulated

through her "set," and the attentions of her friends became quite overwhelming. Katy Brown invited her to her next party on the spot; Mary Kingsley insisted on lending her her watch till recess; and Jenny Snow, a satirical young lady, who had basely twitted Amy upon her limeless state, promptly buried the hatchet and offered to furnish answers to certain appalling sums. But Amy had not forgotten Miss Snow's cutting remarks about "some persons whose noses were not too flat to smell other people's limes, and stuck-up people, who were not too proud to ask for them"; and she instantly crushed "that Snow girl's" hopes by the withering telegram: "You needn't be so polite all of a sudden, for you won't get any."

A distinguished personage happened to visit the school that morning, and Amy's beautifully drawn maps received praise, which honor to her foe rankled in the soul of Miss Snow, and caused Miss March to assume the airs of a studious young peacock. But, alas, alas! pride goes before a fall, and the revengeful Snow turned the tables with disastrous success. No sooner had the guest paid the usual stale compliments, and bowed himself out, than Jenny, under pretense of asking an important question, informed Mr. Davis, the teacher, that Amy March had pickled limes in her desk.

Now Mr. Davis had declared limes a contraband article, and solemnly vowed to publicly ferrule the first person who was found breaking the law. This much-enduring man had succeeded in banishing chewing gum after a long and stormy war, had made a bonfire of the confiscated novels and newspapers, had suppressed a private post office, had forbidden distortions of the face, nicknames, and caricatures, and done all that one man could do to keep half a hundred rebellious girls in order. Boys are trying enough to human patience, goodness knows, but girls are infinitely more so, especially to nervous gentlemen, with tyrannical tempers, and no more talent for teaching than Dr. Blimber. Mr. Davis knew any quantity of Greek, Latin, algebra, and ologies of all sorts, so he was called a fine teacher; and manners, morals, feelings, and examples were not considered of any particular importance. It was a most unfortunate moment for denouncing Amy, and Jenny knew it. Mr. Davis had evidently taken his coffee too strong that morning; there was an east wind, which always affected his neuralgia; and his pupils had not done him the credit which he felt he deserved; therefore, to use the expressive, if not elegant, language of a schoolgirl, "he was as nervous as a witch and as cross as a bear." The word "limes" was like fire to powder; his yellow face flushed, and he rapped on his desk with an energy which made Jenny skip to her seat with unusual rapidity.

"Young ladies, attention, if you please!"

At the stern order the buzz ceased, and fifty pairs of blue, black, gray, and brown eyes were obediently fixed upon his awful countenance.

"Miss March, come to the desk."

Amy rose to comply with outward composure, but a secret fear oppressed her, for the limes weighed upon her conscience.

"Bring with you the limes you have in your desk," was the unexpected command which arrested her before she got out of her seat.

"Don't take all," whispered her neighbor, a young lady of great presence of mind.

Amy hastily shook out half a dozen, and laid the rest down before Mr. Davis, feeling that any man possessing a human heart would relent when that delicious perfume met his nose. Unfortunately, Mr. Davis particularly detested the odor of the fashionable pickle, and disgust added to his wrath.

"Is that all?"

"Not quite," stammered Amy.

"Bring the rest immediately."

With a despairing glance at her set, she obeyed.

"You are sure there are no more?"

"I never lie, sir."

"So I see. Now take these disgusting things two by two, and throw them out of the window."

There was a simultaneous sigh, which created quite a little gust, as the last hope fled, and the treat was ravished from their longing lips. Scarlet with shame and anger, Amy went to and fro six dreadful times; and as each doomed couple— looking oh! so plump and juicy—fell from her reluctant hands, a shout from the street completed the anguish of the girls, for it told them that their feast was being exulted over by the little Irish children, who were their sworn foes. This—this was too much; all flashed indignant or appealing glances at the inexorable Davis, and one passionate lime lover burst into tears.

As Amy returned from her last trip, Mr. Davis gave a portentous "Hem!" and said, in his most impressive manner: "Young ladies, you remember what I said to you a week ago. I am sorry this has happened, but I never allow my rules to be infringed, and I *never* break my word. Miss March, hold out your hand."

Amy started, and put both hands behind her, turning on him an imploring look which pleaded for her better than the words she could not utter. She was rather a favorite with "old Davis," as, of course, he was called, and it's my private belief that he *would* have broken his word if the indignation of one irrepressible young lady had not found vent in a hiss. That hiss, faint as it was, irritated the irascible gentleman, and sealed the culprit's fate.

"Your hand, Miss March!" was the only answer her mute appeal received; and, too proud to cry or beseech, Amy set her teeth, threw back her head defiantly, and bore without flinching several tingling blows on her little palm. They were neither many nor heavy, but that made no difference to her. For the first time in her life she had been struck; and the disgrace, in her eyes, was as deep as if he had knocked her down.

"You will now stand on the platform till recess," said Mr. Davis, resolved to do the thing thoroughly, since he had begun.

That was dreadful. It would have been bad enough to go to her seat, and see the pitying faces of her friends, or the satisfied ones of her few enemies; but to face the whole school, with that shame fresh upon her, seemed impossible, and for a second she felt as if she could only drop down where she stood, and break her heart with crying. A bitter sense of wrong, and the thought of Jenny Snow, helped her to bear it; and, taking the ignominious place, she fixed her eyes on the stove funnel above what now seemed a sea of faces, and stood there, so motionless and white that the girls found it very hard to study with that pathetic figure before them.

During the fifteen minutes that followed, the proud and sensitive little girl suffered a shame and pain which she never forgot. To others it might seem a ludicrous or trivial affair, but to her it was a hard experience; for during the twelve years of her life she had been governed by love alone, and a blow of that sort had never touched her before. The smart of her hand and the ache of her heart were forgotten in the sting of the thought:

"I shall have to tell at home, and they will be so disappointed in me!"

The fifteen minutes seemed an hour; but they came to an end at last, and the word "Recess!" had never seemed so welcome to her before.

"You can go, Miss March," said Mr. Davis, looking, as he felt, uncomfortable.

He did not soon forget the reproachful glance Amy gave him, as she went, without a word to anyone, straight into the anteroom, snatched her things, and left the place "forever," as she passionately declared to herself. She was in a sad state when she got home; and when the older girls arrived, some time later, an indignation meeting was held at once. Mrs. March did not say much, but looked disturbed, and comforted her afflicted little daughter in her tenderest manner. Meg bathed the insulted hand with glycerine and tears; Beth felt that even her beloved kittens would fail as a balm for griefs like this; Jo wrathfully proposed that Mr. Davis be arrested without delay; and Hannah shook her fist at the "villain," and pounded potatoes for dinner as if she had him under her pestle.

No notice was taken of Amy's flight, except by her mates; but the sharp-eyed demoiselles discovered that Mr. Davis was quite benignant in the afternoon, also unusually nervous. Just before school closed, Jo appeared, wearing a grim expression, as she stalked up to the desk, and delivered a letter from her mother; then collected Amy's property, and departed, carefully scraping the mud from her boots on the door mat as if she shook the dust of the place off her feet.

"Yes, you can have a vacation from school, but I want you to study a little every day, with Beth," said Mrs. March, that evening. "I don't approve of corporal punishment, especially for girls. I dislike Mr. Davis's manner of teaching, and don't think the girls you associate with are doing you any good, so I shall ask your father's advice before I send you anywhere else."

"That's good! I wish all the girls would leave, and spoil his old school. It's perfectly maddening to think of those lovely limes," sighed Amy, with the air of a martyr.

"I am not sorry you lost them, for you broke the rules, and deserved some punishment for disobedience," was the severe reply, which rather disappointed the young lady, who expected nothing but sympathy.

"Do you mean you are glad I was disgraced before the whole school?" cried Amy.

"I should not have chosen that way of mending a fault," replied her mother, "but I'm not sure that it won't do you more good than a milder method. You are getting to be rather conceited, my dear, and it is quite time you set about correcting it. You have a good many little gifts and virtues, but there is no need of parading them, for conceit spoils the finest genius. There is not much danger that real talent or goodness will be overlooked long; even if it is, the consciousness of possessing and using it well should satisfy one, and the great charm of all power is modesty."

"So it is!" cried Laurie, who was playing chess in a corner with Jo. "I knew a girl, once, who had a really remarkable talent for music, and she didn't know it; never guessed what sweet little things she composed when she was alone, and wouldn't have believed it if anyone had told her."

"I wish I'd known that nice girl; maybe she would have helped me, I'm so stupid," said Beth, who stood beside him, listening eagerly.

"You do know her, and she helps you better than anyone else could," answered Laurie, looking at her with such mischievous meaning in his merry black eyes that Beth suddenly turned very red, and hid her face in the sofa cushion, quite overcome by such an unexpected discovery.

Jo let Laurie win the game, to pay for that praise of her Beth, who could not be prevailed upon to play for them after her compliment. So Laurie did his best, and sung delightfully, being in a particularly lovely humor, for to the Marches he seldom showed the moody side of his character. When he was gone, Amy, who had been pensive all the evening, said suddenly, as if busy over some new idea:

"Is Laurie an accomplished boy?"

"Yes; he has had an excellent education, and has much talent; he will make a fine man, if not spoilt by petting," replied her mother.

"And he isn't conceited, is he?" asked Amy.

"Not in the least; that is why he is so charming, and we all like him so much."

"I see; it's nice to have accomplishments, and be elegant; but not to show off, or get perked up," said Amy thoughtfully.

"These things are always seen and felt in a person's manner and conversation, if modestly used; but it is not necessary to display them," said Mrs. March.

"Any more than it's proper to wear all your bonnets and gowns and ribbons at once, that folks may know you've got them," added Jo, and the lecture ended in a laugh.

CHAPTER EIGHT

Jo Meets Apollyon

"GIRLS, where are you going?" asked Amy, coming into their room one Saturday afternoon, and finding them getting ready to go out, with an air of secrecy which excited her curiosity.

"Never mind; little girls shouldn't ask questions," returned Jo sharply.

Now if there *is* anything mortifying to our feelings, when we are young, it is to be told that; and to be bidden to "run away, dear," is still more trying to us. Amy bridled up at this insult, and determined to find out the secret, if she teased for an hour. Turning to Meg, who never refused her anything very long, she said coaxingly, "Do tell me! I should think you might let me go, too; for Beth is fussing over her piano, and I haven't got anything to do, and am *so* lonely."

"I can't, dear, because you aren't invited," began Meg, but Jo broke in impatiently, "Now, Meg, be quiet, or you will spoil it all. You can't go, Amy; so don't be a baby, and whine about it."

"You are going somewhere with Laurie, I know you are; you were whispering and laughing together, on the sofa, last night, and you stopped when I came in. Aren't you going with him?"

"Yes, we are; now do be still, and stop bothering."

Amy held her tongue, but used her eyes, and saw Meg slip a fan into her pocket.

"I know! I know! You're going to the theater to see the 'Seven Castles'!" she cried; adding resolutely, "and I *shall* go, for mother said I might see it; and I've got my rag money, and it was mean not to tell me in time."

"Just listen to me a minute and be a good child," said Meg soothingly. "Mother doesn't wish you to go this week, because your eyes are not well enough yet to bear the light of this fairy piece. Next week you can go with Beth and Hannah, and have a nice time."

"I don't like that half as well as going with you and Laurie. Please let me; I've been sick with this cold so long, and shut up, I'm dying for some fun. Do, Meg! I'll be ever so good," pleaded Amy, looking as pathetic as she could.

"Suppose we take her. I don't believe mother would mind, if we bundle her up well," began Meg.

"If she goes, I shan't, and if I don't Laurie won't like it; and it will be very rude, after he invited only us, to go and drag in Amy. I should think she'd hate to poke herself where she isn't wanted," said Jo crossly, for she disliked the trouble of overseeing a fidgety child, when she wanted to enjoy herself.

Her tone and manner angered Amy, who began to put her boots on, saying, in her most aggravating way, "I *shall* go; Meg says I may; and if I pay for myself, Laurie hasn't anything to do with it."

"You can't sit with us, for our seats are reserved, and you mustn't sit alone; so Laurie will give you his place, and that will spoil our pleasure; or he'll get another seat for you, and

that isn't proper, when you weren't asked. You shan't stir a
step; so you may just stay where you are," scolded Jo, crosser
than ever, having just pricked her finger in her hurry.

Sitting on the floor, with one boot on, Amy began to cry,
and Meg to reason with her, when Laurie called from below
and the two girls hurried down, leaving their sister wailing;
for now and then she forgot her grown-up ways, and acted
like a spoilt child. Just as the party was setting out, Amy called
over the banisters, in a threatening tone, "You'll be sorry for
this, Jo March; see if you ain't."

"Fiddlesticks," returned Jo, slamming the door.

They had a charming time, for "The Seven Castles of the
Diamond Lake" were as brilliant and wonderful as heart could
wish. But, in spite of the comical red imps, sparkling elves,
and gorgeous princes and princesses, Jo's pleasure had a drop
of bitterness in it; the fairy queen's yellow curls reminded her
of Amy; and between the acts she amused herself with wondering what her sister would do to make her "sorry for it."
She and Amy had had many lively skirmishes in the course
of their lives, for both had quick tempers and were apt to be
violent when fairly roused. Amy teased Jo and Jo irritated
Amy, and semioccasional explosions occurred, of which both
were much ashamed afterward. Although the older, Jo had
the least self-control, and had hard times trying to curb the
fiery spirit which was continually getting her into trouble; her
anger never lasted long, and, having humbly confessed her
fault, she sincerely repented and tried to do better. Her sisters
used to say that they rather liked to get Jo into a fury, because
she was such an angel afterward. Poor Jo tried desperately to
be good, but her bosom enemy was always ready to flame up
and defeat her; and it took years of patient effort to subdue it.

When they got home, they found Amy reading in the parlor. She assumed an injured air as they came in; never lifted
her eyes from her book or asked a single question. Perhaps curiosity might have conquered resentment, if Beth had not been
there to inquire, and receive a glowing description of the play.
On going up to put away her best hat, Jo's first look was toward the bureau; for, in their last quarrel, Amy had soothed
her feelings by turning Jo's top drawer upside down on the

floor. Everything was in its place, however; and after a hasty glance into her various closets, bags and boxes, Jo decided that Amy had forgiven and forgotten her wrongs.

There Jo was mistaken; for next day she made a discovery which produced a tempest. Meg, Beth, and Amy were sitting together, late in the afternoon, when Jo burst into the room, looking excited, and demanding breathlessly, "Has anyone taken my book?"

Meg and Beth said "No," at once, and looked surprised; Amy poked the fire, and said nothing. Jo saw her color rise, and was down upon her in a minute.

"Amy, you've got it!"

"No, I haven't."

"You know where it is, then!"

"No, I don't."

"That's a fib!" cried Jo, taking her by the shoulders, and looking fierce enough to frighten a much braver child than Amy.

"It isn't. I haven't got it, don't know where it is now, and don't care."

"You know something about it, and you'd better tell at once, or I'll make you," and Jo gave her a slight shake.

"Scold as much as you like, you'll never see your silly old book again," cried Amy, getting excited in her turn.

"Why not?"

"I burnt it up."

"What! My little book I was so fond of, and worked over, and meant to finish before father got home? Have you really burnt it?" said Jo, turning very pale, while her eyes kindled and her hands clutched Amy nervously.

"Yes, I did! I told you I'd make you pay for being so cross yesterday, and I have, so—"

Amy got no further for Jo's hot temper mastered her, and she shook Amy till her teeth chattered in her head; crying, in a passion of grief and anger:

"You wicked, wicked girl! I never can write it again, and I'll never forgive you as long as I live."

Meg flew to rescue Amy, and Beth to pacify Jo, but Jo was quite beside herself; and with a parting box on her sister's ear she rushed out of the room up to the old sofa in the garret, and finished her fight alone.

The storm cleared up below, for Mrs. March came home, and, having heard the story, soon brought Amy to a sense of the wrong she had done her sister. Jo's book was the pride of her heart, and was regarded by her family as a literary sprout of great promise. It was only half a dozen little fairy tales, but Jo had worked over them patiently, putting her whole heart into her work, hoping to make something good enough to print. She had just copied them with great care, and had destroyed the old manuscript, so that Amy's bonfire had consumed the loving work of several years. It seemed a small loss to others, but to Jo it was a dreadful calamity, and she felt that it never could be made up to her. Beth mourned as for a departed kitten, and Meg refused to defend her pet; Mrs. March looked grave and grieved, and Amy felt that no one would love her till she had asked pardon for the act which she now regretted more than any of them.

When the tea bell rang, Jo appeared, looking so grim and unapproachable that it took all Amy's courage to say meekly:

"Please forgive me, Jo; I'm very, very sorry."

"I never shall forgive you" was Jo's stern answer; and, from that moment, she ignored Amy entirely.

No one spoke of the great trouble—not even Mrs. March —for all had learned by experience that when Jo was in that mood words were wasted; and the wisest course was to wait till some little accident or her own generous nature softened Jo's resentment, and healed the breach. It was not a happy evening; for, though they sewed as usual, while their mother read aloud from Bremer, Scott, or Edgeworth, something was wanting, and the sweet home peace was disturbed. They felt this most when singing time came; for Beth could only play, Jo stood dumb as a stone, and Amy broke down, so Meg and mother sung alone. But, in spite of their efforts to be as cheery as larks, the flutelike voices did not seem to chord as well as usual, and all felt out of tune.

As Jo received her good-night kiss, Mrs. March whispered gently:

"My dear, don't let the sun go down upon your anger; forgive each other, help each other, and begin again tomorrow."

Jo wanted to lay her head down on that motherly bosom and cry her grief and anger all away; but tears were an unmanly weakness, and she felt so deeply injured that she really *couldn't* quite forgive yet. So she winked hard, shook her head, and said, gruffly because Amy was listening:

"It was an abominable thing, and she don't deserve to be forgiven."

With that she marched off to bed, and there was no merry or confidential gossip that night.

Amy was much offended that her overtures of peace had been repulsed, and began to wish she had not humbled herself, to feel more injured than ever, and to plume herself on her superior virtue in a way which was particularly exasperating. Jo still looked like a thundercloud, and nothing went well all day. It was bitter cold in the morning; she dropped her precious turnover in the gutter, Aunt March had an attack of fidgets, Meg was pensive, Beth *would* look grieved and wistful when she got home, and Amy kept making remarks about people who were always talking about being good, and yet wouldn't try, when other people set them a virtuous example.

"Everybody is so hateful, I'll ask Laurie to go skating. He is always kind and jolly, and will put me to rights, I know," said Jo to herself, and off she went.

Amy heard the clash of skates, and looked out with an impatient exclamation:

"There! She promised I should go next time, for this is the last ice we shall have. But it's no use to ask such a crosspatch to take me."

"Don't say that; you *were* very naughty, and it *is* hard to forgive the loss of her precious little book; but I think she might do it now, and I guess she will, if you try her at the right minute," said Meg. "Go after them; don't say anything till Jo has got good-natured with Laurie, then take a quiet minute, and just kiss her, or do some kind thing, and I'm sure she'll be friends again, with all her heart."

"I'll try," said Amy, for the advice suited her; and, after a flurry to get ready, she ran after the friends, who were just disappearing over the hill.

It was not far to the river, but both were ready before Amy reached them. Jo saw her coming, and turned her back; Laurie did not see, for he was carefully skating along the shore, sounding the ice, for a warm spell had preceded the cold snap.

"I'll go on to the first bend, and see if it's all right, before we begin to race," Amy heard him say, as he shot away, looking like a young Russian, in his fur-trimmed coat and cap.

Jo heard Amy panting after her run, stamping her feet and blowing her fingers, as she tried to put her skates on; but Jo never turned, and went slowly zigzagging down the river, taking a bitter, unhappy sort of satisfaction in her sister's troubles. She had cherished her anger till it grew strong, and took possession of her, as evil thoughts and feelings always do, unless cast out at once. As Laurie turned the bend, he shouted back:

"Keep near the shore; it is not safe in the middle."

Jo heard, but Amy was just struggling to her feet, and did not catch a word. Jo glanced over her shoulder, and the little demon she was harboring said in her ear:

"No matter whether she heard or not, let her take care of herself."

Laurie had vanished round the bend; Jo was just at the turn, and Amy, far behind, striking out toward the smoother ice in the middle of the river. For a minute Jo stood still, with a strange feeling at her heart; then she resolved to go on, but something held and turned her round, just in time to see Amy throw up her hands and go down, with the sudden crash of rotten ice, the splash of water, and a cry that made Jo's heart stand still with fear. She tried to call Laurie, but her voice was gone; she tried to rush forward, but her feet seemed to have no strength in them; and, for a second, she could only stand motionless, staring, with a terror-stricken face, at the little blue hood above the black water. Something rushed swiftly by her, and Laurie's voice cried out:

"Bring a rail; quick, quick!"

How she did it, she never knew; but for the next few minutes she worked as if possessed, blindly obeying Laurie, who was quite self-possessed, and, lying flat, held Amy up by his arm and hockey, till Jo dragged a rail from the fence, and together they got the child out, more frightened than hurt.

"Now then, we must walk her home as fast as we can; pile our things on her, while I get off these confounded skates," cried Laurie, wrapping his coat round Amy, and tugging away at the straps, which never seemed so intricate before.

Shivering, dripping, and crying, they got Amy home; and, after an exciting time of it, she fell asleep, rolled in blankets, before a hot fire. During the bustle Jo had scarcely spoken; but flown about, looking pale and wild, with her things half off, her dress torn, and her hands cut and bruised by ice and rails, and refractory buckles. When Amy was comfortably asleep, the house quiet, and Mrs. March sitting by the bed, she called Jo to her, and began to bind up the hurt hands.

"Are you sure she is safe?" whispered Jo, looking remorsefully at the golden head, which might have been swept away from her sight forever under the treacherous ice.

"Quite safe, dear; she is not hurt, and won't even take cold, I think, you were so sensible in covering and getting her home quickly," replied her mother cheerfully.

"Laurie did it all; I only let her go. Mother, if she *should* die, it would be my fault"; and Jo dropped down beside the bed, in a passion of penitent tears, telling all that had happened, bitterly condemning her hardness of heart, and sobbing out her gratitude for being spared the heavy punishment which might have come upon her.

"It's my dreadful temper! I try to cure it; I think I have, and then it breaks out worse than ever. Oh, mother, what shall I do? What shall I do?" cried poor Jo, in despair.

"Watch and pray, dear; never get tired of trying; and never think it is impossible to conquer your fault," said Mrs. March, drawing the blowzy head to her shoulder and kissing the wet cheek so tenderly that Jo cried harder than ever.

"You don't know, you can't guess how bad it is! It seems as if I could do anything when I'm in a passion; I get so savage, I could hurt anyone, and enjoy it. I'm afraid I *shall* do something dreadful someday, and spoil my life, and make everybody hate me. Oh, mother, help me, do help me!"

"I will, my child, I will. Don't cry so bitterly, but remember this day and resolve, with all your soul, that you will never know another like it. Jo, dear, we all have our temptations, some far greater than yours, and it often takes us all our lives to conquer them. You think your temper is the worst in the world; but mine used to be just like it."

"Yours, mother? Why, you are never angry!" and, for the moment, Jo forgot remorse in surprise.

"I've been trying to cure it for forty years, and have only succeeded in controlling it. I am angry nearly every day of my life, Jo; but I have learned not to show it; and I still hope to learn not to feel it, though it may take me another forty years to do so."

The patience and the humility of the face she loved so well was a better lesson to Jo than the wisest lecture, the sharpest reproof. She felt comforted at once by the sympathy and confidence given her; the knowledge that her mother had a fault like hers, and tried to mend it, made her own easier to bear and strengthened her resolution to cure it; though forty years seemed rather a long time to watch and pray, to a girl of fifteen.

"Mother, are you angry when you fold your lips tight together, and go out of the room sometimes, when Aunt March scolds or people worry you?" asked Jo, feeling nearer and dearer to her mother than ever before.

"Yes, I've learned to check the hasty words that rise to my lips; and when I feel that they mean to break out against my will, I just go away a minute, and give myself a little shake, for being so weak and wicked," answered Mrs. March, with a sigh and a smile, as she smoothed and fastened up Jo's disheveled hair.

"How did you learn to keep still? That is what troubles me—for the sharp words fly out before I know what I'm about; and the more I say the worse I get, till it is a pleasure to hurt people's feelings, and say dreadful things. Tell me how you do it, Marmee dear."

"My good mother used to help me—"

"As you do us—" interrupted Jo, with a grateful kiss.

"But I lost her when I was a little older than you are, and for years had to struggle on alone, for I was too proud to confess my weakness to anyone else. I had a hard time, Jo, and shed a good many bitter tears over my failures; for, in spite of my efforts, I never seemed to get on. Then your father came, and I was so happy that I found it easy to be good. But by and by, when I had four little daughters round me, and we were poor, then the old trouble began again; for I am not patient by nature, and it tried me very much to see my children wanting anything."

"Poor mother! What helped you then?"

"Your father, Jo. He never loses patience—never doubts or complains—but always hopes, and works, and waits so cheerfully that one is ashamed to do otherwise before him. He helped and comforted me, and showed me that I must try to practice all the virtues I would have my little girls possess, for I was their example. It was easier to try for your sakes than for my own; a startled or surprised look from one of you, when I spoke sharply, rebuked me more than any words could have done; and the love, respect, and confidence of my children was the sweetest reward I could receive for my efforts to be the woman I would have them copy."

"Oh, mother, if I'm ever half as good as you I shall be satisfied," cried Jo, much touched.

"I hope you will be a great deal better, dear; but you must keep watch over your 'bosom enemy,' as father calls it, or it may sadden, if not spoil your life. You have had a warning;

remember it, and try with heart and soul to master this quick
temper, before it brings you greater sorrow and regret than
you have known today."

"I will try, mother; I truly will. But you must help me, remind me, and keep me from flying out. I used to see father
sometimes put his fingers on his lips, and look at you with a
very kind but sober face, and you always folded your lips tight
or went away: was he reminding you then?" asked Jo softly.

"Yes; I asked him to help me so, and he never forgot it,
but saved me from many a sharp word by that little gesture
and kind look."

Jo saw that her mother's eyes filled and her lips trembled,
as she spoke; and, fearing that she had said too much, she
whispered anxiously, "Was it wrong to watch you, and to speak
of it? I didn't mean to be rude, but it's so comfortable to say
all I think to you, and feel so safe and happy here."

"My Jo, you may say anything to your mother, for it is my
greatest happiness and pride to feel that my girls confide in
me, and know how much I love them."

"I thought I'd grieved you."

"No, my dear; but speaking of father reminded me how
much I miss him, how much I owe him, and how faithfully I
should watch and work to keep his little daughters safe and
good for him."

"Yet you told him to go, mother, and didn't cry when he
went, and never complain now, or seem as if you needed any
help," said Jo, wondering.

"I gave my best to the country I love, and kept my tears
till he was gone. Why should I complain, when we both have
merely done our duty and will surely be the happier for it in
the end? If I don't seem to need help, it is because I have a
better friend, even than father, to comfort and sustain me. My
child, the troubles and temptations of your life are beginning,
and may be many; but you can overcome and outlive them all
if you learn to feel the strength and tenderness of your Heavenly Father as you do that of your earthly one. The more you
love and trust Him, the nearer you will feel to Him, and the
less you will depend on human power and wisdom. His love
and care never tire or change, can never be taken from you,

but may become the source of lifelong peace, happiness, and strength. Believe this heartily, and go to God with all your little cares, and hopes, and sins, and sorrows, as freely and confidingly as you come to your mother."

Jo's only answer was to hold her mother close, and, in the silence which followed, the sincerest prayer she had ever prayed left her heart without words; for in that sad, yet happy hour, she had learned not only the bitterness of remorse and despair, but the sweetness of self-denial and self-control; and, led by her mother's hand, she had drawn near to the Friend who welcomes every child with a love stronger than that of any father, tenderer than that of any mother.

Amy stirred, and sighed in her sleep; and, as if eager to begin at once to mend her fault, Jo looked up with an expression on her face which it had never worn before.

"I let the sun go down on my anger; I wouldn't forgive her, and today, if it hadn't been for Laurie, it might have been too late! How could I be so wicked?" said Jo half aloud, as she leaned over her sister, softly stroking the wet hair scattered on the pillow.

As if she heard, Amy opened her eyes, and held out her arms, with a smile that went straight to Jo's heart. Neither said a word, but they hugged one another close, in spite of the blankets, and everything was forgiven and forgotten in one hearty kiss.

CHAPTER NINE

Meg Goes to Vanity Fair

"I DO think it was the most fortunate thing in the world that those children should have the measles just now," said Meg, one April day, as she stood packing the "go abroady" trunk in her room, surrounded by her sisters.

"And so nice of Annie Moffat not to forget her promise. A whole fortnight of fun will be regularly splendid," replied Jo, looking like a windmill, as she folded skirts with her long arms.

"And such lovely weather; I'm so glad of that," added Beth, tidily sorting neck and hair ribbons in her best box, lent for the great occasion.

"I wish I was going to have a fine time, and wear all these nice things," said Amy, with her mouth full of pins, as she artistically replenished her sister's cushion.

"I wish you were all going; but, as you can't, I shall keep my adventures to tell you when I come back. I'm sure it's the least I can do, when you have been so kind, lending me things, and helping me get ready," said Meg, glancing round the room at the very simple outfit, which seemed nearly perfect in her eyes.

"What did mother give you out of the treasure box?" asked Amy, who had not been present at the opening of a certain cedar chest, in which Mrs. March kept a few relics of past splendor, as gifts for her girls when the proper time came.

"A pair of silk stockings, that pretty carved fan, and a lovely blue sash. I wanted the violet silk; but there isn't time to make it over, so I must be contented with my old tarlatan."

"It will look nicely over my new muslin skirt, and the sash will set it off beautifully. I wish I hadn't smashed my coral bracelet, for you might have had it," said Jo, who loved to give and lend, but whose possessions were usually too dilapidated to be of much use.

"There is a lovely old-fashioned pearl set in the treasure box; but mother said real flowers were the prettiest ornament for a young girl, and Laurie promised to send me all I want," replied Meg. "Now, let me see; there's my new gray walking suit—just curl up the feather in my hat, Beth—then my poplin, for Sunday, and the small party—it looks heavy for spring, doesn't it? The violet silk would be so nice; oh, dear!"

"Never mind; you've got the tarlatan for the big party, and you always look like an angel in white," said Amy, brooding over the little store of finery in which her soul delighted.

"It isn't low-necked, and it doesn't sweep enough, but it will have to do. My blue house dress looks so well, turned and freshly trimmed, that I feel as if I'd got a new one. My silk sacque isn't a bit the fashion, and my bonnet doesn't look like Sallie's; I didn't like to say anything, but I was sadly disappointed in my umbrella. I told mother black, with a white handle, but she forgot, and bought a green one, with a yellowish handle. It's strong and neat, so I ought not to complain, but I know I shall feel ashamed of it beside Annie's silk one with a gold top," sighed Meg, surveying the little umbrella with great disfavor.

"Change it," advised Jo.

"I won't be so silly, or hurt Marmee's feelings, when she took so much pains to get my things. It's a nonsensical notion of mine, and I'm not going to give up to it. My silk stockings and two pairs of new gloves are my comfort. You are a dear, to lend me yours, Jo. I feel so rich, and sort of elegant, with two new pairs, and the old ones cleaned up for common"; and Meg took a refreshing peep at her glove box.

"Annie Moffat has blue and pink bows on her nightcaps; would you put some on mine?" she asked, as Beth brought up a pile of snowy muslins, fresh from Hannah's hands.

"No, I wouldn't; for the smart caps won't match the plain gowns, without any trimming on them. Poor folks shouldn't rig," said Jo decidedly.

"I wonder if I shall *ever* be happy enough to have real lace on my clothes, and bows on my caps?" said Meg impatiently.

"You said the other day that you'd be perfectly happy if you could only go to Annie Moffat's," observed Beth, in her quiet way.

"So I did! Well, I *am* happy, and I won't *fret;* but it does seem as if the more one gets the more one wants, doesn't it? There, now, the trays are ready, and everything in but my ball dress, which I shall leave for mother to pack," said Meg, cheering up, as she glanced from the half-filled trunk to the many-times pressed and mended white tarlatan, which she called her "ball dress," with an important air.

The next day was fine, and Meg departed, in style, for a fortnight of novelty and pleasure. Mrs. March had consented to the visit rather reluctantly, fearing that Margaret would come back more discontented than she went. But she had begged so hard, and Sallie had promised to take good care of her, and a little pleasure seemed so delightful after a winter of irksome work, that the mother yielded, and the daughter went to take her first taste of fashionable life.

The Moffats *were* very fashionable, and simple Meg was rather daunted, at first, by the splendor of the house and the elegance of its occupants. But they were kindly people, in spite of the frivolous life they led, and soon put their guest at her ease. Perhaps Meg felt, without understanding why, that they were not particularly cultivated or intelligent people, and that all their gilding could not quite conceal the ordinary material of which they were made. It certainly was agreeable to fare sumptuously, drive in a fine carriage, wear her best frock every day, and do nothing but enjoy herself. It suited her exactly; and soon she began to imitate the manners and conversation of those about her; to put on little airs and graces, use French phrases, crimp her hair, take in her dresses, and talk about the fashions as well as she could. The more she saw of Annie Moffat's pretty things, the more she envied her and sighed to be rich. Home now looked bare and dismal as she thought of it, work grew harder than ever, and she felt that she was a very destitute and much-injured girl, in spite of the new gloves and silk stockings.

She had not much time for repining, however, for the three young girls were busily employed in "having a good time." They shopped, walked, rode, and called all day; went to theaters and operas, or frolicked at home in the evening; for Annie had many friends, and knew how to entertain them. Her older sisters were very fine young ladies, and one was engaged, which was extremely interesting and romantic, Meg thought. Mr. Moffat was a fat, jolly old gentleman, who knew her father; and Mrs. Moffat, a fat jolly old lady, who took as great a fancy to Meg as her daughter had done. Everyone petted her; and "Daisy," as they called her, was in a fair way to have her head turned.

When the evening for the "small party" came, she found that the poplin wouldn't do at all, for the other girls were putting on thin dresses, and making themselves very fine indeed; so out came the tarlatan, looking older, limper, and shabbier than ever beside Sallie's crisp new one. Meg saw the girls glance at it and then at one another, and her cheeks began to burn, for, with all her gentleness, she was very proud. No one said a word about it, but Sallie offered to dress her hair, and Annie to tie her sash, and Belle, the engaged sister, praised her white arms; but in their kindness Meg saw only pity for her poverty, and her heart felt very heavy as she stood by herself, while the others laughed, chattered, and flew about like gauzy butterflies. The hard, bitter feeling was getting pretty bad, when the maid brought in a box of flowers. Before she could speak, Annie had the cover off, and all were exclaiming at the lovely roses, heath, and fern within.

"It's for Belle, of course; George always sends her some, but these are altogether ravishing," cried Annie, with a great sniff.

"They are for Miss March, the man said. And here's a note," put in the maid, holding it out to Meg.

"What fun! Who are they from? Didn't know you had a lover," cried the girls, fluttering about Meg in a high state of curiosity and surprise.

"The note is from mother, and the flowers from Laurie," said Meg simply, yet much gratified that he had not forgotten her.

"Oh, indeed!" said Annie, with a funny look, as Meg slipped the note into her pocket, as a sort of talisman against envy, vanity, and false pride; for the few loving words had done her good, and the flowers cheered her up by their beauty.

Feeling almost happy again, she laid by a few ferns and roses for herself, and quickly made up the rest in dainty bouquets for the breasts, hair, or skirts of her friends, offering them so prettily that Clara, the older sister, told her she was "the sweetest little thing she ever saw," and they looked quite charmed with her small attention. Somehow the kind act finished her despondency; and when all the rest went to show themselves to Mrs. Moffat, she saw a happy, bright-eyed face in the mirror, as she laid her ferns against her rippling hair, and fastened the roses in the dress that didn't strike her as so *very* shabby now.

She enjoyed herself very much that evening, for she danced to her heart's content; everyone was very kind, and she had three compliments. Annie made her sing, and someone said she had a remarkably fine voice; Major Lincoln asked who "the fresh little girl, with the beautiful eyes" was; and Mr. Moffat insisted on dancing with her, because she "didn't dawdle, but had some spring in her," as he gracefully expressed it. So, altogether, she had a very nice time, till she overheard a bit of a conversation which disturbed her extremely. She was sitting just inside the conservatory, waiting for her partner to bring her an ice, when she heard a voice ask, on the other side of the flowery wall:

"How old is he?"

"Sixteen or seventeen, I should say," replied another voice.

"It would be a grand thing for one of those girls, wouldn't it? Sallie says they are very intimate now, and the old man quite dotes on them."

"Mrs. M. has made her plans, I dare say, and will play her cards well, early as it is. The girl evidently doesn't think of it yet," said Mrs. Moffat.

"She told that fib about her mamma, as if she did know, and colored up when the flowers came, quite prettily. Poor thing! She'd be so nice if she was only got up in style. Do you think she'd be offended if we offered to lend her a dress for Thursday?" asked another voice.

"She's proud, but I don't believe she'd mind, for that dowdy tarlatan is all she has got. She may tear it tonight, and that will be a good excuse for offering a decent one."

"We'll see. I shall ask young Laurence, as a compliment to her, and we'll have fun about it afterward."

Here Meg's partner appeared, to find her looking much flushed and rather agitated. She *was* proud, and her pride was useful just then, for it helped her hide her mortification, anger, and disgust at what she had just heard; for, innocent and unsuspicious as she was, she could not help understanding the gossip of her friends. She tried to forget it, but could not, and kept repeating to herself "Mrs. M. has made her plans," "that fib about her mamma," and "dowdy tarlatan" till she was ready to cry, and rush home and tell her troubles and ask for advice. As that was impossible, she did her best to seem gay; and being rather excited, she succeeded so well that no one dreamed what an effort she was making. She was very glad when it was all over, and she was quiet in her bed, where she could think and wonder and fume till her head ached and her hot cheeks were cooled by a few natural tears. Those foolish, yet well-meant words had opened a new world to Meg, and much disturbed the peace of the old one, in which, till now, she had lived as happily as a child. Her innocent friendship with Laurie was spoilt by the silly speeches she had overheard; her faith in her mother was a little shaken by the worldly plans attributed to her by Mrs. Moffat, who judged others by herself; and the sensible resolution to be contented with the simple wardrobe which

suited a poor man's daughter was weakened by the unnecessary pity of girls who thought a shabby dress one of the great
est calamities under heaven.

Poor Meg had a restless night, and got up heavy-eyed, unhappy, half resentful toward her friends, and half ashamed of
herself for not speaking out frankly, and setting everything
right. Everybody dawdled that morning and it was noon before
the girls found energy enough even to take up their worsted
work. Something in the manner of her friends struck Meg at
once; they treated her with more respect, she thought; took
quite a tender interest in what she said, and looked at her with
eyes that plainly betrayed curiosity. All this surprised and flattered her, though she did not understand it till Miss Belle
looked up from her writing, and said, with a sentimental air:

"Daisy dear, I've sent an invitation to your friend, Mr.
Laurence, for Thursday. We should like to know him, and it's
only a proper compliment to you."

Meg colored, but a mischievous fancy to tease the girls
made her reply demurely:

"You are very kind, but I'm afraid he won't come."

"Why not, *chérie?*" asked Miss Belle.

"He's too old."

"My child, what do you mean? What is his age, I beg to
know!" cried Miss Clara.

"Nearly seventy, I believe," answered Meg, counting stitches
to hide the merriment in her eyes.

"You sly creature! Of course we meant the young man," exclaimed Miss Belle, laughing.

"There isn't any; Laurie is only a little boy," and Meg
laughed also at the queer look which the sisters exchanged as
she thus described her supposed lover.

"About your age," Nan said.

"Nearer my sister Jo's; *I* am seventeen in August," returned
Meg, tossing her head.

"It's very nice of him to send you flowers, isn't it?" said
Annie, looking wise about nothing.

"Yes, he often does, to all of us; for their house is full, and
we are so fond of them. My mother and old Mr. Laurence are
friends, you know, so it is quite natural that we children should
play together," and Meg hoped they would say no more.

"It's evident Daisy isn't out yet," said Miss Clara to Belle, with a nod.

"Quite a pastoral state of innocence all around," returned Miss Belle, with a shrug.

"I'm going out to get some little matters for my girls; can I do anything for you, young ladies?" asked Mrs. Moffat, lumbering in, like an elephant, in silk and lace.

"No, thank you, ma'am," replied Sallie. "I've got my new pink silk for Thursday, and don't want a thing."

"Nor I—" began Meg, but stopped, because it occurred to her that she *did* want several things, and could not have them.

"What shall you wear?" asked Sallie.

"My old white one again, if I can mend it fit to be seen; it got sadly torn last night," said Meg, trying to speak quite easily, but feeling very uncomfortable.

"Why don't you send home for another?" said Sallie, who was not an observing young lady.

"I haven't got any other." It cost Meg an effort to say that, but Sallie did not see it, and exclaimed, in amiable surprise:

"Only that? How funny—" She did not finish her speech, for Belle shook her head at her, and broke in, saying kindly:

"Not at all; where is the use of having a lot of dresses when she isn't out? There's no need of sending home, Daisy, even if you had a dozen, for I've got a sweet blue silk laid away, which I've outgrown, and you shall wear it, to please me, won't you, dear?"

"You are very kind, but I don't mind my old dress, if you don't; it does well enough for a little girl like me," said Meg.

"Now do let me please myself by dressing you up in style. I admire to do it, and you'd be a regular little beauty, with a touch here and there. I shan't let anyone see you till you are done, and then we'll burst upon them like Cinderella and her godmother, going to the ball," said Belle, in her persuasive tone.

Meg couldn't refuse the offer so kindly made, for a desire to see if she would be "a little beauty" after touching up caused her to accept, and forget all her former uncomfortable feelings toward the Moffats.

On the Thursday evening, Belle shut herself up with her maid; and, between them, they turned Meg into a fine lady.

They crimped and curled her hair, they polished her neck
and arms with some fragrant powder, touched her lips with
coralline salve, to make them redder, and Hortense would
have added "a *soupçon* of rouge," if Meg had not rebelled.
They laced her into a sky-blue dress, which was so tight she
could hardly breathe, and so low in the neck that modest Meg
blushed at herself in the mirror. A set of silver filigree was
added, bracelets, necklace, brooch, and even earrings, for
Hortense tied them on, with a bit of pink silk, which did not
show. A cluster of tea-rose buds at the bosom, and a ruche, reconciled Meg to the display of her pretty white shoulders, and a
pair of high-heeled blue silk boots satisfied the last wish of
her heart. A laced handkerchief, a plumy fan, and a bouquet
in a silver holder finished her off; and Miss Belle surveyed her
with the satisfaction of a little girl with a newly dressed doll.

"Mademoiselle is *charmante, très jolie*, is she not?" cried
Hortense, clasping her hands in an affected rapture.

"Come and show yourself," said Miss Belle, leading the way
to the room where the others were waiting.

As Meg went rustling after, with her long skirts trailing,
her earrings tinkling, her curls waving, and her heart beating,
she felt as if her "fun" had really begun at last, for the mirror
had plainly told her that she *was* "a little beauty." Her friends
repeated the pleasing phrase enthusiastically; and, for several
minutes, she stood, like the jackdaw in the fable, enjoying her
borrowed plumes, while the rest chattered like a party of mag-
pies.

"While I dress, do you drill her, Nan, in the management
of her skirt, and those French heels, or she will trip herself up.
Take your silver butterfly, and catch up that long curl on the
left side of her head, Clara, and don't any of you disturb the
charming work of my hands," said Belle, as she hurried away,
looking well pleased with her success.

"I'm afraid to go down, I feel so queer and stiff and half
dressed," said Meg to Sallie, as the bell rang and Mrs. Moffat
sent to ask the young ladies to appear at once.

"You don't look a bit like yourself, but you are very nice.
I'm nowhere beside you, for Belle has heaps of taste, and
you're quite French, I assure you. Let your flowers hang; don't

be so careful of them, and be sure you don't trip," returned
Sallie, trying not to care that Meg was prettier than herself.

Keeping that warning carefully in mind, Margaret got
safely downstairs, and sailed into the drawing rooms, where
the Moffats and a few early guests were assembled. She very
soon discovered that there is a charm about fine clothes which
attracts a certain class of people, and secures their respect.
Several young ladies, who had taken no notice of her before,
were very affectionate all of a sudden; several young gentlemen, who had only stared at her at the other party, now not
only stared, but asked to be introduced, and said all manner
of foolish but agreeable things to her; and several old ladies,
who sat on sofas and criticized the rest of the party, inquired
who she was, with an air of interest. She heard Mrs. Moffat reply to one of them:

"Daisy March—father a colonel in the army—one of our first
families, but reverses of fortune, you know; intimate friends of
the Laurences; sweet creature, I assure you; my Ned is quite
wild about her."

"Dear me!" said the old lady, putting up her glass for another observation of Meg, who tried to look as if she had not
heard and been rather shocked at Mrs. Moffat's fibs.

The "queer feeling" did not pass away, but she imagined
herself acting the new part of fine lady, and so got on pretty
well, though the tight dress gave her a side-ache, the train
kept getting under her feet, and she was in constant fear lest
her earrings should fly off and get lost or broken. She was flirting her fan, and laughing at the feeble jokes of a young gentleman who tried to be witty, when she suddenly stopped laughing, and looked confused; for, just opposite, she saw Laurie.
He was staring at her with undisguised surprise, and disapproval also, she thought; for, though he bowed and smiled,
yet something in his honest eyes made her blush, and wish she
had her old dress on. To complete her confusion, she saw Belle
nudge Annie, and both glance from her to Laurie, who, she
was happy to see, looked unusually boyish and shy.

"Silly creatures, to put such thoughts into my head! I won't
care for it, or let it change me a bit," thought Meg, and rustled
across the room to shake hands with her friend.

"I'm glad you came, 1 was afraid you wouldn't," she said, with her most grown-up air.

"Jo wanted me to come, and tell her how you looked, so I did," answered Laurie, without turning his eyes upon her, though he half smiled at her maternal tone.

"What shall you tell her?" asked Meg, full of curiosity to know his opinion of her, yet feeling ill at ease with him for the first time.

"I shall say I didn't know you; for you look so grown up and unlike yourself, I'm quite afraid of you," he said, fumbling at his glove button.

"How absurd of you! The girls dressed me up for fun, and I rather like it. Wouldn't Jo stare if she saw me?" said Meg, bent on making him say whether he thought her improved or not.

"Yes, I think she would," returned Laurie gravely.

"Don't you like me so?" asked Meg.

"No, I don't," was the blunt reply.

"Why not?" in an anxious tone.

He glanced at her frizzled head, bare shoulders, and fantastically trimmed dress, with an expression that abashed her more than his answer, which had not a particle of his usual politeness about it.

"I don't like fuss and feathers."

That was altogether too much from a lad younger than herself; and Meg walked away, saying petulantly:

"You are the rudest boy I ever saw."

Feeling very much ruffled, she went and stood at a quiet window, to cool her cheeks, for the tight dress gave her an uncomfortably brilliant color. As she stood there, Major Lincoln passed by; and, a minute after, she heard him saying to his mother:

"They are making a fool of that little girl; I wanted you to see her, but they have spoilt her entirely; she's nothing but a doll, tonight."

"Oh, dear!" sighed Meg, "I wish I'd been sensible, and worn my own things; then I should not have disgusted other people or felt so uncomfortable and ashamed myself."

She leaned her forehead on the cool pane, and stood half hidden by the curtains, never minding that her favorite waltz had begun, till someone touched her; and, turning, she saw Laurie, looking penitent, as he said, with his very best bow, and his hand out:

"Please forgive my rudeness, and come and dance with me."

"I'm afraid it will be too disagreeable to you," said Meg, trying to look offended, and failing entirely.

"Not a bit of it; I'm dying to do it. Come, I'll be good; I don't like your gown, but I do think you are—just splendid," and he waved his hands, as if words failed to express his admiration.

Meg smiled and relented, and whispered, as they stood waiting to catch the time:

"Take care my skirt don't trip you up; it's the plague of my life, and I was a goose to wear it."

"Pin it round your neck, and then it will be useful," said Laurie, looking down at the little blue boots, which he evidently approved of.

Away they went fleetly and gracefully; for, having practiced at home, they were well matched, and the blithe young couple were a pleasant sight to see, as they twirled merrily round and round, feeling more friendly than ever after their small tiff.

"Laurie, I want you to do me a favor; will you?" said Meg, as he stood fanning her, when her breath gave out, which it did very soon, though she would not own why.

"Won't I!" said Laurie, with alacrity.

"Please don't tell them at home about my dress tonight. They won't understand the joke, and it will worry mother."

"Then why did you do it?" said Laurie's eyes, so plainly that Meg hastily added:

"I shall tell them, myself, all about it, and 'fess to mother how silly I've been. But I'd rather do it myself; so you'll not tell, will you?"

"I'll give you my word I won't; only what shall I say when they ask me?"

"Just say I looked pretty well, and was having a good time."

"I'll say the first, with all my heart; but how about the other?

You don't look as if you were having a good time; are you?" and Laurie looked at her with an expression which made her answer, in a whisper:

"No; not just now. Don't think I'm horrid; I only wanted a little fun, but this sort doesn't pay, I find, and I'm getting tired of it."

"Here comes Ned Moffat; what does he want?" said Laurie, knitting his black brows, as if he did not regard his young host in the light of a pleasant addition to the party.

"He put his name down for three dances, and I suppose he's coming for them. What a bore!" said Meg, assuming a languid air, which amused Laurie immensely.

He did not speak to her again till suppertime, when he saw her drinking champagne with Ned and his friend Fisher, who were behaving "like a pair of fools," as Laurie said to himself, for he felt a brotherly sort of right to watch over the Marches, and fight their battles whenever a defender was needed.

"You'll have a splitting headache tomorrow, if you drink much of that. I wouldn't, Meg; your mother doesn't like it, you know," he whispered, leaning over her chair, as Ned turned to refill her glass, and Fisher stooped to pick up her fan.

"I'm not Meg, tonight; I'm 'a doll,' who does all sorts of crazy things. Tomorrow I shall put away my 'fuss and feathers,' and be desperately good again," she answered, with an affected little laugh.

"Wish tomorrow was here, then," muttered Laurie, walking off, ill pleased at the change he saw in her.

Meg danced and flirted, chattered and giggled, as the other girls did; after supper she undertook the german, and blundered through it, nearly upsetting her partner with her long skirt, and romping in a way that scandalized Laurie, who looked on and meditated a lecture. But he got no chance to deliver it, for Meg kept away from him till he came to say good night.

"Remember!" she said, trying to smile, for the splitting headache had already begun.

"Silence à la mort," replied Laurie, with a melodramatic flourish, as he went away.

This little bit of byplay excited Annie's curiosity; but Meg

was too tired for gossip, and went to bed, feeling as if she had
been to a masquerade, and hadn't enjoyed herself as much as
she expected. She was sick all the next day, and on Saturday
went home, quite used up with her fortnight's fun, and feeling
that she had "sat in the lap of luxury" long enough.

"It does seem pleasant to be quiet, and not have company
manners on all the time. Home *is* a nice place, though it isn't
splendid," said Meg, looking about her with a restful expression as she sat with her mother and Jo on the Sunday
evening.

"I'm glad to hear you say so, dear, for I was afraid home
would seem dull and poor to you, after your fine quarters," replied her mother, who had given her many anxious looks that
day, for motherly eyes are quick to see any change in children's faces.

Meg had told her adventures gaily, and said over and over
what a charming time she had had; but something still seemed
to weigh upon her spirits, and, when the younger girls were
gone to bed, she sat thoughtfully staring at the fire, saying
little, and looking worried. As the clock struck nine, and Jo proposed bed, Meg suddenly left her chair, and, taking Beth's
stool, leaned her elbows on her mother's knee, saying bravely:

"Marmee, I want to 'fess."

"I thought so; what is it, dear?"

"Shall I go away?" asked Jo discreetly.

"Of course not; don't I always tell you everything? I was
ashamed to speak of it before the children, but I want you to
know all the dreadful things I did at the Moffats'."

"We are prepared," said Mrs. March, smiling but looking a
little anxious.

"I told you they dressed me up, but I didn't tell you that they
powdered and squeezed and frizzled, and made me look like a
fashion plate. Laurie thought I wasn't proper; I know he did,
though he didn't say so, and one man called me 'a doll.' I knew
it was silly, but they flattered me, and said I was a beauty, and
quantities of nonsense, so I let them make a fool of me."

"Is that all?" asked Jo, as Mrs. March looked silently at the
downcast face of her pretty daughter, and could not find it in
her heart to blame her little follies.

"No; I drank champagne and romped and tried to flirt, and was altogether abominable," said Meg self-reproachfully.

"There is something more, I think," and Mrs. March smoothed the soft cheek, which suddenly grew rosy, as Meg answered slowly:

"Yes; it's very silly, but I want to tell it, because I hate to have people say and think such things about us and Laurie."

Then she told the various bits of gossip she had heard at the Moffats'; and, as she spoke, Jo saw her mother fold her lips tightly, as if ill pleased that such ideas should be put into Meg's innocent mind.

"Well, if that isn't the greatest rubbish I ever heard," cried Jo indignantly. "Why didn't you pop out and tell them so, on the spot?"

"I couldn't, it was so embarrassing for me. I couldn't help hearing, at first, and then I was so angry and ashamed I didn't remember that I ought to go away."

"Just wait till *I* see Annie Moffat, and I'll show you how to settle such ridiculous stuff. The idea of having 'plans,' and being kind to Laurie, because he's rich, and may marry us by and by! Won't he shout, when I tell him what those silly things say about us poor children?" and Jo laughed, as if, on second thoughts, the thing struck her as a good joke.

"If you tell Laurie, I'll never forgive you! She mustn't, must she, mother?" said Meg, looking distressed.

"No; never repeat that foolish gossip, and forget it as soon as you can," said Mrs. March gravely. "I was very unwise to let you go among people of whom I know so little—kind, I dare say, but worldly, ill-bred, and full of these vulgar ideas about young people. I am more sorry than I can express for the mischief this visit may have done you, Meg."

"Don't be sorry, I won't let it hurt me; I'll forget all the bad, and remember only the good; for I did enjoy a great deal, and thank you very much for letting me go. I'll not be sentimental or dissatisfied, mother; I know I'm a silly little girl, and I'll stay with you till I'm fit to take care of myself. But it *is* nice to be praised and admired, and I can't help saying I like it," said Meg, looking half ashamed of the confession.

"That is perfectly natural, and quite harmless, if the liking

does not become a passion and lead one to do foolish or unmaidenly things. Learn to know and value the praise which is
worth having, and to excite the admiration of excellent people
by being modest as well as pretty, Meg."

Margaret sat thinking a moment, while Jo stood with her
hands behind her, looking both interested and a little perplexed; for it was a new thing to see Meg blushing and talking
about admiration, lovers, and things of that sort; and Jo felt
as if, during that fortnight, her sister had grown up amazingly,
and was drifting away from her into a world where she could
not follow.

"Mother, do you have 'plans,' as Mrs. Moffat said?" asked
Meg bashfully.

"Yes, my dear, I have a great many; all mothers do, but mine
differ somewhat from Mrs. Moffat's, I suspect. I will tell you
some of them, for the time has come when a word may set this
romantic little head and heart of yours right, on a very serious
subject. You are young, Meg, but not too young to understand
me; and mothers' lips are the fittest to speak of such things to
girls like you. Jo, your turn will come in time, perhaps, so
listen to my 'plans,' and help me carry them out, if they are
good."

Jo went and sat on one arm of the chair, looking as if she
thought they were about to join in some very solemn affair.
Holding a hand of each, and watching the two young faces
wistfully, Mrs. March said, in her serious yet cheery way:

"I want my daughters to be beautiful, accomplished, and
good; to be admired, loved, and respected; to have a happy
youth, to be well and wisely married, and to lead useful, pleasant lives, with as little care and sorrow to try them as God sees
fit to send. To be loved and chosen by a good man is the best
and sweetest thing which can happen to a woman; and I sincerely hope my girls may know this beautiful experience. It is
natural to think of it, Meg; right to hope and wait for it, and
wise to prepare for it; so that, when the happy time comes, you
may feel ready for the duties and worthy of the joy. My dear
girls, I *am* ambitious for you, but not to have you make a dash
in the world—marry rich men merely because they are rich, or
have splendid houses, which are not homes because love is

wanting. Money is a needful and precious thing—and, when well used, a noble thing—but I never want you to think it is the first or only prize to strive for. I'd rather see you poor men's wives, if you were happy, beloved, contented, than queens on thrones, without self-respect and peace."

"Poor girls don't stand any chance, Belle says, unless they put themselves forward," sighed Meg.

"Then we'll be old maids," said Jo stoutly.

"Right, Jo; better be happy old maids than unhappy wives, or unmaidenly girls, running about to find husbands," said Mrs. March decidedly. "Don't be troubled, Meg; poverty seldom daunts a sincere lover. Some of the best and most honored women I know were poor girls, but so loveworthy that they were not allowed to be old maids. Leave these things to time; make this home happy, so that you may be fit for homes of your own, if they are offered to you, and contented here if they are not. One thing remember, my girls: mother is always ready to be your confidante, father to be your friend; and both of us trust and hope that our daughters, whether married or single, will be the pride and comfort of our lives."

"We will, Marmee, we will!" cried both, with all their hearts, as she bade them good night.

CHAPTER TEN

The P.C. and P.O.

AS spring came on, a new set of amusements became the fashion, and the lengthening days gave long afternoons for work and play of all sorts. The garden had to be put in order, and each sister had a quarter of the little plot to do what she liked with. Hannah used to say, "I'd know which each of them gardings belonged to, ef I see 'em in Chiny," and so she might, for the girls' tastes differed as much as their characters. Meg's had roses and heliotrope, myrtle, and a little orange tree in it. Jo's bed was never alike two seasons, for she was always trying experiments; this year it was to be a plantation of sunflowers, the seeds of which cheerful and aspiring plant were to feed "Aunt Cockle-top" and her family of chicks. Beth had old-fashioned, fragrant flowers in her garden—sweet peas and mignonette, larkspur, pinks, pansies, and southernwood, with chickweed for the bird, and catnip for the pussies. Amy had a bower in hers—rather small and earwiggy, but very pretty to look at—with honeysuckles and morning-glories hanging their colored horns and bells in graceful wreaths all over it; tall, white lilies, delicate ferns, and as many brilliant, picturesque plants as would consent to blossom there.

Gardening, walks, rows on the river, and flower hunts employed the fine days; and for rainy ones, they had house diversions—some old, some new—all more or less original. One of these was the "P.C."; for, as secret societies were the fashion, it was thought proper to have one; and, as all of the girls admired Dickens, they called themselves the Pickwick Club. With a few interruptions, they had kept this up for a year, and met every Saturday evening in the big garret, on which occasion the ceremonies were as follows: Three chairs were arranged in a row before a table, on which was a lamp, also four white badges, with a big "P.C." in different colors on each, and the weekly newspaper, called "The Pickwick Portfolio," to which all contributed something; while Jo, who reveled in pens and ink, was the editor. At seven o'clock, the four members ascended to the clubroom, tied their badges round their heads, and took their seats with great solemnity. Meg, as the eldest, was Samuel Pickwick; Jo, being of a literary turn, Augustus Snodgrass; Beth, because she was round and rosy, Tracy Tupman; and Amy, who was always trying to do what she couldn't, was Nathaniel Winkle. Pickwick, the president, read the paper, which was filled with original tales, poetry, local news, funny advertisements, and hints, in which they good-naturedly reminded each other of their faults and short-comings. On one occasion, Mr. Pickwick put on a pair of spectacles without any glasses, rapped upon the table, hemmed, and, having stared hard at Mr. Snodgrass, who was tilting back in his chair, till he arranged himself properly, began to read:

"The Pickwick Portfolio"

Poet's Corner

ANNIVERSARY ODE

Again we meet to celebrate
  With badge and solemn rite,
Our fifty-second anniversary,
  In Pickwick Hall, tonight.

We all are here in perfect health,
  None gone from our small
    band;
Again we see each well-known
    face,
  And press each friendly hand.

Our Pickwick, always at his post,
  With reverence we greet,
As, spectacles on nose, he reads
  Our well-filled weekly sheet.

Although he suffers from a cold,
  We joy to hear him speak,
For words of wisdom from him
    fall,
  In spite of croak or squeak.

Old six-foot Snodgrass looms on
    high,
  With elephantine grace,
And beams upon the company,
  With brown and jovial face.

Poetic fire lights up his eye,
  He struggles 'gainst his lot.
Behold ambition on his brow,
  And on his nose a blot!

Next our peaceful Tupman comes,
  So rosy, plump, and sweet,
Who chokes with laughter at the
    puns,
  And tumbles off his seat.

Prim little Winkle too is here,
  With every hair in place,
A model of propriety,
  Though he hates to wash his
    face.

The year is gone, we still unite
  To joke and laugh and read,
And tread the path of literature
  That doth to glory lead.

Long may our paper prosper well,
  Our club unbroken be,
And coming years their blessings
    pour
  On the useful, gay "P.C."
                    A. SNODGRASS

THE MASKED MARRIAGE

A TALE OF VENICE

Gondola after gondola swept up to the marble steps, and left its lovely load to swell the brilliant throng that filled the stately halls of Count de Adelon. Knights and ladies, elves and pages, monks and flower girls, all mingled gaily in the dance. Sweet voices and rich melody filled the air; and so with mirth and music the masquerade went on.

"Has your Highness seen the Lady Viola tonight?" asked a gallant troubadour of the fairy queen who floated down the hall upon his arm.

"Yes; is she not lovely, though so sad! Her dress is well chosen, too, for in a week she weds Count Antonio, whom she passionately hates."

"By my faith, I envy him. Yonder he comes, arrayed like a bridegroom, except the black mask. When that is off we shall see how he regards the fair maid whose heart he cannot win, though her stern father bestows her hand," returned the troubadour.

"'Tis whispered that she loves the young English artist who haunts her steps, and is spurned by the old count," said the lady, as they joined the dance.

The revel was at its height when a priest appeared, and, withdrawing the young pair to an alcove hung with purple velvet, he motioned them to kneel. Instant silence fell upon the gay throng; and not a sound, but the dash of fountains or the rustle of orange groves sleeping in the moonlight, broke the hush as Count de Adelon spoke thus:

"My lords and ladies, pardon the ruse by which I have gathered you here to witness the marriage of my daughter. Father, we wait your services."

All eyes turned toward the bridal party, and a low murmur of amazement went through the throng, for neither bride nor groom removed their masks. Curiosity and wonder possessed all hearts, but respect restrained all tongues till the holy rite was over. Then the eager spectators gathered round the count, demanding an explanation.

"Gladly would I give it if I could; but I only know that it was the whim of my timid Viola, and I yielded to it. Now, my children, let the play end. Unmask, and receive my blessing."

But neither bent the knee; for the young bridegroom replied, in a tone that startled all listeners, as the mask fell, disclosing the noble face of Ferdinand Devereux, the artist lover; and, leaning on the breast where now flashed the star of an English earl, was the lovely Viola radiant with joy and beauty.

"My lord, you scornfully bade me claim your daughter when I could boast as high a name and vast a fortune as the Count Antonio. I can do more; for even your ambitious soul cannot refuse the Earl of Devereux and De Vere, when he gives his ancient name and boundless wealth in return for the beloved hand of this fair lady, now my wife."

The count stood like one changed to stone; and, turning to the bewildered crowd, Ferdinand added, with a gay smile of triumph, "To you, my gallant friends, I can only wish that your wooing may prosper as mine has done; and that you may all win as fair a bride as I have, by this masked marriage."

S. PICKWICK

Why is the P.C. like the Tower of Babel? It is full of unruly members.

THE HISTORY OF A SQUASH

Once upon a time a farmer planted a little seed in his garden, and after a while it sprouted and became a vine, and bore many squashes. One day in October, when they were ripe, he picked one and took it to market. A grocerman bought and put it in his shop. That same morning, a little girl, in a brown hat and blue dress, with a round face and snub nose, went and bought it for her mother. She lugged it home, cut it up, and boiled it in the big pot; mashed some of it, with salt and butter, for dinner; and to the rest she added a pint of milk, two eggs, four spoons of sugar, nutmeg, and some crackers; put it in a deep dish, and baked it till it was brown and nice; and next day it was eaten by a family named March.

T. TUPMAN

MR. PICKWICK, *Sir:* —

I address you upon the subject of sin the sinner I mean is a man named Winkle who makes trouble in his club by laughing and sometimes won't write his piece in this fine paper I hope you will pardon his badness and let him send a French fable because he can't write out of his head as he has so many lessons to do and no brains in future I will try to take time by the fetlock and prepare some work which will be all *commy la fo* that means all right I am in haste as it is nearly school time

Yours respectably,

N. WINKLE

[The above is a manly and handsome acknowledgment of past misdemeanors. If our young friend studied punctuation, it would be well.]

THE PUBLIC BEREAVEMENT

It is our painful duty to record the sudden and mysterious disappearance of our cherished friend, Mrs. Snowball Pat Paw. This lovely and beloved cat was the pet of a large circle of warm and admiring friends; for her beauty attracted all eyes, her graces and virtues endeared her to all hearts, and her loss is deeply felt by the whole community.

When last seen, she was sitting at the gate, watching the butcher's cart; and it is feared that some villain, tempted by her charms, basely stole her. Weeks have passed, but no trace of her has been discovered; and we relinquish all hope, tie a black ribbon to her basket, set aside her dish, and weep for her as one lost to us forever.

A sympathizing friend sends the following gem:

A LAMENT
FOR S. B. PAT PAW

We mourn the loss of our little
  pet,
  And sigh o'er her hapless fate,
For never more by the fire she'll
  sit,
  Nor play by the old green
  gate.

The little grave where her infant
  sleeps
Is 'neath the chestnut tree;
But o'er *her* grave we may not
  weep,
We know not where it may be.

Her empty bed, her idle ball,
  Will never see her more;
No gentle tap, no loving purr
  Is heard at the parlor door.

Another cat comes after her
  mice,
  A cat with a dirty face;
But she does not hunt as our
  darling did,
  Nor play with her airy grace.

Her stealthy paws tread the very
  hall
  Where Snowball used to play,
But she only spits at the dogs
  our pet
So gallantly drove away.

She is useful and mild, and does
  her best,
  But she is not fair to see;
And we cannot give her your
  place, dear,
  Nor worship her as we worship thee.

            A. S.

A SAD ACCIDENT

On Friday last, we were startled by a violent shock in our base-
ment, followed by cries of distress.
On rushing, in a body, to the cellar, we discovered our beloved
President prostrate upon the floor,
having tripped and fallen while
getting wood for domestic purposes. A perfect scene of ruin met
our eyes; for in his fall Mr. Pickwick had plunged his head and
shoulders into a tub of water, upset a keg of soft soap upon his
manly form, and torn his garments
badly. On being removed from
this perilous situation, it was discovered that he had suffered no injury but several bruises; and, we
are happy to add, is now doing
well.

           ED.

ADVERTISEMENTS

MISS ORANTHY BLUGGAGE, the
accomplished Strong-Minded Lec-
turer, will deliver her famous
Lecture on "WOMAN AND HER
POSITION," at Pickwick Hall, next
Saturday Evening, after the usual
performances.

A WEEKLY MEETING will be
held at Kitchen Place, to teach
young ladies how to cook. Hannah
Brown will preside; and all are invited to attend.

THE DUSTPAN SOCIETY will
meet on Wednesday next, and parade in the upper story of the Club
House. All members to appear in
uniform and shoulder their brooms
at nine precisely.

MRS. BETH BOUNCER will open
her new assortment of Doll's Millinery next week. The latest Paris
Fashions have arrived, and orders
are respectfully solicited.

A NEW PLAY will appear at the Barnville Theater, in the course of a few weeks, which will surpass anything ever seen on the American stage. "THE GREEK SLAVE, or Constantine the Avenger," is the name of this thrilling drama!!!

HINTS

If S. P. didn't use so much soap on his hands, he wouldn't always be late at breakfast. A. S. is requested not to whistle in the street. T. T., please don't forget Amy's napkin. N. W. must not fret because his dress has not nine tucks.

WEEKLY REPORT

Meg—Good
Jo—Bad
Beth—Very good
Amy—Middling

As the President finished reading the paper (which I beg leave to assure my readers is a *bona fide* copy of one written by *bona fide* girls once upon a time), a round of applause followed, and then Mr. Snodgrass rose to make a proposition.

"Mr. President and gentlemen," he began, assuming a parliamentary attitude and tone, "I wish to propose the admission of a new member—one who highly deserves the honor, would be deeply grateful for it, and would add immensely to the spirit of the club, the literary value of the paper, and be no end jolly and nice. I propose Mr. Theodore Laurence as an honorary member of the P.C. Come now, do have him."

Jo's sudden change of tone made the girls laugh; but all looked rather anxious, and no one said a word, as Snodgrass took his seat.

"We'll put it to vote," said the President. "All in favor of this motion please to manifest it by saying 'Aye.'"

A loud response from Snodgrass, followed, to everybody's surprise, by a timid one from Beth.

"Contrary minded say 'No.'"

Meg and Amy were contrary minded; and Mr. Winkle rose to say, with great elegance, "We don't wish any boys; they only joke and bounce about. This is a ladies' club, and we wish to be private and proper."

"I'm afraid he'll laugh at our paper. and make fun of us afterward," observed Pickwick, pulling the little curl on her forehead, as she always did when doubtful.

Up rose Snodgrass, very much in earnest. "Sir, I give you my word as a gentleman, Laurie won't do anything of the sort. He likes to write, and he'll give a tone to our contributions, and keep us from being sentimental, don't you see? We can do so little for him, and he does so much for us, I think the least we can do is to offer him a place here, and make him welcome if he comes."

This artful allusion to benefits conferred brought Tupman to his feet, looking as if he had quite made up his mind.

"Yes, we ought to do it, even if we *are* afraid. I say he *may* come, and his grandpa, too, if he likes."

This spirited burst from Beth electrified the club, and Jo left her seat to shake hands approvingly. "Now, then, vote again. Everybody remember it's our Laurie, and say 'Aye!'" cried Snodgrass excitedly.

"Aye! aye! aye!" replied three voices at once.

"Good! Bless you! Now, as there's nothing like 'taking time by the *fetlock*,' as Winkle characteristically observes, allow me to present the new member," and, to the dismay of the rest of

the club, Jo threw open the door of the closet, and displayed
Laurie sitting on a rag bag, flushed and twinkling with suppressed laughter.

"You rogue! you traitor! Jo, how could you?" cried the three
girls, as Snodgrass led her friend triumphantly forth; and, producing both a chair and a badge, installed him in a jiffy.

"The coolness of you two rascals is amazing," began Mr.
Pickwick, trying to get up an awful frown, and only succeeding
in producing an amiable smile. But the new member was equal
to the occasion; and, rising, with a grateful salutation to the
Chair, said, in the most engaging manner, "Mr. President and
ladies—I beg pardon, gentlemen—allow me to introduce myself as Sam Weller the very humble servant of the club."

"Good! good!" cried Jo, pounding with the handle of the old
warming pan on which she leaned.

"My faithful friend and noble patron," continued Laurie,
with a wave of the hand, "who has so flatteringly presented
me, is not to be blamed for the base stratagem of tonight. I
planned it, and she only gave in after lots of teasing."

"Come, now, don't lay it all on yourself; you know I proposed the cupboard," broke in Snodgrass, who was enjoying
the joke amazingly.

"Never you mind what she says. I'm the wretch that did it,
sir," said the new member, with a Welleresque nod to Mr.
Pickwick. "But on my honor, I never will do so again, and
henceforth *dewote* myself to the interest of this immortal
club."

"Hear, hear!" cried Jo, clashing the lid of the warming pan
like a cymbal.

"Go on, go on!" added Winkle and Tupman, while the President bowed benignly.

"I merely wish to say that, as a slight token of my gratitude
for the honor done me, and as a means of promoting friendly
relations between adjoining nations, I have set up a post office
in the hedge in the lower corner of the garden; a fine, spacious
building, with padlocks on the doors, and every convenience
for the mails—also the females, if I may be allowed the expression. It's the old martin house; but I've stopped up the
door, and made the roof open, so it will hold all sorts of things,

and save our valuable time. Letters, manuscripts, books, and bundles can be passed in there; and, as each nation has a key, it will be uncommonly nice, I fancy. Allow me to present the club key; and, with many thanks for your favor, take my seat."

Great applause as Mr. Weller deposited a little key on the table and subsided; the warming pan clashed and waved wildly and it was some time before order could be restored. A long discussion followed, and everyone came out surprising, for everyone did her best; so it was an unusually lively meeting, and did not adjourn till a late hour, when it broke up with three shrill cheers for the new member. No one ever regretted the admittance of Sam Weller, for a more devoted, well-behaved, and jovial member no club could have. He certainly did add "spirit" to the meetings, and "a tone" to the paper; for his orations convulsed his hearers, and his contributions were excellent, being patriotic, classical, comical, or dramatic, but never sentimental. Jo regarded them as worthy of Bacon, Milton, or Shakespeare; and remodeled her own works with good effect, she thought.

The P.O. was a capital little institution, and flourished wonderfully, for nearly as many queer things passed through it as through the real office. Tragedies and cravats, poetry and pickles, garden seeds and long letters, music and gingerbread, rubbers, invitations, scoldings and puppies. The old gentleman liked the fun, and amused himself by sending odd bundles, mysterious messages, and funny telegrams; and his gardener, who was smitten with Hannah's charms, actualy sent a love letter to Jo's care. How they laughed when the secret came out, never dreaming how many love letters that little post office would hold in the years to come!

CHAPTER ELEVEN

Experiments

"THE first of June! The Kings are off to the seashore to-morrow, and I'm free. Three months' vacation—how I shall enjoy it!" exclaimed Meg, coming home one warm day to find Jo laid upon the sofa in an unusual state of exhaustion, while Beth took off her dusty boots, and Amy made lemonade for the refreshment of the whole party.

"Aunt March went today, for which, oh, be joyful!" said Jo. "I was mortally afraid she'd ask me to go with her; if she had, I should have felt as if I ought to do it; but Plumfield is about as gay as a churchyard, you know, and I'd rather be excused. We had a flurry getting the old lady off, and I had a fright every time she spoke to me, for I was in such a hurry to be through that I was uncommonly helpful and sweet, and feared she'd find it impossible to part from me. I quaked till she was fairly in the carriage, and had a final fright, for, as it drove off, she popped out her head, saying, 'Josyphine, won't you—?' I didn't hear any more, for I basely turned and fled; I did actually run, and whisked round the corner, where I felt safe."

"Poor old Jo! She came in looking as if bears were after her," said Beth, as she cuddled her sister's feet with a motherly air.

"Aunt March is a regular sampire, is she not?" observed Amy, tasting her mixture critically.

"She means *vampire*, not seaweed; but it doesn't matter; it's too warm to be particular about one's parts of speech," murmured Jo.

"What shall you do all your vacation?" asked Amy, changing the subject, with tact.

"I shall lie abed late, and do nothing," replied Meg, from the depths of the rocking chair. "I've been routed up early all winter, and had to spend my days working for other people; so now I'm going to rest and revel to my heart's content."

"No," said Jo; "that dozy way wouldn't suit me. I've laid in a heap of books, and I'm going to improve my shining hours reading on my perch in the old apple tree, when I'm not having l—"

"Don't say 'larks'!" implored Amy, as a return snub for the "sampire" correction.

"I'll say 'nightingales,' then, with Laurie; that's proper and appropriate, since he's a warbler."

"Don't let us do any lessons, Beth, for a while, but play all the time, and rest, as the girls mean to," proposed Amy.

"Well, I will, if mother doesn't mind. I want to learn some new songs, and my children need fitting up for the summer; they are dreadfully out of order, and really suffering for clothes."

"May we, mother?" asked Meg, turning to Mrs. March, who sat sewing in what they called "Marmee's corner."

"You may try your experiment for a week, and see how you like it. I think by Saturday night you will find that all play and no work is as bad as all work and no play."

"Oh, dear, no! It will be delicious, I'm sure," said Meg complacently.

"I now propose a toast as my 'friend and pardner, Sairy Gamp,' says. Fun forever, and no grubbing!" cried Jo, rising glass in hand, as the lemonade went round.

They all drank it merrily, and began the experiment by lounging for the rest of the day. Next morning, Meg did not appear till ten o'clock; her solitary breakfast did not taste nice, and the room seemed lonely and untidy; for Jo had not filled the vases, Beth had not dusted, and Amy's books lay scattered about. Nothing was neat and pleasant but "Marmee's corner," which looked as usual and there Meg sat, to "rest and read," which meant yawn, and imagine what pretty summer dresses she would get with her salary. Jo spent the morning on the river, with Laurie, and the afternoon reading and crying over "The Wide, Wide World," up in the apple tree. Beth began by rummaging everything out of the big closet where her family resided; but, getting tired before half done, she left her establishment topsy-turvy, and went to her music, rejoicing that she had no dishes to wash. Amy arranged her bower, put on her best white frock, smoothed her curls, and sat down to draw under the honeysuckles, hoping someone would see and inquire who the young artist was. As no one appeared but an inquisitive daddy longlegs, who examined her work with interest, she went to walk, got caught in a shower, and came home dripping.

At teatime they compared notes, and all agreed that it had been a delightful, though unusually long day. Meg, who went shopping in the afternoon, and got a "sweet blue muslin," had discovered after she had cut the breadths off, that it wouldn't wash, which mishap made her slightly cross. Jo had burnt the skin off her nose boating, and got a raging headache by reading too long. Beth was worried by the confusion of her closet, and the difficulty of learning three or four songs at once; and Amy deeply regretted the damage done her frock, for Katy Brown's party was to be the next day; and now, like Flora McFlimsey, she had "nothing to wear." But these were mere trifles; and they assured their mother that the experiment was working finely. She smiled, said nothing, and, with Hannah's help, did their neglected work, keeping home pleasant and the domestic machinery running smoothly. It was astonishing what a peculiar and uncomfortable state of things was produced by the "resting and reveling" process. The days kept getting longer and longer; the weather was unusually variable, and so were tempers; an unsettled feeling possessed everyone, and Satan found plenty of mischief for the idle hands to do. As the height of luxury, Meg put out some of her sewing, and then found time hang so heavily that she fell to snipping and spoiling her clothes, in her attempts to furbish them up à la Moffat. Jo read till her eyes gave out, and she was sick of books; got so fidgety that even good-natured Laurie had a quarrel with her, and so reduced in spirits that she desperately wished she had gone with Aunt March. Beth got on pretty well, for she was constantly forgetting that it was to be *all play, and no work,* and fell back into her old ways now and then; but something in the air affected her, and, more than once, her tranquillity was much disturbed; so much so that, on one occasion, she actually shook poor dear Joanna, and told her she was "a fright." Amy fared worst of all, for her resources were small; and when her sisters left her to amuse and care for herself she soon found that accomplished and important little self a great burden. She didn't like dolls, fairy tales were childish, and one couldn't draw all the time; tea parties didn't amount to much, neither did picnics, unless very well conducted. "If one could have a fine house, full of nice girls, or go traveling, the summer would be delightful; but to stay at home with three selfish sisters and a grown-up boy was enough to try the patience of a Boaz," complained Miss Malaprop, after several days devoted to pleasure, fretting, and ennui.

No one would own that they were tired of the experiment; but by Friday night each acknowledged to herself that she was glad the week was nearly done. Hoping to impress the lesson more deeply, Mrs. March, who had a good deal of humor, resolved to finish off the trial in an appropriate manner; so she gave Hannah a holiday, and let the girls enjoy the full effect of the play system.

When they got up on Saturday morning, there was no fire in the kitchen, no breakfast in the dining room, and no mother anywhere to be seen.

"Mercy on us, what *has* happened?" cried Jo, staring about her in dismay.

Meg ran upstairs, and soon came back again, looking relieved, but rather bewildered, and a little ashamed.

"Mother isn't sick, only very tired, and she says she is going to stay quietly in her room all day, and let us do the best we can. It's a very queer thing for her to do, she doesn't act a bit like herself; but she says it has been a hard week for her, so we mustn't grumble, but take care of ourselves."

"That's easy enough, and I like the idea; I'm aching for something to do—that is, some new amusement, you know," added Jo quickly.

In fact it *was* an immense relief to them all to have a little work, and they took hold with a will, but soon realized the truth of Hannah's saying, "Housekeeping ain't no joke." There was plenty of food in the larder, and while Beth and Amy set the table, Meg and Jo got breakfast, wondering, as they did so, why servants ever talked about hard work.

"I shall take some up to mother, though she said we were not to think of her, for she'd take care of herself," said Meg, who presided and felt quite matronly behind the teapot.

So a tray was fitted out before anyone began, and taken up, with the cook's compliments. The boiled tea was very bitter, the omelette scorched, and the biscuits speckled with saleratus; but Mrs. March received her repast with thanks, and laughed heartily over it after Jo was gone.

"Poor little souls, they will have a hard time, I'm afraid, but they won't suffer, and it will do them good," she said, producing the more palatable viands with which she had provided herself, and disposing of the bad breakfast, so that their feelings might not be hurt—a motherly little deception, for which they were grateful.

Many were the complaints below, and great the chagrin of the head cook at her failures. "Never mind, I'll get the dinner and be servant; you be mistress, keep your hands nice, see company, and give orders," said Jo, who knew still less than Meg about culinary affairs.

This obliging offer was gladly accepted; and Margaret retired to the parlor, which she hastily put in order by whisking

the litter under the sofa, and shutting the blinds, to save the
trouble of dusting. Jo, with perfect faith in her own powers,
and a friendly desire to make up the quarrel, immediately put
a note in the office, inviting Laurie to dinner.

"You'd better see what you have got before you think of
having company," said Meg, when informed of the hospitable
but rash act.

"Oh, there's corned beef and plenty of potatoes; and I shall
get some asparagus, and a lobster, 'for a relish,' as Hannah
says. We'll have lettuce, and make a salad. I don't know how,
but the book tells. I'll have blancmange and strawberries for
dessert; and coffee, too, if you want to be elegant."

"Don't try too many messes, Jo, for you can't make anything
but gingerbread and molasses candy, fit to eat. I wash my
hands of the dinner party; and, since you have asked Laurie
on your own responsibility, you may just take care of him."

"I don't want you to do anything but be civil to him, and
help with the pudding. You'll give me your advice if I get in
a muddle, won't you?" asked Jo, rather hurt.

"Yes; but I don't know much, except about bread, and a few
trifles. You had better ask mother's leave before you order anything," returned Meg prudently.

"Of course I shall; I'm not a fool," and Jo went off in a huff
at the doubts expressed of her powers.

"Get what you like, and don't disturb me; I'm going out to
dinner, and can't worry about things at home," said Mrs.
March, when Jo spoke to her. "I never enjoyed housekeeping,
and I'm going to take a vacation today, and read, write, go
visiting, and amuse myself."

The unusual spectacle of her busy mother rocking comfortably, and reading, early in the morning, made Jo feel as if
some unnatural phenomenon had occurred; for an eclipse, an
earthquake, or a volcanic eruption would hardly have seemed
stranger.

"Everything is out of sorts, somehow," she said to herself,
going downstairs. "There's Beth crying; that's a sure sign that
something is wrong with this family. If Amy is bothering, I'll
shake her."

Feeling very much out of sorts herself, Jo hurried into the

parlor to find Beth sobbing over Pip, the canary, who lay dead in the cage, with his little claws pathetically extended, as if imploring the food for want of which he had died.

"It's all my fault—I forgot him—there isn't a seed or a drop left. Oh, Pip! Oh, Pip! How could I be so cruel to you?" cried Beth, taking the poor thing in her hands and trying to restore him.

Jo peeped into his half-open eye, felt his little heart, and finding him stiff and cold, shook her head, and offered her domino box for a coffin.

"Put him in the oven, and maybe he will get warm and revive," said Amy hopefully.

"He's been starved, and he shan't be baked, now he's dead. I'll make him a shroud, and he shall be buried in the garden; and I'll never have another bird, never, my Pip' For I am too bad to own one," murmured Beth, sitting on the floor with her pet folded in her hands.

"The funeral shall be this afternoon, and we will all go. Now, don't cry, Bethy; it's a pity, but nothing goes right this week, and Pip has had the worst of the experiment. Make the shroud, and lay him in my box; and, after the dinner party, we'll have a nice little funeral," said Jo, beginning to feel as if she had undertaken a good deal.

Leaving the others to console Beth, she departed to the kitchen, which was in a most discouraging state of confusion. Putting on a big apron, she fell to work, and got the dishes piled up ready for washing, when she discovered that the fire was out.

"Here's a sweet prospect!" muttered Jo, slamming the stove door open, and poking vigorously among the cinders.

Having rekindled the fire, she thought she would go to market while the water heated. The walk revived her spirits; and, flattering herself that she had made good bargains, she trudged home again, after buying a very young lobster, some very old asparagus, and two boxes of acid strawberires. By the time she got cleared up, the dinner arrived, and the stove was red hot. Hannah had left a pan of bread to rise, Meg had worked it up early, set it on the hearth for a second rising, and forgotten it. Meg was entertaining Sallie Gardiner in the parlor, when the door flew open, and a floury, crocky, flushed, and disheveled figure appeared, demanding tartly:

"I say, isn't bread 'riz' enough when it runs over the pans?"

Sallie began to laugh; but Meg nodded, and lifted her eyebrows as high as they would go, which caused the apparition to vanish, and put the sour bread into the oven without further delay. Mrs. March went out, after peeping here and there to see how matters went, also saying a word of comfort to Beth, who sat making a winding sheet, while the dear departed lay in state in the domino box. A strange sense of helplessness fell upon the girls as the gray bonnet vanished round the corner; and despair seized them, when, a few minutes later, Miss Crocker appeared, and said she'd come to dinner. Now, this lady was a thin, yellow spinster, with a sharp nose and inquisitive eyes, who saw everything and gossiped about all she saw. They disliked her, but had been taught to be kind to her, simply because she was old and poor, and had few friends. So Meg gave her the easy chair, and tried to entertain her, while she asked questions, criticized everything, and told stories of the people whom she knew.

Language cannot describe the anxieties, experiences, and exertions which Jo underwent that morning; and the dinner she served up became a standing joke. Fearing to ask any more advice, she did her best alone, and discovered that something more than energy and good will is necessary to make a cook. She boiled the asparagus for an hour, and was grieved to find the heads cooked off and the stalks harder than ever. The bread burnt black; for the salad dressing so aggravated her that she let everything else go till she had convinced herself that she could not make it fit to eat. The lobster was a scarlet mystery to her, but she hammered and poked, till it was unshelled, and its meager proportions concealed in a grove of lettuce leaves. The potatoes had to be hurried, not to keep the asparagus waiting, and were not done at last. The blancmange was lumpy, and the strawberries were not as ripe as they looked, having been skillfully "deaconed."

"Well, they can eat beef, and bread and butter, if they are hungry; only it's mortifying to have to spend your whole morning for nothing," thought Jo, as she rang the bell half an hour later than usual, and stood, hot, tired, and dispirited, surveying the feast spread for Laurie, accustomed to all sorts of elegance, and Miss Crocker, whose curious eyes would mark all failures and whose tattling tongue would report them far and wide.

Poor Jo would gladly have gone under the table, as one thing after another was tasted and left; while Amy giggled, Meg looked distressed, Miss Crocker pursed up her lips, and Laurie talked and laughed with all his might, to give a cheerful tone to the festive scene. Jo's one strong point was the fruit, for she had sugared it well, and had a pitcher of rich cream to eat with it. Her hot cheeks cooled a trifle, and she drew a long breath, as the pretty glass plates went round, and everyone looked graciously at the little rosy islands floating in a sea of cream. Miss Crocker tasted first, made a wry face, and drank some water hastily. Jo, who had refused, thinking there might not be enough, for they dwindled sadly after the picking over, glanced at Laurie, but he was eating away manfully, though there was a slight pucker about his mouth, and he kept his eye fixed on his plate. Amy, who was fond of delicate fare, took a heaping spoonful, choked, hid her face in her napkin, and left the table precipitately.

"Oh, what is it?" exclaimed Jo, trembling.

"Salt, instead of sugar, and the cream is sour," replied Meg, with a tragic gesture.

Jo uttered a groan, and fell back in her chair; remembering that she had given a last hasty powdering to the berries out of the two boxes on the kitchen table, and had neglected to put the milk in the refrigerator. She turned scarlet, and was on the verge of crying, when she met Laurie's eyes, which *would* look merry in spite of his heroic efforts; the comical side of the affair suddenly struck her, and she laughed till the tears ran down her cheeks. So did everyone else, even "Croaker," as the girls called the old lady; and the unfortunate dinner ended gaily, with bread and butter, olives and fun.

"I haven't strength of mind enough to clear up now, so we will sober ourselves with a funeral," said Jo, as they rose; and Miss Crocker made ready to go, being eager to tell the new story at another friend's dinner table.

They did sober themselves, for Beth's sake; Laurie dug a grave under the ferns in the grove, little Pip was laid in with many tears, by his tenderhearted mistress, and covered with moss, while a wreath of violets and chickweed was hung on the stone which bore his epitaph, composed by Jo, while she struggled with the dinner:

> *Here lies Pip March,*
> *Who died the 7th of June;*
> *Loved and lamented sore,*
> *And not forgotten soon.*

At the conclusion of the ceremonies, Beth retired to her room, overcome with emotion and lobster; but there was no place of repose, for the beds were not made, and she found her grief much assuaged by beating up pillows and putting things in order. Meg helped Jo clear away the remains of the feast, which took half the afternoon, and left them so tired that they agreed to be contented with tea and toast for supper. Laurie took Amy to drive, which was a deed of charity, for the sour cream seemed to have had a bad effect upon her temper. Mrs. March came home to find the three older girls hard at work in the middle of the afternoon; and a glance at the closet gave her an idea of the success of one part of the experiment.

Before the housewives could rest, several people called, and there was a scramble to get ready to see them; then tea must be got, errands done; and one or two necessary bits of sewing neglected till the last minute. As twilight fell, dewy and still, one by one they gathered in the porch where the June roses were budding beautifully, and each groaned or sighed as she sat down, as if tired or troubled.

"What a dreadful day this has been!" began Jo, usually the first to speak.

"It has seemed shorter than usual, but *so* uncomfortable," said Meg.

"Not a bit like home," added Amy.

"It can't seem so without Marmee and little Pip," sighed Beth, glancing with full eyes at the empty cage above her head.

"Here's mother, dear, and you shall have another bird to-morrow, if you want it."

As she spoke, Mrs. March came and took her place among them, looking as if her holiday had not been much pleasanter than theirs.

"Are you satisfied with your experiment, girls, or do you want another week of it?" she asked, as Beth nestled up to her and the rest turned toward her with brightening faces, as flowers turn toward the sun.

"I don't!" cried Jo decidedly.

"Nor I," echoed the others.

"You think, then, it is better to have a few duties, and live a little for others, do you?"

"Lounging and larking doesn't pay," observed Jo, shaking her head. "I'm tired of it, and mean to go to work at something right off."

"Suppose you learn plain cooking; that's a useful accomplishment, which no woman should be without," said Mrs. March, laughing inaudibly at the recollection of Jo's dinner party, for she had met Miss Crocker and heard her account of it.

"Mother, did you go away and let everything be, just to see how we'd get on?" cried Meg, who had had suspicions all day.

"Yes; I wanted you to see how the comfort of all depends on each doing her share faithfully. While Hannah and I did your work, you got on pretty well, though I don't think you were very happy or amiable; so I thought, as a little lesson, I would show you what happens when everyone thinks only of herself. Don't you feel that it is pleasanter to help one another, to have daily duties which make leisure sweet when it comes, and to bear and forbear, that home may be comfortable and lovely to us all?"

"We do, mother, we do!" cried the girls.

"Then let me advise you to take up your little burdens again; for though they seem heavy sometimes, they are good for us, and lighten as we learn to carry them. Work is wholesome, and there is plenty for everyone; it keeps us from ennui and mischief, is good for health and spirits, and gives us a sense of power and independence better than money or fashion."

"We'll work like bees, and love it too; see if we don't!" said Jo. "I'll learn plain cooking for my holiday task; and the next dinner party I have shall be a success."

"I'll make the set of shirts for father, instead of letting you do it, Marmee. I can and I will, though I'm not fond of sewing; that will be better than fussing over my own things, which are plenty nice enough as they are," said Meg.

"I'll do my lessons every day, and not spend so much time with my music and dolls. I am a stupid thing, and ought to be studying, not playing," was Beth's resolution; while Amy followed their example by heroically declaring, "I shall learn to make buttonholes, and attend to my parts of speech."

"Very good! Then I am quite satisfied with the experiment, and fancy that we shall not have to repeat it; only don't go to the other extreme, and delve like slaves. Have regular hours for work and play; make each day both useful and pleasant, and prove that you understand the worth of time by employing it well. Then youth will be delightful, old age will bring few regrets, and life become a beautiful success, in spite of poverty."

"We'll remember, mother!" and they did.

CHAPTER TWELVE

Camp Laurence

BETH was postmistress, for, being most at home, she could attend to it regularly, and dearly liked the daily task of unlocking the little door and distributing the mail. One July day she came in with her hands full, and went about the house leaving letters and parcels, like the penny post.

"Here's your posy, mother! Laurie never forgets that," she said, putting the fresh nosegay in the vase that stood in "Marmee's corner," and was kept supplied by the affectionate boy.

"Miss Meg March, one letter and a glove," continued Beth, delivering the articles to her sister, who sat near her mother, stitching wristbands.

"Why, I left a pair over there, and here is only one," said Meg, looking at the gray cotton glove.

"Didn't you drop the other in the garden?"

"No, I'm sure I didn't; for there was only one in the office."

"I hate to have odd gloves! Never mind, the other may be found. My letter is only a translation of the German song I wanted; I think Mr. Brooke did it, for that isn't Laurie's writing."

Mrs. March glanced at Meg, who was looking very pretty in her gingham morning gown, with the little curls blowing about her forehead, and very womanly, as she sat sewing at her little worktable, full of tidy white rolls; so unconscious of the thought in her mother's mind as she sewed and sung, while her fingers flew, and her thoughts were busied with girlish fancies as innocent and fresh as the pansies in her belt, that Mrs. March smiled, and was satisfied.

"Two letters for Doctor Jo, a book, and a funny old hat which covered the whole post office, stuck outside," said Beth, laughing, as she went into the study where Jo sat writing.

"What a sly fellow Laurie is! I said I wished bigger hats were the fashion, because I burn my face every hot day. He said, 'Why mind the fashion? Wear a big hat, and be comfortable!' I said I would if I had one, and he has sent me this, to try me. I'll wear it, for fun, and show him I *don't* care for the fashion," and, hanging the antique broad-brim on a bust of Plato, Jo read her letters.

One from her mother made her cheeks glow and her eyes fill, for it said to her:

My DEAR:

I write a little word to tell you with how much satisfaction I watch your efforts to control your temper. You say nothing about your trials, failures, or successes, and think, perhaps, that no one sees them but the Friend whose help you daily ask, if I may trust the well-worn cover of your guidebook. I, too, have seen them all, and heartily believe in the sincerity of your resolution, since it begins to bear fruit. Go on, dear, patiently and bravely, and always believe that no one sympathizes more tenderly with you than your loving

MOTHER

"That does me good; that's worth millions of money and

pecks of praise. Oh, Marmee, I do try! I will keep on trying,
and not get tired, since I have you to help me."

Laying her head on her arms, Jo wet her little romance
with a few happy tears, for she *had* thought that no one saw
and appreciated her efforts to be good; and this assurance was
doubly precious, doubly encouraging, because unexpected,
and from the person whose commendation she most valued.
Feeling stronger than ever to meet and subdue her Apollyon,
she pinned the note inside her frock, as a shield and a reminder, lest she be taken unaware, and proceeded to open her
other letter, quite ready for either good or bad news. In a big,
dashing hand, Laurie wrote:

DEAR JO,
    What ho!
    Some English girls and boys are coming to see me tomor-
row and I want to have a jolly time. If it's fine, I'm going to
pitch my tent in Longmeadow, and row up the whole crew
to lunch and croquet—have a fire, make messes, gypsy fashion,
and all sorts of larks. They are nice people, and like such
things. Brooke will go, to keep us boys steady, and Kate
Vaughn will play propriety for the girls. I want you all to
come; can't let Beth off, at any price, and nobody shall worry
her. Don't bother about rations—I'll see to that, and everything else—only do come, there's a good fellow!
    In a tearing hurry,
                                          Yours ever,
                                                    LAURIE

"Here's richness!" cried Jo, flying in to tell the news to Meg.
"Of course we can go, mother? It will be such a help to
Laurie, for I can row, and Meg can see to the lunch, and the
children be useful in some way."

"I hope the Vaughns are not fine, grown-up people. Do you
know anything about them, Jo?" asked Meg.

"Only that there are four of them. Kate is older than you,
Fred and Frank (twins) about my age, and a little girl
(Grace) who is nine or ten. Laurie knew them abroad, and
liked the boys; I fancied, from the way he primmed up his

mouth in speaking of her, that he didn't admire Kate much."

"I'm so glad my French print is clean; it's just the thing, and
so becoming!" observed Meg complacently. "Have you anything decent, Jo?"

"Scarlet and gray boating suit, good enough for me. I shall
row and tramp about, so I don't want any starch to think of.
You'll come, Betty?"

"If you won't let any of the boys talk to me."

"Not a boy!"

"I like to please Laurie; and I'm not afraid of Mr. Brooke,
he is so kind; but I don't want to play, or sing, or say anything.
I'll work hard, and not trouble anyone; and you'll take care of
me, Jo, so I'll go."

"That's my good girl; you do try to fight off your shyness,
and I love you for it. Fighting faults isn't easy, as I know; and
a cheery word kind of gives a lift. Thank you, mother," and
Jo gave the thin cheek a grateful kiss, more precious to Mrs.
March than if it had given back the rosy roundness of her
youth.

"I had a box of chocolate drops, and the picture I wanted
to copy," said Amy, showing her mail.

"And I got a note from Mr. Laurence, asking me to come
over and play to him tonight, before the lamps are lighted,
and I shall go," added Beth, whose friendship with the old
gentleman prospered finely.

"Now let's fly around, and do double duty today, so that we
can play tomorrow with free minds," said Jo, preparing to replace her pen with a broom.

When the sun peeped into the girls' room early next morning, to promise them a fine day, he saw a comical sight. Each
had made such preparation for the fete as seemed necessary
and proper. Meg had an extra row of little curl papers across
her forehead, Jo had copiously anointed her afflicted face with
cold cream. Beth had taken Joanna to bed with her to atone
for the approaching separation, and Amy had capped the climax by putting a clothespin on her nose, to uplift the offending feature. It was one of the kind artists use to hold the paper
on their drawing boards, therefore quite appropriate and effective for the purpose to which it was now put. This funny

spectacle appeared to amuse the sun, for he burst out with such radiance that Jo woke up, and roused all her sisters by a hearty laugh at Amy's ornament.

Sunshine and laughter were good omens for a pleasure party, and soon a lively bustle began in both houses. Beth, who was ready first, kept reporting what went on next door, and enlivened her sisters' toilettes by frequent telegrams from the window.

"There goes the man with the tent! I see Mrs. Barker doing up the lunch in a hamper and a great basket. Now Mr. Laurence is looking up at the sky, and the weathercock; I wish he would go, too. There's Laurie, looking like a sailor—nice boy! Oh, mercy me, here's a carriage full of people—a tall lady, a little girl, and two dreadful boys. One is lame; poor thing, he's got a crutch. Laurie didn't tell us that. Be quick, girls, it's getting late. Why, there is Ned Moffat, I do declare. Look, Meg, isn't that the man who bowed to you one day when we were shopping?"

"So it is. How queer that he should come. I thought he was at the Mountains. There is Sallie; I'm glad she got back in time. Am I all right, Jo?" cried Meg, in a flutter.

"A regular daisy. Hold up your dress and put your hat straight; it looks sentimental tipped that way, and will fly off at the first puff. Now, then, come on!"

"Oh, Jo, you are not going to wear that awful hat? It's too absurd! You shall *not* make a guy of yourself," remonstrated Meg, as Jo tied down, with a red ribbon, the broad-brimmed, old-fashioned Leghorn Laurie had sent for a joke.

"I just will, though, for it's capital—so shady, light, and big. It will make fun; and I don't mind being a guy if I'm comfortable." With that Jo marched straight away, and the rest followed—a bright little band of sisters, all looking their best, in summer suits, with happy faces under the jaunty hat brims.

Laurie ran to meet, and present them to his friends, in the most cordial manner. The lawn was the reception room, and for several minutes a lively scene was enacted there. Meg was grateful to see that Miss Kate, though twenty, was dressed with a simplicity which American girls would do well to imitate; and she was much flattered by Mr. Ned's assurances that he came especially to see her. Jo understood why Laurie "primmed up his mouth" when speaking of Kate, for that young lady had a stand-off-don't-touch-me air, which contrasted strongly with the free and easy demeanor of the other girls. Beth took an observation of the new boys, and decided that the lame one was not "dreadful," but gentle and feeble, and she would be kind to him on that account. Amy found Grace a well-mannered, merry little person; and after staring dumbly at one another for a few minutes, they suddenly became very good friends.

Tents, lunch, and croquet utensils having been sent on beforehand, the party was soon embarked, and the two boats pushed off together, leaving Mr. Laurence waving his hat on the shore. Laurie and Jo rowed one boat; Mr. Brooke and Ned the other; while Fred Vaughn, the riotous twin, did his best to upset both by paddling about in a wherry like a disturbed water bug. Jo's funny hat deserved a vote of thanks, for it was of general utility; it broke the ice in the beginning, by producing a laugh; it created quite a refreshing breeze, flapping to and fro as she rowed, and would make an excellent umbrella for the whole party, if a shower came up, she said. Kate looked rather amazed at Jo's proceedings, especially as she exclaimed "Christopher Columbus!" when she lost her oar; and Laurie said, "My dear fellow, did I hurt you?" when he tripped over her feet in taking his place. But after putting up her glass to examine the queer girl several times, Miss Kate decided that she was "odd, but rather clever," and smiled upon her from afar.

Meg, in the other boat, was delightfully situated, face to face with the rowers, who both admired the prospect, and feathered their oars with uncommon "skill and dexterity." Mr. Brooke was a grave, silent young man, with handsome brown eyes and a pleasant voice. Meg liked his quiet manners, and considered him a walking encyclopedia of useful knowledge. He never talked to her much; but he looked at her a good deal, and she felt sure that he did not regard her with aversion. Ned, being in college, of course put on all the airs which Freshmen think it their bounden duty to assume; he was not very wise, but very good-natured, and altogether an excellent person to carry on a picnic. Sallie Gardiner was absorbed in keeping her white piqué dress clean, and chattering with the ubiquitous Fred, who kept Beth in constant terror by his pranks.

It was not far to Longmeadow; but the tent was pitched and the wickets down by the time they arrived. A pleasant green field, with three wide-spreading oaks in the middle, and a smooth strip of turf for croquet.

"Welcome to Camp Laurence!" said the young host, as they landed, with exclamations of delight.

"Brooke is commander in chief; I am commissary general; the other fellows are staff officers; and you, ladies, are company. The tent is for your especial benefit, and that oak is your drawing room; this is the mess room, and the third is the camp kitchen. Now, let's have a game before it gets hot, and then we'll see about dinner."

Frank, Beth, Amy, and Grace sat down to watch the game played by the other eight. Mr. Brooke chose Meg, Kate, and Fred; Laurie took Sallie, Jo, and Ned. The Englishers played well; but the Americans played better, and contested every inch of the ground as strongly as if the spirit of '76 inspired them. Jo and Fred had several skirmishes, and once narrowly escaped high words. Jo was through the last wicket, and had missed the stroke, which failure ruffled her a good deal. Fred was close behind her, and his turn came before hers; he gave a stroke, his ball hit the wicket, and stopped an inch on the wrong side. No one was very near; and running up to examine, he gave it a sly nudge with his toe, which put it just an inch on the right side.

"I'm through! Now, Miss Jo, I'll settle you, and get in first," cried the young gentleman, swinging his mallet for another blow.

"You pushed it; I saw you; it's my turn now," said Jo sharply.

"Upon my word, I didn't move it; it rolled a bit, perhaps, but that is allowed; so stand off, please, and let me have a go at the stake."

"We don't cheat in America, but you can if you choose," said Jo angrily.

"Yankees are a deal the most tricky, everybody knows. There you go!" returned Fred, croqueting her ball far away.

Jo opened her lips to say something rude, but checked herself in time, coloring up to her forehead, and stood a minute, hammering down a wicket with all her might, while Fred hit the stake, and declared himself out with much exultation. She went off to get her ball, and was a long time finding it, among the bushes; but she came back, looking cool and quiet, and waited her turn patiently. It took several strokes to regain the place she had lost; and, when she got there, the other side had nearly won, for Kate's ball was the last but one, and lay near the stake.

"By George, it's all up with us! Good-by, Kate. Miss Jo owes me one, so you are finished," cried Fred excitedly, as they all drew near to see the finish.

"Yankees have a trick of being generous to their enemies," said Jo, with a look that made the lad redden, "especially when they beat them," she added, as, leaving Kate's ball untouched, she won the game by a clever stroke.

Laurie threw up his hat; then remembered that it wouldn't do to exult over the defeat of his guests, and stopped in the middle of a cheer to whisper to his friend:

"Good for you, Jo! He did cheat, I saw him; but we can't tell him so, but he won't do it again, take my word for it."

Meg drew her aside, under pretense of pinning up a loose braid, and said approvingly:

"It was dreadfully provoking, but you kept your temper, and I'm so glad, Jo."

"Don't praise me, Meg, for I could box his ears this minute. I should certainly have boiled over if I hadn't stayed among the nettles till I got my rage under enough to hold my tongue. It's simmering now, so I hope he'll keep out of my way," returned Jo, biting her lips, as she glowered at Fred from under her big hat.

"Time for lunch," said Mr. Brooke, looking at his watch. "Commissary general, will you make the fire and get water, while Miss March, Miss Sallie, and I spread the table? Who can make good coffee?"

"Jo can," said Meg, glad to recommend her sister. So Jo, feeling that her late lessons in cookery were to do her honor, went to preside over the coffeepot, while the children collected dry sticks, and the boys made a fire, and got water from a spring near by. Miss Kate sketched, and Frank talked to Beth, who was making little mats of braided rushes to serve as plates.

The commander in chief and his aides soon spread the

tablecloth with an inviting array of eatables and drinkables, prettily decorated with green leaves. Jo announced that the coffee was ready, and everyone settled themselves to a hearty meal; for youth is seldom dyspeptic, and exercise develops wholesome appetites. A very merry lunch it was; for everything seemed fresh and funny, and frequent peals of laughter startled a venerable horse who fed near by. There was a pleasing inequality in the table, which produced many mishaps to cups and plates; acorns dropped into the milk, little black ants partook of the refreshments without being invited, and fuzzy caterpillars swung down from the tree to see what was going on. Three white-headed children peeped over the fence, and an objectionable dog barked at them from the other side of the river with all his might and main.

"There's salt here, if you prefer it," said Laurie, as he handed Jo a saucer of berries.

"Thank you, I prefer spiders," she replied, fishing up two unwary little ones who had gone to a creamy death.

"How dare you remind me of that horrid dinner party, when yours is so nice in every way?" added Jo, as they both laughed, and ate out of one plate, the china having run short.

"I had an uncommonly good time that day, and haven't got over it yet. This is no credit to me, you know; I don't do anything; it's you and Meg and Brooke who make it go, and I'm no end obliged to you. What shall we do when we can't eat any more?" asked Laurie, feeling that his trump card had been played when lunch was over.

"Have games, till it's cooler. I brought 'Authors,' and I dare say Miss Kate knows something new and nice. Go and ask her; she's company, and you ought to stay with her more."

"Aren't you company too? I thought she'd suit Brooke; but he keeps talking to Meg, and Kate just stares at them through that ridiculous glass of hers. I'm going, so you needn't try to preach propriety, for you can't do it, Jo."

Miss Kate did know several new games; and as the girls would not, and the boys could not, eat any more, they all adjourned to the drawing room to play "Rigmarole."

"One person begins a story, any nonsense you like, and tells as long as he pleases, only taking care to stop short at some exciting point, when the next takes it up and does the same. It's very funny when well done, and makes a perfect jumble of tragical comical stuff to laugh over. Please start it, Mr. Brooke," said Kate, with a commanding air, which surprised Meg, who treated the tutor with as much respect as any other gentleman.

Lying on the grass at the feet of the two young ladies, Mr. Brooke obediently began the story, with the handsome brown eyes steadily fixed upon the sunshiny river.

"Once on a time, a knight went out into the world to seek his fortune, for he had nothing but his sword and his shield. He traveled a long while, nearly eight and twenty years, and had a hard time of it, till he came to the palace of a good old king, who had offered a reward to anyone who would tame and train a fine but unbroken colt, of which he was very fond. The knight agreed to try, and got on slowly but surely; for the colt was a gallant fellow, and soon learned to love his new master, though he was freakish and wild. Every day, when he gave his lessons to this pet of the king's, the knight rode him through the city; and, as he rode, he looked everywhere for a certain beautiful face, which he had seen many times in his dreams, but never found. One day, as he went prancing down a quiet street, he saw at the window of a ruinous castle the lovely face. He was delighted, inquired who lived in this old castle, and was told that several captive princesses were kept there by a spell, and spun all day to lay up money to buy their liberty. The knight wished intensely that he could free them; but he was poor, and could only go by each day, watching for the sweet face, and longing to see it out in the sunshine. At last he resolved to get into the castle and ask how he could help them. He went and knocked; the great door flew open, and he beheld—"

"A ravishingly lovely lady, who exclaimed, with a cry of rapture, 'At last! at last!'" continued Kate, who had read French novels, and admired the style. "'Tis she!' cried Count Gustave, and fell at her feet in an ecstasy of joy. 'Oh, rise!' she said, extending a hand of marble fairness. 'Never, till you tell me how I may rescue you,' swore the knight, still kneeling. 'Alas, my cruel fate condemns me to remain here till my tyrant is

destroyed.' 'Where is the villain?' 'In the mauve salon. Go,
brave heart, and save me from despair.' 'I obey, and return
victorious or dead!' With these thrilling words he rushed away,
and flinging open the door of the mauve salon, was about to
enter, when he received—"

"A stunning blow from the big Greek lexicon, which an old
fellow in a black gown fired at him," said Ned. "Instantly Sir
What's-his-name recovered himself, pitched the tyrant out of
the window, and turned to join the lady, victorious, but with
a bump on his brow; found the door locked, tore up the curtains, made a rope ladder, got halfway down when the ladder
broke, and he went head first into the moat, sixty feet below.
Could swim like a duck, paddled round the castle till he came
to a little door guarded by two stout fellows; knocked their
heads together till they cracked like a couple of nuts; then, by
a trifling exertion of his prodigious strength, he smashed in the
door, went up a pair of stone steps covered with dust a foot
thick, toads as big as your fist, and spiders that would frighten
you into hysterics, Miss March. At the top of these steps he
came plump upon a sight that took his breath away and chilled
his blood—"

"A tall figure, all in white with a veil over its face and a
lamp in its wasted hand," went on Meg. "It beckoned, gliding
noiselessly before him down a corridor as dark and cold as any
tomb. Shadowy effigies in armor stood on either side, a dead
silence reigned, the lamp burned blue, and the ghostly figure
ever and anon turned its face toward him, showing the glitter
of awful eyes through its white veil. They reached a curtained
door, behind which sounded lovely music; he sprang forward
to enter, but the specter plucked him back, and waved threateningly before him a—"

"Snuffbox," said Jo, in a sepulchral tone, which convulsed
the audience. "'Thankee,' said the knight politely, as he took
a pinch, and sneezed seven times so violently that his head fell
off. 'Ha! ha!' laughed the ghost; and having peeped through
the keyhole at the princesses spinning away for dear life, the
evil spirit picked up her victim and put him in a large tin box,
where there were eleven other knights packed together without their heads, like sardines, who all rose and began to—"

"Dance a hornpipe," cut in Fred, as Jo paused for breath; "and, as they danced, the rubbishy old castle turned to a man-of-war in full sail. 'Up with the jib, reef the tops'l halliards, held hard alee, and man the guns!' roared the captain, as a Portuguese pirate hove in sight, with a flag black as ink flying from her foremast. 'Go in and win, my hearties!' says the captain; and a tremendous fight begun. Of course the British beat; they always do."

"No, they don't!" cried Jo, aside.

"Having taken the pirate captain prisoner, sailed slap over the schooner, whose decks were piled with dead, and lee scuppers ran blood, for the order had been 'Cutlasses, and die hard!' 'Bosun's mate, take a bight of the flying-jib sheet, and start this villain if he don't confess his sins double quick,' said the British captain. The Portuguese held his tongue like a brick, and walked the plank, while the jolly tars cheered like mad. But the sly dog dived, came up under the man-of-war, scuttled her, and down she went, with all sail set, 'To the bottom of the sea, sea, sea,' where—"

"Oh, gracious! what *shall* I say?" cried Sallie, as Fred ended his rigmarole, in which he had jumbled together, pell-mell, nautical phrases and facts out of one of his favorite books. "Well, they went to the bottom, and a nice mermaid welcomed them, but was much grieved on finding the box of headless knights, and kindly pickled them in brine, hoping to discover the mystery about them; for, being a woman, she was curious. By and by a diver came down, and the mermaid said, 'I'll give you this box of pearls if you can take it up,' for she wanted to restore the poor things to life, and couldn't raise the heavy load herself. So the diver hoisted it up, and was much disappointed, on opening it, to find no pearls. He left it in a great lonely field, where it was found by a—"

"Little goosegirl, who kept a hundred fat geese in the field," said Amy, when Sallie's invention gave out. "The little girl was sorry for them, and asked an old woman what she should do to help them. 'Your geese will tell you, they know everything,' said the old woman. So she asked what she should use for new heads, since the old ones were lost, and all the geese opened their hundred mouths and screamed—"

" 'Cabbages!' " continued Laurie promptly. " 'Just the thing,'
said the girl, and ran to get twelve fine ones from her garden.
She put them on, the knights revived at once, thanked her, and
went on their way rejoicing, never knowing the difference, for
there were so many other heads like them in the world that no
one thought anything about it. The knight in whom I'm interested went back to find the pretty face, and learned that the
princesses had spun themselves free, and all gone to be married, but one. He was in a great state of mind at that; and
mounting the colt, who stood by him through thick and thin,
rushed to the castle to see which was left. Peeping over the
hedge, he saw the queen of his affections picking flowers in
her garden. 'Will you give me a rose?' said he. 'You must come
and get it. I can't come to you; it isn't proper,' said she, as
sweet as honey. He tried to climb over the hedge, but it
seemed to grow higher and higher; then he tried to push
through, but it grew thicker and thicker, and he was in despair. So he patiently broke twig after twig, till he had made
a little hole, through which he peeped, saying imploringly,
'Let me in! let me in!' But the pretty princess did not seem to
understand, for she picked her roses quietly, and left him to
fight his way in. Whether he did or not, Frank will tell you."

"I can't; I'm not playing, I never do," said Frank, dismayed
at the sentimental predicament out of which he was to rescue
the absurd couple. Beth had disappeared behind Jo, and Grace
was asleep.

"So the poor knight is to be left sticking in the hedge, is
he?" asked Mr. Brooke, still watching the river, and playing
with the wild rose in his buttonhole.

"I guess the princess gave him a posy, and opened the gate,
after a while," said Laurie, smiling to himself, as he threw
acorns at his tutor.

"What a piece of nonsense we have made! With practice we
might do something quite clever. Do you know 'Truth'?" asked
Sallie, after they had laughed over their story.

"I hope so," said Meg soberly.

"The game, I mean?"

"What is it?" said Fred.

"Why, you pile up your hands, choose a number, and draw

out in turn, and the person who draws at the number has to
answer truly any questions put by the rest. It's great fun."

"Let's try it," said Jo, who liked new experiments.

Miss Kate and Mr. Brooke, Meg, and Ned declined, but
Fred, Sallie, Jo, and Laurie piled and drew; and the lot fell to
Laurie.

"Who are your heroes?" asked Jo.

"Grandfather and Napoleon."

"Which lady here do you think prettiest?" said Sallie.

"Margaret."

"Which do you like best?" from Fred.

"Jo, of course."

"What silly questions you ask!" and Jo gave a disdainful
shrug as the rest laughed at Laurie's matter-of-fact tone.

"Try again; Truth isn't a bad game," said Fred.

"It's a very good one for you," retorted Jo, in a low voice.

Her turn came next.

"What is your greatest fault?" asked Fred, by way of testing
in her the virtue he lacked himself.

"A quick temper."

"What do you wish for?" said Laurie.

"A pair of boot lacings," returned Jo, guessing and defeating
his purpose.

"Not a true answer; you must say what you really do want
most."

"Genius; don't you wish you could give it to me, Laurie?"
and she slyly smiled in his disappointed face.

"What virtues do you most admire in a man?" asked Sallie.

"Courage and honesty."

"Now my turn," said Fred, as his hand came last.

"Let's give it to him," whispered Laurie to Jo, who nodded,
and asked at once:

"Didn't you cheat at croquet?"

"Well, yes, a little bit."

"Good! Didn't you take your story out of 'The Sea-Lion'?"
said Laurie.

"Rather."

"Don't you think the English nation perfect in every respect?" asked Sallie.

"I should be ashamed of myself if I didn't."

"He's a true John Bull. Now, Miss Sallie, you shall have a chance without waiting to draw. I'll harrow up your feelings first, by asking if you don't think you are something of a flirt," said Laurie, as Jo nodded to Fred, as a sign that peace was declared.

"You impertinent boy! Of course I'm not," exclaimed Sallie, with an air that proved the contrary.

"What do you hate most?" asked Fred.

"Spiders and rice pudding."

"What do you like best?" asked Jo.

"Dancing and French gloves."

"Well, *I* think Truth is a very silly play; let's have a sensible game of Authors, to refresh our minds," proposed Jo.

Ned, Frank, and the little girls joined in this, and while it went on, the three elders sat apart, talking. Miss Kate took out her sketch again, and Margaret watched her, while Mr. Brooke lay on the grass, with a book, which he did not read.

"How beautifully you do it! I wish I could draw," said Meg, with mingled admiration and regret in her voice.

"Why don't you learn? I should think you had taste and talent for it," replied Miss Kate graciously.

"I haven't time."

"Your mamma prefers other accomplishments, I fancy, so did mine; but I proved to her that I had talent, by taking a few lessons privately, and then she was quite willing I should go on. Can't you do the same with your governess?"

"I have none."

"I forgot; young ladies in America go to school more than with us. Very fine schools they are, too, papa says. You go to a private one, I suppose?"

"I don't go at all; I am a governess myself."

"Oh, indeed!" said Miss Kate; but she might as well have said, "Dear me, how dreadful!" for her tone implied it, and something in her face made Meg color and wish she had not been so frank.

Mr. Brooke looked up, and said quickly, "Young ladies in America love independence as much as their ancestors did, and are admired and respected for supporting themselves."

"Oh, yes; of course it's very nice and proper in them to do so. We have many most respectable and worthy young women who do the same and are employed by the nobility, because, being the daughters of gentlemen, they are both well bred and accomplished, you know," said Miss Kate, in a patronizing tone that hurt Meg's pride and made her work seem not only more distasteful, but degrading.

"Did the German song suit, Miss March?" inquired Mr. Brooke, breaking an awkward pause.

"Oh, yes! It was very sweet, and I'm much obliged to whoever translated it for me," and Meg's downcast face brightened as she spoke.

"Don't you read German?" asked Miss Kate, with a look of surprise.

"Not very well. My father, who taught me, is away, and I don't get on very fast alone, for I've no one to correct my pronunciation."

"Try a little now; here is Schiller's 'Mary Stuart,' and a tutor who loves to teach," and Mr. Brooke laid his book on her lap, with an inviting smile.

"It's so hard I'm afraid to try," said Meg, grateful, but bashful in the presence of the accomplished young lady beside her.

"I'll read a bit to encourage you," and Miss Kate read one of the most beautiful passages, in a perfectly correct but perfectly expressionless manner.

Mr. Brooke made no comment, as she returned the book to Meg, who said innocently:

"I thought it was poetry."

"Some of it is. Try this passage."

There was a queer smile about Mr. Brooke's mouth as he opened at poor Mary's lament.

Meg obediently following the long grass blade which her new tutor used to point with, read slowly and timidly, unconsciously making poetry of the hard words by the soft intonation of her musical voice. Down the page went the green guide, and presently, forgetting her listener in the beauty of the sad scene, Meg read as if alone, giving a little touch of tragedy to the words of the unhappy queen. If she had seen the brown eyes then, she would have stopped short; but she never looked up, and the lesson was not spoiled for her.

"Very well indeed!" said Mr. Brooke, as she paused, quite ignoring her many mistakes, and looking as if he did, indeed, "love to teach."

Miss Kate put up her glass, and, having taken a survey of the little tableau before her, shut her sketchbook, saying, with condescension:

"You've a nice accent, and, in time, will be a clever reader. I advise you to learn, for German is a valuable accomplishment to teachers. I must look after Grace, she is romping," and Miss Kate strolled away, adding to herself, with a shrug, "I didn't come to chaperon a governess, though she *is* young and pretty. What odd people these Yankees are; I'm afraid Laurie will be quite spoilt among them."

"I forgot that English people rather turn up their noses at governesses, and don't treat them as we do," said Meg, looking after the retreating figure with an annoyed expression.

"Tutors, also, have rather a hard time of it there, as I know to my sorrow. There's no place like America for us workers, Miss Margaret," and Mr. Brooke looked so contented and cheerful that Meg was ashamed to lament her hard lot.

"I'm glad I live in it then. I don't like my work, but I get a good deal of satisfaction out of it after all, so I won't complain; I only wish I liked teaching as you do."

"I think you would if you had Laurie for a pupil. I shall be sorry to lose him next year," said Mr. Brooke, busily punching holes in the turf.

"Going to college, I suppose?" Meg's lips asked that question, but her eyes added, "And what becomes of you?"

"Yes; it's high time he went, for he is ready; and as soon as he is off, I shall turn soldier. I am needed."

"I am glad of that!" exclaimed Meg. "I should think every young man would want to go; though it is hard for the mothers and sisters who stay at home," she added sorrowfully.

"I have neither, and very few friends, to care whether I live or die," said Mr. Brooke rather bitterly, as he absently put the dead rose in the hole he had made and covered it up, like a little grave.

"Laurie and his grandfather would care a great deal, and we should all be very sorry to have any harm happen to you," said Meg heartily.

"Thank you; that sounds pleasant," began Mr. Brooke, looking cheerful again; but before he could finish his speech, Ned, mounted on the old horse, came lumbering up to display his equestrian skill before the young ladies, and there was no more quiet that day.

"Don't you love to ride?" asked Grace of Amy, as they stood resting, after a race round the field with the others, led by Ned.

"I dote upon it; my sister Meg used to ride when papa was rich, but we don't keep horses now, except Ellen Tree," added Amy, laughing.

"Tell me about Ellen Tree; is it a donkey?" asked Grace, curiously.

"Why, you see, Jo is crazy about horses, and so am I, but we've only got an old side saddle, and no horse. Out in our garden is an apple tree that has a nice low branch; so Jo put the saddle on it, fixed some reins on the part that turns up, and we bounce away on Ellen Tree whenever we like."

"How funny!" laughed Grace. "I have a pony at home, and ride nearly every day in the park, with Fred and Kate; it's very nice, for my friends go too, and the Row is full of ladies and gentlemen."

"Dear, how charming! I hope I shall go abroad someday; but I'd rather go to Rome than the Row," said Amy, who had not the remotest idea what the Row was and wouldn't have asked for the world.

Frank, sitting just behind the little girls, heard what they were saying, and pushed his crutch away from him with an impatient gesture as he watched the active lads going through all sorts of comical gymnastics. Beth, who was collecting the scattered Author cards, looked up, and said, in her shy yet friendly way:

"I'm afraid you are tired; can I do anything for you?"

"Talk to me, please; it's dull, sitting by myself," answered Frank, who had evidently been used to being made much of at home.

If he had asked her to deliver a Latin oration, it would not

have seemed a more impossible task to bashful Beth; but there
was no place to run to, no Jo to hide behind now, and the poor
boy looked so wistfully at her that she bravely resolved to try.

"What do you like to talk about?" she asked, fumbling over
the cards, and dropping half as she tried to tie them up.

"Well, I like to hear about cricket and boating and hunting,"
said Frank, who had not yet learned to suit his amusements
to his strength.

"My heart, what shall I do? I don't know anything about
them," thought Beth; and, forgetting the boy's misfortune in
her flurry, she said, hoping to make him talk, "I never saw any
hunting, but I suppose you know all about it."

"I did once; but I can never hunt again, for I got hurt leaping a confounded five-barred gate; so there are no more horses
and hounds for me," said Frank, with a sigh that made Beth
hate herself for her innocent blunder.

"Your deer are much prettier than our ugly buffaloes," she
said, turning to the prairies for help, and feeling glad that she
had read one of the boys' books in which Jo delighted.

Buffaloes proved soothing and satisfactory; and, in her ea-
gerness to amuse another, Beth forgot herself, and was quite
unconscious of her sisters' surprise and delight at the unusual
spectacle of Beth talking away to one of the dreadful boys
against whom she had begged protection.

"Bless her heart! She pities him, so she is good to him," said
Jo, beaming at her from the croquet ground.

"I always said she was a little saint," added Meg, as if there
could be no further doubt of it.

"I haven't heard Frank laugh so much for ever so long," said
Grace to Amy, as they sat discussing dolls, and making tea sets
out of the acorn cups.

"My sister Beth is a very *fastidious* girl, when she likes to
be," said Amy, well pleased at Beth's success. She meant
"fascinating," but as Grace didn't know the exact meaning of
either word, "fastidious" sounded well and made a good impression.

An impromptu circus, fox and geese, and an amicable game
of croquet finished the afternoon. At sunset the tent was struck,
hampers packed, wickets pulled up, boats loaded, and the

whole party floated down the river, singing at the tops of their voices. Ned, getting sentimental, warbled a serenade with the pensive refrain:

"Alone, alone, ah! woe, alone,"

and at the lines —

"We each are young, we each have a heart,
Oh, why should we stand thus coldly apart?"

he looked at Meg with such a lackadaisical expression that she laughed outright and spoilt his song.

"How can you be so cruel to me?" he whispered under cover of a lively chorus. "You've kept close to that starched-up Englishwoman all day, and now you snub me."

"I didn't mean to; but you looked so funny I really couldn't help it," replied Meg, passing over the first part of his reproach, for it was quite true that she *had* shunned him, remembering the Moffat party and the talk after it.

Ned was offended, and turned to Sallie for consolation, saying to her rather pettishly, "There isn't a bit of flirt in that girl, is there?"

"Not a particle; but she's a dear," returned Sallie, defending her friend even while confessing her shortcomings.

"She's not a stricken deer, anyway," said Ned, trying to be witty, and succeeding as well as very young gentlemen usually do.

On the lawn, where it had gathered, the little party separated with cordial good nights and good-bys, for the Vaughns were going to Canada. As the four sisters went home through the garden, Miss Kate looked after them, saying, without the patronizing tone in her voice, "In spite of their demonstrative manners, American girls are very nice when one knows them."

"I quite agree with you," said Mr. Brooke.

CHAPTER THIRTEEN

Castles in the Air

LAURIE lay luxuriously swinging to and fro in his hammock, one warm September afternoon, wondering what his neighbors were about, but too lazy to go and find out. He was in one of his moods; for the day had been both unprofitable and unsatisfactory, and he was wishing he could live it over again. The hot weather made him indolent, and he had shirked his studies, tried Mr. Brooke's patience to the utmost, displeased his grandfather by practicing half the afternoon, frightened the maidservants half out of their wits by mischievously hinting that one of his dogs was going mad, and, after high words with the stableman about some fancied neglect of his horse, he had flung himself into his hammock, to fume over the stupidity of the world in general till the peace

The two boats pushed off together

[SEE PAGE 138]

of the lovely day quieted him in spite of himself. Staring up into the green gloom of the horse chestnut trees above him, he dreamed dreams of all sorts, and was just imagining himself tossing on the ocean, in a voyage around the world, when the sound of voices brought him ashore in a flash. Peeping through the meshes of the hammock, he saw the Marches coming out, as if bound on some expedition.

"What in the world are those girls about now?" thought Laurie, opening his sleepy eyes to take a good look, for there was something rather peculiar in the appearance of his neighbors. Each wore a large, flapping hat, a brown linen pouch slung over one shoulder, and carried a long staff. Meg had a cushion, Jo a book, Beth a basket, and Amy a portfolio. All walked quietly through the garden, out at the little back gate, and began to climb the hill that lay between the house and the river.

"Well, that's cool," said Laurie to himself, "to have a picnic and never ask me. They can't be going in the boat, for they haven't got the key. Perhaps they forgot it; I'll take it to them, and see what's going on."

Though possessed of half a dozen hats, it took him some time to find one; then there was a hunt for the key, which was at last discovered in his pocket; so that the girls were quite out of sight when he leaped the fence and ran after them. Taking the shortest way to the boathouse, he waited for them to appear but no one came, and he went up the hill to take an observation. A grove of pines covered one part of it, and from the heart of this green spot came a clearer sound than the soft sigh of the pines or the drowsy chirp of the crickets.

"Here's a landscape!" thought Laurie, peeping through the bushes, and looking wide-awake and good-natured already.

It *was* rather a pretty little picture, for the sisters sat together in the shady nook, with sun and shadow flickering over them, the aromatic wind lifting their hair and cooling their hot cheeks, and all the little wood people going on with their affairs as if these were no strangers but old friends. Meg sat upon her cushion, sewing daintily with her white hands, and looking as fresh and sweet as a rose, in her pink dress, among the green. Beth was sorting the cones that lay thick under the hemlock near by, for she made pretty things of them. Amy was sketching a group of ferns, and Jo was knitting as she read aloud. A shadow passed over the boy's face as he watched them, feeling that he ought to go away, because uninvited; yet lingering because home seemed very lonely, and this quiet party in the woods most attractive to his restless spirit. He stood so still that a squirrel, busy with its harvesting, ran down a pine close beside him, saw him suddenly and skipped back, scolding so shrilly that Beth looked up, espied the wistful face behind the birches, and beckoned with a reassuring smile.

"May I come in, please? Or shall I be a bother?" he asked, advancing slowly.

Meg lifted her eyebrows, but Jo scowled at her defiantly and said, at once, "Of course you may. We should have asked you before, only we thought you wouldn't care for such a girls' game as this."

"I always liked your games; but if Meg doesn't want me, I'll go away."

"I've no objection, if you do something; it's against the rules to be idle here," replied Meg, gravely but graciously.

"Much obliged; I'll do anything if you'll let me stop a bit, for it's as dull as the Desert of Sahara down there. Shall I sew, read, cone, draw, or do all at once? Bring on your bears; I'm ready," and Laurie sat down, with a submissive expression delightful to behold.

"Finish this story while I set my heel," said Jo, handing him the book.

"Yes'm" was the meek answer, as he began, doing his best to prove his gratitude for the favor of an admission into the "Busy Bee Society."

The story was not a long one, and, when it was finished, he ventured to ask a few questions as a reward of merit.

"Please, ma'am, could I inquire if this highly instructive and charming institution is a new one?"

"Would you tell him?" asked Meg of her sisters.

"He'll laugh," said Amy warningly.

"Who cares?" said Jo.

"I guess he'll like it," added Beth.

"Of course I shall! I give you my word I won't laugh. Tell away, Jo, and don't be afraid."

"The idea of being afraid of you! Well, you see we used to play Pilgrim's Progress, and we have been going on with it in earnest, all winter and summer."

"Yes, I know," said Laurie, nodding wisely.

"Who told you?" demanded Jo.

"Spirits."

"No, I did; I wanted to amuse him one night when you were all away, and he was rather dismal. He did like it, so don't scold, Jo," said Beth meekly.

"You can't keep a secret. Never mind; it saves trouble now."

"Go on, please," said Laurie, as Jo became absorbed in her work, looking a trifle displeased.

"Oh, didn't she tell you about this new plan of ours? Well, we have tried not to waste our holiday, but each has had a task and worked at it with a will. The vacation is nearly over, the stints are all done, and we are ever so glad that we didn't dawdle."

"Yes, I should think so," and Laurie thought regretfully of his own idle days.

"Mother likes to have us out of doors as much as possible, so we bring our work here, and have nice times. For the fun of it we bring out things in these bags, wear the old hats, use poles to climb the hill, and play pilgrims, as we used to do years ago. We call this hill the Delectable Mountain, for we can look far away and see the country where we hope to live sometime."

Jo pointed, and Laurie sat up to examine; for through an opening in the wood one could look across the wide, blue river, the meadows on the other side, far over the outskirts of the great city, to the green hills that rose to meet the sky. The sun was low, and the heavens glowed with the splendor of an autumn sunset. Gold and purple clouds lay on the hilltops; and rising high into the ruddy light were silvery white peaks, that shone like the airy spires of some Celestial City.

"How beautiful that is!" said Laurie softly, for he was quick to see and feel beauty of any kind.

"It's often so; and we like to watch it, for it is never the same, but always splendid," replied Amy, wishing she could paint it.

"Jo talks about the country where we hope to live sometime

—the real country, she means, with pigs and chickens and hay-making. It would be nice, but I wish the beautiful country up there was real, and we could ever go to it," said Beth musingly.

"There is a lovelier country even than that, where we *shall* go, by and by, when we are good enough," answered Meg, with her sweet voice.

"It seems so long to wait, so hard to do; I want to fly away at once, as those swallows fly, and go in at that splendid gate."

"You'll get there, Beth, sooner or later; no fear of that," said Jo; "I'm the one that will have to fight and work, and climb and wait, and maybe never get in after all."

"You'll have me for company, if that's any comfort. I shall have to do a deal of traveling before I come in sight of your Celestial City. If I arrive late, you'll say a good word for me, won't you, Beth?"

Something in the boy's face troubled his little friend; but she said cheerfully, with her quiet eyes on the changing clouds, "If people really want to go, and really try all their lives, I think they will get in; for I don't believe there are any locks on that door, or any guards at the gate. I always imagine it is as it is in the picture, where the shining ones stretch out their hands to welcome poor Christian as he comes up from the river."

"Wouldn't it be fun if all the castles in the air which we make could come true, and we could live in them?" said Jo, after a little pause.

"I've made such quantities it would be hard to choose which I'd have," said Laurie, lying flat, and throwing cones at the squirrel who had betrayed him.

"You'd have to take your favorite one. What is it?" asked Meg.

"If I tell mine, will you tell yours?"

"Yes, if the girls will too."

"We will. Now, Laurie."

"After I'd seen as much of the world as I want to, I'd like to settle in Germany, and have just as much music as I choose. I'm to be a famous musician myself, and all creation is to rush to hear me; and I'm never to be bothered about money or business, but just enjoy myself, and live for what I like. That's my favorite castle. What's yours, Meg?"

Margaret seemed to find it a little hard to tell hers, and waved a brake before her face, as if to disperse imaginary gnats, while she said slowly, "I should like a lovely house, full of all sorts of luxurious things—nice food, pretty clothes, handsome furniture, pleasant people, and heaps of money. I am to be mistress of it, and manage it as I like, with plenty of servants, so I never need work a bit. How I should enjoy it! For I wouldn't be idle, but do good, and make everyone love me dearly."

"Wouldn't you have a master for your castle in the air?" asked Laurie slyly.

"I said 'pleasant people,' you know," and Meg carefully tied up her shoe as she spoke, so that no one saw her face.

"Why don't you say you'd have a splendid, wise, good husband, and some angelic little children? You know your castle wouldn't be perfect without," said blunt Jo, who had no tender fancies yet, and rather scorned romance, except in books.

"You'd have nothing but horses, inkstands, and novels in yours," answered Meg petulantly.

"Wouldn't I, though? I'd have a stable full of Arabian steeds, rooms piled with books, and I'd write out of a magic inkstand, so that my works should be as famous as Laurie's music. I want to do something splendid before I go into my castle—something heroic or wonderful, that won't be forgotten after I'm dead. I don't know what, but I'm on the watch for it, and mean to astonish you all, someday. I think I shall write books, and get rich and famous: that would suit me, so that is *my* favorite dream."

"Mine is to stay at home safe with father and mother, and help take care of the family," said Beth contentedly.

"Don't you wish for anything else?" asked Laurie.

"Since I had my little piano, I am perfectly satisfied. I only wish we may all keep well and be together; nothing else."

"I have ever so many wishes; but the pet one is to be an artist, and go to Rome, and do fine pictures, and be the best artist in the whole world" was Amy's modest desire.

"We're an ambitious set, aren't we? Every one of us, but Beth, wants to be rich and famous, and gorgeous in every respect. I do wonder if any of us will ever get our wishes," said Laurie, chewing grass like a meditative calf.

"I've got the key to my castle in the air; but whether I can unlock the door remains to be seen," observed Jo mysteriously.

"I've got the key to mine, but I'm not allowed to try it. Hang college!" muttered Laurie, with an impatient sigh.

"Here's mine!" and Amy waved her pencil.

"I haven't got any," said Meg forlornly.

"Yes, you have," said Laurie at once.

"Where?"

"In your face."

"Nonsense; that's of no use."

"Wait and see if it doesn't bring you something worth having," replied the boy, laughing at the thought of a charming little secret which he fancied he knew.

Meg colored behind the brake, but asked no questions and looked across the river with the same expectant expression which Mr. Brooke had worn when he told the story of the knight.

"If we are all alive ten years hence, let's meet, and see how many of us have got our wishes, or how much nearer we are then than now," said Jo, always ready with a plan.

"Bless me, how old I shall be—twenty-seven!" exclaimed Meg, who felt grown up already, having just reached seventeen.

"You and I will be twenty-six, Teddy, Beth twenty-four, and Amy twenty-two. What a venerable party!" said Jo.

"I hope I shall have done something to be proud of by that time; but I'm such a lazy dog, I'm afraid I shall 'dawdle,' Jo."

"You need a motive, mother says; and when you get it, she is sure you'll work splendidly."

"Is she? By Jupiter I will, if I only get the chance!" cried Laurie, sitting up with sudden energy. "I ought to be satisfied to please grandfather, and I do try, but it's working against the grain, you see, and comes hard. He wants me to be an India merchant, as he was, and I'd rather be shot. I hate tea and silk and spices, and every sort of rubbish his old ships bring, and I don't care how soon they go to the bottom when I own them. Going to college ought to satisfy him, for if I give him four years he ought to let me off from the business; but he's set, and I've got to do just as he did, unless I break away and please myself, as my father did. If there was anyone left to stay with the old gentleman, I'd do it tomorrow."

Laurie spoke excitedly, and looked ready to carry his threat into execution on the slightest provocation; for he was growing up very fast, and, in spite of his indolent ways, had a young man's hatred of subjection, a young man's restless longing to try the world for himself.

"I advise you to sail away in one of your ships, and never come home again till you have tried your own way," said Jo, whose imagination was fired by the thought of such a daring exploit, and whose sympathy was excited by what she called "Teddy's wrongs."

"That's not right, Jo; you mustn't talk in that way, and Laurie mustn't take your bad advice. You should do just what your grandfather wishes, my dear boy," said Meg, in her most maternal tone. "Do your best at college, and, when he sees that you try to please him, I'm sure he won't be hard or unjust to you. As you say, there is no one else to stay with and love him, and you'd never forgive yourself if you left him without his permission. Don't be dismal or fret, but do your duty; and you'll get your reward, as good Mr. Brooke has, by being respected and loved."

"What do you know about him?" asked Laurie, grateful for the good advice, but objecting to the lecture, and glad to turn the conversation from himself, after his unusual outbreak.

"Only what your grandpa told us about him—how he took good care of his own mother till she died, and wouldn't go abroad as tutor to some nice person, because he wouldn't leave her; and how he provides now for an old woman who nursed his mother; and never tells anyone, but is just as generous and patient and good as he can be."

"So he is, dear old fellow!" said Laurie heartily, as Meg paused, looking flushed and earnest with her story. "It's like grandpa to find out all about him, without letting him know, and to tell all his goodness to others, so that they might like him. Brooke couldn't understand why your mother was so kind to him, asking him over with me, and treating him in her beautiful friendly way. He thought she was just perfect, and talked about it for days and days, and went on about you all in flaming style. If ever I do get my wish, you see what I'll do for Brooke."

"Begin to do something now, by not plaguing his life out," said Meg sharply.

"How do you know I do, miss?"

"I can always tell by his face, when he goes away. If you have been good, he looks satisfied and walks briskly; if you have plagued him, he's sober and walks slowly, as if he wanted to go back and do his work better."

"Well, I like that! So you keep an account of my good and bad marks in Brooke's face, do you? I see him bow and smile as he passes your window, but I didn't know you'd got up a telegraph."

"We haven't; don't be angry, and oh, don't tell him I said anything! It was only to show that I cared how you get on, and what is said here is said in confidence, you know," cried Meg, much alarmed at the thought of what might follow from her careless speech.

"I don't tell tales," replied Laurie, with his "high and mighty" air, as Jo called a certain expression which he occasionally wore. "Only if Brooke is

going to be a thermometer, I must mind and have fair weather
for him to report."

"Please don't be offended. I didn't mean to preach or tell
tales or be silly; I only thought Jo was encouraging you in a
feeling which you'd be sorry for, by and by. You are so kind
to us, we feel as if you were our brother, and say just what we
think. Forgive me, I meant it kindly." And Meg offered her
hand with a gesture both affectionate and timid.

Ashamed of his momentary pique, Laurie squeezed the
kind little hand, and said frankly, "I'm the one to be forgiven;
I'm cross, and have been out of sorts all day. I like to have you
tell me my faults and be sisterly, so don't mind if I am grumpy
sometimes; I thank you all the same."

Bent on showing that he was not offended, he made himself as agreeable as possible—wound cotton for Meg, recited
poetry to please Jo, shook down cones for Beth, and helped
Amy with her ferns, proving himself a fit person to belong to
the Busy Bee Society. In the midst of an animated discussion
on the domestic habits of turtles (one of those amiable creatures having strolled up from the river), the faint sound of a
bell warned them that Hannah had put the tea "to draw," and
they would just have time to get home to supper.

"May I come again?" asked Laurie.

"Yes, if you are good, and love your book, as the boys in the
primer are told to do," said Meg, smiling.

"I'll try."

"Then you may come, and I'll teach you to knit as the
Scotchmen do; there's a demand for socks just now," added Jo,
waving hers, like a big blue worsted banner, as they parted at
the gate.

That night, when Beth played to Mr. Laurence in the twilight, Laurie, standing in the shadow of the curtain, listened to
the little David, whose simple music always quieted his moody
spirit, and watched the old man, who sat with his gray head on
his hand, thinking tender thoughts of the dead child he had
loved so much. Remembering the conversation of the afternoon, the boy said to himself, with the resolve to make the
sacrifice cheerfully, "I'll let my castle go, and stay with the
dear old gentleman while he needs me, for I am all he has."

CHAPTER FOURTEEN

Secrets

◆ JO was very busy in the garret, for the October days began to grow chilly, and the afternoons were short. For two or
three hours the sun lay warmly in the high window, showing
Jo seated on the old sofa, writing busily, with her papers
spread out upon a trunk before her, while Scrabble, the pet
rat, promenaded the beams overhead, accompanied by his oldest son, a fine young fellow, who was evidently very proud of
his whiskers. Quite absorbed in her work, Jo scribbled away
till the last page was filled, when she signed her name with a
flourish, and threw down her pen, exclaiming:

"There, I've done my best! If this won't suit I shall have to
wait till I can do better."

Lying back on the sofa, she read the manuscript carefully

through, making dashes here and there, and putting in many exclamation points, which looked like little balloons; then she tied it up with a smart red ribbon, and sat a minute looking at it with a sober, wistful expression, which plainly showed how earnest her work had been. Jo's desk up here was an old tin kitchen, which hung against the wall. In it she kept her papers and a few books, safely shut away from Scrabble, who, being likewise of a literary turn, was fond of making a circulating library of such books as were left in his way, by eating the leaves. From this tin receptacle Jo produced another manuscript; and, putting both in her pocket, crept quietly downstairs, leaving her friends to nibble her pens and taste her ink.

She put on her hat and jacket as noiselessly as possible, and, going to the back entry window, got out upon the roof of a low porch, swung herself down to the grassy bank, and took a roundabout way to the road. Once there, she composed herself, hailed a passing omnibus, and rolled away to town, looking very merry and mysterious.

If anyone had been watching her, he would have thought her movements decidedly peculiar; for, on alighting, she went off at a great pace till she reached a certain number in a certain busy street; having found the place with some difficulty, she went into the doorway, looked up the dirty stairs, and, after standing stock-still a minute, suddenly dived into the street, and walked away as rapidly as she came. This maneuver she repeated several times, to the great amusement of a black-eyed young gentleman lounging in the window of a building opposite. On returning for the third time, Jo gave herself a shake, pulled her hat over her eyes, and walked up the stairs, looking as if she were going to have all her teeth out.

There was a dentist's sign, among others, which adorned the entrance, and, after staring a moment at the pair of artificial jaws which slowly opened and shut to draw attention to a fine set of teeth, the young gentleman put on his coat, took his hat, and went down to post himself in the opposite doorway, saying, with a smile and a shiver:

"It's like her to come alone, but if she has a bad time she'll need someone to help her home."

In ten minutes Jo came running downstairs with a very red

face, and the general appearance of a person who had just passed through a trying ordeal of some sort. When she saw the young gentleman she looked anything but pleased, and passed him with a nod; but he followed, asking with an air of sympathy:

"Did you have a bad time?"

"Not very."

"You got through quickly."

"Yes, thank goodness!"

"Why did you go alone?"

"Didn't want anyone to know."

"You're the oddest fellow I ever saw. How many did you have out?"

Jo looked at her friend as if she did not understand him; then began to laugh, as if mightily amused at something.

"There are two which I want to have come out, but I must wait a week."

"What are you laughing at? You are up to some mischief, too," said Laurie, looking mystified.

"So are you. What were you doing, sir, up in that billiard saloon?"

"Begging your pardon, ma'am, it wasn't a billiard saloon, but a gymnasium, and I was taking a lesson in fencing."

"I'm glad of that."

"Why?"

"You can teach me, and then when we play 'Hamlet,' you can be Laertes, and we'll make a fine thing of the fencing scene."

Laurie burst out with a hearty boy's laugh, which made several passers-by smile in spite of themselves.

"I'll teach you whether we play 'Hamlet' or not; it's grand fun, and will straighten you up capitally. But I don't believe that was your only reason for saying 'I'm glad,' in that decided way; was it, now?"

"No, I was glad that you were not in the saloon, because I hope you never go to such places. Do you?"

"Not often."

"I wish you wouldn't."

"It's no harm, Jo. I have billiards at home, but it's no fun unless you have good players; so, as I'm fond of it, I come sometimes and have a game with Ned Moffat or some of the other fellows."

"Oh, dear, I'm so sorry, for you'll get to liking it better and better, and will waste time and money, and grow like those dreadful boys. I did hope you'd stay respectable, and be a satisfaction to your friends," said Jo, shaking her head.

"Can't a fellow take a little innocent amusement now and then without losing his respectability?" asked Laurie, looking nettled.

"That depends upon how and where he takes it. I don't like Ned and his set, and wish you'd keep out of it. Mother won't let us have him at our house, though he wants to come; and if you grow like him she won't be willing to have us frolic together as we do now."

"Won't she?" asked Laurie anxiously.

"No, she can't bear fashionable young men, and she'd shut us all up in bandboxes rather than have us associate with them."

"Well, she needn't get out her bandboxes yet; I'm not a fashionable party, and don't mean to be; but I do like harmless larks now and then, don't you?"

"Yes, nobody minds them, so lark away, but don't get wild, will you? Or there will be an end of all our good times."

"I'll be a double-distilled saint."

"I can't bear saints: just be a simple, honest, respectable boy, and we'll never desert you. I don't know what I *should* do if you acted like Mr. King's son; he had plenty of money, but didn't know how to spend it, and got tipsy and gambled, and ran away, and forged his father's name, I believe, and was altogether horrid."

"You think I'm likely to do the same? Much obliged."

"No, I don't—oh, *dear,* no!—but I hear people talking about money being such a temptation, and I sometimes wish you were poor; I shouldn't worry then."

"Do you worry about me, Jo?"

"A little, when you look moody or discontented, as you sometimes do; for you've got such a strong will, if you once get started wrong, I'm afraid it would be hard to stop you."

Laurie walked in silence a few minutes, and Jo watched him, wishing she had held her tongue, for his eyes looked angry, though his lips still smiled as if at her warnings.

"Are you going to deliver lectures all the way home?" he asked presently.

"Of course not; why?"

"Because if you are, I'll take a bus; if you are not, I'd like to walk with you, and tell you something very interesting."

"I won't preach any more, and I'd like to hear the news immensely."

"Very well, then; come on. It's a secret, and if I tell you, you must tell me yours."

"I haven't got any," began Jo, but stopped suddenly, remembering that she had.

"You know you have—you can't hide anything; so up and 'fess, or I won't tell," cried Laurie.

"Is your secret a nice one?"

"Oh, isn't it! All about people you know, and such fun! You ought to hear it, and I've been aching to tell it this long time. Come, you begin."

"You'll not say anything about it at home, will you?"

"Not a word."

"And you won't tease me in private?"

"I never tease."

"Yes, you do; you get everything you want out of people. I don't know how you do it, but you are a born wheedler."

"Thank you; fire away."

"Well, I've left two stories with a newspaperman, and he's to give his answer next week," whispered Jo, in her confidant's ear.

"Hurrah for Miss March, the celebrated American authoress!" cried Laurie, throwing up his hat and catching it again, to the great delight of two ducks, four cats, five hens, and half a dozen Irish children; for they were out of the city now.

"Hush! It won't come to anything, I dare say; but I couldn't rest till I had tried, and I said nothing about it, because I didn't want anyone else to be disappointed."

"It won't fail. Why, Jo, your stories are works of Shakespeare, compared to half the rubbish that is published every day. Won't it be fun to see them in print; and shan't we feel proud of our authoress?"

Jo's eyes sparkled, for it is always pleasant to be believed in; and a friend's praise is always sweeter than a dozen newspaper puffs.

"Where's *your* secret? Play fair, Teddy, or I'll never believe in you again," she said, trying to extinguish the brilliant hopes that blazed up at a word of encouragement.

"I may get into a scrape for telling; but I didn't promise not to, so I will, for I never feel easy in my mind till I've told you any plummy bit of news I get. I know where Meg's glove is."

"Is that all?" said Jo, looking disappointed, as Laurie nodded and twinkled, with a face full of mysterious intelligence.

"It's quite enough for the present, as you'll agree when I tell you where it is."

"Tell, then."

Laurie bent, and whispered three words in Jo's ear, which produced a comical change. She stood and stared at him for a minute, looking both surprised and displeased, then walked on, saying sharply, "How do you know?"

"Saw it."

"Where?"

"Pocket."

"All this time?"

"Yes; isn't that romantic?"

"No, it's horrid."

"Don't you like it?"

"Of course I don't. It's ridiculous; it won't be allowed. My patience, what would Meg say?"

"You are not to tell anyone; mind that."

"I didn't promise."

"That was understood, and I trusted you."

"Well, I won't for the present, anyway; but I'm disgusted, and wish you hadn't told me."

"I thought you'd be pleased."

"At the idea of anybody coming to take Meg away? No, thank you."

"You'll feel better about it when somebody comes to take you away."

"I'd like to see anyone try it," cried Jo fiercely.

"So should I!" and Laurie chuckled at the idea.

"I don't think secrets agree with me; I feel rumpled up in my mind since you told me that," said Jo rather ungratefully.

"Race down this hill with me, and you'll be all right," suggested Laurie.

No one was in sight; the smooth road sloped invitingly before her; and finding the temptation irresistible, Jo darted away, soon leaving hat and comb behind her, and scattering hairpins as she ran. Laurie reached the goal first, and was quite satisfied with the success of his treatment; for his Atalanta came panting up, with flying hair, bright eyes, ruddy cheeks, and no signs of dissatisfaction in her face.

"I wish I was a horse; then I could run for miles in this splendid air and not lose my breath. It was capital; but see what a guy it's made me. Go, pick up my things, like a cherub as you are," said Jo, dropping down under a maple tree, which was carpeting the bank with crimson leaves.

Laurie leisurely departed to recover the lost property, and Jo bundled up her braids, hoping no one would pass by till she was tidy again. But someone did pass, and who should it be but Meg, looking particularly ladylike in her state and festival suit, for she had been making calls.

"What in the world are you doing here?" she asked, regarding her disheveled sister with well-bred surprise.

"Getting leaves," meekly answered Jo, sorting the rosy handful she had just swept up.

"And hairpins," added Laurie, throwing half a dozen into Jo's lap. "They grow on this road, Meg; so do combs and brown straw hats."

"You have been running, Jo; how could you? When *will* you stop such romping ways?" said Meg reprovingly, as she settled her cuffs, and smoothed her hair, with which the wind had taken liberties.

"Never till I'm stiff and old, and have to use a crutch. Don't try to make me grow up before my time, Meg; it's hard enough to have you change all of a sudden; let me be a little girl as long as I can."

As she spoke, Jo bent over the leaves to hide the trembling

of her lips, for lately she had felt that Margaret was fast getting to be a woman, and Laurie's secret made her dread the separation which must surely come sometime, and now seemed very near. He saw the trouble in her face, and drew Meg's attention from it by asking quickly, "Where have you been calling, all so fine?"

"At the Gardiners', and Sallie has been telling me all about Belle Moffat's wedding. It was very splendid, and they have gone to spend the winter in Paris. Just think how delightful that must be!"

"Do you envy her, Meg?" said Laurie.

"I'm afraid I do."

"I'm glad of it!" muttered Jo, tying on her hat with a jerk.

"Why?" asked Meg, looking surprised.

"Because if you care much about riches, you will never go and marry a poor man," said Jo, frowning at Laurie, who was mutely warning her to mind what she said.

"I shall never 'go and marry' anyone," observed Meg, walking on with great dignity, while the others followed, laughing, whispering, skipping stones, and "behaving like children," as Meg said to herself, though she might have been tempted to join them if she had not had her best dress on.

For a week or two, Jo behaved so queerly that her sisters were quite bewildered. She rushed to the door when the postman rang; was rude to Mr. Brooke whenever they met; would sit looking at Meg with a woebegone face, occasionally jumping up to shake, and then to kiss her, in a very mysterious manner; Laurie and she were always making signs to one another, and talking about "Spread Eagles," till the girls declared they had both lost their wits. On the second Saturday after Jo got out of the window, Meg, as she sat sewing at her window, was scandalized by the sight of Laurie chasing Jo all over the garden, and finally capturing her in Amy's bower. What went on there, Meg could not see; but shrieks of laughter were heard, followed by the murmur of voices and a great flapping of newspapers.

"What shall we do with that girl? She never *will* behave like a young lady," sighed Meg, as she watched the race with a disapproving face.

"I hope she won't; she is so funny and dear as she is," said Beth, who had never betrayed that she was a little hurt at Jo's having secrets with anyone but her.

"It's very trying, but we never can make her *commy la fo*," added Amy, who sat making some new frills for herself, with her curls tied up in a very becoming way—two agreeable things, which made her feel unusually elegant and ladylike.

In a few minutes Jo bounced in, laid herself on the scfa, and affected to read.

"Have you anything interesting there?" asked Meg with condescension.

"Nothing but a story! Won't amount to much, I guess," returned Jo, carefully keeping the name of the paper out of sight.

"You'd better read it aloud; that will amuse us and keep you out of mischief," said Amy, in her most grown-up tone.

"What's the name?" asked Beth, wondering why Jo kept her face behind the sheet.

"'The Rival Painters.'"

"That sounds well; read it," said Meg.

With a loud "Hem!" and a long breath, Jo began to read very fast. The girls listened with interest, for the tale was romantic, somewhat pathetic, as most of the characters died in the end.

"I like that about the splendid picture" was Amy's approving remark, as Jo paused.

"I prefer the lovering part. Viola and Angelo are two of our favorite names; isn't that queer?" said Meg, wiping her eyes, for the "lovering part" was tragical.

"Who wrote it?" asked Beth, who had caught a glimpse of Jo's face.

The reader suddenly sat up, cast away the paper, displaying a flushed countenance, and, with a funny mixture of solemnity and excitement, replied in a loud voice, "Your sister."

"You?" cried Meg, dropping her work.

"It's very good," said Amy critically.

"I knew it! I knew it! Oh, my Jo, I *am* so proud!" and Beth ran to hug her sister, and exult over this splendid success.

Dear me, how delighted they all were, to be sure! How Meg wouldn't believe it till she saw the words "Miss Jose-

phine March" actually printed in the paper; how graciously
Amy criticized the artistic parts of the story, and offered hints
for a sequel, which unfortunately couldn't be carried out, as
the hero and heroine were dead; how Beth got excited, and
skipped and sung with joy; how Hannah came in to exclaim
"Sakes alive, well, I never!" in great astonishment at "that Jo's
doin's"; how proud Mrs. March was when she knew it; how Jo
laughed with tears in her eyes, as she declared she might as
well be a peacock and done with it; and how the "Spread
Eagle" might be said to flap his wings triumphantly over the
House of March, as the paper passed from hand to hand.

"Tell us all about it." "When did it come?" "How much
did you get for it?" "What *will* father say?" "Won't Laurie
laugh?" cried the family, all in one breath, as they clustered
about Jo; for these foolish, affectionate people made a jubilee
of every little household joy.

"Stop jabbering, girls, and I'll tell you everything," said
Jo, wondering if Miss Burney felt any grander over her "Eve-
lina" than she did over her "Rival Painters." Having told how
she disposed of her tales, Jo added, "And when I went to get
my answer, the man said he liked them both, but didn't pay beginners, only let them print in his paper, and noticed the
stories. It was good practice, he said; and when the beginners
improved, anyone would pay. So I let him have the two stories,
and today this was sent to me, and Laurie caught me with it,
and insisted on seeing it, so I let him; and he said it was
good, and I shall write more, and he's going to get the next
paid for, and I *am* so happy, for in time I may be able to support myself and help the girls."

Jo's breath gave out here; and, wrapping her head in the
paper, she bedewed her little story with a few natural tears;
for to be independent and earn the praise of those she loved
were the dearest wishes of her heart, and this seemed to be
the first step toward that happy end.

CHAPTER FIFTEEN

A Telegram

⤳"NOVEMBER is the most disagreeable month in the whole year," said Margaret, standing at the window one dull afternoon, looking out at the frost-bitten garden.

"That's the reason I was born in it," observed Jo pensively, quite unconscious of the blot on her nose.

"If something very pleasant should happen now, we should think it a delightful month," said Beth, who took a hopeful view of everything, even November.

"I dare say; but nothing pleasant ever *does* happen in this family," said Meg, who was out of sorts. "We go grubbing along day after day, without a bit of change, and very little fun. We might as well be in a treadmill."

"My patience, how blue we are!" cried Jo. "I don't much

wonder, poor dear, for you see other girls having splendid
times, while you grind, grind, year in and year out. Oh, don't
I wish I could manage things for you as I do for my heroines!
You're pretty enough and good enough already, so I'd have
some rich relation leave you a fortune unexpectedly; then
you'd dash out as an heiress, scorn everyone who has slighted
you, go abroad, and come home my Lady Something, in a blaze
of splendor and elegance."

"People don't have fortunes left them in that style nowadays; men have to work, and women to marry for money. It's
a dreadfully unjust world," said Meg bitterly.

"Jo and I are going to make fortunes for you all; just wait
ten years, and see if we don't," said Amy, who sat in a corner
making mud pies, as Hannah called her little clay models of
birds, fruit, and faces.

"Can't wait, and I'm afraid I haven't much faith in ink and
dirt, though I'm grateful for your intentions."

Meg sighed, and turned to the frost-bitten garden again; Jo
groaned, and leaned both elbows on the table in a despondent
attitude, but Amy spatted away energetically; and Beth, who
sat at the other window, said, smiling, "Two pleasant things are
going to happen right away: Marmee is coming down the
street, and Laurie is tramping through the garden as if he had
something nice to tell."

In they both came, Mrs. March with her usual question,
"Any letter from father, girls?" and Laurie to say in his persuasive way, "Won't some of you come for a drive? I've been
working away at mathematics till my head is in a muddle, and
I'm going to freshen my wits by a brisk turn. It's a dull day,
but the air isn't bad, and I'm going to take Brooke home, so it
will be gay inside if it isn't out. Come, Jo, you and Beth will
go, won't you?"

"Of course we will."

"Much obliged, but I'm busy," and Meg whisked out her
workbasket, for she had agreed with her mother that it was
best, for her at least, not to drive often with the young gentleman.

"We three will be ready in a minute," cried Amy, running
away to wash her hands.

"Can I do anything for you, Madam Mother?" asked Laurie, leaning over Mrs. March's chair, with the affectionate look and tone he always gave her.

"No, thank you, except call at the office, if you'll be so kind, dear. It's our day for a letter, and the postman hasn't been. Father is as regular as the sun; there's some delay on the way, perhaps."

A sharp ring interrupted her, and a minute after Hannah came in with a letter.

"It's one of them horrid telegraph things, mum," she said, handling it as if she was afraid it would explode and do some damage.

At the word "telegraph," Mrs. March snatched it, read the two lines it contained, and dropped back into her chair as white as if the little paper had sent a bullet to her heart. Laurie dashed downstairs for water, while Meg and Hannah supported her, and Jo read aloud, in a frightened voice:

"Mrs. March:
Your husband is very ill. Come at once.
                                    S. Hale,
                        Blank Hospital, Washington."

How still the room was as they listened breathlessly, how strangely the day darkened outside, and how suddenly the whole world seemed to change, as the girls gathered about their mother, feeling as if all the happiness and support of their lives was about to be taken from them. Mrs. March was herself again directly; read the message over, and stretched out her arms to her daughters, saying, in a tone they never forgot, "I shall go at once, but it may be too late. Oh, children, children, help me to bear it!"

For several minutes there was nothing but the sound of sobbing in the room, mingled with broken words of comfort, tender assurances of help, and hopeful whispers that died away in tears. Poor Hannah was the first to recover, and with unconscious wisdom she set all the rest a good example; for, with her, work was the panacea for most afflictions.

"The Lord keep the dear man! I won't waste no time a cryin', but git your things ready right away, mum," she said heartily, as she wiped her face on her apron, gave her mistress a warm shake of the hand with her own hard one, and went away, to work like three women in one.

"She's right; there's no time for tears now. Be calm, girls, and let me think."

They tried to be calm, poor things, as their mother sat up, looking pale, but steady, and put away her grief to think and plan for them.

"Where's Laurie?" she asked presently, when she had collected her thoughts, and decided on the first duties to be done.

"Here, ma'am. Oh, let me do something!" cried the boy, hurrying from the next room, whither he had withdrawn, feeling that their first sorrow was too sacred for even his friendly eyes to see.

"Send a telegram saying I will come at once. The next train goes early in the morning. I'll take that."

"What else? The horses are ready; I can go anywhere, do anything," he said, looking ready to fly to the ends of the earth.

"Leave a note at Aunt March's. Jo, give me that pen and paper."

Tearing off the blank side of one of her newly copied pages, Jo drew the table before her mother, well knowing that money for the long, sad journey must be borrowed, and feeling as if she could do anything to add a little to the sum for her father.

"Now go, dear; but don't kill yourself driving at a desperate pace; there is no need of that."

Mrs. March's warning was evidently thrown away; for five minutes later Laurie tore by the window on his own fleet horse, riding as if for his life.

"Jo, run to the rooms, and tell Mrs. King that I can't come. On the way get these things. I'll put them down; they'll be needed, and I must go prepared for nursing. Hospital stores are not always good. Beth, go and ask Mr. Laurence for a couple bottles of old wine: I'm not too proud to beg for father; he shall have the best of everything. Amy, tell Hannah to get down the black trunk; and Meg, come and help me find my things, for I'm half bewildered."

Writing, thinking, and directing all at once might well bewilder the poor lady, and Meg begged her to sit quietly in her

room for a little while, and let them work. Everyone scattered
like leaves before a gust of wind; and the quiet, happy household was broken up as suddenly as if the paper had been an
evil spell.

Mr. Laurence came hurrying back with Beth, bringing
every comfort the kind old gentleman could think of for the
invalid, and friendliest promises of protection for the girls during the mother's absence, which comforted her very much.
There was nothing he didn't offer, from his own dressing gown
to himself as escort. But that last was impossible. Mrs. March
would not hear of the old gentleman's undertaking the long
journey; yet an expression of relief was visible when he spoke
of it, for anxiety ill fits one for traveling. He saw the look, knit
his heavy eyebrows, rubbed his hands, and marched abruptly
away, saying he'd be back directly. No one had time to think
of him again till, as Meg ran through the entry, with a pair of
rubbers in one hand and a cup of tea in the other, she came
suddenly upon Mr. Brooke.

"I'm very sorry to hear of this, Miss March," he said, in the
kind, quiet tone which sounded very pleasantly to her perturbed spirit. "I came to offer myself as escort to your mother.
Mr. Laurence has commissions for me in Washington, and it
will give me real satisfaction to be of service to her there."

Down dropped the rubbers, and the tea was very near
following, as Meg put out her hand, with a face so full of gratitude, that Mr. Brooke would have felt repaid for a much
greater sacrifice than the trifling one of time and comfort which
he was about to make.

"How kind you all are! Mother will accept, I'm sure; and it
will be such a relief to know that she has someone to take care
of her. Thank you very, very much!"

Meg spoke earnestly, and forgot herself entirely till something in the brown eyes looking down at her made her remember the cooling tea, and lead the way into the parlor, saying she
would call her mother.

Everything was arranged by the time Laurie returned with
a note from Aunt March, enclosing the desired sum, and a few
lines repeating what she had often said before—that she had
always told them it was absurd for March to go into the army,

always predicted that no good would come of it, and she hoped they would take her advice next time. Mrs. March put the note in the fire, the money in her purse, and went on with her preparations, with her lips folded tightly, in a way which Jo would have understood if she had been there.

The short afternoon wore away; all the other errands were done, and Meg and her mother busy at some necessary needle-work while Beth and Amy got tea, and Hannah finished her ironing with what she called a "slap and a bang," but still Jo did not come. They began to get anxious; and Laurie went off to find her, for no one ever knew what freak Jo might take into her head. He missed her, however, and she came walking in with a very queer expression of countenance, for there was a mixture of fun and fear, satisfaction and regret, in it, which puzzled the family as much as did the roll of bills she laid before her mother, saying, with a little choke in her voice, "That's my contribution toward making father comfortable and bringing him home!"

"My dear, where did you get it? Twenty-five dollars! Jo, I hope you haven't done anything rash?"

"No, it's mine honestly; I didn't beg, borrow, or steal it. I earned it, and I don't think you'll blame me, for I only sold what was my own."

As she spoke, Jo took off her bonnet, and a general outcry arose, for all her abundant hair was cut short.

"Your hair! Your beautiful hair!" "Oh, Jo, how could you? Your one beauty." "My dear girl, there was no need of this." "She doesn't look like my Jo any more, but I love her dearly for it!"

As everyone exclaimed, and Beth hugged the cropped head tenderly, Jo assumed an indifferent air, which did not deceive anyone a particle, and said, rumpling up the brown bush, and trying to look as if she liked it, "It doesn't affect the fate of the nation, so don't wail, Beth. It will be good for my vanity; I was getting too proud of my wig. It will do my brains good to have that mop taken off; my head feels deliciously light and cool, and the barber said I could soon have a curly crop, which will be boyish, becoming, and easy to keep in order. I'm satisfied; so please take the money, and let's have supper."

"Tell me all about it, Jo. *I* am not quite satisfied, but I can't blame you, for I know how willingly you sacrificed your vanity, as you call it, to your love. But, my dear, it was not necessary, and I'm afraid you will regret it, one of these days," said Mrs. March.

"No, I won't!" returned Jo stoutly, feeling much relieved that her prank was not entirely condemned.

"What made you do it?" asked Amy, who would as soon have thought of cutting off her head as her pretty hair.

"Well, I was wild to do something for father," replied Jo, as they gathered about the table, for healthy young people can eat even in the midst of trouble. "I hate to borrow as much as mother does, and I knew Aunt March would croak; she always does, if you ask for a ninepence. Meg gave all her quarterly salary toward the rent, and I only got some clothes with mine, so I felt wicked, and was bound to have some money, if I sold the nose off my face to get it."

"You needn't feel wicked, my child: you had no winter things, and got the simplest with your own hard earnings," said Mrs. March, with a look that warmed Jo's heart.

"I hadn't the least idea of selling my hair at first, but as I went along I kept thinking what I could do, and feeling as if I'd like to dive into some of the rich stores and help myself. In a barber's window I saw tails of hair with the prices marked; and one black tail, not so thick as mine, was forty dollars. It came over me all of a sudden that I had one thing to make money out of, and without stopping to think, I walked in, asked if they bought hair, and what they would give for mine."

"I don't see how you dared to do it," said Beth, in a tone of awe.

"Oh, he was a little man who looked as if he merely lived to oil his hair. He rather stared, at first, as if he wasn't used to having girls bounce into his shop and ask him to buy their hair. He said he didn't care about mine, it wasn't the fashionable color, and he never paid much for it in the first place; the work put into it made it dear, and so on. It was getting late, and I was afraid, if it wasn't done right away, that I shouldn't have it done at all, and you know when I start to do a thing I hate to give it up; so I begged him to take it, and told him why

I was in such a hurry. It was silly, I dare say, but it changed his mind, for I got rather excited, and told the story in my topsy-turvy way, and his wife heard, and said so kindly:

"'Take it, Thomas, and oblige the young lady; I'd do as much for our Jimmy any day if I had a spire of hair worth selling.'"

"Who was Jimmy?" asked Amy, who liked to have things explained as they went along.

"Her son, she said, who was in the army. How friendly such things make strangers feel, don't they? She talked away all the time the man clipped, and diverted my mind nicely."

"Didn't you feel dreadfully when the first cut came?" asked Meg, with a shiver.

"I took a last look at my hair while the man got his things, and that was the end of it. I never snivel over trifles like that; I will confess, though, I felt queer when I saw the dear old hair laid out on the table, and felt only the short, rough ends on my head. It almost seemed as if I'd an arm or a leg off. The woman saw me look at it, and picked out a long lock for me to keep. I'll give it to you, Marmee, just to remember past glories by; for a crop is so comfortable I don't think I shall ever have a mane again."

Mrs. March folded the wavy chestnut lock, and laid it away with a short gray one in her desk. She only said, "Thank you, deary," but something in her face made the girls change the subject, and talk as cheerfully as they could about Mr. Brooke's kindness, the prospect of a fine day tomorrow, and the happy times they would have when father came home to be nursed.

No one wanted to go to bed when, at ten o'clock, Mrs. March put by the last finished job, and said, "Come, girls." Beth went to the piano, and played the father's favorite hymn; all began bravely, but broke down one by one, till Beth was left alone, singing with all her heart, for her music was always a sweet consoler.

"Go to bed and don't talk, for we must be up early, and shall need all the sleep we can get. Good night, my darlings," said Mrs. March, as the hymn ended, for no one cared to try another.

They kissed her quietly, and went to bed as silently as if the dear invalid lay in the next room. Beth and Amy soon fell

asleep in spite of the great trouble, but Meg lay awake, thinking the most serious thoughts she had ever known in her short
life. Jo lay motionless, and her sister fancied that she was
asleep, till a stifled sob made her exclaim, as she touched a wet
cheek:

"Jo, dear, what is it? Are you crying about father?"

"No, not now."

"What then?"

"My—my hair!" burst out poor Jo, trying vainly to smother
her emotion in the pillow.

It did not sound at all comical to Meg, who kissed and caressed the afflicted heroine in the tenderest manner.

"I'm not sorry," protested Jo, with a choke. "I'd do it again
tomorrow, if I could. It's only the vain selfish part of me that
goes and cries in this silly way. Don't tell anyone, it's all over
now. I thought you were asleep, so I just made a little private
moan for my one beauty. How came you to be awake?"

"I can't sleep, I'm so anxious," said Meg.

"Think about something pleasant, and you'll soon drop off."

"I tried it, but felt wider awake than ever."

"What did you think of?"

"Handsome faces—eyes particularly," answered Meg, smiling to herself, in the dark.

"What color do you like best?"

"Brown—that is, sometimes; blue are lovely."

Jo laughed, and Meg sharply ordered her not to talk, then
amiably promised to make her hair curl, and fell asleep to
dream of living in her castle in the air.

The clocks were striking midnight, and the rooms were
very still, as a figure glided quietly from bed to bed, smoothing
a coverlid here, settling a pillow there, and pausing to look
long and tenderly at each unconscious face, to kiss each with
lips that mutely blessed, and to pray the fervent prayers which
only mothers utter. As she lifted the curtain to look out into the
dreary night, the moon broke suddenly from behind the clouds
and shone upon her like a bright, benignant face, which
seemed to whisper in the silence, "Be comforted, dear soul!
There is always light behind the clouds."

CHAPTER SIXTEEN

Letters

IN the cold gray dawn the sisters lit their lamp, and read their chapter with an earnestness never felt before; for now the shadow of a real trouble had come, the little books were full of help and comfort; and, as they dressed, they agreed to say good-by cheerfully and hopefully, and send their mother on her anxious journey unsaddened by tears or complaints from them. Everything seemed very strange when they went down—so dim and still outside, so full of light and bustle within. Breakfast at that early hour seemed odd, and even Hannah's familiar face looked unnatural as she flew about her kitchen with her nightcap on. The big trunk stood ready in the hall, mother's cloak and bonnet lay on the sofa, and mother herself sat trying to eat, but looking so pale and worn with sleeplessness and anxiety that the girls found it very hard to keep their resolution. Meg's eyes kept filling in spite of herself; Jo was obliged to hide her face in the kitchen roller more than once; and the little girls wore a grave, troubled expression, as if sorrow was a new experience to them.

Nobody talked much, but as the time drew very near, and they sat waiting for the carriage, Mrs. March said to the girls, who were all busied about her, one folding her shawl, another smoothing out the strings of her bonnet, a third putting on her overshoes, and a fourth fastening up her traveling bag:

"Children, I leave you to Hannah's care and Mr. Laurence's protection. Hannah is faithfulness itself, and our good neighbor will guard you as if you were his own. I have no fears for you, yet I am anxious that you should take this trouble rightly. Don't grieve and fret when I am gone, or think that you can comfort yourselves by being idle and trying to forget. Go on with your work as usual, for work is a blessed solace. Hope and keep busy; and whatever happens, remember that you never can be fatherless."

"Yes, mother."

"Meg dear, be prudent, watch over your sisters, consult Hannah, and, in any perplexity, go to Mr. Laurence. Be patient, Jo, don't get despondent or do rash things; write to me often, and be my brave girl, ready to help and cheer us all. Beth, comfort yourself with your music, and be faithful to the little home duties; and you, Amy, help all you can, be obedient, and keep happy safe at home."

"We will, mother, we will!"

The rattle of an approaching carriage made them all start and listen. That was the hard minute, but the girls stood it well: no one cried, no one ran away or uttered a lamentation though their hearts were very heavy as they sent loving messages to father, remembering, as they spoke, that it might be too late to deliver them. They kissed their mother quietly, clung about her tenderly, and tried to wave their hands cheerfully when she drove away.

Laurie and his grandfather came over to see her off, and Mr. Brooke looked so strong and sensible and kind that the girls christened him "Mr. Greatheart" on the spot.

"Good-by, my darlings! God bless and keep us all!" whispered Mrs. March, as she kissed one dear little face after the other, and hurried into the carriage.

As she rolled away, the sun came out, and, looking back, she saw it shining on the group at the gate, like a good omen. They saw it also, and smiled and waved their hands; and the last thing she beheld, as she turned the corner, was the four bright faces, and behind them, like a bodyguard, old Mr. Laurence, faithful Hannah, and devoted Laurie.

"How kind everyone is to us!" she said, turning to find fresh proof of it in the respectful sympathy of the young man's face.

"I don't see how they can help it," returned Mr. Brooke, laughing so infectiously that Mrs. March could not help smiling; and so the long journey began with the good omens of sunshine, smiles, and cheerful words.

"I feel as if there had been an earthquake," said Jo, as their neighbors went home to breakfast, leaving them to rest and refresh themselves.

"It seems as if half the house was gone," added Meg forlornly.

Beth opened her lips to say something, but could only point to the pile of nicely mended hose which lay on mother's table, showing that even in her last hurried moments she had thought and worked for them. It was a little thing, but it went straight to their hearts; and, in spite of their brave resolutions, they all broke down and cried bitterly.

Hannah wisely allowed them to relieve their feelings, and, when the shower showed signs of clearing up, she came to the rescue, armed with a coffeepot.

"Now, my dear young ladies, remember what your ma said, and don't fret. Come and have a cup of coffee all round, and then let's fall to work, and be a credit to the family."

Coffee was a treat, and Hannah showed great tact in making it that morning. No one could resist her persuasive nods, or the fragrant invitation issuing from the nose of the coffeepot. They drew up to the table, exchanged their handkerchiefs for napkins, and in ten minutes were all right again.

"'Hope and keep busy,' that's the motto for us, so let's see who will remember it best. I shall go to Aunt March, as usual. Oh, won't she lecture though!" said Jo, as she sipped with returning spirit.

"I shall go to my Kings, though I'd much rather stay at home and attend to things here," said Meg, wishing she hadn't made her eyes so red.

"No need of that; Beth and I can keep house perfectly well," put in Amy, with an important air.

"Hannah will tell us what to do; and we'll have everything nice when you come home," added Beth, getting out her mop and dishtub without delay.

"I think anxiety is very interesting," observed Amy, eating sugar, pensively.

The girls couldn't help laughing, and felt better for it, though Meg shook her head at the young lady who could find consolation in a sugar bowl.

The sight of the turnovers made Jo sober again; and when the two went out to their daily tasks, they looked sorrowfully back at the window where they were accustomed to see their mother's face. It was gone; but Beth had remembered the little household ceremony, and there she was, nodding away at them like a rosy-faced mandarin.

"That's so like my Beth!" said Jo, waving her hat, with a grateful face. "Good-by, Meggy; I hope the Kings won't train today. Don't fret about father, dear," she added, as they parted.

"And I hope Aunt March won't croak. Your hair *is* becoming, and it looks very boyish and nice," returned Meg, trying not to smile at the curly head, which looked comically small on her tall sister's shoulders.

"That's my only comfort," and, touching her hat à la Laurie, away went Jo, feeling like a shorn sheep on a wintry day.

News from their father comforted the girls very much; for though dangerously ill, the presence of the best and tenderest of nurses had already done him good. Mr. Brooke sent a bulletin every day, and, as the head of the family, Meg insisted on reading the dispatches, which grew more and more cheering as the week passed. At first, everyone was eager to write, and plump envelopes were carefully poked into the letter box by one or other of the sisters, who felt rather important with their Washington correspondence. As one of these packets contained characteristic notes from the party, we will rob an imaginary mail, and read them:

"Good=by, my darlings! God bless and keep us all!"

[SEE PAGE 184]

My Dearest Mother:

It is impossible to tell you how happy your last letter made us, for the news was so good we couldn't help laughing and crying over it. How very kind Mr. Brooke is, and how fortunate that Mr. Laurence's business detains him near you so long, since he is so useful to you and father. The girls are as good as gold. Jo helps me with the sewing, and insists on doing all sorts of hard jobs. I should be afraid she might overdo, if I didn't know that her "moral fit" wouldn't last long. Beth is as regular about her tasks as a clock, and never forgets what you told her. She grieves about father, and looks sober except when she is at her little piano. Amy minds me nicely, and I take great care of her. She does her own hair and I am teaching her to make buttonholes and mend her stockings. She tries very hard, and I know you will be pleased with her improvement when you come. Mr. Laurence watches over us like a motherly old hen, as Jo says; and Laurie is very kind and neighborly. He and Jo keep us merry, for we get pretty blue sometimes, and feel like orphans with you so far away. Hannah is a perfect saint; she does not scold at all, and always calls me Miss "Margaret," which is quite proper, you know, and treats me with respect. We are all well and busy; but we long, day and night, to have you back. Give my dearest love to father, and believe me, ever your own

MEG

This note, prettily written on scented paper, was a great contrast to the next, which was scribbled on a big sheet of thin foreign paper, ornamented with blots and all manner of flourishes and curly-tailed letters:

My Precious Marmee:

Three cheers for dear father! Brooke was a trump to telegraph right off, and let us know the minute he was better. I rushed up garret when the letter came, and tried to thank God for being so good to us; but I could only cry, and say, "I'm glad! I'm glad!" Didn't that do as well as a regular prayer? For I felt a great many in my heart. We have such funny times; and now I can enjoy them, for everyone is so desperately good, it's like living in a nest of turtledoves. You'd laugh to see Meg head the table and try to be motherish. She gets prettier every day, and I'm in love with her sometimes. The children are regular arch-angels, and I—well, I'm Jo, and never shall be anything else. Oh, I must tell you that I came near having a quarrel with Laurie. I freed my mind about a silly little thing, and he was offended. I was right, but didn't speak as I ought, and he marched home, saying he wouldn't come again till I begged pardon. I declared I wouldn't, and got mad. It lasted all day; I felt bad, and wanted you very much. Laurie and I are both so proud, it's hard to beg pardon; but I thought he'd come to it, for I *was* in the right. He didn't come; and just at night I re-membered what you said when Amy fell into the river. I read my little book, felt better, resolved not to let the sun set on *my* anger, and ran over to tell Laurie I was sorry. I met him at the gate, coming for the same thing. We both laughed, begged each other's pardon, and felt all good and comfortable again.

I made a "pome" yesterday, when I was helping Hannah wash; and, as father likes my silly little things, I put it in to amuse him. Give him the lovingest hug that ever was, and kiss yourself a dozen times for your

Topsy-Turvy Jo

A SONG FROM THE SUDS

Queen of my tub, I merrily sing,
*   While the white foam rises high;*
And sturdily wash and rinse and wring,
*   And fasten the clothes to dry;*
Then out in the free fresh air they swing,
*   Under the sunny sky.*

I wish we could wash from our hearts and souls
*   The stains of the week away,*
And let water and air by their magic make
*   Ourselves as pure as they;*
Then on the earth there would be indeed
*   A glorious washing day!*

Along the path of a useful life,
  Will heart's-ease ever bloom;
The busy mind has no time to think
  Of sorrow or care or gloom;
And anxious thoughts may be swept away,
  As we bravely wield a broom.

I am glad a task to me is given,
  To labor at day by day;
For it brings me health and strength and hope,
  And I cheerfully learn to say,—
"Head, you may think, Heart, you may feel,
  But, Hand, you shall work alway!"

DEAR MOTHER:

There is only room for me to send my love, and some pressed pansies from the root I have been keeping safe in the house for father to see. I read every morning, try to be good all day, and sing myself to sleep with father's tune. I can't sing "Land of the Leal" now; it makes me cry. Everyone is very kind, and we are as happy as we can be without you. Amy wants the rest of the page, so I must stop. I didn't forget to cover the holders, and I wind the clock and air the rooms every day.

Kiss dear father on the cheek he calls mine. Oh, do come soon to your loving

LITTLE BETH

MA CHERE MAMMA:

We are all well I do my lessons always and never corroborate the girls—Meg says I mean contradick so I put in both words and you can take the properest. Meg is a great comfort to me and lets me have jelly every night at tea its so good for me Jo says because it keeps me sweet-tempered. Laurie is not as respeckful as he ought to be now I am almost in my teens, he calls me Chick and hurts my feelings by talking French to me very fast when I say Merci or Bon jour as Hattie King does. The sleeves of my blue dress were all worn out, and Meg put in new ones, but the full front came wrong and they are more blue than the dress. I felt bad but did not fret I bear my troubles well but I do wish Hannah would put more starch in my aprons and have buckwheats every day. Can't she? Didn't I make that interrigation point nice? Meg says my punchtuation and spelling are disgraceful and I am mortyfied but dear me I have so many things to do, I can't stop. Adieu, I send heaps of love to Papa.

Your affectionate daughter,
AMY CURTIS MARCH

DEAR MIS MARCH:

I jes drop a line to say we git on fust rate. The girls is clever and fly around right smart. Miss Meg is going to make a proper good housekeeper; she hes the liking for it, and gits the hang of things surprisin quick. Jo doos beat all for going ahead, but she don't stop to calklate fust, and you never know where she's like to bring up. She done out a tub of clothes on Monday, but she starched em afore they was wrenched, and blued a pink calico dress till I thought I should a died a laughing. Beth is the best of little creeters, and a sight of help to me, bein so forehanded and dependable. She tries to learn everything, and really goes to market beyond her years; likewise keeps accounts, with my help, quite wonderful. We have got on very economical so fur; I don't let the girls hev coffee only once a week, according to your wish, and keep em on plain wholesome vittles. Amy does well about frettin, wearin her best clothes and eatin sweet stuff. Mr. Laurie is as full of didoes as usual, and turns the house upside down frequent, but he heartens up the girls, and so I let em have full swing. The old gentleman sends heaps of things, and is rather wearing but means wal, and it aint my place to say nothin. My bread is riz, so no more at this time. I send my duty to Mr. March and hope he's seen the last of his Pewmonia.

Yours Respectful,
HANNAH MULLET

HEAD NURSE OF WARD NO. 2—

All serene on the Rappahannock, troops in fine condition, commissary department well conducted, the Home Guard under Colonel Teddy always on duty, Commander in Chief General Laurence reviews the army daily, Quartermaster Mullet keeps order in camp, and Major Lion does picket duty at night. A salute of twenty-four guns was fired on receipt of good news from Washington, and a dress parade took place at headquarters. Commander in Chief sends best wishes, in which he is heartily joined by

COLONEL TEDDY

DEAR MADAM:

The little girls are all well; Beth and my boy report daily; Hannah is a model servant, and guards pretty Meg like a dragon. Glad the fine weather holds; pray make Brooke useful, and draw on me for funds if expenses exceed your estimate. Don't let your husband want anything. Thank God he is mending.

Your sincere friend and servant,
JAMES LAURENCE

CHAPTER SEVENTEEN

Little Faithful

FOR a week the amount of virtue in the old house would have supplied the neighborhood. It was really amazing, for everyone seemed in a heavenly frame of mind, and self-denial was all the fashion. Relieved of their first anxiety about their father, the girls insensibly relaxed their praiseworthy efforts a little, and began to fall back into the old ways. They did not forget their motto, but hoping and keeping busy seemed to grow easier; and after such tremendous exertions, they felt that Endeavor had deserved a holiday, and gave it a good many.

Jo caught a bad cold through neglect to cover the shorn head enough, and was ordered to stay at home till she was better, for Aunt March didn't like to hear people read with colds in their heads. Jo liked this, and after an energetic rummage from garret to cellar, subsided on the sofa to nurse her cold with arsenicum and books. Amy found that housework and art did not go well together, and returned to her mud pies. Meg went daily to her pupils, and sewed, or thought she did, at home, but much time was spent in writing long letters to her mother, or reading the Washington dispatches over and over. Beth kept on, with only slight relapses into idleness or grieving.

All the little duties were faithfully done each day, and many of her sisters' also, for they were forgetful, and the house seemed like a clock whose pendulum was gone a-visiting. When her heart got heavy with longings for her mother or fears for her father, she went away into a certain closet, hid her face in the folds of a certain dear old gown, and made her little moan and prayed her little prayer quietly by herself. Nobody knew what cheered her up after a sober fit, but everyone felt how sweet and helpful Beth was, and fell into a way of going to her for comfort or advice in their small affairs.

All were unconscious that this experience was a test of character; and, when the first excitement was over, felt that they had done well, and deserved praise. So they did; but their mistake was in ceasing to do well, and they learned this lesson through much anxiety and regret.

"Meg, I wish you'd go and see the Hummels; you know mother told us not to forget them," said Beth, ten days after Mrs. March's departure.

"I'm too tired to go this afternoon," replied Meg, rocking comfortably as she sewed.

"Can't you, Jo?" asked Beth.

"Too stormy for me with my cold."

"I thought it was almost well."

"It's well enough for me to go out with Laurie, but not well enough to go to the Hummels'," said Jo, laughing, but looking a little ashamed of her inconsistency.

"Why don't you go yourself?" asked Meg.

"I have been every day, but the baby is sick, and I don't know what to do for it. Mrs. Hummel goes away to work and Lottchen takes care of it; but it gets sicker and sicker and I think you or Hannah ought to go."

Beth spoke earnestly, and Meg promised she would go to-morrow.

"Ask Hannah for some nice little mess, and take it round, Beth; the air will do you good," said Jo, adding apologetically, "I'd go, but I want to finish my writing."

"My head aches and I'm tired, so I thought maybe some of you would go," said Beth.

"Amy will be in presently, and she will run down for us," suggested Meg.

"Well, I'll rest a little and wait for her."

So Beth lay down on the sofa, the others returned to their work, and the Hummels were forgotten. An hour passed: Amy did not come; Meg went to her room to try on a new dress; Jo was absorbed in her story, and Hannah was sound asleep before the kitchen fire, when Beth quietly put on her hood, filled her basket with odds and ends for the poor children, and went out into the chilly air, with a heavy head and a grieved look in her patient eyes. It was late when she came back, and no one saw her creep upstairs and shut herself into her mother's room. Half an hour later Jo went to "mother's closet" for something, and there found Beth sitting on the medicine chest, looking very grave, with red eyes, and a camphor bottle in her hand.

"Christopher Columbus! What's the matter?" cried Jo, as Beth put out her hand as if to warn her off, and asked quickly:

"You've had the scarlet fever, haven't you?"

"Years ago, when Meg did. Why?"

"Then I'll tell you. Oh, Jo, the baby's dead!"

"What baby?"

"Mrs. Hummel's; it died in my lap before she got home," cried Beth, with a sob.

"My poor dear, how dreadful for you! I ought to have gone," said Jo, taking her sister in her arms as she sat down in her mother's big chair, with a remorseful face.

"It wasn't dreadful, Jo, only so sad! I saw in a minute that it was sicker, but Lottchen said her mother had gone for a doctor, so I took baby and let Lotty rest. It seemed asleep, but all of a sudden it gave a little cry, and trembled, and then lay very still. I tried to warm its feet, and Lotty gave it some milk, but it didn't stir, and I knew it was dead."

"Don't cry, dear! What did you do?"

"I just sat and held it softly till Mrs. Hummel came with the doctor. He said it was dead, and looked at Heinrich and Minna, who have got sore throats. 'Scarlet fever, ma'am. Ought to have called me before,' he said crossly. Mrs. Hummel told him she was poor, and had tried to cure baby herself, but now it was too late, and she could only ask him to help the others, and trust to charity for his pay. He smiled then, and was kinder; but it was very sad, and I cried with them till he turned round, all of a sudden, and told me to go home and take belladonna right away, or I'd have the fever."

"No, you won't!" cried Jo, hugging her close, with a frightened look. "Oh, Beth, if you should be sick I never could forgive myself! What *shall* we do?"

"Don't be frightened, I guess I shan't have it badly. I looked in mother's book, and saw that it begins with headaches, sore throat, and queer feelings like mine, so I did take some belladonna, and I feel better," said Beth, laying her cold hand on her hot forehead, and trying to look well.

"If mother was only at home!" exclaimed Jo, seizing the book, and feeling that Washington was an immense way off. She read a page, looked at Beth, felt her head, peeped into her throat, and then said gravely, "You've been over the baby every day for more than a week, and among the others who are going to have it; so I'm afraid you are going to have it, Beth. I'll call Hannah, she knows all about sickness."

"Don't let Amy come; she never had it, and I should hate to give it to her. Can't you and Meg have it over again?" asked Beth anxiously.

"I guess not; don't care if I do; serves me right, selfish pig, to let you go and stay writing rubbish myself!" muttered Jo, as she went to consult Hannah.

The good soul was wide awake in a minute, and took the lead at once, assuring Jo that there was no need to worry; everyone had scarlet fever, and if rightly treated, nobody died, all of which Jo believed, and felt much relieved as they went up to call Meg.

"Now I'll tell you what we'll do," said Hannah, when she had examined and questioned Beth; "we will have Dr. Bangs, just to take a look at you, dear, and see that we start right; then we'll send Amy off to Aunt March's for a spell, to keep her out of harm's way, and one of you girls can stay at home and amuse Beth for a day or two."

"I shall stay, of course; I'm oldest," began Meg, looking anxious and self-reproachful.

"*I* shall, because it's my fault she is sick; I told mother I'd do the errands, and I haven't," said Jo decidedly.

"Which will you have, Beth? There ain't no need of but one," said Hannah.

"Jo, please," and Beth leaned her head against her sister, with a contented look, which effectually settled that point.

"I'll go and tell Amy," said Meg, feeling a little hurt yet rather relieved, on the whole, for she did not like nursing, and Jo did.

Amy rebelled outright, and passionately declared that she had rather have the fever than go to Aunt March. Meg reasoned, pleaded, and commanded: all in vain. Amy protested that she would *not* go; and Meg left her in despair, to ask Hannah what should be done. Before she came back, Laurie walked into the parlor to find Amy sobbing, with her head in the sofa cushions. She told her story, expecting to be consoled; but Laurie only put his hands in his pockets and walked about the room, whistling softly, as he knit his brows in deep thought. Presently he sat down beside her, and said, in his most wheedlesome tone, "Now be a sensible little woman, and do as they say. No, don't cry, but hear what a jolly plan I've got. You go to Aunt March's, and I'll come and take you out every day, driving or walking, and we'll have capital times. Won't that be better than moping here?"

"I don't wish to be sent off as if I was in the way," began Amy, in an injured voice.

"Bless your heart, child, it's to keep you well. You don't want to be sick, do you?"

"No, I'm sure I don't; but I dare say I shall be, for I've been with Beth all the time."

"That's the very reason you ought to go away at once, so that you may escape it. Change of air and care will keep you well, I dare say; or, if it does not entirely, you will have the fever more lightly. I advise you to be off as soon as you can, for scarlet fever is no joke, miss."

"But it's dull at Aunt March's, and she is so cross," said Amy, looking rather frightened.

"It won't be dull with me popping in every day to tell you how Beth is, and take you out gallivanting. The old lady likes me, and I'll be as sweet as possible to her, so she won't peck at us, whatever we do."

"Will you take me out in the trotting wagon with Puck?"

"On my honor as a gentleman."

"And come every single day?"

"See if I don't."

"And bring me back the minute Beth is well?"

"The identical minute."

"And go to the theater, truly?"

"A dozen theaters, if we may."

"Well—I guess—I will," said Amy slowly.

"Good girl! Call Meg, and tell her you'll give in," said Laurie, with an approving pat, which annoyed Amy more than the "giving in."

Meg and Jo came running down to behold the miracle which had been wrought; and Amy, feeling very precious and self-sacrificing, promised to go, if the doctor said Beth was going to be ill.

"How is the little dear?" asked Laurie; for Beth was his especial pet, and he felt more anxious about her than he liked to show.

"She is lying down on mother's bed, and feels better. The baby's death troubled her, but I dare say she has only got cold. Hannah says she thinks so; but she *looks* worried, and that makes me fidgety," answered Meg.

"What a trying world it is!" said Jo, rumpling up her hair in a fretful sort of way. "No sooner do we get out of one trouble than down comes another. There doesn't seem to be anything to hold on to when mother's gone; so I'm all at sea."

"Well, don't make a porcupine of yourself, it isn't becoming. Settle your wig, Jo, and tell me if I shall telegraph to your mother, or do anything?" asked Laurie, who never had been reconciled to the loss of his friend's one beauty.

"That is what troubles me," said Meg. "I think we ought to tell her if Beth is really ill, but Hannah says we mustn't, for mother can't leave father, and it will only make them anxious.

Beth won't be sick long, and Hannah knows just what to do, and mother said we were to mind her, so I suppose we must, but it doesn't seem quite right to me."

"Hum, well, I can't say; suppose you ask grandfather after the doctor has been."

"We will. Jo, go and get Dr. Bangs at once," commanded Meg; "we can't decide anything till he has been."

"Stay where you are, Jo; I'm errand boy to this establishment," said Laurie, taking up his cap.

"I'm afraid you are busy," began Meg.

"No, I've done my lessons for the day."

"Do you study in vacationtime?" asked Jo.

"I follow the good example my neighbors set me" was Laurie's answer, as he swung himself out of the room.

"I have great hopes of my boy," observed Jo, watching him fly over the fence with an approving smile.

"He does very well—for a boy" was Meg's somewhat ungracious answer, for the subject did not interest her.

Dr. Bangs came, said Beth had symptoms of the fever, but thought she would have it lightly, though he looked sober over the Hummel story. Amy was ordered off at once, and provided with something to ward off danger, she departed in great state, with Jo and Laurie as escort.

Aunt March received them with her usual hospitality.

"What do you want now?" she asked, looking sharply over her spectacles, while the parrot, sitting on the back of her chair, called out:

"Go away. No boys allowed here."

Laurie retired to the window, and Jo told her story.

"No more than I expected if you are allowed to go poking about among poor folk. Amy can stay and make herself useful if she isn't sick, which I've no doubt she will be—looks like it now. Don't cry, child, it worries me to hear people sniff."

Amy *was* on the point of crying, but Laurie slyly pulled the parrot's tail, which caused Polly to utter an astonished croak, and call out:

"Bless my boots!" in such a funny way that she laughed instead.

"What do you hear from your mother?" asked the old lady gruffly.

"Father is much better," replied Jo, trying to keep sober.

"Oh, is he? Well, that won't last long, I fancy; March never had any stamina" was the cheerful reply.

"Ha, ha! never say die, take a pinch of snuff, good-by, good-by!" squalled Polly, dancing on his perch, and clawing at the old lady's cap as Laurie tweaked him in the rear.

"Hold your tongue, you disrespectful old bird! and, Jo, you'd better go at once; it isn't proper to be gadding about so late with a rattle-pated boy like—"

"Hold your tongue, you disrespectful old bird!" cried Polly, tumbling off the chair with a bounce, and running to peck the "rattle-pated" boy, who was shaking with laughter at the last speech.

"I don't think I *can* bear it, but I'll try," thought Amy, as she was left alone with Aunt March.

"Get along, you fright!" screamed Polly; and at that rude speech Amy could not restrain a sniff.

CHAPTER EIGHTEEN

Dark Days

BETH did have the fever, and was much sicker than any-one but Hannah and the doctor suspected. The girls knew nothing about illness, and Mr. Laurence was not allowed to see her, so Hannah had everything all her own way, and busy Dr. Bangs did his best, but left a good deal to the excellent nurse. Meg stayed at home, lest she should infect the Kings, and kept house, feeling very anxious and a little guilty when she wrote letters in which no mention was made of Beth's illness. She could not think it right to deceive her mother, but she had been bidden to mind Hannah, and Hannah wouldn't hear of "Mrs. March bein' told, and worried just for sech a trifle." Jo devoted herself to Beth day and night; not a hard task, for Beth was very patient, and bore her pain uncomplain-

ingly as long as she could control herself. But there came a
time when during the fever fits she began to talk in a hoarse,
broken voice, to play on the coverlet, as if on her beloved little
piano, and try to sing with a throat so swollen that there was
no music left; a time when she did not know the familiar faces
round her, but addressed them by wrong names, and called imploringly for her mother. Then Jo grew frightened, Meg
begged to be allowed to write the truth, and even Hannah said
she "would think of it, though there was no danger *yet*." A
letter from Washington added to their trouble, for Mr. March
had had a relapse, and could not think of coming home for a
long while.

How dark the days seemed now, how sad and lonely the
house, and how heavy were the hearts of the sisters as they
worked and waited, while the shadow of death hovered over
the once happy home! Then it was that Margaret, sitting alone
with tears dropping often on her work, felt how rich she had
been in things more precious than any luxuries money could
buy—in love, protection, peace, and health, the real blessings
of life. Then it was that Jo, living in the darkened room, with
that suffering little sister always before her eyes, and that pathetic voice sounding in her ears, learned to see the beauty
and the sweetness of Beth's nature, to feel how deep and
tender a place she filled in all hearts, and to acknowledge the
worth of Beth's unselfish ambition to live for others, and make
home happy by the exercise of those simple virtues which all
may possess, and which all should love and value more than
talent, wealth, or beauty. And Amy, in her exile, longed eagerly
to be at home, that she might work for Beth, feeling now that
no service would be hard or irksome, and remembering, with
regretful grief, how many neglected tasks those willing hands
had done for her. Laurie haunted the house like a restless
ghost, and Mr. Laurence locked the grand piano, because he
could not bear to be reminded of the young neighbor who used
to make the twilight pleasant for him. Everyone missed Beth.
The milkman, baker, grocer, and butcher inquired how she
did; poor Mrs. Hummel came to beg pardon for her thought-
lessness, and to get a shroud for Minna; the neighbors sent all
sorts of comforts and good wishes, and even those who knew

her best were surprised to find how many friends shy little
Beth had made.

Meanwhile she lay on her bed with old Joanna at her side,
for even in her wanderings she did not forget her forlorn pro-
tégée. She longed for her cats, but would not have them
brought, lest they should get sick; and, in her quiet hours, she

was full of anxiety about Jo. She sent loving messages to Amy,
bade them tell her mother that she would write soon; and often
begged for pencil and paper to try to say a word, that father
might not think she had neglected him. But soon even these
intervals of consciousness ended, and she lay hour after hour,
tossing to and fro, with incoherent words on her lips, or sank
into a heavy sleep which brought her no refreshment. Dr.
Bangs came twice a day, Hannah sat up at night, Meg kept a
telegram in her desk all ready to send off at any minute, and
Jo never stirred from Beth's side.

The first of December was a wintry day indeed to them, for a bitter wind blew, snow fell fast, and the year seemed getting ready for its death. When Dr. Bangs came that morning, he looked long at Beth, held the hot hand in both his own a minute, and laid it gently down, saying in a low tone, to Hannah:

"If Mrs. March *can* leave her husband, she'd better be sent for."

Hannah nodded without speaking, for her lips twitched nervously; Meg dropped down into a chair as the strength seemed to go out of her limbs at the sound of those words; and Jo, after standing with a pale face for a minute, ran to the parlor, snatched up the telegram, and, throwing on her things, rushed out into the storm. She was soon back, and, while noiselessly taking off her cloak, Laurie came in with a letter, saying that Mr. March was mending again. Jo read it thankfully, but the heavy weight did not seem lifted off her heart, and her face was so full of misery that Laurie asked quickly:

"What is it? Is Beth worse?"

"I've sent for mother," said Jo, tugging at her rubber boots with a tragical expression.

"Good for you, Jo! Did you do it on your own responsibility?" asked Laurie, as he seated her in the hall chair, and took off the rebellious boots, seeing how her hands shook.

"No, the doctor told us to."

"Oh, Jo, it's not so bad as that?" cried Laurie, with a startled face.

"Yes, it is; she doesn't know us, she doesn't even talk about the flocks of green doves, as she calls the vine leaves on the wall; she doesn't look like my Beth, and there's nobody to help us bear it; mother and father both gone, and God seems so far away I can't find Him."

As the tears streamed fast down poor Jo's cheeks, she stretched out her hand in a helpless sort of way, as if groping in the dark, and Laurie took it in his, whispering, as well as he could, with a lump in his throat:

"I'm here. Hold on to me, Jo dear!"

She could not speak, but she did "hold on," and the warm grasp of the friendly human hand comforted her sore heart,

and seemed to lead her nearer to the divine arm which alone
could uphold her in her trouble. Laurie longed to say something tender and comfortable, but no fitting words came to
him, so he stood silent, gently stroking her bent head as her
mother used to do. It was the best thing he could have done;
far more soothing than the most eloquent words, for Jo felt
the unspoken sympathy, and, in the silence, learned the sweet
solace which affection administers to sorrow. Soon she dried
the tears which had relieved her, and looked up with a grateful
face.

"Thank you, Teddy, I'm better now; I don't feel so forlorn,
and will try to bear it if it comes."

"Keep hoping for the best; that will help you, Jo. Soon your
mother will be here, and then everything will be right."

"I'm so glad father is better; now she won't feel so bad about
leaving him. Oh, me! It does seem as if all the troubles came in
a heap, and I got the heaviest part on my shoulders," sighed Jo,
spreading her wet handkerchief over her knees to dry.

"Doesn't Meg pull fair?" asked Laurie, looking indignant.

"Oh, yes; she tries to, but she can't love Bethy as I do; and
she won't miss her as I shall. Beth is my conscience, and I *can't*
give her up. I can't! I can't!"

Down went Jo's face into the wet handkerchief, and she
cried despairingly; for she had kept up bravely till now, and
never shed a tear. Laurie drew his hand across his eyes, but
could not speak till he had subdued the choky feeling in his
throat and steadied his lips. It might be unmanly, but he
couldn't help it, and I am glad of it. Presently, as Jo's sobs
quieted, he said hopefully, "I don't think she will die; she's so
good, and we all love her so much, I don't believe God will
take her away yet."

"The good and dear people always do die," groaned Jo, but
she stopped crying, for her friend's words cheered her up in
spite of her own doubts and fears.

"Poor girl, you're worn out. It isn't like you to be forlorn.
Stop a bit; I'll hearten you up in a jiffy."

Laurie went off two stairs at a time, and Jo laid her wearied
head down on Beth's little brown hood, which no one had

thought of moving from the table where she left it. It must have possessed some magic, for the submissive spirit of its gentle owner seemed to enter into Jo; and, when Laurie came running down with a glass of wine, she took it with a smile, and said bravely, "I drink—Health to my Beth! You are a good doctor, Teddy, and *such* a comfortable friend; how can I ever pay you?" she added, as the wine refreshed her body, as the kind words had done her troubled mind.

"I'll send in my bill, by and by; and tonight I'll give you something that will warm the cockles of your heart better than quarts of wine," said Laurie, beaming at her with a face of suppressed satisfaction at something.

"What is it?" cried Jo, forgetting her woes for a minute, in her wonder.

"I telegraphed to your mother yesterday, and Brooke answered she'd come at once, and she'll be here tonight, and everything will be all right. Aren't you glad I did it?"

Laurie spoke very fast, and turned red and excited all in a minute, for he had kept his plot a secret, for fear of disappointing the girls or harming Beth. Jo grew quite white, flew out of her chair, and the moment he stopped speaking she electrified him by throwing her arms round his neck, and crying out, with a joyful cry, "Oh, Laurie! Oh, mother! I *am* so glad!" She did not weep again, but laughed hysterically, and trembled and clung to her friend as if she was a little bewildered by the sudden news.

Laurie, though decidedly amazed, behaved with great presence of mind; he patted her back soothingly, and, finding that she was recovering, followed it up by a bashful kiss or two, which brought Jo round at once. Holding on to the banisters, she put him gently away, saying breathlessly, "Oh, don't! I didn't mean to; it was dreadful of me; but you were such a dear to go and do it in spite of Hannah that I couldn't help flying at you. Tell me all about it, and don't give me wine again; it makes me act so."

"I don't mind," laughed Laurie, as he settled his tie. "Why, you see I got fidgety, and so did grandpa. We thought Hannah was overdoing the authority business, and your mother ought to know. She'd never forgive us if Beth—well, if anything happened, you know. So I got grandpa to say it was high time we did something, and off I pelted to the office yesterday, for the doctor looked sober, and Hannah most took my head off when I proposed a telegram. I never *can* bear to be 'lorded over'; so that settled my mind, and I did it. Your mother will come, I know, and the late train is in at two A.M. I shall go for her; and you've only got to bottle up your rapture, and keep Beth quiet, till that blessed lady gets here."

"Laurie, you're an angel! How shall I ever thank you?"

"Fly at me again; I rather like it," said Laurie, looking mischievous—a thing he had not done for a fortnight.

"No, thank you. I'll do it by proxy, when your grandpa comes. Don't tease, but go home and rest, for you'll be up half the night. Bless you, Teddy, bless you!"

Jo had backed into a corner; and, as she finished her speech she vanished precipitately into the kitchen, where she sat down upon a dresser and told the assembled cats that she was "happy, oh, *so* happy!" while Laurie departed, feeling that he had made rather a neat thing of it.

"That's the interferingest chap I ever see; but I forgive him, and do hope Mrs. March is coming on right away," said Hannah, with an air of relief, when Jo told the good news.

Meg had a quiet rapture, and then brooded over the letter while Jo set the sickroom in order, and Hannah "knocked up a couple of pies in case of company unexpected." A breath of fresh air seemed to blow through the house and something better than sunshine brightened the quiet rooms. Everything appeared to feel the hopeful change; Beth's bird began to chirp again, and a half-blown rose was discovered on Amy's bush in the window; the fires seemed to burn with unusual cheeriness; and every time the girls met, their pale faces broke into smiles as they hugged one another, whispering encouragingly, "Mother's coming, dear! Mother's coming!" Everyone rejoiced but Beth; she lay in that heavy stupor, alike unconscious of hope and joy, doubt and danger. It was a piteous sight—the once rosy face so changed and vacant, the once busy hands so weak and wasted, the once smiling lips quite dumb, and the once pretty, well-kept hair scattered rough and tangled on the

pillow. All day she lay so, only rousing now and then to mutter, "Water!" with lips so parched they could hardly shape the
word; all day Jo and Meg hovered over her, watching, waiting,
hoping, and trusting in God and mother; and all day the snow
fell, the bitter wind raged, and the hours dragged slowly by.
But night came at last; and every time the clock struck, the
sisters, still sitting on either side the bed, looked at each other
with brightening eyes, for each hour brought help nearer. The
doctor had been in to say that some change, for better or
worse, would probably take place about midnight at which
time he would return.

Hannah, quite worn out, lay down on the sofa at the bed's
foot, and fell fast asleep; Mr. Laurence marched to and fro in
the parlor, feeling that he would rather face a rebel battery
than Mrs. March's anxious countenance as she entered; Laurie
lay on the rug, pretending to rest, but staring into the fire with
the thoughtful look which made his black eyes beautifully soft
and clear.

The girls never forgot that night, for no sleep came to them
as they kept their watch, with that dreadful sense of powerless-
ness which comes to us in hours like those.

"If God spares Beth I never will complain again," whispered
Meg earnestly.

"If God spares Beth I'll try to love and serve Him all my
life," answered Jo, with equal fervor.

"I wish I had no heart, it aches so," sighed Meg, after a
pause.

"If life is often as hard as this, I don't see how we ever shall
get through it," added her sister despondently.

Here the clock struck twelve, and both forgot themselves
in watching Beth, for they fancied a change passed over her
wan face. The house was still as death, and nothing but the
wailing of the wind broke the deep hush. Weary Hannah slept
on, and no one but the sisters saw the pale shadow which
seemed to fall upon the little bed. An hour went by, and
nothing happened except Laurie's quiet departure for the station. Another hour—still no one came; and anxious fears of delay in the storm, or accidents by the way, or worst of all, a
great grief at Washington, haunted the poor girls.

It was past two when Jo, who stood at the window thinking how dreary the world looked in its winding sheet of snow, heard a movement by the bed, and, turning quickly, saw Meg kneeling before their mother's easy chair, with her face hidden. A dreadful fear passed coldly over Jo, as she thought, "Beth is dead, and Meg is afraid to tell me."

She was back at her post in an instant; and to her excited eyes a great change seemed to have taken place. The fever flush and the look of pain were gone, and the beloved little face looked so pale and peaceful in its utter repose that Jo felt no desire to weep or to lament. Leaning low over this dearest of her sisters, she kissed the damp forehead with her heart on her lips, and softly whispered, "Good-by, my Beth; good-by!"

As if waked by the stir, Hannah started out of her sleep, hurried to the bed, looked at Beth, felt her hands, listened at her lips, and then, throwing her apron over her head, sat down to rock to and fro, exclaiming, under her breath, "The fever's turned; she's sleepin' nat'ral; her skin's damp, and she breathes easy. Praise be given! Oh, my goodness me!"

Before the girls could believe the happy truth, the doctor came to confirm it. He was a homely man, but they thought his face quite heavenly when he smiled, and said, with a fatherly look at them, "Yes, my dears, I think the little girl will pull through this time. Keep the house quiet; let her sleep, and when she wakes, give her—"

What they were to give, neither heard; for both crept into the dark hall, and sitting on the stairs, held each other close, rejoicing with hearts too full for words. When they went back to be kissed and cuddled by faithful Hannah, they found Beth lying, as she used to do, with her cheek pillowed on her hand, the dreadful pallor gone, and breathing quietly, as if just fallen asleep.

"If mother would only come now!" said Jo, as the winter night began to wane.

"See," said Meg, coming up with a white, half-opened rose, "I thought this would hardly be ready to lay in Beth's hand to-morrow if she—went away from us. But it has blossomed in the night, and now I mean to put it in my vase here, so that when the darling wakes, the first thing she sees will be the little rose, and mother's face."

Never had the sun risen so beautifully, and never had the world seemed so lovely, as it did to the heavy eyes of Meg and Jo, as they looked out in the early morning, when their long, sad vigil was done.

"It looks like a fairy world," said Meg, smiling to herself, as she stood behind the curtain, watching the dazzling sight.

"Hark!" cried Jo, starting to her feet.

Yes, there was a sound of bells at the door below, a cry from Hannah, and then Laurie's voice saying, in a joyful whisper, "Girls, she's come, she's come!"

CHAPTER NINETEEN

Amy's Will

WHILE these things were happening at home, Amy was having hard times at Aunt March's. She felt her exile deeply, and for the first time in her life realized how much she was beloved and petted at home. Aunt March never petted anyone; she did not approve of it; but she meant to be kind, for the well-behaved little girl pleased her very much, and Aunt March had a soft place in her old heart for her nephew's children, though she didn't think proper to confess it. She really did her best to make Amy happy, but, dear me, what mistakes she made! Some old people keep young at heart in spite of wrinkles and gray hairs, can sympathize with children's little cares and joys, make them feel at home, and can hide wise lessons under pleasant plays, giving and receiving friendship

in the sweetest way. But Aunt March had not this gift, and
she worried Amy very much with her rules and orders, her
prim ways, and long, prosy talks. Finding the child more docile and amiable than her sister, the old lady felt it her duty to
try and counteract, as far as possible, the bad effects of her
home freedom and indulgence. So she took Amy in hand, and
taught her as she herself had been taught sixty years ago—a
process which carried dismay to Amy's soul and made her
feel like a fly in the web of a very strict spider.

She had to wash the cups every morning, and polish up the
old-fashioned spoons, the fat silver teapot, and the glasses till
they shone. Then she must dust the room, and what a trying
job that was! Not a speck escaped Aunt March's eye, and all
the furniture had claw legs, and much carving, which was
never dusted to suit. Then Polly must be fed, the lap dog
combed and a dozen trips upstairs and down, to get things, or
deliver orders, for the old lady was very lame, and seldom left
her big chair. After these tiresome labors, she must do her lessons, which was a daily trial of every virtue she possessed.
Then she was allowed one hour for exercise or play, and didn't
she enjoy it? Laurie came every day, and wheedled Aunt
March, till Amy was allowed to go out with him, when they
walked and rode, and had capital times. After dinner, she had
to read aloud, and sit still while the old lady slept, which she
usually did for an hour, as she dropped off over the first page.
Then patchwork or towels appeared, and Amy sewed with
outward meekness and inward rebellion till dusk, when she
was allowed to amuse herself as she liked till teatime. The
evenings were the worst of all, for Aunt March fell to telling
long stories about her youth, which were so unutterably dull
that Amy was always ready to go to bed, intending to cry over
her hard fate, but usually going to sleep before she had
squeezed out more than a tear or two.

If it had not been for Laurie, and old Esther, the maid, she
felt that she never could have got through that dreadful time.
The parrot alone was enough to drive her distracted, for he
soon felt that she did not admire him, and revenged himself by
being as mischievous as possible. He pulled her hair whenever
she came near him, upset his bread and milk to plague her

when she had newly cleaned his cage, made Mop bark by pecking at him while Madam dozed; called her names before company, and behaved in all respects like a reprehensible old bird. Then she could not endure the dog—a fat, cross beast, who snarled and yelped at her when she made his toilette, and who lay on his back, with all his legs in the air and a most idiotic expression of countenance when he wanted something to eat, which was about a dozen times a day. The cook was bad-tempered, the old coachman deaf, and Esther the only one who ever took any notice of the young lady.

Esther was a Frenchwoman, who had lived with "Madame," as she called her mistress, for many years, and who rather tyrannized over the old lady, who could not get along without her. Her real name was Estelle, but Aunt March ordered her to change it, and she obeyed, on condition that she was never asked to change her religion. She took a fancy to Mademoiselle, and amused her very much, with odd stories of her life in France, when Amy sat with her while she got up Madame's laces. She also allowed her to roam about the great house, and examine the curious and pretty things stored away in the big wardrobes and the ancient chests; for Aunt March hoarded like a magpie. Amy's chief delight was an Indian cabinet, full of queer drawers, little pigeonholes, and secret places, in which were kept all sorts of ornaments, some precious, some merely curious, all more or less antique. To examine and arrange these things gave Amy great satisfaction, especially the jewel cases, in which, on velvet cushions, reposed the ornaments which had adorned a belle forty years ago. There was the garnet set which Aunt March wore when she came out, the pearls her father gave her on her wedding day, her lover's diamonds, the jet mourning rings and pins, the queer lockets, with portraits of dead friends, and weeping willows made of hair inside; the baby bracelets her one little daughter had worn; Uncle March's big watch, with the red seal so many childish hands had played with, and in a box, all by itself, lay Aunt March's wedding ring, too small now for her fat finger, but put carefully away like the most precious jewel of them all.

"Which would Mademoiselle choose if she had her will?"

asked Esther, who always sat near to watch over and lock up the valuables.

"I like the diamonds best, but there is no necklace among them, and I'm fond of necklaces, they are so becoming. I should choose this if I might," replied Amy, looking with great admiration at a string of gold and ebony beads, from which hung a heavy cross of the same.

"I, too, covet that, but not as a necklace; ah, no! to me it is a rosary, and as such I should use it like a good Catholic," said Esther, eying the handsome thing wistfully.

"Is it meant to use as you use the string of good-smelling wooden beads hanging over your glass?" asked Amy.

"Truly, yes, to pray with. It would be pleasing to the saints if one used so fine a rosary as this, instead of wearing it as a vain bijou."

"You seem to take a great deal of comfort in your prayers, Esther, and always come down looking quiet and satisfied. I wish I could."

"If Mademoiselle was a Catholic, she would find true comfort; but, as that is not to be, it would be well if you went apart each day, to meditate and pray, as did the good mistress whom I served before Madame. She had a little chapel, and in it found solacement for much trouble."

"Would it be right for me to do so too?" asked Amy, who, in her loneliness, felt the need of help of some sort, and found that she was apt to forget her little book, now that Beth was not there to remind her of it.

"It would be excellent and charming; and I shall gladly arrange the little dressing room for you if you like it. Say nothing to Madame, but when she sleeps go you and sit alone a while to think good thoughts, and pray the dear God to preserve your sister."

Esther was truly pious, and quite sincere in her advice; for she had an affectionate heart, and felt much for the sisters in their anxiety. Amy liked the idea, and gave her leave to arrange the light closet next her room, hoping it would do her good.

"I wish I knew where all these pretty things would go when

Aunt March dies," she said, as she slowly replaced the shining rosary, and shut the jewel cases one by one.

"To you and your sisters. I know it; Madame confides in me; I witnessed her will, and it is to be so," whispered Esther, smiling.

"How nice! But I wish she'd let us have them now. Pro-cras-ti-nation is not agreeable," observed Amy, taking a last look at the diamonds.

"It is too soon yet for the young ladies to wear these things. The first one who is affianced will have the pearls—Madame has said it; and I have a fancy that the little turquoise ring will be given to you when you go, for Madame approves your good behavior and charming manners."

"Do you think so? Oh, I'll be a lamb, if I can only have that lovely ring! It's ever so much prettier than Kitty Bryant's. I do like Aunt March, after all," and Amy tried on the blue ring with a delighted face, and a firm resolve to earn it.

From that day she was a model of obedience, and the old lady complacently admired the success of her training. Esther fitted up the closet with a little table, placed a footstool before it, and over it a picture taken from one of the shut-up rooms. She thought it was of no great value, but, being appropriate, she borrowed it, well knowing that Madame would never know it, nor care if she did. It was, however, a very valuable copy of one of the famous pictures of the world, and Amy's beauty-loving eyes were never tired of looking up at the sweet face of the divine mother, while tender thoughts of her own were busy at her heart. On the table she laid her little Testament and hymnbook, kept a vase always full of the best flowers Laurie brought her, and came every day to "sit alone, thinking good thoughts, and praying the dear God to preserve her sister." Esther had given her a rosary of black beads, with a silver cross, but Amy hung it up and did not use it, feeling doubtful as to its fitness for Protestant prayers.

The little girl was very sincere in all this, for, being left alone outside the safe home nest, she felt the need of some kind hand to hold by so sorely that she instinctively turned to the strong and tender Friend, whose fatherly love most closely surrounds His little children. She missed her mother's help to understand and rule herself, but having been taught where to

look, she did her best to find the way, and walk in it confidingly. But Amy was a young pilgrim, and just now her burden
seemed very heavy. She tried to forget herself, to keep cheerful, and be satisfied with doing right, though no one saw or
praised her for it. In her first effort at being very, very good,
she decided to make her will, as Aunt March had done; so that
if she *did* fall ill and die, her possessions might be justly and
generously divided. It cost her a pang even to think of giving
up the little treasures which in her eyes were as precious as
the old lady's jewels.

During one of her play hours she wrote out the important
document as well as she could, with some help from Esther as
to certain legal terms, and,
when the good-natured
Frenchwoman had signed
her name, Amy felt re-
lieved, and laid it by to
show Laurie, whom she
wanted as a second wit-
ness. As it was a rainy day,
she went upstairs to amuse
herself in one of the large

chambers, and took Polly with her for company. In this room there was a wardrobe full of old-fashioned costumes, with which Esther allowed her to play, and it was her favorite amusement to array herself in the faded brocades, and parade up and down before the long mirror, making stately curtsies, and sweeping her train about, with a rustle which delighted her ears. So busy was she on this day that she did not hear Laurie's ring, nor see his face peeping in at her, as she gravely promenaded to and fro, flirting her fan and tossing her head, on which she wore a great pink turban, contrasting oddly with her blue brocade dress and yellow quilted petticoat. She was obliged to walk carefully, for she had on high-heeled shoes, and, as Laurie told Jo afterward, it was a comical sight to see her mince along in her gay suit, with Polly sidling and bridling just behind her, imitating her as well as he could, and occasionally stopping to laugh or exclaim, "Ain't we fine? Get along, you fright! Hold your tongue! Kiss me, dear! Ha, ha!"

Having with difficulty restrained an explosion of merriment, lest it should offend her majesty, Laurie tapped, and was graciously received.

"Sit down and rest while I put these things away; then I want to consult you about a very serious matter," said Amy, when she had shown her splendor, and driven Polly into a corner. "That bird is the trial of my life," she continued, removing the pink mountain from her head, while Laurie seated himself astride of a chair. "Yesterday, when aunt was asleep, and I was trying to be as still as a mouse, Polly began to squall and flap about in his cage; so I went to let him out, and found a big spider there. I poked it out, and it ran under the bookcase; Polly marched straight after it, stooped down and peeped under the bookcase, saying, in his funny way, with a cock of his eye, 'Come out and take a walk, my dear.' I *couldn't* help laughing, which made Poll swear, and aunt woke up and scolded us both."

"Did the spider accept the old fellow's invitation?" asked Laurie, yawning.

"Yes; out it came, and away ran Polly, frightened to death, and scrambled up on aunt's chair, calling out, 'Catch her! catch her! catch her!' as I chased the spider."

"That's a lie! Oh, lor!" cried the parrot, pecking at Laurie's toes.

"I'd wring your neck if you were mine, you old torment," cried Laurie, shaking his fist at the bird, who put his head on one side, and gravely croaked, "Allyluyer! Bless your buttons, dear!"

"Now I'm ready," said Amy, shutting the wardrobe, and taking a paper out of her pocket. "I want you to read that, please, and tell me if it is legal and right. I felt that I ought to do it, for life is uncertain and I don't want any ill feeling over my tomb."

Laurie bit his lips, and turning a little from the pensive speaker, read the following document, with praiseworthy gravity, considering the spelling:

MY LAST WILL AND TESTMENT

I, Amy Curtis March, being in my sane mind, do give and bequeethe all my earthly property—viz. to wit:—namely

To my father, my best pictures, sketches, maps, and works of art, including frames. Also my $100, to do what he likes with.

To my mother, all my clothes, except the blue apron with pockets—also my likeness, and my medal, with much love.

To my dear sister Margaret, I give my turkquoise ring (if I get it), also my green box with the doves on it, also my piece of real lace for her neck, and my sketch of her as a memorial of her "little girl."

To Jo I leave my breastpin, the one mended with sealing wax, also my bronze inkstand—she lost the cover—and my most precious plaster rabbit, because I am sorry I burnt up her story.

To Beth (if she lives after me) I give my dolls and the little bureau, my fan, my linen collars and my new slippers if she can wear them being thin when she gets well. And I herewith also leave her my regret that I ever made fun of old Joanna.

To my friend and neighbor Theodore Laurence I bequeethe my paper marshay portfolio, my clay model of a horse though he did say it hadn't any neck. Also in return for his great kindness in the hour of affliction any one of my artistic works he likes, Notre Dame is the best.

To our venerable benefactor Mr. Laurence I leave my purple box with a looking glass in the cover which will be nice for his pens and remind him of the departed girl who thanks him for his favors to her family, specially Beth.

I wish my favorite playmate Kitty Bryant to have the blue silk apron and my gold-bead ring with a kiss.

To Hannah I give the bandbox she wanted and all the patch work I leave hoping she "will remember me, when it you see."

And now having disposed of my most valuable property I hope all will be satisfied and not blame the dead. I forgive everyone, and trust we may all meet when the trump shall sound. Amen.

To this will and testament I set my hand and seal on this 20th day of Nov. Anni Domino 1861.

AMY CURTIS MARCH

Witnesses: { ESTELLE VALNOR
              { THEODORE LAURENCE

The last name was written in pencil, and Amy explained that he was to rewrite it in ink, and seal it up for her properly.

"What put it into your head? Did anyone tell you about Beth's giving away her things?" asked Laurie soberly, as Amy laid a bit of red tape, with sealing wax, a taper, and a standish before him.

She explained; and then asked anxiously, "What about Beth?"

"I'm sorry I spoke; but as I did, I'll tell you. She felt so ill one day that she told Jo she wanted to give her piano to Meg, her cats to you, and the poor old doll to Jo, who would love it for her sake. She was sorry she had so little to give, and left locks of hair to the rest of us, and her best love to grandpa. *She* never thought of a will."

Laurie was signing and sealing as he spoke, and did not look up till a great tear dropped on the paper. Amy's face was full of trouble; but she only said, "Don't people put sort of postscripts to their wills, sometimes?"

"Yes; 'codicils,' they call them."

"Put one in mine then—that I wish *all* my curls cut off, and given round to my friends. I forgot it; but I want it done, though it will spoil my looks."

Laurie added it, smiling at Amy's last and greatest sacrifice. Then he amused her for an hour, and was much interested in all her trials. But when he came to go, Amy held him back to whisper, with trembling lips, "Is there really any danger about Beth?"

"I'm afraid there is; but we must hope for the best, so don't cry, dear," and Laurie put his arm about her with a brotherly gesture which was very comforting.

When he had gone, she went to her little chapel, and, sitting in the twilight, prayed for Beth, with streaming tears and an aching heart, feeling that a million turquoise rings would not console her for the loss of her gentle little sister.

CHAPTER TWENTY

Confidential

I DON'T think I have any words in which to tell the meeting of the mother and daughters; such hours are beautiful to live, but very hard to describe, so I will leave it to the imagination of my readers, merely saying that the house was full of genuine happiness, and that Meg's tender hope was realized; for when Beth woke from that long, healing sleep, the first objects on which her eyes fell *were* the little rose and mother's face. Too weak to wonder at anything, she only smiled, and nestled close into the loving arms about her, feeling that the hungry longing was satisfied at last. Then she slept again, and the girls waited upon their mother, for she would not unclasp the thin hand which clung to hers even in sleep.

Hannah had "dished up" an astonishing breakfast for the traveler, finding it impossible to vent her excitement in any other way; and Meg and Jo fed their mother like dutiful young storks, while they listened to her whispered account of father's state, Mr. Brooke's promise to stay and nurse him, the delays which the storm occasioned on the homeward journey, and the unspeakable comfort Laurie's hopeful face had given her when she arrived, worn out with fatigue, anxiety, and cold.

What a strange, yet pleasant day that was, so brilliant and gay without, for all the world seemed abroad to welcome the first snow; so quiet and reposeful within, for everyone slept, spent with watching, and a Sabbath stillness reigned through the house, while nodding Hannah mounted guard at the door. With a blissful sense of burdens lifted off, Meg and Jo closed their weary eyes, and lay at rest, like storm-beaten boats, safe at anchor in a quiet harbor. Mrs. March would not leave Beth's side, but rested in the big chair, waking often to look at, touch, and brood over her child, like a miser over some recovered treasure.

Laurie, meanwhile, posted off to comfort Amy, and told his story so well that Aunt March actually "sniffed" herself, and never once said "I told you so." Amy came out so strong on this occasion that I think the good thoughts in the little chapel really began to bear fruit. She dried her tears quickly, calmly restrained her impatience to see her mother, and never even thought of the turquoise ring, when the old lady heartily agreed in Laurie's opinion, that she behaved "like a capital little woman." Even Polly seemed impressed, for he called her "good girl," blessed her buttons, and begged her to "come and take a walk, dear" in his most affable tone. She would very gladly have gone out to enjoy the bright wintry weather; but discovering that Laurie was dropping with sleep in spite of manful efforts to conceal the fact, she persuaded him to rest on the sofa, while she wrote a note to her mother. She was a long time about it; and, when she returned, he was stretched out with both arms under his head, sound asleep, while Aunt March had pulled down the curtains, and sat doing nothing in an unusual fit of benignity.

After a while, they began to think he was not going to wake till night, and I'm not sure that he would, had he not been effectually roused by Amy's cry of joy at sight of her mother. There probably were a good many happy little girls in and about the city that day, but it is my private opinion that Amy was the happiest of all, when she sat in her mother's lap and told her trials, receiving consolation and compensation in the shape of approving smiles and fond caresses. They were alone together in the chapel, to which her mother did not object when its purpose was explained to her.

"On the contrary, I like it very much, dear," looking from the dusty rosary to the well-worn little book, and the lovely picture with its garland of evergreen. "It is an excellent plan to have some place where we can go to be quiet, when things vex or grieve us. There are a good many hard times in this life of ours, but we can always bear them if we ask help in the right way. I think my little girl is learning this?"

"Yes, mother; and when I go home I mean to have a corner in the big closet to put my books, and the copy of that picture which I've tried to make. The woman's face is not good—it's too beautiful for me to draw—but the baby is done better, and I love it very much. I like to think He was a little child once, for then I don't seem so far away, and that helps me."

As Amy pointed to the smiling Christ child on his mother's knee, Mrs. March saw something on the lifted hand that made her smile. She said nothing, but Amy understood the look, and, after a minute's pause, she added gravely:

"I wanted to speak to you about this, but I forgot it. Aunt gave me the ring today; she called me to her and kissed me, and put it on my finger, and said I was a credit to her, and she'd like to keep me always. She gave that funny guard to keep the turquoise on, as it's too big. I'd like to wear them, mother; can I?"

"They are very pretty, but I think you're rather too young for such ornaments, Amy," said Mrs. March, looking at the plump little hand, with the band of sky-blue stones on the forefinger, and the quaint guard, formed of two tiny, golden hands clasped together.

"I'll try not to be vain," said Amy. "I don't think I like it only because it's so pretty; but I want to wear it as the girl in the story wore her bracelet, to remind me of something."

"Do you mean Aunt March?" asked her mother, laughing.

"No, to remind me not to be selfish." Amy looked so earnest and sincere about it that her mother stopped laughing, and listened respectfully to the little plan.

"'I've thought a great deal lately about my 'bundle of naughties,' and being selfish is the largest one in it; so I'm going to try hard to cure it, if I can. Beth isn't selfish, and that's the reason everyone loves her and feels so bad at the thought of losing her. People wouldn't feel half so bad about me if I was sick, and I don't deserve to have them! But I'd like to be loved and missed by a great many friends, so I'm going to try and be like Beth all I can. I'm apt to forget my resolutions; but if I had something always about me to remind me, I guess I should do better. May I try this way?'

"Yes; but I have more faith in the corner of the big closet. Wear your ring, dear, and do your best; I think you will prosper, for the sincere wish to be good is half the battle. Now I must go back to Beth. Keep up your heart, little daughter, and we will soon have you home again."

That evening, while Meg was writing to her father, to report the traveler's safe arrival, Jo slipped upstairs into Beth's room and, finding her mother in her usual place, stood a minute twisting her fingers in her hair, with a worried gesture and an undecided look.

"What is it, deary?" asked Mrs. March, holding out her hand, with a face which invited confidence.

"I want to tell you something, mother."

"About Meg?"

"How quickly you guessed! Yes, it's about her, and though it's a little thing it fidgets me."

"Beth is asleep; speak low, and tell me all about it. That Moffat hasn't been here, I hope?" asked Mrs. March rather sharply.

"No, I should have shut the door in his face if he had," said Jo, settling herself on the floor at her mother's feet. "Last summer Meg left a pair of gloves over at the Laurences', and only one was returned. We forgot all about it, till Teddy told me that Mr. Brooke had it. He kept it in his waistcoat pocket and once it fell out, and Teddy joked him about it, and Mr. Brooke owned that he liked Meg, but didn't dare say so, she was so young and he so poor. Now, isn't it a *dread*ful state of things?"

"Do you think Meg cares for him?" asked Mrs. March, with an anxious look.

"Mercy me! I don't know anything about love and such nonsense!" cried Jo, with a funny mixture of interest and contempt. "In novels, the girls show it by starting and blushing, fainting away, growing thin, and acting like fools. Now Meg does not do anything of the sort: she eats and drinks and sleeps, like a sensible creature; she looks straight in my face when I talk about that man, and only blushes a little bit when Teddy jokes about lovers. I forbid him to do it, but he doesn't mind me as he ought."

"Then you fancy that Meg is *not* interested in John?"

"Who?" cried Jo, staring.

"Mr. Brooke. I call him 'John' now; we fell into the way of doing so at the hospital, and he likes it."

"Oh, dear! I know you'll take his part; he's been good to father, and you won't send him away, but let Meg marry him, if she wants to. Mean thing, to go petting papa and helping you, just to wheedle you into liking him!" and Jo pulled her hair again with a wrathful tweak.

"My dear, don't get angry about it, and I will tell you how it happened. John went with me at Mr. Laurence's request, and was so devoted to poor father that we couldn't help getting fond of him. He was perfectly open and honorable about Meg, for he told us he loved her, but would earn a comfortable home before he asked her to marry him. He only wanted our leave to love her and work for her, and the right to make her love him if he could. He is a truly excellent young man, and we could not refuse to listen to him; but I will not consent to Meg's engaging herself so young."

"Of course not; it would be idiotic! I knew there was mischief brewing! I felt it; and now it's worse than I imagined. I just wish I could marry Meg myself, and keep her safe in the family."

This odd arrangement made Mrs. March smile; but she said gravely, "Jo, I confide in you, and don't wish you to say anything to Meg yet. When John comes back, and I see them together, I can judge better of her feelings toward him."

"She'll see his in those handsome eyes that she talks about, and then it will be all up with her. She's got such a soft heart, it will melt like butter in the sun if anyone looks sentimentally at her. She read the short reports he sent more than she did your letters and pinched me when I spoke of it, and likes brown eyes, and doesn't think John an ugly name, and she'll go and fall in love, and there's an end of peace and fun, and cozy times together. I see it all! They'll go lovering around the house, and we shall have to dodge; Meg will be absorbed, and no good to me any more; Brooke will scratch up a fortune somehow, carry her off, and make a hole in the family; and I shall break my heart, and everything will be abominably uncomfortable. Oh, dear me! Why weren't we all boys? Then there wouldn't be any bother."

Jo leaned her chin on her knees, in a disconsolate attitude, and shook her fist at the reprehensible John. Mrs. March sighed, and Jo looked up with an air of relief.

"You don't like it, mother? I'm glad of it. Let's send him about his business, and not tell Meg a word of it, but all be happy together as we always have been."

"I did wrong to sigh, Jo. It is natural and right you should all go to homes of your own, in time; but I do want to keep my girls as long as I can; and I am sorry that this happened so soon, for Meg is only seventeen, and it will be some years before John can make a home for her. Your father and I have agreed that she shall not bind herself in any way, nor be married, before twenty. If she and John love one another, they can wait, and test the love by doing so. She is conscientious, and I have no fear of her treating him unkindly. My pretty, tender-hearted girl! I hope things will go happily with her."

"Hadn't you rather have her marry a rich man?" asked Jo, as her mother's voice faltered a little over the last words.

"Money is a good and useful thing, Jo; and I hope my girls will never feel the need of it too bitterly, nor be tempted by too much. I should like to know that John was firmly established in some good business, which gave him an income large enough to keep free from debt and make Meg comfortable. I'm not ambitious for a splendid fortune, a fashionable position, or a great name for my girls. If rank and money come with love and virtue, also, I should accept them gratefully, and enjoy your good fortune; but I know, by experience, how much genuine happiness can be had in a plain little house, where the daily bread is earned, and some privations give sweetness to the few pleasures. I am content to see Meg begin humbly, for, if I am not mistaken, she will be rich in the possession of a good man's heart, and that is better than a fortune."

"I understand, mother, and quite agree; but I'm disappointed about Meg, for I'd planned to have her marry Teddy by and by, and sit in the lap of luxury all her days. Wouldn't it be nice?" asked Jo, looking up, with a brighter face.

"He is younger than she, you know," began Mrs. March; but Jo broke in:

"Only a little; he's old for his age, and tall; and can be quite grown up in his manners if he likes. Then he's rich and generous and good, and loves us all; and I say it's a pity my plan is spoilt."

"I'm afraid Laurie is hardly grown up enough for Meg, and altogether too much of a weathercock, just now, for anyone to depend on. Don't make plans, Jo; but let time and their own hearts mate your friends. We can't meddle safely in such matters, and had better not get 'romantic rubbish,' as you call it, into our heads, lest it spoil our friendship."

"Well, I won't; but I hate to see things going all crisscross and getting snarled up, when a pull here and a snip there would straighten it out. I wish wearing flatirons on our heads would keep us from growing up. But buds will be roses, and kittens, cats—more's the pity!"

"What's that about flatirons and cats?" asked Meg, as she crept into the room, with the finished letter in her hand.

"Only one of my stupid speeches. I'm going to bed; come, Peggy," said Jo, unfolding herself, like an animated puzzle.

"Quite right, and beautifully written. Please add that I send my love to John," said Mrs. March, as she glanced over the letter, and gave it back.

"Do you call him 'John'?" asked Meg, smiling, with her innocent eyes looking down into her mother's.

"Yes; he has been like a son to us, and we are very fond of him," replied Mrs. March, returning the look with a keen one.

"I'm glad of that, he is so lonely. Good night, mother dear. It is so inexpressibly comfortable to have you here" was Meg's quiet answer.

The kiss her mother gave her was a very tender one; and, as she went away, Mrs. March said, with a mixture of satisfaction and regret, "She does not love John yet, but will soon learn to."

CHAPTER TWENTY-ONE

Laurie Makes Mischief, and Jo Makes Peace

JO'S face was a study next day, for the secret rather weighed upon her, and she found it hard not to look mysterious and important. Meg observed it, but did not trouble herself to make inquiries, for she had learned that the best way to manage Jo was by the law of contraries so she felt sure of being told everything if she did not ask. She was rather surprised, therefore, when the silence remained unbroken, and Jo assumed a patronizing air, which decidedly aggravated Meg, who in turn assumed an air of dignified reserve, and devoted herself to her mother. This left Jo to her own devices; for Mrs. March had taken her place as nurse, and bade her rest, exercise, and amuse herself after her long confinement. Amy being gone, Laurie was her only refuge; and, much as she enjoyed his society, she rather dreaded him just then, for he was an incorrigible tease, and she feared he would coax her secret from her.

She was quite right; for the mischief-loving lad no sooner suspected a mystery than he set himself to find it out, and led Jo a trying life of it. He wheedled, bribed, ridiculed, threatened, and scolded; affected indifference, that he might surprise the truth from her; declared he knew, then that he didn't care; and at last, by dint of perseverance, he satisfied himself that it concerned Meg and Mr. Brooke. Feeling indignant that he was not taken into his tutor's confidence, he set his wits to work to devise some proper retaliation for the slight.

Meg meanwhile had apparently forgotten the matter and was absorbed in preparations for her father's return; but all of a sudden a change seemed to come over her, and, for a day or two, she was quite unlike herself. She started when spoken to, blushed when looked at, was very quiet, and sat over her sewing, with a timid, troubled look on her face. To her mother's inquiries she answered that she was quite well, and Jo's she silenced by begging to be let alone.

"She feels it in the air—love, I mean—and she's going very fast. She's got most of the symptoms—is twittery and cross, doesn't eat, lies awake, and mopes in corners. I caught her singing that song he gave her, and once she said 'John,' as you do, and then turned red as a poppy. Whatever shall we do?" said Jo, looking ready for any measures, however violent.

"Nothing but wait. Let her alone, be kind and patient, and father's coming will settle everything," replied her mother.

"Here's a note to you, Meg, all sealed up. How odd! Teddy never seals mine," said Jo, next day, as she distributed the contents of the little post office.

Mrs. March and Jo were deep in their own affairs, when a sound from Meg made them look up to see her staring at her note, with a frightened face.

"My child, what is it?" cried her mother, running to her while Jo tried to take the paper which had done the mischief.

"It's all a mistake—he didn't send it. Oh, Jo, how could you

do it?" and Meg hid her face in her hands, crying as if her
heart was quite broken.

"Me! I've done nothing! What's she talking about?" cried
Jo, bewildered.

Meg's mild eyes kindled with anger as she pulled a crumpled note from her pocket, and threw it at Jo, saying reproachfully:

"You wrote it, and that bad boy helped you. How could you
be so rude, so mean, and cruel to us both?"

Jo hardly heard her, for she and her mother were reading
the note, which was written in a peculiar hand.

MY DEAREST MARGARET:

I can no longer restrain my passion, and must know my
fate before I return. I dare not tell your parents yet, but I think
they would consent if they knew that we adored one another.
Mr. Laurence will help me to some good place, and then, my
sweet girl, you will make me happy. I implore you to say nothing to your family yet, but to send one word of hope through
Laurie to

Your devoted JOHN

"Oh, the little villain! That's the way he meant to pay me for
keeping my word to mother. I'll give him a hearty scolding,
and bring him over to beg pardon," cried Jo, burning to exe-
cute immediate justice. But her mother held her back, saying,
with a look she seldom wore:

"Stop, Jo, you must clear yourself first. You have played so
many pranks that I am afraid you have had a hand in this."

"On my word, mother, I haven't! I never saw that note before, and don't know anything about it, as true as I live!" said
Jo, so earnestly that they believed her. "If I *had* taken a part in
it I'd have done it better than this, and have written a sensible
note. I should think you'd have known Mr. Brooke wouldn't
write such stuff as that," she added, scornfully tossing down
the paper.

"It's like his writing," faltered Meg, comparing it with the
note in her hand.

"Oh, Meg, you didn't answer it?" cried Mrs. March quickly.

"Yes, I did!" and Meg hid her face again, overcome with
shame.

"Here's a scrape! *Do* let me bring that wicked boy over to explain, and be lectured. I can't rest till I get hold of him," and Jo made for the door again.

"Hush! Let me manage this, for it is worse than I thought. Margaret, tell me the whole story," commanded Mrs. March, sitting down by Meg, yet keeping hold of Jo, lest she should fly off.

"I received the first letter from Laurie, who didn't look as if he knew anything about it," began Meg, without looking up. "I was worried at first, and meant to tell you; then I remembered how you liked Mr. Brooke, so I thought you wouldn't mind if I kept my little secret for a few days. I'm so silly that I liked to think no one knew; and, while I was deciding what to say, I felt like the girls in books, who have such things to do. Forgive me, mother, I'm paid for my silliness now; I never can look him in the face again."

"What did you say to him?" asked Mrs. March.

"I only said I was too young to do anything about it yet; that I didn't wish to have secrets from you, and he must speak to father. I was very grateful for his kindness, and would be his friend, but nothing more, for a long while."

Mrs. March smiled, as if well pleased, and Jo clapped her hands, exclaiming, with a laugh:

"You are almost equal to Caroline Percy, who was a pattern of prudence! Tell on, Meg. What did he say to that?"

"He writes in a different way entirely, telling me that he never sent any love letter at all, and is very sorry that my roguish sister, Jo, should take such liberties with our names. It's very kind and respectful, but think how dreadful for me!"

Meg leaned against her mother, looking the image of despair, and Jo tramped about the room calling Laurie names. All of a sudden she stopped, caught up the two notes, and, after looking at them closely, said decidedly, "I don't believe Brooke ever saw either of these letters. Teddy wrote both, and keeps yours to crow over me with, because I wouldn't tell him my secret."

"Don't have any secrets, Jo; tell it to mother, and keep out of trouble, as I should have done," said Meg warningly.

"Bless you, child! Mother told me."

"That will do, Jo. I'll comfort Meg while you go and get

Laurie. I shall sift the matter to the bottom and put a stop to such pranks at once."

Away ran Jo, and Mrs. March gently told Meg Mr. Brooke's real feelings. "Now, dear, what are your own? Do you love him enough to wait till he can make a home for you, or will you keep yourself quite free for the present?"

"I've been so scared and worried, I don't want to have anything to do with lovers for a long while—perhaps never," answered Meg petulantly. "If John *doesn't* know anything about this nonsense, don't tell him, and make Jo and Laurie hold their tongues. I won't be deceived and plagued and made a fool of —it's a shame!"

Seeing that Meg's usually gentle temper was roused and her pride hurt by this mischievous joke, Mrs. March soothed her by promises of entire silence, and great discretion for the future. The instant Laurie's step was heard in the hall, Meg fled into the study, and Mrs. March received the culprit alone. Jo had not told him why he was wanted, fearing he wouldn't come; but he knew the minute he saw Mrs. March's face and stood twirling his hat, with a guilty air which convicted him at once. Jo was dismissed, but chose to march up and down the hall like a sentinel, having some fear that the prisoner might bolt. The sound of voices in the parlor rose and fell for half an hour; but what happened during that interview the girls never knew.

When they were called in, Laurie was standing by their mother, with such a penitent face that Jo forgave him on the spot, but did not think it wise to betray the fact. Meg received his humble apology, and was much comforted by the assurance that Brooke knew nothing of the joke.

"I'll never tell him to my dying day—wild horses shan't drag it out of me; so you'll forgive me, Meg, and I'll do anything to show how out-and-out sorry I am," he added, looking very much ashamed of himself.

"I'll try; but it was a very ungentlemanly thing to do. I didn't think you could be so sly and malicious, Laurie," replied Meg, trying to hide her maidenly confusion under a gravely reproachful air.

"It was altogether abominable, and I don't deserve to be spoken to for a month; but you will, though, won't you?" and Laurie folded his hands together with such an imploring gesture, as he spoke in his irresistibly persuasive tone, that it was impossible to frown upon him, in spite of his scandalous behavior. Meg pardoned him, and Mrs. March's grave face relaxed, in spite of her efforts to keep sober, when she heard him declare that he would atone for his sins by all sorts of penances, and abase himself like a worm before the injured damsel.

Jo stood aloof, meanwhile, trying to harden her heart against him, and succeeding only in primming up her face in an expression of entire disapprobation. Laurie looked at her once or twice, but, as she showed no signs of relenting, he felt injured, and turned his back on her till the others were done with him, when he made her a low bow, and walked off without a word.

As soon as he had gone, she wished she had been more forgiving; and when Meg and her mother went upstairs, she felt lonely and longed for Teddy. After resisting for some time, she yielded to the impulse, and, armed with a book to return, went over to the big house.

"Is Mr. Laurence in?" asked Jo, of a housemaid, who was coming downstairs.

"Yes, miss; but I don't believe he's seeable just yet."

"Why not? Is he ill?"

"La, no, miss, but he's had a scene with Mr. Laurie, who is in one of his tantrums about something, which vexes the old gentleman so I dursn't go nigh him."

"Where is Laurie?"

"Shut up in his room, and he won't answer, though I've been a-tapping. I don't know what's to become of the dinner, for it's ready and there's no one to eat it."

"I'll go and see what the matter is. I'm not afraid of either of them."

Up went Jo, and knocked smartly on the door of Laurie's little study.

"Stop that, or I'll open the door and make you!" called out the young gentleman, in a threatening tone.

Jo immediately knocked again; the door flew open, and in she bounced, before Laurie could recover from his surprise. Seeing that he really *was* out of temper, Jo, who knew how to manage him, assumed a contrite expression, and going artistically down upon her knees, said meekly, "Please forgive me for being so cross. I came to make it up, and can't go away till I have."

"It's all right. Get up, and don't be a goose, Jo" was the cavalier reply to her petition.

"Thank you; I will. Could I ask what's the matter? You don't look exactly easy in your mind."

"I've been shaken, and I won't bear it!" growled Laurie indignantly.

"Who did it?" demanded Jo.

"Grandfather; if it had been anyone else I'd have—" and the injured youth finished his sentence by an energetic gesture of the right arm.

"That's nothing; I often shake you, and you don't mind," said Jo soothingly.

"Pooh! You're a girl, and it's fun, but I'll allow no man to shake *me*."

"I don't think anyone would care to try it, if you looked as much like a thundercloud as you do now. Why were you treated so?"

"Just because I wouldn't say what your mother wanted me for. I'd promised not to tell, and of course I wasn't going to break my word."

"Couldn't you satisfy your grandpa in any other way?"

"No; he *would* have the truth, the whole truth, and nothing but the truth. I'd have told my part of the scrape, if I could without bringing Meg in. As I couldn't, I held my tongue, and bore the scolding till the old gentleman collared me. Then I got angry, and bolted, for fear I should forget myself."

"It wasn't nice, but he's sorry, I know; so go down and make up. I'll help you."

"Hanged if I do! I'm not going to be lectured and pummeled by everyone, just for a bit of a frolic. I *was* sorry about Meg, and begged pardon like a man; but I won't do it again, when I wasn't in the wrong."

"He didn't know that."

"He ought to trust me, and not act as if I was a baby. It's no use, Jo; he's got to learn that I'm able to take care of myself, and don't need anyone's apron string to hold on by."

"What pepper pots you are!" sighed Jo. "How do you mean to settle this affair?"

"Well, he ought to beg pardon, and believe me when I say I can't tell him what the fuss's about."

"Bless you, he won't do that."

"I won't go down till he does."

"Now, Teddy, be sensible; let it pass, and I'll explain what I can. You can't stay here, so what's the use of being melodramatic?"

"I don't intend to stay here long, anyway. I'll slip off and take a journey somewhere, and when grandpa misses me he'll come around fast enough."

"I dare say; but you ought not to go and worry him."

"Don't preach. I'll go to Washington and see Brooke; it's gay there, and I'll enjoy myself after the troubles."

"What fun you'd have! I wish I could run off too," said Jo, forgetting her part of Mentor in lively visions of martial life at the capital.

"Come on, then! Why not? You go and surprise your father, and I'll stir up old Brooke. It would be a glorious joke; let's do it, Jo. We'll leave a letter saying we are all right, and trot off at once. I've got money enough; it will do you good, and be no harm, as you go to your father."

For a moment Jo looked as if she would agree; for, wild as the plan was, it just suited her. She was tired of care and confinement, longed for change, and thoughts of her father blended temptingly with the novel charms of camps and hospitals, liberty and fun. Her eyes kindled as they turned wistfully toward the window, but they fell on the old house opposite and she shook her head with sorrowful decision.

"If I was a boy, we'd run away together, and have a capital time; but as I'm a miserable girl, I must be proper, and stop at home. Don't tempt me, Teddy, it's a crazy plan."

"That's the fun of it," began Laurie, who had got a willful fit on him, and was possessed to break out of bounds in some way.

"Hold your tongue!" cried Jo, covering her ears. " 'Prunes and prisms' are my doom, and I may as well make up my mind to it. I came here to moralize, not to hear about things that make me skip to think of."

"I know Meg would wet-blanket such a proposal, but I thought you had more spirit," began Laurie insinuatingly.

"Bad boy, be quiet! Sit down and think of your own sins; don't go making me add to mine. If I get your grandpa to apologize for the shaking, will you give up running away?" asked Jo seriously.

"Yes, but you won't do it," answered Laurie, who wished "to make up," but felt that his outraged dignity must be appeased first.

"If I can manage the young one I can the old one," muttered Jo, as she walked away, leaving Laurie bent over a railroad map, with his head propped up on both hands.

"Come in!" and Mr. Laurence's gruff voice sounded gruffer than ever, as Jo tapped at his door.

"It's only me, sir, come to return a book," she said blandly as she entered.

"Want any more?" asked the old gentleman, looking grim and vexed, but trying not to show it.

"Yes, please. I like old Sam so well, I think I'll try the second volume," returned Jo, hoping to propitiate him by accepting a second dose of Boswell's "Johnson," as he had recommended that lively work.

The shaggy eyebrows unbent a little, as he rolled the steps toward the shelf where the Johnsonian literature was placed. Jo skipped up, and, sitting on the top step, affected to be searching for her book, but was really wondering how best to introduce the dangerous object of her visit. Mr. Laurence seemed to suspect that something was brewing in her mind; for, after taking several brisk turns about the room, he faced round on her, speaking so abruptly that "Rasselas" tumbled face downward on the floor.

"What has that boy been about? Don't try to shield him. I know he has been in mischief by the way he acted when he came home. I can't get a word from him; and when I threatened to shake the truth out of him he bolted upstairs, and locked himself into his room."

"He did do wrong, but we forgave him, and all promised not to say a word to anyone," began Jo reluctantly.

"That won't do; he shall not shelter himself behind a promise from you softhearted girls. If he's done anything amiss, he shall confess, beg pardon, and be punished. Out with it, Jo, I won't be kept in the dark."

Mr. Laurence looked so alarming and spoke so sharply that Jo would have gladly run away if she could, but she was perched aloft on the steps, and he stood at the foot, a lion in the path, so she had to stay and brave it out.

"Indeed, sir, I cannot tell! Mother forbade it. Laurie has confessed, asked pardon, and been punished quite enough. We don't keep silence to shield him, but someone else, and it will make more trouble if you interfere. Please don't: it was partly my fault, but it's all right now; so let's forget it, and talk about the 'Rambler,' or something pleasant."

"Hang the 'Rambler'! Come down and give me your word that this harum-scarum boy of mine hasn't done anything ungrateful or impertinent. If he has, after all your kindness to him, I'll thrash him with my own hands."

The threat sounded awful, but did not alarm Jo, for she knew the irascible old gentleman would never lift a finger against his grandson, whatever he might say to the contrary. She obediently descended, and made as light of the prank as she could without betraying Meg or forgetting the truth.

"Hum—ha—well, if the boy held his tongue because he promised, and not from obstinacy, I'll forgive him. He's a stubborn fellow, and hard to manage," said Mr. Laurence, rubbing up his hair till it looked as if he had been out in a gale and smoothing the frown from his brow with an air of relief.

"So am I; but a kind word will govern me when all the king's horses and all the king's men couldn't," said Jo, trying to say a kind word for her friend, who seemed to get out of one scrape only to fall into another.

"You think I'm not kind to him, hey?" was the sharp answer.

"Oh, dear, no, sir; you are rather too kind sometimes, and then just a trifle hasty when he tries your patience. Don't you think you are?"

Jo was determined to have it out now, and tried to look quite placid, though she quaked a little after her bold speech. To her great relief and surprise, the old gentleman only threw his spectacles onto the table with a rattle, and exclaimed frankly:

"You're right, girl, I am! I love the boy, but he tries my patience past bearing, and I don't know how it will end, if we go on so."

"I'll tell you, he'll run away." Jo was sorry for that speech the minute it was made; she meant to warn him that Laurie would not bear much restraint, and hoped he would be more forbearing with the lad.

Mr. Laurence's ruddy face changed suddenly, and he sat down, with a troubled glance at the picture of a handsome man which hung over his table. It was Laurie's father, who *had* run away in his youth and married against the imperious old man's will. Jo fancied he remembered and regretted the past, and she wished she had held her tongue.

"He won't do it unless he is very much worried, and only threatens it sometimes, when he gets tired of studying. I often think I should like to, especially since my hair was cut; so, if you ever miss us, you may advertise for two boys, and look among the ships bound for India."

She laughed as she spoke, and Mr. Laurence looked relieved, evidently taking the whole as a joke.

"You hussy, how dare you talk in that way? Where's your respect for me, and your proper bringing up? Bless the boys and girls! What torments they are; yet we can't do without them," he said, pinching her cheeks good-humoredly. "Go and bring that boy down to his dinner, tell him it's all right, and advise him not to put on tragedy airs with his grandfather. I won't bear it."

"He won't come, sir; he feels badly because you didn't believe him when he said he couldn't tell. I think the shaking hurt his feelings very much."

Jo tried to look pathetic, but must have failed for Mr. Laurence began to laugh, and she knew the day was won.

"I'm sorry for that, and ought to thank him for not shaking *me*, I suppose. What the dickens does the fellow expect?" and the old gentleman looked a trifle ashamed of his own testiness.

"If I were you, I'd write him an apology, sir. He says he won't come down till he has one, and talks about Washington, and goes on in an absurd way. A formal apology will make him see how foolish he is, and bring him down quite amiable. Try it; he likes fun, and this way is better than talking. I'll carry it up, and teach him his duty."

Mr. Laurence gave her a sharp look, and put on his spectacles, saying slowly, "You're a sly puss, but I don't mind being

managed by you and Beth. Here, give me a bit of paper, and
let us have done with this nonsense."

The note was written in the terms which one gentleman
would use to another after offering some deep insult. Jo
dropped a kiss on top of Mr. Laurence's bald head and ran up

to slip the apology under Laurie's door, advising him, through
the keyhole, to be submissive, decorous, and a few other agreeable impossibilities. Finding the door locked again, she left the
note to do its work, and was going quietly away, when the
young gentleman slid down the banisters, and waited for her
at the bottom, saying, with his most virtuous expression of
countenance, "What a good fellow you are, Jo! Did you get
blown up?" he added, laughing.

"No; he was pretty mild, on the whole."

"Ah! I got it all round; even you cast me off over there, and
I felt just ready to go to the deuce," he began apologetically.

"Don't talk in that way; turn over a new leaf and begin
again, Teddy, my son."

"I keep turning over new leaves, and spoiling them, as I used to spoil my copybooks; and I make so many beginnings there never will be an end," he said dolefully.

"Go and eat your dinner; you'll feel better after it. Men always croak when they are hungry," and Jo whisked out at the front door after that.

"That's a 'label' on my 'sect,'" answered Laurie, quoting Amy, as he went to partake of humble pie dutifully with his grandfather, who was quite saintly in temper and overwhelmingly respectful in manner all the rest of the day.

Everyone thought the matter ended and the little cloud blown over; but the mischief was done, for, though others forgot it, Meg remembered. She never alluded to a certain person, but she thought of him a good deal, dreamed dreams more than ever; and once Jo rummaging her sister's desk for stamps found a bit of paper scribbled over with the words, "Mrs. John Brooke," whereat she groaned tragically and cast it into the fire, feeling that Laurie's prank had hastened the evil day for her.

CHAPTER TWENTY-TWO

Pleasant Meadows

LIKE sunshine after storm were the peaceful weeks which followed. The invalids improved rapidly, and Mr. March began to talk of returning early in the new year. Beth was soon able to lie on the study sofa all day, amusing herself with the well-beloved cats, at first, and, in time, with doll's sewing, which had fallen sadly behindhand. Her once active limbs were so stiff and feeble that Jo took her a daily airing about the house in her strong arms. Meg cheerfully blackened and burnt her white hands cooking delicate messes for "the dear," while Amy, a loyal slave of the ring, celebrated her return by giving away as many of her treasures as she could prevail on her sisters to accept.

As Christmas approached, the usual mysteries began to haunt the house and Jo frequently convulsed the family by proposing utterly impossible or magnificently absurd ceremonies, in honor of this unusually merry Christmas. Laurie was equally impracticable, and would have had bonfires, skyrockets, and triumphal arches if he had had his own way. After many skirmishes and snubbings, the ambitious pair were considered effectually quenched and went about with forlorn faces, which were rather belied by explosions of laughter when the two got together.

Several days of unusually mild weather fitly ushered in a splendid Christmas Day. Hannah "felt in her bones" that it was going to be an unusually fine day, and she proved herself a true prophetess, for everybody and everything seemed bound to produce a grand success. To begin with, Mr. March wrote that he would soon be with them; then Beth felt uncommonly well that morning, and, being dressed in her mother's gift—a soft crimson merino wrapper—was borne in triumph to the window to behold the offering of Jo and Laurie. The Unquenchables had done their best to be worthy of the name, for, like elves, they had worked by night and conjured up a comical surprise. Out in the garden stood a stately snow maiden, crowned with holly, bearing a basket of fruit and flowers in one hand, a great roll of new music in the other, a perfect rainbow of an Afghan round her chilly shoulders, and a Christmas card issuing from her lips on a pink paper streamer:

THE JUNGFRAU TO BETH

God bless you, dear Queen Bess!
  May nothing you dismay,
But health and peace and happiness
  Be yours, this Christmas Day.

Here's fruit to feed our busy bee,
  And flowers for her nose;
Here's music for her pianee,
  An Afghan for her toes.

A portrait of Joanna, see,
By Raphael No. 2,
Who labored with great industry
To make it fair and true.

Accept a ribbon red, I beg,
For Madam Purrer's tail;
And ice cream made by lovely Peg —
A Mont Blanc in a pail.

Their dearest love my makers laid
Within my breast of snow:
Accept it, and the Alpine maid,
From Laurie and from Jo.

How Beth laughed when she saw it, how Laurie ran up and down to bring in the gifts, and what ridiculous speeches Jo made as she presented them!

"I'm so full of happiness that, if father was only here, I couldn't hold one drop more," said Beth, quite sighing with contentment as Jo carried her off to the study to rest after the excitement, and to refresh herself with some of the delicious grapes the Jungfrau had sent her.

"So am I," added Jo, slapping the pocket wherein reposed the long-desired "Undine and Sintram."

"I'm sure I am," echoed Amy, poring over the engraved copy of the Madonna and Child, which her mother had given her, in a pretty frame.

"Of course I am!" cried Meg, smoothing the silvery folds of her first silk dress; for Mr. Laurence had insisted on giving it.

"How can *I* be otherwise?" said Mrs. March gratefully, as her eyes went from her husband's letter to Beth's smiling face and her hand caressed the brooch made of gray and golden, chestnut and dark brown hair, which the girls had just fastened on her breast.

Now and then, in this workaday world, things do happen in the delightful storybook fashion, and what a comfort that is. Half an hour after everyone had said that they were so happy they could only hold one drop more, the drop came. Laurie opened the parlor door, and popped his head in very quietly. He might just as well have turned a somersault and uttered an Indian war whoop; for his face was so full of suppressed excitement and his voice so treacherously joyful, that everyone jumped up, though he only said, in a queer, breathless voice, "Here's another Christmas present for the March family."

Before the words were well out of his mouth, he was whisked away somehow, and in his place appeared a tall man, muffled up to the eyes, leaning on the arm of another tall man, who tried to say something and couldn't. Of course there was a general stampede; and for several minutes everybody seemed to lose their wits, for the strangest things were done, and no one said a word. Mr. March became invisible in the embrace of four pairs of loving arms; Jo disgraced herself by nearly fainting away, and had to be doctored by Laurie in the china closet; Mr. Brooke kissed Meg entirely by mistake, as he somewhat incoherently explained; and Amy, the dignified, tumbled over a stool, and, never stopping to get up, hugged and cried over her father's boots in the most touching manner. Mrs. March was the first to recover herself, and held up her hand with a warning, "Hush! Remember Beth!"

But it was too late; the study door flew open, the little red wrapper appeared on the threshold—joy put strength into the feeble limbs—and Beth ran straight into her father's arms. Never mind what happened just after that; for the full hearts overflowed, washing away the bitterness of the past, and leaving only the sweetness of the present.

It was not at all romantic, but a hearty laugh set everybody straight again, for Hannah was discovered behind the door, sobbing over the fat turkey, which she had forgotten to put down when she rushed up from the kitchen. As the laugh subsided, Mrs. March began to thank Mr. Brooke for his faithful care of her husband, at which Mr. Brooke suddenly remembered that Mr. March needed rest, and, seizing Laurie, he precipitately retired. Then the two invalids were ordered to repose, which they did, by both sitting in one big chair, and talking hard.

Mr. March told how he had longed to surprise them, and how, when the fine weather came, he had been allowed by his doctor to take advantage of it; how devoted Brooke had been, and how he was altogether a most estimable and upright young man. Why Mr. March paused a minute just there, and, after a glance at Meg, who was violently poking the fire, looked at his wife with an inquiring lift of his eyebrows, I leave you to imagine; also why Mrs. March gently nodded her head, and asked, rather abruptly, if he wouldn't have something to eat. Jo saw and understood the look; and she stalked grimly away to get wine and beef tea, muttering to herself, as she slammed the door, "I hate estimable young men with brown eyes!"

There never *was* such a Christmas dinner as they had that day. The fat turkey was a sight to behold, when Hannah served him up, stuffed, browned, and decorated; so was the plum pudding, which quite melted in one's mouth; likewise the jellies, in which Amy reveled like a fly in a honey pot. Everything turned out well, which was a mercy, Hannah said, "For my mind was that flustered, mum, that it's a merrycle I didn't roast the pudding, and stuff the turkey with raisins, let alone bilin' of it in a cloth."

Mr. Laurence and his grandson dined with them, also Mr. Brooke—at whom Jo glowered darkly, to Laurie's infinite amusement. Two easy chairs stood side by side at the head of the table, in which sat Beth and her father, feasting modestly on chicken and a little fruit. They drank healths, told stories, sung songs, "reminisced," as the old folks say, and had a thoroughly good time. A sleigh ride had been planned, but the girls would not leave their father; so the guests departed early, and, as the twilight gathered, the happy family sat together round the fire.

"Just a year ago we were groaning over the dismal Christmas we expected to have. Do you remember?" asked Jo, breaking a short pause which had followed a long conversation about many things.

"Rather a pleasant year on the whole!" said Meg, smiling at the fire, and congratulating herself on having treated Mr. Brooke with dignity.

"I think it's been a pretty hard one," observed Amy, watching the light shine on her ring with thoughtful eyes.

"I'm glad it's over, because we've got you back," whispered Beth, who sat on her father's knee.

"Rather a rough road for you to travel, my little pilgrims, especially the latter part of it. But you have got on bravely; and I think the burdens are in a fair way to tumble off very soon," said Mr. March, looking with fatherly satisfaction at the four young faces gathered round him.

"How do you know? Did mother tell you?" asked Jo.

"Not much; straws show which way the wind blows, and I've made several discoveries today."

"Oh, tell us what they are!" cried Meg, who sat beside him.

"Here is one," and taking up the hand which lay on the arm of his chair, he pointed to the roughened forefinger, a burn on the back, and two or three little hard spots on the palm. "I remember a time when this hand was white and smooth, and your first care was to keep it so. It was very pretty then, but to me it is much prettier now—for in these seeming blemishes I read a little history. A burnt offering has been made of vanity; this hardened palm has earned something better than blisters; and I'm sure the sewing done by these pricked fingers will last a long time, so much good will went into the stitches. Meg, my dear, I value the womanly skill which keeps home happy more than white hands or fashionable accomplishments. I'm proud to shake this good, industrious little hand, and hope I shall not soon be asked to give it away."

If Meg had wanted a reward for hours of patient labor, she received it in a hearty pressure of her father's hand and the approving smile he gave her.

"What about Jo? Please say something nice; for she has tried so hard, and been so very, very good to me," said Beth in her father's ear.

He laughed, and looked across at the tall girl who sat opposite, with an unusually mild expression in her brown face.

"In spite of the curly crop, I don't see the 'son Jo' whom I left a year ago," said Mr. March. "I see a young lady who pins her collar straight, laces her boots neatly, and neither whistles, talks slang, nor lies on the rug as she used to do. Her face is rather thin and pale, just now, with watching and anxiety; but

I like to look at it, for it has grown gentler, and her voice is lower; she doesn't bounce, but moves quietly, and takes care of a certain little person in a motherly way which delights me. I rather miss my wild girl; but if I get a strong, helpful, tender-hearted woman in her place, I shall feel quite satisfied. I don't know whether the shearing sobered our black sheep, but I do know that in all Washington I couldn't find anything beautiful enough to be bought with the five and twenty dollars which my good girl sent me."

Jo's keen eyes were rather dim for a minute, and her thin face grew rosy in the firelight, as she received her father's praise, feeling that she did deserve a portion of it.

"Now Beth," said Amy, longing for her turn, but ready to wait.

"There's so little of her, I'm afraid to say much, for fear she will slip away altogether, though she is not so shy as she used to be," began their father cheerfully; but recollecting how nearly he *had* lost her, he held her close, saying tenderly, with her cheek against his own, "I've got you safe, my Beth, and I'll keep you so, please God."

After a minute's silence, he looked down at Amy, who sat on the cricket at his feet, and said, with a caress of the shining hair:

"I observed that Amy took drumsticks at dinner, ran errands for her mother all the afternoon, gave Meg her place tonight, and has waited on everyone with patience and good humor. I also observe that she does not fret much nor look in the glass, and has not even mentioned a very pretty ring which she wears; so I conclude that she has learned to think of other people more and of herself less, and has decided to try and mold her character as carefully as she molds her little clay figures. I am glad of this; for though I should be very proud of a grace-ful statue made by her, I shall be infinitely prouder of a lovable daughter, with a talent for making life beautiful to herself and others."

"What are you thinking of, Beth?" asked Jo, when Amy had thanked her father and told about her ring.

"I read in 'Pilgrim's Progress' today, how, after many trou-bles, Christian and Hopeful came to a pleasant green meadow, where lilies bloomed all the year round, and there they rested happily, as we do now, before they went on to their journey's end," answered Beth; adding, as she slipped out of her father's arms, and went slowly to the instrument, "It's singing time now, and I want to be in my old place. I'll try to sing the song of the shepherd boy which the Pilgrims heard. I made the music for father, because he likes the verses."

So, sitting at the dear little piano, Beth softly touched the keys, and, in the sweet voice they had never thought to hear again, sang to her own accompaniment the quaint hymn, which was a singularly fitting song for her:

> *"He that is down need fear no fall,*
> *He that is low no pride;*
> *He that is humble ever shall*
> *Have God to be his guide.*
>
> *"I am content with what I have,*
> *Little be it or much;*
> *And, Lord! contentment still I crave,*
> *Because Thou savest such.*
>
> *"Fullness to them a burden is,*
> *That go on pilgrimage;*
> *Here little, and hereafter bliss,*
> *Is best from age to age!"*

CHAPTER TWENTY-THREE

Aunt March Settles the Question

LIKE bees swarming after their queen, mother and daughters hovered about Mr. March the next day, neglecting everything to look at wait upon, and listen to the new invalid, who was in a fair way to be killed by kindness. As he sat propped up in a big chair by Beth's sofa, with the other three close by, and Hannah popping in her head now and then, "to peek at the dear man," nothing seemed needed to complete their happiness. But something *was* needed, and the elder ones felt it, though none confessed the fact. Mr. and Mrs. March looked at one another with an anxious expression, as their eyes followed Meg. Jo had sudden fits of sobriety, and was seen to shake her

fist at Mr. Brooke's umbrella, which had been left in the hall;
Meg was absent-minded, shy, and silent, started when the bell
rang, and colored when John's name was mentioned; Amy said,
"Everyone seemed waiting for something, and couldn't settle
down, which was queer, since father was safe at home," and
Beth innocently wondered why their neighbors didn't run over
as usual.

Laurie went by in the afternoon, and, seeing Meg at the
window, seemed suddenly possessed with a melodramatic fit,
for he fell down upon one knee in the snow, beat his breast,
tore his hair, and clasped his hands imploringly, as if begging
some boon; and when Meg told him to behave himself and go
away, he wrung imaginary tears out of his handkerchief, and
staggered round the corner as if in utter despair.

"What does the goose mean?" said Meg, laughing and trying
to look unconscious.

"He's showing you how your John will go on by and by.
Touching, isn't it?" answered Jo scornfully.

"Don't say *my John*, it isn't proper or true," but Meg's voice
lingered over the words as if they sounded pleasant to her.
"Please don't plague me, Jo; I've told you I don't care *much*
about him, and there isn't to be anything said, but we are all to
be friendly, and go on as before."

"We can't, for something *has* been said, and Laurie's mischief has spoilt you for me. I see it, and so does mother; you
are not like your old self a bit, and seem ever so far away from
me. I don't mean to plague you, and will bear it like a man,
but I do wish it was all settled. I hate to wait; so if you mean
ever to do it, make haste and have it over quickly," said Jo
pettishly.

"*I* can't say or do anything till he speaks, and he won't because father said I was too young," began Meg, bending over
her work with a queer little smile, which suggested that she did
not quite agree with her father on that point.

"If he did speak, you wouldn't know what to say, but would
cry or blush, or let him have his own way, instead of giving a
good, decided No."

"I'm not so silly and weak as you think. I know just what I
should say, for I've planned it all, so I needn't be taken una-

wares; there's no knowing what may happen, and I wished to be prepared."

Jo couldn't help smiling at the important air which Meg had unconsciously assumed, and which was as becoming as the pretty color varying in her cheeks.

"Would you mind telling me what you'd say?" asked Jo more respectfully.

"Not at all; you are sixteen now, quite old enough to be my confidante, and my experience will be useful to you by and by, perhaps, in your own affairs of this sort."

"Don't mean to have any; it's fun to watch other people philander, but I should feel like a fool doing it myself," said Jo, looking alarmed at the thought.

"I think not, if you liked anyone very much, and he liked you." Meg spoke as if to herself, and glanced out at the lane where she had often seen lovers walking together in the summer twilight.

"I thought you were going to tell your speech to that man," said Jo, rudely shortening her sister's little reverie.

"Oh, I should merely say, quite calmly and decidedly, 'Thank you, Mr. Brooke, you are very kind, but I agree with father that I am too young to enter into any engagement at present, so please say no more, but let us be friends as we were.'"

"Hum! That's stiff and cool enough. I don't believe you'll ever say it, and I know he won't be satisfied if you do. If he goes on like the rejected lovers in books, you'll give in rather than hurt his feelings."

"No, I won't. I shall tell him I've made up my mind, and shall walk out of the room with dignity."

Meg rose as she spoke, and was just going to rehearse the dignified exit when a step in the hall made her fly into her seat and begin to sew as if her life depended on finishing that particular seam in a given time. Jo smothered a laugh at the sudden change, and, when someone gave a modest tap, opened the door with a grim aspect, which was anything but hospitable.

"Good afternoon. I came to get my umbrella—that is, to see how your father finds himself today," said Mr. Brooke, getting

"I only want to know if you care for me a little."

a trifle confused as his eye went from one telltale face to the other.

"It's very well, he's in the rack, I'll get him, and tell it you are here," and having jumbled her father and the umbrella well together in her reply, Jo slipped out of the room to give Meg a chance to make her speech and air her dignity. But the instant she vanished, Meg began to sidle toward the door, murmuring:

"Mother will like to see you. Pray sit down, I'll call her."

"Don't go; are you afraid of me, Margaret?" and Mr. Brooke looked so hurt that Meg thought she must have done something very rude. She blushed up to the little curls on her forehead, for he had never called her Margaret before, and she was surprised to find how natural and sweet it seemed to hear him say it. Anxious to appear friendly and at her ease, she put out her hand with a confiding gesture, and said gratefully:

"How can I be afraid when you have been so kind to father? I only wish I could thank you for it."

"Shall I tell you how?" asked Mr. Brooke, holding the small hand fast in both his own, and looking down at Meg with so much love in the brown eyes that her heart began to flutter, and she both longed to run away and to stop and listen.

"Oh, no, please don't—I'd rather not," she said, trying to withdraw her hand, and looking frightened in spite of her denial.

"I won't trouble you, I only want to know if you care for me a little, Meg. I love you so much, dear," added Mr. Brooke tenderly.

This was the moment for the calm, proper speech, but Meg didn't make it; she forgot every word of it, hung her head, and answered, "I don't know," so softly that John had to stoop down to catch the foolish little reply.

He seemed to think it was worth the trouble, for he smiled to himself as if quite satisfied, pressed the plump hand gratefully, and said, in his most persuasive tone, "Will you try and find out? I want to know so much; for I can't go to work with any heart until I learn whether I am to have my reward in the end or not."

"I'm too young," faltered Meg, wondering why she was so fluttered, yet rather enjoying it.

"I'll wait; and in the meantime, you could be learning to like me. Would it be a very hard lesson, dear?"

"Not if I chose to learn it, but—"

"Please choose to learn, Meg. I love to teach, and this is easier than German," broke in John, getting possession of the other hand, so that she had no way of hiding her face, as he bent to look into it.

His tone was properly beseeching; but, stealing a shy look at him, Meg saw that his eyes were merry as well as tender, and that he wore the satisfied smile of one who had no doubt of his success. This nettled her; Annie Moffat's foolish lessons in coquetry came into her mind, and the love of power, which sleeps in the bosoms of the best of little women, woke up all of a sudden and took possession of her. She felt excited and strange, and, not knowing what else to do, followed a capricious impulse, and, withdrawing her hands, said petulantly, "I *don't* choose. Please go away and let me be!"

Poor Mr. Brooke looked as if his lovely castle in the air was tumbling about his ears, for he had never seen Meg in such a mood before, and it rather bewildered him.

"Do you really mean that?" he asked anxiously, following her as she walked away.

"Yes, I do; I don't want to be worried about such things. Father says I needn't; it's too soon and I'd rather not."

"Mayn't I hope you'll change your mind by and by? I'll wait, and say nothing till you have had more time. Don't play with me, Meg. I didn't think that of you."

"Don't think of me at all. I'd rather you wouldn't," said Meg, taking a naughty satisfaction in trying her lover's patience and her own power.

He was grave and pale now, and looked decidedly more like the novel heroes whom she admired; but he neither slapped his forehead nor tramped about the room, as they did; he just stood looking at her so wistfully, so tenderly, that she found her heart relenting in spite of her. What would have happened next I cannot say, if Aunt March had not come hobbling in at this interesting minute.

The old lady couldn't resist her longing to see her nephew; for she had met Laurie as she took her airing, and, hearing of Mr. March's arrival, drove straight out to see him. The family were all busy in the back part of the house, and she had made her way quietly in, hoping to surprise them. She did surprise two of them so much that Meg started as if she had seen a ghost, and Mr. Brooke vanished into the study.

"Bless me, what's all this?" cried the old lady, with a rap of her cane, as she glanced from the pale young gentleman to the scarlet young lady.

"It's father's friend. I'm *so* surprised to see you!" stammered Meg, feeling that she was in for a lecture now.

"That's evident," returned Aunt March, sitting down. "But what is father's friend saying to make you look like a peony? There's mischief going on, and I insist upon knowing what it it," with another rap.

"We were merely talking. Mr. Brooke came for his umbrella," began Meg, wishing that Mr. Brooke and the umbrella were safely out of the house.

"Brooke? That boy's tutor? Ah! I understand now. I know all about it. Jo blundered into a wrong message in one of your father's letters, and I made her tell me. You haven't gone and accepted him, child?" cried Aunt March, looking scandalized.

"Hush! He'll hear. Shan't I call mother?" said Meg, much troubled.

"Not yet. I've something to say to you, and I must free my mind at once. Tell me, do you mean to marry this Cook? If you do, not one penny of my money ever goes to you. Remember that, and be a sensible girl," said the old lady impressively.

Now Aunt March possessed in perfection the art of rousing the spirit of opposition in the gentlest people, and enjoyed doing it. The best of us have a spice of perversity in us, especially when we are young and in love. If Aunt March had begged Meg to accept John Brooke, she would probably have declared she couldn't think of it; but as she was peremptorily ordered *not* to like him, she immediately made up her mind that she would. Inclination as well as perversity made the decision easy, and, being already much excited, Meg opposed the old lady with unusual spirit.

"I shall marry whom I please, Aunt March, and you can leave your money to anyone you like," she said, nodding her head with a resolute air.

"Highty tighty! Is that the way you take my advice, miss? You'll be sorry for it, by and by, when you've tried love in a cottage, and found it a failure."

"It can't be a worse one than some people find in big houses," retorted Meg.

Aunt March put on her glasses and took a look at the girl, for she did not know her in this new mood. Meg hardly knew herself, she felt so brave and independent—so glad to defend John, and assert her right to love him if she liked. Aunt March saw that she had begun wrong, and, after a little pause, made a fresh start, saying, as mildly as she could, "Now, Meg, my dear, be reasonable and take my advice. I mean it kindly, and don't want you to spoil your whole life by making a mistake at the beginning. You ought to marry well, and help your family; it's your duty to make a rich match, and it ought to be impressed upon you."

"Father and mother don't think so; they like John, though he *is* poor."

"Your parents, my dear, have no more worldly wisdom than two babies."

"I'm glad of it," cried Meg stoutly.

Aunt March took no notice, but went on with her lecture. "This Rook is poor, and hasn't got any rich relations, has he?"

"No; but he has many warm friends."

"You can't live on friends; try it, and see how cool they'll grow. He hasn't any business, has he?"

"Not yet; Mr. Laurence is going to help him."

"That won't last long. James Laurence is a crotchety old fellow, and not to be depended on. So you intend to marry a man without money, position, or business, and go on working harder than you do now, when you might be comfortable all your days by minding me and doing better? I thought you had more sense, Meg."

"I couldn't do better if I waited half my life! John is good and wise; he's got heaps of talent; he's willing to work, and sure to get on, he's so energetic and brave. Everyone likes and respects him, and I'm proud to think he cares for me, though I'm so poor and young and silly," said Meg, looking prettier than ever in her earnestness.

"He knows *you* have got rich relations, child; that's the secret of his liking, I suspect."

"Aunt March, how dare you say such a thing? John is above such meanness, and I won't listen to you a minute if you talk so," cried Meg indignantly, forgetting everything but the injustice of the old lady's suspicions. "My John wouldn't marry for money any more than I would. We are willing to work, and we mean to wait. I'm not afraid of being poor, for I've been happy so far, and I know I shall be with him, because he loves me, and I—"

Meg stopped there, remembering all of a sudden that she hadn't made up her mind; that she had told "her John" to go away, and that he might be overhearing her inconsistent remarks.

Aunt March was very angry, for she had set her heart on having her pretty niece make a fine match, and something in the girl's happy young face made the lonely old woman feel both sad and sour.

"Well, I wash my hands of the whole affair! You are a willful child, and you've lost more than you know by this piece of folly. No, I won't stop; I'm disappointed in you, and haven't spirits to see your father now. Don't expect anything from me when you are married; your Mr. Book's friends must take care of you. I'm done with you forever."

And, slamming the door in Meg's face, Aunt March drove off in high dudgeon. She seemed to take all the girl's courage with her; for, when left alone, Meg stood a moment, undecided whether to laugh or cry. Before she could make up her mind, she was taken possession of by Mr. Brooke, who said, all in one breath, "I couldn't help hearing, Meg. Thank you for defending me, and Aunt March for proving that you *do* care for me a little bit."

"I didn't know how much, till she abused you," began Meg.

"And I needn't go away, but may stay and be happy, may I, dear?"

Here was another fine chance to make the crushing speech

and the stately exit, but Meg never thought of doing either, and disgraced herself forever in Jo's eyes by meekly whispering, "Yes, John," and hiding her face on Mr. Brooke's waistcoat.

Fifteen minutes after Aunt March's departure, Jo came softly downstairs, paused an instant at the parlor door, and hearing no sound within, nodded and smiled, with a satisfied expression, saying to herself, "She has sent him away as we planned, and that affair is settled. I'll go and hear the fun, and have a good laugh over it."

But poor Jo never got her laugh, for she was transfixed upon the threshold by a spectacle which held her there, staring with her mouth nearly as wide open as her eyes. Going in to exult over a fallen enemy, and to praise a strong-minded sister for the banishment of an objectionable lover, it certainly *was* a shock to behold the aforesaid enemy serenely sitting on the sofa, with the strong-minded sister enthroned upon his knee, and wearing an expression of the most abject submission. Jo gave a sort of gasp, as if a cold shower bath had suddenly fallen upon her—for such an unexpected turning of the tables actually took her breath away. At the odd sound, the lovers turned and saw her. Meg jumped up, looking both proud and shy; but "that man," as Jo called him, actually laughed, and said coolly, as he kissed the astonished newcomer, "Sister Jo, congratulate us!"

That was adding insult to injury—it was altogether too much—and, making some wild demonstration with her hands, Jo vanished without a word. Rushing upstairs, she startled the invalids by exclaiming tragically, as she burst into the room, "Oh, *do* somebody go down quick; John Brooke is acting dreadfully and Meg likes it!"

Mr. and Mrs. March left the room with speed; and, casting herself upon the bed, Jo cried and scolded tempestuously as she told the awful news to Beth and Amy. The little girls, however, considered it a most agreeable and interesting event, and Jo got little comfort from them; so she went up to her refuge in the garret, and confided her troubles to the rats.

Nobody ever knew what went on in the parlor that afternoon; but a great deal of talking was done, and quiet Mr.

Brooke astonished his friends by the eloquence and spirit with which he pleaded his suit, told his plans, and persuaded them to arrange everything just as he wanted.

The tea bell rang before he had finished describing the paradise which he meant to earn for Meg, and he proudly took her in to supper, both looking so happy that Jo hadn't the heart to be jealous or dismal. Amy was very much impressed by John's devotion and Meg's dignity, Beth beamed at them from a distance, while Mr. and Mrs. March surveyed the young couple with such tender satisfaction that it was perfectly evident Aunt March was right in calling them as "unworldly as a pair of babies." No one ate much, but everyone looked very happy, and the old room seemed to brighten up amazingly when the first romance of the family began there.

"You can't say nothing pleasant ever happens now, can you, Meg?" said Amy, trying to decide how she would group the lovers in the sketch she was planning to make.

"No, I'm sure I can't. How much has happened since I said that! It seems a year ago," answered Meg, who was in a blissful dream, lifted far above such common things as bread and butter.

"The joys come close upon the sorrows this time, and I rather think the changes have begun," said Mrs. March. "In most families there comes, now and then, a year full of events; this has been such an one, but it ends well, after all."

"Hope the next will end better," muttered Jo, who found it very hard to see Meg absorbed in a stranger before her face; for Jo loved a few persons very dearly, and dreaded to have their affection lost or lessened in any way.

"I hope the third year from this *will* end better; I mean it shall if I live to work out my plans," said Mr. Brooke, smiling at Meg as if everything had become possible to him now.

"Doesn't it seem very long to wait?" asked Amy, who was in a hurry for the wedding.

"I've got so much to learn before I shall be ready, it seems a short time to me," answered Meg, with a sweet gravity in her face never seen there before.

"You have only to wait; *I* am to do the work," said John, beginning his labors by picking up Meg's napkin, with an expression which caused Jo to shake her head, and then say to herself, with an air of relief, as the front door banged, "Here comes Laurie. Now we shall have a little sensible conversation."

But Jo was mistaken; for Laurie came prancing in, overflowing with spirits, bearing a great bridal-looking bouquet for "Mrs. John Brooke," and evidently laboring under the delusion that the whole affair had been brought about by his excellent management.

"I knew Brooke would have it all his own way, he always does; for when he makes up his mind to accomplish anything, it's done, though the sky falls," said Laurie, when he had presented his offering and his congratulations.

"Much obliged for that recommendation. I take it as a good omen for the future, and invite you to my wedding on the spot," answered Mr. Brooke, who felt at peace with all mankind, even his mischievous pupil.

"I'll come if I'm at the ends of the earth; for the sight of Jo's face alone, on that occasion, would be worth a long journey. You don't look festive, ma'am; what's the matter?" asked Laurie, following her into a corner of the parlor, whither all had adjourned to greet Mr. Laurence.

"I don't approve of the match, but I've made up my mind to bear it, and shall not say a word against it," said Jo solemnly. "You can't know how hard it is for me to give up Meg," she continued, with a little quiver in her voice.

"You don't give her up. You only go halves," said Laurie consolingly.

"It never can be the same again. I've lost my dearest friend," sighed Jo.

"You've got me, anyhow. I'm not good for much, I know; but I'll stand by you, Jo, all the days of my life, upon my word I will!" and Laurie meant what he said.

"I know you will, and I'm ever so much obliged; you are always a great comfort to me, Teddy," returned Jo, gratefully shaking hands.

"Well, now, don't be dismal, there's a good fellow. It's all right, you see. Meg is happy; Brooke will fly round and get settled immediately; grandpa will attend to him, and it will be very jolly to see Meg in her own little house. We'll have capital times after she is gone, for I shall be through college before long, and then we'll go abroad, or some nice trip or other. Wouldn't that console you?"

"I rather think it would; but there's no knowing what may happen in three years," said Jo thoughtfully.

"That's true. Don't you wish you could take a look forward and see where we shall all be then? I do," returned Laurie.

"I think not, for I might see something sad; and everyone looks so happy now, I don't believe they could be much improved," and Jo's eyes went slowly round the room, brightening as they looked, for the prospect was a pleasant one.

Father and mother sat together, quietly reliving the first chapter of the romance which for them began some twenty years ago. Amy was drawing the lovers, who sat apart in a beautiful world of their own, the light of which touched their faces with a grace the little artist could not copy. Beth lay on her sofa, talking cheerily with her old friend, who held her little hand as if he felt that it possessed the power to lead him along the peaceful way she walked. Jo lounged in her favorite low seat, with the grave, quiet look which best became her; and Laurie, leaning on the back of her chair, his chin on a level with her curly head, smiled with his friendliest aspect, and nodded at her in the long glass which reflected them both.

So grouped, the curtain falls upon Meg, Jo, Beth, and Amy. Whether it ever rises again depends upon the reception given to the first act of the domestic drama called "LITTLE WOMEN."

Little Women
PART SECOND

CHAPTER TWENTY-FOUR

Gossip

IN order that we may start afresh, and go to Meg's wedding with free minds, it will be well to begin with a little gossip about the Marches. And here let me promise that if any of the elders think there is too much "lovering" in the story, as I fear they may (I'm not afraid the young folks will make that objection), I can only say with Mrs. March, "What *can* you expect when I have four gay girls in the house, and a dashing young neighbor over the way?"

The three years that have passed have brought but few changes to the quiet family. The war is over, and Mr. March safely at home, busy with his books and the small parish which found in him a minister by nature as by grace—a quiet, studious man, rich in the wisdom that is better than learning, the charity that calls all mankind "brother," the piety that blossoms into character, making it august and lovely.

These attributes, in spite of poverty and the strict integrity which shut him out from the more worldly successes, attracted to him many admirable persons, as naturally as sweet herbs draw bees, and as naturally he gave them the honey into which fifty years of hard experience had distilled no bitter drop. Earnest young men found the gray-headed scholar as young at heart as they; thoughtful or troubled women instinctively brought their doubts and sorrows to him, sure of finding the gentlest sympathy, the wisest counsel; sinners told their sins to the purehearted old man, and were both rebuked and saved; gifted men found a companion in him; ambitious men caught glimpses of nobler ambitions than their own; and even worldlings confessed that his beliefs were beautiful and true, although "they wouldn't pay."

To outsiders, the five energetic women seemed to rule the house, and so they did in many things; but the quiet scholar, sitting among his books, was still the head of the family, the household conscience, anchor, and comforter; for to him the busy, anxious women always turned in troublous times, finding him, in the truest sense of those sacred words, husband and father.

The girls gave their hearts into their mother's keeping, their souls into their father's; and to both parents, who lived and labored so faithfuly for them, they gave a love that grew with their growth, and bound them tenderly together by the sweetest tie which blesses life and outlives death.

Mrs. March is as brisk and cheery, though rather grayer, than when we saw her last, and just now so absorbed in Meg's affairs that the hospitals and homes, still full of wounded "boys" and soldiers' widows, decidedly miss the motherly missionary's visits.

John Brooke did his duty manfully for a year, got wounded, was sent home, and not allowed to return. He received no stars or bars, but he deserved them, for he cheerfully risked all he had; and life and love are very precious when both are in full bloom. Perfectly resigned to his discharge, he devoted himself to getting well, preparing for business, and earning a home for Meg. With the good sense and sturdy independence that characterized him, he refused Mr. Laurence's more generous offers, and accepted the place of bookkeeper, feeling better satisfied to begin with an honestly earned salary than by running any risks with borrowed money.

Meg had spent the time in working as well as waiting, growing womanly in character, wise in housewifely arts, and prettier than ever; for love is a great beautifier. She had her girlish ambitions and hopes, and felt some disappointment at the humble way in which the new life must begin. Ned Moffat had just married Sallie Gardiner, and Meg couldn't help contrasting their fine house and carriage, many gifts, and splendid outfit with her own, and secretly wishing she could have the same. But somehow envy and discontent soon vanished when she thought of all the patient love and labor John had put into the little home awaiting her; and when they sat together in the twilight, talking over their small plans, the future always grew so beautiful and bright that she forgot Sallie's splendor and felt herself the richest, happiest girl in Christendom.

Jo never went back to Aunt March, for the old lady took such a fancy to Amy that she bribed her with the offer of drawing lessons from one of the best teachers going; and for the sake of this advantage, Amy would have served a far harder mistress. So she gave her mornings to duty, her afternoons to pleasure, and prospered finely. Jo, meantime, devoted herself to literature and Beth, who remained delicate long after the fever was a thing of the past. Not an invalid exactly, but never again the rosy, healthy creature she had been; yet always hopeful, happy, and serene, busy with the quiet duties she loved, everyone's friend, and an angel in the house, long before those who loved her most had learned to know it.

As long as the "Spread Eagle" paid her a dollar a column for her "rubbish," as she called it, Jo felt herself a woman of means, and spun her little romances diligently. But great plans fermented in her busy brain and ambitious mind, and the old tin kitchen in the garret held a slowly increasing pile of blotted manuscript, which was one day to place the name of March upon the roll of fame.

Laurie, having dutifully gone to college to please his grandfather, was now getting through it in the easiest possible manner to please himself. A universal favorite, thanks to money, manners, much talent, and the kindest heart that ever got its owner into scrapes by trying to get other people out of them, he stood in great danger of being spoilt, and probably would have been, like many another promising boy, if he had not possessed a talisman against evil in the memory of the kind old man who was bound up in his success, the motherly friend who watched over him as if he were her son, and last, but not least by any means, the knowledge that four innocent girls loved, admired, and believed in him with all their hearts.

Being only "a glorious human boy," of course he frolicked and flirted, grew dandified, aquatic, sentimental, or gymnastic, as college fashions ordained; hazed and was hazed, talked slang, and more than once came perilously near suspension and expulsion. But as high spirits and the love of fun were the causes of these pranks, he always managed to save himself by frank confession, honorable atonement, or the irresistible power of persuasion which he possessed in perfection. In fact, he rather prided himself on his narrow escapes, and liked to thrill the girls with graphic accounts of his triumphs over wrathful tutors, dignified professors, and vanquished enemies. The "men of my class" were heroes in the eyes of the girls, who never wearied of the exploits of "our fellows," and were frequently allowed to bask in the smiles of these great creatures, when Laurie brought them home with him.

Amy especially enjoyed this high honor, and became quite a belle among them; for her ladyship early felt and learned to use the gift of fascination with which she was endowed. Meg was too much absorbed in her private and particular John to care for any other lords of creation, and Beth too shy to do more than peep at them, and wonder how Amy dared to order them about so; but Jo felt quite in her element, and found it very difficult to refrain from imitating the gentlemanly attitudes, phrases, and feats, which seemed more natural to her than the decorums prescribed for young ladies. They all liked Jo immensely, but never fell in love with her, though very few escaped without paying the tribute of a sentimental sigh or two at Amy's shrine. And speaking of sentiment brings us very naturally to the "Dovecote."

That was the name of the little brown house which Mr.
Brooke had prepared for Meg's first home. Laurie had christened it, saying it was highly appropriate to the gentle lovers,
who "went on together like a pair of turtledoves, with first a
bill and then a coo." It was a tiny house, with a little garden
behind, and a lawn about as big as a pocket handkerchief in
front. Here Meg meant to have a fountain, shrubbery, and a
profusion of lovely flowers; though just at present, the fountain
was represented by a weather-beaten urn, very like a dilapidated slop bowl; the shrubbery consisted of several young
larches, undecided whether to live or die; and the profusion of
flowers was merely hinted by regiments of sticks, to show

where seeds were planted. But inside, it was altogether charming, and the happy bride saw no fault from garret to cellar. To be sure, the hall was so narrow, it was fortunate that they had no piano, for one never could have been got in whole; the dining room was so small that six people were a tight fit; and the kitchen stairs seemed built for the express purpose of precipitating both servants and china pell-mell into the coalbin. But once get used to these slight blemishes, and nothing could be more complete, for good sense and good taste had presided over the furnishings, and the result was highly satisfactory. There were no marble-topped tables, long mirrors, or lace curtains in the little parlor, but simple furniture, plenty of books, a fine picture or two, a stand of flowers in the bay window, and, scattered all about, the pretty gifts which came from friendly hands, and were the fairer for the loving messages they brought.

I don't think the Parian Psyche Laurie gave lost any of its beauty because John put up the bracket it stood upon; that any upholsterer could have draped the plain muslin curtains more gracefully than Amy's artistic hand; or that any storeroom was ever better provided with good wishes, merry words, and happy hopes, than that in which Jo and her mother put away Meg's few boxes, barrels, and bundles; and I am morally certain that the spandy-new kitchen never *could* have looked so cozy and neat if Hannah had not arranged every pot and pan a dozen times over, and laid the fire all ready for lighting, the minute "Mis Brooke came home." I also doubt if any young matron ever began life with so rich a supply of dusters, holders, and piece bags; for Beth made enough to last till the silver wedding came round, and invented three different kinds of dishcloths for the express service of the bridal china.

People who hire all these things done for them never know what they lose; for the homeliest tasks get beautified if loving hands do them, and Meg found so many proofs of this that everything in her small nest, from the kitchen roller to the silver vase on her parlor table, was eloquent of home love and tender forethought.

What happy times they had planning together, what solemn shopping excursions; what funny mistakes they made, and what shouts of laughter arose over Laurie's ridiculous bargains. In his love of jokes, this young gentleman, though nearly through college, was as much of a boy as ever. His last whim had been to bring with him, on his weekly visits, some new, useful, and ingenious article for the young housekeeper. Now a bag of remarkable clothespins; next, a wonderful nutmeg grater, which fell to pieces at the first trial; a knife cleaner that spoilt all the knives; or a sweeper that picked the nap neatly off the carpet, and left the dirt; laborsaving soap that took the skin off one's hands; infallible cements which stuck firmly to nothing but the fingers of the deluded buyer; and every kind of tinware, from a toy savings bank for odd pennies to a wonderful boiler, which would wash articles in its own steam, with every prospect of exploding in the process.

In vain Meg begged him to stop. John laughed at him, and Jo called him "Mr. Toodles." He was possessed with a mania for patronizing Yankee ingenuity, and seeing his friends fitly furnished forth. So each week beheld some fresh absurdity.

Everything was done at last, even to Amy's arranging different colored soaps to match the different colored rooms, and Beth's setting the table for the first meal.

"Are you satisfied? Does it seem like home, and do you feel as if you should be happy here?" asked Mrs. March, as she and her daughter went through the new kingdom, arm in arm; for just then they seemed to cling together more tenderly than ever.

"Yes, mother, perfectly satisfied, thanks to you all, and *so* happy that I can't talk about it," answered Meg, with a look that was better than words.

"If she only had a servant or two it would be all right," said Amy, coming out of the parlor, where she had been trying to decide whether the bronze Mercury looked best on the whatnot or the mantelpiece.

"Mother and I have talked it over, and I have made up my mind to try her way first. There will be so little to do that, with Lotty to run my errands and help me here and there, I shall only have enough work to keep me from getting lazy or homesick," answered Meg tranquilly.

"Sallie Moffat has four," began Amy.

"If Meg had four the house wouldn't hold them, and master and missis would have to camp in the garden," broke in Jo, who, enveloped in a big blue pinafore, was giving the last polish to the door handles.

"Sallie isn't a poor man's wife, and many maids are in keeping with her fine establishment. Meg and John begin humbly, but I have a feeling that there will be quite as much happiness in the little house as in the big one. It's a great mistake for young girls like Meg to leave themselves nothing to do but dress, give orders, and gossip. When I was first married, I used to long for my new clothes to wear out or get torn, so that I might have the pleasure of mending them; for I got heartily sick of doing fancywork and tending my pocket handkerchief."

"Why didn't you go into the kitchen and make messes, as Sallie says she does, to amuse herself, though they never turn out well, and the servants laugh at her?" said Meg.

"I did, after a while; not to 'mess,' but to learn of Hannah how things should be done, that my servants need *not* laugh at me. It was play then; but there came a time when I was truly grateful that I not only possessed the will but the power to cook wholesome food for my little girls, and help myself when I could no longer afford to hire help. You begin at the other end, Meg dear; but the lessons you learn now will be of use to you by and by, when John is a richer man, for the mistress of a house, however splendid, should know how work ought to be done, if she wishes to be well and honestly served."

"Yes, mother, I'm sure of that," said Meg, listening respectfully to the little lecture; for the best of women will hold forth upon the all-absorbing subject of housekeeping. "Do you know I like this room most of all in my baby-house," added Meg, a minute after, as they went upstairs, and she looked into her well-stored linen closet.

Beth was there, laying the snowy piles smoothly on the shelves, and exulting over the goodly array. All three laughed as Meg spoke; for that linen closet was a joke. You see, after having said that if Meg married "that Brooke" she shouldn't have a cent of her money, Aunt March was rather in a quandary, when time had appeased her wrath and made her repent her vow. She never broke her word, and was much exercised in her mind how to get round it, and at last devised a plan whereby she could satisfy herself. Mrs. Carrol, Florence's mamma, was ordered to buy, have made, and marked, a generous supply of house and table linen, and send it as *her* present, all of which was faithfuly done; but the secret leaked out, and was greatly enjoyed by the family; for Aunt March tried **to** look utterly unconscious, and insisted that she could give nothing but the old-fashioned pearls long promised to the first bride.

"That's a housewifely taste which I am glad to see. I had a young friend who set up housekeeping with six sheets, but she had finger bowls for company, and that satisfied her," said Mrs. March, patting the damask tablecloths, with a truly feminine appreciation of their fineness.

"I haven't a single finger bowl, but this is a 'set out' that will last me all my days, Hannah says," and Meg looked quite contented, as well she might.

"Toodles is coming," cried Jo from below; and they all went down to meet Laurie, whose weekly visit was an important event in their quiet lives.

A tall, broad-shouldered young fellow, with a cropped head, a felt-basin of a hat, and a flyaway coat, came tramping down the road at a great pace, walked over the low fence without stopping to open the gate, straight up to Mrs. March, with both hands out, and a hearty:

"Here I am, mother! Yes, it's all right."

The last words were in answer to the look the elder lady gave him; a kindly questioning look, which the handsome eyes met so frankly that the little ceremony closed, as usual, with a motherly kiss.

"For Mrs. John Brooke, with the maker's congratulations and compliments. Bless you, Beth! What a refreshing spectacle you are, Jo. Amy, you are getting altogether too handsome for a single lady."

As Laurie spoke, he delivered a brown paper parcel to Meg, pulled Beth's hair ribbon, stared at Jo's big pinafore, and fell into an attitude of mock rapture before Amy, then shook hands all round, and everyone began to talk.

"Where is John?" asked Meg anxiously.

"Stopped to get the license for tomorrow, ma'am."

"Which side won the last match, Teddy?" inquired Jo, who persisted in feeling an interest in manly sports despite her nineteen years.

"Ours, of course. Wish you'd been there to see."

"How is the lovely Miss Randal?" asked Amy, with a significant smile.

"More cruel than ever; don't you see how I'm pining away?" and Laurie gave his broad chest a sounding slap and heaved a melodramatic sigh.

"What's the last joke? Undo the bundle and see, Meg," said Beth, eying the knobby parcel with curiosity.

"It's a useful thing to have in the house in case of fire or thieves," observed Laurie, as a watchman's rattle appeared, amid the laughter of the girls.

"Any time when John is away, and you get frightened, Mrs. Meg, just swing that out of the front window, and it will rouse the neighborhood in a jiffy. Nice thing, isn't it?" and Laurie gave them a sample of its powers that made them cover up their ears.

"There's gratitude for you! And speaking of gratitude reminds me to mention that you may thank Hannah for saving your wedding cake from destruction. I saw it going into your house as I came by, and if she hadn't defended it manfully, I'd have had a pick at it, for it looked like a remarkably plummy one."

"I wonder if you will ever grow up, Laurie," said Meg in a matronly tone.

"I'm doing my best, ma'am, but can't get much higher, I'm afraid, as six feet is about all men can do in these degenerate days," responded the young gentleman, whose head was about level with the little chandelier.

"I suppose it would be profanation to eat anything in this spick-and-span new bower, so, as I'm tremendously hungry, I propose an adjournment," he added presently.

"Mother and I are going to wait for John. There are some last things to settle," said Meg, bustling away.

"Beth and I are going over to Kitty Bryant's to get more flowers for tomorrow," added Amy, tying a picturesque hat over her picturesque curls, and enjoying the effect as much as anybody.

"Come, Jo, don't desert a fellow. I'm in such a state of exhaustion I can't get home without help. Don't take off your apron, whatever you do; it's peculiarly becoming," said Laurie, as Jo bestowed his especial aversion in her capacious pocket, and offered him her arm to support his feeble steps.

"Now, Teddy, I want to talk seriously to you about tomorrow," began Jo, as they strolled away together. "You *must* promise to behave well, and not cut up any pranks, and spoil our plans."

"Not a prank."

"And don't say funny things when we ought to be sober."

"I never do; you are the one for that."

"And I implore you not to look at me during the ceremony; I shall certainly laugh if you do."

"You won't see me; you'll be crying so hard that the thick fog round you will obscure the prospect."

"I never cry unless for some great affliction."

"Such as fellows going to college, hey?" cut in Laurie, with a suggestive laugh.

"Don't be a peacock. I only moaned a trifle to keep the girls company."

"Exactly. I say, Jo, how is grandpa this week; pretty amiable?"

"Very. Why, have you got into a scrape, and want to know how he'll take it?" asked Jo rather sharply.

"Now, Jo, do you think I'd look your mother in the face, and say 'All right,' if it wasn't?" and Laurie stopped short, with an injured air.

"No, I don't."

"Then don't go and be suspicious; I only want some money," said Laurie, walking on again, appeased by her hearty tone.

"You spend a great deal, Teddy."

"Bless you, *I* don't spend it; it spends itself, somehow, and is gone before I know it."

"You are so generous and kindhearted that you let people

borrow, and can't say 'No' to anyone. We heard about Henshaw, and all you did for him. If you always spent money in that way, no one would blame you," said Jo warmly.

"Oh, he made a mountain out of a molehill. You wouldn't have me let that fine fellow work himself to death just for the want of a little help, when he is worth a dozen of us lazy chaps, would you?"

"Of course not; but I don't see the use of your having seventeen waistcoats, endless neckties, and a new hat every time you come home. I thought you'd got over the dandy period; but every now and then it breaks out in a new spot. Just now it's the fashion to be hideous—to make your head look like a scrubbing brush, wear a strait jacket, orange gloves, and clumping, square-toed boots. If it was cheap ugliness, I'd say nothing; but it costs as much as the other, and I don't get any satisfaction out of it."

Laurie threw back his head and laughed so heartily at this attack that the felt-basin fell off, and Jo walked on it, which insult only afforded him an opportunity for expatiating on the advantages of a rough-and-ready costume, as he folded up the maltreated hat, and stuffed it into his pocket.

"Don't lecture any more, there's a good soul! I have enough all through the week, and like to enjoy myself when I come home. I'll get myself up regardless of expense, tomorrow, and be a satisfaction to my friends."

"I'll leave you in peace if you'll only let your hair grow. I'm not aristocratic, but I do object to being seen with a person who looks like a young prize fighter," observed Jo severely.

"This unassuming style promotes study; that's why we adopt it," returned Laurie, who certainly could not be accused of vanity, having voluntarily sacrificed a handsome curly crop to the demand for quarter-of-an-inch-long stubble.

"By the way, Jo, I think that little Parker is really getting desperate about Amy. He talks of her constantly, writes poetry, and moons about in a most suspicious manner. He'd better nip his little passion in the bud, hadn't he?" added Laurie, in a confidential, elder-brotherly tone, after a minute's silence.

"Of course he had; we don't want any more marrying in the family for years to come. Mercy on us, what *are* the children thinking of?" and Jo looked as much scandalized as if Amy and little Parker were not yet in their teens.

"It's a fast age, and I don't know what we are coming to, ma'am. You are a mere infant, but you'll go next, Jo, and we'll be left lamenting," said Laurie, shaking his head over the degeneracy of the times.

"Don't be alarmed; I'm not one of the agreeable sort. Nobody will want me, and it's a mercy, for there should always be one old maid in a family."

"You won't give anyone a chance," said Laurie, with a sidelong glance, and a little more color than before in his sunburnt face. "You won't show the soft side of your character, and if a fellow gets a peep at it by accident, and can't help showing that he likes it, you treat him as Mrs. Gummidge did her sweetheart—throw cold water over him—and get so thorny no one dares touch or look at you."

"I don't like that sort of thing; I'm too busy to be worried with nonsense, and I think it's dreadful to break up families so. Now don't say any more about it; Meg's wedding has turned all our heads, and we talk of nothing but lovers and such absurdities. I don't wish to get cross, so let's change the subject," and Jo looked quite ready to fling cold water on the slightest provocation.

Whatever his feelings might have been, Laurie found a vent for them in a long, low whistle, and the fearful prediction, as they parted at the gate, "Mark my words, Jo, you'll go next."

CHAPTER TWENTY-FIVE

The First Wedding

THE June roses over the porch were awake bright and early on that morning, rejoicing with all their hearts in the cloudless sunshine, like friendly little neighbors, as they were. Quite flushed with excitement were their ruddy faces, as they swung in the wind, whispering to one another what they had seen; for some peeped in at the dining-room windows, where the feast was spread, some climbed up to nod and smile at the sisters as they dressed the bride, others waved a welcome to those who came and went on various errands in garden, porch, and hall, and all, from the rosiest full-blown flower to the palest baby bud, offered their tribute of beauty and fragrance to the gentle mistress who had loved and tended them so long.

Meg looked very like a rose herself; for all that was best

and sweetest in heart and soul seemed to bloom into her face
that day, making it fair and tender, with a charm more beautiful than beauty. Neither silk, lace, nor orange flowers would
she have. "I don't want to look strange or fixed up today," she
said. "I don't want a fashionable wedding, but only those about
me whom I love, and to them I wish to look and be my familiar
self."

So she made her wedding gown herself, sewing into it the
tender hopes and innocent romances of a girlish heart. Her
sisters braided up her pretty hair, and the only ornaments she
wore were the lilies of the valley which "her John" liked best
of all the flowers that grew.

"You *do* look just like our own dear Meg, only so very sweet
and lovely that I should hug you if it wouldn't crumple your
dress," cried Amy, surveying her with delight, when all was
done.

"Then I am satisfied. But please hug and kiss me, everyone,
and don't mind my dress; I want a great many crumples of this
sort put into it today," and Meg opened her arms to her sisters,
who clung about her with April faces for a minute, feeling
that the new love had not changed the old.

"Now I'm going to tie John's cravat for him, and then to
stay a few minutes with father quietly in the study," and Meg
ran down to perform these little ceremonies, and then to follow
her mother wherever she went, conscious that, in spite of the
smiles on the motherly face, there was a secret sorrow hid in
the motherly heart at the flight of the first bird from the nest.

As the younger girls stand together, giving the last touches
to their simple toilette, it may be a good time to tell of a few
changes which three years have brought in their appearance,
for all are looking their best just now.

Jo's angles are much softened; she has learned to carry herself with ease, if not grace. The curly crop has lengthened into
a thick coil, more becoming to the small head atop of the tall
figure. There is a fresh color in her brown cheeks, a soft shine
in her eyes, and only gentle words fall from her sharp tongue
today.

Beth has grown slender, pale, and more quiet than ever; the
beautiful, kind eyes are larger, and in them lies an expression

that saddens one, although it is not sad itself. It is the shadow of pain which touches the young face with such pathetic patience; but Beth seldom complains, and always speaks hopefully of "being better soon."

Amy is with truth considered "the flower of the family," for at sixteen she has the air and bearing of a full-grown woman —not beautiful, but possessed of that indescribable charm called grace. One saw it in the lines of her figure, the make and motion of her hands, the flow of her dress, the droop of her hair—unconscious, yet harmonious, and as attractive to many as beauty itself. Amy's nose still afflicted her, for it never *would* grow Grecian; so did her mouth, being too wide, and having a decided chin. These offending features gave character to her whole face, but she never could see it, and consoled herself with her wonderfully fair complexion, keen blue eyes, and curls, more golden and abundant than ever.

All three wore suits of thin silver gray (their best gowns for the summer), with blush roses in hair and bosom; and all three looked just what they were—fresh-faced, happyhearted girls, pausing a moment in their busy lives to read with wistful eyes the sweetest chapter in the romance of womanhood.

There were to be no ceremonious performances, everything was to be as natural and homelike as possible; so when Aunt March arrived, she was scandalized to see the bride come running to welcome and lead her in, to find the bridegroom fastening up a garland that had fallen down, and to catch a glimpse of the paternal minister marching upstairs with a grave countenance, and a wine bottle under each arm.

"Upon my word, here's a state of things!" cried the old lady, taking the seat of honor prepared for her, and settling the folds of her lavender moiré with a great rustle. "You oughtn't to be seen till the last minute, child."

"I'm not a show, aunty, and no one is coming to stare at me, to criticize my dress, or count the cost of my luncheon. I'm too happy to care what anyone says or thinks, and I'm going to have my little wedding just as I like it. John dear, here's your hammer," and away went Meg to help "that man" in his highly improper employment.

Mr. Brooke didn't even say "Thank you," but as he stooped

for the unromantic too!, he kissed his little bride behind the folding door, with a look that made Aunt March whisk out her pocket handkerchief, with a sudden dew in her sharp old eyes.

A crash, a cry, and a laugh from Laurie, accompanied by the indecorous exclamation, "Jupiter Ammon! Jo's upset the cake again!" caused a momentary flurry, which was hardly over when a flock of cousins arrived and "the party came in," as Beth used to say when a child.

"Don't let that young giant come near me; he worries me worse than mosquitoes," whispered the old lady to Amy, as the rooms filled, and Laurie's black head towered above the rest.

"He has promised to be very good today, and he *can* be perfectly elegant if he likes," returned Amy, gliding away to warn Hercules to beware of the dragon, which warning caused him to haunt the old lady with a devotion that nearly distracted her.

There was no bridal procession, but a sudden silence fell upon the room as Mr. March and the young pair took their places under the green arch. Mother and sisters gathered close, as if loath to give Meg up; the fatherly voice broke more than once, which only seemed to make the service more beautiful and solemn; the bridegroom's hand trembled visibly, and no one heard his replies; but Meg looked straight up in her husband's eyes, and said, "I will!" with such tender trust in her own face and voice that her mother's heart rejoiced, and Aunt March sniffed audibly.

Jo did *not* cry, though she was very near it once, and was only saved from a demonstration by the consciousness that Laurie was staring fixedly at her, with a comical mixture of merriment and emotion in his wicked black eyes. Beth kept her face hidden on her mother's shoulder, but Amy stood like a graceful statue, with a most becoming ray of sunshine touching her white forehead and the flower in her hair.

It wasn't at all the thing, I'm afraid, but the minute she was fairly married, Meg cried, "The first kiss for Marmee!" and, turning, gave it with her heart on her lips. During the next fifteen minutes she looked more like a rose than ever, for everyone availed themselves of their privileges to the fullest extent, from Mr. Laurence to old Hannah, who, adorned with a headdress fearfully and wonderfully made, fell upon her in the hall, crying, with a sob and a chuckle, "Bless you, deary, a hundred times! The cake ain't hurt a mite, and everything looks lovely."

Everybody cleared up after that, and said something brilliant, or tried to, which did just as well, for laughter is ready when hearts are light. There was no display of gifts, for they were already in the little house, nor was there an elaborate breakfast, but a plentiful lunch of cake and fruit, dressed with flowers. Mr. Laurence and Aunt March shrugged and smiled at one another when water, lemonade, and coffee were found to be the only sorts of nectar which the three Hebes carried round. No one said anything, however, till Laurie, who insisted on serving the bride, appeared before her, with a loaded salver in his hand and a puzzled expression on his face.

"Has Jo smashed all the bottles by accident," he whispered, "or am I merely laboring under a delusion that I saw some lying about loose this morning?"

"No; your grandfather kindly offered us his best, and Aunt March actually sent some, but father put away a little for Beth, and dispatched the rest to the Soldiers' Home. You know he thinks that wine should be used only in illness, and mother says that neither she nor her daughters will ever offer it to any young man under her roof."

Meg spoke seriously, and expected to see Laurie frown or laugh; but he did neither, for after a quick look at her, he said,

in his impetuous way, "I like that! For I've seen enough harm done to wish other women would think as you do."

"You are not made wise by experience, I hope?" and there was an anxious accent in Meg's voice.

"No; I give you my word for it. Don't think too well of me, either; this is not one of my temptations. Being brought up where wine is as common as water, and almost as harmless, I don't care for it; but when a pretty girl offers it, one doesn't like to refuse, you see."

"But you will, for the sake of others, if not for your own. Come, Laurie, promise, and give me one more reason to call this the happiest day of my life."

A demand so sudden and so serious made the young man hesitate a moment, for ridicule is often harder to bear than self-denial. Meg knew that if he gave the promise he would keep it at all costs; and, feeling her power, used it as a woman may for her friend's good. She did not speak, but she looked up at him with a face made very eloquent by happiness, and a smile which said, "No one can refuse me anything today."

Laurie certainly could not; and, with an answering smile, he gave her his hand, saying heartily, "I promise, Mrs. Brooke!"

"I thank you, very, very much."

"And I drink 'long life to your resolution,' Teddy," cried Jo, baptizing him with a splash of lemonade, as she waved her glass, and beamed approvingly upon him.

So the toast was drunk, the pledge made, and loyally kept, in spite of many temptations; for, with instinctive wisdom, the girls had seized a happy moment to do their friend a service for which he thanked them all his life.

After lunch, people strolled about, by twos and threes, through house and garden, enjoying the sunshine without and within. Meg and John happened to be standing together in the middle of the grass plot, when Laurie was seized with an inspiration which put the finishing touch to this unfashionable wedding.

"All the married people take hands and dance round the new-made husband and wife, as the Germans do, while we bachelors and spinsters prance in couples outside!" cried Laurie, promenading down the path with Amy, with such infectious spirit and skill that everyone else followed their example without a murmur. Mr. and Mrs. March, Aunt and Uncle Carrol, began it; others rapidly joined in; even Sallie Moffat, after a moment's hesitation, threw her train over her arm, and whisked Ned into the ring. But the crowning joke was Mr. Laurence and Aunt March; for when the stately old gentleman chasséd solemnly up to the old lady, she just tucked her cane under her arm, and hopped briskly away to join hands with the rest, and dance about the bridal pair, while the young folks pervaded the garden, like butterflies on a midsummer day.

Want of breath brought the impromptu ball to a close, and than people began to go.

"I wish you well, my dear, I heartily wish you well; but I think you'll be sorry for it," said Aunt March to Meg, adding to the bridegroom, as he led her to the carriage, "You've got a treasure, young man, see that you deserve it."

"That is the prettiest wedding I've been to for an age, Ned, and I don't see why, for there wasn't a bit of style about it," observed Mrs. Moffat to her husband, as they drove away.

The young pair took their places under the arch

"Laurie, my lad, if you ever want to indulge in this sort of thing, get one of those little girls to help you, and I shall be perfectly satisfied," said Mr. Laurence, settling himself in his easy chair to rest, after the excitement of the morning.

"I'll do my best to gratify you, sir" was Laurie's unusually dutiful reply, as he carefully unpinned the posy Jo had put in his buttonhole.

The little house was not far away, and the only bridal journey Meg had was the quiet walk with John, from the old home to the new. When she came down, looking like a pretty Quakeress in her dove-colored suit and straw bonnet tied with white, they all gathered about her to say "good-by" as tenderly as if she had been going to make the grand tour.

"Don't feel that I am separated from you, Marmee dear, or that I love you any the less for loving John so much," she said, clinging to her mother, with full eyes, for a moment. "I shall come every day, father, and expect to keep my old place in all your hearts, though I *am* married. Beth is going to be with me a great deal, and the other girls will drop in now and then to laugh at my housekeeping struggles. Thank you all for my happy wedding day. Good-by, good-by!"

They stood watching her, with faces full of love and hope and tender pride, as she walked away, leaning on her husband's arm, with her hands full of flowers, and the June sunshine brightening her happy face—and so Meg's married life began.

CHAPTER TWENTY-SIX

Artistic Attempts

IT takes people a long time to learn the difference between talent and genius, especially ambitious young men and women. Amy was learning this distinction through much tribulation; for, mistaking enthusiasm for inspiration, she attempted every branch of art with youthful audacity. For a long time there was a lull in the "mud-pie" business, and she devoted herself to the finest pen-and-ink drawing, in which she showed such taste and skill that her graceful handiwork proved both pleasant and profitable. But overstrained eyes soon caused pen and ink to be laid aside for a bold attempt at poker sketching.

While this attack lasted, the family lived in constant fear of a conflagration, for the odor of burning wood pervaded the house at all hours; smoke issued from attic and shed with alarming frequency, red-hot pokers lay about promiscuously, and Hannah never went to bed without a pail of water and the dinner bell at her door, in case of fire. Raphael's face was found boldly executed on the underside of the molding board, and Bacchus on the head of a beer barrel; a chanting cherub adorned the cover of the sugar bucket, and attempts to portray Romeo and Juliet supplied kindlings for some time.

From fire to oil was a natural transition for burnt fingers, and Amy fell to painting with undiminished ardor. An artist friend fitted her out with his castoff palettes, brushes, and colors; and she daubed away, producing pastoral and marine views such as were never seen on land or sea. Her monstrosities in the way of cattle would have taken prizes at an agricultural fair; and the perilous pitching of her vessels would have produced seasickness in the most nautical observer, if the utter disregard to all known rules of shipbuilding and rigging had not convulsed him with laughter at the first glance. Swarthy boys and dark-eyed Madonnas, staring at you from one corner of the studio, suggested Murillo; oily-brown shadows of faces, with a lurid streak in the wrong place, meant Rembrandt; buxom ladies and dropsical infants, Rubens; and Turner appeared in tempests of blue thunder, orange lightning, brown rain, and purple clouds, with a tomato-colored splash in the middle, which might be the sun or a buoy, a sailor's shirt or a king's robe, as the spectator pleased.

Charcoal portraits came next; and the entire family hung in a row, looking as wild and crocky as if just evoked from a coalbin. Softened into crayon sketches, they did better; for the likenesses were good, and Amy's hair, Jo's nose, Meg's mouth, and Laurie's eyes were pronounced "wonderfully fine." A return to clay and plaster followed, and ghostly casts of her acquaintances haunted corners of the house or tumbled off closet shelves on to people's heads. Children were enticed in as models, till their incoherent accounts of her mysterious doings caused Miss Amy to be regarded in the light of a young ogress. Her efforts in this line, however, were brought to an abrupt close by an untoward accident, which quenched her ardor. Other models failing her for a time, she undertook to cast her own pretty foot, and the family were one day alarmed by an unearthly bumping and screaming, and running to the rescue, found the young enthusiast hopping wildly about the shed, with her foot held fast in a panful of plaster, which had hardened with unexpected rapidity. With much difficulty and some danger she was dug out; for Jo was so overcome with laughter while she excavated that her knife went too far, cut the poor foot, and left a lasting memorial of one artistic attempt, at least.

After this Amy subsided, till a mania for sketching from nature set her to haunting river, field, and wood for picturesque studies, and sighing for ruins to copy. She caught endless colds sitting on damp grass to book "a delicious bit," composed of a stone, a stump, one mushroom, and a broken mullein-stalk or "a heavenly mass of clouds," that looked like a choice display of feather beds when done. She sacrificed her complexion floating on the river in the midsummer sun, to study light and shade, and got a wrinkle over her nose trying after "points of sight," or whatever the squint-and-string performance is called.

If "genius is eternal patience," as Michelangelo affirms, Amy certainly had some claim to the divine attribute, for she persevered in spite of all obstacles, failures, and discouragements, firmly believing that in time she should do something worthy to be called "high art."

She was learning, doing, and enjoying other things, meanwhile, for she had resolved to be an attractive and accomplished woman, even if she never became a great artist. Here she succeeded better; for she was one of those happily created beings who please without effort, make friends everywhere, and take life so gracefully and easily that less fortunate souls are tempted to believe that such are born under a lucky star. Everybody liked her, for among her good gifts was tact. She had an instinctive sense of what was pleasing and proper, always said the right thing to the right person, did just what suited the time and place, and was so self-possessed that her sisters used to say, "If Amy went to court without any rehearsal beforehand, she'd know exactly what to do."

One of her weaknesses was a desire to move in "our best society," without being quite sure what the *best* really was.

Money, position, fashionable accomplishments, and elegant manners were most desirable things in her eyes, and she liked to associate with those who possessed them, often mistaking the false for the true, and admiring what was not admirable. Never forgetting that by birth she was a gentlewoman, she cultivated her aristocratic tastes and feelings, so that when the opportunity came she might be ready to take the place from which poverty now excluded her.

"My lady," as her friends called her, sincerely desired to be a genuine lady, and was so at heart, but had yet to learn that money cannot buy refinement of nature, that rank does not always confer nobility, and that true breeding makes itself felt in spite of external drawbacks.

"I want to ask a favor of you, mamma," Amy said, coming in, with an important air, one day.

"Well, little girl, what is it?" replied her mother, in whose eyes the stately young lady still remained "the baby."

"Our drawing class breaks up next week, and before the girls separate for the summer, I want to ask them out here for a day. They are wild to see the river, sketch the broken bridge, and copy some of the things they admire in my book. They have been very kind to me in many ways, and I am grateful, for they are all rich, and know I am poor, yet they never made any difference."

"Why should they?" and Mrs. March put the question with what the girls called her "Maria Theresa air."

"You know as well as I that it *does* make a difference with nearly everyone, so don't ruffle up, like a dear, motherly hen, when your chickens get pecked by smarter birds; the ugly duckling turned out a swan, you know," and Amy smiled without bitterness, for she possessed a happy temper and hopeful spirit.

Mrs. March laughed, and smoothed down her maternal pride as she asked:

"Well, my swan, what is your plan?"

"I should like to ask the girls out to lunch next week, to take them a drive to the places they want to see, a row on the river, perhaps, and make a little artistic fete for them."

"That looks feasible. What do you want for lunch? Cake,

sandwiches, fruit, and coffee will be all that is necessary, I suppose?"

"Oh, dear, no! we must have cold tongue and chicken. French chocolate and ice cream, besides. The girls are used to such things, and I want my lunch to be proper and elegant, though I *do* work for my living."

"How many young ladies are there?" asked her mother, beginning to look sober.

"Twelve or fourteen in the class, but I dare say they won't all come."

"Bless me, child, you will have to charter an omnibus to carry them about."

"Why, mother, how *can* you think of such a thing? Not more than six or eight will probably come, so I shall hire a beach wagon, and borrow Mr. Laurence's cherry-bounce." (Hannah's pronunciation of charabanc.)

"All this will be expensive, Amy."

"Not very; I've calculated the cost, and I'll pay for it myself."

"Don't you think, dear, that as these girls are used to such things, and the best we can do will be nothing new, that some simpler plan would be pleasanter to them, as a change, if nothing more, and much better for us than buying or borrowing what we don't need, and attempting a style not in keeping with our circumstances?"

"If I can't have it as I like, I don't care to have it at all. I know that I can carry it out perfectly well, if you and the girls will help a little; and I don't see why I can't if I'm willing to pay for it," said Amy, with the decision which opposition was apt to change into obstinacy.

Mrs. March knew that experience was an excellent teacher, and when it was possible she left her children to learn alone the lessons which she would gladly have made easier, if they had not objected to taking advice as much as they did salts and senna.

"Very well, Amy; if your heart is set upon it, and you see your way through without too great an outlay of money, time, and temper, I'll say no more. Talk it over with the girls, and whichever way you decide, I'll do my best to help you."

"Thanks, mother; you are always *so* kind," and away went Amy to lay her plan before her sisters.

Meg agreed at once, and promised her aid, gladly offering anything she possessed, from her little house itself to her very best salt spoons. But Jo frowned upon the whole project, and would have nothing to do with it at first.

"Why in the world should you spend your money, worry your family, and turn the house upside down for a parcel of girls who don't care a sixpence for you? I thought you had too much pride and sense to truckle to any mortal woman just because she wears French boots and rides in a coupé," said Jo, who, being called from the tragical climax of her novel, was not in the best mood for social enterprises.

"I *don't* truckle, and I hate being patronized as much as you do!" returned Amy indignantly, for the two still jangled when such questions arose. "The girls do care for me, and I for them, and there's a great deal of kindness and sense and talent among them, in spite of what you call fashionable nonsense. You don't care to make people like you, to go into good society, and cultivate your manners and tastes. I do, and I mean to make the most of every chance that comes. *You* can go through the world with your elbows out and your nose in the air, and call it independence, if you like. That's not my way."

When Amy whetted her tongue and freed her mind she usually got the best of it, for she seldom failed to have common sense on her side, while Jo carried her love of liberty and hate of conventionalities to such an unlimited extent that she naturally found herself worsted in an argument. Amy's definition of Jo's idea of independence was such a good hit that both burst out laughing, and the discussion took a more amiable turn. Much against her will, Jo at length consented to sacrifice a day to Mrs. Grundy, and help her sister through what she regarded as a "nonsensical business."

The invitations were sent, nearly all accepted, and the following Monday was set apart for the grand event. Hannah was out of humor because her week's work was deranged, and prophesied that "ef the washin' and ironin' warn't done reg'lar nothin' would go well anywheres." This hitch in the mainspring of the domestic machinery had a bad effect upon the whole concern; but Amy's motto was "Nil desperandum," and having made up her mind what to do, she proceeded to do it in spite of all obstacles. To begin with, Hannah's cooking didn't turn out well: the chicken was tough, the tongue too salt, and the chocolate wouldn't froth properly. Then the cake and ice cost more than Amy expected, so did the wagon; and various other expenses, which seemed trifling at the outset, counted up rather alarmingly afterward. Beth got cold and took to her bed, Meg had an unusual number of callers to keep her at home, and Jo was in such a divided state of mind that her breakages, accidents, and mistakes were uncommonly numerous, serious, and trying.

"If it hadn't been for mother I never should have got through," as Amy declared afterward, and gratefully remembered when "the best joke of the season" was entirely forgotten by everybody else.

If it was not fair on Monday, the young ladies were to come on Tuesday—an arrangement which aggravated Jo and Hannah to the last degree. On Monday morning the weather was in that undecided state which is more exasperating than a steady pour. It drizzled a little, shone a little, blew a little, and didn't make up its mind till it was too late for anyone else to make up theirs. Amy was up at dawn, hustling people out of their beds and through their breakfasts, that the house might be got in order. The parlor struck her as looking uncommonly shabby; but without stopping to sigh for what she had not, she skillfully made the best of what she had, arranging chairs over the worn places in the carpet, covering stains on the walls with pictures framed in ivy, and filling up empty corners with home-made statuary, which gave an artistic air to the room, as did the lovely vases of flowers Jo scattered about.

The lunch looked charming; and as she surveyed it, she sincerely hoped it would taste good, and that the borrowed glass, china, and silver would get safely home again. The carriages were promised, Meg and mother were all ready to do the honors, Beth was able to help Hannah behind the scenes, Jo had engaged to be as lively and amiable as an absent mind, an aching head, and a very decided disapproval of everybody and everything would allow, and, as she wearily dressed,

Amy cheered herself with anticipations of the happy moment, when, lunch safely over, she should drive away with her friends for an afternoon of artistic delights; for the "cherry-bounce" and the broken bridge were her strong points.

Then came two hours of suspense, during which she vibrated from parlor to porch, while public opinion varied like the weathercock. A smart shower at eleven had evidently quenched the enthusiasm of the young ladies who were to arrive at twelve, for nobody came; and at two the exhausted family sat down in a blaze of sunshine to consume the perishable portions of the feast, that nothing might be lost.

"No doubt about the weather today; they will certainly come, so we must fly round and be ready for them," said Amy, as the sun woke her next morning. She spoke briskly, but in her secret soul she wished she had said nothing about Tuesday, for her interest, like her cake, was getting a little stale.

"I can't get any lobsters, so you will have to do without salad today," said Mr. March, coming in half an hour later with an expression of placid despair.

"Use the chicken, then; the toughness won't matter in a salad," advised his wife.

"Hannah left it on the kitchen table a minute, and the kittens got at it. I'm very sorry, Amy," added Beth, who was still a patroness of cats.

"Then I *must* have a lobster, for tongue alone won't do," said Amy decidedly.

"Shall I rush into town and demand one?" asked Jo, with the magnanimity of a martyr.

"You'd come bringing it home under your arm, without any paper, just to try me. I'll go myself," answered Amy, whose temper was beginning to fail.

Shrouded in a thick veil and armed with a genteel traveling basket, she departed, feeling that a cool drive would soothe her ruffled spirit, and fit her for the labors of the day. After some delay, the object of her desire was procured, likewise a bottle of dressing, to prevent further loss of time at home, and off she drove again, well pleased with her own forethought.

As the omnibus contained only one other passenger, a sleepy old lady, Amy pocketed her veil, and beguiled the tedium of the way by trying to find out where all her money had gone to. So busy was she with her card full of refractory figures that she did not observe a newcomer, who entered without stopping the vehicle till a masculine voice said, "Good morning, Miss March," and, looking up, she beheld one of Laurie's most elegant college friends. Fervently hoping that he would get out before she did, Amy utterly ignored the basket at her feet, and, congratulating herself that she had on her new traveling dress, returned the young man's greeting with her usual suavity and spirit.

They got on excellently; for Amy's chief care was soon set at rest by learning that the gentleman would leave first, and she was chatting away in a peculiarly lofty strain when the old lady got out. In stumbling to the door, she upset the basket, and—oh, horror!—the lobster, in all its vulgar size and brilliancy, was revealed to the highborn eyes of a Tudor.

"By Jove, she's forgotten her dinner!" cried the unconscious youth, poking the scarlet monster into its place with his cane, and preparing to hand out the basket after the old lady.

"Please don't—it's—it's mine," murmured Amy, with a face nearly as red as her fish.

"Oh, really, I beg pardon; it's an uncommonly fine one, isn't it?" said Tudor, with great presence of mind and an air of sober interest that did credit to his breeding.

Amy recovered herself in a breath, set her basket boldly on the seat, and said, laughing:

"Don't you wish you were to have some of the salad he's to make, and to see the charming young ladies who are to eat it?"

Now that was tact, for two of the ruling foibles of the masculine mind were touched: the lobster was instantly surrounded by a halo of pleasing reminiscences, and curiosity about "the charming young ladies" diverted his mind from the comical mishap.

"I suppose he'll laugh and joke over it with Laurie, but I shan't see them; that's a comfort," thought Amy, as Tudor bowed and departed.

She did not mention this meeting at home (though she discovered that, thanks to the upset, her new dress was much damaged by the rivulets of dressing that meandered down the skirt), but went through with the preparations which now seemed more irksome than before; and at twelve o'clock all was ready again. Feeling that the neighbors were interested in her movements, she wished to efface the memory of yesterday's failure by a grand success today; so she ordered the "cherry-bounce," and drove away in state to meet and escort her guests to the banquet.

"There's the rumble, they're coming! I'll go into the porch to meet them; it looks hospitable, and I want the poor child to have a good time after all her trouble," said Mrs. March, suiting the action to the word. But after one glance she retired, with an indescribable expression, for, looking quite lost in the big carriage, sat Amy and one young lady.

"Run, Beth, and help Hannah clear half the things off the table; it will be too absurd to put a luncheon for twelve before a single girl," cried Jo, hurrying away to the lower regions, too excited to stop even for a laugh.

In came Amy, quite calm, and delightfully cordial to the one guest who had kept her promise; the rest of the family, being of a dramatic turn, played their parts equally well, and Miss Eliott found them a most hilarious set; for it was impossible to entirely control the merriment which possessed them. The remodeled lunch being gaily partaken of, the studio and garden visited, and art discussed with enthusiasm, Amy ordered a buggy (alas for the elegant cherry-bounce!) and drove her friend quietly about the neighborhood till sunset, when "the party went out."

As she came walking in, looking very tired, but as composed as ever, she observed that every vestige of the unfortunate fete had disappeared, except a suspicious pucker about the corners of Jo's mouth.

"You've had a lovely afternoon for your drive, dear," said her mother, as respectfully as if the whole twelve had come

"Miss Eliott is a very sweet girl, and seemed to enjoy herself, I thought," observed Beth, with unusual warmth.

"Could you spare me some of your cake? I really need some, I have so much company, and I can't make such delicious stuff as yours," asked Meg soberly.

"Take it all; I'm the only one here who likes sweet things,

and it will mold before I can dispose of it," answered Amy, thinking with a sigh of the generous store she had laid in for such an end as this.

"It's a pity Laurie isn't here to help us," began Jo, as they sat down to ice cream and salad for the second time in two days.

A warning look from her mother checked any further remarks, and the whole family ate in heroic silence, till Mr. March mildly observed, "Salad was one of the favorite dishes of the ancients, and Evelyn"—here a general explosion of laughter cut short the "history of sallets," to the great surprise of the learned gentleman.

"Bundle everything into a basket and send it to the Hummels: Germans like messes. I'm sick of the sight of this; and there's no reason you should all die of a surfeit because I've been a fool," cried Amy, wiping her eyes.

"I thought I *should* have died when I saw you two girls rattling about in the what-you-call-it, like two little kernels in a very big nutshell, and mother waiting in state to receive the throng," sighed Jo, quite spent with laughter.

"I'm very sorry you were disappointed, dear, but we all did our best to satisfy you," said Mrs. March, in a tone full of motherly regret.

"I *am* satisfied; I've done what I undertook, and it's not my fault that it failed; I comfort myself with that," said Amy, with a little quaver in her voice. "I thank you all very much for helping me, and I'll thank you still more if you won't allude to it for a month, at least."

No one did for several months; but the word "fete" always produced a general smile, and Laurie's birthday gift to Amy was a tiny coral lobster in the shape of a charm for her watch guard.

CHAPTER TWENTY-SEVEN

Literary Lessons

FORTUNE suddenly smiled upon Jo, and dropped a good-luck penny in her path. Not a golden penny, exactly, but I doubt if half a million would have given more real happiness than did the little sum that came to her in this wise.

Every few weeks she would shut herself up in her room, put on her scribbling suit, and "fall into a vortex," as she expressed it, writing away at her novel with all her heart and soul, for till that was finished she could find no peace. Her "scribbling suit" consisted of a black woolen pinafore on which she could wipe her pen at will, and a cap of the same material, adorned with a cheerful red bow, into which she bundled her hair when the decks were cleared for action. This cap was a beacon to the inquiring eyes of her family, who during these periods kept their distance, merely popping in their heads semioccasionally, to ask, with interest, "Does genius burn, Jo?" They did not always venture even to ask this question, but took an observation of the cap and judged accordingly. If this expressive article of dress was drawn low upon the forehead, it was a sign that hard work was going on; in exciting moments it was pushed rakishly askew; and when despair seized the author it was plucked wholly off, and cast upon the floor. At such times the intruder silently withdrew; and not until the red bow was seen gaily erect upon the gifted brow did anyone dare address Jo.

She did not think herself a genius by any means; but when the writing fit came on, she gave herself up to it with entire abandon, and led a blissful life, unconscious of want, care or bad weather, while she sat safe and happy in an imaginary world, full of friends almost as real and dear to her as any in the flesh. Sleep forsook her eyes, meals stood untasted, day and night were all too short to enjoy the happiness which blessed her only at such times, and made these hours worth living, even if they bore no other fruit. The divine afflatus usually lasted a week or two, and then she emerged from her "vortex" hungry, sleepy, cross, or despondent.

She was just recovering from one of these attacks when she was prevailed upon to escort Miss Crocker to a lecture, and in return for her virtue was rewarded with a new idea. It was a People's Course, the lecture on the Pyramids, and Jo rather wondered at the choice of such a subject for such an audience, but took it for granted that some great social evil would be remedied or some great want supplied by unfolding the glories of the Pharaohs to an audience whose thoughts were busy with the price of coal and flour, and whose lives were spent in trying to solve harder riddles than that of the Sphinx.

They were early; and while Miss Crocker set the heel of her stocking Jo amused herself by examining the faces of the people who occupied the seat with them. On her left were two matrons, with massive foreheads, and bonnets to match, discussing Woman's Rights and making tatting. Beyond sat a pair of humble lovers, artlessly holding each other by the hand, a somber spinster eating peppermints out of a paper bag, and an old gentleman taking his preparatory nap behind a yellow bandanna. On her right, her only neighbor was a studious-looking lad absorbed in a newspaper.

It was a pictorial sheet, and Jo examined the work of art nearest her, idly wondering what unfortuitous concatenation of circumstances needed the melodramatic illustration of an Indian in full war costume, tumbling over a precipice with a wolf at his throat, while two infuriated young gentlemen, with unnaturally small feet and big eyes, were stabbing each other close by, and a disheveled female was flying away in the background with her mouth wide open. Pausing to turn a page, the lad saw her looking, and, with boyish good nature, offered half his paper, saying bluntly, "Want to read it? That's a first-rate story."

Jo accepted it with a smile, for she had never outgrown her liking for lads, and soon found herself involved in the usual labyrinth of love, mystery, and murder, for the story belonged to that class of light literature in which the passions have a holiday, and when the author's invention fails, a grand catastrophe clears the stage of one half the *dramatis personae*, leaving the other half to exult over their downfall.

"Prime, isn't it?" asked the boy, as her eye went down the last paragraph of her portion.

"I think you and I could do as well as that if we tried," returned Jo, amused at his admiration of the trash.

"I should think I was a pretty lucky chap if I could. She makes a good living out of such stories, they say," and he pointed to the name of Mrs. S.L.A.N.G. Northbury, under the title of the tale.

"Do you know her?" asked Jo, with sudden interest.

"No; but I read all her pieces, and I know a fellow who works in the office where this paper is printed."

"Do you say she makes a good living out of stories like this?" and Jo looked more respectfully at the agitated group and thickly sprinkled exclamation points that adorned the page.

"Guess she does! She knows just what folks like, and gets paid well for writing it."

Here the lecture began, but Jo heard very little of it, for while Professor Sands was prosing away about Belzoni,

Cheops, scarabei, and hieroglyphics, she was covertly taking
down the address of the paper, and boldly resolving to try for
the hundred-dollar prize offered in its columns for a sensational story. By the time the lecture ended and the audience
awoke, she had built up a splendid fortune for herself (not
the first founded upon paper), and was already deep in the
concoction of her story, being unable to decide whether the
duel should come before the elopement or after the murder.

She said nothing of her plan at home, but fell to work next
day, much to the disquiet of her mother, who always looked a
little anxious when "genius took to burning." Jo had never
tried this style before, contenting herself with very mild
romances for the "Spread Eagle." Her theatrical experience
and miscellaneous reading were of service now, for they gave
her some idea of dramatic effect, and supplied plot, language,
and costumes. Her story was as full of desperation and despair
as her limited acquaintance with those uncomfortable emotions enabled her to make it, and, having located it in Lisbon,
she wound up with an earthquake, as a striking and appropriate denouement. The manuscript was privately dispatched, accompanied by a note, modestly saying that if the tale didn't
get the prize, which the writer hardly dared expect, she would
be very glad to receive any sum it might be considered worth.

Six weeks is a long time to wait, and a still longer time for
a girl to keep a secret; but Jo did both, and was just beginning
to give up all hope of ever seeing her manuscript again when
a letter arrived which almost took her breath away; for on
opening it, a check for a hundred dollars fell into her lap. For
a minute she stared at it as if it had been a snake, then she read
her letter and began to cry. If the amiable gentleman who
wrote that kindly note could have known what intense happiness he was giving a fellow creature, I think he would devote
his leisure hours, if he has any, to that amusement; for Jo
valued the letter more than the money, because it was encouraging; and after years of effort it was *so* pleasant to find
that she had learned to do something, though it was only to
write a sensation story.

A prouder young woman was seldom seen than she, when,
having composed herself, she electrified the family by appear-

ing before them with the letter in one hand, the check in the other, announcing that she had won the prize. Of course there was a great jubilee, and when the story came everyone read and praised it; though after her father had told her that the language was good, the romance fresh and hearty, and the tragedy quite thrilling, he shook his head, and said in his un-worldly way:

"You can do better than this, Jo. Aim at the highest, and never mind the money."

"*I* think the money is the best part of it. What *will* you do with such a fortune?" asked Amy, regarding the magic slip of paper with a reverential eye.

"Send Beth and mother to the seaside for a month or two," answered Jo promptly.

"Oh, how splendid! No, I can't do it, dear, it would be so selfish," cried Beth, who had clapped her thin hands, and taken a long breath, as if pining for fresh ocean breezes; then stopped herself, and motioned away the check which her sister waved before her.

"Ah, but you shall go, I've set my heart on it; that's what I tried for, and that's why I suc-ceeded. I never get on when I think of myself alone, so it will help me to work for you, don't you see? Besides, Marmee needs the change, and she won't leave you, so you *must* go. Won't it be fun to see you come home

plump and rosy again? Hurrah for Doctor Jo, who always cures her patients!"

To the seaside they went, after much discussion; and though Beth didn't come home as plump and rosy as could be desired, she was much better, while Mrs. March declared she felt ten years younger; so Jo was satisfied with the investment of her prize money, and fell to work with a cheery spirit, bent on earning more of those delightful checks. She did earn several that year, and began to feel herself a power in the house; for by the magic of a pen, her "rubbish" turned into comforts for them all. "The Duke's Daughter" paid the butcher's bill, "A Phantom Hand" put down a new carpet, and the "Curse of the Coventrys" proved the blessing of the Marches in the way of groceries and gowns.

Wealth is certainly a most desirable thing, but poverty has its sunny side, and one of the sweet uses of adversity is the genuine satisfaction which comes from hearty work of head or hand; and to the inspiration of necessity we owe half the wise, beautiful, and useful blessings of the world. Jo enjoyed a taste of this satisfaction, and ceased to envy richer girls, taking great comfort in the knowledge that she could supply her own wants, and need ask no one for a penny.

Little notice was taken of her stories, but they found a market; and, encouraged by this fact, she resolved to make a bold stroke for fame and fortune. Having copied her novel for the fourth time, read it to all her confidential friends, and submitted it with fear and trembling to three publishers, she at last disposed of it, on condition that she would cut it down one third, and omit all the parts which she particularly admired.

"Now I must either bundle it back into my tin kitchen to mold, pay for printing it myself, or chop it up to suit purchasers, and get what I can for it. Fame is a very good thing to have in the house, but cash is more convenient; so I wish to take the sense of the meeting on this important subject," said Jo, calling a family council.

"Don't spoil your book, my girl, for there is more in it than you know, and the idea is well worked out. Let it wait and ripen" was her father's advice; and he practiced as he preached, having waited patiently thirty years for fruit of his own to ripen, and being in no haste to gather it, even now, when it was sweet and mellow.

"It seems to me that Jo will profit more by making the trial than by waiting," said Mrs. March. "Criticism is the best test of such work, for it will show her both unsuspected merits and faults, and help her to do better next time. We are too partial; but the praise and blame of outsiders will prove useful, even if she gets but little money."

"Yes," said Jo, knitting her brows, "that's just it; I've been fussing over the thing so long, I really don't know whether it's good, bad, or indifferent. It will be a great help to have cool, impartial persons take a look at it, and tell me what they think of it."

"I wouldn't leave out a word of it; you'll spoil it if you do, for the interest of the story is more in the minds than in the actions of the people, and it will be all a muddle if you don't explain as you go on," said Meg, who firmly believed that this book was the most remarkable novel ever written.

"But Mr. Allen says, 'Leave out the explanations, make it brief and dramatic, and let the characters tell the story,'" interrupted Jo, turning to the publisher's note.

"Do as he tells you; he knows what will sell, and we don't. Make a good, popular book, and get as much money as you can. By and by, when you've got a name, you can afford to digress, and have philosophical and metaphysical people in your novels," said Amy, who took a strictly practical view of the subject.

"Well," said Jo, laughing, "if my people *are* 'philosophical and metaphysical,' it isn't my fault, for I know nothing about such things, except what I hear father say, sometimes. If I've got some of his wise ideas jumbled up with my romance, so much the better for me. Now, Beth, what do you say?"

"I should so like to see it printed *soon*" was all Beth said, and smiled in saying it; but there was an unconscious emphasis on the last word, and a wistful look in the eyes that never lost their childlike candor, which chilled Jo's heart for a minute with a foreboding fear, and decided her to make her little venture "soon."

So, with Spartan firmness, the young authoress laid her first-born on her table, and chopped it up as ruthlessly as any ogre. In the hope of pleasing everyone, she took everyone's advice and, like the old man and his donkey in the fable, suited nobody.

Her father liked the metaphysical streak which had unconsciously got into it; so that was allowed to remain, though she had her doubts about it. Her mother thought that there *was* a trifle too much description; out, therefore, it nearly all came and with it many necessary links in the story. Meg admired the tragedy; so Jo piled up the agony to suit her, while Amy objected to the fun, and, with the best intentions in life, Jo quenched the sprightly scenes which relieved the somber character of the story. Then, to complete the ruin, she cut it down one-third, and confidingly sent the poor little romance, like a picked robin, out into the big, busy world, to try its fate.

Well, it was printed, and she got three hundred dollars for it; likewise plenty of praise and blame, both so much greater than she expected that she was thrown into a state of bewilderment, from which it took her some time to recover.

"You said, mother, that criticism would help me; but how can it, when it's so contradictory that I don't know whether I've written a promising book or broken all the Ten Commandments?" cried poor Jo, turning over a heap of notices, the perusal of which filled her with pride and joy one minute, and wrath and dire dismay the next. "This man says 'An exquisite book, full of truth, beauty, and earnestness; all is sweet, pure, and healthy,'" continued the perplexed authoress. "The next, 'The theory of the book is bad, full of morbid fancies, spiritualistic ideas, and unnatural characters.' Now, as I had no theory of any kind, don't believe in spiritualism, and copied my characters from life, I don't see how this critic *can* be right. Another says, 'It's one of the best American novels which has appeared for years' (I know better than that); and the next asserts that 'though it is original, and written with great force and feeling, it is a dangerous book.' 'Tisn't! Some make fun of it, some overpraise, and nearly all insist that I had a deep theory to expound, when I only wrote it for the pleasure and the

money. I wish I'd printed it whole or not at all, for I do hate
to be so misjudged."

Her family and friends administered comfort and commendation liberally; yet it was a hard time for sensitive, high-spir-
ited Jo, who meant so well and had apparently done so ill.
But it did her good, for those whose opinion had real value
gave her the criticism which is an author's best education; and
when the first soreness was over, she could laugh at her poor
little book, yet believe in it still, and feel herself the wiser and
stronger for the buffeting she had received.

"Not being a genius, like Keats, it won't kill me," she said
stoutly; "and I've got the joke on my side, after all; for the
parts that were taken straight out of real life are denounced as
impossible and absurd, and the scenes that I made up out of
my own silly head are pronounced 'charmingly natural, tender,
and true.' So I'll comfort myself with that; and when I'm ready,
I'll up again and take another."

CHAPTER TWENTY-EIGHT

Domestic Experiences

LIKE most other young matrons, Meg began her married life with the determination to be a model housekeeper. John should find home a paradise; he should always see a smiling face, should fare sumptuously every day, and never know the loss of a button. She brought so much love, energy, and cheerfulness to the work that she could not but succeed, in spite of some obstacles. Her paradise was not a tranquil one, for the little woman fussed, was overanxious to please, and bustled about like a true Martha, cumbered with many cares. She was too tired, sometimes, even to smile; John grew dyspeptic after a course of dainty dishes, and ungratefully demanded plain fare. As for buttons, she soon learned to wonder where they went, to shake her head over the carelessness of men, and to threaten to make him sew them on himself, and then see if *his* work would stand impatient tugs and clumsy fingers any better than hers.

They were very happy, even after they discovered that they couldn't live on love alone. John did not find Meg's beauty diminished, though she beamed at him from behind the familiar coffeepot; nor did Meg miss any of the romance from the daily parting, when her husband followed up his kiss with the tender inquiry, "Shall I send home veal or mutton for dinner, darling?" The little house ceased to be a glorified bower, but it became a home, and the young couple soon felt that it was a change for the better. At first they played keep-house, and frolicked over it like children; then John took steadily to business, feeling the cares of the head of a family upon his shoulders; and Meg laid by her cambric wrappers, put on a big apron, and fell to work, as before said, with more energy than discretion.

While the cooking mania lasted she went through Mrs. Cornelius's Receipt Book as if it were a mathematical exercise, working out the problems with patience and care. Sometimes her family were invited in to help eat up a too bounteous feast of successes, or Lotty would be privately dispatched with a batch of failures, which were to be concealed from all eyes in the convenient stomachs of the little Hummels. An evening with John over the account books usually produced a temporary lull in the culinary enthusiasm, and a frugal fit would ensue, during which the poor man was put through a course of bread pudding, hash, and warmed-over coffee, which tried his soul, although he bore it with praiseworthy fortitude. Before the golden mean was found, however, Meg added to her domestic possessions what young couples seldom get on long without—a family jar.

Fired with a housewifely wish to see her storeroom stocked with homemade preserves, she undertook to put up her own currant jelly. John was requested to order home a dozen or so of little pots, and an extra quantity of sugar, for their own currants were ripe, and were to be attended to at once. As John firmly believed that "my wife" was equal to anything, and took a natural pride in her skill, he resolved that she should be gratified, and their only crop of fruit laid by in a most pleasing form for winter use. Home came four dozen delightful little pots, half a barrel of sugar, and a small boy to pick the currants for her. With her pretty hair tucked into a little cap, arms bared to the elbow, and a checked apron which had a coquettish look in spite of the bib, the young housewife fell to work, feeling no doubts about her success; for hadn't she seen Hannah do it hundreds of times? The array of pots rather amazed her at first, but John was so fond of jelly, and the nice little jars would look so well on the top shelf, that Meg resolved to fill them all, and spent a long day picking, boiling, straining, and fussing over her jelly. She did her best; she asked the advice of Mrs. Cornelius; she racked her brain to remember what Hannah did that she had left undone; she reboiled, resugared, and re-strained, but that dreadful stuff wouldn't *jell*.

She longed to run home, bib and all, and ask mother to lend a hand, but John and she had agreed that they would never annoy anyone with their private worries, experiments, or quarrels. They had laughed over that last word as if the idea it suggested was a most preposterous one; but they had held to their resolve, and whenever they could get on without help they did so, and no one interfered, for Mrs. March had advised the plan. So Meg wrestled alone with the refractory sweetmeats all that hot summer day, and at five o'clock sat down in her topsy-turvy kitchen, wrung her bedaubed hands, lifted up her voice and wept.

Now, in the first flush of the new life, she had often said: "My husband shall always feel free to bring a friend home whenever he likes. I shall always be prepared; there shall be no flurry, no scolding, no discomfort, but a neat house, a cheerful wife, and a good dinner. John, dear, never stop to ask my leave, invite whom you please, and be sure of a welcome from me."

How charming that was, to be sure! John quite glowed with pride to hear her say it, and felt what a blessed thing it was to have a superior wife. But, although they had had company from time to time, it never happened to be unexpected, and Meg had never had an opportunity to distinguish herself till now. It always happens so in this vale of tears; there is an inevitability about such things which we can only wonder at, deplore, and bear as we best can.

If John had not forgotten all about the jelly, it really would have been unpardonable in him to choose that day, of all the days in the year, to bring a friend home to dinner unexpectedly. Congratulating himself that a handsome repast had been ordered that morning, feeling sure that it would be ready on the minute, and indulging in pleasant anticipations of the charming effect it would produce, when his pretty wife came running out to meet him, he escorted his friend to his mansion with the irrespressible satisfaction of a young host and husband.

It is a world of disappointments, as John discovered when he reached the Dovecote. The front door usually stood hospitably open; now it was not only shut, but locked, and yesterday's mud still adorned the steps. The parlor windows were closed and curtained, no picture of the pretty wife sewing on the piazza, in white, with a distracting little bow in her hair, or a bright-eyed hostess, smiling a shy welcome as she greeted her guest. Nothing of the sort, for not a soul appeared, but a sanguinary-looking boy asleep under the currant bushes.

"I'm afraid something has happened. Step into the garden, Scott, while I look up Mrs. Brooke," said John, alarmed at the silence and solitude.

Round the house he hurried, led by a pungent smell of burnt sugar, and Mr. Scott strolled after him, with a queer look on his face. He paused discreetly at a distance when Brooke disappeared; but he could both see and hear, and, being a bachelor, enjoyed the prospect mightily.

In the kitchen reigned confusion and despair; one edition of jelly was trickled from pot to pot, another lay upon the floor, and a third was burning gaily on the stove. Lotty, with Teutonic phlegm, was calmly eating bread and currant wine, for the jelly was still in a hopelessly liquid state, while Mrs. Brooke, with her apron over her head, sat sobbing dismally.

"My dearest girl, what is the matter?" cried John, rushing in, with awful visions of scalded hands, sudden news of affliction, and secret consternation at the thought of the guest in the garden.

"Oh, John, I *am* so tired and hot and cross and worried! I've been at it till I'm all worn out. Do come and help me or I *shall* die!" and the exhausted housewife cast herself upon his breast, giving him a sweet welcome in every sense of the word, for her pinafore had been baptized at the same time as the floor.

"What worries you, dear? Has anything dreadful happened?" asked the anxious John, tenderly kissing the crown of the little cap, which was all askew.

"Yes," sobbed Meg despairingly.

"Tell me quick, then. Don't cry, I can bear anything better than that. Out with it, love."

"The—the jelly won't jell and I don't know what to do!"

John Brooke laughed then as he never dared to laugh afterward; and the derisive Scott smiled involuntarily as he heard the hearty peal, which put the finishing stroke to poor Meg's woe.

"Is that all? Fling it out of the window, and don't bother any more about it. I'll buy you quarts if you want it; but for heaven's sake don't have hysterics, for I've brought Jack Scott home to dinner, and—"

John got no further, for Meg cast him off, and clasped her hands with a tragic gesture as she fell into a chair, exclaiming in a tone of mingled indignation, reproach, and dismay:

"A man to dinner, and everything in a mess! John Brooke, how *could* you do such a thing?"

"Hush, he's in the garden! I forgot the confounded jelly, but it can't be helped now," said John, surveying the prospect with an anxious eye.

"You ought to have sent word, or told me this morning, and you ought to have remembered how busy I was," continued Meg petulantly; for even turtledoves will peck when ruffled.

"I didn't know it this morning, and there was no time to send word, for I met him on the way out. I never thought of asking leave, when you have always told me to do as I liked. I never tried it before, and hang me if I ever do again!" added John with an aggrieved air.

"I should hope not! Take him away at once; I can't see him, and there isn't any dinner."

"Well, I like that! Where's the beef and vegetables I sent

home, and the pudding you promised?" cried John, rushing to
the larder.

"I hadn't time to cook anything; I meant to dine at mother's.
I'm sorry, but I was *so* busy," and Meg's tears began again.

John was a mild man, but he was human; and after a long
day's work, to come home tired, hungry, and hopeful, to find
a chaotic house, an empty table, and a cross wife was not exactly conducive to repose of mind or manner. He restrained
himself, however, and the little squall would have blown over
but for one unlucky word.

"It's a scrape, I acknowledge; but if you will lend a hand,
we'll pull through, and have a good time yet. Don't cry, dear,
but just exert yourself a bit, and knock us up something to eat.
We're both as hungry as hunters, so we shan't mind what it is.
Give us the cold meat, and bread and cheese; we won't ask for
jelly."

He meant it for a good-natured joke; but that one word
sealed his fate. Meg thought it was *too* cruel to hint about her
sad failure, and the last atom of patience vanished as he spoke.

"You must get yourself out of the scrape as you can; I'm too
used up to 'exert' myself for anyone. It's like a man to propose
a bone and vulgar bread and cheese for company. I won't have
anything of the sort in my house. Take that Scott up to mother's, and tell him I'm away, sick, dead—anything. I won't see
him, and you two can laugh at me and my jelly as much as
you like: you won't have anything else here," and having delivered her defiance all in one breath, Meg cast away her pinafore, and precipitately left the field to bemoan herself in her
own room.

What those two creatures did in her absence, she never
knew; but Mr. Scott was not taken "up to mother's," and when
Meg descended, after they had strolled away together, she
found traces of a promiscuous lunch which filled her with horror. Lotty reported that they had eaten "a much, and greatly
laughed, and the master bid her throw away all the sweet
stuff, and hide the pots."

Meg longed to go and tell mother; but a sense of shame at
her own shortcomings, of loyalty to John, "who might be cruel,
but nobody should know it," restrained her; and after a sum-

mary clearing up, she dressed herself prettily, and sat down to wait for John to come and be forgiven.

Unfortunately, John didn't come, not seeing the matter in that light. He had carried it off as a good joke with Scott, excused his little wife as well as he could, and played the host so hospitably that his friend enjoyed the impromptu dinner, and promised to come again. But John was angry, though he did not show it; he felt that Meg had got him into a scrape, and then deserted him in his hour of need. "It wasn't fair to tell a man to bring folks home any time, with perfect freedom, and when he took you at your word, to flare up and blame him, and leave him in the lurch, to be laughed at or pitied. No, by George, it wasn't! And Meg must know it." He had fumed inwardly during the feast, but when the flurry was over, and he strolled home, after seeing Scott off, a milder mood came over him. "Poor little thing! It was hard upon her when she tried so heartily to please me. She was wrong, of course, but then she was young. I must be patient and teach her." He hoped she had not gone home—he hated gossip and interference. For a minute he was ruffled again at the mere thought of it; and then the fear that Meg would cry herself sick softened his heart, and sent him on at a quicker pace, resolving to be calm and kind, but firm, quite firm, and show her where she had failed in her duty to her spouse.

Meg likewise resolved to be "calm and kind, but firm," and show *him* his duty. She longed to run to meet him, and beg pardon, and be kissed and comforted, as she was sure of being; but, of course, she did nothing of the sort, and when she saw John coming, began to hum quite naturally, as she rocked and sewed, like a lady of leisure in her best parlor.

John was a little disappointed not to find a tender Niobe; but, feeling that his dignity demanded the first apology, he made none, only came leisurely in, and laid himself upon the sofa, with the singularly relevant remark:

"We are going to have a new moon, my dear."

"I've no objection" was Meg's equally soothing remark.

A few other topics of general interest were introduced by Mr. Brooke, and wet-blanketed by Mrs. Brooke, and conversation languished. John went to one window, unfolded his paper, and wrapped himself in it, figuratively speaking. Meg went to the other window, and sewed as if new rosettes for her slippers were among the necessaries of life. Neither spoke; both looked quite "calm and firm," and both felt desperately uncomfortable.

"Oh dear," thought Meg, "married life is very trying, and does need infinite patience, as well as love, as mother says."

The word "mother" suggested other maternal counsels given long ago, and received with unbelieving protests.

"John is a good man, but he has his faults, and you must learn to see and bear with them, remembering your own. He is very decided, but never will be obstinate, if you reason kindly, not oppose impatiently. He is very accurate, and particular about the truth—a good trait, though you call him 'fussy.' Never deceive him by look or word, Meg, and he will give you the confidence you deserve, the support you need. He has a temper, not like ours—one flash, and then all over—but the white, still anger, that is seldom stirred, but once kindled, is hard to quench. Be careful, very careful, not to wake this anger against yourself, for peace and happiness depend on keeping his respect. Watch yourself, be the first to ask pardon if you both err, and guard against the little piques, misunderstandings, and hasty words that often pave the way for bitter sorrow and regret."

These words came back to Meg, as she sat sewing in the sunset, especially the last. This was the first serious disagreement; her own hasty speeches sounded both silly and unkind, as she recalled them, her own anger looked childish now, and thoughts of poor John coming home to such a scene quite melted her heart. She glanced at him with tears in her eyes, but he did not see them; she put down her work and got up, thinking, "I *will* be the first to say, 'Forgive me,'" but he did not seem to hear her; she went very slowly across the room, for pride was hard to swallow, and stood by him, but he did not turn his head. For a minute she felt as if she really couldn't do it; then came the thought, "This is the beginning, I'll do my part, and have nothing to reproach myself with," and stooping down, she softly kissed her husband on the forehead. Of course that settled it; the penitent kiss was better than a world of words, and John had her on his knee in a minute, saying tenderly:

"It was too bad to laugh at the poor little jelly pots. Forgive me, dear, I never will again!"

But he did, oh, bless you, yes, hundreds of times, and so did Meg, both declaring that it was the sweetest jelly they ever made; for family peace was preserved in that little family jar.

After this, Meg had Mr. Scott to dinner by special invitation, and served him up a pleasant feast without a cooked wife for the first course; on which occasion she was so gay and gracious, and made everything go off so charmingly, that Mr. Scott told John he was a happy fellow, and shook his head over the hardships of bachelorhood all the way home.

In the autumn, new trials and experiences came to Meg. Sallie Moffat renewed her friendship, was always running out for a dish of gossip at the little house, or inviting "that poor dear" to come in and spend the day at the big house. It was pleasant, for in dull weather Meg often felt lonely; all were busy at home, John absent till night, and nothing to do but sew, or read, or potter about. So it naturally fell out that Meg got into the way of gadding and gossiping with her friend. Seeing Sallie's pretty things made her long for such, and pity herself because she had not got them. Sallie was very kind and often offered her the coveted trifles; but Meg declined them, knowing that John wouldn't like it; and then this foolish little woman went and did what John disliked infinitely worse.

She knew her husband's income, and she loved to feel that he trusted her, not only with his happiness, but what some men seem to value more—his money. She knew where it was, was free to take what she liked, and all he asked was that she should keep account of every penny, pay bills once a month, and remember that she was a poor man's wife. Till now, she had done well, been prudent and exact, kept his little account books neatly, and showed them to him monthly without fear. But that autumn the serpent got into Meg's paradise, and tempted her, like many a modern Eve, not with apples, but with dress. Meg didn't like to be pitied and made to feel poor; it irritated her, but she was ashamed to confess it, and now and then she tried to console herself by buying something pretty, so that Sallie needn't think she had to economize. She always felt wicked after it, for the pretty things were seldom necessaries; but then they cost so little, it wasn't worth worrying about; so the trifles increased unconsciously, and in the shopping excursions she was no longer a passive looker-on.

But the trifles cost more than one would imagine; and when she cast up her accounts at the end of the month, the sum total rather scared her. John was busy that month, and left the bills to her; the next month he was absent; but the third he had a grand quarterly settling up, and Meg never forgot it. A few days before she had done a dreadful thing, and it weighed upon her conscience. Sallie had been buying silks, and Meg longed for a new one—just a handsome light one for parties. her black silk was so common, and thin things for evening wear were only proper for girls. Aunt March usually gave the sisters a present of twenty-five dollars apiece at New Year's; that was only a month to wait, and here was a lovely violet silk going at a bargain, and she had the money, if she only dared to take it. John always said what was his was hers; but would he think it right to spend not only the prospective five and twenty, but another five and twenty out of the household fund? That was the question. Sallie had urged her to do it, had offered to loan the money, and with the best intentions in life, had tempted Meg beyond her strengh. In an evil moment the shopman held up the lovely, shimmering folds, and said, "A bargain, I assure you, ma'am." She answered, "I'll take it," and it was cut off and paid for, and Sallie had exulted, and she had laughed as if it were a thing of no consequence, and driven away, feeling as if she had stolen something and the police were after her.

When she got home, she tried to assuage the pangs of remorse by spreading forth the lovely silk; but it looked less silvery now, didn't become her, after all, and the words "fifty dollars" seemed stamped like a pattern down each breadth. She put it away; but it haunted her, not delightfully, as a new dress should, but dreadfully, like the ghost of a folly that was not easily laid. When John got out his books that night, Meg's heart sank, and, for the first time in her married life, she was afraid of her husband. The kind, brown eyes looked as if they could be stern; and though he was unusually merry, she fancied he had found her out, but didn't mean to let her know it. The house bills were all paid, the books all in order. John had praised her, and was undoing the old pocketbook which they called the "bank," when Meg, knowing that it was quite empty, stopped his hand, saying nervously:

"You haven't seen my private expense book yet."

John never asked to see it; but she always insisted on his doing so, and used to enjoy his masculine amazement at the queer things women wanted, and made him guess what "piping" was, demand fiercely the meaning of a "hug-me-tight," or wonder how a little thing composed of three rosebuds, a bit of velvet, and a pair of strings, could possibly be a bonnet, and cost five or six dollars. That night he looked as if he would like the fun of quizzing her figures and pretending to be horrified at her extravagance, as he often did, being particularly proud of his prudent wife.

The little book was brought slowly out, and laid down before him. Meg got behind his chair under pretense of smoothing the wrinkles out of his tired forehead, and standing there, she said, with her panic increasing with every word:

"John, dear, I'm ashamed to show you my book, for I've really been dreadfully extravagant lately. I go about so much I must have things, you know, and Sallie advised my getting it, so I did; and my New Year's money will partly pay for it: but I was sorry after I'd done it, for I knew you'd think it wrong in me."

John laughed, and drew her round beside him, saying good-humoredly, "Don't go and hide. I won't beat you if you *have* got a pair of killing boots; I'm rather proud of my wife's feet, and don't mind if she does pay eight or nine dollars for her boots, if they are good ones."

That had been one of her last "trifles," and John's eye had fallen on it as he spoke. "Oh, what *will* he say when he comes to that awful fifty dollars!" thought Meg, with a shiver.

"It's worse than boots, it's a silk dress," she said, with the calmness of desperation, for she wanted the worst over.

"Well, dear, what is the 'dem'd total,' as Mr. Mantalini says?"

That didn't sound like John, and she knew he was looking

up at her with the straightforward look that she had always been ready to meet and answer with one as frank till now. She turned the page and her head at the same time, pointing to the sum which would have been bad enough without the fifty, but which was appalling to her with that added. For a minute the room was very still; then John said slowly—but she could feel it cost him an effort to express no displeasure:

"Well, I don't know that fifty is much for a dress, with all the furbelows and notions you have to have to finish it off these days."

"It isn't made or trimmed," sighed Meg faintly, for a sudden recollection of the cost still to be incurred quite overwhelmed her.

"Twenty-five yards of silk seems a good deal to cover one small woman, but I've no doubt my wife will look as fine as Ned Moffat's when she gets it on," said John dryly.

"I know you are angry, John, but I can't help it. I don't mean to waste your money, and I didn't think those little things would count up so. I can't resist them when I see Sallie buying all she wants, and pitying me because I don't. I try to be contented, but it is hard, and I'm tired of being poor."

The last words were spoken so low she thought he did not hear them, but he did, and they wounded him deeply, for he had denied himself many pleasures for Meg's sake. She could have bitten her tongue out the minute she had said it, for John pushed the books away, and got up, saying with a little quiver in his voice, "I was afraid of this; I do my best, Meg." If he had scolded her, or even shaken her, it would not have broken her heart like those few words. She ran to him and held him close, crying, with repentant tears, "Oh, John, my dear, kind, hard-working boy, I didn't mean it! It was so wicked, so untrue and ungrateful, how could I say it! Oh, how could I say it!"

He was very kind, forgave her readily, and did not utter one reproach; but Meg knew that she had done and said a thing which would not be forgotten soon, although he might never allude to it again. She had promised to love him for better or for worse; and then she, his wife, had reproached him with his poverty, after spending his earnings recklessly. It was dreadful; and the worst of it was John went on so quietly afterward, just as if nothing had happened, except that he stayed in town later, and worked at night when she had gone to cry herself to sleep. A week of remorse nearly made Meg sick; and the discovery that John had countermanded the order for his new greatcoat reduced her to a state of despair which was pathetic to behold. He had simply said, in answer to her surprised inquiries as to the change, "I can't afford it, my dear."

Meg said no more, but a few minutes after he found her in the hall, with her face buried in the old greatcoat, crying as if her heart would break.

They had a long talk that night, and Meg learned to love her husband better for his poverty, because it seemed to have made a man of him, given him the strength and courage to fight his own way, and taught him a tender patience with which to bear and comfort the natural longings and failures of those he loved.

Next day she put her pride in her pocket, went to Sallie, told the truth, and asked her to buy the silk as a favor. The good-natured Mrs. Moffat willingly did so, and had the delicacy not to make her a present of it immediately afterward. Then Meg ordered home the greatcoat, and when John arrived, she put it on, and asked him how he liked her new silk gown. One can imagine what answer he made, how he received his present, and what a blissful state of things ensued. John came home early, Meg gadded no more; and that greatcoat was put on in the morning by a very happy husband, and taken off at night by a most devoted little wife. So the year rolled round, and at midsummer there came to Meg a new experience—the deepest and tenderest of a woman's life.

Laurie came sneaking into the kitchen of the Dovecote, one Saturday, with an excited face, and was received with the clash of cymbals; for Hannah clapped her hands with a saucepan in one and the cover in the other.

"How's the little mamma? Where is everybody? Why didn't you tell me before I came home?" began Laurie, in a loud whisper.

"Happy as a queen, the dear! Every soul of 'em is upstairs a-worshipin'; we didn't want no hurrycanes round. Now you go into the parlor, and I'll send 'em down to you," with which somewhat involved reply Hannah vanished, chuckling ecstatically.

Presently Jo appeared, proudly bearing a flannel bundle laid forth upon a large pillow. Jo's face was very sober, but her eyes twinkled, and there was an odd sound in her voice of repressed emotion of some sort.

"Shut your eyes and hold out your arms," she said invitingly.

Laurie backed precipitately into a corner, and put his hands behind him with an imploring gesture: "No, thank you, I'd rather not. I shall drop it or smash it, as sure as fate."

"Then you shan't see your nevvy," said Jo decidedly, turning as if to go.

"I will, I will! Only you must be responsible for damages," and, obeying orders, Laurie heroically shut his eyes while something was put into his arms. A peal of laughter from Jo, Amy, Mrs. March, Hannah, and John caused him to open them the next minute, to find himself invested with two babies instead of one.

No wonder they laughed, for the expression on his face was droll enough to convulse a Quaker, as he stood and stared wildly from the unconscious innocents to the hilarious spectators, with such dismay that Jo sat down on the floor and screamed.

"Twins, by Jupiter!" was all he said for a minute; then, turning to the women with an appealing look that was comically piteous, he added, "Take 'em quick, somebody! I'm going to laugh, and I shall drop 'em."

John rescued his babies, and marched up and down, with one on each arm, as if already initiated into the mysteries of baby tending, while Laurie laughed till the tears ran down his cheeks.

"It's the best joke of the season, isn't it? I wouldn't have you told, for I set my heart on surprising you, and I flatter myself I've done it," said Jo, when she got her breath.

"I never was more staggered in my life. Isn't it fun? Are they boys? What are you going to name them? Let's have another look. Hold me up, Jo; for upon my life it's one too many for me," returned Laurie, regarding the infants with the air of a big, benevolent Newfoundland looking at a pair of infantile kittens.

"Boy and girl. Aren't they beauties?" said the proud papa, beaming upon the little red squirmers as if they were unfledged angels.

"Most remarkable children I ever saw. Which is which?" and Laurie bent like a well sweep to examine the prodigies.

"Amy put a blue ribbon on the boy and a pink on the girl, French fashion, so you can always tell. Besides, one has blue eyes and one brown. Kiss them, Uncle Teddy," said wicked Jo.

"I'm afraid they mightn't like it," began Laurie, with unusual timidity in such matters.

"Of course they will; they are used to it now. Do it this minute, sir!" commanded Jo, fearing he might propose a proxy.

Laurie screwed up his face, and obeyed with a gingerly peck at each little cheek that produced another laugh, and made the babies squeal.

"There, I knew they didn't like it! That's the boy; see him kick; he hits out with his fists like a good one. Now then,

young Brooke, pitch into a man of your own size, will you?"
cried Laurie, delighted with a poke in the face from a tiny
fist, flapping aimlessly about.

"He's to be named John Laurence, and the girl Margaret,
after mother and grandmother. We shall call her Daisy, so as
not to have two Megs, and I suppose the mannie will be Jack,
unless we find a better name," said Amy, with auntlike interest.

"Name him demijohn, and call him 'Demi' for short," said
Laurie.

"Daisy and Demi—just the thing! I *knew* Teddy would do
it," cried Jo, clapping her hands.

Teddy certainly had done it that time, for the babies were
"Daisy" and "Demi" to the end of the chapter.

CHAPTER TWENTY-NINE

Calls

"COME, Jo, it's time."

"For what?"

"You don't mean to say you have forgotten that you promised to make half a dozen calls with me today?"

"I've done a good many rash and foolish things in my life, but I don't think I ever was mad enough to say I'd make six calls in one day, when a single one upsets me for a week."

"Yes, you did; it was a bargain between us. I was to finish the crayon of Beth for you, and you were to go properly with me, and return our neighbors' visits."

"If it was fair—that was in the bond; and I stand to the letter of my bond, Shylock. There is a pile of clouds in the east; it's *not* fair, and I don't go."

"Now, that's shirking. It's a lovely day, no prospect of rain and you pride yourself on keeping promises; so be honorable, come and do your duty, and then be at peace for another six months."

At that minute Jo was particularly absorbed in dressmaking, for she was mantuamaker general to the family, and took especial credit to herself because she could use a needle as well as a pen. It was very provoking to be arrested in the act of a first trying on, and ordered out to make calls in her best array, on a warm July day. She hated calls of the formal sort, and never made any till Amy compelled her with a bargain, bribe, or promise. In the present instance, there was no escape; and having clashed her scissors rebelliously, while protesting that she smelt thunder, she gave in, put away her work, and taking up her hat and gloves with an air of resignation, told Amy the victim was ready.

"Jo March, you are perverse enough to provoke a saint. You don't intend to make calls in that state, I hope," cried Amy, surveying her with amazement.

"Why not? I'm neat and cool and comfortable; quite proper for a dusty walk on a warm day. If people care more for my clothes than they do for me, I don't wish to see them. You can dress for both, and be as elegant as you please: it pays for you to be fine; it doesn't for me, and furbelows only worry me."

"Oh, dear!" sighed Amy. "Now she's in a contrary fit and will drive me distracted before I can get her properly ready. I'm sure it's no pleasure to me to go today, but it is a debt we owe society, and there's no one to pay it but you and me. I'll do anything for you, Jo, if you'll only dress yourself nicely, and come and help me do the civil. You can talk so well, look so aristocratic in your best things, and behave so beautifully, if you try, that I'm proud of you. I'm afraid to go alone; do come and take care of me."

"You're an artful little puss to flatter and wheedle your cross old sister in that way. The idea of my being aristocratic and well bred, and your being afraid to go anywhere alone! I don't know which is the most absurd. Well, I'll go if I must, and do my best. You shall be commander of the expedition, and I'll obey blindly; will that satisfy you?" said Jo, with a sudden change from perversity to lamblike submission.

"You're a perfect cherub! Now put on all your best things,

and I'll tell you how to behave at each place, so that you will make a good impression. I want people to like you, and they would if you'd only try to be a little more agreeable. Do your hair the pretty way, and put the pink rose in your bonnet; it's becoming, and you look too sober in your plain suit. Take your light gloves and the embroidered handkerchief. We'll stop at Meg's, and borrow her white sunshade, and then you can have my dove-colored one."

While Amy dressed, she issued orders, and Jo obeyed them; not without entering her protest, however, for she sighed as she rustled into her new organdy, frowned darkly at herself as she tied her bonnet strings in an irreproachable bow, wrestled viciously with pins as she put on her collar, wrinkled up her features generally as she shook out the handkerchief, whose embroidery was as irritating to her nose as the present mission was to her feelings; and when she had squeezed her hands into tight gloves with three buttons and a tassel, as the last touch of elegance, she turned to Amy with an imbecile expression of countenance, saying meekly:

"I'm perfectly miserable; but if you consider me present-able, I die happy."

"You are highly satisfactory; turn slowly round, and let me get a careful view." Jo revolved, and Amy gave a touch here and there, then fell back, with her head on one side, observing, graciously, "Yes, you'll do; your head is all I could ask, for that white bonnet *with* the rose is quite ravishing. Hold back your shoulders, and carry your hands easily, no matter if your gloves do pinch. There's one thing you can do well, Jo, that is, wear a shawl—I can't; but it's very nice to see you, and I'm so glad Aunt March gave you that lovely one; it's simple, but handsome, and those folds over the arm are really artistic. Is the point of my mantle in the middle, and have I looped my dress evenly? I like to show my boots, for my feet are pretty, though my nose isn't."

"You are a thing of beauty and a joy forever," said Jo, look-ing through her hand with the air of a connoisseur at the blue feather against the gold hair. "Am I to drag my best dress through the dust, or loop it up, please, ma'am?"

"Hold it up when you walk, but drop it in the house; the sweeping style suits you best, and you must learn to trail your skirts gracefully. You haven't half buttoned one cuff; do it at once. You'll never look finished if you are not careful about the little details, for they make up the pleasing whole."

Jo sighed, and proceeded to burst the buttons off her glove in doing up her cuff; but at last both were ready, and sailed away, looking as "pretty as picters," Hannah said, as she hung out of the upper window to watch them.

"Now, Jo dear, the Chesters consider themselves very elegant people, so I want you to put on your best deportment. Don't make any of your abrupt remarks; or do anything odd, will you? Just be calm, cool, and quiet—that's safe and ladylike; and you can easily do it for fifteen minutes," said Amy, as they approached the first place, having borrowed the white parasol and been inspected by Meg, with a baby on each arm.

"Let me see. 'Calm, cool, and quiet'—yes, I think I can promise that. I've played the part of a prim young lady on the stage, and I'll try it off. My powers are great, as you shall see; so be easy in your mind, my child."

Amy looked relieved, but naughty Jo took her at her word; for, during the first call, she sat with every limb gracefully composed, every fold correctly draped, calm as a summer sea, cool as a snowbank, and as silent as a sphinx. In vain Mrs. Chester alluded to her "charming novel," and the Misses Chester introduced parties, picnics, the opera, and the fashions; each and all were answered by a smile, a bow, and a demure "Yes" or "No," with the chill on. In vain Amy telegraphed the word "Talk," tried to draw her out, and administered covert pokes with her foot. Jo sat as if blandly unconscious of it all, with deportment like Maud's face, "icily regular, splendidly dull."

"What a haughty, uninteresting creature that oldest Miss March is!" was the unfortunately audible remark of one of the ladies, as the door closed upon their guests. Jo laughed noiselessly all through the hall, but Amy looked disgusted at the failure of her instructions, and very naturally laid the blame upon Jo.

"How could you mistake me so? I merely meant you to be properly dignified and composed, and you made yourself a perfect stock and stone. Try to be sociable at the Lambs', gossip as other girls do, and be interested in dress and flirtations and whatever nonsense comes up. They move in the best society, and are valuable persons for us to know, and I wouldn't fail to make a good impression there for anything."

"I'll be agreeable; I'll gossip and giggle, and have horrors and raptures over any trifle you like. I rather enjoy this, and now I'll imitate what is called 'a charming girl'; I can do it, for I have May Chester as a model, and I'll improve upon her. See if the Lambs don't say, 'What a lively, nice creature that Jo March is!'"

Amy felt anxious, as well she might, for when Jo turned freakish there was no knowing where she would stop. Amy's face was a study when she saw her sister skim into the next drawing room, kiss all the young ladies with effusion, beam graciously upon the young gentlemen, and join in the chat with a spirit which amazed the beholder. Amy was taken possession of by Mrs. Lamb, with whom she was a favorite, and forced to hear a long account of Lucretia's last attack, while three delightful young gentlemen hovered near, waiting for a pause when they might rush in and rescue her. So situated, she was powerless to check Jo, who seemed possessed by a spirit of mischief, and talked away as volubly as the old lady. A knot of heads gathered about her, and Amy strained her ears to hear what was going on; for broken sentences filled her with alarm, round eyes and uplifted hands tormented her with curiosity, and frequent peals of laughter made her wild to share the fun. One may imagine her suffering on overhearing fragments of this sort of conversation:

"She rides splendidly—who taught her?"

"No one; she used to practice mounting, holding the reins, and sitting straight on an old saddle in a tree. Now she rides anything, for she doesn't know what fear is, and the stableman lets her have horses cheap, because she trains them to carry ladies so well. She has such a passion for it, I often tell her if everything else fails she can be a horse breaker, and get her living so."

At this awful speech Amy contained herself with difficulty, for the impression was being given that she was rather a fast young lady, which was her especial aversion. But what could she do? For the old lady was in the middle of her story, and

long before it was done Jo was off again, making more droll
revelations, and committing still more fearful blunders.

"Yes, Amy was in despair that day, for all the good beasts
were gone, and of three left, one was lame, one blind, and the
other so balky that you had to put dirt in his mouth before he
would start. Nice animal for a pleasure party, wasn't it?"

"Which did she choose?" asked one of the laughing gentlemen, who enjoyed the subject.

"None of them; she heard of a young horse at the farmhouse
over the river, and, though a lady had never ridden him, she
resolved to try, because he was handsome and spirited. Her
struggles were really pathetic; there was no one to bring the
horse to the saddle, so she took the saddle to the horse. My
dear creature, she actually rowed it over the river, put it on
her head, and marched up to the barn to the utter amazement
of the old man!"

"Did she ride the horse?"

"Of course she did, and had a capital time. I expected to see
her brought home in fragments, but she managed him perfectly, and was the life of the party."

"Well, I call that plucky!" and young Mr. Lamb turned an
approving glance upon Amy, wondering what his mother
could be saying to make the girl look so red and uncomfortable.

She was still redder and more uncomfortable a moment
after, when a sudden turn in the conversation introduced the
subject of dress. One of the young ladies asked Jo where she
got the pretty drab hat she wore to the picnic; and stupid Jo,
instead of mentioning the place where it was bought two years
ago, must needs answer, with unnecessary frankness, "Oh,
Amy painted it; you can't buy those soft shades, so we paint
ours any color we like. It's a great comfort to have an artistic
sister."

"Isn't that an original idea?" cried Miss Lamb, who found
Jo great fun.

"That's nothing compared to some of her brilliant performances. There's nothing the child can't do. Why, she wanted a
pair of blue boots for Sallie's party, so she just painted her
soiled white ones the loveliest shade of sky blue you ever saw,

and they looked exactly like satin," added Jo, with an air of pride in her sister's accomplishments that exasperated Amy till she felt that it would be a relief to throw her card case at her.

"We read a story of yours the other day, and enjoyed it very much," observed the elder Miss Lamb, wishing to compliment the literary lady, who did not look the character just then, it must be confessed.

Any mention of her "works" always had a bad effect upon Jo, who either grew rigid and looked offended, or changed the subject with a brusque remark, as now. "Sorry you could find nothing better to read. I write that rubbish because it sells, and ordinary people like it. Are you going to New York this winter?"

As Miss Lamb had "enjoyed" the story, this speech was not exactly grateful or complimentary. The minute it was made Jo saw her mistake; but fearing to make the matter worse, suddenly remembered that it was for her to make the first move toward departure, and did so with an abruptness that left three people with half-finished sentences in their mouths.

"Amy, we *must* go. *Good*-by, dear; *do* come and see us; we are *pining* for a visit. I don't dare to ask *you*, Mr. Lamb; but if you *should* come, I don't think I shall have the heart to send you away."

Jo said this with such a droll imitation of May Chester's gushing style that Amy got out of the room as rapidly as possible, feeling a strong desire to laugh and cry at the same time.

"Didn't I do that well?" asked Jo, with a satisfied air, as they walked away.

"Nothing could have been worse" was Amy's crushing reply. "What possessed you to tell those stories about my saddle, and the hats and boots, and all the rest of it?"

"Why, it's funny, and amuses people. They know we are poor, so it's no use pretending that we have grooms, buy three or four hats a season, and have things as easy and fine as they do."

"You needn't go and tell them all our little shifts, and expose our poverty in that perfectly unnecessary way. You haven't a bit of proper pride, and never will learn when to hold your tongue and when to speak," said Amy despairingly.

Poor Jo looked abashed, and silently chafed the end of her nose with the stiff handkerchief, as if performing a penance for her misdemeanors.

"How shall I behave here?" she asked, as they approached the third mansion.

"Just as you please; I wash my hands of you" was Amy's short answer.

"Then I'll enjoy myself. The boys are at home, and we'll have a comfortable time. Goodness knows I need a little change, for elegance has a bad effect upon my constitution," returned Jo gruffly, being disturbed by her failures to suit.

An enthusiastic welcome from three big boys and several pretty children speedily soothed her ruffled feelings; and, leaving Amy to entertain the hostess and Mr. Tudor, who happened to be calling likewise, Jo devoted herself to the young folks, and found the change refreshing. She listened to college stories with deep interest, caressed pointers and poodles without a murmur, agreed heartily that "Tom Brown was a brick," regardless of the improper form of praise; and when one lad proposed a visit to his turtle tank, she went with an alacrity which caused mamma to smile upon her as that motherly lady settled the cap which was left in a ruinous condition by filial hugs, bearlike but affectionate, and dearer to her than the most faultless coiffures from the hands of an inspired Frenchwoman.

Leaving her sister to her own devices, Amy proceeded to enjoy herself to her heart's content. Mr. Tudor's uncle had married an English lady who was third cousin to a living lord, and Amy regarded the whole family with great respect; for, in spite of her American birth and breeding she possessed that reverence for titles which haunts the best of us—that unacknowledged loyalty to the early faith in kings which set the most democratic nation under the sun in a ferment at the coming of a royal yellow-haired laddie, some years ago, and which still has something to do with the love the young country bears the old, like that of a big son for an imperious little mother, who held him while she could, and let him go with a farewell scolding when he rebelled. But even the satisfaction of talking with a distant connection of the British nobility did not render

Amy forgetful of time; and when the proper number of minutes had passed, she reluctantly tore herself from this aristocratic society, and looked about for Jo, fervently hoping that her incorrigible sister would not be found in any position which should bring disgrace upon the name of March.

It might have been worse, but Amy considered it bad; for Jo sat on the grass, with an encampment of boys about her, and a dirty-footed dog reposing on the skirt of her state and festival dress, as she related one of Laurie's pranks to her admiring audience. One small child was poking turtles with Amy's cherished parasol, a second was eating gingerbread over Jo's best bonnet, and a third playing ball with her gloves. But all were enjoying themselves; and when Jo collected her damaged property to go, her escort accompanied her, begging her to come again, "it was such fun to hear about Laurie's larks."

"Capital boys, aren't they? I feel quite young and brisk again after that," said Jo, strolling along with her hands behind her, partly from habit, partly to conceal the bespattered parasol.

"Why do you always avoid Mr. Tudor?" asked Amy, wisely refraining from any comment upon Jo's dilapidated appearance.

"Don't like him; he puts on airs, snubs his sisters, worries his father, and doesn't speak respectfully of his mother. Laurie says he is fast, and *I* don't consider him a desirable acquaintance; so I let him alone."

"You might treat him civilly, at least. You gave him a cool nod; and just now you bowed and smiled in the politest way to Tommy Chamberlain, whose father keeps a grocery store. If you had just reversed the nod and the bow, it would have been right," said Amy reprovingly.

"No, it wouldn't," returned perverse Jo; "I neither like, respect, nor admire Tudor, though his grandfather's uncle's nephew's niece *was* third cousin to a lord. Tommy is poor and bashful and good and very clever; I think well of him, and like to show that I do, for he *is* a gentleman in spite of the brown paper parcels."

"It's no use trying to argue with you—" began Amy.

"Not the least, my dear," interrupted Jo; "so let us look amiable, and drop a card here, as the Kings are evidently out, for which I'm deeply grateful."

The family card case having done its duty, the girls walked on, and Jo uttered another thanksgiving on reaching the fifth house, and being told that the young ladies were engaged.

"Now let us go home, and never mind Aunt March today. We can run down there any time, and it's really a pity to trail through the dust in our best bibs and tuckers, when we are tired and cross."

"Speak for yourself, if you please. Aunt likes to have us pay her the compliment of coming in style, and making a formal call; it's a little thing to do, but it gives her pleasure, and I don't believe it will hurt your things half so much as letting dirty dogs and clumping boys spoil them. Stoop down, and let me take the crumbs off your bonnet."

"What a good girl you are, Amy!" said Jo, with a repentant glance from her own damaged costume to that of her sister, which was fresh and spotless still. "I wish it was as easy for me to do little things to please people as it is for you. I think of them, but it takes too much time to do them; so I wait for a chance to confer a great favor, and let the small ones slip; but they tell best in the end, I fancy."

Amy smiled, and was mollified at once, saying with a maternal air:

"Women should learn to be agreeable, particularly poor ones; for they have no other way of repaying the kindnesses they receive. If you'd remember that, and practice it, you'd be better liked than I am, because there is more of you."

"I'm a crotchety old thing, and always shall be, but I'm willing to own that you are right; only it's easier for me to risk my life for a person than to be pleasant to him when I don't feel like it. It's a great misfortune to have such strong likes and dislikes, isn't it?"

"It's a greater not to be able to hide them. I don't mind saying that I don't approve of Tudor any more than you do; but I'm not called upon to tell him so; neither are you, and there is no use in making yourself disagreeable because he is."

"But I think girls ought to show when they disapprove of young men; and how can they do it except by their manners? Preaching does not do any good, as I know to my sorrow, since

I've had Teddy to manage; but there are many little ways in which I can influence him without a word, and I say we *ought* to do it to others if we can."

"Teddy is a remarkable boy, and can't be taken as a sample of other boys," said Amy, in a tone of solemn conviction, which would have convulsed the "remarkable boy," if he had heard it. "If we were belles, or women of wealth and position, we might do something, perhaps; but for us to frown at one set of young gentlemen because we don't approve of them, and smile upon another set because we do, wouldn't have a particle of effect, and we should only be considered odd and puritanical."

"So we are to countenance things and people which we detest, merely because we are not belles and millionaires, are we? That's a nice sort of morality."

"I can't argue about it, I only know that it's the way of the world; and people who set themselves against it only get laughed at for their pains. I don't like reformers, and I hope you will never try to be one."

"I do like them, and I shall be one if I can; for, in spite of the laughing, the world would never get on without them. We can't agree about that, for you belong to the old set and I to the new: you will get on the best, but I shall have the liveliest time of it. I should rather enjoy the brickbats and hooting, I think."

"Well, compose yourself now, and don't worry aunt with your new ideas."

"I'll try not to, but I'm always possessed to burst out with some particularly blunt speech or revolutionary sentiment before her; it's my doom, and I can't help it."

They found Aunt Carrol with the old lady, both absorbed in some very interesting subject; but they dropped it as the girls came in, with a conscious look which betrayed that they had been talking about their nieces. Jo was not in a good humor, and the perverse fit returned; but Amy, who had virtuously done her duty, kept her temper, and pleased everybody, was in a most angelic frame of mind. This amiable spirit was felt at once, and both aunts "my deared" her affectionately, looking what they afterwards said emphatically—"That child improves every day."

"Are you going to help about the fair, dear?" asked Mrs. Carrol, as Amy sat down beside her with the confiding air elderly people like so well in the young.

"Yes, aunt. Mrs. Chester asked me if I would, and I offered to tend a table, as I have nothing but my time to give."

"I'm not," put in Jo decidedly. "I hate to be patronized, and the Chesters think it's a great favor to allow us to help with their highly connected fair. I wonder you consented, Amy: they only want you to work."

"I am willing to work: it's for the freedmen as well as the Chesters, and I think it very kind of them to let me share the labor and the fun. Patronage does not trouble me when it is well meant."

"Quite right and proper. I like your grateful spirit, my dear; it's a pleasure to help people who appreciate our efforts: some do not, and that is trying," observed Aunt March, looking over her spectacles at Jo, who sat apart, rocking herself, with a somewhat morose expression.

If Jo had only known what a great happiness was wavering in the balance for one of them, she would have turned dove-like in a minute; but, unfortunately, we don't have windows in our breasts, and cannot see what goes on in the minds of our friends; better for us that we cannot as a general thing, but now and then it would be such a comfort, such a saving of time and temper. By her next speech, Jo deprived herself of several years of pleasure, and received a timely lesson in the art of holding her tongue.

"I don't like favors; they oppress and make me feel like a slave. I'd rather do everything for myself, and be perfectly independent."

"Ahem!" coughed Aunt Carrol softly, with a look at Aunt March.

"I told you so," said Aunt March, with a decided nod to Aunt Carrol.

Mercifully unconscious of what she had done, Jo sat with her nose in the air, and a revolutionary aspect which was anything but inviting.

"Do you speak French, dear?" asked Mrs. Carrol, laying her hand on Amy's.

"Pretty well, thanks to Aunt March who lets Esther talk to

me as often as I like," replied Amy, with a grateful look, which caused the old lady to smile affably.

"How are you about languages?" asked Mrs. Carrol of Jo.

"Don't know a word; I'm very stupid about studying anything; can't bear French, it's such a slippery, silly sort of language" was the brusque reply.

Another look passed between the ladies, and Aunt March said to Amy, "You are quite strong and well, now, dear, I believe? Eyes don't trouble you any more, do they?"

"Not at all, thank you, ma'am. I'm very well, and mean to do great things next winter, so that I may be ready for Rome, whenever that joyful time arrives."

"Good girl. You deserve to go, and I'm sure you will someday," said Aunt March, with an approving pat on the head, as Amy picked up her ball for her.

> *"Crosspatch, draw the latch,*
> *Sit by the fire and spin,"*

squalled Polly, bending down from his perch on the back of her chair to peep into Jo's face, with such a comical air of impertinent inquiry that it was impossible to help laughing.

"Most observing bird," said the old lady.

"Come and take a walk, my dear?" cried Polly, hopping toward the china closet, with a look suggestive of lump sugar.

"Thank you, I will. Come, Amy," and Jo brought the visit to an end, feeling more strongly than ever that calls did have a bad effect upon her constitution. She shook hands in a gentlemanly manner, but Amy kissed both aunts, and the girls departed, leaving behind them the impression of shadow and sunshine; which impression caused Aunt March to say, as they vanished:

"You'd better do it, Mary; I'll supply the money," and Aunt Carrol to reply decidedly, "I certainly will, if her father and mother consent."

CHAPTER THIRTY

Consequences

🙝 MRS. CHESTER'S fair was so very elegant and select that it was considered a great honor by the young ladies of the neighborhood to be invited to take a table, and everyone was much interested in the matter. Amy was asked, but Jo was not, which was fortunate for all parties, as her elbows were decidedly akimbo at this period of her life, and it took a good many hard knocks to teach her how to get on easily. The "haughty, uninteresting creature" was let severely alone; but Amy's talent and taste were duly complimented by the offer of the art table, and she exerted herself to prepare and secure appropriate and valuable contributions to it.

Everything went on smoothly till the day before the fair opened; then there occurred one of the little skirmishes which it is almost impossible to avoid, when some five and twenty women, old and young, with all their private piques and prejudices, try to work together.

May Chester was rather jealous of Amy because the latter was a greater favorite than herself; and, just at this time, several trifling circumstances occurred to increase the feeling. Amy's dainty pen-and-ink work entirely eclipsed May's painted vases—that was one thorn; then the all-conquering Tudor had danced four times with Amy, at a late party, and only once with May—that was thorn number two; but the chief grievance that rankled in her soul, and gave her an excuse for her unfriendly conduct, was a rumor which some obliging gossip had whispered to her, that the March girls had made fun of her at the Lambs'. All the blame of this should have fallen upon Jo for her naughty imitation had been too lifelike to escape detection, and the frolicsome Lambs had permitted the joke to escape. No hint of this had reached the culprits, however, and Amy's dismay can be imagined when, the very evening before the fair, as she was putting the last touches to her pretty table, Mrs. Chester, who, of course, resented the supposed ridicule of her daughter, said, in a bland tone, but with a cold look:

"I find, dear, that there is some feeling among the young ladies about giving this table to anyone but my girls. As this is the most prominent, and some say the most attractive table of all, and they are the chief getters-up of the fair, it is thought best for them to take this place. I'm sorry, but I know you are too sincerely interested in the cause to mind a little personal disappointment, and you shall have another table if you like."

Mrs. Chester had fancied beforehand that it would be easy to deliver this little speech; but when the time came, she found it rather difficult to utter it naturally, with Amy's unsuspicious eyes looking straight at her, full of surprise and trouble.

Amy felt that there was something behind this, but could not guess what, and said quietly, feeling hurt, and showing that she did:

"Perhaps you had rather I took no table at all?"

"Now, my dear, don't have any ill feeling, I beg; it's merely a matter of expediency, you see; my girls will naturally take the lead, and this table is considered their proper place. *I* think it very appropriate to you, and feel very grateful for your efforts to make it so pretty; but we must give up our private wishes, of course, and I will see that y⸍ ᵌave a good place elsewhere. Wouldn't you like the flower table? The little girls undertook it, but they are discouraged. You could make a charming thing of it, and the flower table is always attractive, you know."

"Especially to gentlemen," added May, with a look which enlightened Amy as to one cause of her sudden fall from favor. She colored angrily, but took no other notice of that girlish sarcasm, and answered, with unexpected amiability:

"It shall be as you please, Mrs. Chester. I'll give up my place here at once, and attend to the flowers, if you like."

"You can put your own things on your own table, if you prefer," began May, feeling a little conscience-stricken, as she

looked at the pretty racks, the painted shells, and quaint illu-
minations Amy had so carefully made and so gracefully arranged. She meant it kindly, but Amy mistook her meaning,
and said quickly:

"Oh, certainly, if they are in your way," and sweeping her
contributions into her apron, pell-mell, she walked off, feeling
that herself and her works of art had been insulted past for-
giveness.

"Now, she's mad. Oh, dear, I wish I hadn't asked you to
speak, mamma," said May, looking disconsolately at the empty
spaces on her table.

"Girls' quarrels are soon over," returned her mother, feeling
a trifle ashamed of her own part in this one, as well she might.

The little girls hailed Amy and her treasures with delight,
which cordial reception somewhat soothed her perturbed
spirit, and she fell to work, determined to succeed florally, if
she could not artistically. But everything seemed against her:
it was late, and she was tired; everyone was too busy with
their own affairs to help her; and the little girls were only hin-
drances, for the dears fussed and chattered like so many mag-
pies, making a great deal of confusion in their artless efforts to
preserve the most perfect order. The evergreen arch wouldn't
stay firm after she got it up, but wiggled and threatened to
tumble down on her head when the hanging baskets were
filled; her best tile got a splash of water, which left a sepia tear
on the Cupid's cheek; she bruised her hands with hammering,
and got cold working in a draught, which last affliction filled
her with apprehensions for the morrow. Any girl reader who
has suffered like afflictions will sympathize with poor Amy,
and wish her well through her task.

There was great indignation at home when she told her
story that evening. Her mother said it was a shame, but told
her she had done right; Beth declared she wouldn't go to the
fair at all; and Jo demanded why she didn't take all her pretty
things and leave those mean people to get on without her.

"Because they are mean is no reason why I should be. I hate
such things, and though I think I've a right to be hurt, I don't
intend to show it. They will feel that more than angry speeches
or huffy actions, won't they, Marmee?"

"That's the right spirit, my dear; a kiss for a blow is always best, though it's not very easy to give it sometimes," said her mother, with the air of one who had learned the difference between preaching and practicing.

In spite of various very natural temptations to resent and retaliate, Amy adhered to her resolution all the next day, bent on conquering her enemy by kindness. She began well, thanks to a silent reminder that came to her unexpectedly, but most opportunely. As she arranged her table that morning, while the little girls were in an anteroom filling the baskets, she took up her pet production—a little book, the antique cover of which her father had found among his treasures, and in which, on leaves of vellum, she had beautifully illuminated different texts. As she turned the pages, rich in dainty devices, with very pardonable pride, her eye fell upon one verse that made her stop and think. Framed in a brilliant scrollwork of scarlet, blue, and gold, with little spirits of good will helping one another up and down among the thorns and flowers, were the words "Thou shalt love thy neighbor as thyself."

"I ought, but I don't," thought Amy, as her eye went from the bright page to May's discontented face behind the big vases, that could not hide the vacancies her pretty work had once filled. Amy stood a minute, turning the leaves in her hand, reading on each some sweet rebuke for all heartburnings and uncharitableness of spirit. Many wise and true sermons are preached us every day by unconscious ministers in street, school, office, or home; even a fair table may become a pulpit, if it can offer the good and helpful words which are never out of season. Amy's conscience preached her a little sermon from that text, then and there; and she did what many of us do not always do—took the sermon to heart, and straightway put it in practice.

A group of girls were standing by May's table, admiring the pretty things, and talking over the change of saleswomen. They dropped their voices, but Amy knew they were speaking of her, hearing one side of the story and judging accordingly. It was not pleasant, but a better spirit had come over her, and presently a chance offered for proving it. She heard May say sorrowfully:

"It's too bad, for there is no time to make other things, and I don't want to fill up with odds and ends. The table was just complete then; now it's spoilt."

"I dare say she'd put them back if you asked her," suggested someone.

"How could I after all the fuss?" began May, but she did not finish, for Amy's voice came across the hall, saying pleasantly:

"You may have them, and welcome, without asking, if you want them. I was just thinking I'd offer to put them back, for they belong to your table rather than mine. Here they are; please take them, and forgive me if I was hasty in carrying them away last night."

As she spoke, Amy returned her contribution, with a nod and a smile, and hurried away again, feeling that it was easier to do a friendly thing than it was to stay and be thanked for it.

"Now, I call that lovely of her, don't you?" cried one girl.

May's answer was inaudible; but another young lady, whose temper was evidently a little soured by making lemonade, added, with a disagreeable laugh, "Very lovely; for she knew she couldn't sell them at her own table."

Now that was hard; when we make little sacrifices we like to have them appreciated, at least; and for a minute Amy was sorry she had done it, feeling that virtue was not always its own reward. But it is—as she presently discovered; for her spirits began to rise, and her table to blossom under her skillful hands; the girls were very kind, and that one little act seemed to have cleared the atmosphere amazingly.

It was a very long day, and a hard one to Amy, as she sat behind her table, often quite alone, for the little girls deserted very soon: few cared to buy flowers in summer, and her bouquets began to droop long before night.

The art table *was* the most attractive in the room; there was a crowd about it all day long, and the tenders were constantly flying to and fro with important faces and rattling moneyboxes. Amy often looked wistfully across, longing to be there, where she felt at home and happy, instead of in a corner with nothing to do. It might seem no hardship to some of us; but to a pretty, blithe young girl, it was not only tedious, but very trying; and the thought of being found there in the evening by her family, and Laurie and his friends, made it a real martyrdom.

She did not go home till night, and then she looked so pale and quiet that they knew the day had been a hard one, though she made no complaint, and did not even tell what she had done. Her mother gave her an extra cordial cup of tea, Beth helped her dress, and made a charming little wreath for her hair, while Jo astonished her family by getting herself up with unusual care, and hinting darkly that the tables were about to be turned.

"Don't do anything rude, pray, Jo. I won't have any fuss made, so let it all pass, and behave yourself," begged Amy, as she departed early, hoping to find a reinforcement of flowers to refresh her poor little table.

"I merely intend to make myself entrancingly agreeable to everyone I know, and to keep them in your corner as long as possible. Teddy and his boys will lend a hand, and we'll have a good time yet," returned Jo, leaning over the gate to watch for Laurie. Presently the familiar tramp was heard in the dusk, and she ran out to meet him.

"Is that my boy?"

"As sure as this is my girl!" and Laurie tucked her hand under his arm, with the air of a man whose every wish was gratified.

"Oh, Teddy, such doings!" and Jo told Amy's wrongs with sisterly zeal.

"A flock of our fellows are going to drive over by and by, and I'll be hanged if I don't make them buy every flower she's got, and camp down before her table afterward," said Laurie, espousing her cause with warmth.

"The flowers are not at all nice, Amy says, and the fresh ones may not arrive in time. I don't wish to be unjust or sus-picious, but I shouldn't wonder if they never came at all. When people do one mean thing they are very likely to do another," observed Jo, in a disgusted tone.

"Didn't Hayes give you the best out of our gardens? I told him to."

"I didn't know that; he forgot, I suppose; and, as your

grandpa was poorly, I didn't like to worry him by asking, though I did want some."

"Now, Jo, how could you think there was any need of asking! They are just as much yours as mine. Don't we always go halves in everything?" began Laurie, in the tone that always made Jo turn thorny.

"Gracious, I hope not! Half of some of your things wouldn't fit me at all. But we mustn't stand philandering here; I've got to help Amy, so you go and make yourself splendid; and if you'll be so very kind as to let Hayes take a few nice flowers up to the hall, I'll bless you forever."

"Couldn't you do it now?" asked Laurie, so suggestively that Jo shut the gate in his face with inhospitable haste, and called through the bars, "Go away, Teddy; I'm busy."

Thanks to the conspirators, the tables *were* turned that night.

Hayes sent up a wilderness of flowers, with a lovely basket, arranged in his best manner, for a centerpiece; then the March family turned out en masse, and Jo exerted herself to some purpose, for people not only came, but stayed, laughing at her nonsense, admiring Amy's taste, and apparently enjoying themselves very much. Laurie and his friends gallantly threw themselves into the breach, bought up the bouquets, encamped before the table, and made that corner the liveliest spot in the room. Amy was in her element now, and, out of gratitude, if nothing more, was as sprightly and gracious as possible—coming to the conclusion about that time that virtue *was* its own reward after all.

Jo behaved herself with exemplary propriety; and when Amy was happily surrounded by her guard of honor, Jo circulated about the hall, picking up various bits of gossip, which enlightened her upon the subject of the Chester change of base. She reproached herself for her share of the ill feeling, and resolved to exonerate Amy as soon as possible; she also discovered what Amy had done about the things in the morning, and considered her a model of magnanimity. As she passed the art table, she glanced over it for her sister's things, but saw no signs of them. "Tucked away out of sight, I dare say," thought Jo, who could forgive her own wrongs, but hotly resented any insult offered to her family.

"Good evening, Miss Jo. How does Amy get on?" asked May, with a conciliatory air, for she wanted to show that she also could be generous.

"She has sold everything she had that was worth selling and now she is enjoying herself. The flower table is always attractive, you know, 'especially to gentlemen.'"

Jo *couldn't* resist giving that little slap, but May took it so meekly she regretted it a minute after, and fell to praising the great vases, which still remained unsold.

"Is Amy's illumination anywhere about? I took a fancy to buy that for father," said Jo, very anxious to learn the fate of her sister's work.

"Everything of Amy's sold long ago; I took care that the right people saw them, and they made a nice little sum of money for us," returned May, who had overcome sundry small temptations, as well as Amy, that day.

Much gratified, Jo rushed back to tell the good news; and Amy looked both touched and surprised by the report of May's words and manner.

"Now, gentlemen, I want you to go and do your duty by the other tables as generously as you have by mine—especially the art table," she said, ordering out "Teddy's Own," as the girls called the college friends.

" 'Charge, Chester, charge!' is the motto for that table; but do your duty like men, and you'll get your money's worth of *art* in every sense of the word," said the irrepressible Jo, as the devoted phalanx prepared to take the field.

"To hear is to obey, but March is fairer far than May," said little Parker, making a frantic effort to be both witty and tender, and getting promptly quenched by Laurie, who said, "Very well, my son, for a small boy!" and walked him off, with a paternal pat on the head.

"Buy the vases," whispered Amy to Laurie, as a final heaping of coals of fire on her enemy's head.

To May's great delight, Mr. Laurence not only bought the vases, but pervaded the hall with one under each arm. The

other gentleman speculated with equal rashness in all sorts of
frail trifles, and wandered helplessly about afterward, burdened with wax flowers, painted fans, filigree portfolios, and
other useful and appropriate purchases.

Aunt Carrol was there, heard the story, looked pleased,
and said something to Mrs. March in a corner, which made the
latter lady beam with satisfaction, and watch Amy with a face
full of mingled pride and anxiety, though she did not betray
the cause of her pleasure till several days later.

The fair was pronounced a success; and when May bade
Amy good night, she did not "gush" as usual, but gave her an
affectionate kiss, and a look which said, "Forgive and forget."
That satisfied Amy; and when she got home she found the
vases paraded on the parlor chimney piece, with a great
bouquet in each. "The reward of merit for a magnanimous
March," as Laurie announced with a flourish.

"You've a deal more principle and generosity and nobleness
of character than I ever gave you credit for, Amy. You've behaved sweetly, and I respect you with all my heart," said Jo
warmly, as they brushed their hair together late that night.

"Yes, we all do, and love her for being so ready to forgive.
It must have been dreadfully hard, after working so long, and
setting your heart on selling your own pretty things. I don't
believe I could have done it as kindly as you did," added Beth
from her pillow.

"Why, girls, you needn't praise me so; I only did as I'd be
done by. You laugh at me when I say I want to be a lady, but
I mean a true gentlewoman in mind and manners, and I try
to do it as far as I know how. I can't explain exactly, but I
want to be above the little meannesses and follies and faults
that spoil so many women. I'm far from it now, but I do my
best, and hope in time to be what mother is."

Amy spoke earnestly, and Jo said, with a cordial hug:

"I understand now what you mean, and I'll never laugh at
you again. You are getting on faster than you think, and I'll
take lessons of you in true politeness, for you've learned the
secret, I believe. Try away, deary; you'll get your reward
someday, and no one will be more delighted than I shall."

A week later Amy did get her reward, and poor Jo found it

hard to be delighted. A letter came from Aunt Carrol, and
Mrs. March's face was illuminated to such a degree, when she
read it, that Jo and Beth, who were with her, demanded what
the glad tidings were.

"Aunt Carrol is going abroad next month, and wants—"

"Me to go with her!" burst in Jo, flying out of her chair in
an uncontrollable rapture.

"No, dear, not you; it's Amy."

"Oh, mother! she's too young; it's my turn first. I've wanted
it so long—it would do me so much good, and be so altogether
splendid—I *must* go."

"I'm afraid it's impossible, Jo. Aunt says Amy, decidedly,
and it is not for us to dictate when she offers such a favor."

"It's always so. Amy has all the fun and I have all the work.
It isn't fair, oh, it isn't fair," cried Jo passionately.

"I'm afraid it is partly your own fault, dear. When Aunt
spoke to me the other day, she regretted your blunt manners
and too independent spirit; and here she writes, as if quoting
something you had said—'I planned at first to ask Jo; but as
"favors burden her" and she "hates French," I think I won't
venture to invite her. Amy is more docile, will make a good
companion for Flo, and receive gratefully any help the trip
may give her.'"

"Oh, my tongue, my abominable tongue! Why can't I learn
to keep it quiet?" groaned Jo, remembering words which had
been her undoing. When she had heard the explanation of the
quoted phrases, Mrs. March said sorrowfully:

"I wish you could have gone, but there is no hope of it this
time; so try to bear it cheerfully, and don't sadden Amy's pleasure by reproaches or regrets."

"I'll try," said Jo, winking hard, as she knelt down to pick
up the basket she had joyfully upset. "I'll take a leaf out of her
book, and try not only to seem glad, but to be so, and not
grudge her one minute of happiness; but it won't be easy, for
it is a dreadful disappointment," and poor Jo bedewed the
little fat pincushion she held with several very bitter tears.

"Jo, dear, I'm very selfish, but I couldn't spare you, and I'm
glad you are not going quite yet," whispered Beth, embracing
her, basket and all, with such a clinging touch and loving face,

that Jo felt comforted in spite of the sharp regret that made her want to box her own ears, and humbly beg Aunt Carrol to burden her with this favor, and see how gratefully she would bear it.

By the time Amy came in, Jo was able to take her part in the family jubilation; not quite as heartily as usual, perhaps, but without repinings at Amy's good fortune. The young lady herself received the news as tidings of great joy, went about in a solemn sort of rapture, and began to sort her colors and pack her pencils that evening, leaving such trifles as clothes, money, and passports to those less absorbed in visions of art than herself.

"It isn't a mere pleasure trip to me, girls," she said impressively, as she scraped her best palette. "It will decide my career; for if I have any genius, I shall find it out in Rome, and will do something to prove it."

"Suppose you haven't?" said Jo, sewing away, with red eyes, at the new collars which were to be handed over to Amy.

"Then I shall come home and teach drawing for my living," replied the aspirant for fame, with philosophic composure; but she made a wry face at the prospect, and scratched away at her palette as if bent on vigorous measures before she gave up her hopes.

"No, you won't; you hate hard work, and you'll marry some rich man, and come home to sit in the lap of luxury all your days," said Jo.

"Your predictions sometimes come to pass, but I don't believe that one will. I'm sure I wish it would, for if I can't be an artist myself, I should like to be able to help those who are," said Amy, smiling, as if the part of Lady Bountiful would suit her better than that of a poor drawing teacher.

"Hum!" said Jo, with a sigh. "If you wish it you'll have it, for your wishes are always granted—mine never."

"Would you like to go?" asked Amy, thoughtfully patting her nose with her knife.

"Rather!"

"Well, in a year or two I'll send for you, and we'll dig in the Forum for relics, and carry out all the plans we've made so many times."

"Thank you; I'll remind you of your promise when that joyful day comes, if it ever does," returned Jo, accepting the vague but magnificent offer as gratefully as she could.

There was not much time for preparation, and the house was in a ferment till Amy was off. Jo bore up very well till the last flutter of blue ribbon vanished, when she retired to her refuge, the garret, and cried till she couldn't cry any more. Amy likewise bore up stoutly till the steamer sailed; then, just as the gangway was about to be withdrawn, it suddenly came over her that a whole ocean was soon to roll between her and those who loved her best, and she clung to Laurie, the last lingerer, saying with a sob:

"Oh, take care of them for me; and if anything should happen—"

"I will, dear, I will; and if anything happens, I'll come and comfort you," whispered Laurie, little dreaming that he would be called upon to keep his word.

So Amy sailed away to find the old world, which is always new and beautiful to young eyes, while her father and friend watched her from the shore, fervently hoping that none but gentle fortunes would befall the happyhearted girl, who waved her hand to them till they could see nothing but the summer sunshine dazzling on the sea.

CHAPTER THIRTY-ONE

Our Foreign Correspondent

DEAREST PEOPLE:

Here I really sit at a front window of the Bath Hotel, Piccadilly. It's not a fashionable place, but uncle stopped here years ago, and won't go anywhere else; however, we don't mean to stay long, so it's no great matter. Oh, I can't begin to tell you how I enjoy it all! I never can, so I'll only give you bits out of my notebook, for I've done nothing but sketch and scribble since I started.

I sent a line from Halifax, when I felt pretty miserable, but after that I got on delightfully, seldom ill, on deck all day, with plenty of pleasant people to amuse me. Everyone was very kind to me, especially the officers. Don't laugh, Jo; gentlemen really are very necessary aboard ship, to hold on to, or to wait upon one; and as they have nothing to do, it's a mercy to make them useful, otherwise they would smoke themselves to death, I'm afraid.

Aunt and Flo were poorly all the way, and liked to be let alone, so when I had done what I could for them, I went and enjoyed myself. Such walks on deck, such sunsets, such splendid air and waves! It was almost as exciting as riding a fast horse, when we went rushing on so grandly. I wish Beth could have come, it would have done her so much good; as for Jo, she would have gone up and sat on the main-top jib, or whatever the high thing is called, made friends with the engineers, and tooted on the captain's speaking trumpet, she'd have been in such a state of rapture.

It was all heavenly, but I was glad to see the Irish coast, and found it very lovely, so green and sunny, with brown cabins here and there, ruins on some of the hills, and gentlemen's country seats in the valleys, with deer feeding in the parks. It was early in the morning, but I didn't regret getting up to see it, for the bay was full of little boats, the shore *so* picturesque, and a rosy sky overhead. I never shall forget it.

At Queenstown one of my new acquaintances left us— Mr. Lennox—and when I said something about the Lakes of Killarney, he sighed and sung, with a look at me—

> *"Oh, have you e'er heard of Kate Kearney?*
> *She lives on the banks of Killarney;*
> *From the glance of her eye,*
> *Shun danger and fly,*
> *For fatal's the glance of Kate Kearney."*

Wasn't that nonsensical?

We only stopped at Liverpool a few hours. It's a dirty, noisy place, and I was glad to leave it. Uncle rushed out and bought a pair of dogskin gloves, some ugly, thick shoes, and an umbrella, and got shaved à la mutton chop, the first thing. Then he flattered himself that he looked like a true Briton; but the first time he had the mud cleaned off his shoes, the little bootblack knew that an American stood in them, and said, with a grin, "There yer har, sir. I've give 'em the latest Yankee shine." It amused uncle immensely. Oh, I *must* tell you what that absurd Lennox did! He got his friend Ward, who came on with us, to order a bouquet for me, and the first thing I saw in my room was a lovely one, with "Robert Lennox's compliments" on the card. Wasn't that fun, girls? I like traveling.

I never shall get to London if I don't hurry. The trip was like riding through a long picture gallery, full of lovely landscapes. The farmhouses were my delight; with thatched roofs, ivy up to the eaves, latticed windows, and stout women with rosy children at the doors. The very cattle looked more tranquil than ours, as they stood knee-deep in clover, and the hens had a contented cluck, as if they never got nervous, like Yankee biddies. Such perfect color I never saw—the grass so green, sky so blue, grain so yellow, wood so dark—I was in a rapture all the way. So was Flo; and we kept bouncing from one side to the other, trying to see everything while we were whisking along at the rate of sixty miles an hour. Aunt was tired and went to sleep, but uncle read his guidebook, and wouldn't be astonished at anything. This is the way we went on: Amy, flying up—"Oh, that must be Kenilworth, that gray place

among the trees!" Flo, darting to my window—"How sweet!
We must go there sometime, won't we, papa?" Uncle, calmly
admiring his boots—"No, my dear, not unless you want beer;
that's a brewery."

A pause—then Flo cried out, "Bless me, there's a gallows
and a man going up." "Where, where?" shrieks Amy, staring
out at two tall posts with a crossbeam and some dangling
chains. "A colliery," remarks uncle, with a twinkle of the eye.
"Here's a lovely flock of lambs all lying down," says Amy.
"See, papa, aren't they pretty!" adds Flo sentimentally.
"Geese, young ladies," returns uncle, in a tone that keeps us
quiet till Flo settles down to enjoy "The Flirtations of Capt.
Cavendish," and I have the scenery all to myself.

Of course it rained when we got to London, and there was
nothing to be seen but fog and umbrellas. We rested, un-
packed, and shopped a little between showers. Aunt Mary got
me some new things, for I came off in such a hurry I wasn't
half ready. A white hat and blue feather, a muslin dress to
match, and the loveliest mantle you ever saw. Shopping in Re-
gent Street is perfectly splendid; things seem so cheap—nice

ribbons only sixpence a yard. I laid in a stock, but shall get my gloves in Paris. Doesn't that sound sort of elegant and rich?

Flo and I, for the fun of it, ordered a hansom cab, while aunt and uncle were out, and went for a drive, though we learned afterward that it wasn't the thing for young ladies to ride in them alone. It was so droll! For when we were shut in by the wooden apron, the man drove so fast that Flo was frightened, and told me to stop him. But he was up outside behind somewhere, and I couldn't get at him. He didn't hear me call, nor see me flap my parasol in front, and there we were, quite helpless, rattling away, and whirling around corners at a breakneck pace. At last, in my despair, I saw a little door in the roof, and on poking it open, a red eye appeared, and a beery voice said:

"Now then, mum?"

I gave my order as soberly as I could, and slamming down the door, with an "Aye, aye, mum," the man made his horse walk, as if going to a funeral. I poked again, and said, "A little faster," then off he went, helter-skelter, as before, and we resigned ourselves to our fate.

Today was fair, and we went to Hyde Park, close by, for we are more aristocratic than we look. The Duke of Devonshire lives near. I often see his footmen lounging at the back gate; and the Duke of Wellington's house is not far off. Such sights as I saw, my dear! It was as good as Punch, for there were fat dowagers rolling about in their red and yellow coaches, with gorgeous Jeameses in silk stockings and velvet coats, up behind, and powdered coachmen in front. Smart maids, with the rosiest children I ever saw; handsome girls, looking half asleep; dandies, in queer English hats and lavender kids, lounging about, and tall soldiers, in short red jackets and muffin caps stuck on one side, looking so funny I longed to sketch them.

Rotten Row means *"Route de Roi,"* or the king's way; but now it's more like a riding school than anything else. The horses are splendid, and the men, especially the grooms, ride well; but the women are stiff, and bounce, which isn't according to our rules. I longed to show them a tearing American gallop, for they trotted solemnly up and down, in their scant habits and high hats, looking like the women in a toy Noah's Ark. Everyone rides—old men, stout ladies, little children—and the young folks do a deal of flirting here; I saw a pair exchange rosebuds, for it's the thing to wear one in the buttonhole, and I thought it rather a nice little idea.

In the P.M. to Westminster Abbey; but don't expect me to describe it, that's impossible—so I'll only say it was sublime! This evening we are going to see Fletcher, which will be an appropriate end to the happiest day of my life.

Midnight

It's very late, but I can't let my letter go in the morning without telling you what happened last evening. Who do you think came in, as we were at tea? Laurie's English friends, Fred and Frank Vaughn! I was *so* surprised, for I shouldn't have known them but for the cards. Both are tall fellows, with whiskers; Fred handsome in the English style, and Frank much better, for he only limps slightly, and uses no crutches. They had heard from Laurie where we were to be, and came to ask us to their house; but uncle won't go, so we shall return the call, and see them as we can. They went to the theater with us, and we did have *such* a good time, for Frank devoted himself to Flo, and Fred and I talked over past, present, and future fun as if we had known each other all our days. Tell Beth Frank asked for her, and was sorry to hear of her ill-health. Fred laughed when I spoke of Jo, and sent his "respectful compliments to the big hat." Neither of them had forgotten Camp Laurence, or the fun we had there. What ages ago it seems, doesn't it?

Aunt is tapping on the wall for the third time, so I *must* stop. I really feel like a dissipated London fine lady, writing here so late, with my room full of pretty things, and my head a jumble of parks, theaters, new gowns, and gallant creatures, who say "Ah!" and twirl their blond mustaches with the true English lordliness. I long to see you all, and in spite of my nonsense am, as ever, your loving   Amy

DEAR GIRLS:

In my last I told you about our London visit—how kind the Vaughns were, and what pleasant parties they made for us. I enjoyed the trips to Hampton Court and the Kensington Museum more than anything else—for at Hampton I saw Raphael's cartoons, and, at the Museum, rooms full of pictures by Turner, Lawrence, Reynolds, Hogarth, and the other great creatures. The day in Richmond Park was charming, for we had a regular English picnic, and I had more splendid oaks and groups of deer than I could copy; also heard a nightingale, and saw larks go up. We "did" London to our hearts' content, thanks to Fred and Frank, and were sorry to go away; for though English people are slow to take you in, when they once make up their minds to do it they cannot be outdone in hospitality, I think. The Vaughns hope to meet us in Rome next winter, and I shall be dreadfully disappointed if they don't, for Grace and I are great friends, and the boys very nice fellows—especially Fred.

Well, we were hardly settled here, when he turned up again, saying he had come for a holiday, and was going to Switzerland. Aunt looked sober at first, but he was so cool about it she couldn't say a word; and now we get on nicely, and are very glad he came, for he speaks French like a native, and I don't know what we should do without him. Uncle doesn't know ten words, and insists on talking English very loud, as if that would make people understand him. Aunt's pronunciation is old-fashioned, and Flo and I, though we flattered ourselves that we knew a good deal, find we don't, and are very grateful to have Fred do the *"parley vooing,"* as uncle calls it.

Such delightful times as we are having! Sightseeing from morning till night, stopping for nice lunches in the gay cafés, and meeting with all sorts of droll adventures. Rainy days I spend in the Louvre, reveling in pictures. Jo would turn up her naughty nose at some of the finest, because she has no soul for art; but *I* have, and I'm cultivating eye and taste as fast as I can. She would like the relics of great people better, for I've seen her Napoleon's cocked hat and gray coat, his baby's cradle and his old toothbrush; also Marie Antoinette's little shoe, the ring of St. Denis, Charlemagne's sword, and many other interesting things. I'll talk for hours about them when I come, but haven't time to write.

The Palais Royal is a heavenly place—so full of *bijouterie* and lovely things that I'm nearly distracted because I can't buy them. Fred wanted to get me some, but of course I didn't allow it. Then the Bois and the Champs-Elysées are *très magnifique*. I've seen the imperial family several times—the emperor an ugly, hard-looking man, the empress pale and pretty, but dressed in bad taste, *I* thought—purple dress, green hat and yellow gloves. Little Nap is a handsome boy, who sits chatting to his tutor, and kisses his hand to the people as he passes in his four-horse barouche, with postilions in red satin jackets, and a mounted guard before and behind.

We often walk in the Tuileries Gardens, for they are lovely, though the antique Luxembourg Gardens suit me better. Père la Chaise is very curious, for many of the tombs are like small rooms, and, looking in, one sees a table, with images or pictures of the dead, and chairs for the mourners to sit in when they come to lament. That is so Frenchy.

Our rooms are on the Rue de Rivoli, and, sitting in the balcony, we look up and down the long, brilliant street. It is so pleasant that we spend our evenings talking there, when too tired with our day's work to go out. Fred is very entertaining, and is altogether the most agreeable young man I ever knew—except Laurie, whose manners are more charming. I wish Fred was dark, for I don't fancy light men; however, the Vaughns are very rich, and come of an excellent family, so I won't find fault with their yellow hair, as my own is yellower.

Next week we are off to Germany and Switzerland; and as we shall travel fast, I shall only be able to give you hasty letters. I keep my diary, and try to "remember correctly and describe clearly all that I see and admire," as father advised. It is good practice for me, and, with my sketchbook, will give you a better idea of my tour than these scribbles.

Adieu; I embrace you tenderly.

Votre Amie

MY DEAR MAMMA:

Having a quiet hour before we leave for Berne, I'll try to tell you what has happened, for some of it is very important, as you will see.

The sail up the Rhine was perfect, and I just sat and enjoyed it with all my might. Get father's old guidebooks, and read about it; I haven't words beautiful enough to describe it. At Coblentz we had a lovely time, for some students from Bonn, with whom Fred got acquainted on the boat, gave us a serenade. It was a moonlight night, and, about one o'clock, Flo and I were waked by the most delicious music under our windows. We flew up, and hid behind the curtains; but sly peeps showed us Fred and the students singing away down below. It was the most romantic thing I ever saw—the river, the bridge, the boats, the great fortress opposite, moonlight everywhere, and music fit to melt a heart of stone.

When they were done we threw down some flowers, and saw them scramble for them, kiss their hands to the invisible ladies, and go laughing away—to smoke and drink beer, I suppose. Next morning Fred showed me one of the crumpled flowers in his vest pocket, and looked very sentimental. I laughed at him, and said I didn't throw it, but Flo, which seemed to disgust him, for he tossed it out of the window, and turned sensible again. I'm afraid I'm going to have trouble with that boy, it begins to look like it.

The Baths at Nassau were very gay, so was Baden-Baden, where Fred lost some money, and I scolded him. He needs someone to look after him when Frank is not with him. Kate said once she hoped he'd marry soon, and I quite agree with her that it would be well for him. Frankfort was delightful; I saw Goethe's house, Schiller's statue, and Dannecker's famous "Ariadne." It was very lovely, but I should have enjoyed it more if I had known the story better. I didn't like to ask, as everyone knew it or pretended they did. I wish Jo would tell me all about it; I ought to have read more, for I find I don't know anything, and it mortifies me.

Now comes the serious part—for it happened here, and

Fred is just gone. He has been so kind and jolly that we all got quite fond of him; I never thought of anything but a travel-ing friendship, till the serenade night. Since then I've begun to feel that the moonlight walks, balcony talks, and daily ad-ventures were something more to him than fun. I haven't flirted, mother, truly, but remembered what you said to me, and have done my very best. I can't help it if people like me; I don't try to make them, and it worries me if I don't care for them, though Jo says I haven't got any heart. Now I know mother will shake her head, and the girls say, "Oh, the merce-nary little wretch!" but I've made up my mind, and, if Fred asks me, I shall accept him, though I'm not madly in love. I like him, and we get on comfortably together. He is handsome, young, clever enough, and very rich—ever so much richer than the Laurences. I don't think his family would object, and I should be very happy, for they are all kind, well-bred, gen-erous people, and they like me. Fred, as the eldest twin, will have the estate, I suppose, and such a splendid one as it is! A city house in a fashionable street, not so showy as our big houses, but twice as comfortable, and full of solid luxury, such as English people believe in. I like it, for it's genuine. I've seen the plate, the family jewels, the old servants, and pictures of the country place, with its park, great house, lovely grounds, and fine horses. Oh, it would be all I should ask! And I'd rather have it than any title such as girls snap up so readily, and find nothing behind. I may be mercenary, but I hate pov-erty, and don't mean to bear it a minute longer than I can help. One of us *must* marry well; Meg didn't, Jo won't, Beth can't yet, so I shall, and make everything cozy all round. I wouldn't marry a man I hated or despised. You may be sure of that, and, though Fred is not my model hero, he does very well, and, in time, I should get fond enough of him if he was very fond of me, and let me do just as I liked. So I've been turning the matter over in my mind the last week, for it was impossible to help seeing that Fred liked me. He said nothing, but little things showed it; he never goes with Flo, always gets on my side of the carriage, table, or promenade, looks senti-mental when we are alone, and frowns at anyone else who ventures to speak to me. Yesterday, at dinner, when an Austrian officer stared at us, and then said something to his friend —a rakish-looking baron—about *"ein wunderschönes Blöndchen,"* Fred looked as fierce as a lion, and cut his meat so savagely, it nearly flew off his plate. He isn't one of the cool, stiff Englishmen, but is rather peppery, for he has Scotch blood in him, as one might guess from his bonnie blue eyes.

Well, last evening we went up to the castle about sunset— at least all of us but Fred, who was to meet us there, after going to the Poste Restante for letters. We had a charming time poking about the ruins, the vaults where the monster tun is, and the beautiful gardens made by the elector, long ago, for his English wife. I liked the great terrace best, for the view was divine; so, while the rest went to see the rooms inside, I sat there trying to sketch the gray stone lion's head on the wall, with scarlet woodbine sprays hanging round it. I felt as if I'd got into a romance, sitting there, watching the Neckar rolling through the valley, listening to the music of the Austrian band below, and waiting for my lover, like a real storybook girl. I had a feeling that something was going to happen, and I was ready for it. I didn't feel blushy or quaky, but quite cool, and only a little excited.

By and by I heard Fred's voice, and then he came hurrying through the great arch to find me. He looked so troubled that I forgot all about myself, and asked what the matter was. He said he'd just got a letter begging him to come home, for Frank was very ill; so he was going at once, in the night train, and only had time to say good-by. I was very sorry for him, and disappointed for myself, but only for a minute, because he said, as he shook hands—and said it in a way that I could not mistake—"I shall soon come back; you won't forget me, Amy?"

I didn't promise, but I looked at him, and he seemed satisfied, and there was no time for anything but messages and good-bys, for he was off in an hour, and we all miss him very much. I know he wanted to speak, but I think, from something he once hinted, that he had promised his father not to do anything of the sort yet awhile, for he is a rash boy, and the old gentleman dreads a foreign daughter-in-law. We shall soon meet in Rome; and then, if I don't change my mind, I'll say "Yes, thank you," when he says "Will you, please?"

Of course this is all *very private*, but I wished you to know what was going on. Don't be anxious about me; remember I am your "prudent Amy," and be sure I will do nothing rashly. Send me as much advice as you like; I'll use it if I can. I wish I could see you for a good talk, Marmee. Love and trust me.

Ever your

AMY

CHAPTER THIRTY-TWO

Tender Troubles

"JO, I'm anxious about Beth."

"Why, mother, she has seemed unusually well since the babies came."

"It's not her health that troubles me now; it's her spirits. I'm sure there is something on her mind, and I want you to discover what it is."

"What makes you think so, mother?"

"She sits alone a good deal, and doesn't talk to her father as much as she used. I found her crying over the babies the other day. When she sings, the songs are always sad ones, and now and then I see a look in her face that I don't understand. This isn't like Beth, and it worries me."

"Have you asked her about it?"

"I have tried once or twice; but she either evaded my questions or looked so distressed that I stopped. I never force my children's confidence, and I seldom have to wait for it long."

Mrs. March glanced at Jo as she spoke, but the face opposite seemed quite unconscious of any secret disquietude but Beth's, and, after sewing thoughtfully for a minute, Jo said:

"I think she is growing up, and so begins to dream dreams, and have hopes and fears and fidgets, without knowing why, or being able to explain them. Why, mother, Beth's eighteen, but we don't realize it, and treat her like a child, forgetting she's a woman."

"So she is. Dear heart, how fast you do grow up," returned her mother, with a sigh and a smile.

"Can't be helped, Marmee, so you must resign yourself to all sorts of worries, and let your birds hop out of the nest, one by one. I promise never to hop very far, if that is any comfort to you."

"It's a great comfort, Jo; I always feel strong when you are at home, now Meg is gone. Beth is too feeble and Amy too young to depend upon; but when the tug comes, you are always ready."

"Why, you know I don't mind hard jobs much, and there must always be one scrub in a family. Amy is splendid in fine works, and I'm not; but I feel in my element when all the carpets are to be taken up, or half the family fall sick at once. Amy is distinguishing herself abroad; but if anything is amiss at home, I'm your man."

"I leave Beth to your hands, then, for she will open her tender little heart to her Jo sooner than to anyone else. Be very kind, and don't let her think anyone watches or talks about her. If she only would get quite strong and cheerful again, I shouldn't have a wish in the world."

"Happy woman! I've got heaps."

"My dear, what are they?"

"I'll settle Bethy's troubles, and then I'll tell you mine. They are not very wearing, so they'll keep," and Jo stitched away, with a wise nod which set her mother's heart at rest about her, for the present at least.

While apparently absorbed in her own affairs, Jo watched Beth; and, after many conflicting conjectures, finally settled upon one which seemed to explain the change in her. A slight incident gave Jo the clue to the mystery, she thought, and lively fancy, loving heart did the rest. She was affecting to write busily one Saturday afternoon, when she and Beth were alone together; yet as she scribbled, she kept her eye on her sister, who seemed unusually quiet. Sitting at the window, Beth's work often dropped into her lap, and she leaned her head upon her hand, in a dejected attitude, while her eyes rested on the dull, autumnal landscape. Suddenly someone passed below, whistling like an operatic blackbird, and a voice called out:

"All serene! Coming in tonight."

Beth started, leaned forward, smiled and nodded, watched the passer-by till his quick tramp died away, then said softly as if to herself:

"How strong and well and happy that dear boy looks."

"Hum!" said Jo, still intent upon her sister's face; for the bright color faded as quickly as it came, the smile vanished and presently a tear lay shining on the window ledge. Beth whisked it off, and glanced apprehensively at Jo; but she was scratching away at a tremendous rate, apparently engrossed in "Olympia's Oath." The instant Beth turned, Jo began her watch again, saw Beth's hand go quietly to her eyes more than once, and, in her half-averted face, read a tender sorrow that made her own eyes fill. Fearing to betray herself, she slipped away, murmuring something about needing more paper.

"Mercy on me, Beth loves Laurie!" she said, sitting down in her own room, pale with the shock of the discovery which she believed she had just made. "I never dreamt of such a thing. What *will* mother say? I wonder if"—there Jo stopped, and turned scarlet with a sudden thought. "If he shouldn't love back again, how dreadful it would be. He must; I'll make him!" and she shook her head threateningly at the picture of the mischievous-looking boy laughing at her from the wall. "Oh, dear, we *are* growing up with a vengeance. Here's Meg married and a mamma, Amy flourishing away at Paris, and Beth in love. I'm the only one that has sense enough to keep out of mischief." Jo thought intently for a minute, with her eyes fixed on the picture; then she smoothed out her wrinkled forehead, and said, with a decided nod at the face opposite, "No, thank you, sir; you're very charming, but you've no more stability than a weathercock; so you needn't write touching notes, and smile in that insinuating way, for it won't do a bit of good, and I won't have it."

Then she sighed, and fell into a reverie, from which she did not wake till the early twilight sent her down to take new observations, which only confirmed her suspicion. Though Laurie flirted with Amy and joked with Jo, his manner to Beth had always been peculiarly kind and gentle, but so was everybody's; therefore, no one thought of imagining that he cared more for her than for the others. Indeed, a general impression had prevailed in the family, of late, that "our boy" was getting fonder than ever of Jo, who, however, wouldn't hear a word upon the subject, and scolded violently if anyone dared to suggest it. If they had known the various tender passages of the past year, or rather attempts at tender passages which had been nipped in the bud, they would have had the immense satisfaction of saying, "I told you so." But Jo hated "philandering," and wouldn't allow it, always having a joke or a smile ready at the least sign of impending danger.

When Laurie first went to college, he fell in love about once a month; but these small flames were as brief as ardent, did no damage, and much amused Jo, who took great interest in the alternations of hope, despair, and resignation, which were confided to her in their weekly conferences. But there came a time when Laurie ceased to worship at many shrines, hinted darkly at one all-absorbing passion, and indulged occasionally in Byronic fits of gloom. Then he avoided the tender subject altogether, wrote philosophical notes to Jo, turned studious, and gave out that he was going to "dig," intending to graduate in a blaze of glory. This suited the young lady better than twilight confidences, tender pressures of the hand, and eloquent glances of the eye; for with Jo, brain developed earlier than heart, and she preferred imaginary heroes to real ones, because, when tired of them, the former could be shut up in the tin kitchen till called for, and the latter were less manageable.

Things were in this state when the grand discovery was

made, and Jo watched Laurie that night as she had never done before. If she had not got the new idea into her head, she would have seen nothing unusual in the fact that Beth was very quiet, and Laurie very kind to her. But having given the rein to her lively fancy, it galloped away with her at a great pace; and common sense, being rather weakened by a long course of romance writing, did not come to the rescue. As usual, Beth lay on the sofa, and Laurie sat in a low chair close by, amusing her with all sorts of gossip; for she depended on her weekly "spin," and he never disappointed her. But that evening, Jo fancied that Beth's eyes rested on the lively, dark face beside her with peculiar pleasure, and that she listened with intense interest to an account of some exciting cricket match, though the phrases "caught off a tice," "stumped off his ground," and "the leg hit for three," were as intelligible to her as Sanskrit. She also fancied, having set her heart upon seeing it, that she saw a certain increase of gentleness in Laurie's manner, that he dropped his voice now and then, laughed less than usual, was a little absent-minded, and settled the afghan over Beth's feet with an assiduity that was really almost tender.

"Who knows? Stranger things have happened," thought Jo, as she fussed about the room. "She will make quite an angel of him, and he will make life delightfully easy and pleasant for the dear, if they only love each other. I don't see how he can help it; and I do believe he would if the rest of us were out of the way."

As everyone *was* out of the way but herself, Jo began to feel that she ought to dispose of herself with all speed. But where should she go? And burning to lay herself upon the shrine of sisterly devotion, she sat down to settle that point.

Now, the old sofa was a regular patriarch of a sofa—long, broad, well cushioned, and low; a trifle shabby, as well it might be, for the girls had slept and sprawled on it as babies, fished over the back, rode on the arms, and had menageries under it as children, and rested tired heads, dreamed dreams, and listened to tender talk on it as young women. They all loved it, for it was a family refuge, and one corner had always been Jo's favorite lounging place. Among the many pillows that

adorned the venerable couch was one, hard, round, covered
with prickly horse hair and furnished with a knobby button
at each end; this repulsive pillow was her especial property,
being used as a weapon of defense, a barricade, or a stern
preventive of too much slumber.

Laurie knew this pillow well, and had cause to regard it
with deep aversion, having been unmercifully pummeled with
it in former days when romping was allowed, and now frequently debarred by it from taking the seat he most coveted,
next to Jo in the sofa corner. If "the sausage," as they called it,
stood on an end, it was a sign that he might approach and repose; but if it lay flat across the sofa, woe to the man, woman,
or child who dared disturb it! That evening Jo forgot to barricade her corner, and had not been in her seat five minutes,
before a massive form appeared beside her, and, with both
arms spread over the sofa back, both long legs stretched out
before him, Laurie exclaimed, with a sigh of satisfaction:

"Now, *this* is filling at the price."

"No slang," snapped Jo, slamming down the pillow. But it
was too late, there was no room for it; and coasting on to the
floor, it disappeared in a most mysterious manner.

"Come, Jo, don't be thorny. After studying himself to a
skeleton all the week, a fellow deserves petting, and ought to
get it."

"Beth will pet you; I'm busy."

"No, she's not to be bothered with me; but you like that sort
of thing, unless you've suddenly lost your taste for it. Have
you? Do you hate your boy, and want to fire pillows at him?"

Anything more wheedlesome than that touching appeal
was seldom heard, but Jo quenched "her boy" by turning on
him with the stern query:

"How many bouquets have you sent Miss Randal this week?"

"Not one, upon my word. She's engaged. Now then."

"I'm glad of it; that's one of your foolish extravagances—
sending flowers and things to girls for whom you don't care
two pins," continued Jo reprovingly.

"Sensible girls, for whom I do care whole papers of pins,
won't let me send them 'flowers and things,' so what can I do?
My feelings must have a *went*."

"Mother doesn't approve of flirting, even in fun; and you do flirt desperately, Teddy."

"I'd give anything if I could answer, 'So do you.' As I can't, I'll merely say that I don't see any harm in that pleasant little game, if all parties understand that it's only play."

"Well, it does look pleasant, but I can't learn how it's done. I've tried, because one feels awkward in company, not to do as everybody else is doing; but I don't seem to get on," said Jo, forgetting to play Mentor.

"Take lessons of Amy; she has a regular talent for it."

"Yes, she does it very prettily, and never seems to go too far. I suppose it's natural to some people to please without trying, and others to always say and do the wrong thing in the wrong place."

"I'm glad you can't flirt; it's really refreshing to see a sensible, straightforward girl, who can be jolly and kind without making a fool of herself. Between ourselves, Jo, some of the girls I know really do go on at such a rate I'm ashamed of them. They don't mean any harm, I'm sure; but if they knew how we fellows talked about them afterward, they'd mend their ways, I fancy."

"They do the same; and, as their tongues are the sharpest, you fellows get the worst of it, for you are as silly as they, every bit. If you behaved properly, they would; but, knowing you like their nonsense, they keep it up, and then you blame them."

"Much you know about it, ma'am," said Laurie, in a superior tone. "We don't like romps and flirts, though we may act as if we did sometimes. The pretty, modest girls are never talked about, except respectfully, among gentlemen. Bless your innocent soul! If you could be in my place for a month you'd see things that would astonish you a trifle. Upon my word, when I see one of those harum-scarum girls, I always want to say with our friend Cock Robin:

"'Out upon you, fie upon you,
    Bold-faced jig!'"

It was impossible to help laughing at the funny conflict between Laurie's chivalrous reluctance to speak ill of womankind and his very natural dislike of the unfeminine folly of which fashionable society showed him many samples. Jo knew that "young Laurence" was regarded as a most eligible *parti* by worldly mammas, was much smiled upon by their daughters, and flattered enough by ladies of all ages to make a coxcomb of him; so she watched him rather jealously, fearing he would be spoilt, and rejoiced more than she confessed to find that he still believed in modest girls. Returning suddenly to her admonitory tone, she said, dropping her voice, "If you *must* have a 'went,' Teddy, go and devote yourself to one of the 'pretty modest girls' whom you do respect, and not waste your time with the silly ones."

"You really advise it?" and Laurie looked at her with an odd mixture of anxiety and merriment in his face.

"Yes, I do; but you'd better wait till you are through college, on the whole, and be fitting yourself for the place meantime. You're not half good enough for—well, whoever the modest girl may be," and Jo looked a little queer likewise, for a name had almost escaped her.

"That I'm not!" acquiesced Laurie, with an expression of humility quite new to him, as he dropped his eyes and absently wound Jo's apron tassel round his finger.

"Mercy on us, this will never do," thought Jo; adding aloud. "Go and sing to me. I'm dying for some music, and always like yours."

"I'd rather stay here, thank you."

"Well, you can't; there isn't room. Go and make yourself useful, since you are too big to be ornamental. I thought you hated to be tied to a woman's apron string?" retorted Jo, quoting certain rebellious words of his own.

"Ah, that depends on who wears the apron!" and Laurie gave an audacious tweak at the tassel.

"Are you going?" demanded Jo, diving for the pillow.

He fled at once, and the minute it was well "Up with the bonnets of bonnie Dundee," she slipped away, to return no more till the young gentleman had departed in high dudgeon.

Jo lay long awake that night, and was just dropping off when the sound of a stifled sob made her fly to Beth's bedside, with the anxious inquiry, "What is it, dear?"

"I thought you were asleep," sobbed Beth.

"Is it the old pain, my precious?"

"No; it's a new one; but I can bear it," and Beth tried to check her tears.

"Tell me all about it, and let me cure it as I often did the other."

"You can't; there is no cure." There Beth's voice gave way, and, clinging to her sister, she cried so despairingly that Jo was frightened.

"Where is it? Shall I call mother?"

Beth did not answer the first question; but in the dark one

hand went involuntarily to her heart, as if the pain were there;
with the other she held Jo fast, whispering eagerly, "No, no,
don't call her, don't tell her. I shall be better soon. Lie down
here and 'poor' my head. I'll be quiet, and go to sleep; indeed
I will."

Jo obeyed; but as her hand went softly to and fro across
Beth's hot forehead and wet eyelids, her heart was very full,
and she longed to speak. But young as she was, Jo had learned
that hearts, like flowers, cannot be rudely handled, but must
open naturally; so, though she believed she knew the cause of
Beth's new pain, she only said, in her tenderest tone, "Does
anything trouble you, deary?"

"Yes, Jo," after a long pause.

"Wouldn't it comfort you to tell me what it is?"

"Not now, not yet."

"Then I won't ask; but remember, Beth, that mother and Jo
are always glad to hear and help you, if they can."

"I know it. I'll tell you by and by."

"Is the pain better now?"

"Oh, yes, much better. You are so comfortable, Jo!"

"Go to sleep, dear; I'll stay with you."

So cheek to cheek they fell asleep, and on the morrow Beth
seemed quite herself again; for at eighteen, neither heads nor
hearts ache long, and a loving word can medicine most ills.

But Jo had made up her mind, and, after pondering over a
project for some days, she confided it to her mother.

"You asked me the other day what my wishes were. I'll tell
you one of them, Marmee," she began, as they sat alone together. "I want to go away somewhere this winter for a
change."

"Why, Jo?" and her mother looked up quickly, as if the
words suggested a double meaning.

With her eyes on her work, Jo answered soberly, "I want
something new; I feel restless, and anxious to be seeing, doing,
and learning more than I am. I brood too much over my own
small affairs, and need stirring up, so, as I can be spared this
winter, I'd like to hop a little way, and try my wings."

"Where will you hop?"

"To New York. I had a bright idea yesterday, and this is it.

You know Mrs. Kirke wrote to you for some respectable young person to teach her children and sew. It's rather hard to find just the thing, but I think I should suit if I tried."

"My dear, go out to service in that great boardinghouse!" And Mrs. March looked surprised, but not displeased.

"It's not exactly going out to service; for Mrs. Kirke is your friend—the kindest soul that ever lived—and would make things pleasant for me, I know. Her family is separate from the rest, and no one knows me there. Don't care if they do; it's honest work, and I'm not ashamed of it."

"Nor I; but your writing?"

"All the better for the change. I shall see and hear new things, get new ideas, and, even if I haven't much time there, I shall bring home quantities of new material for my rubbish."

"I have no doubt of it; but are these your only reasons for this sudden fancy?"

"No, mother."

"May I know the others?"

Jo looked up and Jo looked down, then said slowly, with sudden color in her cheeks, "It may be vain and wrong to say it, but—I'm afraid—Laurie is getting too fond of me."

"Then you don't care for him in the way it is evident he begins to care for you?" and Mrs. March looked anxious as she put the question.

"Mercy, no! I love the dear boy, as I always have, and am immensely proud of him; but as for anything more, it's out of the question."

"I'm glad of that, Jo."

"Why, please?"

"Because, dear, I don't think you are suited to one another. As friends you are very happy, and your frequent quarrels soon blow over; but I fear you would both rebel if you were mated for life. You are too much alike and too fond of freedom, not to mention hot tempers and strong wills, to get on happily together, in a relation which needs infinite patience and forbearance, as well as love."

"That's just the feeling I had, though I couldn't express it. I'm glad you think he is only beginning to care for me. It would trouble me sadly to make him unhappy; for I couldn't fall in love with the dear fellow merely out of gratitude, could I?"

"You are sure of his feeling for you?"

The color deepened in Jo's cheeks, as she answered, with the look of mingled pleasure, pride, and pain which young girls wear when speaking of first lovers:

"I'm afraid it is so, mother; he hasn't said anything, but he looks a great deal. I think I had better go away before it comes to anything."

"I agree with you, and if it can be managed you shall go."

Jo looked relieved, and, after a pause, said, smiling, "How Mrs. Moffat would wonder at your want of management, if she knew; and how she will rejoice that Annie still may hope."

"Ah, Jo, mothers may differ in their management, but the hope is the same in all—the desire to see their children happy. Meg is so, and I am content with her success. You I leave to enjoy your liberty till you tire of it; for only then will you find that there is something sweeter. Amy is my chief care now, but her good sense will help her. For Beth, I indulge no hopes except that she may be well. By the way, she seems brighter this last day or two. Have you spoken to her?"

"Yes; she owned she had a trouble, and promised to tell me by and by. I said no more, for I think I know it," and Jo told her little story.

Mrs. March shook her head, and did not take so romantic a view of the case, but looked grave, and repeated her opinion that, for Laurie's sake, Jo should go away for a time.

"Let us say nothing about it to him till the plan is settled; then I'll run away before he can collect his wits and be tragical. Beth must think I'm going to please myself, as I am, for I can't talk about Laurie to her; but she can pet and comfort him after I'm gone, and so cure him of this romantic notion. He's been through so many little trials of the sort, he's used to it, and will soon get over his lovelornity."

Jo spoke hopefully, but could not rid herself of the foreboding fear that this "little trial" would be harder than the others, and that Laurie would not get over his "lovelornity" as easily as heretofore.

The plan was talked over in a family council, and agreed upon; for Mrs. Kirke gladly accepted Jo, and promised to make a pleasant home for her. The teaching would render her independent; and such leisure as she got might be made profitable by writing, while the new scenes and society would be both useful and agreeable. Jo liked the prospect and was eager to be gone, for the home nest was growing too narrow for her restless nature and adventurous spirit. When all was settled, with fear and trembling she told Laurie; but to her surprise he took it very quietly. He had been graver than usual of late, but very pleasant; and, when jokingly accused of turning over a new leaf, he answered soberly, "So I am; and I mean this one shall stay turned."

Jo was very much relieved that one of his virtuous fits should come on just then, and made her preparations with a lightened heart—for Beth seemed more cheerful—and hoped she was doing the best for all.

"One thing I leave to your especial care," she said, the night before she left.

"You mean your papers?" asked Beth.

"No, my boy. Be very good to him, won't you?"

"Of course I will; but I can't fill your place, and he'll miss you sadly."

"It won't hurt him; so remember, I leave him in your charge to plague, pet, and keep in order."

"I'll do my best, for your sake," promised Beth, wondering why Jo looked at her so queerly.

When Laurie said "Good-by," he whispered significantly, "It won't do a bit of good, Jo. My eye is on you; so mind what you do, or I'll come and bring you home."

CHAPTER THIRTY-THREE

Jo's Journal

ᗡᐧDEAR MARMEE AND BETH:

I'm going to write you a regular volume, for I've got heaps
to tell you, though I'm not a fine young lady traveling on the
continent. When I lost sight of father's dear old face, I felt a
trifle blue, and might have shed a briny drop or two, if an
Irish lady with four small children, all crying more or less,
hadn't diverted my mind; for I amused myself by dropping
gingerbread nuts over the seat every time they opened their
mouths to roar.

Soon the sun came out, and taking it as a good omen, I
cleared up likewise, and enjoyed my journey with all my heart.

Mrs. Kirke welcomed me so kindly I felt at home at once,

even in that big house full of strangers. She gave me a funny little sky-parlor—all she had; but there is a stove in it, and a nice table in a sunny window, so I can sit here and write whenever I like. A fine view and a church tower opposite atone for the many stairs, and I took a fancy to my den on the spot. The nursery, where I am to teach and sew, is a pleasant room next to Mrs. Kirke's private parlor, and the two little girls are pretty children—rather spoilt, I fancy, but they took to me after telling them "The Seven Bad Pigs!" and I've no doubt I shall make a model governess.

I am to have my meals with the children, if I prefer it to the great table, and for the present I do, for I *am* bashful, though no one will believe it.

"Now, my dear, make yourself at home," said Mrs. K. in her motherly way; "I'm on the drive from morning to night, as you may suppose with such a family; but a great anxiety will be off my mind if I know the children are safe with you. My rooms are always open to you, and your own shall be as comfortable as I can make it. There are some pleasant people in the house if you feel sociable, and your evenings are always free. Come to me if anything goes wrong, and be as happy as you can. There's the tea bell; I must run and change my cap"; and off she bustled, leaving me to settle myself in my new nest.

As I went downstairs, soon after, I saw something I liked. The flights are very long in this tall house, and as I stood waiting at the head of the third one for a little servantgirl to lumber up, I saw a gentleman come along behind her, take the heavy hod of coal out of her hand, carry it all the way up, put it down at a door near by, and walk away, saying, with a kind nod and a foreign accent:

"It goes better so. The little back is too young to haf such heaviness."

Wasn't it good of him? I like such things, for, as father says, trifles show character. When I mentioned it to Mrs. K., that evening, she laughed, and said:

"That must have been Professor Bhaer; he's always doing things of that sort."

Mrs. K. told me he was from Berlin; very learned and good,

but poor as a church mouse, and gives lessons to support himself and two little orphan nephews whom he is educating here,
according to the wishes of his sister, who married an American.
Not a very romantic story, but it interested me; and I was glad
to hear that Mrs. K. lends him her parlor for some of his
scholars. There is a glass door between it and the nursery, and
I mean to peep at him, and then I'll tell you how he looks. He's
almost forty, so it's no harm, Marmee.

After tea and a go-to-bed romp with the little girls, I attacked the big workbasket, and had a quiet evening with my
new friend. I shall keep a journal-letter, and send it once a
week; so good night, and more tomorrow.

Tuesday Eve

Had a lively time in my seminary, this morning, for the
children acted like Sancho; and at one time I really thought I
should shake them all round. Some good angel inspired me to
try gymnastics, and I kept it up till they were glad to sit down
and keep still. After luncheon, the girl took them out for a
walk, and I went to my needlework, like little Mabel, "with a
willing mind." I was thanking my stars that I'd learned to make
nice buttonholes, when the parlor door opened and shut and
someone began to hum:

"Kennst du das land,"

like a big bumblebee. It was dreadfully improper, I know, but
I couldn't resist the temptation; and lifting one end of the
curtain before the glass door, I peeped in. Professor Bhaer was
there; and while he arranged his books, I took a good look at
him. A regular German—rather stout, with brown hair tumbled
all over his head, a bushy beard, good nose, the kindest eyes I
ever saw, and a splendid big voice that does one's ears good,
after our sharp or slipshod American gabble. His clothes were
rusty, his hands were large, and he hadn't a really handsome
feature in his face, except his beautiful teeth; yet I liked him,
for he had a fine head; his linen was very nice, and he looked
like a gentleman, though two buttons were off his coat, and
there was a patch on one shoe. He looked sober in spite of his

humming, till he went to the window to turn the hyacinth bulbs toward the sun, and stroke the cat, who received him like an old friend. Then he smiled; and when a tap came at the door, called out in a loud, brisk tone:

"Herein!"

I was just going to run, when I caught sight of a morsel of a child carrying a big book, and stopped to see what was going on.

"Me wants my Bhaer," said the mite, slamming down her book, and running to meet him.

"Thou shalt haf thy Bhaer; come, then, and take a goot hug from him, my Tina," said the professor, catching her up, with a laugh, and holding her so high over his head that she had to stoop her little face to kiss him.

"Now me mus tuddy my lessin," went on the funny little thing; so he put her up at the table, opened the great dictionary she had brought, and gave her a paper and pencil, and she scribbled away, turning a leaf now and then, and passing her little fat finger down the page, as if finding a word, so soberly that I nearly betrayed myself by a laugh, while Mr. Bhaer stood stroking her pretty hair, with a fatherly look, that made me think she must be his own, though she looked more French than German.

Another knock and the appearance of two young ladies sent me back to my work, and there I virtuously remained through all the noise and gabbling that went on next door. One of the girls kept laughing affectedly, and saying, "Now, professor," in a coquettish tone, and the other pronounced her German with an accent that must have made it hard for him to keep sober.

Both seemed to try his patience sorely; for more than once I heard him say emphatically, "No, no, it is *not* so; you haf not listened to what I say"; and once there was a loud rap, as if he struck the table with his book, followed by the despairing exclamation, "Prut! It all goes bad this day."

Poor man, I pitied him; and when the girls were gone, took just one more peep, to see if he survived it. He seemed to have thrown himself back in his chair, tired out, and sat there with his eyes shut till the clock struck two, when he jumped up, put his books in his pocket, as if ready for another lesson, and taking little Tina, who had fallen asleep on the sofa, in his arms, he carried her quietly away. I fancy he has a hard life of it.

Mrs. Kirke asked me if I wouldn't go down to the five, o'clock dinner; and, feeling a little bit homesick, I thought I would, just to see what sort of people are under the same roof with me. So I made myself respectable, and tried to slip in behind Mrs. Kirke; but as she is short, and I'm tall, my efforts at concealment were rather a failure. She gave me a seat by her, and after my face had cooled off I plucked up courage and looked about me. The long table was full, and everyone intent on getting their dinner—the gentlemen especially, who seemed to be eating on time, for they *bolted* in every sense of the word, vanishing as soon as they were done. There was the usual assortment of young men absorbed in themselves; young couples absorbed in each other; married ladies in their babies, and old gentlemen in politics. I don't think I shall care to have much to do with any of them, except one sweet-faced maiden lady who looks as if she had something in her.

Cast away at the very bottom of the table was the professor, shouting answers to the questions of a very inquisitive, deaf old gentleman on one side, and talking philosophy with a Frenchman on the other. If Amy had been here, she'd have turned her back on him forever, because, sad to relate, he had a great appetite, and shoveled in his dinner in a manner which would have horrified "her ladyship." I didn't mind, for I like "to see folks eat with a relish," as Hannah says, and the poor man must have needed a deal of food after teaching idiots all day.

As I went upstairs after dinner, two of the young men were settling their hats before the hall mirror, and I heard one say low to the other, "Who's the new party?"

"Governess, or something of that sort."

"What the deuce is she at our table for?"

"Friend of the old lady's."

"Handsome head, but no style."

"Not a bit of it. Give us a light and come on."

I felt angry at first, and then I didn't care, for a governess is as good as a clerk, and I've got sense, if I haven't style, which is more than some people have, judging from the remarks of the elegant beings who clattered away, smoking like bad chimneys. I hate ordinary people!

Thursday

Yesterday was a quiet day, spent in teaching, sewing, and writing in my little room, which is very cozy, with a light and fire. I picked up a few bits of news, and was introduced to the professor. It seems that Tina is the child of the Frenchwoman who does the fine ironing in the laundry here. The little thing has lost her heart to Mr. Bhaer, and follows him about the house like a dog whenever he is at home, which delights him, as he is very fond of children, though a "bacheldore." Kitty and Minnie Kirke likewise regard him with affection, and tell all sorts of stories about the plays he invents, the presents he brings, and the splendid tales he tells. The young men quiz him, it seems, call him Old Fritz, Lager Beer, Ursa Major, and make all manner of jokes on his name. But he enjoys it like a boy, Mrs. K. says, and takes it so good-naturedly that they all like him, in spite of his foreign ways.

The maiden lady is a Miss Norton—rich, cultivated, and kind. She spoke to me at dinner today (for I went to table again, it's such fun to watch people) and asked me to come and see her at her room. She has fine books and pictures, knows interesting persons, and seems friendly; so I shall make myself agreeable, for I *do* want to get into good society, only it isn't the same sort that Amy likes.

I was in our parlor last evening, when Mr. Bhaer came in with some newspapers for Mrs. Kirke. She wasn't there, but Minnie, who is a little old woman, introduced me very prettily: "This is mamma's friend, Miss March."

"Yes; and she's jolly and we like her lots," added Kitty, who is an *enfant terrible*.

We both bowed, and then we laughed, for the prim introduction and the blunt addition were rather a comical contrast.

"Ah, yes, I hear these naughty ones go to vex you, Mees Marsch. If so again, call at me and I come," he said, with a threatening frown that delighted the little wretches.

I promised I would, and he departed; but it seems as if I was doomed to see a good deal of him, for today, as I passed his door on my way out, by accident I knocked against it with my umbrella. It flew open, and there he stood in his dressing gown, with a big blue sock in one hand, and a darning needle in the other; he didn't seem at all ashamed of it, for when I explained and hurried on, he waved his hand, sock and all, saying in his loud, cheerful way:

"You haf a fine day to make your walk. Bon voyage, mademoiselle."

I laughed all the way downstairs; but it was a little pathetic, also, to think of the poor man having to mend his own clothes. The German gentlemen embroider, I know; but darning hose is another thing, and not so pretty.

Saturday

Nothing has happened to write about, except a call on Miss Norton, who has a room full of lovely things, and who was very charming, for she showed me all her treasures, and asked me if I would sometimes go with her to lectures and concerts, as her escort—if I enjoyed them. She put it as a favor, but I'm sure Mrs. Kirke has told her about us, and she does it out of kindness to me. I'm as proud as Lucifer, but such favors from such people don't burden me, and I accepted gratefully.

When I got back to the nursery there was such an uproar in the parlor that I looked in; and there was Mr. Bhaer down on his hands and knees, with Tina on his back, Kitty leading him with a jump rope, and Minnie feeding two small boys with seedcakes, as they roared and ramped in cages built of chairs.

"We are playing *nargerie*," explained Kitty.

"Dis is mine effalunt!" added Tina, holding on by the professor's hair.

"Mamma always allows us to do what we like Saturday afternoons, when Franz and Emil come, doesn't she, Mr. Bhaer?" said Minnie.

The "effalunt" sat up, looking as much in earnest as any of them, and said soberly to me:

"I gif you my wort it is so. If we make too large a noise you shall say 'Hush!' to us, and we go more softly."

I promised to do so, but left the door open, and enjoyed the fun as much as they did—for a more glorious frolic I never witnessed. They played tag and soldiers, danced and sung, and when it began to grow dark they all piled on to the sofa about the professor, while he told charming fairy stories of the storks on the chimneytops, and the little "kobolds," who ride the snowflakes as they fall. I wish Americans were as simple and natural as Germans, don't you?

I'm so fond of writing, I should go spinning on forever if motives of economy didn't stop me; for though I've used thin paper and written fine, I tremble to think of the stamps this long letter will need. Pray forward Amy's as soon as you can spare them. My small news will sound very flat after her splendors, but you will like them, I know. Is Teddy studying so hard that he can't find time to write to his friends? Take good care of him for me, Beth, and tell me about the babies, and give heaps of love to everyone.

From your faithful   Jo

P.S. On reading over my letter it strikes me as rather Bhaery; but I am always interested in odd people, and I really had nothing else to write about. Bless you!

DECEMBER

MY PRECIOUS BETSEY:

As this is to be a scribble-scrabble letter, I direct it to you, for it may amuse you, and give you some idea of my goings-on; for, though quiet, they are rather amusing, for which, oh, be joyful! After what Amy would call Herculaneum efforts, in the way of mental and moral agriculture, my young ideas begin to shoot and my little twigs to bend as I would wish. They are not so interesting to me as Tina and the boys, but I do my duty by them, and they are fond of me. Franz and Emil are jolly little lads, quite after my own heart; for the mixture of German and American spirit in them produces a constant state of effervescence. Saturday afternoons are riotous times, whether spent in the house or out; for on pleasant days they all go to walk, like a seminary, with the professor and myself to keep order; and then such fun!

We are very good friends now, and I've begun to take lessons. I really couldn't help it, and it all came about in such a

droll way that I must tell you. To begin at the beginning, Mrs.
Kirke called to me, one day, as I passed Mr. Bhaer's room,
where she was rummaging.

"Did you ever see such a den, my dear? Just come and help
me put these books to rights, for I've turned everything upside
down, trying to discover what he has done with the six new
handkerchiefs I gave him not long ago."

I went in, and while we worked I looked about me, for it
was "a den," to be sure. Books and papers everywhere; a
broken meerschaum, and an old flute over the mantelpiece as
if done with; a ragged bird, without any tail, chirped on one
window seat, and a box of white mice adorned the other; half-
finished boats and bits of string lay among the manuscripts;
dirty little boots stood drying before the fire; and traces of the
dearly beloved boys, for whom he makes a slave of himself,
were to be seen all over the room. After a grand rummage three
of the missing articles were found—one over the bird cage, one
covered with ink, and a third burnt brown, having been used
as a holder.

"Such a man!" laughed good-natured Mrs. K., as she put the
relics in the rag bag. "I suppose the others are torn up to rig
ships, bandage cut fingers, or make kite-tails. It's dreadful, but
I can't scold him; he's so absent-minded and good-natured, he
lets those boys ride over him roughshod. I agreed to do his
washing and mending, but he forgets to give out his things and
I forget to look them over, so he comes to a sad pass sometimes."

"Let me mend them," I said. "I don't mind it, and he needn't
know. I'd like to—he's so kind to me about bringing my letters
and lending books."

So I have got his things in order, and knit heels into two
pairs of the socks—for they were boggled out of shape with his
queer darns. Nothing was said, and I hoped he wouldn't find
it out, but one day last week he caught me at it. Hearing the
lessons he gives to others has interested and amused me so
much that I took a fancy to learn; for Tina runs in and out,
leaving the door open, and I can hear. I had been sitting near
this door, finishing off the last sock, and trying to understand
what he said to a new scholar, who is as stupid as I am. The

girl had gone, and I thought he had also, it was so still, and I was busily gabbling over a verb, and rocking to and fro in a most absurd way, when a little crow made me look up, and there was Mr. Bhaer looking and laughing quietly, while he made signs to Tina not to betray him.

"So!" he said, as I stopped and stared like a goose, "you peep at me, I peep at you, and that is not bad; but see, I am not pleasanting when I say, haf you a wish for German?"

"Yes; but you are too busy. I am too stupid to learn," I blundered out, red as a peony.

"Prut! We will make the time, and we fail not to find the sense. At efening I shall gif a little lesson with much gladness; for, look you, Mees Marsch, I haf this debt to pay," and he pointed to my work. "'Yes,' they say to one another, these so kind ladies, 'he is a stupid old fellow; he will see not what we do; he will never opserve that his sock heels go not in holes any more, he will think his buttons grow out new when they fall, and believe that strings make theirselves.' Ah! but I haf an eye, and I see much. I haf a heart, and I feel the thanks for this. Come, a little lesson then and now, or no more good fairy works for me and mine."

Of course I couldn't say anything after that, and as it really is a splendid opportunity, I made the bargain, and we began. I took four lessons, and then I stuck fast in a grammatical bog. The professor was very patient with me, but it must have been a torment to him, and now and then he'd look at me with such an expression of mild despair that it was a toss-up with me whether to laugh or cry. I tried both ways; and when it came to a sniff of utter mortification and woe, he just threw the grammar onto the floor, and marched out of the room. I felt myself disgraced and deserted forever, but didn't blame him a particle, and was scrambling my papers together, meaning to rush upstairs and shake myself hard, when in he came, as brisk and beaming as if I'd covered myself with glory.

"Now we shall try a new way. You and I will read these pleasant little Märchen together, and dig no more in that dry book, that goes in the corner for making us trouble."

He spoke so kindly, and opened Hans Andersen's fairy tales so invitingly before me, that I was more ashamed than ever, and went at my lesson in a neck-or-nothing style that seemed to amuse him immensely. I forgot my bashfulness, and pegged away (no other word will express it) with all my might, tumbling over long words, pronouncing according to the inspiration of the minute, and doing my very best. When I finished reading my first page, and stopped for breath, he clapped his hands and cried out, in his hearty way, "Das ist gut! Now we go well! My turn. I do him in German; gif me your ear." And away he went, rumbling out the words with his strong voice, and a relish which was good to see as well as hear. Fortunately the story was the "Constant Tin Soldier," which is droll, you know, so I could laugh—and I did—though I didn't understand half he read, for I couldn't help it, he was so earnest, I so excited, and the whole thing so comical.

After that we got on better, and now I read my lessons pretty well; for this way of studying suits me, and I can see that the grammar gets tucked into the tales and poetry as one gives pills in jelly. I like it very much, and he doesn't seem tired of it yet—which is very good of him, isn't it? I mean to give him something on Christmas, for I dare not offer money. Tell me something nice, Marmee.

I'm glad Laurie seems so happy and busy, that he has given up smoking, and lets his hair grow. You see Beth manages him better than I did. I'm not jealous, dear; do your best, only don't make a saint of him. I'm afraid I couldn't like him without a spice of human naughtiness. Read him bits of my letters. I haven't time to write much, and that will do just as well. Thank Heaven, Beth continues so comfortable.

JANUARY

A Happy New Year to you all, my dearest family, which of course includes Mr. L. and a young man by the name of Teddy. I can't tell you how much I enjoyed your Christmas bundle, for I didn't get it till night, and had given up hoping. Your letter came in the morning, but you said nothing about a parcel, meaning it for a surprise; so I was disappointed, for I'd had a "kind of feeling" that you wouldn't forget me. I felt a little low in my mind, as I sat up in my room, after tea; and when the big, muddy, battered-looking bundle was brought to me, I just hugged it, and pranced. It was so *homey* and refreshing that I sat down on the floor and read and looked and ate and laughed and cried, in my usual absurd way. The things were just what I wanted, and all the better for being made instead of bought. Beth's new "ink bib" was capital; and Hannah's box of hard gingerbread will be a treasure. I'll be sure and wear the nice flannels you sent, Marmee, and read carefully the books father has marked. Thank you all, heaps and heaps.

Speaking of books reminds me that I'm getting rich in that line, for, on New Year's Day, Mr. Bhaer gave me a fine Shakespeare. It is one that he values much, and I've often admired it, set up in the place of honor, with his German Bible, Plato, Homer, and Milton; so you may imagine how I felt when he brought it down, without its cover, and showed me my name in it, "from your friend Friedrich Bhaer."

"You say often you wish a library: here I gif you one; for between these lids (he meant covers) is many books in one. Read him well, and he will help you much; for the study of character in this book will help you to read it in the world and paint it with your pen."

I thanked him as well as I could, and talk now about "my library," as if I had a hundred books. I never knew how much there was in Shakespeare before; but then I never had a Bhaer to explain it to me. Now *don't* laugh at his horrid name; it isn't pronounced either Bear or Beer, as people *will* say it, but something between the two, as only Germans can give it. I'm glad you both like what I tell you about him, and hope you will know him someday. Mother would admire his warm heart, father his wise head. I admire both, and feel rich in my new "friend Friedrich Bhaer."

Not having much money, or knowing what he'd like, I got several little things, and put them about the room, where he would find them unexpectedly. They were useful, pretty, or funny—a new standish on his table, a little vase for his flowers —he always has one, or a bit of green in a glass, to keep him fresh, he says—and a holder for his blower, so that he needn't burn up what Amy calls "mouchoirs." I made it like those Beth invented—a big butterfly with a fat body, and black and yellow wings, worsted feelers, and bead eyes. It took his fancy immensely, and he put it on his mantelpiece, as an article of *vertu;* so it was rather a failure, after all. Poor as he is, he didn't forget a servant or a child in the house; and not a soul here, from the French laundrywoman to Miss Norton, forgot him. I was so glad of that.

They got up a masquerade, and had a gay time New Year's Eve. I didn't mean to go down, having no dress; but at the last minute, Mrs. Kirke remembered some old brocades, and Miss Norton lent me lace and feathers; so I dressed up as Mrs. Malaprop, and sailed in with a mask on. No one knew me, for I disguised my voice, and no one dreamed the silent, haughty Miss March (for they think I am very stiff and cool, most of them; and so I am to whippersnappers) could dance and dress, and burst out into a "nice derangement of epitaphs, like an allegory on the banks of the Nile." I enjoyed it very much; and when we unmasked, it was fun to see them stare at me. I heard one of the young men tell another that he knew I'd been an actress; in fact, he thought he remembered seeing me at one of the minor theaters. Meg will relish that joke. Mr. Bhaer was Nick Bottom, and Tina was Titania—a perfect little fairy in his arms. To see them dance was "quite a landscape," to use a Teddyism.

I had a very happy New Year, after all; and when I thought it over in my room, I felt as if I was getting on a little in spite of my many failures; for I'm cheerful all the time now, work with a will, and take more interest in other people than I used to, which is satisfactory. Bless you all! Ever your loving

Jo

CHAPTER THIRTY-FOUR

A Friend

THOUGH very happy in the social atmosphere about her, and very busy with the daily work that earned her bread, and made it sweeter for the effort, Jo still found time for literary labors. The purpose which now took possession of her was a natural one to a poor and ambitious girl; but the means she took to gain her end were not the best. She saw that money conferred power; money and power, therefore, she resolved to have; not to be used for herself alone, but for those whom she loved more than self.

The dream of filling home with comforts, giving Beth everything she wanted, from strawberries in winter to an organ in her bedroom; going abroad herself, and always having *more* than enough, so that she might indulge in the luxury of charity, had been for years Jo's most cherished castle in the air.

The prize-story experience had seemed to open a way which might, after long traveling and much uphill work lead to this delightful *château en Espagne*. But the novel disaster quenched her courage for a time, for public opinion is a giant which has frightened stouterhearted Jacks on bigger beanstalks than hers. Like that immortal hero, she reposed awhile after the first attempt, which resulted in a tumble, and the least lovely of the giant's treasures, if I remember rightly. But the "up again and take another" spirit was as strong in Jo as in Jack, so she scrambled up, on the shady side this time, and got more booty, but nearly left behind her what was far more precious than the moneybags.

She took to writing sensation stories; for in those dark ages even all-perfect America read rubbish. She told no one, but concocted a "thrilling tale," and boldly carried it herself to Mr. Dashwood, editor of the "Weekly Volcano." She had never read "Sartor Resartus," but she had a womanly instinct that clothes possess an influence more powerful over many than the worth of character or the magic of manners. So she dressed herself in her best, and, trying to persuade herself that she was neither excited nor nervous, bravely climbed two pairs of dark and dirty stairs to find herself in a disorderly room, a cloud of cigar smoke, and the presence of three gentlemen, sitting with their heels rather higher than their hats, which articles of dress none of them took the trouble to remove on her appearance. Somewhat daunted by this reception, Jo hesitated on the threshold, murmuring in much embarrassment—"Excuse me, I was looking for the 'Weekly Volcano' office; I wished to see Mr. Dashwood."

Down went the highest pair of heels, up rose the smokiest gentleman, and, carefully cherishing his cigar between his fingers, he advanced, with a nod, and a countenance expressive of nothing but sleep. Feeling that she must get through the matter somehow, Jo produced her manuscript, and, blushing redder and redder with each sentence, blundered out fragments of the little speech carefully prepared for the occasion.

"A friend of mine desired me to offer—a story—just as an experiment—would like your opinion—be glad to write more if this suits."

While she blushed and blundered, Mr. Dashwood had taken the manuscript, and was turning over the leaves with a pair of rather dirty fingers, and casting critical glances up and down the neat pages.

"Not a first attempt, I take it?" observing that the pages were numbered, covered only on one side, and not tied up with a ribbon—sure sign of a novice.

"No, sir; she has had some experience, and got a prize for a tale in the 'Blarneystone Banner.'"

"Oh, did she?" and Mr. Dashwood gave Jo a quick look, which seemed to take note of everything she had on, from the

bow in her bonnet to the buttons on her boots. "Well, you can leave it, if you like. We've more of this sort of thing on hand than we know what to do with at present; but I'll run my eye over it, and give you an answer next week."

Now, Jo did *not* like to leave it, for Mr. Dashwood didn't suit her at all; but, under the circumstances, there was nothing for her to do but bow and walk away, looking particularly tall and dignified, as she was apt to do when nettled or abashed. Just then she was both; for it was perfectly evident, from the knowing glances exchanged among the gentlemen, that her little fiction of "my friend" was considered a good joke; and a laugh, produced by some inaudible remark of the editor, as he closed the door, completed her discomfiture. Half resolving never to return, she went home, and worked off her irritation by stitching pinafores vigorously; and in an hour or two was cool enough to laugh over the scene, and long for next week.

When she went again, Mr. Dashwood was alone, whereat she rejoiced; Mr. Dashwood was much wider awake than before, which was agreeable; and Mr. Dashwood was not too deeply absorbed in a cigar to remember his manners: so the second interview was much more comfortable than the first.

"We'll take this" (editors never say I) "if you don't object to a few alterations. It's too long, but omitting the passages I've marked will make it just the right length," he said, in a businesslike tone.

Jo hardly knew her own ms. again, so crumpled and underscored were its pages and paragraphs; but, feeling as a tender parent might on being asked to cut off her baby's legs in order that it might fit into a new cradle, she looked at the marked passages, and was surprised to find that all the moral reflections —which she had carefully put in as ballast for much romance —had been stricken out.

"But, sir, I thought every story should have some sort of a moral, so I took care to have a few of my sinners repent."

Mr. Dashwood's editorial gravity relaxed into a smile, for Jo had forgotten her "friend," and spoken as only an author could.

"People want to be amused, not preached at, you know. Morals don't sell nowadays," which was not quite a correct statement, by the way.

"You think it would do with these alterations, then?"

"Yes; it's a new plot, and pretty well worked up—language good, and so on" was Mr. Dashwood's affable reply.

"What do you—that is, what compensation—" began Jo, not exactly knowing how to express herself.

"Oh, yes, well, we give from twenty-five to thirty for things of this sort. Pay when it comes out," returned Mr. Dashwood, as if that point had escaped him; such trifles often do escape the editorial mind, it is said.

"Very well; you can have it," said Jo, handing back the story with a satisfied air; for, after the dollar-a-column work, even twenty-five dollars seemed good pay.

"Shall I tell my friend you will take another if she has one better than this?" asked Jo, unconscious of the little slip of the tongue, and emboldened by her success.

"Well, we'll look at it; can't promise to take it. Tell her to make it short and spicy, and never mind the moral. What name would your friend like to put to it?" in a careless tone.

"None at all, if you please; she doesn't wish her name to appear, and has no nom de plume," said Jo, blushing in spite of herself.

"Just as she likes, of course. The tale will be out next week; will you call for the money, or shall I send it?" asked Mr. Dashwood, who felt a natural desire to know who his new contributor might be.

"I'll call. Good morning, sir."

As she departed, Mr. Dashwood put up his feet, with the graceful remark, "Poor and proud, as usual, but she'll do."

Following Mr. Dashwood's directions, and making Mrs. Northbury her model, Jo rashly took a plunge into the frothy sea of sensational literature; but, thanks to the life preserver thrown her by a friend, she came up again, not much worse for her ducking.

Like most young scribblers, she went abroad for her characters and scenery; and banditti, counts, gypsies, nuns, and duchesses appeared upon her stage, and played their parts with as much accuracy and spirit as could be expected. Her readers were not particular about such trifles as grammar, punctuation, and probability, and Mr. Dashwood graciously permitted her to fill his columns at the lowest prices, not think-

ing it necessary to tell her that the real cause of his hospitality
was the fact that one of his hacks, on being offered higher
wages, had basely left him in the lurch.

She soon became interested in her work, for her emaciated
purse grew stout, and the little hoard she was making to take
Beth to the mountains next summer grew slowly but surely as
the weeks passed. One thing disturbed her satisfaction, and
that was that she did not tell them at home. She had a feeling
that father and mother would not approve, and preferred to
have her own way first, and beg pardon afterward. It was easy
to keep her secret, for no name appeared with her stories. Mr.
Dashwood had, of course, found it out very soon, but promised
to be dumb; and, for a wonder, kept his word.

She thought it would do her no harm, for she sincerely
meant to write nothing of which she should be ashamed, and
quieted all pricks of conscience by anticipations of the happy
minute when she should show her earnings and laugh over her
well-kept secret.

But Mr. Dashwood rejected any but thrilling tales; and, as
thrills could not be produced except by harrowing up the
souls of the readers, history and romance, land and sea, science
and art, police records and lunatic asylums had to be ransacked
for the purpose. Jo soon found that her innocent experience
had given her but few glimpses of the tragic world which
underlies society; so, regarding it in a business light, she set
about supplying her deficiencies with characteristic energy.
Eager to find material for stories, and bent on making them
original in plot, if not masterly in execution, she searched
newspapers for accidents, incidents, and crimes; she excited the
suspicion of public librarians by asking for works on poisons;
she studied faces in the street, and characters, good, bad, and
indifferent, all about her; she delved in the dust of ancient
times for facts or fictions so old that they were as good as new,
and introduced herself to folly, sin, and misery, as well as her
limited opportunities allowed. She thought she was prospering
finely; but, unconsciously, she was beginning to desecrate some
of the womanliest attributes of a woman's character. She was
living in bad society; and, imaginary though it was, its influence affected her, for she was feeding heart and fancy on
dangerous and unsubstantial food, and was fast brushing the

innocent bloom from her nature by a premature acquaintance with the darker side of life, which comes soon enough to all of us.

She was beginning to feel rather than see this, for much describing of other people's passions and feelings set her to studying and speculating about her own—a morbid amusement, in which healthy young minds do not voluntarily indulge. Wrongdoing always brings its own punishment; and, when Jo most needed hers, she got it.

I don't know whether the study of Shakespeare helped her to read character, or the natural instinct of a woman for what was honest, brave, and strong; but while endowing her imaginary heroes with every perfection under the sun, Jo was discovering a live hero, who interested her in spite of many human imperfections. Mr. Bhaer, in one of their conversations, had advised her to study simple, true, and lovely characters, wherever she found them, as good training for a writer. Jo took him at his word, for she coolly turned round and studied him—a proceeding which would have much surprised him, had he known it, for the worthy professor was very humble in his own conceit.

Why everybody liked him was what puzzled Jo, at first. He was neither rich nor great, young nor handsome; in no respect what is called fascinating, imposing, or brilliant; and yet he was as attractive as a genial fire, and people seemed to gather about him as naturally as about a warm hearth. He was poor, yet always appeared to be giving something away; a stranger, yet everyone was his friend; no longer young, but as happy-hearted as a boy; plain and peculiar, yet his face looked beautiful to many, and his oddities were freely forgiven for his sake. Jo often watched him, trying to discover the charm, and, at last, decided that it was benevolence which worked the miracle. If he had any sorrow, "it sat with its head under its wing," and he turned only his sunny side to the world. There were lines upon his forehead, but Time seemed to have touched him gently, remembering how kind he was to others. The pleasant curves about his mouth were the memorials of many friendly words and cheery laughs; his eyes were never cold or hard, and his big hand had a warm, strong grasp that was more expressive than words.

His very clothes seemed to partake of the hospitable nature of the wearer. They looked as if they were at ease, and liked to make him comfortable; his capacious waistcoat was suggestive of a large heart underneath; his rusty coat had a social air, and the baggy pockets plainly proved that little hands often went in empty and came out full; his very boots were benevolent and his collar never stiff and raspy like other people's.

"That's it!" said Jo to herself, when she at length discovered that genuine good will toward one's fellow men could beautify and dignify even a stout German teacher, who shoveled in his dinner, darned his own socks, and was burdened with the name of Bhaer.

Jo valued goodness highly, but she also possessed a most feminine respect for intellect, and a little discovery which she made about the professor added much to her regard for him. He never spoke of himself, and no one ever knew that in his native city he had been a man much honored and esteemed for learning and integrity, till a countryman came to see him, and in a conversation with Miss Norton, divulged the pleasing fact. From her Jo learned it, and liked it all the better because Mr. Bhaer had never told it. She felt proud to know that he was an honored professor in Berlin, though only a poor language master in America; and his homely, hard-working life was much beautified by the spice of romance which this discovery gave it.

Another and a better gift than intellect was shown her in a most unexpected manner. Miss Norton had the entree into literary society, which Jo would have had no chance of seeing but for her. The solitary woman felt an interest in the ambitious girl, and kindly conferred many favors of this sort both on Jo and the professor. She took them with her, one night, to a select symposium, held in honor of several celebrities.

Jo went prepared to bow down and adore the mighty ones whom she had worshiped with youthful enthusiasm afar off. But her reverence for genius received a severe shock that night, and it took her some time to recover from the discovery that the great creatures were only men and women after all.

Imagine her dismay, on stealing a glance of timid admiration at the poet whose lines suggested an ethereal being fed on "spirit, fire, and dew," to behold him devouring his supper with an ardor which flushed his intellectual countenance. Turning as from a fallen idol, she made other discoveries which rapidly dispelled her romantic illusions. The great novelist vibrated between two decanters with the regularity of a pendulum; the famous divine flirted openly with one of the Madame de Staëls of the age, who looked daggers at another Corinne, who was amiably satirizing her, after outmaneuvering her in efforts to absorb the profound philosopher, who imbibed tea Johnsonianly and appeared to slumber, the loquacity of the lady rendering speech impossible. The scientific celebrities, forgetting their mollusks and glacial periods, gossiped about art, while devoting themselves to oysters and ices with characteristic energy; the young musician, who was charming the city like a second Orpheus, talked horses; and the specimen of the British nobility present happened to be the most ordinary man of the party.

Before the evening was half over, Jo felt so completely *désillusionnée,* that she sat down in a corner to recover herself. Mr. Bhaer soon joined her, looking rather out of his element, and presently several of the philosophers, each mounted on his hobby, came ambling up to hold an intellectual tournament in the recess. The conversation was miles beyond Jo's comprehension, but she enjoyed it, though Kant and Hegel were unknown gods, the Subjective and Objective unintelligible terms; and the only thing "evolved from her inner consciousness" was a bad headache after it was all over. It dawned upon her gradually that the world was being picked to pieces, and put together on new and, according to the talkers, on infinitely better principles than before; that religion was in a fair way to be reasoned into nothingness, and intellect was to be the only God. Jo knew nothing about philosophy or metaphysics of any sort, but a curious excitement, half pleasurable, half painful, came over her, as she listened with a sense of being turned adrift into time and space, like a young balloon out on a holiday.

She looked round to see how the professor liked it, and

found him looking at her with the grimmest expression she had ever seen him wear. He shook his head, and beckoned her to come away; but she was fascinated, just then, by the freedom of Speculative Philosophy, and kept her seat, trying to find out what the wise gentlemen intended to rely upon after they had annihilated all the old beliefs.

Now, Mr. Bhaer was a diffident man, and slow to offer his own opinions, not because they were unsettled, but too sincere and earnest to be lightly spoken. As he glanced from Jo to several other young people, attracted by the brilliancy of the philosophical pyrotechnics, he knit his brows, and longed to speak, fearing that some inflammable young soul would be led astray by the rockets, to find, when the display was over, that they had only an empty stick or a scorched hand.

He bore it as long as he could; but when he was appealed to for an opinion, he blazed up with honest indignation, and defended religion with all the eloquence of truth—an eloquence which made his broken English musical and his plain face beautiful. He had a hard fight, for the wise men argued well, but he didn't know when he was beaten, and stood to his colors like a man. Somehow, as he talked, the world got right again to Jo; the old beliefs, that had lasted so long, seemed better than the new; God was not a blind force, and immortality was not a pretty fable, but a blessed fact. She felt as if she had solid ground under her feet again; and when Mr. Bhaer paused, outtalked but not one whit convinced, Jo wanted to clap her hands and thank him.

She did neither; but she remembered this scene, and gave the professor her heartiest respect, for she knew it cost him an effort to speak out then and there, because his conscience would not let him be silent. She began to see that character is a better possession than money, rank, intellect, or beauty, and to feel that if greatness is what a wise man has defined it to be, "truth, reverence, and good will," then her friend Friedrich Bhaer was not only good, but great.

This belief strengthened daily. She valued his esteem, she coveted his respect, she wanted to be worthy of his friendship; and, just when the wish was sincerest, she came near losing everything. It all grew out of a cocked hat; for one evening the professor came in to give Jo her lesson, with a paper soldier cap on his head, which Tina had put there, and he had forgotten to take off.

"It's evident he doesn't look in his glass before coming down," thought Jo, with a smile, as he said "Goot efening" and sat soberly down, quite unconscious of the ludicrous contrast between his subject and his headgear, for he was going to read her the "Death of Wallenstein."

She said nothing at first, for she liked to hear him laugh out his big hearty laugh, when anything funny happened, so she left him to discover it for himself, and presently forgot all about it; for to hear a German read Schiller is rather an absorbing occupation. After the reading came the lesson, which was a lively one, for Jo was in a gay mood that night, and the cocked hat kept her eyes dancing with merriment. The professor didn't know what to make of her, and stopped at last, to ask, with an air of mild surprise that was irresistible:

"Mees Marsch, for what do you laugh in your master's face? Haf you no respect for me, that you go on so bad?"

"How can I be respectful, sir, when you forget to take your hat off?" said Jo.

Lifting his hand to his head, the absent-minded professor gravely felt and removed the little cocked hat, looked at it a minute, and then threw back his head, and laughed like a merry bass viol.

"Ah! I see him now; it is that imp Tina who makes me a fool with my cap. Well, it is nothing; but see you, if this lesson goes not well, you too shall wear him."

But the lesson did not go at all for a few minutes, because Mr. Bhaer caught sight of a picture on the hat, and, unfolding it, said, with an air of great disgust:

"I wish these papers did not come into the house; they are not for children to see, nor young people to read. It is not well, and I haf no patience with those who make this harm."

Jo glanced at the sheet, and saw a pleasing illustration composed of a lunatic, a corpse, a villain, and a viper. She did not like it; but the impulse that made her turn it over was not of displeasure, but fear, because, for a minute, she fancied the paper was the "Volcano." It was not, however, and her panic subsided as she remembered that, even if it had been, and one of her own tales in it, there would have been no name to betray her. She had betrayed herself, however, by a look and a blush; for, though an absent man, the professor saw a good deal more than people fancied. He knew that Jo wrote, and had met her down among the newspaper offices more than once; but as she never spoke of it, he asked no questions, in spite of a strong desire to see her work. Now it occurred to him that she was doing what she was ashamed to own, and it troubled him. He did not say to himself, "It is none of my business; I've no right to say anything," as many people would have done; he only remembered that she was young and poor, a girl far away from mother's love and father's care; and he was moved to help her with an impulse as quick and natural as that which would prompt him to put out his hand to save a baby from a puddle. All this flashed through his mind in a minute, but not a trace of it appeared in his face; and by the time the paper was turned, and Jo's needle threaded, he was ready to say quite naturally, but very gravely:

"Yes, you are right to put it from you. I do not like to think that good young girls should see such things. They are made pleasant to some, but I would more rather give my boys gunpowder to play with than this bad trash."

"All may not be bad, only silly, you know; and if there is a demand for it, I don't see any harm in supplying it. Many very respectable people make an honest living out of what are called sensation stories," said Jo, scratching gathers so energetically that a row of little slits followed her pin.

"There is a demand for whisky, but I think you and I do not care to sell it. If the respectable people knew what harm they did, they would not feel that the living *was* honest. They haf no right to put poison in the sugar plum, and let the small ones eat it. No; they should think a little, and sweep mud in the street before they do this thing."

Mr. Bhaer spoke warmly, and walked to the fire, crumpling the paper in his hands. Jo sat still, looking as if the fire had come to her; for her cheeks burned long after the cocked hat had turned to smoke, and gone harmlessly up the chimney.

"I should like much to send all the rest after him," muttered the professor. coming back with a relieved air.

Jo thought what a blaze her pile of papers upstairs would make, and her hard-earned money lay rather heavily on her conscience at that minute. Then she thought consolingly to herself, "Mine are not like that; they are only silly, never bad, so I won't be worried," and taking up her book, she said, with a studious face:

"Shall we go on, sir? I'll be very good and proper now."

"I shall hope so" was all he said, but he meant more than she imagined; and the grave, kind look he gave her made her feel as if the words "Weekly Volcano" were printed in large type on her forehead.

As soon as she went to her room, she got out her papers, and carefully reread every one of her stories. Being a little shortsighted, Mr. Bhaer sometimes used eyeglasses, and Jo had tried them once, smiling to see how they magnified the fine print of her book; now she seemed to have got on the professor's mental or moral spectacles also; for the faults of these poor stories glared at her dreadfully and filled her with dismay.

"They *are* trash, and will soon be worse than trash if I go on; for each is more sensational than the last. I've gone blindly on, hurting myself and other people, for the sake of money; I know it's so, for I can't read this stuff in sober earnest without being horribly ashamed of it; and what *should* I do if they were seen at home, or Mr. Bhaer got hold of them?"

Jo turned hot at the bare idea, and stuffed the whole bundle into her stove, nearly setting her chimney afire with the blaze.

"Yes, that's the best place for such inflammable nonsense; I'd better burn the house down, I suppose, than let other people blow themselves up with my gunpowder," she thought, as she watched the "Demon of the Jura" whisk away, a little black cinder with fiery eyes.

But when nothing remained of all her three months' work except a heap of ashes, and the money in her lap, Jo looked sober, as she sat on the floor, wondering what she ought to do about her wages.

"I think I haven't done much harm *yet,* and may keep this to pay for my time," she said, after a long meditation, adding impatiently, "I almost wish I hadn't any conscience, it's so inconvenient. If I didn't care about doing right and didn't feel uncomfortable when doing wrong, I should get on capitally.

I can't help wishing sometimes that father and mother hadn't been so particular about such things."

Ah, Jo, instead of wishing that, thank God that "father and mother *were* particular," and pity from your heart those who have no such guardians to hedge them round with principles which may seem like prison walls to impatient youth, but which will prove sure foundations to build character upon in womanhood.

Jo wrote no more sensational stories, deciding that the money did not pay for her share of the sensation; but, going to the other extreme, as is the way with people of her stamp, she took a course of Mrs. Sherwood, Miss Edgeworth, and Hannah More; and then produced a tale which might have been more properly called an essay or a sermon, so intensely moral was it. She had her doubts about it from the beginning; for her lively fancy and girlish romance felt as ill at ease in the new style as she would have done masquerading in the stiff and cumbrous costume of the last century. She sent this didactic gem to several markets, but it found no purchaser; and she was inclined to agree with Mr. Dashwood, that morals didn't sell.

Then she tried a child's story, which she could easily have disposed of if she had not been mercenary enough to demand filthy lucre for it. The only person who offered enough to make it worth while to try juvenile literature was a worthy gentleman who felt it his mission to convert all the world to his particular belief. But much as she liked to write for children, Jo could not consent to depict all her naughty boys as being eaten by bears or tossed by mad bulls, because they did not go to a particular Sabbath school, nor all the good infants, who did go, as rewarded by every kind of bliss, from gilded gingerbread to escorts of angels, when they departed this life with psalms or sermons on their lisping tongues. So nothing came of these trials; and Jo corked up her inkstand, and said, in a fit of very wholesome humility:

"I don't know anything; I'll wait till I do before I try again, and meantime 'sweep mud in the street,' if I can't do better; that's honest, at least," which decision proved that her second tumble down the beanstalk had done her some good.

While these internal revolutions were going on, her external life had been as busy and uneventful as usual; and if she sometimes looked serious or a little sad no one observed it but Professor Bhaer. He did it so quietly that Jo never knew he was watching to see if she would accept and profit by his reproof; but she stood the test, and he was satisfied; for, though no words passed between them, he knew that she had given up writing. Not only did he guess it by the fact that the second finger of her right hand was no longer inky, but she spent her evenings downstairs now, was met no more among newspaper offices, and studied with a dogged patience, which assured him that she was bent on occupying her mind with something useful, if not pleasant.

He helped her in many ways, proving himself a true friend, and Jo was happy; for, while her pen lay idle, she was learning other lessons besides German, and laying a foundation for the sensation story of her own life.

It was a pleasant winter and a long one, for she did not leave Mrs. Kirke till June. Everyone seemed sorry when the time came; the children were inconsolable, and Mr. Bhaer's hair stuck straight up all over his head, for he always rumpled it wildly when disturbed in mind.

"Going home? Ah, you are happy that you haf a home to go in," he said, when she told him, and sat silently pulling his beard in the corner, while she held a little levee on that last evening.

She was going early, so she bade them all good-by overnight; and when his turn came, she said warmly:

"Now, sir, you won't forget to come and see us, if you ever travel our way, will you? I'll never forgive you if you do, for I want them all to know my friend."

"Do you? Shall I come?" he asked, looking down at her with an eager expression which she did not see.

"Yes, come next month; Laurie graduates then, and you'd enjoy Commencement as something new."

"That is your best friend of whom you speak?" he said, in an altered tone.

"Yes, my boy Teddy; I'm very proud of him, and should like you to see him."

Jo looked up then, quite unconscious of anything but her own pleasure at the prospect of showing them to one another.

Something in Mr. Bhaer's face suddenly recalled the fact that she might find Laurie more than a "best friend," and, simply because she particularly wished not to look as if anything was the matter, she involuntarily began to blush; and the more she tried not to, the redder she grew. If it had not been for Tina on her knee, she didn't know what would have become of her. Fortunately, the child was moved to hug her; so she managed to hide her face an instant, hoping the professor did not see it. But he did, and his own changed again from that momentary anxiety to its usual expression, as he said cordially:

"I fear I shall not make the time for that, but I wish the friend much success, and you all happiness. Gott bless you!" and with that, he shook hands warmly, shouldered Tina, and went away.

But after the boys were abed, he sat long before his fire, with the tired look on his face, and the *heimweh*, or homesickness, lying heavy at his heart. Once, when he remembered Jo, as she sat with the little child in her lap and that new softness in her face, he leaned his head on his hands a minute, and then roamed about the room, as if in search of something that he could not find.

"It is not for me; I must not hope it now," he said to himself, with a sigh that was almost a groan; then, as if reproaching himself for the longing that he could not repress, he went and kissed the two tousled heads upon the pillow, took down his seldom-used meerschaum, and opened his Plato.

He did his best, and did it manfully; but I don't think he found that a pair of rampant boys, a pipe, or even the divine Plato were very satisfactory substitutes for wife and child and home.

Early as it was, he was at the station, next morning, to see Jo off; and, thanks to him, she began her solitary journey with the pleasant memory of a familiar face smiling its farewell, a bunch of violets to keep her company, and, best of all, the happy thought:

"Well, the winter's gone, and I've written no books, earned no fortune; but I've made a friend worth having and I'll try to keep him all my life."

CHAPTER THIRTY-FIVE

Heartache

WHATEVER his motive might have been, Laurie studied to some purpose that year, for he graduated with honor, and gave the Latin oration with the grace of a Phillips and the eloquence of a Demosthenes, so his friends said. They were all there, his grandfather—oh, so proud!—Mr. and Mrs. March, John and Meg, Jo and Beth, and all exulted over him with the sincere admiration which boys make light of at the time, but fail to win from the world by any aftertriumphs.

"I've got to stay for this confounded supper, but I shall be home early tomorrow; you'll come and meet me as usual, girls?" Laurie said, as he put the sisters into the carriage after the joys of the day were over. He said "girls," but he meant Jo, for she was the only one who kept up the old custom; she had not the heart to refuse her splendid, successful boy anything, and answered warmly:

"I'll come, Teddy, rain or shine, and march before you, playing, 'Hail, the conquering hero comes,' on a jew's-harp."

Laurie thanked her with a look that made her think, in a sudden panic, "Oh, deary me! I know he'll say something, and then what shall I do?"

Evening meditation and morning work somewhat allayed her fears, and having decided that she wouldn't be vain enough to think people were going to propose when she had given them every reason to know what her answer would be, she set forth at the appointed time, hoping Teddy wouldn't do anything to make her hurt his poor little feelings. A call at Meg's, and a refreshing sniff and sip at the Daisy and Demijohn, still further fortified her for the tête-à-tête, but when she saw a stalwart figure looming in the distance, she had a strong desire to turn about and run away.

"Where's the jew's-harp, Jo?" cried Laurie, as soon as he was within speaking distance.

"I forgot it," and Jo took heart again, for that salutation could not be called loverlike.

She always used to take his arm on these occasions, now she did not, and he made no complaint, which was a bad sign, but talked on rapidly about all sorts of faraway subjects, till they turned from the road into the little path that led homeward through the grove. Then he walked more slowly, suddenly lost his fine flow of language, and, now and then, a dreadful pause occurred. To rescue the conversation from one of the wells of silence into which it kept falling, Jo said hastily:

"Now you must have a good long holiday!"

"I intend to."

Something in his resolute tone made Jo look up quickly to find him looking down at her with an expression that assured her the dreaded moment had come, and made her put out her hand with an imploring:

"No, Teddy, please don't!"

"I will, and you *must* hear me. It's no use, Jo; we've got to have it out, and the sooner the better for both of us," he answered, getting flushed and excited all at once.

"Say what you like then; I'll listen," said Jo, with a desperate sort of patience.

Laurie was a young lover, but he was in earnest, and meant to "have it out" if he died in the attempt; so he plunged into the subject with characteristic impetuosity, saying in a voice that *would* get choky now and then, in spite of manful efforts to keep it steady:

"I've loved you ever since I've known you, Jo; couldn't help it, you've been so good to me. I've tried to show it, but you wouldn't let me; now I'm going to make you hear, and give me an answer, for I *can't* go on so any longer."

"I wanted to save you this! I thought you'd understand—" began Jo, finding it a great deal harder than she expected.

"I know you did; but girls are so queer you never know what they mean. They say 'No' when they mean 'Yes,' and drive a man out of his wits just for the fun of it," returned Laurie, entrenching himself behind an undeniable fact.

"*I* don't. I never wanted to make you care for me so, and I went away to keep you from it if I could."

"I thought so; it was like you, but it was no use. I only loved you all the more, and I worked hard to please you, and I gave up billiards and everything you didn't like, and waited and never complained, for I hoped you'd love me, though I'm not half good enough—" Here there was a choke that couldn't be controlled, so he decapitated buttercups while he cleared his "confounded throat."

"Yes, you are; you're a great deal too good for me, and I'm grateful to you, and so proud and fond of you, I don't see why I can't love you as you want me to. I've tried, but I can't change the feeling, and it would be a lie to say I do when I don't."

"Really, truly, Jo?"

He stopped short, and caught both her hands as he put his question with a look that she did not soon forget.

"Really, truly, dear."

They were in the grove now, close by the stile; and when the last words fell reluctantly from Jo's lips, Laurie dropped her hands and turned as if to go on, but for once in his life that fence was too much for him; so he just laid his head down on the mossy post, and stood so still that Jo was frightened.

"Oh, Teddy, I'm sorry, so desperately sorry, I could kill myself if it would do any good! I wish you wouldn't take it so hard. I can't help it; you know it's impossible for people to make themselves love other people if they don't," cried Jo, inelegantly but remorsefully, as she softly patted his shoulder, remembering the time when he had comforted her so long ago.

"They do sometimes," said a muffled voice from the post.

"I don't believe it's the right sort of love, and I'd rather not try it" was the decided answer.

There was a long pause, while a blackbird sung blithely on the willow by the river, and the tall grass rustled in the wind. Presently Jo said very soberly, as she sat down on the step of the stile:

"Laurie, I want to tell you something."

He started as if he had been shot, threw up his head, and cried out, in a fierce tone:

"*Don't* tell me that, Jo, I can't bear it now!"

"Tell what?" she asked, wondering at his violence.

"That you love that old man."

"What old man?" demanded Jo, thinking he must mean his grandfather.

"That devilish professor you were always writing about. If you say you love him, I know I shall do something desperate," and he looked as if he would keep his word, as he clenched his hands, with a wrathful spark in his eyes.

Jo wanted to laugh, but restrained herself, and said warmly, for she, too, was getting excited with all this:

"Don't swear, Teddy! He isn't old, nor anything bad, but good and kind, and the best friend I've got, next to you. Pray, don't fly into a passion; I want to be kind, but I know I shall get angry if you abuse my professor. I haven't the least idea of loving him or anybody else."

"But you will after a while, and then what will become of me?"

"You'll love someone else too, like a sensible boy, and forget all this trouble."

"I *can't* love anyone else; and I'll never forget you, Jo, never, never!" with a stamp to emphasize his passionate words.

"What *shall* I do with him?" sighed Jo, finding that emotions were more unmanageable than she expected. "You haven't heard what I wanted to tell you. Sit down and listen; for indeed I want to do right and make you happy," she said, hoping to soothe him with a little reason, which proved that she knew nothing about love.

Seeing a ray of hope in that last speech, Laurie threw himself down on the grass at her feet, leaned his arm on the lower step of the stile, and looked up at her with an expectant face. Now that arrangement was not conducive to calm speech or clear thought on Jo's part; for how *could* she say hard things to her boy while he watched her with eyes full of love and longing, and lashes still wet with the bitter drop or two her hardness of heart had wrung from him? She gently turned his head away, saying, as she stroked the wavy hair which had been allowed to grow for her sake—how touching that was, to be sure!—

"I agree with mother that you and I are not suited to each other, because our quick tempers and strong wills would probably make us very miserable, if we were so foolish as to—" Jo paused a little over the last word, but Laurie uttered it with a rapturous expression:

"Marry—no, we shouldn't! If you loved me, Jo, I should be a perfect saint, for you could make me anything you like."

"No, I can't. I've tried it and failed, and I won't risk our happiness by such a serious experiment. We don't agree and we never shall; so we'll be good friends all our lives, but we won't go and do anything rash."

"Yes, but we will if we get the chance," muttered Laurie rebelliously.

"Now do be reasonable, and take a sensible view of the case," implored Jo, almost at her wit's end.

"I won't be reasonable; I don't want to take what you call 'a sensible view'; it won't help me, and it only makes you harder. I don't believe you've got any heart."

"I wish I hadn't!"

There was a little quiver in Jo's voice, and, thinking it a good omen, Laurie turned round, bringing all his persuasive powers to bear as he said, in the wheedlesome tone that had never been so dangerously wheedlesome before:

"Don't disappoint us, dear! Everyone expects it. Grandpa has set his heart upon it, your people like it, and I can't get on without you. Say you will, and let's be happy. Do, do!"

Not until months afterward did Jo understand how she had the strength of mind to hold fast to the resolution she had made when she decided that she did not love her boy, and never could. It was very hard to do, but she did it, knowing that delay was both useless and cruel.

"I can't say 'Yes' truly, so I won't say it at all. You'll see that I'm right, by and by, and thank me for it—" she began solemnly.

"I'll be hanged if I do!" and Laurie bounced up off the grass, burning with indignation at the bare idea.

"Yes, you will!" persisted Jo. "You'll get over this after a while, and find some lovely, accomplished girl, who will adore you, and make a fine mistress for your fine house. I shouldn't. I'm homely and awkward and odd and old, and you'd be ashamed of me, and we should quarrel—we can't help it even now, you see—and I shouldn't like elegant society and you would, and you'd hate my scribbling, and I couldn't get on without it, and we should be unhappy, and wish we hadn't done it, and everything would be horrid!"

"Anything more?" asked Laurie, finding it hard to listen patiently to this prophetic burst.

"Nothing more, except that I don't believe I shall ever marry. I'm happy as I am, and love my liberty too well to be in any hurry to give it up for any mortal man."

"I know better!" broke in Laurie. "You think so now; but there'll come a time when you *will* care for somebody, and you'll love him tremendously, and live and die for him. I know you will, it's your way, and I shall have to stand by and see it," and the despairing lover cast his hat upon the ground with a gesture that would have seemed comical, if his face had not been so tragical.

"Yes, I *will* live and die for him, if he ever comes and makes

me love him in spite of myself, and you must do the best you
can!" cried Jo, losing patience with poor Teddy. "I've done my
best, but you *won't* be reasonable, and it's selfish of you to keep
teasing for what I can't give. I shall always be fond of you,
very fond indeed, as a friend, but I'll never marry you; and the
sooner you believe it the better for both of us—so now!"

That speech was like fire to gunpowder. Laurie looked at
her a minute as if he did not quite know what to do with himself, then turned sharply away, saying, in a desperate sort of
tone:

"You'll be sorry someday, Jo."

"Oh, where are you going?" she cried, for his face frightened her.

"To the devil!" was the consoling answer.

For a minute Jo's heart stood still, as he swung himself
down the bank, toward the river; but it takes much folly, sin,
or misery to send a young man to a violent death, and Laurie
was not one of the weak sort who are conquered by a single
failure. He had no thought of a melodramatic plunge, but
some blind instinct led him to fling hat and coat into his boat,
and row away with all his might, making better time up the
river than he had done in many a race. Jo drew a long breath
and unclasped her hands as she watched the poor fellow trying to outstrip the trouble which he carried in his heart.

"That will do him good, and he'll come home in such a tender, penitent state of mind, that I shan't dare to see him," she
said; adding, as she went slowly home, feeling as if she had
murdered some innocent thing, and buried it under the leaves:

"Now I must go and prepare Mr. Laurence to be very kind
to my poor boy. I wish he'd love Beth; perhaps he may, in
time, but I begin to think I was mistaken about her. Oh, dear,
how can girls like to have lovers and refuse them. I think it's
dreadful."

Being sure that no one could do it so well as herself, she
went straight to Mr. Laurence and told the hard story bravely
through, and then broke down, crying so dismally over her
own insensibility that the kind old gentleman, though sorely
disappointed, did not utter a reproach. He found it difficult to
understand how any girl could help loving Laurie, and hoped

she would change her mind, but he knew even better than Jo that love cannot be forced, so he shook his head sadly and resolved to carry his boy out of harm's way; for Young Impetuosity's parting words to Jo disturbed him more than he would confess.

When Laurie came home, dead tired but quite composed, his grandfather met him as if he knew nothing, and kept up the delusion very successfully for an hour or two. But when they sat together in the twilight, the time they used to enjoy so much, it was hard work for the old man to ramble on as usual, and harder still for the young one to listen to praises of the last year's success, which to him now seemed love's labor lost. He bore it as long as he could, then went to his piano, and began to play. The windows were open; and Jo, walking in the garden with Beth, for once understood music better than her sister, for he played the "Sonata Pathétique," and played it as he never did before.

"That's very fine, I dare say, but it's sad enough to make one cry; give us something gayer, lad," said Mr. Laurence, whose kind old heart was full of sympathy, which he longed to show but knew not how.

Laurie dashed into a livelier strain, played stormily for several minutes, and would have got through bravely, if, in a momentary lull, Mrs. March's voice had not been heard calling:

"Jo, dear, come in; I want you."

Just what Laurie longed to say, with a different meaning! As he listened, he lost his place; the music ended with a broken chord, and the musician sat silent in the dark.

"I can't stand this," muttered the old gentleman. Up he got, groped his way to the piano, laid a kind hand on either of the broad shoulders, and said as gently as a woman:

"I know, my boy, I know."

No answer for an instant; then Laurie asked sharply:

"Who told you?"

"Jo herself."

"Then there's an end of it!" and he shook off his grandfather's hands with an impatient motion; for, though grateful for the sympathy, his man's pride could not bear a man's pity.

"Not quite; I want to say one thing, and then there shall be

an end of it," returned Mr. Laurence, with unusual mildness. "You won't care to stay at home just now, perhaps?"

"I don't intend to run away from a girl. Jo can't prevent my seeing her, and I shall stay and do it as long as I like," interrupted Laurie, in a defiant tone.

"Not if you are the gentleman I think you. I'm disappointed, but the girl can't help it; and the only thing left for you to do is to go away for a time. Where will you go?"

"Anywhere. I don't care what becomes of me," and Laurie got up with a reckless laugh that grated on his grandfather's ear.

"Take it like a man, and don't do anything rash, for God's sake. Why not go abroad, as you planned, and forget it?"

"I can't."

"But you've been wild to go, and I promised you should when you got through college."

"Ah, but I didn't mean to go alone!" and Laurie walked fast through the room, with an expression which it was well his grandfather did not see.

"I don't ask you to go alone; there's someone ready and glad to go with you, anywhere in the world."

"Who, sir?" stopping to listen.

"Myself."

Laurie come back as quickly as he went, and put out his hand, saying huskily:

"I'm a selfish brute; but—you know—grandfather—"

"Lord help me, yes, I do know, for I've been through it all before, once in my own young days, and then with your father. Now, my dear boy, just sit quietly down and hear my plan. It's all settled, and can be carried out at once," said Mr. Laurence, keeping hold of the young man, as if fearful that he would break away, as his father had done before him.

"Well, sir, what is it?" and Laurie sat down, without a sign of interest in face or voice.

"There is business in London that needs looking after; I meant you should attend to it; but I can do it better myself, and things here will get on very well with Brooke to manage them. My partners do almost everything; I'm merely holding on till you take my place, and can be off at any time."

'But you hate traveling, sir; I can't ask it of you at your age," began Laurie, who was grateful for the sacrifice, but much preferred to go alone, if he went at all.

The old gentleman knew that perfectly well, and particularly desired to prevent it; for the mood in which he found his grandson assured him that it would not be wise to leave him

"Oh, Teddy, I wish you wouldn't take it so hard!"

[SEE PAGE 404]

to his own devices. So, stifling a natural regret at the thought of the home comforts he would leave behind him, he said stoutly:

"Bless your soul, I'm not superannuated yet. I quite enjoy the idea; it will do me good, and my old bones won't suffer, for traveling nowadays is almost as easy as sitting in a chair."

A restless movement from Laurie suggested that *his* chair was not easy, or that he did not like the plan, and made the old man add hastily:

"I don't mean to be a marplot or a burden; I go because I think you'd feel happier than if I was left behind. I don't intend to gad about with you, but leave you free to go where you like, while I amuse myself in my own way. I've friends in London and Paris, and should like to visit them; meantime you can go to Italy, Germany, Switzerland, where you will, and enjoy pictures, music, scenery, and adventures to your heart's content."

Now, Laurie felt just then that his heart was entirely broken, and the world a howling wilderness; but at the sound of certain words which the old gentleman artfully introduced into his closing sentence, the broken heart gave an unexpected leap, and a green oasis or two suddenly appeared in the howling wilderness. He sighed, and then said, in a spiritless tone:

"Just as you like, sir; it doesn't matter where I go or what I do."

"It does to me, remember that, my lad; I give you entire liberty, but I trust you to make an honest use of it. Promise me that, Laurie."

"Anything you like, sir."

"Good," thought the old gentleman. "You don't care now, but there'll come a time when that promise will keep you out of mischief, or I'm much mistaken."

Being an energetic individual, Mr. Laurence struck while the iron was hot; and before the blighted being recovered spirit enough to rebel, they were off. During the time necessary for preparation, Laurie bore himself as young gentlemen usually do in such cases. He was moody, irritable, and pensive by turns; lost his appetite, neglected his dress, and devoted much time to playing tempestuously on his piano; avoided Jo, but consoled himself by staring at her from his window, with a tragical face that haunted her dreams by night, and oppressed her with a heavy sense of guilt by day. Unlike some sufferers, he never spoke of his unrequited passion, and would allow no one, not even Mrs. March, to attempt consolation or offer sympathy. On some accounts, this was a relief to his friends; but the weeks before his departure were very uncomfortable, and everyone rejoiced that the "poor, dear fellow was going away to forget his trouble, and come home happy." Of course, he smiled darkly at their delusion, but passed it by, with the sad superiority of one who knew that his fidelity, like his love, was unalterable.

When the parting came he affected high spirits, to conceal certain inconvenient emotions which seemed inclined to assert themselves. This gaiety did not impose upon anybody, but they tried to look as if it did, for his sake, and he got on very well till Mrs. March kissed him, with a whisper full of motherly solicitude; then, feeling that he was going very fast, he hastily embraced them all around, not forgetting the afflicted Hannah, and ran downstairs as if for his life. Jo followed a minute after to wave her hand to him if he looked round. He did look round, came back, put his arms about her, as she stood on the step above him, and looked up at her with a face that made his short appeal both eloquent and pathetic.

"Oh, Jo, can't you?"

"Teddy, dear, I wish I could!"

That was all, except a little pause; then Laurie straightened himself up, said, "It's all right, never mind," and went away without another word. Ah, but it wasn't all right, and Jo *did* mind; for while the curly head lay on her arm a minute after her hard answer, she felt as if she had stabbed her dearest friend; and when he left her without a look behind him, she knew that the boy Laurie never would come again.

CHAPTER THIRTY-SIX

Beth's Secret

WHEN Jo came home that spring, she had been struck with the change in Beth. No one spoke of it or seemed aware of it, for it had come too gradually to startle those who saw her daily; but to eyes sharpened by absence, it was very plain; and a heavy weight fell on Jo's heart as she saw her sister's face. It was no paler and but little thinner than in the autumn; yet there was a strange, transparent look about it, as if the mortal was being slowly refined away, and the immortal shining through the frail flesh with an indescribably pathetic beauty. Jo saw and felt it, but said nothing at the time and soon the first impression lost much of its power; for Beth seemed happy, no one appeared to doubt that she was better; and presently, in other cares, Jo for a time forgot her fear.

But when Laurie was gone, and peace prevailed again, the vague anxiety returned and haunted her. She had confessed her sins and been forgiven; but when she showed her savings and proposed the mountain trip, Beth had thanked her heartily, but begged not to go so far away from home. Another little visit to the seashore would suit her better, and, as grandma could not be prevailed upon to leave the babies, Jo took Beth down to the quiet place, where she could live much in the open air, and let the fresh sea breezes blow a little color into her pale cheeks.

It was not a fashionable place, but, even among the pleasant people there the girls made few friends, preferring to live for one another. Beth was too shy to enjoy society, and Jo too wrapped up in her to care for anyone else; so they were all in all to each other, and came and went quite unconscious of the interest they excited in those about them, who watched with sympathetic eyes the strong sister and the feeble one, always together, as if they felt instinctively that a long separation was not far away.

They did feel it, yet neither spoke of it; for often between ourselves and those nearest and dearest to us there exists a reserve which it is very hard to overcome. Jo felt as if a veil had fallen between her heart and Beth's; but when she put out her hand to lift it up, there seemed something sacred in the silence, and waited for Beth to speak. She wondered, and was thankful also, that her parents did not seem to see what she saw; and, during the quiet weeks, when the shadow grew so plain to her, she said nothing of it to those at home, believing that it would tell itself when Beth came back no better. She wondered still more if her sister really guessed the hard truth, and what thoughts were passing through her mind during the long hours when she lay on the warm rocks, with her head in Jo's lap, while the winds blew healthfully over her, and the sea made music at her feet.

One day Beth told her. Jo thought she was asleep, she lay so still; and, putting down her book, sat looking at her with wistful eyes, trying to see signs of hope in the faint color on Beth's cheeks. But she could not find enough to satisfy her, for the cheeks were very thin, and the hands seemed too feeble to hold even the rosy little shells they had been gathering. It came to her then more bitterly than ever that Beth was slowly drifting away from her, and her arms instinctively tightened their hold upon the dearest treasure she possessed. For a minute her eyes were too dim for seeing, and, when they cleared, Beth was looking up at her so tenderly that there was hardly any need for her to say:

"Jo, dear, I'm glad you know it. I've tried to tell you, but I couldn't."

There was no answer except her sister's cheek against her own, not even tears; for when most deeply moved, Jo did not cry. She was the weaker, then, and Beth tried to comfort and sustain her, with her arms about her, and the soothing words she whispered in her ear.

"I've known it for a good while, dear, and, now I'm used to it, it isn't hard to think of or to bear. Try to see it so, and don't be troubled about me, because it's best; indeed it is."

"Is this what made you so unhappy in the autumn, Beth? You did not feel it then, and keep it to yourself so long, did you?" asked Jo, refusing to see or say that it *was* best, but glad to know that Laurie had no part in Beth's trouble.

"Yes, I gave up hoping then, but I didn't like to own it. I tried to think it was a sick fancy, and would not let it trouble anyone. But when I saw you all so well and strong, and full of happy plans, it was hard to feel that I could never be like you, and then I was miserable, Jo."

"Oh, Beth, and you didn't tell me, didn't let me comfort and help you! How could you shut me out, and bear it all alone?"

Jo's voice was full of tender reproach, and her heart ached to think of the solitary struggle that must have gone on while Beth learned to say good-by to health, love, and life, and take up her cross so cheerfully.

"Perhaps it was wrong, but I tried to do right; I wasn't sure, no one said anything, and I hoped I was mistaken. It would have been selfish to frighten you all when Marmee was so anxious about Meg, and Amy away, and you so happy with Laurie —at least, I thought so then."

"And I thought that you loved him, Beth, and I went away because I couldn't," cried Jo, glad to say all the truth.

Beth looked so amazed at the idea that Jo smiled in spite
of her pain, and added softly:

"Then you didn't, deary? I was afraid it was so, and imagined your poor little heart full of lovelornity all that while."

"Why, Jo, how could I, when he was so fond of you?" asked
Beth, as innocently as a child. "I do love him dearly; he is so
good to me, how can J help it? But he never could be anything
to me but my brother. I hope he truly will be, sometime."

"Not through me," said Jo decidedly. "Amy is left for him,
and they would suit excellently; but I have no heart for such
things, now. I don't care what becomes of anybody but you,
Beth. You *must* get well."

"I want to, oh, so much! I try, but every day I lose a little,
and feel more sure that I shall never gain it back. It's like the
tide, Jo, when it turns, it goes slowly, but it can't be stopped."

"It *shall* be stopped, your tide must not turn so soon, nineteen is too young. Beth, I can't let you go. I'll work and pray
and fight against it. I'll keep you in spite of everything; there
must be ways, it can't be too late. God won't be so cruel as to
take you from me," cried poor Jo rebelliously, for her spirit
was far less piously submissive than Beth's.

Simple, sincere people seldom speak much of their piety;
it shows itself in acts, rather than in words, and has more influence than homilies or protestations. Beth could not reason
upon or explain the faith that gave her courage and patience
to give up life, and cheerfully wait for death. Like a confiding
child, she asked no questions, but left everything to God and
nature, Father and mother of us all, feeling sure that they, and
they only, could teach and strengthen heart and spirit for this
life and the life to come. She did not rebuke Jo with saintly
speeches, only loved her better for her passionate affection,
and clung more closely to the dear human love, from which
our Father never means us to be weaned, but through which
He draws us closer to Himself. She could not say "I'm glad
to go," for life was very sweet to her; she could only sob out
"I try to be willing," while she held fast to Jo, as the first bitter
wave of this great sorrow broke over them together.

By and by Beth said, with recovered serenity:

"You'll tell them this when we go home?"

"I think they will see it without words," sighed Jo; for now it seemed to her that Beth changed every day.

"Perhaps not; I've heard that the people who love best are often blindest to such things. If they don't see it, you will tell them for me. I don't want any secrets, and it's kinder to prepare them. Meg has John and the babies to comfort her, but you must stand by father and mother, won't you, Jo?"

"If I can, but, Beth, I don't give up yet; I'm going to believe that it *is* a sick fancy; and not let you think it's true," said Jo, trying to speak cheerfully.

Beth lay a minute thinking, and then said in her quiet way: "I don't know how to express myself, and shouldn't try to anyone but you, because I can't speak out, except to my Jo. I only mean to say that I have a feeling that it never was intended I should live long. I'm not like the rest of you; I never made any plans about what I'd do when I grew up; I never thought of being married, as you all did. I couldn't seem to imagine myself anything but stupid little Beth, trotting about at home, of no use anywhere but there. I never wanted to go away and the hard part now is the leaving you all. I'm not afraid, but it seems as if I should be homesick for you even in heaven."

Jo could not speak; and for several minutes there was no sound but the sigh of the wind and the lapping of the tide. A white-winged gull flew by, with the flash of sunshine on its silvery breast; Beth watched it till it vanished, and her eyes were full of sadness. A little gray-coated sand bird came tripping over the beach, "peeping" softly to itself, as if enjoying the sun and sea; it came quite close to Beth, looked at her with a friendly eye, and sat upon a warm stone, dressing its wet feathers, quite at home. Beth smiled, and felt comforted, for the tiny thing seemed to offer its small friendship, and remind her that a pleasant world was still to be enjoyed.

"Dear little bird! See, Jo, how tame it is. I like peeps better than the gulls: they are not so wild and handsome, but they seem happy, confiding little things. I used to call them my birds, last summer; and mother said they reminded her of me — busy, quaker-colored creatures, always near the shore, and always chirping that contented little song of theirs. You are the gull, Jo, strong and wild, fond of the storm and the wind, flying far out to sea, and happy all alone. Meg is the turtledove, and Amy is like the lark she writes about, trying to get up among the clouds, but always dropping down into its nest again. Dear little girl! She's so ambitious, but her heart is good and tender; and no matter how high she flies, she never will forget home. I hope I shall see her again, but she seems *so* far away."

"She is coming in the spring, and I mean that you shall be all ready to see and enjoy her. I'm going to have you well and rosy by that time," began Jo, feeling that of all the changes in Beth, the talking change was the greatest, for it seemed to cost no effort now, and she thought aloud in a way quite unlike bashful Beth.

"Jo dear, don't hope any more; it won't do any good, I'm sure of that. We won't be miserable, but enjoy being together while we wait. We'll have happy times, for I don't suffer much, and I think the tide will go out easily, if you help me."

Jo leaned down to kiss the tranquil face; and with that silent kiss, she dedicated herself soul and body to Beth.

She was right; there was no need of any words when they got home, for father and mother saw plainly, now, what they had prayed to be saved from seeing. Tired with her short journey, Beth went at once to bed, saying how glad she was to be at home; and when Jo went down, she found that she would be spared the hard task of telling Beth's secret. Her father stood leaning his head on the mantelpiece, and did not turn as she came in; but her mother stretched out her arms as if for help, and Jo went to comfort her without a word.

CHAPTER THIRTY-SEVEN

New Impressions

AT three o'clock in the afternoon, all the fashionable world at Nice may be seen on the Promenade des Anglais—a charming place; for the wide walk, bordered with palms, flowers, and tropical shrubs, is bounded on one side by the sea, on the other by the grand drive, lined with hotels and villas, while beyond lie orange orchards and the hills. Many nations are represented, many languages spoken, many costumes worn; and, on a sunny day, the spectacle is as gay and brilliant as a carnival. Haughty English, lively French, sober Germans, handsome Spaniards, ugly Russians, meek Jews, free-and-easy Americans, all drive, sit, or saunter here, chatting over the news, and criticizing the latest celebrity who has arrived—

Ristori or Dickens, Victor Emmanuel or the Queen of the Sandwich Islands. The equipages are as varied as the company, and attract as much attention, especially the low basket barouches in which ladies drive themselves, with a pair of dashing ponies, gay nets to keep their voluminous flounces from overflowing the diminutive vehicles, and little grooms on the perch behind.

Along this walk, on Christmas Day, a tall young man walked slowly, with his hands behind him, and a somewhat absent expression of countenance. He looked like an Italian, was dressed like an Englishman, and had the independent air of an American—a combination which caused sundry pairs of feminine eyes to look approvingly after him, and sundry dandies in black velvet suits, with rose-colored neckties, buff gloves, and orange flowers in their buttonholes, to shrug their shoulders, and then envy him his inches. There were plenty of pretty faces to admire, but the young man took little notice of them, except to glance, now and then, at some blonde girl, or lady in blue. Presently he strolled out of the promenade, and stood a moment at the crossing, as if undecided whether to go and listen to the band in the Jardin Publique, or to wander along the beach toward Castle Hill. The quick trot of ponies' feet made him look up, as one of the little carriages, containing a single lady, came rapidly down the street. The lady was young, blonde, and dressed in blue. He stared a minute, then his whole face woke up, and waving his hat like a boy, he hurried forward to meet her.

"Oh, Laurie, is it really you? I thought you'd never come!" cried Amy, dropping the reins, and holding out both hands, to the great scandalization of a French mamma, who hastened her daughter's steps, lest she should be demoralized by beholding the free manners of these "mad English."

"I was detained by the way, but I promised to spend Christmas with you, and here I am."

"How is your grandfather? When did you come? Where are you staying?"

"Very well—last night—at the Chauvain. I called at your hotel, but you were all out."

"I have so much to say, I don't know where to begin! Get

in, and we can talk at our ease; I was going for a drive, and
longing for company. Flo's saving up for tonight."

"What happens then, a ball?"

"A Christmas party at our hotel. There are many Americans
there, and they give it in honor of the day. You'll go with us,
of course? Aunt will be charmed."

"Thank you. Where now?" asked Laurie, leaning back and
folding his arms, a proceeding which suited Amy, who preferred to drive; for her parasol whip and blue reins over the
white ponies' backs, afforded her infinite satisfaction.

"I'm going to the banker's first, for letters, and then to Castle
Hill; the view is so lovely, and I like to feed the peacocks.
Have you ever been there?"

"Often, years ago; but I don't mind having a look at it."

"Now tell me all about yourself. The last I heard of you,
your grandfather wrote that he expected you from Berlin."

"Yes, I spent a month there, and then joined him in Paris,
where he has settled for the winter. He has friends there, and
finds plenty to amuse him; so I go and come and we get on
capitally."

"That's a sociable arrangement," said Amy, missing something in Laurie's manner, though she couldn't tell what.

"Why, you see he hates to travel, and I hate to keep still; so
we each suit ourselves, and there is no trouble. I am often with
him, and he enjoys my adventures, while I like to feel that
someone is glad to see me when I get back from my wanderings. Dirty old hole, isn't it?" he added, with a look of disgust,
as they drove along the boulevard to the Place Napoleon, in
the old city.

"The dirt is picturesque, so I don't mind. The river and the
hills are delicious, and these glimpses of the narrow cross
streets are my delight. Now we shall have to wait for that procession to pass; it's going to the Church of St. John."

While Laurie listlessly watched the procession of priests
under their canopies, white-veiled nuns bearing lighted tapers,
and some brotherhood in blue, chanting as they walked, Amy
watched him, and felt a new sort of shyness steal over her; for
he was changed, and she could not find the merry-faced boy
she left in the moody-looking man beside her. He was hand-

somer than ever, and greatly improved, she thought; but now
that the flush of pleasure at meeting her was over, he looked
tired and spiritless—not sick, nor exactly unhappy, but older
and graver than a year or two of prosperous life should have
made him. She couldn't understand it, and did not venture to
ask questions; so she shook her head, and touched up her
ponies, as the procession wound away across the arches of the
Paglioni bridge, and vanished in the church.

"*Que pensez-vous?*" she said, airing her French, which had
improved in quantity, if not in quality, since she came abroad.

"That mademoiselle has made good use of her time, and the
result is charming," replied Laurie, bowing, with his hand on
his heart, and an admiring look.

She blushed with pleasure, but somehow the compliment
did not satisfy her like the blunt praises he used to give her at
home, when he promenaded round her on festival occasions,
and told her she was "altogether jolly," with a hearty smile
and an approving pat on the head. She didn't like the new one;
for, though not blasé, it sounded indifferent in spite of the
look.

"If that's the way he's going to grow up, I wish he'd stay a
boy," she thought, with a curious sense of disappointment and
discomfort, trying meantime to seem quite easy and gay.

At Avigdor's she found the precious home letters, and, giving the reins to Laurie, read them luxuriously, as they wound
up the shady road between green hedges, where tea roses
bloomed as freshly as in June.

"Beth is very poorly, mother says. I often think I ought to
go home, but they all say 'stay'; so I do, for I shall never have
another chance like this," said Amy, looking sober over one
page.

"I think you are right there; you could do nothing at home,
and it is a great comfort to them to know that you are well and
happy, and enjoying so much, my dear."

He drew a little nearer, and looked more like his old self,
as he said that; and the fear that sometimes weighed on Amy's
heart was lightened, for the look, the act, the brotherly "my
dear," seemed to assure her that if any trouble did come, she
would not be alone in a strange land. Presently she laughed,

and showed him a small sketch of Jo in her scribbling suit, with the bow rampantly erect upon her cap, and issuing from her mouth the words "Genius burns!"

Laurie smiled, took it, put it in his vest pocket, "to keep it from blowing away," and listened with interest to the lively letter Amy read him.

"This will be a regularly merry Christmas to me, with presents in the morning, you and letters in the afternoon, and a party at night," said Amy, as they alighted among the ruins of the old fort, and a flock of splendid peacocks came trooping about them, tamely waiting to be fed. While Amy stood laughing on the bank above him as she scattered crumbs to the brilliant birds, Laurie looked at her as she had looked at him, with a natural curiosity to see what changes time and absence had wrought. He found nothing to perplex or disappoint, much to admire and approve; for, overlooking a few little affectations of speech and manner, she was as sprightly and graceful as ever, with the addition of that indescribable something in dress and bearing which we call elegance. Always mature for her age, she had gained a certain aplomb in both carriage and conversation, which made her seem more of a woman of the world than she was; but her old petulance now and then showed itself, her strong will still held its own, and her native frankness was unspoiled by foreign polish.

Laurie did not read all this while he watched her feed the peacocks, but he saw enough to satisfy and interest him, and carried away a pretty little picture of a bright-faced girl standing in the sunshine, which brought out the soft hue of her dress, the fresh color of her cheeks, the golden gloss of her hair, and made her a prominent figure in the pleasant scene.

As they came up on to the stone plateau that crowns the hill, Amy waved her hand as if welcoming him to her favorite haunt, and said, pointing here and there:

"Do you remember the Cathedral and the Corso, the fishermen dragging their nets in the bay, and the lovely road to Villa Franca, Schubert's Tower, just below, and best of all, that speck far out to sea which they say is Corsica?"

"I remember; it's not much changed," he answered, without enthusiasm.

"What Jo would give for a sight of that famous speck!" said Amy, feeling in good spirits, and anxious to see him so also.

"Yes" was all he said, but he turned and strained his eyes to see the island which a greater usurper than even Napoleon now made interesting in his sight.

"Take a good look at it for her sake, and then come and tell me what you have been doing with yourself all this while," said Amy, seating herself, ready for a good talk.

But she did not get it; for, though he joined her, and answered all her questions freely, she could only learn that he had roved about the Continent and been to Greece. So, after idling away an hour, they drove home again; and, having paid his respects to Mrs. Carrol, Laurie left them, promising to return in the evening.

It must be recorded of Amy that she deliberately "prinked" that night. Time and absence had done its work on both the young people; she had seen her old friend in a new light, not as "our boy," but as a handsome and agreeable man, and she was conscious of a very natural desire to find favor in his sight. Amy knew her good points, and made the most of them, with the taste and skill which is a fortune to a poor and pretty woman.

Tarlatan and tulle were cheap at Nice, so she enveloped herself in them on such occasions, and, following the sensible English fashion of simple dress for young girls, got up charming little toilettes with fresh flowers, a few trinkets, and all manner of dainty devices, which were both inexpensive and effective. It must be confessed that the artist sometimes got possession of the woman, and indulged in antique coiffures, statuesque attitudes, and classic draperies. But, dear heart, we all have our little weaknesses, and find it easy to pardon such in the young, who satisfy our eyes with their comeliness and keep our hearts merry with their artless vanities.

"I do want him to think I look well, and tell them so at home," said Amy to herself, as she put on Flo's old white silk ball dress, and covered it with a cloud of fresh illusion, out of which her white shoulders and golden head emerged with a most artistic effect. Her hair she had the sense to let alone, after gathering up the thick waves and curls into a Hebelike knot at the back of her head.

"It's not the fashion, but it's becoming, and I can't afford to make a fright of myself," she used to say, when advised to frizzle, puff, or braid, as the latest style commanded.

Having no ornaments fine enough for this important occasion, Amy looped her fleecy skirts with rosy clusters of azalea, and framed the white shoulders in delicate green vines. Remembering the painted boots, she surveyed her white satin slippers with girlish satisfaction, and chasséd down the room, admiring her aristocratic feet all by herself.

"My new fan just matches my flowers, my gloves fit to a charm, and the real lace on aunt's *mouchoir* gives an air to my whole dress. If I only had a classical nose and mouth I should be perfectly happy," she said, surveying herself with a critical eye, and a candle in each hand.

In spite of this affliction, she looked unusually gay and graceful as she glided away; she seldom ran—it did not suit her style, she thought, for, being tall, the stately and Junoesque was more appropriate than the sportive or piquante. She walked up and down the long saloon while waiting for Laurie, and once arranged herself under the chandelier, which had a good effect upon her hair; then she thought better of it, and went away to the other end of the room, as if ashamed of the girlish desire to have the first view a propitious one. It so happened that she could not have done a better thing, for Laurie came in so quietly she did not hear him; and, as she stood at the distant window, with her head half turned, and one hand gathering up her dress, the slender, white figure against the red curtains was as effective as a well-placed statue.

"Good evening, Diana!" said Laurie, with the look of satisfaction she liked to see in his eyes when they rested on her.

"Good evening, Apollo!" she answered, smiling back at him, for he, too, looked unusually debonair, and the thought of entering the ballroom on the arm of such a personable man caused Amy to pity the four plain Misses Davis from the bottom of her heart.

"Here are your flowers; I arranged them myself, remembering that you didn't like what Hannah calls a 'sot bookay,'" said Laurie, handing her a delicate nosegay, in a holder that she had long coveted as she daily passed it in Cardiglia's window.

"How kind you are!" she exclaimed gratefully. "If I'd known you were coming I'd have had something ready for you today, though not as pretty as this, I'm afraid."

"Thank you; it isn't what it should be, but you have improved it," he added, as she snapped the silver bracelet on her wrist.

"Please don't."

"I thought you liked that sort of thing?"

"Not from you; it doesn't sound natural, and I like your old bluntness better."

"I'm glad of it," he answered, with a look of relief; then buttoned her gloves for her, and asked if his tie was straight, just as he used to do when they went to parties together, at home.

The company assembled in the long *salle à manger*, that evening, was such as one sees nowhere but on the Continent. The hospitable Americans had invited every acquaintance they had in Nice, and, having no prejudice against titles, secured a few to add luster to their Christmas ball.

A Russian prince condescended to sit in a corner for an hour and talk with a massive lady, dressed like Hamlet's mother, in black velvet, with a pearl bridle under her chin. A Polish count, aged eighteen, devoted himself to the ladies, who pronounced him "a fascinating dear," and a German Serene Something, having come for the supper alone, roamed vaguely about seeking what he might devour. Baron Rothschild's private secretary, a tall man, in tight boots, affably beamed upon the world, as if his master's name crowned him with a golden halo; a stout Frenchman, who knew the Emperor, came to indulge his mania for dancing, and Lady de Jones, a British matron, adorned the scene with her little family of eight. Of course, there were many light-footed, and shrill-voiced American girls, handsome, lifeless-looking English ditto, and a few plain but piquante French demoiselles; likewise the usual set of traveling young gentlemen, who disported themselves gaily, while mammas of all nations lined the walls, and smiled upon them benignly when they danced with their daughters.

Any young girl can imagine Amy's state of mind when she "took the stage" that night, leaning on Laurie's arm. She knew she looked well, she loved to dance, she felt that her foot was on her native heath in a ballroom, and enjoyed the delightful sense of power which comes when young girls first discover the new and lovely kingdom they are born to rule by virtue of beauty, youth, and womanhood. She did pity the Davis girls, who were awkward, plain, and destitute of escort, except a grim papa and three grimmer maiden aunts, and she bowed to them in her friendliest manner as she passed; which was good of her, as it permitted them to see her dress, and burn with curiosity to know who her distinguished-looking friend might be. With the first burst of the band, Amy's color rose, her eyes began to sparkle, and her feet to tap the floor impatiently; for she danced well, and wanted Laurie to know it; therefore the shock she received can better be imagined than described, when he said in a perfectly tranquil tone:

"Do you care to dance?"

"One usually does at a ball."

Her amazed look and quick answer caused Laurie to repair his error as fast as possible.

"I meant the first dance. May I have the honor?"

"I can give you one if I put off the count. He dances divinely; but he will excuse me, as you are an old friend," said Amy, hoping that the name would have a good effect, and show Laurie that she was not to be trifled with.

"Nice little boy, but rather a short Pole to support

> "A daughter of the gods,
> Divinely tall, and most divinely fair,"

was all the satisfaction she got, however.

The set in which they found themselves was composed of English, and Amy was compelled to walk decorously through a cotillon, feeling all the while as if she could dance the tarantella with a relish. Laurie resigned her to the "nice little boy," and went to do his duty to Flo, without securing Amy for the joys to come, which reprehensible want of forethought was properly punished, for she immediately engaged herself till supper, meaning to relent if he then gave any signs of penitence. She showed him her ball book with demure satisfaction when he strolled, instead of rushing, up to claim her for the next, a glorious polka-redowa; but his polite regrets didn't impose upon her, and when she galloped away with the count she saw Laurie sit down by her aunt with an actual expression of relief.

That was unpardonable; and Amy took no more notice of him for a long while, except a word now and then when she came to her chaperon, between the dances, for a necessary pin or a moment's rest. Her anger had a good effect, however, for she hid it under a smiling face, and seemed unusually blithe and brilliant. Laurie's eyes followed her with pleasure, for she neither romped nor sauntered, but danced with spirit and grace, making the delightsome pastime what it should be. He very naturally fell to studying her from this new point of view; and, before the evening was half over, had decided that "little Amy was going to make a very charming woman."

It was a lively scene, for soon the spirit of the social season took possession of everyone, and Christmas merriment made all faces shine, hearts happy, and heels light. The musicians fiddled, tooted, and banged as if they enjoyed it; everybody danced who could, and those who couldn't admired their neighbors with uncommon warmth. The air was dark with Davises, and many Joneses gamboled like a flock of young giraffes. The golden secretary darted through the room like a meteor, with a dashing Frenchwoman, who carpeted the floor with her pink satin train. The Serene Teuton found the supper table, and was happy, eating steadily through the bill of fare, and dismayed the garçons by the ravages he committed. But the Emperor's friend covered himself with glory, for he danced everything, whether he knew it or not, and introduced impromptu pirouettes when the figures bewildered him. The boyish abandon of that stout man was charming to behold; for, though he "carried weight," he danced like an India-rubber ball. He ran, he flew, he pranced; his face glowed, his bald head shone; his coattails waved wildly, his pumps actually twinkled in the air, and when the music stopped, he wiped the drops from his brow, and beamed upon his fellow men like a French Pickwick without glasses.

Amy and her Pole distinguished themselves by equal enthusiasm, but more graceful agility; and Laurie found himself involuntarily keeping time to the rhythmic rise and fall of the

white slippers as they flew by as indefatigably as if winged.
When little Vladimir finally relinquished her, with assurances
that he was "desolated to leave so early," she was ready to rest,
and see how her recreant knight had borne his punishment.

It had been successful; for, at three and twenty blighted
affections find a balm in friendly society, and young nerves
will thrill, young blood dance, and healthy young spirits rise,
when subjected to the enchantment of beauty, light, music,
and motion. Laurie had a waked-up look as he rose to give her
his seat; and when he hurried away to bring her some supper,
she said to herself, with a satisfied smile:

"Ah, I thought that would do him good!"

"You look like Balzac's 'Femme peinte par elle même,'" he
said, as he fanned her with one hand and held her coffee cup
in the other.

"My rouge won't come off," and Amy rubbed her brilliant
cheek, and showed him her white glove with a sober simplicity that made him laugh outright.

"What do you call this stuff?" he asked, touching a fold of
her dress that had blown over his knee.

"Illusion."

"Good name for it; it's very pretty—new thing, isn't it?"

"It's as old as the hills; you have seen it on dozens of girls,
and you never found out that it was pretty till now—*stupide!*"

"I never saw it on you before, which accounts for the mistake, you see."

"None of that, it is forbidden; I'd rather take coffee than
compliments just now. No, don't lounge, it makes me nervous."

Laurie sat bolt upright, and meekly took her empty plate,
feeling an odd sort of pleasure in having "little Amy" order
him about; for she had lost her shyness now, and felt an irresistible desire to trample on him, as girls have a delightful way
of doing when lords of creation show any signs of subjection.

"Where did you learn all this sort of thing?" he asked, with
a quizzical look.

"As 'this sort of thing' is rather a vague expression, would
you kindly explain?" returned Amy, knowing perfectly well
what he meant, but wickedly leaving him to describe what is
indescribable.

"Well—the general air, the style, the self-possession, the—
the—illusion—you know," laughed Laurie, breaking down, and
helping himself out of his quandary with the new word.

Amy was gratified, but, of course, didn't show it, and demurely answered, "Foreign life polishes one in spite of one's
self; I study as well as play; and as for this"—with a little gesture toward her dress—"why, tulle is cheap, posies to be had
for nothing, and I am used to making the most of my poor
little things."

Amy rather regretted that last sentence, fearing it wasn't in
good taste; but Laurie liked her the better for it, and found
himself both admiring and respecting the brave patience that
made the most of opportunity, and the cheerful spirit that covered poverty with flowers. Amy did not know why he looked
at her so kindly, nor why he filled up her book with his own
name, and devoted himself to her for the rest of the evening,
in the most delightful manner; but the impulse that wrought
this agreeable change was the result of one of the new impres-
sions which both of them were unconsciously giving and receiving.

CHAPTER THIRTY-EIGHT

On the Shelf

IN France the young girls have a dull time of it till they are married, when *"Vive la liberté"* becomes their motto. In America, as everyone knows, girls early sign the declaration of independence, and enjoy their freedom with republican zest; but the young matrons usually abdicate with the first heir to the throne, and go into a seclusion almost as close as a French nunnery, though by no means as quiet. Whether they like it or not, they are virtually put upon the shelf as soon as the wedding excitement is over, and most of them might exclaim, as did a very pretty woman the other day, "I'm as handsome as ever, but no one takes any notice of me because I'm married."

Not being a belle or even a fashionable lady, Meg did not experience this affliction till her babies were a year old, for in her little world primitive customs prevailed, and she found herself more admired and beloved than ever.

A; she was a womanly little woman, the maternal instinct was very strong, and she was entirely absorbed in her children, to the utter exclusion of everything and everybody else. Day and night she brooded over them with tireless devotion and anxiety, leaving John to the tender mercies of the help, for an Irish lady now presided over the kitchen department. Being a domestic man, John decidedly missed the wifely attentions he had been accustomed to receive; but, as he adored his babies, he cheerfully relinquished his comfort for a time, supposing, with masculine ignorance, that peace would soon be restored. But three months passed, and there was no return or repose; Meg looked worn and nervous, the babies absorbed every minute of her time, the house was neglected, and Kitty, the cook, who took life "aisy," kept him on short commons. When he went out in the morning he was bewildered by small commissions for the captive mamma; if he came gaily in at night, eager to embrace his family, he was quenched by a "Hush! They are just asleep after worrying all day." If he proposed a little amusement at home, "No, it would disturb the babies." If he hinted at a lecture or concert, he was answered with a reproachful look, and a decided "Leave my children for pleasure, never!" His sleep was broken by infant wails and visions of a phantom figure pacing noiselessly to and fro in the watches of the night; his meals were interrupted by the frequent flight of the presiding genius, who deserted him, half helped, if a muffled chirp sounded from the nest above; and when he read his paper of an evening, Demi's colic got into the shipping list, and Daisy's fall affected the price of stocks, for Mrs. Brooke was only interested in domestic news.

The poor man was very uncomfortable, for the children had bereft him of his wife; home was merely a nursery, and the perpetual "hushing" made him feel like a brutal intruder whenever he entered the sacred precincts of Babyland. He bore it very patiently for six months, and, when no signs of amendment appeared, he did what other paternal exiles do—tried to get a little comfort elsewhere. Scott had married and gone to housekeeping not far off, and John fell into the way of running over for an hour or two of an evening, when his own parlor was empty and his own wife singing lullabies that seemed to have no end. Mrs. Scott was a lively, pretty girl, with nothing to do but be agreeable, and she performed her mission most successfully. The parlor was always bright and attractive, the chessboard ready, the piano in tune, plenty of gay gossip, and a nice little supper set forth in tempting style.

John would have preferred his own fireside if it had not been so lonely; but as it was, he gratefully took the next best thing, and enjoyed his neighbor's society.

Meg rather approved of the new arrangement at first, and found it a relief to know that John was having a good time instead of dozing in the parlor or tramping about the house and waking the children. But by and by, when the teething worry was over, and the idols went to sleep at proper hours, leaving mamma time to rest, she began to miss John, and find her workbasket dull company, when he was not sitting opposite in his old dressing gown, comfortably scorching his slippers on the fender. She would not ask him to stay at home, but felt injured because he did not know that she wanted him without being told, entirely forgetting the many evenings he had waited for her in vain. She was nervous and worn out with watching and worry, and in that unreasonable frame of mind which the best of mothers occasionally experience when domestic cares oppress them. Want of exercise robs them of cheerfulness, and too much devotion to that idol of American women, the teapot, makes them feel as if they were all nerve and no muscle.

"Yes," she would say, looking in the glass, "I'm getting old and ugly; John doesn't find me interesting any longer, so he leaves his faded wife and goes to see his pretty neighbor, who has no incumbrances. Well, the babies love me; they don't care if I am thin and pale, and haven't time to crimp my hair; they are my comfort, and someday John will see what I've gladly sacrificed for them, won't he, my precious?"

To which pathetic appeal Daisy would answer with a coo, or Demi with a crow, and Meg would put by her lamentations for a maternal revel, which soothed her solitude for the time being. But the pain increased as politics absorbed John, who was always running over to discuss interesting points with Scott, quite unconscious that Meg missed him. Not a word did she say, however, till her mother found her in tears one day, and insisted on knowing what the matter was, for Meg's drooping spirits had not escaped her observation.

"I wouldn't tell anyone except you, mother; but I really do need advice, for if John goes on so much longer I might as well be widowed," replied Mrs. Brooke, drying her tears on Daisy's bib, with an injured air.

"Goes on how, my dear?" asked her mother anxiously.

"He's away all day, and at night, when I want to see him, he is continually going over to the Scotts'. It isn't fair that I should have the hardest work, and never any amusement. Men are very selfish, even the best of them."

"So are women; don't blame John till you see where you are wrong yourself."

"But it can't be right for him to neglect me."

"Don't you neglect him?"

"Why, mother, I thought you'd take my part!"

"So I do, as far as sympathizing goes; but I think the fault is yours, Meg."

"I don't see how."

"Let me show you. Did John ever neglect you, as you call it, while you made it a point to give him your society of an evening, his only leisure time?"

"No; but I can't do it now, with two babies to tend."

"I think you could, dear; and I think you ought. May I speak quite freely, and will you remember that it's mother who blames as well as mother who sympathizes?"

"Indeed, I will! Speak to me as if I were little Meg again. I often feel as if I needed teaching more than ever since these babies look to me for everything."

Meg drew her low chair beside her mother's, and, with a little interruption in either lap, the two women rocked and talked lovingly together, feeling that the tie of motherhood made them more one than ever.

"You have only made the mistake that most young wives make—forgotten your duty to your husband in your love for your children. A very natural and forgivable mistake, Meg, but one that had better be remedied before you take to different ways; for children should draw you nearer than ever, not separate you, as if they were all yours and John had nothing to do but support them. I've seen it for some weeks, but have not spoken, feeling sure it would come right in time."

"I'm afraid it won't. If I ask him to stay, he'll think I'm jealous; and I wouldn't insult him by such an idea. He doesn't see that I want him, and I don't know how to tell him without words."

"Make it so pleasant he won't want to go away. My dear, he's longing for his little home; but it isn't home without you, and you are always in the nursery."

"Oughtn't I to be there?"

"Not all the time; too much confinement makes you nervous, and then you are unfitted for everything. Besides, you owe something to John as well as to the babies; don't neglect husband for children, don't shut him out of the nursery, but teach him how to help in it. His place is there as well as yours, and the children need him; let him feel that he has his part to do, and he will do it gladly and faithfully, and it will be better for you all."

"You really think so, mother?"

"I know it, Meg, for I've tried it; and I seldom give advice unless I've proved its practicability. When you and Jo were little, I went on just as you are, feeling as if I didn't do my duty unless I devoted myself wholly to you. Poor father took to his books, after I had refused all offers of help, and left me to try my experiment alone. I struggled along as well as I could, but Jo was too much for me. I nearly spoilt her by indulgence. You were poorly, and I worried about you till I fell sick myself. Then father came to the rescue, quietly managed everything, and made himself so helpful that I saw my mistake, and never have been able to get on without him since. That is the secret of our home happiness: he does not let business wean him from the little cares and duties that affect us all, and I try not to let domestic worries destroy my interest in his pursuits. We each do our part alone in many things, but at home we work together, always."

"It is so, mother; and my great wish is to be to my husband

and children what you have been to yours. Show me how; I'll do anything you say."

"You always were my docile daughter. Well, dear, if I were you, I'd let John have more to do with the management of Demi, for the boy needs training, and it's none too soon to begin. Then I'd do what I have often proposed, let Hannah come and help you; she is a capital nurse, and you may trust the precious babies to her while you do more housework. You need the exercise, Hannah would enjoy the rest, and John would find his wife again. Get out more; keep cheerful as well as busy, for you are the sunshine-maker of the family, and if you get dismal there is no fair weather. Then I'd try to take an interest in whatever John likes—talk with him, let him read to you, exchange ideas, and help each other in that way. Don't shut yourself up in a bandbox because you are a woman, but understand what is going on, and educate yourself to take your part in the world's work, for it all affects you and yours."

"John is so sensible, I'm afraid he will think I'm stupid if I ask questions about politics and things."

"I don't believe he would; love covers a multitude of sins, and of whom could you ask more freely than of him? Try it, and see if he doesn't find your society far more agreeable than Mrs. Scott's suppers."

"I will. Poor John! I'm afraid I *have* neglected him sadly, but I thought I was right, and he never said anything."

"He tried not to be selfish, but he *has* felt rather forlorn, I fancy. This is just the time, Meg, when young married people are apt to grow apart, and the very time when they ought to be most together; for the first tenderness soon wears off, unless care is taken to preserve it; and no time is so beautiful and precious to parents as the first years of the little lives given them to train. Don't let John be a stranger to the babies, for they will do more to keep him safe and happy in this world of trial and temptation than anything else, and through them you will learn to know and love one another as you should. Now, dear, good-by; think over mother's preachment, act upon it if it seems good, and God bless you all!"

Meg did think it over, found it good, and acted upon it, though the first attempt was not made exactly as she planned to have it. Of course the children tyrannized over her, and ruled the house as soon as they found out that kicking and squalling brought them whatever they wanted. Mamma was an abject slave to their caprices, but papa was not so easily subjugated, and occasionally afflicted his tender spouse by an attempt at paternal discipline with his obstreperous son. For Demi inherited a trifle of his sire's firmness of character—we won't call it obstinacy—and when he made up his little mind to have or to do anything, all the king's horses and all the king's men could not change that pertinacious little mind. Mamma thought the dear too young to be taught to conquer his prejudices, but papa believed that it never was too soon to learn obedience; so Master Demi early discovered that when he undertook to "wrastle" with "parpar," he always got the worst of it; yet, like the Englishman, Baby respected the man who conquered him, and loved the father whose grave "No, no," was more impressive than all mamma's love pats.

A few days after the talk with her mother, Meg resolved to try a social evening with John; so she ordered a nice supper, set the parlor in order, dressed herself prettily, and put the children to bed early, that nothing should interfere with her experiment. But, unfortunately, Demi's most unconquerable prejudice was against going to bed, and that night he decided to go on a rampage; so poor Meg sung and rocked, told stories and tried every sleep-provoking wile she could devise, but all in vain, the big eyes wouldn't shut; and long after Daisy had gone to bye-low, like the chubby little bunch of good nature she was, naughty Demi lay staring at the light, with the most discouragingly wide-awake expression of countenance.

"Will Demi lie still like a good boy, while mamma runs down and gives poor papa his tea?" asked Meg, as the hall door softly closed, and the well-known step went tiptoeing into the dining room.

"Me has tea!" said Demi, preparing to join in the revel.

"No; but I'll save you some little cakies for breakfast, if you'll go bye-bye like Daisy. Will you, lovey?"

"'Iss!" and Demi shut his eyes tight, as if to catch sleep and hurry the desired day.

Taking advantage of the propitious moment, Meg slipped

away, and ran down to greet her husband with a smiling face,
and the little blue bow in her hair which was his especial admiration. He saw it at once, and said, with pleased surprise:

"Why, little mother, how gay we are tonight. Do you expect
company? Is it a birthday, anniversary, or anything?"

"No; I'm tired of being a dowdy, so I dressed up as a change.
You always make yourself nice for table, no matter how tired
you are; so why shouldn't I when I have the time?"

"I do it out of respect to you, my dear," said the old-fashioned John.

"Ditto, ditto, Mr. Brooke," laughed Meg, looking young and
pretty again, as she nodded to him over the teapot.

"Well, it's altogether delightful, and like old times. This
tastes right. I drink your health, dear." And John sipped his
tea with an air of reposeful rapture, which was of very short
duration, however; for, as he put down his cup, the door handle rattled mysteriously, and a little voice was heard, saying
impatiently:

"Opy doy; me's tummin!"

"It's that naughty boy. I told him to go to sleep alone, and
here he is, downstairs, getting his death a-cold pattering over
that canvas," said Meg, answering the call.

"Mornin' now," announced Demi, in a joyful tone, as he entered, with his long nightgown gracefully festooned over his
arm, and every curl bobbing gaily as he pranced about the
table, eying the "cakies" with loving glances.

"No, it isn't morning yet. You must go to bed, and not trouble poor mamma; then you can have the little cake with sugar
on it."

"Me loves parpar," said the artful one, preparing to climb
the paternal knee, and revel in forbidden joys. But John shook
his head, and said to Meg:

"If you told him to stay up there, and go to sleep alone,
make him do it, or he will never learn to mind you."

"Yes, of course. Come, Demi," and Meg led her son away,
feeling a strong desire to spank the little marplot who hopped
beside her, laboring under the delusion that the bribe was to
be administered as soon as they reached the nursery.

Nor was he disappointed; for that shortsighted woman actually gave him a lump of sugar, tucked him into his bed, and forbade any more promenades till morning.

"Iss!" said Demi the perjured, blissfully sucking his sugar and regarding his first attempt as eminently successful.

Meg returned to her place, and supper was progressing pleasantly, when the little ghost walked again, and exposed the maternal delinquencies by boldly demanding:

"More sudar, marmar."

"Now this won't do," said John, hardening his heart against the engaging little sinner. "We shall never know any peace till that child learns to go to bed properly. You have made a slave of yourself long enough; give him one lesson, and then there will be an end of it. Put him in his bed and leave him, Meg."

"He won't stay there; he never does, unless I sit by him."

"I'll manage him. Demi, go upstairs, and get into your bed, as mamma bids you."

"S'ant!" replied the young rebel, helping himself to the coveted cakie, and beginning to eat the same with calm audacity.

"You must never say that to papa; I shall carry you if you don't go by yourself."

"Go 'way; me don't love parpar," and Demi retired to his mother's skirts for protection.

But even that refuge proved unavailing, for he was delivered over to the enemy, with a "Be gentle with him, John," which struck the culprit with dismay; for when mamma deserted him, then the judgment day was at hand. Bereft of his cake, defrauded of his frolic, and borne away by a strong hand to that detested bed, poor Demi could not restrain his wrath, but openly defied papa, and kicked and screamed lustily all the way upstairs. The minute he was put into bed on one side, he rolled out on the other, and made for the door, only to be ignominiously caught up by the tail of his little toga, and put back again, which lively performance was kept up till the young man's strength gave out, when he devoted himself to roaring at the top of his voice. The vocal exercise usually conquered Meg; but John sat as unmoved as the post which is popularly believed to be deaf. No coaxing, no sugar, no lullaby, no story, even the light was put out, and only the red glow of the fire enlivened the "big dark" which Demi regarded with curiosity rather than fear. This new order of things dis-gusted him, and he howled dismally for "marmar," as his an-gry passions subsided, and recollections of his tender bond-woman returned to the captive autocrat. The plaintive wail which succeeded the passionate roar went to Meg's heart, and she ran up to say beseechingly:

"Let me stay with him; he'll be good, now, John."

"No, my dear, I've told him he must go to sleep, as you bid him; and he must, if I stay here all night."

"But he'll cry himself sick," pleaded Meg, reproaching her-self for deserting her boy.

"No, he won't, he's so tired he will soon drop off, and then the matter is settled; for he will understand that he has got to mind. Don't interfere; I'll manage him."

"He's my child, and I can't have his spirit broken by harsh-ness."

"He's my child, and I won't have his temper spoilt by in-dulgence. Go down, my dear, and leave the boy to me."

When John spoke in that masterful tone, Meg always obeyed, and never regretted her docility.

"Please let me kiss him once, John?"

"Certainly. Demi, say good night to mamma, and let her go and rest, for she is very tired with taking care of you all day."

Meg always insisted upon it that the kiss won the victory; for after it was given, Demi sobbed more quietly, and lay quite still at the bottom of the bed, whither he had wriggled in his anguish of mind.

"Poor little man, he's worn out with sleep and crying. I'll cover him up, and then go and set Meg's heart at rest," thought John, creeping to the bedside, hoping to find his rebellious heir asleep.

But he wasn't; for the moment his father peeped at him, Demi's eyes opened, his little chin began to quiver, and he put up his arms, saying, with a penitent hiccough, "Me's dood, now."

Sitting on the stairs, outside, Meg wondered at the long silence which followed the uproar; and, after imagining all sorts of impossible accidents, she slipped into the room, to set

her fears at rest. Demi lay fast asleep; not in his usual spread-eagle attitude, but in a subdued bunch, cuddled close in the circle of his father's arm and holding his father's finger, as if he felt that justice was tempered with mercy, and had gone to sleep a sadder and a wiser baby. So held, John had waited with womanly patience till the little hand relaxed its hold; and, while waiting, had fallen asleep, more tired by that tussle with his son than with his whole day's work.

As Meg stood watching the two faces on the pillow, she smiled to herself, and then slipped away again, saying, in a satisfied tone:

"I never need fear that John will be too harsh with my babies: he *does* know how to manage them, and will be a great help, for Demi *is* getting too much for me."

When John came down at last, expecting to find a pensive or reproachful wife, he was agreeably surprised to find Meg placidly trimming a bonnet, and to be greeted with the request to read something about the election, if he was not too tired. John saw in a minute that a revolution of some kind was going on, but wisely asked no questions, knowing that Meg was such a transparent little person, she couldn't keep a secret to save her life, and therefore the clew would soon appear. He read a long debate with the most amiable readiness and then explained in his most lucid manner, while Meg tried to look deeply interested, to ask intelligent questions, and keep her thoughts from wandering from the state of the nation to the state of her bonnet. In her secret soul, however, she decided that politics were as bad as mathematics, and that the mission of politicians seemed to be calling each other names; but she kept these feminine ideas to herself, and when John paused shook her head, and said with what she thought diplomatic ambiguity:

"Well, I really don't see what we are coming to."

John laughed and watched her for a minute, as she poised a pretty little preparation of lace and flowers on her hand, and regarded it with the genuine interest which his harangue had failed to waken.

"She is trying to like politics for my sake, so I'll try and like millinery for hers, that's only fair," thought John the Just, adding aloud:

"That's very pretty; is it what you call a breakfast cap?"

"My dear man, it's a bonnet! My very best go-to-concert-and-theater bonnet."

"I beg your pardon; it was so small, I naturally mistook it for one of the flyaway things you sometimes wear. How do you keep it on?"

"These bits of lace are fastened under the chin with a rose-

bud, so," and Meg illustrated by putting on the bonnet and regarding him with an air of calm satisfaction that was irresistible.

"It's a love of a bonnet, but I prefer the face inside, for it
looks young and happy again," and John kissed the smiling
face, to the great detriment of the rosebud under the chin.

"I'm glad you like it, for I want you to take me to one of the
new concerts some night; I really need some music to put me
in tune. Will you, please?"

"Of course I will, with all my heart, or anywhere else you
like. You have been shut up so long, it will do you no end of
good, and I shall enjoy it, of all things. What put it into your
head, little mother?"

"Well, I had a talk with Marmee the other day, and told her
how nervous and cross and out of sorts I felt, and she said I
needed change and less care: so Hannah is to help me with
the children, and I'm to see to things about the house more,
and now and then have a little fun, just to keep me from getting to be a fidgety, broken-down old woman before my time.
It's only an experiment, John, and I want to try it for your sake
as much as for mine, because I've neglected you shamefully
lately, and I'm going to make home what it used to be, if I can.
You don't object, I hope?"

Never mind what John said, or what a very narrow escape
the little bonnet had from utter ruin; all that we have any business to know is that John did *not* appear to object, judging
from the changes which gradually took place in the house and
its inmates. It was not all Paradise by any means, but everyone
was better for the division of labor system; the children throve
under the paternal rule, for accurate, steadfast John brought
order and obedience into Babydom, while Meg recovered her
spirits and composed her nerves by plenty of wholesome exercise, a little pleasure, and much confidential conversation with
her sensible husband. Home grew homelike again, and John
had no wish to leave it, unless he took Meg with him. The
Scotts came to the Brookes' now, and everyone found the little
house a cheerful place, full of happiness, content, and family
love. Even gay Sallie Moffat liked to go there. "It is always so
quiet and pleasant here; it does me good, Meg," she used to

say, looking about with wistful eyes, as if trying to discover the charm, that she might use it in her great house, full of splendid loneliness; for there were no riotous, sunny-faced babies there, and Ned lived in a world of his own, where there was no place for her.

This household happiness did not come all at once, but John and Meg had found the key to it, and each year of married life taught them how to use it, unlocking the treasuries of real home love and mutual helpfulness, which the poorest may possess, and the richest cannot buy. This is the sort of shelf on which young wives and mothers may consent to be laid, safe from the restless fret and fever of the world, finding loyal lovers in the little sons and daughters who cling to them, undaunted by sorrow, poverty, or age; walking side by side, through fair and stormy weather, with a faithful friend, who is, in the true sense of the good old Saxon word, the "houseband," and learning, as Meg learned, that a woman's happiest kingdom is home, her highest honor the art of ruling it not as a queen, but as a wise wife and mother.

CHAPTER THIRTY-NINE

Lazy Laurence

LAURIE went to Nice intending to stay a week, and remained a month. He was tired of wandering about alone, and Amy's familiar presence seemed to give a homelike charm to the foreign scenes in which she bore a part. He rather missed the "petting" he used to receive, and enjoyed a taste of it again; for no attentions, however flattering, from strangers were half so pleasant as the sisterly adoration of the girls at home. Amy never would pet him like the others, but she was very glad to see him now, and quite clung to him, feeling that he was the representative of the dear family for whom she longed more than she would confess. They naturally took comfort in each other's society, and were much together, riding, walking, dancing, or dawdling, for, at Nice, no one can be very industrious during the gay season. But, while apparently amusing themselves in the most careless fashion, they were half consciously making discoveries and forming opinions about each other. Amy rose daily in the estimation of her friend, but he sunk in hers, and each felt the truth before a word was spoken. Amy tried to please, and succeeded, for she was grateful for the many pleasures he gave her, and repaid him with the little services to which womanly women know how to lend an indescribable charm. Laurie made no effort of any kind, but just let himself drift along as comfortably as possible, trying to forget, and feeling that all women owed him a kind word because one had been cold to him. It cost him no effort to be generous, and he would have given Amy all the trinkets in Nice if she would have taken them; but, at the same time, he felt that he could not change the opinion she was forming of him, and he rather dreaded the keen blue eyes that seemed to watch him with such half-sorrowful, half-scornful surprise.

"All the rest have gone to Monaco for the day; I preferred to stay at home and write letters. They are done now, and I am going to Valrosa to sketch; will you come?" said Amy, as she joined Laurie one lovely day when he lounged in as usual, about noon.

"Well, yes; but isn't it rather warm for such a long walk?" he answered slowly, for the shaded salon looked inviting, after the glare without.

"I'm going to have the little carriage, and Baptiste can drive, so you'll have nothing to do but hold your umbrella and keep your gloves nice," returned Amy, with a sarcastic glance at the immaculate kids, which were a weak point with Laurie.

"Then I'll go with pleasure," and he put out his hand for her sketchbook. But she tucked it under her arm with a sharp—

"Don't trouble yourself; it's no exertion to me, but *you* don't look equal to it."

Laurie lifted his eyebrows, and followed at a leisurely pace as she ran downstairs; but when they got into the carriage he took the reins himself, and left little Baptiste nothing to do but fold his arms and fall asleep on his perch.

The two never quarreled—Amy was too well bred, and just now Laurie was too lazy; so, in a minute he peeped under her hat brim with an inquiring air; she answered with a smile, and they went on together in the most amicable manner.

It was a lovely drive, along winding roads rich in the picturesque scenes that delight beauty-loving eyes. Here an ancient monastery, whence the solemn chanting of the monks came down to them. There a barelegged shepherd, in wooden shoes, pointed hat, and rough jacket over one shoulder, sat piping on a stone, while his goats skipped among the rocks or lay at his feet. Meek, mouse-colored donkeys, laden with panniers of freshly cut grass, passed by, with a pretty girl in a *capaline* sitting between the green piles, or an old woman spinning with a distaff as she went. Brown, soft-eyed children ran out from the quaint stone hovels to offer nosegays, or bunches of oranges still on the bough. Gnarled olive trees covered the hills with their dusky foliage, fruit hung golden in the orchard, and great scarlet anemones fringed the roadside; while beyond green slopes and craggy heights, the Maritime Alps rose sharp and white against the blue Italian sky.

Valrosa well deserved its name, for, in that climate of perpetual summer, roses blossomed everywhere. They overhung the archway, thrust themselves between the bars of the great gate with a sweet welcome to passers-by, and lined the avenue, winding through lemon trees and feathery palms up to the villa on the hill. Every shadowy nook, where seats invited one to stop and rest, was a mass of bloom; every cool grotto had its marble nymph smiling from a veil of flowers; and every fountain reflected crimson, white, or pale pink roses, leaning down to smile at their own beauty. Roses covered the walls of the house, draped the cornices, climbed the pillars, and ran riot over the balustrade of the wide terrace, whence one looked down on the sunny Mediterranean, and the white-walled city on its shore.

"This is a regular honeymoon Paradise, isn't it? Did you ever see such roses?" asked Amy, pausing on the terrace to enjoy the view, and a luxurious whiff of perfume that came wandering by.

"No, nor felt such thorns," returned Laurie, with his thumb in his mouth, after a vain attempt to capture a solitary scarlet flower that grew just beyond his reach.

"Try lower down, and pick those that have no thorns," said Amy, gathering three of the tiny cream-colored ones that starred the wall behind her. She put them in his buttonhole, as a peace offering, and he stood a minute looking down at them with a curious expression, for in the Italian part of his nature there was a touch of superstition, and he was just then in that state of half-sweet, half-bitter melancholy, when imaginative young men find significance in trifles, and food for romance everywhere. He had thought of Jo in reaching after the thorny red rose, for vivid flowers became her, and she had often worn ones like that from the greenhouse at home. The pale roses Amy gave him were the sort that the Italians lay in dead hands, never in bridal wreaths, and, for a moment, he wondered if the omen was for Jo or for himself; but the next instant his American common sense got the better of sentimentality, and he laughed a heartier laugh than Amy had heard since he came.

"It's good advice; you'd better take it and save your fingers," she said, thinking her speech amused him.

"Thank you, I will," he answered in jest, and a few months later he did it in earnest.

"Laurie, when are you going to your grandfather?" she asked presently, as she settled herself on a rustic seat.

"Very soon."

"You have said that a dozen times within the last three weeks."

"I dare say; short answers save trouble."

"He expects you, and you really ought to go."

"Hospitable creature! I know it."

"Then why don't you do it?"

"Natural depravity, I suppose."

"Natural indolence, you mean. It's really dreadful!" and Amy looked severe.

"Not so bad as it seems, for I should only plague him if I went, so I might as well stay, and plague you a little longer, you can bear it better; in fact, I think it agrees with you excellently," and Laurie composed himself for a lounge on the broad ledge of the balustrade.

Amy shook her head, and opened her sketchbook with an air of resignation; but she had made up her mind to lecture "that boy," and in a minute she began again.

"What are you doing just now?"

"Watching lizards."

"No, no; I mean what do you intend and wish to do?"

"Smoke a cigarette, if you'll allow me."

"How provoking you are! I don't approve of cigars, and I will only allow it on condition that you let me put you into my sketch; I need a figure."

"With all the pleasure in life. How will you have me—full length or three-quarters, on my head or my heels? I should respectfully suggest a recumbent posture, then put yourself in also, and call it *'Dolce far niente.'*"

"Stay as you are, and go to sleep if you like. *I* intend to work hard," said Amy, in her most energetic tone.

"What delightful enthusiasm!" and he leaned against a tall urn with an air of entire satisfaction.

"What would Jo say if she saw you now?" asked Amy impatiently, hoping to stir him up by the mention of her still more energetic sister's name.

"As usual. 'Go away, Teddy, I'm busy!'" He laughed as he spoke, but the laugh was not natural, and a shade passed over his face, for the utterance of the familiar name touched the wound that was not healed yet. Both tone and shadow struck Amy, for she had seen and heard them before, and now she looked up in time to catch a new expression on Laurie's face— a hard, bitter look, full of pain, dissatisfaction, and regret. It was gone before she could study it, and the listless expression back again. She watched him for a moment with artistic pleasure, thinking how like an Italian he looked, as he lay basking in the sun with uncovered head, and eyes full of southern dreaminess; for he seemed to have forgotten her, and fallen into a reverie.

"You look like the effigy of a young knight asleep on his tomb," she said, carefully tracing the well-cut profile defined against the dark stone.

"Wish I was!"

"That's a foolish wish, unless you have spoilt your life. You are so changed, I sometimes think—" There Amy stopped, with a half-timid, half-wistful look, more significant than her unfinished speech.

Laurie saw and understood the affectionate anxiety which she hesitated to express, and looking straight into her eyes, said; just as he used to say it to her mother:

"It's all right, ma'am."

That satisfied her and set at rest tne doubts that had begun to worry her lately. It also touched her, and she showed that it did, by the cordial tone in which she said:

"I'm glad of that! I didn't think you'd been a very bad boy, but I fancied you might have wasted money at that wicked Baden-Baden, lost your heart to some charming Frenchwoman with a husband, or got into some of the scrapes that young men seem to consider a necessary part of a foreign tour. Don't stay out there in the sun; come and lie on the grass here, and 'let us be friendly,' as Jo used to say when we got in the sofa corner and told secrets."

Laurie obediently threw himself down on the turf, and began to amuse himself by sticking daisies into the ribbons of Amy's hat, that lay there.

"I'm all ready for the secrets," and he glanced up with a decided expression of interest in his eyes.

"I've none to tell; you may begin."

"Haven't one to bless myself with. I thought perhaps you'd had some news from home."

"You have heard all that has come lately. Don't you hear often? I fancied Jo would send you volumes."

"She's very busy; I'm roving about so, it's impossible to be regular, you know. When do you begin your great work of art, Raphaella?" he asked, changing the subject abruptly after another pause, in which he had been wondering if Amy knew his secret, and wanted to talk about it.

"Never," she answered, with a despondent but decided air. "Rome took all the vanity out of me; for after seeing the wonders there, I felt too insignificant to live, and gave up all my foolish hopes in despair."

"Why should you, with so much energy and talent?"

"That's just why—because talent isn't genius, and no amount of energy can make it so. I want to be great, or nothing. I won't be a commonplace dauber, so I don't intend to try any more."

"And what are you going to do with yourself now, if I may ask?"

"Polish up my other talents, and be an ornament to society, if I get the chance."

It was a characteristic speech, and sounded daring; but audacity becomes young people, and Amy's ambition had a good foundation. Laurie smiled, but he liked the spirit with which she took up a new purpose when a long-cherished one died, and spent no time lamenting.

"Good! And here is where Fred Vaughn comes in, I fancy."

Amy preserved a discreet silence, but there was a conscious look in her downcast face, that made Laurie sit up and say gravely:

"Now I'm going to play brother, and ask questions. May I?"

"I don't promise to answer."

"Your face will, if your tongue won't. You aren't woman of the world enough yet to hide your feelings, my dear. I heard rumors about Fred and you last year, and it's my private opinion that, if he had not been called home so suddenly and detained so long, something would have come of it—hey?"

"That's not for me to say" was Amy's prim reply; but her lips would smile, and there was a traitorous sparkle of the eye, which betrayed that she knew her power and enjoyed the knowledge.

"You are not engaged, I hope?" and Laurie looked very elder-brotherly and grave all of a sudden.

"No."

"But you will be, if he comes back and goes properly down upon his knees, won't you?"

"Very likely."

"Then you are fond of old Fred?"

"I could be, if I tried."

"But you don't intend to try till the proper moment? Bless my soul, what unearthly prudence! He's a good fellow, Amy, but not the man I fancied you'd like."

"He is rich, a gentleman, and has delightful manners," began Amy, trying to be quite cool and dignified, but feeling a little ashamed of herself, in spite of the sincerity of her intentions.

"I understand; queens of society can't get on without money, so you mean to make a good match, and start in that way? Quite right and proper, as the world goes, but it sounds odd from the lips of one of your mother's girls."

"True, nevertheless."

A short speech, but the quiet decision with which it was uttered contrasted curiously with the young speaker. Laurie felt this instinctively, and laid himself down again, with a sense of disappointment which he could not explain. His look and silence, as well as a certain inward self-disapproval, ruffled Amy, and made her resolve to deliver her lecture without delay.

"I wish you'd do me the favor to rouse yourself a little," she said sharply.

"Do it for me, there's a dear girl."

"I could, if I tried," and she looked as if she would like doing it in the most summary style.

"Try, then; I give you leave," returned Laurie, who enjoyed having someone to tease, after his long abstinence from his favorite pastime.

"You'd be angry in five minutes."

"I'm never angry with you. It takes two flints to make a fire: you are as cool and soft as snow."

"You don't know what I can do; snow produces a glow and a tingle, if applied rightly. Your indifference is half affectation, and a good stirring up would prove it."

"Stir away; it won't hurt me and it may amuse you, as the big man said when his little wife beat him. Regard me in the light of a husband or a carpet, and beat till you are tired, if that sort of exercise agrees with you."

Being decidedly nettled herself, and longing to see him shake off the apathy that so altered him, Amy sharpened both tongue and pencil, and began:

"Flo and I have got a new name for you; it's 'Lazy Laurence.' How do you like it?"

She thought it would annoy him; but he only folded his arms under his head, with an imperturbable "That's not bad. Thank you, ladies."

"Do you want to know what I honestly think of you?"

"Pining to be told."

"Well, I despise you."

If she had even said "I hate you," in a petulant or coquettish tone, he would have laughed, and rather liked it; but the

grave, almost sad, accent of her voice made him open his eyes
and ask quickly:

"Why, if you please?"

"Because, with every chance for being good, useful, and
happy, you are faulty, lazy, and miserable."

"Strong language, mademoiselle."

"If you like it, I'll go on."

"Pray do; it's quite interesting."

"I thought you'd find it so; selfish people always like to talk
about themselves."

"Am *I* selfish?" The question slipped out involuntarily and
in a tone of surprise, for the one virtue on which he prided
himself was generosity.

"Yes, very selfish," continued Amy, in a calm, cool voice,
twice as effective, just then, as an angry one. "I'll show you
how, for I've studied you while we have been frolicking, and
I'm not at all satisfied with you. Here you have been abroad
nearly six months, and done nothing but waste time and money
and disappoint your friends."

"Isn't a fellow to have any pleasure after a four years' grind?"

"You don't look as if you'd had much; at any rate, you are
none the better for it, as far as I can see. I said, when we first
met, that you had improved. Now I take it all back, for I don't
think you half so nice as when I left you at home. You have
grown abominably lazy; you like gossip, and waste time on
frivolous things; you are contented to be petted and admired
by silly people, instead of being loved and respected by wise
ones. With money, talent, position, health, and beauty—ah,
you like that, Old Vanity! but it's the truth, so I can't help saying it—with all these splendid things to use and enjoy, you
can find nothing to do but dawdle; and, instead of being the
man you might and ought to be, you are only—" There she
stopped, with a look that had both pain and pity in it.

"St. Laurence on a gridiron," added Laurie, blandly finishing
the sentence. But the lecture began to take effect, for there was
a wide-awake sparkle in his eyes now, and a half-angry, half-
injured expression replaced the former indifference.

"I supposed you'd take it so. You men tell us we are angels,
and say we can make you what we will; but the instant we

honestly try to do you good, you laugh at us, and won't listen, which proves how much your flattery is worth." Amy spoke bitterly, and turned her back on the exasperating martyr at her feet.

In a minute a hand came down over the page, so that she could not draw, and Laurie's voice said, with a droll imitation of a penitent child:

"I will be good, oh, I will be good!"

But Amy did not laugh, for she was in earnest; and, tapping on the outspread hand with her pencil, said soberly:

"Aren't you ashamed of a hand like that? It's as soft and white as a woman's, and looks as if it never did anything but wear Jouvin's best gloves, and pick flowers for ladies. You are not a dandy, thank Heaven! so I'm glad to see there are no diamonds or big seal rings on it, only the little old one Jo gave you so long ago. Dear soul, I wish she was here to help me!"

"So do I!"

The hand vanished as suddenly as it came, and there was energy enough in the echo of her wish to suit even Amy. She glanced down at him with a new thought in her mind; but he was lying with his hat half over his face, as if for shade, and his mustache hid his mouth. She only saw his chest rise and fall, with a long breath that might have been a sigh, and the hand that wore the ring nestled down into the grass, as if to hide something too precious or too tender to be spoken of. All in a minute various hints and trifles assumed shape and significance in Amy's mind, and told her what her sister never had confided to her. She remembered that Laurie never spoke voluntarily of Jo; she recalled the shadow on his face just now, the change in his character, and the wearing of the little old ring, which was no ornament to a handsome hand. Girls are quick to read such signs and feel their eloquence. Amy had fancied that perhaps a love trouble was at the bottom of the alteration, and now she was sure of it. Her keen eyes filled, and, when she spoke again, it was in a voice that could be beautifully soft and kind when she chose to make it so.

"I know I have no right to talk so to you, Laurie; and if you weren't the sweetest-tempered fellow in the world, you'd be very angry with me. But we are all so fond and proud of you,

I couldn't bear to think they should be disappointed in you
at home as I have been, though, perhaps, they would understand the change better than I do."

"I think they would" came from under the hat, in a grim
tone, quite as touching as a broken one.

"They ought to have told me, and not let me go blundering
and scolding, when I should have been more kind and patient
than ever. I never did like that Miss Randal, and now I hate
her!" said artful Amy, wishing to be sure of her facts this time.

"Hang Miss Randal!" and Laurie knocked the hat off his
face with a look that left no doubt of his sentiments toward
that young lady.

"I beg pardon; I thought—" and there she paused diplo-
matically.

"No, you didn't; you knew perfectly well I never cared for
anyone but Jo." Laurie said that in his old, impetuous tone, and
turned his face away as he spoke.

"I did think so; but as they never said anything about it, and
you came away, I supposed I was mistaken. And Jo wouldn't
be kind to you? Why, I was sure she loved you dearly."

"She *was* kind, but not in the right way; and it's lucky for
her she didn't love me, if I'm the good-for-nothing fellow you
think me. It's her fault, though, and you may tell her so."

The hard, bitter look came back again as he said that, and
it troubled Amy, for she did not know what balm to apply.

"I was wrong, I didn't know. I'm very sorry I was so cross,
but I can't help wishing you'd bear it better, Teddy dear."

"Don't, that's her name for me!" and Laurie put up his hand
with a quick gesture to stop the words spoken in Jo's half-
kind, half-reproachful tone. "Wait till you've tried it yourself,"
he added, in a low voice, as he pulled up the grass by the
handful.

"I'd take it manfully, and be respected if I couldn't be loved,"
said Amy, with the decision of one who knew nothing about it.

Now, Laurie flattered himself that he *had* borne it remarkably well, making no moan, asking no sympathy, and taking
his trouble away to live it down alone. Amy's lecture put the
matter in a new light, and for the first time it did look weak
and selfish to lose heart at the first failure, and shut himself

up in moody indifference. He felt as if suddenly shaken out of a pensive dream, and found it impossible to go to sleep again. Presently he sat up, and asked slowly:

"Do you think Jo would despise me as you do?"

"Yes, if she saw you now. She hates lazy people. Why don't you do something splendid, and *make* her love you?"

"I did my best, but it was no use."

"Graduating well, you mean? That was no more than you ought to have done, for your grandfather's sake. It would have been shameful to fail after spending so much time and money, when everyone knew you *could* do well."

"I did fail, say what you will, for Jo wouldn't love me," began Laurie, leaning his head on his hand in a despondent attitude.

"No, you didn't, and you'll say so in the end, for it did you good, and proved that you could do something if you tried. If you'd only set about another task of some sort, you'd soon be your hearty, happy self again, and forget your trouble."

"That's impossible."

"Try it and see. You needn't shrug your shoulders, and think, 'Much she knows about such things.' I don't pretend to be wise, but I *am* observing, and I see a great deal more than you'd imagine. I'm interested in other people's experiences and inconsistencies; and, though I can't explain, I remember and use them for my own benefit. Love Jo all your days, if you choose, but don't let it spoil you, for it's wicked to throw away so many good gifts because you can't have the one you want. There, I won't lecture any more, for I know you'll wake up and be a man in spite of that hardhearted girl."

Neither spoke for several minutes. Laurie sat turning the little ring on his finger, and Amy put the last touches to the hasty sketch she had been working at while she talked. Presently she put it on his knee, merely saying:

"How do you like that?"

He looked and then he smiled, as he could not well help doing, for it was capitally done—the long, lazy figure on the grass, with listless face, half-shut eyes, and one hand holding a cigar, from which came the little wreath of smoke that encircled the dreamer's head.

"How well you draw!" he said, with genuine surprise and pleasure at her skill, adding, with a half-laugh:

"Yes, that's me."

"As you are: this is as you were," and Amy laid another sketch beside the one he held.

It was not nearly so well done, but there was life and spirit in it which atoned for many faults, and it recalled the past so vividly that a sudden change swept over the young man's face as he looked. Only a rough sketch of Laurie taming a horse; hat and coat were off, and every line of the active figure, resolute face, and commanding attitude, was full of energy and meaning. The handsome brute, just subdued, stood arching his neck under the tightly drawn rein, with one foot impatiently pawing the ground, and ears pricked up as if listening for the voice that had mastered him. In the ruffled mane, the rider's breezy hair and erect attitude, there was a suggestion of suddenly arrested motion, of strength, courage, and youthful buoyancy, that contrasted sharply with the supine grace of the *"Dolce far niente"* sketch. Laurie said nothing; but, as his eye went from one to the other, Amy saw him flush up and fold his lips together as if he read and accepted the little lesson she had given him. That satisfied her; and, without waiting for him to speak, she said, in her sprightly way:

"Don't you remember the day you played Rarey with Puck, and we all looked on? Meg and Beth were frightened, but Jo clapped and pranced, and I sat on the fence and drew you. I found that sketch in my portfolio the other day, touched it up, and kept it to show you."

"Much obliged. You've improved immensely since then, and I congratulate you. May I venture to suggest in 'a honeymoon Paradise' that five o'clock is the dinner hour at your hotel?"

Laurie rose as he spoke, returned the pictures with a smile and a bow, and looked at his watch, as if to remind her that even moral lectures should have an end. He tried to resume his former easy, indifferent air, but it *was* an affectation now, for the rousing had been more efficacious than he would confess. Amy felt the shade of coldness in his manner, and said to herself:

"Now I've offended him. Well, if it does him good, I'm glad;

if it makes him hate me, I'm sorry; but it's true, and I can't take back a word of it."

They laughed and chatted all the way home; and little Baptiste, up behind, thought that monsieur and mademoiselle were in charming spirits. But both felt ill at ease; the friendly frankness was disturbed, the sunshine had a shadow over it, and, despite their apparent gaiety, there was a secret discontent in the heart of each.

"Shall we see you this evening, *mon frère?*" asked Amy, as they parted at her aunt's door.

"Unfortunately I have an engagement. *Au revoir, mademoiselle,*" and Laurie bent as if to kiss her hand, in the foreign fashion, which became him better than many men. Something in his face made Amy say quickly and warmly:

"No; be yourself with me, Laurie, and part in the good old way. I'd rather have a hearty English handshake than all the sentimental salutations in France."

"Good-by, dear," and with these words, uttered in the tone she liked, Laurie left her, after a handshake almost painful in its heartiness.

Next morning, instead of the usual call, Amy received a note which made her smile at the beginning and sigh at the end:

MY DEAR MENTOR:
Please make my adieux to your aunt, and exult within yourself, for "Lazy Laurence" has gone to his grandpa, like the best of boys. A pleasant winter to you, and may the gods grant you a blissful honeymoon at Valrosa! I think Fred would be benefited by a rouser. Tell him so, with my congratulations.
Yours gratefully,
TELEMACHUS

"Good boy! I'm glad he's gone," said Amy, with an approving smile; the next minute her face fell as she glanced about the empty room, adding, with an involuntary sigh:

"Yes, I *am* glad, but how I shall miss him!"

CHAPTER FORTY

The Valley of the Shadow

WHEN the first bitterness was over, the family accepted the inevitable, and tried to bear it cheerfully, helping one another by the increased affection which comes to bind households tenderly together in times of trouble. They put away their grief, and each did his or her part toward making that last year a happy one.

The pleasantest room in the house was set apart for Beth, and in it was gathered everything that she most loved—flowers, pictures, her piano, the little worktable, and the beloved pussies. Father's best books found their way there, mother's easy chair, Jo's desk, Amy's finest sketches; and every day Meg brought her babies on a loving pilgrimage, to make sunshine for Aunty Beth. John quietly set apart a little sum, that he might enjoy the pleasure of keeping the invalid supplied with the fruit she loved and longed for; old Hannah never wearied of concocting dainty dishes to tempt a capricious appetite, dropping tears as she worked; and from across the sea came little gifts and cheerful letters, seeming to bring breaths of warmth and fragrance from lands that know no winter.

Here, cherished like a household saint in its shrine, sat Beth, tranquil and busy as ever; for nothing could change the sweet, unselfish nature, and even while preparing to leave life, she tried to make it happier for those who should remain behind. The feeble fingers were never idle, and one of her pleasures was to make little things for the school children daily passing to and fro—to drop a pair of mittens from her window for a pair of purple hands, a needlebook for some small mother of many dolls, penwipers for young penmen toiling through forests of pothooks, scrapbooks for picture-loving eyes, and all manner of pleasant devices, till the reluctant climbers up the ladder of learning found their way strewn with flowers, as it were, and came to regard the gentle giver as a sort of fairy godmother, who sat above there, and showered down gifts miraculously suited to their tastes and needs. If Beth had wanted any reward, she found it in the bright little faces always turned up to her window, with nods and smiles, and the droll little letters which came to her, full of blots and gratitude.

The first few months were very happy ones, and Beth often used to look round, and say "How beautiful this is!" as they all sat together in her sunny room, the babies kicking and crowing on the floor, mother and sisters working near, and father reading, in his pleasant voice, from the wise old books which seemed rich in good and comfortable words, as applicable now as when written centuries ago; a little chapel, where a paternal priest taught his flock the hard lessons all must learn, trying to show them that hope can comfort love, and faith make resignation possible. Simple sermons, that went straight to the souls of those who listened; for the father's heart was in the minister's religion, and the frequent falter in the voice gave a double eloquence to the words he spoke or read.

It was well for all that this peaceful time was given them as preparation for the sad hours to come; for, by and by, Beth said the needle was "so heavy," and put it down forever; talking wearied her, faces troubled her, pain claimed her for its own, and her tranquil spirit was sorrowfully perturbed by the ills that vexed her feeble flesh. Ah, me! Such heavy days, such long, long nights, such aching hearts and imploring prayers, when those who loved her best were forced to see the thin hands stretched out to them beseechingly, to hear the bitter cry "Help me, help me!" and to feel that there was no help. A sad eclipse of the serene soul, a sharp struggle of the young life with death; but both were mercifully brief, and then, the natural rebellion over, the old peace returned more beautiful than ever. With the wreck of her frail body, Beth's soul grew strong; and, though she said little, those about her felt that she was ready, saw that the first pilgrim called was likewise the fittest, and waited with her on the shore, trying to see the Shining Ones coming to receive her when she crossed the river.

Jo had never left her for an hour since Beth had said, "I feel stronger when you are here." She slept on a couch in the room, waking often to renew the fire, to feed, lift, or wait upon the patient creature who seldom asked for anything, and "tried not to be a trouble." All day she haunted the room, jealous of any other nurse, and prouder of being chosen then than of any honor her life ever brought her. Precious and helpful hours for Jo, for now her heart received the teaching that it needed: lessons in patience were so sweetly taught her that she could not fail to learn them; charity for all, the lovely spirit that can forgive and truly forget unkindness, the loyalty to duty that makes the hardest easy, and the sincere faith that fears nothing, but trusts undoubtingly.

Often, when she woke, Jo found Beth reading in her wellworn little book, heard her singing softly, to beguile the sleepless night, or saw her lean her face upon her hands, while slow tears dropped through the transparent fingers; and Jo would lie watching her, with thoughts too deep for tears, feeling that Beth, in her simple, unselfish way, was trying to wean herself from the dear old life, and fit herself for the life to come, by sacred words of comfort, quiet prayers, and the music she loved so well.

Seeing this did more for Jo than the wisest sermons, the

saintliest hymns, the most fervent prayers that any voice could utter; for, with eyes made clear by many tears, and a heart softened by the tenderest sorrow, she recognized the beauty of her sister's life—uneventful, unambitious, yet full of the genuine virtues which "smell sweet, and blossom in the dust," the self-forgetfulness that makes the humblest on earth re-membered soonest in heaven, the true success which is possible to all.

One night, when Beth looked among the books upon her table, to find something to make her forget the mortal weariness that was almost as hard to bear as pain, as she turned the leaves of her old favorite "Pilgrim's Progress," she found a little paper, scribbled over in Jo's hand. The name caught her eye, and the blurred look of the lines made her sure that tears had fallen on it.

"Poor Jo! She's fast asleep, so I won't wake her to ask leave; she shows me all her things, and I don't think she'll mind if I look at this," thought Beth, with a glance at her sister, who lay on the rug, with the tongs beside her, ready to wake up the minute the log fell apart.

MY BETH

Sitting patient in the shadow
  Till the blessed light shall come,
A serene and saintly presence
  Sanctifies our troubled home.
Earthly joys and hopes and sorrows
  Break like ripples on the strand
Of the deep and solemn river
  Where her willing feet now stand.

Oh my sister, passing from me,
  Out of human care and strife,
Leave me, as a gift, those virtues
  Which have beautified your life.
Dear, bequeath me that great patience
  Which has power to sustain
A cheerful, uncomplaining spirit
  In its prison-house of pain.

Give me, for I need it sorely,
Of that courage, wise and sweet,
Which has made the path of duty
Green beneath your willing feet.
Give me that unselfish nature,
That with charity divine
Can pardon wrong for love's dear sake—
Meek heart, forgive me mine!

Thus our parting daily loseth
Something of its bitter pain,
And while learning this hard lesson,
My great loss becomes my gain.
For the touch of grief will render
My wild nature more serene,
Give to life new aspirations—
A new trust in the unseen.

Henceforth, safe across the river,
I shall see forevermore
A beloved, household spirit
Waiting for me on the shore.
Hope and faith, born of my sorrow,
Guardian angels shall become,
And the sister gone before me
By their hands shall lead me home.

Blurred and blotted, faulty and feeble, as the lines were, they brought a look of inexpressible comfort to Beth's face, for her one regret had been that she had done so little; and this seemed to assure her that her life had not been useless, that her death would not bring the despair she feared. As she sat with the paper folded between her hands, the charred log fell asunder. Jo started up, revived the blaze, and crept to the bedside, hoping Beth slept.

"Not asleep, but so happy, dear. See, I found this and read it; I knew you wouldn't care. Have I been all that to you, Jo?" she asked, with wistful, humble earnestness.

"Oh, Beth, so much, so much!" and Jo's head went down upon the pillow, beside her sister's.

"Then I don't feel as if I'd wasted my life. I'm not so good as you make me, but I *have* tried to do right; and now, when it's too late to begin even to do better, it's such a comfort to know that someone loves me so much, and feels as if I'd helped them."

"More than anyone in the world, Beth. I used to think I couldn't let you go; but I'm learning to feel that I don't lose you; that you'll be more to me than ever, and death can't part us, though it seems to."

"I know it cannot, and I don't fear it any longer, for I'm sure I shall be your Beth still, to love and help you more than ever. You must take my place, Jo, and be everything to father and mother when I'm gone. They will turn to you, don't fail them; and if it's hard to work alone, remember that I don't forget you, and that you'll be happier in doing that than writing splendid books or seeing all the world; for love is the only thing that we can carry with us when we go, and it makes the end so easy."

"I'll try, Beth," and then and there Jo renounced her old ambition, pledged herself to a new and better one, acknowledging the poverty of other desires, and feeling the blessed solace of a belief in the immortality of love.

So the spring days came and went, the sky grew clearer, the earth greener, the flowers were up fair and early, and the birds came back in time to say good-by to Beth, who, like a tired but trustful child, clung to the hands that had led her all her life, as father and mother guided her tenderly through the Valley of the Shadow, and gave her up to God.

Seldom, except in books, do the dying utter memorable words, see visions, or depart with beatified countenances; and those who have sped many parting souls know that to most the end comes as naturally and simply as sleep. As Beth had hoped, the "tide went out easily," and in the dark hour before the dawn, on the bosom where she had drawn her first breath, she quietly drew her last, with no farewell but one loving look, one little sigh.

With tears and prayers and tender hands, mother and sisters made her ready for the long sleep that pain would never mar again, seeing with grateful eyes the beautiful serenity that soon replaced the pathetic patience that had wrung their hearts so long, and feeling, with reverent joy, that to their darling death was a benignant angel, not a phantom full of dread.

When morning came, for the first time in many months the fire was out, Jo's place was empty, and the room was very still. But a bird sang blithely on a budding bough, close by, the snowdrops blossomed freshly at the window, and the spring sunshine streamed in like a benediction over the placid face upon the pillow—a face so full of painless peace that those who loved it best smiled through their tears, and thanked God that Beth was well at last.

CHAPTER FORTY-ONE

Learning to Forget

AMY'S lecture did Laurie good, though, of course, he did not own it till long afterwards; men seldom do, for when women are the advisers, the lords of creation don't take the advice till they have persuaded themselves that it is just what they intended to do; then they act upon it, and, if it succeeds, they give the weaker vessel half the credit of it; if it fails, they generously give her the whole. Laurie went back to his grandfather, and was so dutifully devoted for several weeks that the old gentleman declared the climate of Nice had improved him wonderfully, and he had better try it again. There was nothing the young gentleman would have liked better, but elephants could not have dragged him back after the scolding he had received; pride forbid, and whenever the longing grew very strong, he fortified his resolution by repeating the words that had made the deepest impression, "I despise you." "Go and do something splendid that will *make* her love you."

Laurie turned the matter over in his mind so often that he soon brought himself to confess that he *had* been selfish and lazy; but then when a man has a great sorrow, he should be indulged in all sorts of vagaries till he has lived it down. He felt that his blighted affections were quite dead now; and, though he should never cease to be a faithful mourner, there was no occasion to wear his weeds ostentatiously. Jo *wouldn't* love him, but he might *make* her respect and admire him by doing something which should prove that a girl's "No" had not spoilt his life. He had always meant to do something, and Amy's advice was quite unnecessary. He had only been waiting till the aforesaid blighted affections were decently interred; that being done, he felt that he was ready to "hide his stricken heart, and still toil on."

As Goethe, when he had a joy or a grief, put it into a song, so Laurie resolved to embalm his love-sorrow in music, and compose a Requiem which should harrow up Jo's soul and melt the heart of every hearer. Therefore the next time the old gentleman found him getting restless and moody, and ordered him off, he went to Vienna, where he had musical friends, and fell to work with a firm determination to distinguish himself. But, whether the sorrow was too vast to be embodied in music or music too ethereal to uplift a mortal woe, he soon discovered that the Requiem was beyond him, just at present. It was evident that his mind was not in working order yet, and his ideas needed clarifying; for often in the middle of a plaintive strain, he would find himself humming a dancing tune that vividly recalled the Christmas ball at Nice, especially the stout Frenchman, and put an effectual stop to tragic composition for the time being.

Then he tried an Opera, for nothing seemed impossible in the beginning; but here, again, unforeseen difficulties beset him. He wanted Jo for his heroine, and called upon his memory to supply him with tender recollections and romantic visions of his love. But memory turned traitor; and, as if possessed by the perverse spirit of the girl, would only recall Jo's oddities, faults, and freaks, would only show her in the most unsentimental aspects—beating mats with her head tied up in a bandanna, barricading herself with the sofa pillow, or throwing cold water over his passion à la Gummidge—and an irresistible laugh spoilt the pensive picture he was endeavoring to paint. Jo wouldn't be put into the Opera at any price, and he had to give her up with a "Bless that girl, what a torment she is!" and to clutch his hair, as became a distracted composer.

When he looked about him for another and a less intractable damsel to immortalize in melody, memory produced one with the most obliging readiness. This phantom wore many faces, but it always had golden hair, was enveloped in a diaphanous cloud, and floated airily before his mind's eye in a pleasing chaos of roses, peacocks, white ponies, and blue ribbons. He did not give the complacent wraith any name, but he took her for his heroine, and grew quite fond of her, as well he might; for he gifted her with every gift and grace under the sun, and escorted her, unscathed, through trials which would have annihilated any mortal woman.

Thanks to this inspiration, he got on swimmingly for a time, but gradually the work lost its charm, and he forgot to compose, while he sat musing, pen in hand, or roamed about the gay city to get new ideas and refresh his mind, which seemed to be in a somewhat unsettled state that winter. He did not do much, but he thought a great deal and was conscious of a change of some sort going on in spite of himself. "It's genius simmering, perhaps. I'll let it simmer, and see what comes of it," he said, with a secret suspicion, all the while, that it wasn't genius, but something far more common. Whatever it was, it simmered to some purpose, for he grew more and more discontented with his desultory life, began to long for some real and earnest work to go at, soul and body, and finally came to the wise conclusion that everyone who loved music was not a composer. Returning from one of Mozart's grand operas, splendidly performed at the Royal Theatre, he looked over his own, played a few of the best parts, sat staring up at the busts of Mendelssohn, Beethoven, and Bach, who stared benignly back again; then suddenly he tore up his music sheets, one by one, and, as the last fluttered out of his hand, he said soberly to himself:

"She is right! Talent isn't genius, and you can't make it so. That music has taken the vanity out of me as Rome took it out of her, and I won't be a humbug any longer. Now what shall I do?"

That seemed a hard question to answer, and Laurie began to wish he had to work for his daily bread. Now, if ever, occurred an eligible opportunity for "going to the devil," as he once forcibly expressed it, for he had plenty of money and nothing to do, and Satan is proverbially fond of providing employment for full and idle hands. The poor fellow had temptations enough from without and from within, but he withstood them pretty well; for, much as he valued liberty, he valued good faith and confidence more, so his promise to his grandfather, and his desire to be able to look honestly into the eyes of the women who loved him, and say "All's well," kept him safe and steady.

Very likely some Mrs. Grundy will observe, "I don't believe it; boys will be boys, young men must sow their wild oats, and women must not expect miracles." I dare say *you* don't, Mrs. Grundy, but it's true nevertheless. Women work a good many miracles, and I have a persuasion that they may perform even that of raising the standard of manhood by refusing to echo such sayings. Let the boys be boys, the longer the better, and let the young men sow their wild oats if they must; but mothers, sisters, and friends may help to make the crop a small one, and keep many tares from spoiling the harvest, by believing, and showing that they believe, in the possibility of loyalty to the virtues which make men manliest in good women's eyes. If it *is* a feminine delusion, leave us to enjoy it while we may, for without it half the beauty and the romance of life is lost, and sorrowful forebodings would embitter all our hopes of the brave, tenderhearted little lads, who still love their mothers better than themselves, and are not ashamed to own it.

Laurie thought that the task of forgetting his love for Jo would absorb all his powers for years; but, to his great surprise, he discovered it grew easier every day. He refused to believe it at first, got angry with himself, and couldn't understand it; but these hearts of ours are curious and contrary things, and time and nature work their will in spite of us. Laurie's heart *wouldn't* ache; the wound persisted in healing with a rapidity that astonished him, and, instead of trying to forget, he found himself trying to remember. He had not foreseen this turn of affairs, and was not prepared for it. He was disgusted with himself, surprised at his own fickleness, and full of a queer mixture of disappointment and relief that he could recover from such a tremendous blow so soon. He carefully stirred up the embers of his lost love, but they refused to burst into a blaze: there was only a comfortable glow that warmed and did him good without putting him into a fever, and he was reluctantly obliged to confess that the boyish passion was slowly subsiding into a more tranquil sentiment, very tender, a little sad and resentful still, but that was sure to pass away in time, leaving a brotherly affection which would last unbroken to the end.

As the word "brotherly" passed through his mind in one of these reveries, he smiled, and glanced up at the picture of Mozart that was before him:

"Well, he was a great man; and when he couldn't have one sister he took the other, and was happy."

Laurie did not utter the words, but he thought them; and the next instant kissed the little old ring, saying to himself:

"No, I won't! I haven't forgotten, I never can. I'll try again, and if that fails, why, then—"

Leaving his sentence unfinished, he seized pen and paper and wrote to Jo, telling her that he could not settle to anything while there was the least hope of her changing her mind. Couldn't she, wouldn't she, and let him come home and be happy? While waiting for an answer he did nothing, but he did it energetically, for he was in a fever of impatience. It came at last, and settled his mind effectually on one point, for Jo decidedly couldn't and wouldn't. She was wrapped up in Beth, and never wished to hear the word "love" again. Then she begged him to be happy with somebody else, but always to keep a little corner of his heart for his loving sister Jo. In a postscript she desired him not to tell Amy that Beth was worse; she was coming home in the spring, and there was no need of saddening the remainder of her stay. That would be time enough, please God, but Laurie must write to her often, and not let her feel lonely, homesick, or anxious.

"So I will, at once. Poor little girl; it will be a sad going home for her, I'm afraid," and Laurie opened his desk, as if writing to Amy had been the proper conclusion of the sentence left unfinished some weeks before.

But he did not write the letter that day; for, as he rummaged out his best paper, he came across something which changed his purpose. Tumbling about in one part of the desk, among bills, passports, and business documents of various kinds were several of Jo's letters, and in another compartment were three notes from Amy, carefully tied up with one of her blue ribbons, and sweetly suggestive of the little dead roses put away inside. With a half-repentant, half-amused expression, Laurie gathered up all Jo's letters, smoothed, folded, and put them neatly into a small drawer of the desk, stood a minute turning the ring thoughtfully on his finger, then slowly drew it off, laid it with the letters, locked the drawer, and went out to hear High Mass at St. Stefan's, feeling as if there had been a funeral; and, though not overwhelmed with affliction, this seemed a more proper way to spend the rest of the day than in writing letters to charming young ladies.

The letter went very soon, however, and was promptly answered, for Amy *was* homesick, and confessed it in the most delightfully confiding manner. The correspondence flourished famously, and letters flew to and fro, with unfailing regularity, all through the early spring. Laurie sold his busts, made allumettes of his opera, and went back to Paris, hoping somebody would arrive before long. He wanted desperately to go to Nice, but would not till he was asked; and Amy would not ask him, for just then she was having little experiences of her own, which made her rather wish to avoid the quizzical eyes of "our boy."

Fred Vaughn had returned, and put the question to which she had once decided to answer, "Yes, thank you," but now she said, "No, thank you," kindly but steadily; for, when the time came, her courage failed her, and she found that something more than money and position was needed to satisfy the new longing that filled her heart so full of tender hopes and fears. The words, "Fred is a good fellow, but not at all the man I fancied you would ever like," and Laurie's face when he uttered them kept returning to her as pertinaciously as her own did when she said in a look, if not in words, "I shall marry for money." It troubled her to remember that now, she wished she could take it back, it sounded so unwomanly. She didn't want Laurie to think her a heartless, worldly creature; she didn't care to be a queen of society now half so much as she did to be a lovable woman; she was so glad he didn't hate her for the dreadful things she said, but took them so beautifully, and was kinder than ever. His letters were such a comfort, for the home letters were very irregular, and were not half so satisfactory as his when they did come. It was not only a pleasure, but a duty to answer them, for the poor fellow was forlorn, and needed petting, since Jo persisted in being stonyhearted. She ought to have made an effort, and tried to love him; it couldn't be very hard, many people would be proud and glad to have such a dear boy care for them; but Jo never would act like other girls, so there was nothing to do but be very kind, and treat him like a brother.

If all brothers were treated as well as Laurie was at this period, they would be a much happier race of beings than they are. Amy never lectured now; she asked his opinion on all subjects; she was interested in everything he did, made charming little presents for him, and sent him two letters a week, full of lively gossip, sisterly confidences, and captivating sketches of the lovely scenes about her. As few brothers are complimented by having their letters carried about in their sisters' pockets, read and reread diligently, cried over when short, kissed when long, and treasured carefully, we will not hint that Amy did any of these fond and foolish things. But she certainly did grow a little pale and pensive that spring, lost much of her relish for society, and went out sketching alone a good deal. She never had much to show when she came home, but was studying nature, I dare say, while she sat for hours, with her hands folded, on the terrace at Valrosa, or absently sketched any fancy that occurred to her—a stalwart knight carved on a tomb, a young man asleep in the grass, with his hat over his eyes, or a curly-haired girl in gorgeous array, promenading down a ballroom on the arm of a tall gentleman, both faces being left a blur according to the last fashion in art, which was safe, but not altogether satisfactory.

Her aunt thought that she regretted her answer to Fred;

and, finding denials useless and explanations impossible, Amy left her to think what she liked, taking care that Laurie should know that Fred had gone to Egypt. That was all, but he understood it, and looked relieved, as he said to himself, with a venerable air:

"I was sure she would think better of it. Poor fellow! I've been through it all, and I can sympathize."

With that he heaved a great sigh, and then, as if he had discharged his duty to the past, put his feet up on the sofa, and enjoyed Amy's letter luxuriously.

While these changes were going on abroad, trouble had come at home; but the letter telling that Beth was failing never reached Amy, and when the next found her, the grass was green above her sister. The sad news met her at Vevay, for the heat had driven them from Nice in May, and they had traveled slowly to Switzerland, by way of Genoa and the Italian lakes. She bore it very well, and quietly submitted to the family decree that she should not shorten her visit, for, since it was too late to say good-by to Beth, she had better stay, and let absence soften her sorrow. But her heart was very heavy; she longed to be at home, and every day looked wistfully across the lake, waiting for Laurie to come and comfort her.

He did come very soon; for the same mail brought letters to them both, but he was in Germany, and it took some days to reach him. The moment he read it, he packed his knapsack, bade adieu to his fellow pedestrians, and was off to keep his promise, with a heart full of joy and sorrow, hope and suspense.

He knew Vevay well; and as soon as the boat touched the little quay, he hurried along the shore to La Tour, where the Carrols were living *en pension*. The *garçon* was in despair that the whole family had gone to take a promenade on the lake; but no, the blonde mademoiselle might be in the château garden. If monsieur would give himself the pain of sitting down, a flash of time should present her. But monsieur could not wait even a "flash of time," and, in the middle of the speech, departed to find mademoiselle himself.

A pleasant old garden on the borders of the lovely lake, with chestnuts rustling overhead, ivy climbing everywhere,

The boat went smoothly through the water

[SEE PAGE 479]

and the black shadow of the tower falling far across the sunny
water. At one corner of the wide, low wall was a seat, and here
Amy often câme to read or work, or console herself with the
beauty all about her. She was sitting here that day, leaning her
head on her hands, with a homesick heart and heavy eyes,
thinking of Beth, and wondering why Laurie did not come.
She did not hear him cross the courtyard beyond, nor see him
pause in the archway that led from the subterranean path into
the garden. He stood a minute, looking at her with new eyes,
seeing what no one had ever seen before—the tender side of
Amy's character. Everything about her mutely suggested love
and sorrow—the blotted letters in her lap, the black ribbon
that tied up her hair, the womanly pain and patience in her
face; even the little ebony cross at her throat seemed pathetic
to Laurie, for he had given it to her, and she wore it as her only
ornament. If he had any doubts about the reception she would
give him, they were set at rest the minute she looked up and
saw him; for, dropping everything, she ran to him, exclaiming
in a tone of unmistakable love and longing:

"Oh, Laurie, Laurie, I knew you'd come to me!"

I think everything was said and settled then; for, as they
stood together quite silent for a moment, with the dark head
bent down protectingly over the light one, Amy felt that no
one could comfort and sustain her so well as Laurie, and
Laurie decided that Amy was the only woman in the world
who could fill Jo's place, and make him happy. He did not tell
her so; but she was not disappointed, for both felt the truth,
were satisfied, and gladly left the rest to silence.

In a minute Amy went back to her place; and, while she
dried her tears, Laurie gathered up the scattered papers, finding in the sight of sundry well-worn letters and suggestive
sketches good omens for the future. As he sat down beside her,
Amy felt shy again, and turned rosy red at the recollection of
her impulsive greeting.

"I couldn't help it; I felt so lonely and sad, and was so very
glad to see you. It was such a surprise to look up and find you,
just as I was beginning to fear you wouldn't come," she said,
trying in vain to speak quite naturally.

"I came the minute I heard. I wish I could say something to

comfort you for the loss of dear little Beth; but I can only feel, and—" He could not get any further, for he, too, turned bashful all of a sudden and did not quite know what to say. He longed to lay Amy's head down on his shoulder, and tell her to have a good cry, but he did not dare; so took her hand instead, and gave it a sympathetic squeeze that was better than words.

"You needn't say anything; this comforts me," she said softly. "Beth is well and happy, and I mustn't wish her back; but I dread the going home, much as I long to see them all. We won't talk about it now, for it makes me cry, and I want to enjoy you while you stay. You needn't go right back, need you?"

"Not if you want me, dear."

"I do, so much. Aunt and Flo are very kind; but you seem like one of the family, and it would be so comfortable to have you for a little while."

Amy spoke and looked so like a homesick child, whose heart was full, that Laurie forgot his bashfulness all at once, and gave her just what she wanted—the petting she was used to and the cheerful conversation she needed.

"Poor little soul, you look as if you'd grieved yourself half sick! I'm going to take care of you, so don't cry any more, but come and walk about with me; the wind is too chilly for you to sit still," he said, in the half-caressing, half-commanding way that Amy liked, as he tied on her hat, drew her arm through his, and began to pace up and down the sunny walk, under the new-leaved chestnuts. He felt more at ease upon his legs; and Amy found it very pleasant to have a strong arm to lean upon, a familiar face to smile at her, and a kind voice to talk delightfully for her alone.

The quaint old garden had sheltered many pairs of lovers, and seemed expressly made for them, so sunny and secluded was it, with nothing but the tower to overlook them, and the wide lake to carry away the echo of their words, as it rippled by below. For an hour this new pair walked and talked, or rested on the wall, enjoying the sweet influences which gave such a charm to time and place; and when an unromantic dinner bell warned them away, Amy felt as if she left her burden of loneliness and sorrow behind her in the château garden.

The moment Mrs. Carrol saw the girl's altered face, she was illuminated with a new idea, and exclaimed to herself, "Now I understand it all—the child has been pining for young Laurence. Bless my heart, I never thought of such a thing!"

With praiseworthy discretion, the good lady said nothing, and betrayed no sign of enlightenment; but cordially urged Laurie to stay, and begged Amy to enjoy his society, for it would do her more good than so much solitude. Amy was a model of docility; and, as her aunt was a good deal occupied with Flo, she was left to entertain her friend, and did it with more than her usual success.

At Nice, Laurie had lounged and Amy had scolded; at Vevay, Laurie was never idle, but always walking, riding, boating, or studying, in the most energetic manner, while Amy admired everything he did, and followed his example as far and as fast as she could. He said the change was owing to the climate, and she did not contradict him, being glad of a like excuse for her own recovered health and spirits.

The invigorating air did them both good, and much exercise worked wholesome changes in minds as well as bodies. They seemed to get clearer views of life and duty up there among the everlasting hills; the fresh winds blew away desponding doubts, delusive fancies, and moody mists; the warm spring sunshine brought out all sorts of aspiring ideas, tender hopes, and happy thoughts; the lake seemed to wash away the troubles of the past, and the grand old mountains to look benignly down upon them, saying, "Little children, love one another."

In spite of the new sorrow, it was a very happy time, so happy that Laurie could not bear to disturb it by a word. It took him a little while to recover from his surprise at the rapid cure of his first, and, as he had firmly believed, his last and only love. He consoled himself for the seeming disloyalty by the thought that Jo's sister was almost the same as Jo's self, and the conviction that it would have been impossible to love any other woman but Amy so soon and so well. His first wooing had been of the tempestuous order, and he looked back upon it as if through a long vista of years, with a feeling of compassion blended with regret. He was not ashamed of it, but put it away as one of the bitter-sweet experiences of his life, for which he could be grateful when the pain was over. His second wooing he resolved should be as calm and simple as possible; there was no need of having a scene, hardly any need of telling Amy that he loved her; she knew it without words, and had given him his answer long ago. It all came about so naturally that no one could complain, and he knew that everybody would be pleased, even Jo. But when our first little passion has been crushed, we are apt to be wary and slow in making a second trial; so Laurie let the days pass, enjoying every hour, and leaving to chance the utterance of the word that would put an end to the first and sweetest part of his new romance.

He had rather imagined that the denouement would take place in the château garden by moonlight, and in the most graceful and decorous manner; but it turned out exactly the reverse, for the matter was settled on the lake, at noonday, in a few blunt words. They had been floating about all the morning, from gloomy St. Gingolf to sunny Montreux, with the Alps of Savoy on one side, Mont St. Bernard and the Dent du Midi on the other, pretty Vevay in the valley, and Lausanne upon the hill beyond, a cloudless blue sky overhead, and the bluer lake below, dotted with the picturesque boats that looked like white-winged gulls.

They had been talking of Bonnivard, as they glided past Chillon, and of Rousseau, as they looked up at Clarens, where he wrote his "Héloïse." Neither had read it, but they knew it was a love story, and each privately wondered if it was half as interesting as their own. Amy had been dabbling her hand in the water during the little pause that fell between them, and, when she looked up, Laurie was leaning on his oars, with an expression in his eyes that made her say hastily, merely for the sake of saying something:

"You must be tired; rest a little, and let me row; it will do me good; for, since you came, I have been altogether lazy and luxurious."

"I'm not tired; but you may take an oar, if you like. There's room enough, though I have to sit nearly in the middle, else the boat won't trim," returned Laurie, as if he rather liked the arrangement.

Feeling that she had not mended matters much, Amy took the offered third of a seat, shook her hair over her face, and accepted an oar. She rowed as well as she did many other things; and, though she used both hands, and Laurie but one, the oars kept time, and the boat went smoothly through the water.

"How well we pull together, don't we?" said Amy, who objected to silence just then.

"So well that I wish we might always pull in the same boat. Will you, Amy?" very tenderly.

"Yes, Laurie," very low.

Then they both stopped rowing, and unconsciously added a pretty little tableau of human love and happiness to the dissolving views reflected in the lake.

CHAPTER FORTY-TWO

All Alone

IT was easy to promise self-abnegation when self was wrapped up in another, and heart and soul were purified by a sweet example; but when the helpful voice was silent, the daily lesson over, the beloved presence gone, and nothing remained but loneliness and grief, then Jo found her promise very hard to keep. How could she "comfort father and mother," when her own heart ached with a ceaseless longing for her sister; how could she "make the house cheerful," when all its light and warmth and beauty seemed to have deserted it when Beth left the old home for the new; and where in all the world could she "find some useful, happy work to do," that would take the place of the loving service which had been its own reward? She tried in a blind, hopeless way to do her duty, secretly rebelling against it all the while, for it seemed unjust that her few joys should be lessened, her burdens made heavier, and life get harder and harder as she toiled along. Some people seemed to get all sunshine, and some all shadow; it was not fair, for she tried more than Amy to be good, but never got any reward, only disappointment, trouble, and hard work.

Poor Jo, these were dark days to her, for something like despair came over her when she thought of spending all her life in that quiet house, devoted to humdrum cares, a few small pleasures, and the duty that never seemed to grow any easier. "I can't do it. I wasn't meant for a life like this, and I know I shall break away and do something desperate if somebody don't come and help me," she said to herself when her first efforts failed, and she fell into the moody, miserable state of mind which often comes when strong wills have to yield to the inevitable.

But someone did come and help her, though Jo did not recognize her good angels at once, because they wore familiar shapes, and used the simple spells best fitted to poor humanity. Often she started up at night, thinking Beth called her; and when the sight of the little empty bed made her cry with the bitter cry of an unsubmissive sorrow, "Oh, Beth, come back, come back!" she did not stretch out her yearning arms in vain; for, as quick to hear her sobbing as she had been to hear her sister's faintest whisper, her mother came to comfort her, not with words only, but the patient tenderness that soothes by a touch, tears that were mute reminders of a greater grief than Jo's, and broken whispers, more eloquent than prayers, because hopeful resignation went hand in hand with natural sorrow. Sacred moments, when heart talked to heart in the silence of the night, turning affliction to a blessing, which chastened grief and strengthened love. Feeling this, Jo's burden seemed easier to bear, duty grew sweeter, and life looked more endurable, seen from the safe shelter of her mother's arms.

When aching heart was a little comforted, troubled mind likewise found help; for one day she went to the study, and, leaning over the good gray head lifted to welcome her with a tranquil smile, she said, very humbly:

"Father, talk to me as you did to Beth. I need it more than she did, for I'm all wrong."

"My dear, nothing can comfort me like this," he answered, with a falter in his voice, and both arms round her, as if he, too, needed help, and did not fear to ask it.

Then, sitting in Beth's little chair close beside him, Jo told her troubles—the resentful sorrow for her loss, the fruitless efforts that discouraged her, the want of faith that made life look so dark, and all the sad bewilderment which we call despair. She gave him entire confidence, he gave her the help she needed, and both found consolation in the act; for the time had come when they could talk together not only as father and daughter, but as man and woman, able and glad to serve each other with mutual sympathy as well as mutual love. Happy, thoughtful times there in the old study which Jo called "the church of one member," and from which she came with fresh courage, recovered cheerfulness, and a more submissive spirit; for the parents who had taught one child to meet death without fear, were trying now to teach another to accept life without despondency or distrust, and to use its beautiful opportunities with gratitude and power.

Other helps had Jo—humble, wholesome duties and delights that would not be denied their part in serving her, and which she slowly learned to see and value. Brooms and dishcloths never could be as distasteful as they once had been, for Beth had presided over both; and something of her housewifely spirit seemed to linger round the little mop and the old brush, that was never thrown away. As she used them, Jo found herself humming the songs Beth used to hum, imitating Beth's orderly ways, and giving the little touches here and there that kept everything fresh and cozy, which was the first step toward making home happy, though she didn't know it, till Hannah said with an approving squeeze of the hand:

"You thoughtful creter, you're determined we shan't miss that dear lamb ef you can help it. We don't say much, but we see it, and the Lord will bless you for't, see ef He don't."

As they sat sewing together, Jo discovered how much improved her sister Meg was; how well she could talk, how much she knew about good, womanly impulses, thoughts, and feelings, how happy she was in husband and children, and how much they were all doing for each other.

"Marriage is an excellent thing, after all. I wonder if I should blossom out half as well as you have, if I tried it?" said Jo, as she constructed a kite for Demi, in the topsy-turvy nursery.

"It's just what you need to bring out the tender, womanly half of your nature, Jo. You are like a chestnut bur, prickly outside, but silk-soft within, and a sweet kernel, if one can only

get at it. Love will make you show your heart someday, and then the rough bur will fall off."

"Frost opens the chestnut burs, ma'am, and it takes a good shake to bring them down. Boys go nutting, and I don't care to be bagged by them," returned Jo, pasting away at the kite which no wind that blows would ever carry up, for Daisy had tied herself on as a bob.

Meg laughed, for she was glad to see a glimmer of Jo's old spirit, but she felt it her duty to enforce her opinion by every argument in her power; and the sisterly chats were not wasted, especially as two of Meg's most effective arguments were the babies, whom Jo loved tenderly. Grief is the best opener for some hearts, and Jo's was nearly ready for the bag: a little more sunshine to ripen the nut, then, not a boy's impatient shake, but a man's hand reached up to pick it gently from the bur, and find the kernel sound and sweet. If she had suspected this, she would have shut up tight, and been more prickly than ever; fortunately she wasn't thinking about herself, so, when the time came, down she dropped.

Now, if she had been the heroine of a moral storybook, she ought at this period of her life to have become quite saintly, renounced the world, and gone about doing good in a mortified bonnet, with tracts in her pocket. But, you see, Jo wasn't a heroine; she was only a struggling human girl, like hundreds of others, and she just acted out her nature, being sad, cross, listless, or energetic, as the mood suggested. It's highly virtuous to say we'll be good, but we can't do it all at once, and it takes a long pull, a strong pull, and a pull all together, before some of us even get our feet set in the right way. Jo had got so far, she was learning to do her duty, and to feel unhappy if she did not; but to do it cheerfully—ah, that was another thing! She had often said she wanted to do something splendid, no matter how hard; and now she had her wish, for what could be more beautiful than to devote her life to father and mother, trying to make home as happy to them as they had to her? And, if difficulties were necessary to increase the splendor of the effort, what could be harder for a restless, ambitious girl than to give up her own hopes, plans, and desires, and cheerfully live for others?

Providence had taken her at her word; here was the task,

not what she had expected, but better, because self had no part in it: now, could she do it? She decided that she would try; and, in her first attempt, she found the helps I have suggested. Still another was given her, and she took it, not as a reward, but as a comfort, as Christian took the refreshment afforded by the little arbor where he rested, as he climbed the hill called Difficulty.

"Why don't you write? That always used to make you happy," said her mother, once, when the desponding fit overshadowed Jo.

"I've no heart to write, and if I had, nobody cares for my things."

"We do; write something for us, and never mind the rest of the world. Try it, dear; I'm sure it would do you good, and please us very much."

"Don't believe I can," but Jo got out her desk, and began to overhaul her half-finished manuscripts.

An hour afterwards her mother peeped in, and there she was, scratching away, with her black pinafore on, and an absorbed expression, which caused Mrs. March to smile and slip away, well pleased with the success of her suggestion. Jo never knew how it happened, but something got into that story that went straight to the hearts of those who read it; for, when her family had laughed and cried over it, her father sent it, much against her will, to one of the popular magazines, and, to her utter surprise, it was not only paid for, but others requested. Letters from several persons, whose praise was honor, followed the appearance of the little story, newspapers copied it, and strangers as well as friends admired it. For a small thing it was a great success; and Jo was more astonished than when her novel was commended and condemned all at once.

"I don't understand it. What *can* there be in a simple little story like that, to make people praise it so?" she said, quite bewildered.

"There is truth in it, Jo, that's the secret; humor and pathos make it alive, and you have found your style at last. You wrote with no thought of fame or money, and put your heart into it, my daughter; you have had the bitter, now comes the sweet. Do your best, and grow as happy as we are in your success."

"If there *is* anything good or true in what I write, it isn't mine; I owe it all to you and mother and to Beth," said Jo, more touched by her father's words than by any amount of praise from the world.

So, taught by love and sorrow, Jo wrote her little stories, and sent them away to make friends for themselves and her, finding it a very charitable world to such humble wanderers; for they were kindly welcomed, and sent home comfortable tokens to their mother, like dutiful children whom good fortune overtakes.

When Amy and Laurie wrote of their engagement, Mrs. March feared that Jo would find it difficult to rejoice over it, but her fears were soon set at rest; for, though Jo looked grave at first, she took it very quietly, and was full of hopes and plans for "the children" before she read the letter twice. It was a sort of written duet, wherein each glorified the other in loverlike fashion, very pleasant to read and satisfactory to think of, for no one had any objection to make.

"You like it, mother?" said Jo, as they laid down the closely written sheets, and looked at one another.

"Yes, I hoped it would be so, ever since Amy wrote that she had refused Fred. I felt sure then that something better than what you call the 'mercenary spirit' had come over her, and a hint here and there in her letters made me suspect that love and Laurie would win the day."

"How sharp you are, Marmee, and how silent! You never said a word to me."

"Mothers have need of sharp eyes and discreet tongues when they have girls to manage. I was half afraid to put the idea into your head, lest you should write and congratulate them before the thing was settled."

"I'm not the scatterbrain I was; you may trust me, I'm sober and sensible enough for anyone's confidante now."

"So you are, dear, and I should have made you mine, only I fancied it might pain you to learn that your Teddy loved anyone else."

"Now, mother, did you really think I could be so silly and selfish, after I'd refused his love, when it was freshest, if not best?"

"I knew you were sincere then, Jo, but lately I have thought that if he came back, and asked again, you might, perhaps, feel like giving another answer. Forgive me, dear, I can't help seeing that you are very lonely, and sometimes there is a hungry look in your eyes that goes to my heart; so I fancied that your boy might fill the empty place if he tried now."

"No, mother, it is better as it is, and I'm glad Amy has learned to love him. But you are right in one thing: I *am* lonely, and perhaps if Teddy had tried again I might have said 'Yes,' not because I love him any more, but because I care more to be loved than when he went away."

"I'm glad of that, Jo, for it shows that you are getting on. There are plenty to love you, so try to be satisfied with father and mother, sisters and brothers, friends and babies, till the best lover of all comes to give you your reward."

"Mothers are the *best* lovers in the world: but I don't mind whispering to Marmee that I'd like to try all kinds. It's very curious, but the more I try to satisfy myself with all sorts of natural affections, the more I seem to want. I'd no idea hearts could take in so many; mine is so elastic, it never seems full now, and I used to be quite contented with my family. I don't understand it."

"I do!" and Mrs. March smiled her wise smile, as Jo turned back the leaves to read what Amy said of Laurie.

"It is so beautiful to be loved as Laurie loves me; he isn't sentimental, doesn't say much about it, but I see and feel it in all he says and does, and it makes me so happy and so humble that I don't seem to be the same girl I was. I never knew how good and generous and tender he was till now, for he lets me read his heart, and I find it full of noble impulses and hopes and purposes, and am so proud to know it's mine. He says he feels as if he 'could make a prosperous voyage now with me aboard as mate, and lots of love for ballast.' I pray he may, and try to be all he believes me, for I love my gallant captain with all my heart and soul and might, and never will desert him, while God lets us be together. Oh, mother, I never knew how much like heaven this world could be, when two people love and live for one another!"

"And that's our cool, reserved, and worldly Amy! Truly, love does work miracles. How very, very happy they must be!" And

Jo laid the rustling sheets together with a careful hand, as one might shut the covers of a lovely romance, which holds the reader fast till the end comes, and he finds himself alone in the workaday world again.

By and by Jo roamed away upstairs, for it was rainy, and she could not walk. A restless spirit possessed her, and the old feeling came again, not bitter as it once was, but a sorrowfully patient wonder why one sister should have all she asked, the other nothing. It was not true; she knew that, and tried to put it away, but the natural craving for affection was strong, and Amy's happiness woke the hungry longing for someone to "love with heart and soul, and cling to while God let them be together."

Up in the garret, where Jo's unquiet wanderings ended, stood four little wooden chests in a row, each marked with its owner's name and each filled with relics of the childhood and girlhood ended now for all. Jo glanced into them, and when she came to her own, leaned her chin on the edge, and stared absently at the chaotic collection, till a bundle of old exercise books caught her eye. She drew them out, turned them over, and relived that pleasant winter at kind Mrs. Kirke's. She had smiled at first, then she looked thoughtful, next sad, and when she came to a little message written in the professor's hand, her lips began to tremble, the books slid out of her lap, and she sat looking at the friendly words, as if they took a new meaning, and touched a tender spot in her heart.

"Wait for me, my friend. I may be a little late, but I shall surely come."

Oh, if he only would! So kind, so good, so patient with me always, my dear old Fritz, I didn't value him half enough when I had him, but now how I should love to see him, for everyone seems going away from me, and I'm all alone.

And holding the little paper fast, as if it were a promise yet to be fulfilled, Jo laid her head down on a comfortable rag bag, and cried, as if in opposition to the rain pattering on the roof.

Was it all self-pity, loneliness, or low spirits? or was it the waking up of a sentiment which had bided its time as patiently as its inspirer? Who shall say?

CHAPTER FORTY-THREE

Surprises

JO was alone in the twilight, lying on the old sofa, looking at the fire, and thinking. It was her favorite way of spending the hour of dusk; no one disturbed her, and she used to lie there on Beth's little red pillow, planning stories, dreaming dreams, or thinking tender thoughts of the sister who never seemed far away. Her face looked tired, grave, and rather sad; for tomorrow was her birthday, and she was thinking how fast the years went by, how old she was getting, and how little she seemed to have accomplished. Almost twenty-five, and nothing to show for it. Jo was mistaken in that; there was a good deal to show, and by and by she saw, and was grateful for it.

"An old maid, that's what I'm to be. A literary spinster, with a pen for a spouse, a family of stories for children, and twenty

years hence a morsel of fame, perhaps; when, like poor Johnson, I'm old, and can't enjoy it, solitary, and can't share it, independent, and don't need it. Well, I needn't be a sour saint
nor a selfish sinner; and, I dare say, old maids are very comfortable when they get used to it; but—" and there Jo sighed, as
if the prospect was not inviting.

It seldom is, at first, and thirty seems the end of all things
to five and twenty; but it's not so bad as it looks, and one can
get on quite happily if one has something in one's self to fall
back upon. At twenty-five, girls begin to talk about being old
maids, but secretly resolve that they never will be; at thirty
they say nothing about it, but quietly accept the fact, and, if
sensible, console themselves by remembering that they have
twenty more useful, happy years, in which they may be learning to grow old gracefully. Don't laugh at the spinsters, dear
girls, for often very tender, tragical romances are hidden away
in the hearts that beat so quietly under the sober gowns, and
many silent sacrifices of youth, health, ambition, love itself,
make the faded faces beautiful in God's sight. Even the sad,
sour sisters should be kindly dealt with, because they have
missed the sweetest part of life, if for no other reason; and,
looking at them with compassion, not contempt, girls in their
bloom should remember that they too may miss the blossom-
time; that rosy cheeks don't last forever, that silver threads will
come in the bonnie brown hair, and that, by and by, kindness
and respect will be as sweet as love and admiration now.

Gentlemen, which means boys, be courteous to the old
maids, no matter how poor and plain and prim, for the only
chivalry worth having is that which is the readiest to pay def-
erence to the old, protect the feeble, and serve womankind, regardless of rank, age, or color. Just recollect the good aunts
who have not only lectured and fussed, but nursed and petted,
too often without thanks; the scrapes they have helped you out
of, the "tips" they have given you from their small store, the
stitches the patient old fingers have set for you, the steps the
willing old feet have taken, and gratefully pay the dear old
ladies the little attentions that women love to receive as long
as they live. The bright-eyed girls are quick to see such traits,

and will like you all the better for them; and if death, almost
the only power that can part mother and son, should rob you
of yours, you will be sure to find a tender welcome and maternal cherishing from some Aunt Priscilla, who has kept the
warmest corner of her lonely old heart for "the best nevvy in
the world."

Jo must have fallen asleep (as I dare say my reader has
during this little homily), for suddenly Laurie's ghost seemed
to stand before her—a substantial, lifelike ghost—leaning over
her, with the very look he used to wear when he felt a good
deal and didn't like to show it. But, like Jenny in the ballad—

She could not think it he,

and lay staring up at him in startled silence, till he stooped and
kissed her. Then she knew him, and flew up, crying joyfully:

"Oh, my Teddy! Oh, my Teddy!"

"Dear Jo, you are glad to see me, then?"

"Glad! My blessed boy, words can't express my gladness.
Where's Amy?"

"Your mother has got her down at Meg's. We stopped there
by the way, and there was no getting my wife out of their
clutches."

"Your what?" cried Jo, for Laurie uttered those two words
with an unconscious pride and satisfaction which betrayed
him.

"Oh, the dickens! Now I've done it!" and he looked so guilty
that Jo was down upon him like a flash.

"You've gone and got married!"

"Yes, please, but I never will again," and he went down upon his knees, with a penitent clasping of hands, and a face full
of mischief, mirth, and triumph.

"Actually married?"

"Very much so, thank you."

"Mercy on us! What dreadful thing will you do next?" and
Jo fell into her seat with a gasp.

"A characteristic, but not exactly complimentary congratula-
tion," returned Laurie, still in an abject attitude, but beaming
with satisfaction.

"What can you expect, when you take one's breath away, creeping in like a burglar, and letting cats out of bags like that? Get up, you ridiculous boy, and tell me all about it."

"Not a word, unless you let me come in my old place, and promise not to barricade."

Jo laughed at that as she had not done for many a long day, and patted the sofa invitingly, as she said, in a cordial tone:

"The old pillow is up garret, and we don't need it now; so, come and 'fess, Teddy."

"How good it sounds to hear you say 'Teddy'! No one ever calls me that but you," and Laurie sat down, with an air of great content.

"What does Amy call you?"

"My lord."

"That's like her. Well, you look it," and Jo's eyes plainly betrayed that she found her boy comelier than ever.

The pillow was gone, but there *was* a barricade, nevertheless—a natural one, raised by time, absence, and change of heart. Both felt it, and for a minute looked at one another as if that invisible barrier cast a little shadow over them. It was gone directly, however, for Laurie said, with a vain attempt at dignity:

"Don't I look like a married man and the head of a family?"

"Not a bit, and you never will. You've grown bigger and bonnier, but you are the same scapegrace as ever."

"Now, really, Jo, you ought to treat me with more respect," began Laurie, who enjoyed it all immensely.

"How can I, when the mere idea of you, married and settled, is so irresistibly funny that I can't keep sober!" answered Jo, smiling all over her face, so infectiously that they had another laugh, and then settled down for a good talk, quite in the pleasant old fashion.

"It's no use your going out in the cold to get Amy, for they are all coming up presently. I couldn't wait; I wanted to be the one to tell you the grand surprise, and have 'first skim,' as we used to say when we squabbled about the cream."

"Of course you did, and spoilt your story by beginning at the wrong end. Now, start right, and tell me how it all happened; I'm pining to know."

"Well, I did it to please Amy," began Laurie, with a twinkle that made Jo exclaim:

"Fib number one; Amy did it to please you. Go on, and tell the truth, if you can, sir."

"Now, she's beginning to marm it; isn't it jolly to hear her?" said Laurie to the fire, and the fire glowed and sparkled as if it quite agreed. "It's all the same, you know, she and I being one. We planned to come home with the Carrols, a month or more ago, but they suddenly changed their minds, and decided to pass another winter in Paris. But grandpa wanted to come home; he went to please me, and I couldn't let him go alone, neither could I leave Amy; and Mrs. Carrol had got English notions about chaperons and such nonsense, and wouldn't let Amy come with us. So I just settled the difficulty by saying, 'Let's be married, and then we can do as we like.' "

"Of course you did; you always have things to suit you."

"Not always," and something in Laurie's voice made Jo say hastily:

"How did you ever get aunt to agree?"

"It was hard work; but, between us, we talked her over, for we had heaps of good reasons on our side. There wasn't time to write and ask leave, but you all liked it, had consented to it by and by, and it was only 'taking Time by the fetlock,' as my wife says."

"Aren't we proud of those words, and don't we like to say them?" interrupted Jo, addressing the fire in her turn, and watching with delight the happy light it seemed to kindle in the eyes that had been so tragically gloomy when she saw them last.

"A trifle, perhaps; she's such a captivating little woman I can't help being proud of her. Well, then, uncle and aunt were there to play propriety; we were so absorbed in one another we were of no mortal use apart, and that charming arrangement would make everything easy all round; so we did it."

"When, where, how?" asked Jo, in a fever of feminine interest and curiosity, for she could not realize it a particle.

"Six weeks ago, at the American consul's, in Paris; a very quiet wedding, of course, for even in our happiness we didn't forget dear little Beth."

Jo put her hand in his as he said that, and Laurie gently smoothed the little red pillow, which he remembered well.

"Why didn't you let us know afterward?" asked Jo, in a quieter tone, when they had sat quite still a minute.

"We wanted to surprise you; we thought we were coming directly home, at first; but the dear old gentleman, as soon as we were married, found he couldn't be ready under a month, at least, and sent us off to spend our honeymoon wherever we liked. Amy had once called Valrosa a regular honeymoon home, so we went there, and were as happy as people are but once in their lives. My faith, wasn't it love among the roses!"

Laurie seemed to forget Jo for a minute, and Jo was glad of it; for the fact that he told her these things so freely and naturally assured her that he had quite forgiven and forgotten. She tried to draw away her hand; but, as if he guessed the thought that prompted the half-involuntary impulse, Laurie held it fast, and said, with a manly gravity she had never seen in him before:

"Jo dear, I want to say one thing, and then we'll put it by forever. As I told you in my letter, when I wrote that Amy had been so kind to me, I never shall stop loving you; but the love is altered, and I have learned to see that it is better as it is. Amy and you change places in my heart, that's all. I think it was meant to be so, and would have come about naturally, if I had waited, as you tried to make me; but I never could be patient, and so I got a heartache. I was a boy then, headstrong and violent; and it took a hard lesson to show me my mistake. For it *was* one, Jo, as you said, and I found it out, after making a fool of myself. Upon my word, I was so tumbled up in my mind, at one time, that I didn't know which I loved best, you or Amy, and tried to love both alike; but I couldn't and when I saw her in Switzerland, everything seemed to clear up all at once. You both got into your right places, and I felt sure that it was well off with the old love before it was on with the new; that I could honestly share my heart between sister Jo and wife Amy, and love them both dearly. Will you believe it, and go back to the happy old times when we first knew one another?"

"I'll believe it, with all my heart; but, Teddy, we never can be boy and girl again: the happy old times can't come back, and we mustn't expect it. We are man and woman now, with sober work to do, for playtime is over, and we must give up frolicking. I'm sure you feel this; I see the change in you, and you'll find it in me. I shall miss my boy, but I shall love the man as much, and admire him more, because he means to be what I hoped he would. We can't be little playmates any longer, but we will be brother and sister, to love and help one another all our lives, won't we, Laurie?"

He did not say a word, but took the hand she offered him, and laid his face down on it for a minute, feeling that out of the grave of a boyish passion there had risen a beautiful, strong friendship to bless them both. Presently Jo said cheerfully, for she didn't want the coming home to be a sad one:

"I can't make it true that you children are really married, and going to set up housekeeping. Why, it seems only yesterday that I was buttoning Amy's pinafore, and pulling your hair when you teased. Mercy me, how time does fly!"

"As one of the children is older than yourself, you needn't talk so like a grandma. I flatter myself I'm a 'gentleman growed,' as Peggotty said of David; and when you see Amy, you'll find her rather a precocious infant," said Laurie, looking amused at her maternal air.

"You may be a little older in years, but I'm ever so much older in feeling, Teddy. Women always are; and this last year has been such a hard one that I feel forty."

"Poor Jo! We left you to bear it alone, while we went pleasuring. You *are* older; here's a line, and there's another; unless you smile, your eyes look sad, and when I touched the cushion, just now, I found a tear on it. You've had a great deal to bear, and had to bear it all alone. What a selfish beast I've been!" and Laurie pulled his own hair, with a remorseful look.

But Jo only turned over the traitorous pillow, and answered, in a tone which she tried to make quite cheerful:

"No, I had father and mother to help me, the dear babies to comfort me, and the thought that you and Amy were safe and happy, to make the troubles here easier to bear. I *am* lonely, sometimes, but I dare say it's good for me, and—"

"You never shall be again," broke in Laurie, putting his arm about her, as if to fence out every human ill. "Amy and I can't get on without you, so you must come and teach 'the children' to keep house, and go halves in everything, just as we used to do, and let us pet you, and all be blissfully happy and friendly together."

"If I shouldn't be in the way, it would be very pleasant. I begin to feel quite young already; for, somehow, all my troubles seemed to fly away when you came. You always were a comfort, Teddy," and Jo leaned her head on his shoulder, just as she did years ago, when Beth lay ill, and Laurie told her to hold onto him.

He looked down at her, wondering if she remembered the time, but Jo was smiling to herself, as if, in truth, her troubles *had* all vanished at his coming.

"You are the same Jo still, dropping tears about one minute, and laughing the next. You look a little wicked now; what is it, grandma?"

"I was wondering how you and Amy get on together."

"Like angels!"

"Yes, of course, at first; but which rules?"

"I don't mind telling you that she does, now; at least I let her think so—it pleases her, you know. By and by we shall take turns, for marriage, they say, halves one's rights and doubles one's duties."

"You'll go on as you begin, and Amy will rule you all the days of your life."

"Well, she does it so imperceptibly that I don't think I shall mind much. She is the sort of woman who knows how to rule well; in fact, I rather like it, for she winds one round her finger as softly and prettily as a skein of silk, and makes you feel as if she was doing you a favor all the while."

"That ever I should live to see you a henpecked husband and enjoying it!" cried Jo, with uplifted hands.

It was good to see Laurie square his shoulders, and smile with masculine scorn at that insinuation, as he replied, with his "high and mighty" air:

"Amy is too well bred for that, and I am not the sort of man to submit to it. My wife and I respect ourselves and one another too much ever to tyrannize or quarrel."

Jo liked that, and thought the new dignity very becoming, but the boy seemed changing very fast into the man, and regret mingled with her pleasure.

"I am sure of that; Amy and you never did quarrel as we

used to. She is the sun and I the wind, in the fable, and the sun managed the man best, you remember."

"She can blow him up as well as shine on him," laughed Laurie. "Such a lecture as I got at Nice! I give you my word it was a deal worse than any of your scoldings—a regular rouser. I'll tell you all about it sometime—*she* never will, because, after telling me that she despised and was ashamed of me; she lost her heart to the despicable party and married the good-for-nothing."

"What baseness! Well, if she abuses you, come to me, and I'll defend you."

"I look as if I needed it, don't I?" said Laurie, getting up and striking an attitude which suddenly changed from the imposing to the rapturous, as Amy's voice was heard calling:

"Where is she? Where's my dear old Jo?"

In trooped the whole family, and everyone was hugged and kissed all over again, and, after several vain attempts, the three wanderers were set down to be looked at and exulted over. Mr. Laurence, hale and hearty as ever, was quite as much improved as the others by his foreign tour, for the crustiness seemed to be nearly gone, and the old-fashioned courtliness had received a polish which made it kindlier than ever. It was good to see him beam at "my children," as he called the young pair; it was better still to see Amy pay him the daughterly duty and affection which completely won his old heart; and best of all, to watch Laurie revolve about the two, as if never tired of enjoying the pretty picture they made.

The minute she put her eyes upon Amy, Meg became conscious that her own dress hadn't a Parisian air, that young Mrs. Moffat would be entirely eclipsed by young Mrs. Laurence, and that "her ladyship" was altogether a most elegant and graceful woman. Jo thought, as she watched the pair, "How well they look together! I was right, and Laurie has found the beautiful, accomplished girl who will become his home better than clumsy old Jo, and be a pride, not a torment to him." Mrs. March and her husband smiled and nodded at each other with happy faces, for they saw that their youngest had done well, not only in worldly things, but the better wealth of love, confidence, and happiness.

For Amy's face was full of the soft brightness which betokens a peaceful heart, her voice had a new tenderness in it, and the cool, prim carriage was changed to a gentle dignity, both womanly and winning. No little affectations marred it, and the cordial sweetness of her manner was more charming than the new beauty or the old grace, for it stamped her at once with the unmistakable sign of the true gentlewoman she had hoped to become.

"Love has done much for our little girl," said her mother softly.

"She has had a good example before her all her life, my dear," Mr. March whispered back, with a loving look at the worn face and gray head beside him.

Daisy found it impossible to keep her eyes off her "pitty aunty," but attached herself like a lap dog to the wonderful chatelaine full of delightful charms. Demi paused to consider the new relationship before he compromised himself by the rash acceptance of a bribe, which took the tempting form of a family of wooden bears from Berne. A flank movement produced an unconditional surrender, however, for Laurie knew where to have him.

"Young man, when I first had the honor of making your acquaintance you hit me in the face: now I demand the satisfaction of a gentleman," and with that the tall uncle proceeded to toss and tousle the small nephew in a way that damaged his philosophical dignity as much as it delighted his boyish soul.

"Blest if she ain't in silk from head to foot? Ain't it a relishin' sight to see her settin' there as fine as a fiddle, and hear folks calling little Amy Mis Laurence?" muttered old Hannah, who could not resist frequent "peeks" through the slide as she set the table in a most decidedly promiscuous manner.

Mercy on us, how they did talk! First one, then the other, then all burst out together, trying to tell the history of three years in half an hour. It was fortunate that tea was at hand, to produce a lull and provide refreshment, for they would have been hoarse and faint if they had gone on much longer. Such a happy procession as filed away into the little dining room! Mr. March proudly escorted "Mrs. Laurence"; Mrs. March as proudly leaned on the arm of "my son"; the old gentleman took

Jo, with a whispered "You must be my girl now," and a glance at the empty corner by the fire, that made Jo whisper back, with trembling lips, "I'll try to fill her place, sir."

The twins pranced behind, feeling that the millennium was at hand, for everyone was so busy with the newcomers that they were left to revel at their own sweet will, and you may be sure they made the most of the opportunity. Didn't they steal sips of tea, stuff gingerbread *ad libitum*, get a hot biscuit apiece, and, as a crowning trespass, didn't they each whisk a captivating little tart into their tiny pockets, there to stick and crumble treacherously, teaching them that both human nature and pastry are frail? Burdened with the guilty consciousness of the sequestered tarts, and fearing that Dodo's sharp eyes would pierce the thin disguise of cambric and merino which hid their booty, the little sinners attached themselves to "Dranpa," who hadn't his spectacles on. Amy, who was handed about like refreshments, returned to the parlor on Father Laurence's arm; the others paired off as before, and this arrangement left Jo companionless. She did not mind it at the minute, for she lingered to answer Hannah's eager inquiry:

"Will Miss Amy ride in her coop (coupé) and use all them lovely silver dishes that's stored away over yander?"

"Shouldn't wonder if she drove six white horses, ate off gold plate, and wore diamonds and point lace every day. Teddy thinks nothing too good for her," returned Jo with infinite satisfaction.

"No more there is! Will you have hash or fishballs for breakfast?" asked Hannah, who wisely mingled poetry and prose.

"I don't care," and Jo shut the door, feeling that food was an uncongenial topic just then. She stood a minute looking at the party vanishing above, and, as Demi's short plaid legs toiled up the last stair, a sudden sense of loneliness came over her so strongly that she looked about her with dim eyes, as if to find something to lean upon, for even Teddy had deserted her. If she had known what birthday gift was coming every minute nearer and nearer, she would not have said to herself, "I'll weep a little weep when I go to bed; it won't do to be dismal now." Then she drew her hand over her eyes—for one of her boyish habits was never to know where her handkerchief was

—and had just managed to call up a smile when there came a
knock at the porch door.

She opened it with hospitable haste, and started as if another ghost had come to surprise her; for there stood a tall
bearded gentleman, beaming on her from the darkness like a
midnight sun.

"Oh, Mr. Bhaer, I *am* so glad to see you!" cried Jo, with a
clutch, as if she feared the night would swallow him up before
she could get him in.

"And I to see Mees Marsch—but no, you haf a party—" and
the professor paused as the sound of voices and the tap of
dancing feet came down to them.

"No, we haven't, only the family. My sister and friends have
just come home, and we are all very happy. Come in, and make
one of us."

Though a very social man, I think Mr. Bhaer would have
gone decorously away, and come again another day; but how
could he, when Jo shut the door behind him, and bereft him of
his hat? Perhaps her face had something to do with it, for she
forgot to hide her joy at seeing him, and showed it with a

frankness that proved irresistible to the solitary man, whose welcome far exceeded his boldest hopes.

"If I shall not be Monsieur de Trop, I will so gladly see them all. You haf been ill, my friend?"

He put the question abruptly, for, as Jo hung up his coat, the light fell on her face, and he saw a change in it.

"Not ill, but tired and sorrowful. We have had trouble since I saw you last."

"Ah, yes, I know. My heart was sore for you when I heard that!" and he shook hands again, with such a sympathetic face that Jo felt as if no comfort could equal the look of the kind eyes, the grasp of the big, warm hand.

"Father, mother, this is my friend, Professor Bhaer," she said, with a face and tone of such irrepressible pride and pleasure that she might as well have blown a trumpet and opened the door with a flourish.

If the stranger had had any doubts about his reception, they were set at rest in a minute by the cordial welcome he received. Everyone greeted him kindly, for Jo's sake at first, but very soon they liked him for his own. They could not help it, for he carried the talisman that opens all hearts, and these simple people warmed to him at once, feeling even the more friendly because he was poor; for poverty enriches those who live above it and is a sure passport to truly hospitable spirits. Mr. Bhaer sat looking about him with the air of a traveler who knocks at a strange door, and, when it opens, finds himself at home. The children went to him like bees to a honey pot; and, establishing themselves on each knee, proceeded to captivate him by rifling his pockets, pulling his beard, and investigating his watch, with juvenile audacity. The women telegraphed their approval to one another, and Mr. March, feeling that he had got a kindred spirit, opened his choicest stores for his guest's benefit, while silent John listened and enjoyed the talk, but said not a word, and Mr. Laurence found it impossible to go to sleep.

If Jo had not been otherwise engaged, Laurie's behavior would have amused her; for a faint twinge, not of jealousy, but something like suspicion caused that gentleman to stand aloof at first, and observe the newcomer with brotherly circumspection. But it did not last long. He got interested in spite of himself, and, before he knew it, was drawn into the circle; for Mr. Bhaer talked well in this genial atmosphere, and did himself justice. He seldom spoke to Laurie, but looked at him often, and a shadow would pass across his face, as if regretting his own lost youth, as he watched the young man in his prime. Then his eye would turn to Jo so wistfully that she would have surely answered the mute inquiry if she had seen it; but Jo had her own eyes to take care of, and, feeling that they could not be trusted, she prudently kept them on the little sock she was knitting, like a model maiden aunt.

A stealthy glance now and then refreshed her like sips of fresh water after a dusty walk, for the sidelong peeps showed her several propitious omens. Mr. Bhaer's face had lost the absent-minded expression, and looked all alive with interest in the present moment, actually young and handsome, she thought, forgetting to compare him with Laurie, as she usually did strange men, to their great detriment. Then he seemed quite inspired, though the burial customs of the ancients, to which the conversation had strayed, might not be considered an exhilarating topic. Jo quite glowed with triumph when Teddy got quenched in an argument, and thought to herself, as she watched her father's absorbed face, "How he would enjoy having such a man as my professor to talk with every day!" Lastly, Mr. Bhaer was dressed in a new suit of black, which made him look more like a gentleman than ever. His bushy hair had been cut and smoothly brushed, but didn't stay in order long, for, in exciting moments, he rumpled it up in the droll way he used to do; and Jo liked it rampantly erect better than flat, because she thought it gave his fine forehead a Jove-like aspect. Poor Jo, how she did glorify that plain man, as she sat knitting away so quietly, yet letting nothing escape her, not even the fact that Mr. Bhaer actually had gold sleeve buttons in his immaculate wristbands!

"Dear old fellow! He couldn't have got himself up with more care if he'd been going a-wooing," said Jo to herself; and then a sudden thought, born of the words, made her blush so dreadfully that she had to drop her ball, and go down after it to hide her face.

The maneuver did not succeed as well as she expected, however; for, though just in the act of setting fire to a funeral pile, the professor dropped his torch, metaphorically speaking, and made a dive after the little blue ball. Of course they bumped their heads smartly together, saw stars, and both came up flushed and laughing, without the ball, to resume their seats, wishing they had not left them.

Nobody knew where the evening went to; for Hannah skillfully abstracted the babies at an early hour, nodding like two rosy poppies, and Mr. Laurence went home to rest. The others sat round the fire, talking away, utterly regardless of the lapse of time, till Meg, whose maternal mind was impressed with a firm conviction that Daisy had tumbled out of bed and Demi set his nightgown afire studying the structure of matches, made a move to go.

"We must have our sing, in the good old way, for we are all together again once more," said Jo, feeling that a good shout would be a safe and pleasant vent for the jubilant emotions of her soul.

They were not *all* there. But no one found the words thoughtless or untrue; for Beth still seemed among them, a peaceful presence, invisible, but dearer than ever, since death could not break the household league that love made indissoluble. The little chair stood in its old place; the tidy basket, with the bit of work she left unfinished when the needle grew "so heavy," was still on its accustomed shelf; the beloved instrument, seldom touched now, had not been moved; and above it Beth's face, serene and smiling, as in the early days, looked down upon them, seeming to say, "Be happy. I am here."

"Play something, Amy. Let them hear how much you have improved," said Laurie, with pardonable pride in his promising pupil.

But Amy whispered, with full eyes, as she twirled the faded stool:

"Not tonight, dear. I can't show off tonight."

But she did show something better than brilliancy or skill; for she sung Beth's songs with a tender music in her voice which the best master could not have taught, and touched the

listeners' hearts with a sweeter power than any other inspiration could have given her. The room was very still, when the
clear voice failed suddenly at the last line of Beth's favorite
hymn. It was hard to say —

> *"Earth hath no sorrow that heaven cannot heal,"*

and Amy leaned against her husband, who stood behind her,
feeling that her welcome home was not quite perfect without
Beth's kiss.

"Now, we must finish with Mignon's song; for Mr. Bhaer
sings that," said Jo, before the pause grew painful. And Mr.
Bhaer cleared his throat with a gratified "Hem!" as he stepped
into the corner where Jo stood, saying:

"You will sing with me? We go excellently well together."

A pleasing fiction, by the way; for Jo had no more idea of
music than a grasshopper. But she would have consented if
he had proposed to sing a whole opera, and warbled away,
blissfully regardless of time and tune. It didn't much matter;
for Mr. Bhaer sang like a true German, heartily and well; and
Jo soon subsided into a subdued hum, that she might listen to
the mellow voice that seemed to sing for her alone.

> *"Know'st thou the land where the citron blooms,"*

used to be the professor's favorite line, for "das land" meant
Germany to him; but now he seemed to dwell, with peculiar
warmth and melody, upon the words —

> *"There, oh, there, might I with thee,*
> *Oh, my beloved, go!"*

and one listener was so thrilled by the tender invitation that
she longed to say she did know the land, and would joyfully
depart thither whenever he liked.

The song was considered a great success, and the singer retired covered with laurels. But a few minutes afterward, he
forgot his manners entirely, and stared at Amy putting on her
bonnet; for she had been introduced simply as "my sister," and
no one called her by her new name since he came. He forgot
himself still further when Laurie said, in his most gracious
manner, at parting:

"My wife and I are very glad to meet you, sir. Please remember that there is always a welcome waiting for you over the way."

Then the professor thanked him so heartily, and looked so suddenly illuminated with satisfaction, that Laurie thought him the most delightfully demonstrative old fellow he ever met.

"I too shall go; but I shall gladly come again, if you will gif me leave, dear madame, for a little business in the city will keep me here some days."

He spoke to Mrs. March, but he looked at Jo; and the mother's voice gave as cordial an assent as did the daughter's eyes; for Mrs. March was not so blind to her children's interest as Mrs. Moffat supposed.

"I suspect that is a wise man," remarked Mr. March, with placid satisfaction, from the hearthrug, after the last guest had gone.

"I know he is a good one," added Mrs. March, with decided approval, as she wound up the clock.

"I thought you'd like him" was all Jo said, as she slipped away to her bed.

She wondered what the business was that brought Mr. Bhaer to the city, and finally decided that he had been appointed to some great honor, somewhere, but had been too modest to mention the fact. If she had seen his face when, safe in his own room, he looked at the picture of a severe and rigid young lady, with a good deal of hair, who appeared to be gazing darkly into futurity, it might have thrown some light upon the subject, especially when he turned off the gas, and kissed the picture in the dark.

CHAPTER FORTY-FOUR

My Lord and Lady

"PLEASE, Madame Mother, could you lend me my wife for half an hour? The luggage has come, and I've been making hay of Amy's Paris finery, trying to find some things I want," said Laurie, coming in the next day to find Mrs. Laurence sitting in her mother's lap, as if being made "the baby" again.

"Certainly. Go, dear; I forget that you have any home but this," said Mrs. March, pressing the white hand that wore the wedding ring, as if asking pardon for her maternal covetousness.

"I shouldn't have come over if I could have helped it; but I can't get on without my little woman any more than a—"

"Weathercock can without wind," suggested Jo, as he paused for a simile; Jo had grown quite her own saucy self again since Teddy came home.

Looking up, she saw Mr. Bhaer looking down

[SEE PAGE 522]

"Exactly; for Amy keeps me pointing due west most of the time, with only an occasional whiffle round to the south, and I haven't had an easterly spell since I was married; don't know anything about the north, but am altogether salubrious and balmy, hey, my lady?"

"Lovely weather so far; I don't know how long it will last, but I'm not afraid of storms, for I'm learning how to sail my ship. Come home, dear, and I'll find your bootjack; I suppose that's what you are rummaging after among my things. Men are *so* helpless, mother," said Amy, with a matronly air, which delighted her husband.

"What are you going to do with yourselves after you get settled?" asked Jo, buttoning Amy's cloak as she used to button her pinafores.

"We have our plans; we don't mean to say much about them yet, because we are such very new brooms, but we don't intend to be idle. I'm going into business with a devotion that shall delight grandfather, and prove to him that I'm not spoilt. I need something of the sort to keep me steady. I'm tired of dawdling, and mean to work like a man."

"And Amy, what is she going to do?" asked Mrs. March, well pleased at Laurie's decision, and the energy with which he spoke.

"After doing the civil all round, and airing our best bonnet, we shall astonish you by the elegant hospitalities of our mansion, the brilliant society we shall draw about us, and the beneficial influence we shall exert over the world at large. That's about it, isn't it, Madame Récamier?" asked Laurie, with a quizzical look at Amy.

"Time will show. Come away, impertinence, and don't shock my family by calling me names before their faces," answered Amy, resolving that there should be a home with a good wife in it before she set up a salon as a queen of society.

"How happy those children seem together!" observed Mr. March, finding it difficult to become absorbed in his Aristotle after the young couple had gone.

"Yes, and I think it will last," added Mrs. March, with the restful expression of a pilot who has brought a ship safely into port.

"I know it will. Happy Amy," and Jo sighed, then smiled

brightly as Professor Bhaer opened the gate with an impatient push.

Later in the evening, when his mind had been set at rest about the bootjack, Laurie said suddenly to his wife, who was flitting about, arranging her new art treasures:

"Mrs. Laurence."

"My lord!"

"That man intends to marry our Jo!"

"I hope so; don't you, dear?"

"Well, my love, I consider him a trump, in the fullest sense of that expressive word, but I do wish he was a little younger and a good deal richer."

"Now, Laurie, don't be too fastidious and worldly-minded. If they love one another it doesn't matter a particle how old they are nor how poor. Women *never* should marry for money—" Amy caught herself up short as the words escaped her and looked at her husband, who replied, with malicious gravity:

"Certainly not, though you do hear charming girls say that they intend to do it sometimes. If my memory serves me, you once thought it your duty to make a rich match; that accounts, perhaps, for your marrying a good-for-nothing like me."

"Oh, my dearest boy, don't, don't say that! I forgot you were rich when I said 'Yes.' I'd have married you if you hadn't a penny, and I sometimes wish you were poor that I might show how much I love you," and Amy, who was very dignified in public and very fond in private, gave convincing proofs of the truth of her words.

"You don't really think I am such a mercenary creature as I tried to be once, do you? It would break my heart if you didn't believe that I'd gladly pull in the same boat with you, even if you had to get your living by rowing on the lake."

"Am I an idiot and a brute? How could I think so, when you refused a richer man for me, and won't let me give you half I want to now, when I have the right? Girls do it every day, poor things, and are taught to think it is their only salvation; but you had better lessons, and, though I trembled for you at one time, I was not disappointed, for the daughter was true to the mother's teaching. I told mamma so yesterday, and she looked as glad and grateful as if I'd given her a check for a million, to be spent in charity. You are not listening to my moral remarks, Mrs. Laurence," and Laurie paused, for Amy's eyes had an absent look, though fixed upon his face.

"Yes, I am, and admiring the dimple in your chin at the same time. I don't wish to make you vain, but I must confess that I'm prouder of my handsome husband than of all his money. Don't laugh, but your nose is *such* a comfort to me," and Amy softly caressed the well-cut feature with artistic satisfaction.

Laurie had received many compliments in his life, but never one that suited him better, as he plainly showed though he did laugh at his wife's peculiar taste, while she said slowly:

"May I ask you a question, dear?"

"Of course you may."

"Shall you care if Jo does marry Mr. Bhaer?"

"Oh, that's the trouble, is it? I thought there was something in the dimple that didn't suit you. Not being a dog in the manger, but the happiest fellow alive, I assure you I can dance at Jo's wedding with a heart as light as my heels. Do you doubt it, my darling?"

Amy looked up at him, and was satisfied; her last little jealous fear vanished forever, and she thanked him, with a face full of love and confidence.

"I wish we could do something for that capital old professor. Couldn't we invent a rich relation, who shall obligingly die out there in Germany, and leave him a tidy little fortune?" said Laurie, when they began to pace up and down the long drawing room, arm in arm, as they were fond of doing, in memory of the château garden.

"Jo would find us out, and spoil it all; she is very proud of him, just as he is, and said yesterday that she thought poverty was a beautiful thing."

"Bless her dear heart! She won't think so when she has a literary husband, and a dozen little professors and professorins to support. We won't interfere now, but watch our chance, and do them a good turn in spite of themselves. I owe Jo for a part of my education, and she believes in people's paying their honest debts, so I'll get round her in that way."

"How delightful it is to be able to help others, isn't it? That was always one of my dreams, to have the power of giving freely; and, thanks to you, the dream has come true."

"Ah! We'll do quantities of good, won't we? There's one sort of poverty that I particularly like to help. Out-and-out beggars get taken care of, but poor gentlefolks fare badly, because they won't ask, and people don't dare to offer charity; yet there are a thousand ways of helping them, if one only knows how to do it so delicately that it does not offend: I must say, I like to serve a decayed gentleman better than a blarneying beggar; I suppose it's wrong, but I do, though it is harder."

"Because it takes a gentleman to do it," added the other member of the domestic admiration society.

"Thank you, I'm afraid I don't deserve that pretty compliment. But I was going to say that while I was dawdling about abroad, I saw a good many talented young fellows making all sorts of sacrifices, and enduring real hardships, that they might realize their dreams. Splendid fellows, some of them, working like heroes, poor and friendless, but so full of courage, patience, and ambition, that I was ashamed of myself, and longed to give them a right good lift. Those are people whom it's a satisfaction to help, for if they've got genius, it's an honor to be allowed to serve them, and not let it be lost or delayed for want of fuel to keep the pot boiling; if they haven't it's a pleasure to comfort the poor souls, and keep them from despair when they find it out."

"Yes, indeed; and there's another class who can't ask, and who suffer in silence. I know something of it, for I belonged to it before you made a princess of me, as the king does the beggarmaid in the old story. Ambitious girls have a hard time, Laurie, and often have to see youth, health, and precious opportunities go by, just for want of a little help at the right minute. People have been very kind to me; and whenever I see girls struggling along, as we used to do, I want to put out my hand and help them, as I was helped."

"And so you shall, like an angel as you are!" cried Laurie, resolving, with a glow of philanthropic zeal, to found and endow an institution for the express benefit of young women with artistic tendencies. "Rich people have no right to sit down and enjoy themselves, or let their money accumulate for others to waste. It's not half so sensible to leave legacies when one dies as it is to use the money wisely while alive, and enjoy making one's fellow creatures happy with it. We'll have a good time ourselves, and add an extra relish to our own pleasure by giving other people a generous taste. Will you be a little Dorcas, going about emptying a big basket of comforts, and filling it up with good deeds?"

"With all my heart, if you will be a brave St. Martin, stopping, as you ride gallantly through the world, to share your cloak with the beggar."

"It's a bargain, and we shall get the best of it!"

So the young pair shook hands upon it, and then paced happily on again, feeling that their pleasant home was more homelike because they hoped to brighten other homes, believing that their own feet would walk more uprightly along the flowery path before them, if they smoothed rough ways for other feet, and feeling that their hearts were more closely knit together by a love which could tenderly remember those less blest than they.

CHAPTER FORTY-FIVE

Daisy and Demi

I CANNOT feel that I have done my duty as humble historian of the March family, without devoting at least one chapter to the two most precious and important members of it. Daisy and Demi had now arrived at years of discretion; for in this fast age babies of three or four assert their rights, and get them, too, which is more than many of their elders do. If there ever were a pair of twins in danger of being utterly spoilt by adoration, it was these prattling Brookes. Of course they were the most remarkable children ever born, as will be shown when I mention that they walked at eight months, talked fluently at twelve months, and at two years they took their places at table, and behaved with a propriety which charmed all beholders. At three, Daisy demanded a "needler," and actually made a bag with four stitches in it; she likewise set up housekeeping in the sideboard, and managed a microscopic cooking stove with a skill that brought tears of pride to Hannah's eyes, while Demi learned his letters with his grandfather, who invented a new mode of teaching the alphabet by forming the letters with his arms and legs, thus uniting gymnastics for head and heels. The boy early developed a mechanical genius which delighted his father and distracted his mother, for he tried to imitate every machine he saw, and kept the nursery in a chaotic condition, with his "sewinsheen"—a mysterious structure of string, chairs, clothespins, and spools, for wheels to go "wound and wound"; also a basket hung over the back of a big chair, in which he vainly tried to hoist his too confiding sister, who, with feminine devotion, allowed her little head to be bumped till rescued, when the young inventor indignantly remarked, "Why, marmar, dat's my lellywaiter, and me's trying to pull her up."

Though utterly unlike in character, the twins got on remarkably well together, and seldom quarreled more than thrice a day. Of course, Demi tyrannized over Daisy, and gallantly defended her from every other aggressor; while Daisy made a galley slave of herself, and adored her brother as the one perfect being in the world. A rosy, chubby, sunshiny little soul was Daisy, who found her way to everybody's heart, and nestled there. One of the captivating children, who seem made to be kissed and cuddled, adorned and adored like little goddesses, and produced for general approval on all festive occasions. Her small virtues were so sweet that she would have been quite angelic if a few small naughtinesses had not kept her delightfully human. It was all fair weather in her world, and every morning she scrambled up to the window in her little nightgown to look out, and say, no matter whether it rained or shone, "Oh, pitty day, oh, pitty day!" Everyone was a friend, and she offered kisses to a stranger so confidingly that the most inveterate bachelor relented, and baby lovers became faithful worshipers.

"Me loves evvybody," she once said, opening her arms, with her spoon in one hand, and her mug in the other, as if eager to embrace and nourish the whole world.

As she grew, her mother began to feel that the Dovecote would be blest by the presence of an inmate as serene and loving as that which had helped to make the old house home, and to pray that she might be spared a loss like that which had lately taught them how long they had entertained an angel unawares. Her grandfather often called her "Beth," and her grandmother watched over her with untiring devotion, as if trying to atone for some past mistake, which no eye but her own could see.

Demi, like a true Yankee, was of an inquiring turn, wanting to know everything, and often getting much disturbed because he could not get satisfactory answers to his perpetual "What for?"

He also possessed a philosophic bent, to the great delight of his grandfather, who used to hold Socratic conversations with him, in which the precocious pupil occasionally posed as his teacher, to the undisguised satisfaction of the women-folk.

"What makes my legs go, dranpa?" asked the young philosopher, surveying those active portions of his frame with a meditative air, while resting after a go-to-bed frolic one night.

"It's your little mind, Demi," replied the sage, stroking the yellow head respectfully.

"What is a little mine?"

"It is something which makes your body move, as the spring made the wheels go in my watch when I showed it to you."

"Open me; I want to see it go wound."

"I can't do that any more than you could open the watch. God winds you up, and you go till He stops you."

"Does I?" and Demi's brown eyes grew big and bright as he took in the new thought. "Is I wounded up like the watch?"

"Yes; but I can't show you how; for it is done when we don't see."

Demi felt of his back, as if expecting to find it like that of the watch, and then gravely remarked:

"I dess Dod does it when I's asleep."

A careful explanation followed, to which he listened so attentively that his anxious grandmother said:

"My dear, do you think it wise to talk about such things to that baby? He's getting great bumps over his eyes, and learning to ask the most unanswerable questions."

"If he is old enough to ask the questions he is old enough to receive true answers. I am not putting the thoughts into his head, but helping him unfold those already there. These children are wiser than we are, and I have no doubt the boy understands every word I have said to him. Now, Demi, tell me where you keep your mind."

If the boy had replied, like Alcibiades, "By the gods, Socrates, I cannot tell," his grandfather would not have been surprised; but when, after standing a moment on one leg, like a meditative young stork, he answered, in a tone of calm conviction, "In my little belly," the old gentleman could only join in grandma's laugh, and dismiss the class in metaphysics.

There might have been cause for maternal anxiety, if Demi had not given convincing proofs that he was a true boy, as well as a budding philosopher; for, often, after a discussion which caused Hannah to prophesy, with ominous nods, "That child ain't long for this world," he would turn about and set her fears at rest by some of the pranks with which dear, dirty, naughty little rascals distract and delight their parents' souls.

Meg made many moral rules, and tried to keep them; but what mother was ever proof against the winning wiles, the ingenious evasions, or the tranquil audacity of the miniature men and women who so early show themselves accomplished Artful Dodgers?

"No more raisins, Demi, they'll make you sick," says mamma to the young person, who offers his services in the kitchen with unfailing regularity on plum-pudding day.

"Me likes to be sick."

"I don't want to have you, so run away and help Daisy make pattycakes."

He reluctantly departs, but his wrongs weigh upon his spirit; and, by and by, when an opportunity comes to redress them, he outwits mamma by a shrewd bargain.

"Now you have been good children, and I'll play anything you like," says Meg, as she leads her assistant cooks upstairs, when the pudding is safely bouncing in the pot.

"Truly, marmar?" asks Demi, with a brilliant idea in his well-powdered head.

"Yes, truly; anything you say," replies the shortsighted parent, preparing herself to sing "The Three Little Kittens" half a dozen times over, or to take her family to "Buy a penny bun," regardless of wind or limb. But Demi corners her by the cool reply:

"Then we'll go and eat up all the raisins."

Aunt Dodo was chief playmate and confidante of both children, and the trio turned the little house topsy-turvy. Aunt Amy was as yet only a name to them, Aunt Beth soon faded into a pleasantly vague memory, but Aunt Dodo was a living reality, and they made the most of her, for which compliment she was deeply grateful. But when Mr. Bhaer came, Jo neglected her playfellows, and dismay and desolation fell upon their little souls. Daisy, who was fond of going about peddling kisses, lost her best customer and became bankrupt; Demi, with infantile penetration, soon discovered that Dodo liked to play with "the bear-man" better than she did with him; but, though hurt, he concealed his anguish, for he hadn't the heart to insult a rival who kept a mine of chocolate drops in his waistcoat pocket, and a watch that could be taken out of its case and freely shaken by ardent admirers.

Some persons might have considered these pleasing liberties as bribes; but Demi didn't see it in that light, and continued to patronize the bear-man with pensive affability, while Daisy bestowed her small affections upon him at the third call, and considered his shoulder her throne, his arm her refuge, his gifts treasures of surpassing worth.

Gentlemen are sometimes seized with sudden fits of admiration for the young relatives of ladies whom they honor with their regard; but this counterfeit philoprogenitiveness sits uneasily upon them, and does not deceive anybody a particle. Mr. Bhaer's devotion was sincere, however likewise effective — for honesty is the best policy in love as in law; he was one of the men who are at home with children, and looked particularly well when little faces made a pleasant contrast with his manly one. His business, whatever it was, detained him from day to day, but evening seldom failed to bring him out to see—

well, he always asked for Mr. March, so I suppose *he* was the attraction. The excellent papa labored under the delusion that he was, and reveled in long discussions with the kindred spirit, till a chance remark of his more observing grandson suddenly enlightened him.

Mr. Bhaer came in one evening to pause on the threshold of the study, astonished by the spectacle that met his eye. Prone upon the floor lay Mr. March, with his respectable legs in the air, and beside him, likewise prone, was Demi, trying to imitate the attitude with his own short, scarlet-stockinged legs, both grovelers so seriously absorbed that they were unconscious of spectators, till Mr. Bhaer laughed his sonorous laugh, and Jo cried out, with a scandalized face:

"Father, father, here's the professor!"

Down went the black legs and up came the gray head, as the preceptor said, with undisturbed dignity:

"Good evening, Mr. Bhaer. Excuse me for a moment; we are just finishing our lesson. Now, Demi, make the letter and tell its name."

"I knows him!" and, after a few convulsive efforts, the red legs took the shape of a pair of compasses, and the intelligent pupil triumphantly shouted, "It's a We, dranpa, it's a We!"

"He's a born Weller," laughed Jo, as her parent gathered himself up, and her nephew tried to stand on his head, as the only mode of expressing his satisfaction that school was over.

"What have you been at today, bübchen?" asked Mr. Bhaer, picking up the gymnast.

"Me went to see little Mary."

"And what did you do there?"

"I kissed her," began Demi, with artless frankness.

"Prut! Thou beginnest early. What did the little Mary say to that?" asked Mr. Bhaer, continuing to confess the young sinner, who stood upon his knee, exploring the waistcoat pocket.

"Oh, she liked it, and she kissed me, and I liked it. *Don't* little boys like little girls?" added Demi, with his mouth full, and an air of bland satisfaction.

"You precocious chick! Who put that into your head?" said Jo, enjoying the innocent revelations as much as the professor.

" 'Tisn't in mine head; it's in mine mouf," answered literal Demi, putting out his tongue, with a chocolate drop on it, thinking she alluded to confectionery, not ideas.

"Thou shouldst save some for the little friend: sweets to the sweets, manling," and Mr. Bhaer offered Jo some, with a look that made her wonder if chocolate was not the nectar drunk by the gods. Demi also saw the smile, was impressed by it, and artlessly inquired:

"Do great boys like great girls, too, 'fessor?"

Like young Washington, Mr. Bhaer "couldn't tell a lie"; so he gave the somewhat vague reply that he believed they did sometimes, in a tone that made Mr. March put down his clothesbrush, glance at Jo's retiring face, and then sink into his chair, looking as if the "precocious chick" had put an idea into *his* head that was both sweet and sour.

Why Dodo, when she caught him in the china closet half an hour afterward, nearly squeezed the breath out of his little body with a tender embrace, instead of shaking him for being there, and why she followed up this novel performance by the unexpected gift of a big slice of bread and jelly, remained one of the problems over which Demi puzzled his small wits, and was forced to leave unsolved forever.

CHAPTER FORTY-SIX

Under the Umbrella

WHILE Laurie and Amy were taking conjugal strolls over velvet carpets, as they set their house in order, and planned a blissful future, Mr. Bhaer and Jo were enjoying promenades of a different sort, along muddy roads and sodden fields.

"I always do take a walk toward evening, and I don't know why I should give it up, just because I often happen to meet the professor on his way out," said Jo to herself, after two or three encounters; for, though there were two paths to Meg's, whichever one she took she was sure to meet him, either going or returning. He was always walking rapidly, and never seemed to see her till quite close, when he would look as if his shortsighted eyes had failed to recognize the approaching lady till that moment. Then, if she was going to Meg's, he always had something for the babies; if her face was turned home-

ward, he had merely strolled down to see the river, and was
just about returning, unless they were tired of his frequent
calls.

Under the circumstances, what could Jo do but greet him
civilly, and invite him in? If she *was* tired of his visits, she
concealed her weariness with perfect skill, and took care that
there should be coffee for supper, "as Friedrich—I mean Mr.
Bhaer—doesn't like tea."

By the second week, everyone knew perfectly well what
was going on, yet everyone tried to look as if they were stone-
blind to the changes in Jo's face. They never asked why she
sang about her work, did up her hair three times a day, and got
so blooming with her evening exercise; and no one seemed to
have the slightest suspicion that Professor Bhaer, while talking
philosophy with the father, was giving the daughter lessons
in love.

Jo couldn't even lose her heart in a decorous manner, but
sternly tried to quench her feelings; and failing to do so, led a
somewhat agitated life. She was mortally afraid of being
laughed at for surrendering, after her many and vehement
declarations of independence. Laurie was her especial dread;
but, thanks to the new manager, he behaved with praiseworthy
propriety, never called Mr. Bhaer "a capital old fellow" in
public, never alluded, in the remotest manner, to Jo's improved
appearance, or expressed the least surprise at seeing the professor's hat on the Marches' hall table nearly every evening.
But he exulted in private and longed for the time to come
when he could give Jo a piece of plate, with a bear and a
ragged staff on it as an appropriate coat of arms.

For a fortnight, the professor came and went with loverlike
regularity; then he stayed away for three whole days, and
made no sign—a proceeding which caused everybody to look
sober, and Jo to become pensive, at first, and then—alas for
romance!—very cross.

"Disgusted, I dare say, and gone home as suddenly as he
came. It's nothing to me, of course; but I *should* think he would
have come and bid us good-by, like a gentleman," she said to
herself, with a despairing look at the gate, as she put on her
things for the customary walk, one dull afternoon.

"You'd better take the little umbrella, dear; it looks like rain," said her mother, observing that she had on her new bonnet, but not alluding to the fact.

"Yes, Marmee; do you want anything in town? I've got to run in and get some paper," returned Jo, pulling out the bow under her chin before the glass as an excuse for not looking at her mother.

"Yes; I want some twilled silesia, a paper of number nine needles, and two yards of narrow lavender ribbon. Have you got your thick boots on, and something warm under your cloak?"

"I believe so," answered Jo absently.

"If you happen to meet Mr. Bhaer, bring him home to tea. I quite long to see the dear man," added Mrs. March.

Jo heard *that*, but made no answer, except to kiss her mother, and walk rapidly away, thinking with a glow of gratitude, in spite of her heartache:

"How good she is to me. What *do* girls do who haven't any mothers to help them through their troubles?"

The dry-goods stores were not down among the counting-houses, banks, and wholesale warerooms, where gentlemen most do congregate; but Jo found herself in that part of the city before she did a single errand, loitering along as if waiting for someone, examining engineering instruments in one window and samples of wool in another, with most unfeminine interest; tumbling over barrels, being half smothered by descending bales, and hustled unceremoniously by busy men who looked as if they wondered "how the deuce she got there." A drop of rain on her cheek recalled her thoughts from baffled hopes to ruined ribbons; for the drops continued to fall, and, being a woman as well as a lover, she felt that, though it was too late to save her heart, she might her bonnet. Now she remembered the little umbrella, which she had forgotten to take in her hurry to be off; but regret was unavailing, and nothing could be done but borrow one or submit to a drenching. She looked up at the lowering sky, down at the crimson bow already flecked with black, forward along the muddy street, then one long, lingering look behind, at a certain grimy warehouse, with "Hoffmann, Swartz, & Co." over the door, and said to herself, with a sternly reproachful air:

"It serves me right! What business had I to put on all my best things and come philandering down here, hoping to see the professor? Jo, I'm ashamed of you! No, you shall *not* go there to borrow an umbrella, or find out where he is, from his friends. You shall trudge away, and do your errands in the rain; and if you catch your death and ruin your bonnet, it's no more than you deserve. Now then!"

With that she rushed across the street so impetuously that she narrowly escaped annihilation from a passing truck, and precipitated herself into the arms of a stately old gentleman, who said, "I beg pardon, ma'am," and looked mortally offended. Somewhat daunted, Jo righted herself, spread her handkerchief over the devoted ribbons, and, putting temptation behind her, hurried on, with increasing dampness about the ankles, and much clashing of umbrellas overhead. The fact that a somewhat dilapidated blue one remained stationary above the unprotected bonnet, attracted her attention; and, looking up, she saw Mr. Bhaer looking down.

"I feel to know the strong-minded lady who goes so bravely under many horse noses, and so fast through much mud. What do you down here, my friend?"

"I'm shopping."

Mr. Bhaer smiled, as he glanced from the pickle factory on one side to the wholesale hide and leather concern on the other; but he only said politely:

"You haf no umbrella. May I go also, and take for you the bundles?"

"Yes, thank you."

Jo's cheeks were as red as her ribbon, and she wondered what he thought of her; but she didn't care, for in a minute she found herself walking away arm in arm with her professor, feeling as if the sun had suddenly burst out with uncommon brilliancy, that the world was all right again, and that one thoroughly happy woman was paddling through the wet that day.

"We thought you had gone," said Jo hastily, for she knew he was looking at her. Her bonnet wasn't big enough to hide her face, and she feared he might think the joy it betrayed unmaidenly.

"Did you believe that I should go with no farewell to those who haf been so heavenly kind to me?" he asked so reproachfully that she felt as if she had insulted him by the suggestion, and answered heartily:

"No, I didn't; I knew you were busy about your own affairs, but we rather missed you—father and mother especially."

"And you?"

"I'm always glad to see you, sir."

In her anxiety to keep her voice quite calm, Jo made it rather cool, and the frosty little monosyllable at the end seemed to chill the professor, for his smile vanished, as he said gravely:

"I thank you, and come one time more before I go."

"You *are* going, then?"

"I haf no longer any business here; it is done."

"Successfully, I hope?" said Jo, for the bitterness of disappointment was in that short reply of his.

"I ought to think so, for I haf a way opened to me by which I can make my bread and gif my Jünglings much help."

"Tell me, please! I like to know all about the—the boys," said Jo eagerly.

"That is so kind, I gladly tell you. My friends find for me a place in a college, where I teach as at home, and earn enough to make the way smooth for Franz and Emil. For this I should be grateful, should I not?"

"Indeed, you should. How splendid it will be to have you doing what you like, and be able to see you often, and the boys!" cried Jo, clinging to the lads as an excuse for the satisfaction she could not help betraying.

"Ah! but we shall not meet often, I fear; this place is at the West."

"So far away!" and Jo left her skirts to their fate, as if it didn't matter now what became of her clothes or herself.

Mr. Bhaer could read several languages, but he had not learned to read women yet. He flattered himself that he knew Jo pretty well, and was, therefore, much amazed by the contradictions of voice, face, and manner, which she showed him in rapid succession that day, for she was in half a dozen different moods in the course of half an hour. When she met him she looked surprised, though it was impossible to help suspecting that she had come for that express purpose. When he offered her his arm, she took it with a look that filled him with delight; but when he asked if she missed him, she gave such a chilly, formal reply that despair fell upon him. On learning his good fortune she almost clapped her hands: was the joy all for the boys? Then, on hearing his destination, she said, "So far away!" in a tone of despair that lifted him on to a pinnacle of hope; but the next minute she tumbled him down again by observing, like one entirely absorbed in the matter:

"Here's the place for my errands; will you come in? It won't take long."

Jo rather prided herself upon her shopping capabilities, and particularly wished to impress her escort with the neatness and dispatch with which she would accomplish the business. But, owing to the flutter she was in, everything went amiss; she upset the tray of needles, forgot the silesia was to be "twilled" till it was cut off, gave the wrong change, and covered herself with confusion by asking for lavender ribbon at the calico counter. Mr. Bhaer stood by, watching her blush and blunder; and, as he watched her, his own bewilderment seemed to subside, for he was beginning to see that on some occasions women, like dreams, go by contraries.

When they came out, he put the parcel under his arm with a more cheerful aspect, and splashed through the puddles as if he rather enjoyed it, on the whole.

"Should we not do a little what you call shopping for the babies, and haf a farewell feast tonight if I go for my last call at your so pleasant home?" he asked, stopping before a window full of fruit and flowers.

"What will we buy?" said Jo, ignoring the latter part of his speech, and sniffing the mingled odors with an affectation of delight as they went in.

"May they haf oranges and figs?" asked Mr. Bhaer, with a paternal air.

"They eat them when they can get them."

"Do you care for nuts?"

"Like a squirrel."

"Hamburg grapes; yes, we shall surely drink to the Fatherland in those?"

Jo frowned upon that piece of extravagance, and asked why he didn't buy a frail of dates, a cask of raisins, and a bag of almonds, and done with it? Whereat Mr. Bhaer confiscated her purse, produced his own, and finished the marketing by buying several pounds of grapes, a pot of rosy daisies, and a pretty jar of honey, to be regarded in the light of a demijohn. Then, distorting his pockets with the knobby bundles, and giving her the flowers to hold, he put up the old umbrella, and they traveled on again.

"Mees Marsch, I haf a great favor to ask of you," began the professor, after a moist promenade of half a block.

"Yes, sir," and Jo's heart began to beat so hard she was afraid he would hear it.

"I am bold to say it in spite of the rain, because so short a time remains to me."

"Yes, sir," and Jo nearly crushed the small flower-pot with the sudden squeeze she gave it.

"I wish to get a little dress for my Tina, and I am too stupid to go alone. Will you kindly gif me a word of taste and help?"

"Yes, sir," and Jo felt as calm and cool, all of a sudden, as if she had stepped into a refrigerator.

"Perhaps also a shawl for Tina's mother, she is so poor and sick, and the husband is such a care. Yes, yes, a thick, warm shawl would be a friendly thing to take the little mother."

"I'll do it with pleasure, Mr. Bhaer." . . . "I'm going very fast and he's getting dearer every minute," added Jo to herself; then, with a mental shake, she entered into the business with an energy which was pleasant to behold.

Mr. Bhaer left it all to her, so she chose a pretty gown for Tina, and then ordered out the shawls. The clerk, being a married man, condescended to take an interest in the couple, who appeared to be shopping for their family.

"Your lady may prefer this; it's a superior article, a most desirable color, quite chaste and genteel," he said, shaking out a comfortable gray shawl, and throwing it over Jo's shoulders.

"Does this suit you, Mr. Bhaer?" she asked, turning her back to him, and feeling deeply grateful for the chance of hiding her face.

"Excellently well; we will haf it," answered the professor, smiling to himself as he paid for it, while Jo continued to rummage the counters like a confirmed bargain hunter.

"Now shall we go home?" he asked, as if the words were very pleasant to him.

"Yes; it's late, and I'm so tired." Jo's voice was more pathetic than she knew; for now the sun seemed to have gone in as suddenly as it came out, the world grew muddy and miserable again, and for the first time she discovered that her feet were cold, her head ached, and that her heart was colder than the former, fuller of pain than the latter. Mr. Bhaer was going away; he only cared for her as a friend; it was all a mistake, and the sooner it was over the better. With this idea in her head, she hailed an approaching omnibus with such a hasty gesture that the daisies flew out of the pot and were badly damaged.

"This is not our omniboos," said the professor, waving the loaded vehicle away, and stooping to pick up the poor little flowers.

"I beg your pardon, I didn't see the name distinctly. Never mind, I can walk. I'm used to plodding in the mud," returned Jo, winking hard, because she would have died rather than openly wipe her eyes.

Mr. Bhaer saw the drops on her cheeks, though she turned her head away; the sight seemed to touch him very much, for, suddenly stooping down, he asked in a tone that meant a great deal:

"Heart's dearest, why do you cry?"

Now, if Jo had not been new to this sort of thing she would have said she wasn't crying, had a cold in her head, or told any other feminine fib proper to the occasion; instead of which the undignified creature answered, with an irrepressible sob:

"Because you are going away."

"Ach, mein Gott, that is *so* good!" cried Mr. Bhaer, managing to clasp his hands in spite of the umbrella and the bundles. "Jo, I haf nothing but much love to gif you; I came to see if you could care for it, and I waited to be sure that I was something more than a friend. Am I? Can you make a little place in your heart for old Fritz?" he added, all in one breath.

"Oh, yes!" said Jo; and he was quite satisfied, for she folded both hands over his arm, and looked up at him with an expression that plainly showed how happy she would be to walk through life beside him, even though she had no better shelter than the old umbrella, if he carried it.

It was certainly proposing under difficulties, for, even if he had desired to do so, Mr. Bhaer could not go down upon his knees, on account of the mud; neither could he offer Jo his hand, except figuratively, for both were full; much less could he indulge in tender demonstrations in the open street, though he was near it; so the only way in which he could express his rapture was to look at her, with an expression which glorified his face to such a degree that there actually seemed to be little rainbows in the drops that sparkled on his beard. If he had not loved Jo very much, I don't think he could have done it *then*, for she looked far from lovely, with her skirts in a deplorable state, her rubber boots splashed to the ankle, and her bonnet a ruin. Fortunately, Mr. Bhaer considered her the most beautiful woman living, and she found him more "Jovelike" than ever, though his hat brim was quite limp with the little rills trickling thence upon his shoulders (for he held the umbrella all over Jo), and every finger of his gloves needed mending.

Passers-by probably thought them a pair of harmless lunatics, for they entirely forgot to hail a bus, and strolled leisurely along, oblivious of deepening dusk and fog. Little they cared what anybody thought, for they were enjoying the happy hour that seldom comes but once in any life, the magical moment which bestows youth on the old, beauty on the plain, wealth on the poor, and gives human hearts a foretaste of heaven. The professor looked as if he had conquered a kingdom, and the world had nothing more to offer him in the way of bliss; while Jo trudged beside him, feeling as if her place had always been there, and wondering how she ever could have chosen any other lot. Of course, she was the first to speak—intelligibly, I mean, for the emotional remarks which followed her impetuous "Oh, yes!" were not of a coherent or reportable character.

"Friedrich, why didn't you—"

"Ah, heaven, she gifs me the name that no one speaks since Minna died!" cried the professor, pausing in a puddle to regard her with grateful delight.

"I always call you so to myself—I forgot; but I won't, unless you like it."

"Like it? It is more sweet to me than I can tell. Say 'thou,' also, and I shall say your language is almost as beautiful as mine."

"Isn't 'thou' a little sentimental?" asked Jo, privately thinking it a lovely monosyllable.

"Sentimental? Yes. Thank Gott, we Germans believe in sentiment, and keep ourselves young mit it. Your English 'you' is so cold, say 'thou,' heart's dearest, it means so much to me," pleaded Mr. Bhaer, more like a romantic student than a grave professor.

"Well, then, why didn't thou tell me all this sooner?" asked Jo bashfully.

"Now I shall haf to show thee all my heart, and I so gladly will, because thou must take care of it hereafter. See, then, my Jo—ah, the dear, funny little name!—I had a wish to tell you something the day I said good-by, in New York; but I thought the handsome friend was betrothed to thee, and so I spoke not. Wouldst thou have said 'Yes,' then, if I *had* spoken?"

"I don't know; I'm afraid not, for I didn't have any heart just then."

"Prut! That I do not believe. It was asleep till the fairy prince came through the wood, and waked it up. Ah, well, 'Die erste Liebe ist die beste,' but that I should not expect."

"Yes, the first love *is* the best; so be contented, for I never had another. Teddy was only a boy, and soon got over his little fancy," said Jo, anxious to correct the professor's mistake.

"Good! Then I shall rest happy, and be sure that thou givest me all. I haf waited so long, I am grown selfish, as thou wilt find, professorin."

"I like that," cried Jo, delighted with her new name. "Now tell me what brought you, at last, just when I most wanted you?"

"This," and Mr. Bhaer took a little worn paper out of his waistcoat pocket.

Jo unfolded it, and looked much abashed, for it was one of her own contributions to a paper that paid for poetry, which accounted for her sending it an occasional attempt.

"How could that bring you?" she asked, wondering what he meant.

"I found it by chance; I knew it by the names and the initials, and in it there was one little verse that seemed to call me. Read and find him; I will see that you go not in the wet."

Jo obeyed, and hastily skimmed through the lines which she had christened:

IN THE GARRET

Four little chests all in a row,
Dim with dust, and worn by time,
All fashioned and filled, long ago,
By children now in their prime.
Four little keys hung side by side,
With faded ribbons, brave and gay
When fastened there, with childish pride
Long ago, on a rainy day.

Four little names, one on each lid,
  Carved out by a boyish hand,
And underneath there lieth hid
  Histories of a happy band
Once playing here, and pausing oft
  To hear the sweet refrain,
That came and went on the roof aloft,
  In the falling summer rain.

"Meg" on the first lid, smooth and fair.
  I look in with loving eyes,
For folded here, with well-known care,
  A goodly gathering lies,
The record of a peaceful life—
  Gifts to gentle child and girl,
A bridal gown, lines to a wife,
  A tiny shoe, a baby curl.
No toys in this first chest remain,
  For all are carried away,
In their old age, to join again
  In another small Meg's play.
Ah, happy mother! well I know
  You hear, like a sweet refrain,
Lullabies ever soft and low
  In the falling summer rain.

"Jo" on the next lid, scratched and worn,
  And within a motley store
Of headless dolls, of schoolbooks torn,
  Birds and beasts that speak no more;
Spoils brought home from the fairy ground
  Only trod by youthful feet,
Dreams of a future never found,
  Memories of a past still sweet;
Half-writ poems, stories wild,
  April letters, warm and cold,
Diaries of a willful child,
  Hints of a woman early old;

A woman in a lonely home,
　　Hearing, like a sad refrain—
"Be worthy, love, and love will come,"
　　In the falling summer rain.

My Beth! the dust is always swept
　　From the lid that bears your name,
As if by loving eyes that wept,
　　By careful hands that often came.
Death canonized for us one saint,
　　Ever less human than divine,
And still we lay, with tender plaint,
　　Relics in this household shrine--
The silver bell, so seldom rung,
　　The little cap which last she wore,
The fair, dead Catherine that hung
　　By angels borne above her door;
The songs she sang, without lament,
　　In her prison-house of pain,
Forever are they sweetly blent
　　With the falling summer rain.

Upon the last lid's polished field—
　　Legend now both fair and true—
A gallant knight bears on his shield,
　　"Amy," in letters gold and blue.
Within lie snoods that bound her hair,
　　Slippers that have danced their last,
Faded flowers laid by with care,
　　Fans whose airy toils are past;
Gay valentines, all ardent flames,
　　Trifles that have borne their part
In girlish hopes and fears and shames,
　　The record of a maiden heart
Now learning fairer, truer spells,
　　Hearing, like a blithe refrain,
The silver sound of bridal bells
　　In falling summer rain.

Four little chests all in a row,
 Dim with dust, and worn by time,
Four women, taught by weal and woe
 To love and labor in their prime.

Four sisters, parted for an hour,
 None lost, one only gone before,
Made by love's immortal power,
 Nearest and dearest evermore.

Oh, when these hidden stores of ours
 Lie open to the Father's sight,
May they be rich in golden hours,
 Deeds that show fairer for the light,

Lives whose brave music long shall ring,
 Like a spirit-stirring strain,
Souls that shall gladly soar and sing
 In the long sunshine after rain.

                                    J. M.

"It's very bad poetry, but I felt it when I wrote it, one day when I was very lonely, and had a good cry on a rag bag. I never thought it would go where it could tell tales," said Jo, tearing up the verses the professor had treasured so long.

"Let it go, it has done its duty, and I will haf a fresh one when I read all the brown book in which she keeps her little secrets," said Mr. Bhaer, with a smile, as he watched the fragments fly away on the wind. "Yes," he added earnestly, "I read that, and I think to myself, she has a sorrow, she is lonely, she would find comfort in true love. I haf a heart full, full for her; shall I not go and say, 'If this is not too poor a thing to gif for what I shall hope to receive, take it in Gott's name'?"

"And so you came to find that it was not too poor, but the one precious thing I needed," whispered Jo.

"I had no courage to think that at first, heavenly kind as was your welcome to me. But soon I began to hope, and then I said, 'I will haf her if I die for it,' and so I will!" cried Mr. Bhaer, with a defiant nod, as if the walls of mist closing round them were barriers which he was to surmount or valiantly knock down.

Jo thought that was splendid, and resolved to be worthy of

her knight, though he did not come prancing on a charger in gorgeous array.

"What made you stay away so long?" she asked presently, finding it so pleasant to ask confidential questions and get delightful answers that she could not keep silent.

"It was not easy, but I could not find the heart to take you from that so happy home until I could haf a prospect of one to give you, after much time, perhaps, and hard work. How could I ask you to gif up so much for a poor old fellow, who has no fortune but a little learning?"

"I'm glad you *are* poor; I couldn't bear a rich husband," said Jo decidedly, adding, in a softer tone, "Don't fear poverty; I've known it long enough to lose my dread and be happy working for those I love; and don't call yourself old—forty is the prime of life. I couldn't help loving you if you were seventy!"

The professor found that so touching that he would have been glad of his handkerchief, if he could have got at it; as he couldn't, Jo wiped his eyes for him, and said, laughing, as she took away a bundle or two:

"I may be strong-minded, but no one can say I'm out of my

sphere now, for woman's special mission is supposed to be drying tears and bearing burdens. I'm to carry my share, Friedrich, and help to earn the home. Make up your mind to that, or I'll never go," she added resolutely, as he tried to reclaim his load.

"We shall see. Haf you patience to wait a long time, Jo? I must go away and do my work alone. I must help my boys first, because, even for you, I may not break my word to Minna. Can you forgif that, and be happy while we hope and wait?"

"Yes, I know I can; for we love one another, and that makes all the rest easy to bear. I have my duty, also, and my work. I couldn't enjoy myself if I neglected them even for you, so there's no need of hurry or impatience. You can do your part out West, I can do mine here, and both be happy hoping for the best, and leaving the future to be as God wills."

"Ah! thou gifest me such hope and courage, and I haf nothing to gif back but a full heart and these empty hands," cried the professor, quite overcome.

Jo never, never would learn to be proper; for when he said that as they stood upon the steps, she just put both hands into his, whispering tenderly, "Not empty now," and, stooping down, kissed her Friedrich under the umbrella. It was dreadful, but she would have done it if the flock of draggletailed sparrows on the hedge had been human beings, for she was very far gone indeed, and quite regardless of everything but her own happiness. Though it came in such a very simple guise, that was the crowning moment of both their lives, when, turning from the night and storm and loneliness to the household light and warmth and peace waiting to receive them, with a glad "Welcome home!" Jo led her lover in, and shut the door.

CHAPTER FORTY-SEVEN

Harvesttime

FOR a year Jo and her professor worked and waited, hoped and loved, met occasionally, and wrote such voluminous letters that the rise in the price of paper was accounted for, Laurie said. The second year began rather soberly, for their prospects did not brighten, and Aunt March died suddenly. But when their first sorrow was over—for they loved the old lady in spite of her sharp tongue—they found they had cause for rejoicing, for she had left Plumfield to Jo, which made all sorts of joyful things possible.

"It's a fine old place, and will bring a handsome sum; for of course you intend to sell it," said Laurie, as they were all talking the matter over, some weeks later.

"No, I don't," was Jo's decided answer, as she petted the fat poodle, whom she had adopted, out of respect to his former mistress.

"You don't mean to live there?"

"Yes, I do."

"But, my dear girl, it's an immense house, and will take a power of money to keep it in order. The garden and orchard alone need two or three men, and farming isn't in Bhaer's line, I take it."

"He'll try his hand at it there, if I propose it."

"And you expect to live on the produce of the place? Well, that sounds paradisiacal, but you'll find it desperate hard work."

"The crop we are going to raise is a profitable one," and Jo laughed.

"Of what is this fine crop to consist, ma'am?"

"Boys. I want to open a school for little lads—a good, happy, homelike school, with me to take care of them, and Fritz to teach them."

"There's a truly Joian plan for you! Isn't that just like her?" cried Laurie, appealing to the family, who looked as much surprised as he.

"I like it," said Mrs. March decidedly.

"So do I," added her husband, who welcomed the thought of a chance for trying the Socratic method of education on modern youth.

"It will be an immense care for Jo," said Meg, stroking the head of her one all-absorbing son.

"Jo can do it, and be happy in it. It's a splendid idea. Tell us all about it," cried Mr. Laurence, who had been longing to lend the lovers a hand, but knew that they would refuse his help.

"I knew you'd stand by me, sir. Amy does too—I see it in her eyes, though she prudently waits to turn it over in her mind before she speaks. Now, my dear people," continued Jo earnestly, "just understand that this isn't a new idea of mine, but a long-cherished plan. Before my Fritz came, I used to think how, when I'd made my fortune, and no one needed me at home, I'd hire a big house, and pick up some poor, forlorn little lads, who hadn't any mothers, and take care of them, and make life jolly for them before it was too late. I see so many going to ruin for want of help at the right minute; I love so to do anything for them; I seem to feel their wants, and sympathize with their troubles, and, oh, *I* should *so* like to be a mother to them!"

Mrs. March held out her hand to Jo, who took it, smiling, with tears in her eyes, and went on in the old enthusiastic way, which they had not seen for a long while.

"I told my plan to Fritz once, and he said it was just what he would like, and agreed to try it when we got rich. Bless his dear heart, he's been doing it all his life—helping poor boys, I mean, not getting rich; that he'll never be; money doesn't stay in his pocket long enough to lay up any. But now, thanks to my good old aunt, who loved me better than ever I deserved, *I'm* rich, at least I feel so, and we can live at Plumfield perfectly well, if we have a flourishing school. It's just the place for boys, the house is big, and the furniture strong and plain. There's plenty of room for dozens inside, and splendid grounds outside. They could help in the garden and orchard: such work is healthy, isn't it, sir? Then Fritz can train and teach in his own way, and father will help him. I can feed and nurse and pet and scold them; and mother will be my stand-by. I've always longed for lots of boys, and never had enough; now I can fill the house full, and revel in the little dears to my heart's content. Think what luxury—Plumfield my own, and a wilderness of boys to enjoy it with me!"

As Jo waved her hands, and gave a sigh of rapture, the family went off into a gale of merriment, and Mr. Laurence laughed till they thought he'd have an apoplectic fit.

"I don't see anything funny," she said gravely, when she could be heard. "Nothing could be more natural or proper than for my professor to open a school, and for me to prefer to reside on my own estate."

"She is putting on airs already," said Laurie, who regarded the idea in the light of a capital joke. "But may I inquire how you intend to support the establishment? If all the pupils are little ragamuffins, I'm afraid your crop won't be profitable in a worldly sense, Mrs. Bhaer."

"Now don't be a wet blanket, Teddy. Of course I shall have rich pupils, also—perhaps begin with such altogether; then, when I've got a start, I can take a ragamuffin or two, just for a relish. Rich people's children often need care and comfort, as well as poor. I've seen unfortunate little creatures left to servants, or backward ones pushed forward, when it's real cruelty. Some are naughty through mismanagement or neglect, and some lose their mothers. Besides, the best have to get through the hobbledehoy age, and that's the very time they need most patience and kindness. People laugh at them, and hustle them about, try to keep them out of sight, and expect them to turn, all at once, from pretty children into fine young men. They don't complain much—plucky little souls—but they feel it. I've been through something of it, and I know all about it. I've a special interest in such young bears, and like to show them that I see the warm, honest, well-meaning boys' hearts, in spite of the clumsy arms and legs and the topsy-turvy heads. I've had experience, too, for haven't I brought up one boy to be a pride and honor to his family?"

"I'll testify that you tried to do it," said Laurie, with a grateful look.

"And I've succeeded beyond my hopes; for here you are, a steady, sensible businessman, doing heaps of good with your money, and laying up the blessings of the poor, instead of dollars. But you are not merely a businessman: you love good and beautiful things, enjoy them yourself, and let others go halves, as you always did in the old times. I *am* proud of you, Teddy, for you get better every year, and everyone feels it, though you won't let them say so. Yes, and when I have my flock, I'll just point to you, and say, 'There's your model, my lads.'"

Poor Laurie didn't know where to look; for, man though he was, something of the old bashfulness came over him as this burst of praise made all faces turn approvingly upon him.

"I say, Jo, that's rather too much," he began, just in his old boyish way. "You have all done more for me than I can ever thank you for, except by doing my best not to disappoint you. You have rather cast me off lately, Jo, but I've had the best of help, nevertheless; so, if I've got on at all, you may thank these two for it," and he laid one hand gently on his grandfather's white head, the other on Amy's golden one, for the three were never far apart.

"I do think that families are the most beautiful things in all the world!" burst out Jo, who was in an unusually uplifted frame of mind just then. "When I have one of my own, I hope it will be as happy as the three I know and love the best. If John and my Fritz were only here, it would be quite a little heaven on earth," she added more quietly. And that night, when she went to her room, after a blissful evening of family counsels, hopes, and plans, her heart was so full of happiness that she could only calm it by kneeling beside the empty bed always near her own, and thinking tender thoughts of Beth.

It was a very astonishing year altogether, for things seemed to happen in an unusually rapid and delightful manner. Almost before she knew where she was, Jo found herself married and settled at Plumfield. Then a family of six or seven boys sprung up like mushrooms, and flourished surprisingly, poor boys as well as rich; for Mr. Laurence was continually finding some touching case of destitution, and begging the Bhaers to take pity on the child, and he would gladly pay a trifle for its support. In this way the sly old gentleman got round proud Jo, and furnished her with the style of boy in which she most delighted.

Of course it was uphill work at first, and Jo made queer mistakes; but the wise professor steered her safely into calmer waters, and the most rampant ragamuffin was conquered in the end. How Jo did enjoy her "wilderness of boys," and how poor, dear Aunt March would have lamented had she been there to see the sacred precincts of prim, well-ordered Plumfield overrun with Toms, Dicks, and Harrys! There was a sort of poetic justice about it, after all, for the old lady had been the terror of the boys for miles round; and now the exiles feasted freely on forbidden plums, kicked up the gravel with profane boots unreproved, and played cricket in the big field where the irritable "cow with a crumpled horn" used to invite rash youths to come and be tossed. It became a sort of boys' paradise, and Laurie suggested that it should be called the "Bhaer-garten," as a compliment to its master and appropriate to its inhabitants.

It never was a fashionable school, and the professor did not lay up a fortune; but it *was* just what Jo intended it to be—

"a happy, homelike place for boys, who needed teaching, care, and kindness." Every room in the big house was soon full; every little plot in the garden soon had its owner; a regular menagerie appeared in barn and shed, for pet animals were allowed; and, three times a day, Jo smiled at her Fritz from the head of a long table lined on either side with rows of happy young faces, which all turned to her with affectionate eyes, confiding words, and grateful hearts, full of love for "Mother Bhaer." She had boys enough now, and did not tire of them, though they were not angels, by any means, and some of them caused both professor and professorin much trouble and anxiety. But her faith in the good spot which exists in the heart of the naughtiest, sauciest, most tantalizing little ragamuffin gave her patience, skill, and, in time, success; for no mortal boy could hold out long with Father Bhaer shining on him as benevolently as the sun, and Mother Bhaer forgiving him seventy times seven. Very precious to Jo was the friendship of the lads; their penitent sniffs and whispers after wrongdoing; their droll or touching little confidences; their pleasant enthusiasms, hopes, and plans; even their misfortunes, for they only

endeared them to her all the more. There were slow boys and bashful boys; feeble boys and riotous boys; boys that lisped and boys that stuttered; one or two lame ones; and a merry little quadroon, who could not be taken in elsewhere, but who was welcome to the "Bhaer-garten," though some people predicted that his admission would ruin the school.

Yes; Jo was a very happy woman there, in spite of hard work, much anxiety, and a perpetual racket. She enjoyed it heartily, and found the applause of her boys more satisfying than any praise of the world; for now she told no stories except to her flock of enthusiastic believers and admirers. As the years went on, two little lads of her own came to increase her happiness—Rob, named for grandpa, and Teddy, a happy-go-lucky baby, who seemed to have inherited his papa's sunshiny temper as well as his mother's lively spirit. How they ever grew up alive in that whirlpool of boys was a mystery to their grandma and aunts; but they flourished like dandelions in spring, and their rough nurses loved and served them well.

There were a great many holidays at Plumfield, and one of the most delightful was the yearly apple picking; for then the

Marches, Laurences, Brookes, and Bhaers turned out in full force, and made a day of it. Five years after Jo's wedding, one of these fruitful festivals occurred—a mellow October day, when the air was full of an exhilarating freshness which made the spirits rise, and the blood dance healthily in the veins. The old orchard wore its holiday attire; goldenrod and asters fringed the mossy walls; grasshoppers skipped briskly in the sere grass, and crickets chirped like fairy pipers at a feast; squirrels were busy with their small harvesting; birds twittered their adieux from the alders in the lane; and every tree stood ready to send down its shower of red or yellow apples at the first shake. Everybody was there; everybody laughed and sang, climbed up and tumbled down; everybody declared that there never had been such a perfect day or such a jolly set to enjoy it; and everyone gave themselves up to the simple pleasures of the hour as freely as if there were no such thing as care or sorrow in the world.

Mr. March strolled placidly about, quoting Tusser, Cowley, and Columella to Mr. Laurence, while enjoying—

"The gentle apple's winey juice."

The professor charged up and down the green aisles like a stout Teutonic knight, with a pole for a lance, leading on the boys, who made a hook and ladder company of themselves, and performed wonders in the way of ground and lofty tumbling. Laurie devoted himself to the little ones, rode his small daughter in a bushel basket, took Daisy up among the birds' nests, and kept adventurous Rob from breaking his neck. Mrs. March and Meg sat among the apple piles like a pair of Pomonas, sorting the contributions that kept pouring in; while Amy, with a beautiful motherly expression in her face, sketched the various groups, and watched over one pale lad, who sat adoring her with his little crutch beside him.

Jo was in her element that day, and rushed about, with her gown pinned up, her hat anywhere but on her head, and her baby tucked under her arm, ready for any lively adventure which might turn up. Little Teddy bore a charmed life, for nothing ever happened to him, and Jo never felt any anxiety when he was whisked up into a tree by one lad, galloped off

on the back of another, or supplied with sour russets by his
indulgent papa, who labored under the Germanic delusion that
babies could digest anything, from pickled cabbage to buttons,
nails, and their own small shoes. She knew that little Ted
would turn up again in time, safe and rosy, dirty and serene,
and she always received him back with a hearty welcome, for
Jo loved her babies tenderly.

At four o'clock a lull took place, and baskets remained
empty, while the apple pickers rested, and compared rents and
bruises. Then Jo and Meg, with a detachment of the bigger
boys, set forth the supper on the grass, for an out-of-door tea
was always the crowning joy of the day. The land literally
flowed with milk and honey on such occasions, for the lads
were not required to sit at table, but allowed to partake of refreshment as they liked—freedom being the sauce best loved
by the boyish soul. They availed themselves of the rare privi-
lege to the fullest extent, for some tried the pleasing experiment of drinking milk while standing on their heads, others
lent a charm to leapfrog by eating pie in the pauses of the
game, cookies were sown broadcast over the field, and apple
turnovers roosted in the trees like a new style of bird. The little
girls had a private tea party, and Ted roved among the edibles
at his own sweet will.

When no one could eat any more, the professor proposed
the first regular toast, which was always drunk at such times—
"Aunt March, God bless her!" A toast heartily given by the
good man, who never forgot how much he owed her, and
quietly drunk by the boys, who had been taught to keep her
memory green.

"Now, grandma's sixtieth birthday! Long life to her, with
three times three!"

That was given with a will, as you may well believe; and
the cheering once begun, it was hard to stop it. Everybody's
health was proposed, from Mr. Laurence, who was considered
their special patron, to the astonished guinea pig, who had
strayed from its proper sphere in search of its young master.
Demi, as the oldest grandchild, then presented the queen of
the day with various gifts, so numerous that they were transported to the festive scene in a wheelbarrow. Funny presents,

some of them, but what would have been defects to other eyes were ornaments to grandma's—for the children's gifts were all their own. Every stitch Daisy's patient little fingers had put into the handkerchiefs she hemmed was better than embroidery to Mrs. March; Demi's shoe box was a miracle of mechanical skill, though the cover wouldn't shut; Rob's footstool had a wiggle in its uneven legs, that she declared was very soothing; and no page of the costly book Amy's child gave her was so fair as that on which appeared, in tipsy capitals, the words —"To dear Grandma, from her little Beth."

During this ceremony the boys had mysteriously disappeared; and, when Mrs. March had tried to thank her children, and broken down, while Teddy wiped her eyes on his pinafore, the professor suddenly began to sing. Then, from above him, voice after voice took up the words, and from tree to tree echoed the music of the unseen choir, as the boys sang, with all their hearts, the little song Jo had written, Laurie set to music, and the professor trained his lads to give with the best effect. This was something altogether new, and it proved a grand success; for Mrs. March couldn't get over her surprise, and insisted on shaking hands with every one of the featherless birds, from tall Franz and Emil to the little quadroon, who had the sweetest voice of all.

After this, the boys dispersed for a final lark, leaving Mrs. March and her daughters under the festival tree.

"I don't think I ever ought to call myself 'Unlucky Jo' again, when my greatest wish has been so beautifully gratified," said Mrs. Bhaer, taking Teddy's little fist out of the milk pitcher, in which he was rapturously churning.

"And yet your life is very different from the one you pictured so long ago. Do you remember our castles in the air?" asked Amy, smiling as she watched Laurie and John playing cricket with the boys.

"Dear fellows! It does my heart good to see them forget business, and frolic for a day," answered Jo, who now spoke in a maternal way of all mankind. "Yes, I remember; but the life I wanted then seems selfish, lonely, and cold to me now. I haven't given up the hope that I may write a good book yet, but I can wait, and I'm sure it will be all the better for such experiences and illustrations as these," and Jo pointed from the lively lads in the distance to her father, leaning on the professor's arm, as they walked to and fro in the sunshine, deep in one of the conversations which both enjoyed so much, and then to her mother, sitting enthroned among her daughters, with their children in her lap and at her feet, as if all found help and happiness in the face which never could grow old to them.

"My castle was the most nearly realized of all. I asked for splendid things, to be sure, but in my heart I knew I should be satisfied, if I had a little home, and John, and some dear children like these. I've got them all, thank God, and am the happiest woman in the world," and Meg laid her hand on her tall boy's head, with a face full of tender and devout content.

"My castle is very different from what I planned, but I would not alter it, though, like Jo, I don't relinquish all my artistic hopes, or confine myself to helping others fulfill their dreams of duty. I've begun to model a figure of baby, and Laurie says it is the best thing I've ever done. I think so myself, and mean to do it in marble, so that, whatever happens, I may at least keep the image of my little angel."

As Amy spoke, a great tear dropped on the golden hair of the sleeping child in her arms; for her one well-beloved daughter was a frail little creature and the dread of losing her was the shadow over Amy's sunshine. This cross was doing much for both father and mother, for one love and sorrow bound them closely together. Amy's nature was growing sweeter, deeper, and more tender; Laurie was growing more serious, strong, and firm; and both were learning that beauty, youth, good fortune, even love itself, cannot keep care and pain, loss and sorrow, from the most blest; for—

> *"Into each life some rain must fall,*
> *Some days must be dark and sad and dreary."*

"She is growing better, I am sure of it, my dear. Don't despond, but hope and keep happy," said Mrs. March, as tenderhearted Daisy stooped from her knee, to lay her rosy cheek against her little cousin's pale one.

"I never ought to, while I have you to cheer me up, Marmee, and Laurie to take more than half of every burden," replied

Amy warmly. "He never lets me see his anxiety, but is so sweet and patient with me, so devoted to Beth, and such a stay and comfort to me always, that I can't love him enough. So, in spite of my one cross, I can say with Meg, 'Thank God, I'm a happy woman.'"

"There's no need for me to say it, for everyone can see that I'm far happier than I deserve," added Jo, glancing from her good husband to her chubby children, tumbling on the grass beside her. "Fritz is getting gray and stout; I'm growing as thin as a shadow, and am thirty; we never shall be rich, and Plum-field may burn up any night, for that incorrigible Tommy Banks *will* smoke sweet-fern cigars under the bedclothes, though he's set himself afire three times already. But in spite of these unromantic facts, I have nothing to complain of, and never was so jolly in my life. Excuse the remark, but living among boys, I can't help using their expressions now and then."

"Yes, Jo, I think your harvest will be a good one," began Mrs. March, frightening away a big black cricket that was staring Teddy out of countenance.

"Not half so good as yours, mother. Here it is, and we never can thank you enough for the patient sowing and reaping you have done," cried Jo, with the loving impetuosity which she never could outgrow.

"I hope there will be more wheat and fewer tares every year," said Amy softly.

"A large sheaf, but I know there's room in your heart for it, Marmee dear," added Meg's tender voice.

Touched to the heart, Mrs. March could only stretch out her arms, as if to gather children and grandchildren to herself, and say, with face and voice full of motherly love, gratitude, and humility:

"Oh, my girls, however long you may live, I never can wish you a greater happiness than this!"

THE BEAUTIFUL
Illustrated Junior Library
EDITIONS

* Available in paperback.

Hands Up Education is a non-profit organization and international community of practice, creating and sharing high-quality teaching resources. The core focus of our work is on Latin and Classics for a modern curriculum.

All income generated by SUBURANI will be invested in supporting Classics teaching in schools around the world.

Authored and published by Hands Up Education Community Interest Company.

First published in 2020.
2nd printing 2021.
3rd printing 2022.

All papers used in this book have been sourced from sustainable forests.

Library of Congress Cataloguing in Publication Data.
British Library Cataloguing in Publication Data.
A catalogue record for this book is available from the British Library.

Paperback edition ISBN 978-1-912870-02-8
Hardcover edition ISBN 978-1-912870-03-5

Printed in the United Kingdom.

Hands Up Education Community Interest Company 133-134 Bradley Road, Little Thurlow, Haverhill, CB9 7HZ, United Kingdom.
www.hands-up-education.org, contact@hands-up-education.org

Contents

CALEDONIA

*Oceanus
Septentrionalis*

HIBERNIA

BRITANNIA

Camulodunum

Londinium

*Aquae
Sulis*

GERMANIA

*Oceanus
Atlanticus*

GERMANIA
INFERIOR

GALLIA
BELGICA

GALLIA LUGDUNENSIS

GERMANIA
SUPERIOR

RAETIA

NORICUM

PANNONIA

DACIA

GALLIA
AQUITANICA

Lugdunum

ALPES
POENINAE

ALPES
COTTIAE

ALPES
MARITIMAE

GALLIA
NARBONENSIS

Arelate

ITALIA

Mare Adriaticum

DALMATIA

MOESIA

CORSICA

HISPANIA
TARRACONENSIS

Roma

Pompeii

Brundisium

MACEDONIA

LUSITANIA

Conimbriga

BALEARES

SARDINIA

Athenae

BAETICA

SICILIA

Syracusae

ACHAEA

Carthago

MAURETANIA
TINGITANA

MAURETANIA CAESARIENSIS

AFRICA

Mare Internum

GAETULIA

CYRENAICA

N
W   E
S

0   250   500   750   1000 MILES

SCALE (APPROXIMATE)

SARMATIA

Pontus Euxinus

THRACIA

BITHYNIA ET PONTUS

Pergamum

GALATIA

CAPPADOCIA

ASIA

Ephesus

LYCIA ET
PAMPHYLIA

CILICIA

MESOPOTAMIA

CRETA

CYPRUS

SYRIA
Palmyra

IUDAEA

Alexandria
AEGYPTUS

ARABIA

Arabicus Sinus

The Roman Empire
AD 64

According to legend, Rome was founded as a small village in 753 BC. By AD 64, when our stories begin, Rome had grown into a huge city, and its armies had conquered a vast empire. Rome controlled lands in areas we now think of as North Africa, the Middle East, Asia, and Europe.

Population

Approximately one million people lived in Rome itself, but between 50 and 100 million people lived in the empire it governed. Some of those people lived in cities, but most lived in small towns, villages, and on farms.

Provinces

The Romans organized their empire into provinces, each under the control of a governor. The shape and size of a province was influenced by natural features (such as mountain ranges or large rivers) and by the location of local peoples and cultures.

Mare Internum

Rome's empire centered around the Internal Sea (*Mare Internum*), which we now call the Mediterranean Sea (the sea in the middle of the land). As it was often quicker to travel by sea than by land, the Mare Internum helped to link together the various peoples and goods of the Empire.

Roads and rivers

To help people, goods, and armies move around the Empire more easily, the Romans built a network of over 50,000 miles of roads. Major rivers, such as the Rhône and the Rhine, also played an important part in the movement of goods.

Information

The Romans built a system of staging posts, where riders with government messages could change horses and rest overnight if necessary. In normal situations it was more important that a message arrived safely than that it arrived quickly, and messengers usually traveled about 30 miles in a day. However, if a message was urgent riders could cover over 100 miles in a single day.

AMPHITHEATER
OF NERO

BATHS
OF
NERO

FIELD OF MARS

PANTHEON

TEMPLE OF ISIS
AND SERAPIS

BATHS
OF
AGRIPPA

SAEPTA
JULIA

THEATER
OF
POMPEY

BRIDGE OF AGRIPPA

BRIDGE OF AURELIUS

RIVER TIBER

CIRCUS
FLAMINIUS

THEATER
OF
BALBUS

THEATER
OF
MARCELLUS

TEMPLE
OF
JUPITER OPTIMUS
MAXIMUS

CAPITOLINE
HILL

TIBER
ISLAND

TEMPLE OF
ASCLEPIUS

BRIDGE OF AEMILIUS

FORUM
BOARIUM

AVENTINE
HILL

N

W   E

S

0   1/4   1/2   3/4   1 MILE

SCALE (APPROXIMATE)

ARCH OF CLAUDIUS

AQUA VIRGO

QUIRINAL HILL

ROME
AD 64

VIMINAL HILL

VIA FLAMINIA

FORUM OF AUGUSTUS

FORUM OF CAESAR

ROMAN FORUM

SUBURA

GREAT DRAIN

SACRED WAY

ESQUILINE HILL

DOMUS TRANSITORIA

PALATINE HILL

AQUA CLAUDIA

IMPERIAL PALACES

CIRCUS MAXIMUS

Chapter 1: Subūra

Sabīna

1 ego sum Sabīna.

2

ego in Subūrā habitō. ego sum in īnsulā.

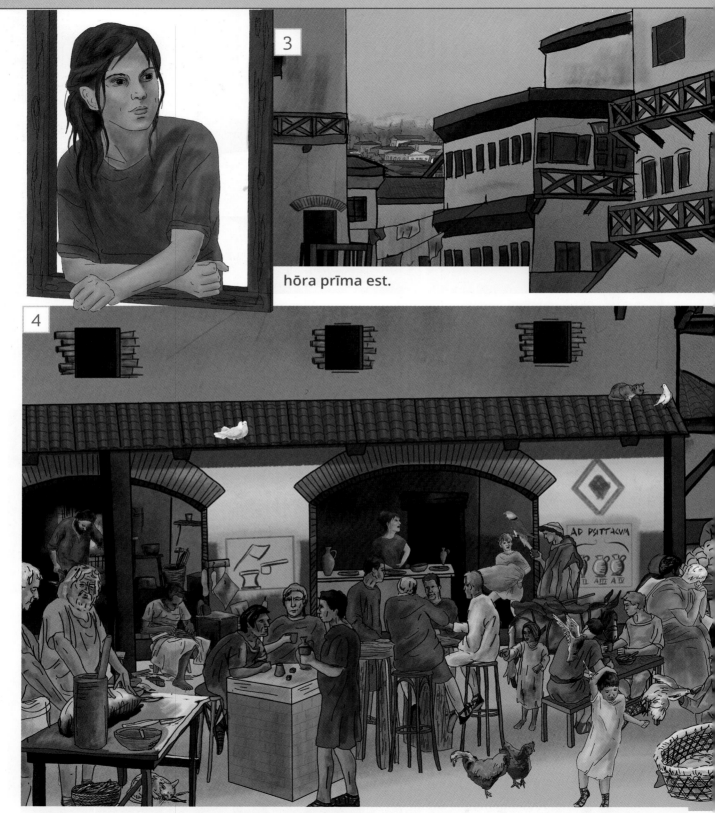

3

hōra prīma est.

4

Subūra nōn est quiēta.   Subūra est clāmōsa.

popīna est in Subūrā.

Rūfīna est in popīnā. Rūfīna in popīnā labōrat.

pater meus est Faustus.

> Rūfīna, ubi es tū?
> tū dormīs?

FAVSTVS EST FVR

pater in īnsulā labōrat.   pater est … negōtiātor.

> salvē, frāter! ego nōn dormiō.
> hōra prīma est.
> ego sum in popīnā.

Rūfīna est amita mea.

19 certē ego labōrō.

ego sum in cellā.

20 ego in cellā legō. ego nōn labōrō.

21 hercle!

amita intrat! pater intrat!

22 Sabīna legit!

23 tū es mendāx! tū es mendāx!

certē Sabīna est mendāx!

īnsula est clāmōsa. Subūra nōn est quiēta.

The Subura

Sabina and her family are living in the Subura, a densely populated district near the center of Rome, in AD 64. Here huge numbers of people lived packed together in multistory apartment buildings, and the population density was probably greater than that of modern London or New York. As well as being a residential area, the Subura was a center of trade and manufacturing. Its narrow, crooked streets were notorious for noise, bustle, and dirt.

At night the streets were unlit, and violence and crime were common. Many of the streets had no sidewalks and were too narrow for traffic. In order to reduce congestion in the wider streets, wheeled traffic (with the exception of carts carrying building material) was banned in the city for most of the daylight hours.

tū errās clāmōsā in Subūrā.
You wander about in the rowdy Subura.

The poet Martial wrote this to his friend. Martial came from Spain to live in Rome in AD 64.

Few apartment buildings from ancient times survive in Rome. This image shows a road in Ostia, the harbor town near Rome.

Juvenal was a poet living in Rome in the late first century AD. In his poems he attacks the vices of Roman society and complains of the difficulties of living in Rome. Here he describes the risks of walking around the city at night:

Now think about the dangers at night:
what a great distance it is for a tile to fall
from the top of the roof and hit you on the head;
how often a broken pot drops from a window;
how hard it hits the sidewalk,
chipping and cracking the stones.
If you go out to dinner without making your will,
people might think you are lazy,
that you don't take into account the possibility
of sudden disaster. There are just as many
chances of dying as there are open windows
above you as you walk past at night.
And so, you should hope and pray, as you pass by,
that the tenants are satisfied
with emptying out their full chamber pots.

A busy street in modern Naples (above), and a street with apartment buildings from Ostia (below).

How similar do you think a street in the Subura might have been to these two?

QUESTIONS

1. According to Juvenal in this passage, why was it dangerous to walk around Rome at night?

2. How reliable do you think Juvenal's description is?

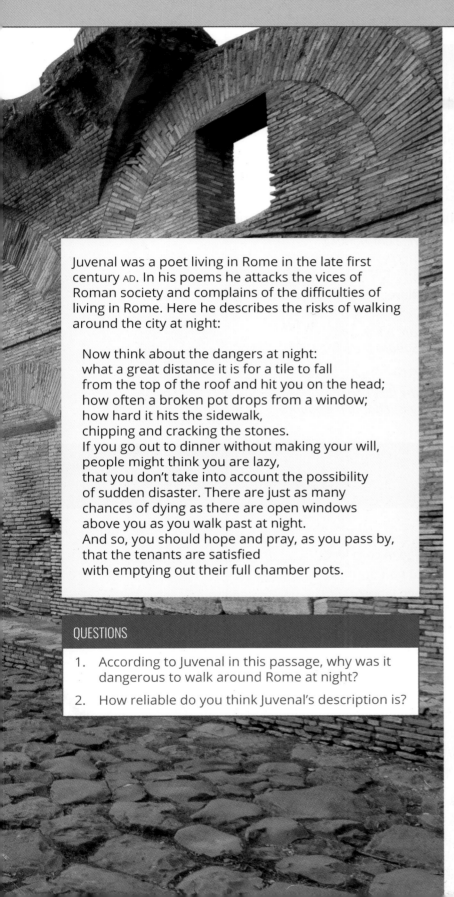

LANGUAGE NOTE 1: WHO'S DOING WHAT?

1. Look at these sentences:

   ego semper labōrō.   **ego in Subūrā habitō.**

   tū in īnsulā labōrās?   **tū in popīnā dormīs.**

   amita in popīnā labōrat.   **Sabīna in īnsulā legit.**

2. In Latin, the **ending** of the verb tells us who is carrying out the action.

-ō	e.g. **ego labōrō**	*I work, I am working*
-s	e.g. **tū dormīs**	*you sleep, you are sleeping*
-t	e.g. **pater intrat**	*the father enters, the father is entering*

3. The verb in the following sentences follows a slightly different pattern:

ego sum Sabīna.	*I am Sabina.*
tū es mendāx.	*You are a liar.*
Subūra est clāmōsa.	*The Subura is rowdy.*

4. Note that **est** can mean *is*, *it is*, or *there is*:

hōra prīma est.	*It is the first hour.*
popīna est in Subūrā.	*There is a bar in the Subura.*

LANGUAGE PRACTICE

1. Translate these sentences:

   a. ego in īnsulā habitō.   **d.** ego in cellā legō.

   b. tū in popīnā labōrās.   **e.** tū nōn dormīs.

   c. Sabīna intrat.   **f.** ego labōrō.

2. Translate these sentences:

   a. ego sum in īnsulā.

   b. negōtiātor in Subūrā est.

   c. tū es in popīnā.

   d. Subūra nōn est quiēta.

This image shows a 100 ft high firewall built from nearly indestructible volcanic rock. The wall separated the Forum of Augustus, of which the remains can be seen in the foreground, from the Subura. The wall ensured fires couldn't spread to the Forum from the apartment buildings of the Subura, and also created a physical barrier between the grand, marble Forum and the cramped and dirty Subura behind it.

The population of the city of Rome

Come, look at this mass of people, for whom the roofs of the vast city of Rome can barely provide shelter. The majority of them are away from their homeland. They have flocked here from their rural towns and cities, from all over the world. Some were brought here by ambition, others by the need to run for office, or as an ambassador, or to enjoy the luxuries of city life, a good education, or the public games. Others have come because of a friendship, or on business, for which there are great opportunities here. If you ask them all, 'Where are you from?', you'll find that the majority of them have left their homes to come to this greatest and most beautiful city, though it wasn't their home city.

Seneca, Letter to his mother Helvia.

In AD 64 about one million people lived in the city of Rome, making it the largest city in the western world until London in 1801. All these people lived in a relatively small city. The fact that a large part of the city was taken up by temples, palaces, fora, theaters, circuses, and the great town residences of the rich and powerful, meant that the majority of the population lived in densely populated areas. Probably the most famous of these neighborhoods was the Subura.

Coming to Rome

Rome attracted people both from nearby regions in Italy and from the farthest reaches of the Empire. Wealthy people might have come to Rome to undertake a career in politics, ordinary people might have been attracted by the employment opportunities in the large city, and the very poor might have arrived in the hope of receiving the free grain dole that the emperor gave out. The largest group by far, however, were enslaved people. They came to Rome against their will and most of them were then sold at the many slave markets in the city.

A multicultural city?

It is hard to work out what percentage of Rome's population had migrated to the city, rather than being born there. Estimates of the total number of immigrants vary from 6% to 30%, so possibly as much as a third of the city's inhabitants were not from Rome originally. And a much larger percentage of the population would have had parents or grandparents who weren't from Rome.

Although many people moved to Rome from elsewhere, it is hard to know how multicultural the city would have felt to a modern observer. A wide variety of cultural and religious practices from across the Empire flourished among the immigrants living in the city, and Romans of all backgrounds embraced their new traditions and religions. Judging from the records that survive, it seems that people did not often state where they came from. This suggests, perhaps, that it was not considered particularly important to them. The extent to which immigrants and their descendants felt like outsiders, or slotted seamlessly into a multicultural melting pot of peoples, is nearly impossible to know.

QUESTIONS

1. What opinion do you think Seneca has of the newcomers to the city?

2. Compare the makeup and density of Rome's population to that of your own town.

Seneca, a well-known Roman intellectual, was tutor and adviser to the young Emperor Nero during the early part of his reign.

Lūcīlius

hōra octāva est. Subūra nōn est quiēta. Subūra est clāmōsa.
Faustus est in īnsulā. fīlia est in popīnā. Sabīna in popīnā labōrat.
servus est in viā. servus prō lectīcā ambulat. iuvenis est in lectīcā.
iuvenis est Lūcīlius. mendīcus est in viā. mendīcus est Mānius.

Mānius	salvē! ego sum mendīcus!	5
servus	tū nōbīs obstās!	

octāva *eighth*

servus *slave, enslaved person (male)*
in viā *in the road*
prō lectīcā *in front of the/a litter*
ambulat *walks*
iuvenis *young person*
mendīcus *beggar*
nōbīs obstās *you are in our way*

Sabīna ē popīnā exit.

Sabīna   Mānius est senex!

Lūcīlius ē lectīcā exit. hercle! tēgula cadit.

Sabīna   cavē!   10

tēgula in viā cadit. Lūcīlius est perterritus.

Sabīna   Subūra est perīculōsa! certē tū in Subūrā nōn habitās.

Lūcīlius ērubēscit. Sabīna rīdet. Mānius nōn rīdet.

ē popīnā exit *comes out of the bar*
senex *old person*

tēgula cadit *a roof tile falls, is falling*
cavē *look out!*

perterritus *terrified*

perīculōsa *dangerous*

ērubēscit *blushes*
rīdet *laughs*

Replica Roman roof tiles.

Women at work

Some women, like Rufina, worked outside the home. It is difficult to know how many women did work, and how much of the work in Rome was done by women (whether enslaved or free). This is because there is relatively little evidence for women working. This may just be because of a bias in the way Romans represented working women, though it might also suggest that it was less common for a woman to have a job.

The lack of evidence might be explained by the fact that many women must have been occupied with having and raising children and domestic work, such as making clothes. Many probably helped in their family business, but this could go unrecorded in our evidence. However, we do also know about women in specialist occupations, such as textile-workers, doctors, and artisans, as well as about women doing jobs usually associated with men (fish sellers, innkeepers, barbers). Additionally, there were women working as performers, dancers, and sex workers.

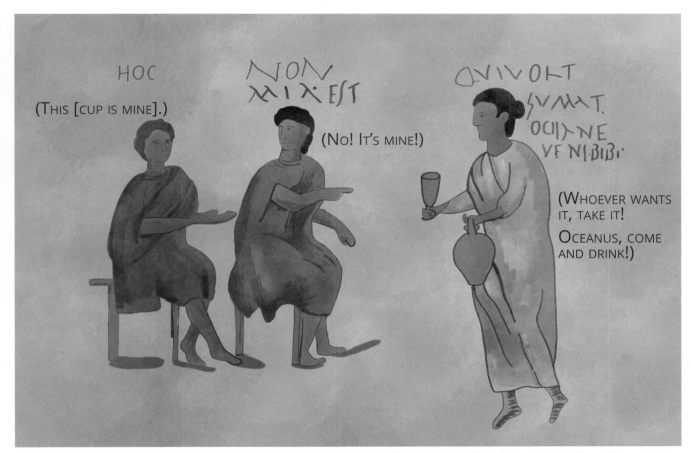

*Drawing of a wall painting from a **popīna** in Pompeii, in Italy.*

QUESTION
What do you think the role of the woman is? Is she a serving woman, a customer, the owner, or someone else entirely?

Living in an insula

The Latin word for an apartment building is *īnsula*, which literally means 'island'. The apartment buildings probably got this name because the separate buildings surrounded on all sides by streets resembled islands surrounded by sea.

Like the vast majority of Rome's population, Sabina's family lived in a rented apartment in a multistory building. Only the very wealthy owned their own house. Sabina's father was the landlord of an insula. Faustus didn't own the building; the owner would be a rich man who had bought the insula as an investment. The landlord was responsible for managing the property and collecting rent from the other tenants. Rents in Rome were extremely high, so evictions for non-payment must have been commonplace.

High rent wasn't the only problem tenants faced. Many of the buildings were flimsily built, with foundations which were not strong enough to support the structure. As a result, these ramshackle buildings often collapsed or caught fire.

Rich and poor lived in the same building. Unlike modern high-rise apartment buildings where the penthouse is often the most desirable apartment, in a Roman insula the best accommodation was on the first and second floors, while the poorest tenants had rooms on the upper floors and in the attics. The risks from fire and collapse were greater on the upper floors. Moreover, there was no running water on the upper floors, so the tenants at the top had to collect water from the public fountains and carry it up several flights of stairs. The rooms at the top were dark and, in winter, they could have been very cold. The windows did not have glass, so the only protection from the wind and rain was wooden shutters or curtains. Some tenants owned a portable heater (*foculus*), which would have heated the room by burning wood or charcoal, creating a very smoky atmosphere.

The first floor of an insula was often divided into shops and workshops, which had openings facing onto the street. These units sometimes had a backroom or a mezzanine floor where the

The inhabitants of the insula would have used oil lamps to light their rooms. They usually burned olive oil, as it was widely available.

This ceramic oil lamp is decorated with a charioteer driving a two-horse chariot.

shopkeeper or craftsman and his family lived – very cramped quarters for a family. (A mezzanine is a half-floor, between the first and the second floor, which was accessed by a ladder.) There were all kinds of shops and workshops in the Subura – bakers, barbers, cobblers, and many others – and lots of places selling food and drink either to eat in

Sanitation was poor. Although some first-floor and possibly second-floor apartments had lavatories, for the most part people used chamber pots, urinated in the street, or went to one of the public lavatories. There were giant clay pots in the street for collecting urine and emptying chamber pots, and other waste went into the sewer.

Above: inside of the remains of an insula in Rome, built just a short distance from the temples of the Capitoline Hill.

There was often no running water in the insula, so people would have to collect water from public fountains (like this one from Pompeii, in Italy).

or to take away. Many apartments had very limited cooking facilities, perhaps an open fire, or none at all, so if people wanted cooked food they had to eat out. Many people would have survived on a diet of bread, cheese, and fruit.

For most of its inhabitants, life in Rome was dangerous, unpredictable, and, compared with what we are used to, unsanitary. As accommodation was so cramped and cooking facilities limited, most people would have spent a lot of time outside, so public spaces and amenities were very important.

LANGUAGE NOTE 2: READING LATIN

1. Look at these sentences:

> **ego in Subūrā habitō.**
> *I live in the Subura.*

> **Sabīna in popīnā labōrat.**
> *Sabina is working in the bar.*

The Latin sentences tell us **who** is carrying out the action, then **where**, then **what** they're doing. The English sentences tell us **who** is carrying out the action, then **what** they're doing, then **where**.

2. Look at these sentences:

> **Sabīna est in cellā.**
> *Sabina is in the room.*

> **ego sum in Subūrā.**
> *I am in the Subura.*

In these Latin sentences, the order of the words in the Latin and the English is the same.

3. When you are reading Latin, try to read it from left to right and get used to the order in which the information comes.

4. If you are translating into English from Latin, you will need to make your English sound natural.

LANGUAGE PRACTICE

3. Complete the sentences with a correct choice from the box, then translate your sentences.

ego	tū	ambulat	habitō	iuvenis	dormīs

a. .... in lectīcā dormit.

b. .... labōrās, soror?

c. ego in Subūrā ....

d. .... nōn sum in cellā.

e. Sabīna in viā ....

f. tū in īnsulā ....

*Sign advertising wines for sale at a popina in Herculaneum, in Italy. The popina is called **ad cucumās** (at the cooking pots).*

*Four different wines are sold, at 4, 3, 4, and 2 **assēs** (pence) per **sextārius** (about half a liter).*

nox

nox est. Sabīna in cellā est. Subūra nōn est quiēta.
Sabīna nōn dormit.

turba in popīnā est. Rūfīna in popīnā labōrat. Faustus in popīnā bibit.
fūr quoque in popīnā est. fūr est pauper.

Faustus	Rūfīna! ubi es tū, soror?	5
Rūfīna	quid est, frāter?	
Faustus	fūr est in popīnā!	
Rūfīna	quid? fūr est in popīnā? ubi est fūr?	
Faustus	tū es fūr! vīnum est nimium cārum!	
Rūfīna	tū es asinus, frāter. vīnum nōn est nimium cārum. tū nimium bibis!	10

Faustus ērubēscit. turba rīdet. fūr quoque rīdet. popīna est clāmōsa.
turba nōn est cauta. fūr nōn est pauper.

nox *night*

turba *crowd*
bibit *drinks, is drinking*
fūr *thief*
quoque *also*
pauper *poor*
soror *sister*
quid est? *what is it?*

vīnum *wine*
nimium *too (much)*
cārum *expensive*
asinus *fool, donkey*

cauta *careful, cautious*

Left: a popina in Pompeii, with vats sunk into the bar.

Right: a wall painting from Pompeii, showing people playing dice in a popina.

*Sabina's aunt runs a popina, a bar which sold drinks and food for people to take away, eat on the street, or consume inside. Romans drank wine, which they mixed with water. In a popina the wine was stored in jars (**amphorae**), and then transferred to jugs for serving. Hot food was cooked on a stove and probably served from the pan.*

Rome in AD 64

Beginnings

The origins of Rome are shrouded in mystery. The original settlement expanded from a secure hilltop location, gradually absorbing its neighbors until it dominated the whole Italian peninsula.

The descendants of those early settlers wanted to create a date for the foundation of their city. Using calculations based on the four-year cycle of the ancient Olympic Games, the Romans chose the year 753 BC for the beginning of Rome. They even selected a date: to this day modern Romans celebrate their city's birthday on April 21. By the time Emperor Augustus established one-man rule in 27 BC, more than 700 years later, Rome was the center of a vast empire (see the map on pages 2–3).

Nero

In AD 54 the teenage Nero became the fifth emperor. The title of emperor always passed down through the male line, because women could not hold political office in Rome. However, some female members of the imperial household, including Nero's mother Agrippina, exercised considerable power.

By the time our story begins, Nero has been emperor for ten years. The early part of his reign was relatively stable. The young emperor was under Agrippina's control and supervised by two advisers: the philosopher and intellectual Seneca (see page 15) and a military commander called Burrus. Violent uprisings at opposite ends of the Empire were successfully put down, and in Rome Nero behaved as a generous and benevolent ruler.

Nero was also a great supporter of the arts. Unusually for an emperor, he took part in plays himself, and he gave poetry and musical performances. He was also a fan of sports, and on occasion drove chariots in races (where his competitors let him win).

However, there was another side to Nero's character, and he did not cope well with the power available to an emperor. His behavior became more erratic and cruel, and on his orders increasing numbers of people (usually those who displeased him or he felt were a threat) were exiled or killed. Just five years into his reign, he even had his mother killed, possibly because she disapproved of an affair he was having, or because he resented her attempts to control him. Perhaps it was a combination of the two. From that point on, he set few boundaries on his own behavior.

Nevertheless, Nero's support for arts and sports made him popular with much of the population of the Empire, particularly the poor, who benefited most from the spending on entertainment. Others felt that it was not appropriate for an emperor to act in plays or take part in chariot races. Some wealthier Romans resented his legal and tax reforms which benefited the common people.

Most of our information about Nero comes from Roman historians, who themselves belonged to the wealthy upper classes and were hostile to Nero. However, like us, Romans were a broad mix of people, with a range of views and interests. In AD 64 different individuals would have had varying opinions about their city and their emperor.

*Gold coin with the head of Nero, from AD 66. It is printed with the words IMP NERO CAESAR AVGVSTVS. IMP is an abbreviation of **imperātor**, which means 'emperor'.*

The abbreviation AD stands for *Annō Dominī* (meaning 'in the year of our Lord'). We use it to indicate a year after the traditional date of the birth of Jesus Christ. A year BC is 'before Christ'. AD is not the only Latin abbreviation that we still use in English. Can you think of any others?

753 BC	27 BC	AD 54	AD 64
Traditional foundation of the city of Rome.	Augustus becomes sole ruler of the Roman Empire.	Nero becomes emperor at the age of 16.	The year our story begins. How old is Rome?

Chapter 2: Rōma

Via Flāminia

equus in viā prōcēdit.   Giscō equum dūcit.

turba est in viā.   Giscō turbam vituperat.

4 st! Giscō!
fīlius dormit.

Catia fīlium tenet.

5 canis est Celer.
Celer in sepulcrō stat.

6 Giscō Celerem vocat.

7

pauper est in sepulcrō. canis pauperem videt.

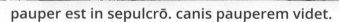

8

bau! au!

pauper canem vituperat.

9 vah!
Celer est amīcus!
tū amīcum habēs!

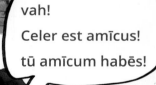

10 īnfāns nōn dormit.
Giscō īnfantem tenet.

11 ecce! arcus est in viā!
arcus est magnificus!

12 Catia arcum videt.

imperātor quoque est magnificus.
tū imperātōrem vidēs?

imperātor est ...
Claudius.

15 Catia nōn est laeta.
Catia est Britannica.

13 īnfāns est laetus.

14 Giscō Catiam ānxiē spectat.

dominus meus īnsulam
in Subūrā habet.
īnsula est optima.
dominus est Faustus.

16 salvē! ego sum Currāx.
tū cellam quaeris?

certē ego cellam quaerō.

servus Giscōnem salūtat.   Giscō servum salūtat.

First impressions

As Gisco and Catia approached Rome along the Via Flaminia, they passed the Field of Mars (*Campus Martius*), named after the god of war because it was originally where soldiers did military training. Later it was used as a recreational space, but over the years temples, monuments commemorating Roman victories, and other grand buildings were constructed there.

On the Field of Mars, Catia and Gisco would have seen monuments and gardens. One of the most impressive was the Altar of Peace (*Āra Pācis*), which had been built by the first emperor, Augustus. Next to this was a huge obelisk from Egypt, which acted as a sundial. Its shadow fell across the center of the marble altar on Augustus' birthday.

They then passed through the Arch of Claudius which was built into the Aqua Virgo, one of the aqueducts which brought water into the city. In this area were the city's largest public bathing complexes. One of these, the Baths of Nero, had been completed only two years before, in AD 62, and surpassed all others in size and grandeur. There were also theaters, temples, and Nero's wooden amphitheater.

As they got closer, the Temple of Jupiter Optimus Maximus (Jupiter the Best and Greatest) on the Capitoline Hill would have loomed above them. Coming round the side of the Capitoline Hill, they would enter the heart of the city, the Roman Forum.

The obelisk now stands in the Piazza di Montecitorio in Rome.

The Arch of Claudius was built to celebrate Emperor Claudius' conquest of Britain in AD 43. The arch has not survived, but we can get an idea of what it looked like from this coin.

A Roman road (the Via Appia) lined with tombs, as it is now. Roman tombs were placed beside the roads outside the city boundary to separate the dead from the living.

The Ara Pacis was decorated with reliefs of processions, the imperial family, Roman gods, and important scenes from Rome's legendary beginnings.

A Roman aqueduct. This one is in Segovia, in Spain.

QUESTION

What impression would walking into Rome along the Via Flaminia have made on visitors and newcomers?

The growth of Rome

By the time of our story, Rome was a large, bustling city and the center of a huge empire. It began as a tiny village on the River Tiber, and over centuries it grew into a mass of winding alleys punctuated with grand open spaces.

Location, location, location

The site of the earliest settlement is often said to have been the Palatine Hill, which provided a good defensive position. As Rome grew, it expanded into the surrounding hills. Famously, Rome was built on seven hills (in fact there are more): the Palatine, Capitoline, Esquiline, Aventine, Quirinal, Viminal, and Caelian. According to legend, the Palatine Hill was the home of Rome's founder, Romulus. It later became the place where the emperors' palaces were built. About 15 miles downriver was Rome's harbor, Ostia. From there, ships brought goods upriver to the docks in Rome near Tiber Island.

Water and waste

The Great Drain (*Cloāca Maxima*) was constructed in about 600 BC to drain the marshy land that lay between the hills of Rome. It was originally an open-air canal, but the Romans later covered it over and constructed a sewage system to remove waste from the city into the Tiber. Aqueducts supplied the city with fresh water from springs in the surrounding countryside. This abundance of water was a key factor in maintaining the growing population of Rome, and soon came to symbolize power and wealth.

All roads lead to Rome?

By the first century AD Rome was at the center of a huge empire. A network of roads linked Rome to the cities of the Empire. Although large quantities of food and building materials were imported by sea, they were also transported via the well-maintained roads leading into Rome. These roads also enabled traders and laborers to come into the city each day from the surrounding countryside.

The Via Flaminia, one of the roads out of Rome to the north, was a route that was often taken to and from northern Gaul (France) and Britannia (Britain). The Via Appia went south to Brundisium on the

A model of the earliest settlement on the Palatine Hill.

south-east coast of Italy. From here travelers could sail on to Greece and the East. The Via Aurelia left Rome to the west, crossing the Tiber at the Aemilian bridge and following the coast through north-west Italy and into southern Gaul.

> In my opinion, the three most impressive achievements which best display the greatness of Rome's Empire are the aqueducts, paved roads, and sewers.
>
> *Dionysius of Halicarnassus*

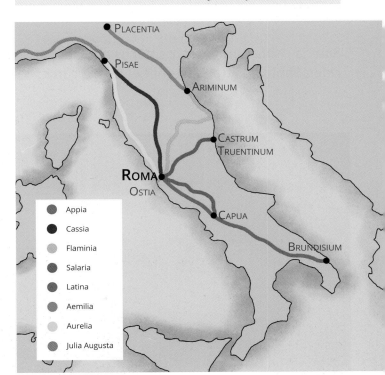

Appia
Cassia
Flaminia
Salaria
Latina
Aemilia
Aurelia
Julia Augusta

The main routes in and out of Rome.

Forum Boārium

clāmor est in popīnā. Rūfīna ē popīnā exit. Rūfīna Sabīnam vocat.

Rūfīna	Sabīna! psittacus nōn adest!

Sabīna Quārtillam vocat. Quārtilla est ancilla. Sabīna cum Quārtillā psittacum quaerit.

Sabīna cum Quārtillā ad Forum Boārium venit. mercātor est in   5
forō. mercātor cibum habet. mercātor cibum vēndit.

mercātor	ego multum cibum habeō! cibus meus est optimus!

mercātōrem intentē spectat Quārtilla. mercātor psittacum habet.

Quārtilla	salvē, mercātor! tū psittacum habēs. tū psittacum vēndis?
mercātor	minimē, ego cibum vēndō. psittacus est meus. 10
psittacus	tū es mendāx! tū es mendāx!
Sabīna	certē tū es mendāx! tū es fūr!

Sabīna psittacum vocat. psittacus ad Sabīnam volitat. Quārtilla rīdet. Sabīna psittacum tenet et ē forō currit.

Forum Boārium
  Forum Boarium (cattle market)

clāmor *noise, shouting*

psittacus *parrot*
adest *is here*
ancilla *slave, enslaved person (female)*
cum *with*
ad *to*
venit *comes*
mercātor *merchant*
cibum *food*
vēndit *sells*
multum *much, a lot of*
intentē *carefully*

volitat *flies*
et *and*
currit *runs*

The Cloaca Maxima ran under the city from the north-east, through the Roman Forum, and into the River Tiber at the Forum Boarium. It drained excess water and removed waste and sewage. Other smaller sewers were connected to the Cloaca Maxima, serving public toilets, baths, and public buildings. Romans believed that the goddess Cloacina looked after the sewer.

What was a forum?

At the center of most Roman towns there was a forum, a rectangular open space surrounded by buildings and colonnades (covered walkways), similar to a square or piazza in a modern city. Originally a forum was a marketplace, with stalls selling food, clothes, pots and pans, jewelry, and all the other things people needed.

Owing to the size of the city, Rome had many fora spread across its different neighborhoods. People from all classes of society gathered in the fora to shop, conduct business such as banking, socialize, or visit temples and public buildings. Some fora were used mostly for public business and ceremonies. In these, lawyers argued cases in the law courts, candidates up for election made speeches, religious processions and ceremonies took place, and the emperor made appearances.

Rome also had fora which specialized in the sale of certain foods such as fish, pork, herbs and vegetables, and wine. One such market was the *Forum Boārium*, close to the docks at Tiber Island. Originally the cattle market (the Latin word for 'cow' is *bōs*), it grew into an important commercial center. It was also a religious center, home to several temples.

As the population of the city grew, more fora were constructed, and several of these were built by emperors and powerful men. The general Julius Caesar built a new forum attached to the Roman Forum, and Emperor Augustus built another forum next to this a few decades later. The emperors Vespasian, Nerva, and Trajan built a further three new fora, creating a network of linked imperial fora in the heart of Rome. These fora, with their grand temples, monuments, and public buildings, were constructed at the emperor's expense. They showed off to all who visited them the wealth, power, and generosity of the emperor.

QUESTIONS

1. What buildings and activities can you spot in this image?

2. Compare market squares in towns today with the fora in Rome. To what extent do you think they fulfill the same functions?

Market square in the town of Mantua, Italy.

LANGUAGE NOTE 1: NOMINATIVE AND ACCUSATIVE CASES

1.   Look at the following sentences:

> **Catia fīlium tenet. Giscō Catiam spectat.**
> *Catia is holding her son. Gisco looks at Catia.*

> **equus in viā prōcēdit. Giscō equum dūcit.**
> *The horse walks along the road. Gisco leads the horse.*

> **canis in sepulcrō stat. Giscō canem vocat.**
> *The dog is standing on the tomb. Gisco calls his dog.*

2.   In Latin, the endings of **nouns** change as their role in the sentence changes. If they are carrying out the action they have one ending, and if they are receiving the action of the verb they have a different ending. We call these different forms of nouns 'cases'.

3.   When a noun is carrying out the action, we say it is in the **nominative case**.

Rūfīna Sabīnam vocat.	*Rufina calls Sabina.*
Lūcīlius ērubēscit.	*Lucilius is blushing.*
mercātor cibum vēndit.	*The merchant is selling food.*

4.   When a noun is receiving the action of the verb, we say it is in the **accusative case**.

Giscō cellam quaerit.	*Gisco is looking for a room.*
ego cibum vēndo.	*I'm selling food.*
Sabīna clāmōrem audit.	*Sabina hears a noise.*

In Latin, the order of information is usually, but not always, nominative accusative verb:

> **Catia fīlium tenet.**
> **tū mendīcum vidēs.**
> **Giscō canem vocat.**
> **mercātōrem spectat Quārtilla.**

In the last example, how can you tell that it's Quartilla who is watching the merchant, rather than the merchant watching Quartilla? Why might the writer have changed the usual order of information?

Forum Rōmānum

Rōmānum *Roman*

Faustus cum servō Forum Rōmānum intrat. servus est Lūcriō.
Forum Rōmānum est clāmōsum.

cūria est in Forō Rōmānō. prō cūriā Lūcriō senātōrem videt.
magnum servum habet senātor.

Lūcriō	ecce! senātor adest. tū magnam pecūniam dēbēs ...	5
Faustus	hercle!	

Faustus cum Lūcriōne ad basilicam festīnat. sed senātor Faustum prō
basilicā videt. senātor cum magnō servō ad basilicam ambulat.

senātor	salvē, negōtiātor! tū pecūniam meam habēs?	
Faustus	salvē, senātor! ego pēnsiōnem nōn habeō, sed ...	10
senātor	quid tū dīcis?	
Lūcriō	Faustus pecūniam semper trādit. Faustus nōn est fūr.	

senātor signum dat. magnus servus Lūcriōnem verberat. Lūcriō cadit.

Faustus	pecūniam nōn habeō!	
senātor	tū pecūniam nōn habēs, sed fīliam habēs. ego	15
	ancillam quaerō. cavē, negōtiātor. urbs est perīculōsa.	

senātor ē forō exit. Faustus perterritus est.

cūria *Senate House*
senātōrem *senator (wealthy politician)*
magnum *big, large*
pecūniam *money, sum of money*
dēbēs *owe*
basilicam *hall*
festīnat *hurries*
sed *but*
pēnsiōnem *rent (payable by Faustus to the owner of the insula)*
dīcis *say*
trādit *hands over*
signum dat *gives a signal*
verberat *beats, hits*

urbs *city*

Photograph taken in the Roman Forum, showing the floor and column bases of the Basilica Aemilia in the foreground, and the side of the Senate House behind it. The Basilica Aemilia was a large hall where bankers and merchants conducted business.

The Forum Romanum

The Roman Forum (*Forum Rōmānum*) was an open square surrounded by magnificent buildings. It was the political, religious, and commercial center of Rome and the whole Empire. People of all classes, both inhabitants of the city and visitors, came to the Forum to socialize, engage in public and private business, worship, listen to speeches, watch processions, and just to gaze in amazement at the splendor of the public buildings. Rome was a city of contrasts, and one of the biggest contrasts was between the grandeur of its public spaces and the poverty of the streets and buildings where the majority of people lived and worked.

A **basilica** was a large public hall. There were two stretching along the sides of the Forum Romanum. Their colonnaded fronts provided shade for people to walk and socialize. The Basilica Julia (*below*) housed the law courts. The Basilica Aemilia was a place for bankers and merchants to conduct business. The entire building was faced with marble and the front was decorated with sculptures; a frieze showed scenes from early Roman legend and history, including the abandonment of Romulus and Remus.

Concordia was the goddess who symbolized unity among the different classes of the Roman people. Her temple was a lavishly decorated marble building, and some of it still survives.

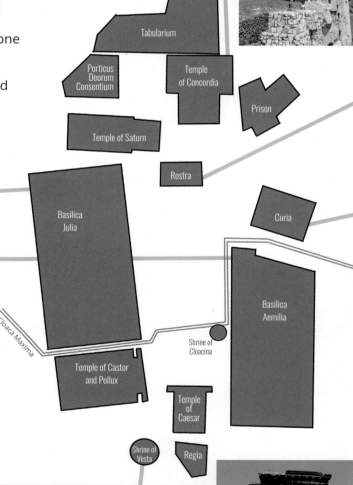

Vesta was the goddess of the hearth and of fire. Roman temples were usually rectangular, but the shrine of Vesta was a small circular building. Inside the shrine was the sacred fire, which symbolized the survival and prosperity of Rome and was never allowed to go out.

The Golden Milestone (*mīliārium aureum*) was a tall column in the Forum Romanum which marked the starting point of the network of roads which radiated from Rome to all parts of Italy and the Empire. The distances to the cities of the Empire were inscribed on it in gilded bronze letters. It was erected by Emperor Augustus as a symbol that Rome was the center of the Empire. Its location in the Forum is not known.

I'll show you where you'll easily find every sort of man, … whether it's a wicked man or a virtuous one that you seek, honest or dishonest. If you want to find a perjurer, go to the *Curia*, for a liar and a boaster, go to the *Shrine of Cloacina*. At the old shops are those who lend or borrow money, and behind the *Temple of Castor and Pollux* are those you trust at your peril.

This extract from a comedy by Plautus gives an impression of the variety of people in the Forum Romanum.

The **Rostra** was a high stone platform. The emperor and his family stood on the Rostra to show themselves to the people and to make speeches.

The **Curia** was the Senate House, where the emperor and Senate met to discuss affairs of government. The building which now stands in the Forum Romanum (*below*) is a later restoration.

A reconstruction of the Forum Romanum, facing the Temple of Concordia with the Capitoline behind.

The Forum Romanum today, facing the remains of the Temple of Concordia.

LANGUAGE NOTE 2: DECLENSIONS

1. Some Latin nouns end -**a** in the nominative and -**am** in the accusative case:

Nominative:	**Rūfīna**	**hōra**	**turba**	**īnsula**
Accusative:	**Rūfīnam**	**hōram**	**turbam**	**īnsulam**

These are known as **first declension** nouns.

2. Some Latin nouns end -**us** in the nominative and -**um** in the accusative case:

Nominative:	**Faustus**	**amīcus**	**cibus**	**servus**
Accusative:	**Faustum**	**amīcum**	**cibum**	**servum**

This group of nouns is known as the **second declension**.

3. Other Latin nouns, which have a variety of endings in the nominative case and end -**em** in the accusative case, are **third declension**:

Nominative:	**Giscō**	**īnfāns**	**canis**	**imperātor**
Accusative:	**Giscōnem**	**īnfantem**	**canem**	**imperātōrem**

LANGUAGE PRACTICE

1. Copy each sentence below, completing the ending of the noun. Then translate each sentence. Use the language note above for help with the noun endings.

    a. Giscō can... videt.

    b. Rūfīn... amīcum vocat.

    c. mercātor cib... vēndit.

    d. amīc... Faustum salūtat.

    e. ego īnsul... spectō.

    f. tū īnfan... tenēs.

cella

Currāx per urbem festīnat. servus Giscōnem et Catiam ad Subūram dūcit. servum Rūfīna videt.

Rūfīna   salvē, Currāx!

Currāx   veterānus cellam quaerit, domina. veterānus est Giscō.
              Giscō uxōrem et fīlium habet. et canis est Celer.   5

fīlium tenet Catia. marītus Celerem mulcet. Rūfīna Giscōnem et uxōrem salūtat. Rūfīna īnfantem laudat, sed canem ānxiē spectat. Rūfīna vīnum et multum cibum portat. Catia cibum cōnsūmit.

Catia   cibus est optimus, Rūfīna!

Currāx Giscōnem ad cellam dūcit. Currāx cellam laudat.   10

Currāx   cella est quiētissima. cella aspectum optimum habet.
              cella est ...

Giscō   parva et obscūra!

subitō cadit tēgula et columba per rīmam volitat. Celer lātrat.
magnus mūs per iānuam currit.   15

Giscō   mūs in cellā habitat. cella nōn est optima, sed tū es
              negōtiātor optimus, Currāx!

per	*through*
domina	*mistress*
veterānus	*veteran, retired soldier*
uxōrem	*wife*
marītus	*husband*
mulcet	*strokes*
laudat	*praises*
portat	*carries, brings*
cōnsūmit	*eats*
aspectum	*view*
parva	*small*
obscūra	*dark*
subitō	*suddenly*
columba	*dove*
rīmam	*hole, crack*
lātrat	*barks*
mūs	*rat*
iānuam	*door*

A cup showing a hunting dog.

LANGUAGE NOTE 3: GENDER OF NOUNS

1. All Latin nouns have a gender. They are masculine, feminine, or neuter.

2. Almost all **first declension** nouns are **feminine**, e.g. **īnsula** (*apartment building*) and **turba** (*crowd*).

3. Most **second declension** nouns are **masculine**, e.g. **cibus** (*food*) and **equus** (*horse*).

Some second declension nouns end **-um** in both the nominative and the accusative cases, e.g. **vīnum** (*wine*) and **forum** (*marketplace*). These nouns are **neuter** and we will study them further in Chapter 4.

4. Some **third declension** nouns are **masculine**, some are **feminine**, and some are **neuter**. For example, **clāmor** (*noise*) is masculine, **nox** (*night*) is feminine, and **caput** (*head*) is neuter.

5. When you look up a noun in the dictionary, its gender is indicated by *m.*, *f.*, or *n.*

LANGUAGE PRACTICE

2. Using the dictionary on pages 283–296, write down the declension and gender of each noun.

For example: **amita,** 1st declension, feminine.

- **a.** psittacus
- **b.** soror
- **c.** cloāca
- **d.** mercātor
- **e.** sepulcrum
- **f.** hōra

3. Select the correct form of the noun to complete each sentence, then translate.

      a. ego .... videō.   (equus, equum)

      b. .... canem vocat.   (servus, servum)

      c. tū .... habēs?   (pecūnia, pecūniam)

      d. .... in popīnā sedet.   (senex, senem)

      e. .... Faustus audit.   (clāmor, clāmōrem)

4. Select the correct form of the verb to complete each sentence, then translate.

      a. ego cibum ....   (habet, habeō, habēs)

      b. Mānius in viā ....   (sedēs, sedeō, sedet)

      c. tū in popīnā ....   (labōrat, labōrās, labōrō)

      d. ego in Subūrā ....   (habitō, habitat, habitās)

      e. Faustus īnsulam ....   (intrō, intrās, intrat)

*Fragments from the **Fōrma Urbis Rōmae**, the map of the city of Rome.*

The Forma Urbis Romae was an enormous map, measuring about 60 x 43 ft and created around AD 211. Inscribed on stone was the plan of every architectural feature in the ancient city, from large public monuments to small shops. Only 10–15% of the original stone map survives, broken into 1,186 pieces.

Romulus and Remus

The story goes that, long before Rome existed, refugees from the Trojan War founded a hilltop town in Italy, which they called Alba Longa. Hundreds of years later the leader of the town, Numitor, was driven out by his brother. Numitor's only child, Rhea Silvia, was forced to become a priestess and forbidden to have any children, so that Numitor would have no more descendants.

However, Rhea Silvia was visited by the god Mars (or so the story goes) and later gave birth to twin sons, Romulus and Remus. They were sent to be drowned, 12 miles away in the River Tiber. What then happened to those boys is the story of the foundation of Rome.

- Read or listen to the myth of Romulus and Remus – there are many versions!

SOURCE 1

Altar to Mars and Venus.

The Wolf

Look at Source 1. What aspects of the myth can you see on the altar? The Romans celebrated the idea that Romulus and Remus were suckled by a wolf, in a cave now known as the Lupercal (in Latin, *lupa* means wolf). If you were writing a foundation story about a civilization, why might you have the founders suckled by a wolf, and in a cave? Later, the twins were brought up in the fields by a shepherd. How might that part of the story help poorer Romans relate to them? The shepherd's name, by the way, was Faustulus, 'Little Faustus'.

SOURCE 2   Remus jumped over Romulus' new walls, mocking his brother. Romulus, in anger, killed his brother and added: 'The same fate awaits anyone else who crosses my walls.'   *Livy*

Fratricide

Read Source 2. Romulus killed his brother, an act known as fratricide. Do you think it is a problem that Rome's founder committed fratricide? Livy was writing at the time when Rome had recently endured many years of civil war (where Romans fought and killed other Romans), and already had a vast empire. How does Romulus' murder of his brother fit into that context? What message do Romulus' words send out to other nations?

Ancestors

The twins' mother, Rhea Silvia, was descended from Aeneas, a Trojan prince who was himself the son of Venus, goddess of love. Their father was Mars, god of war. Why might the Romans want to create the idea that they were descended from these two deities? What characteristics would you expect from people who were the children of Venus and Mars?

SOURCE 3   All myths and legends have an element of truth.
Alfonsina Russo, Italian archaeologist.

Myth, legend, or history?

Look at Source 3. The story of Romulus and Remus is a myth. It isn't true, but some people feel that parts of it may be. Archaeological evidence shows that there was a settlement on the Palatine Hill at the time of the mythological foundation of Rome (753 BC). Which aspects of the myth do you think may be based on fact? Which are fiction? Is it easy to tell? What is the difference between myth, legend, and history?

RESEARCH

Find out more about:
- Other foundation myths for Rome. Why might there be more than one story?
- The Trojans and the Trojan War. How does the story of Rome connect with the story of Troy?
- Foundation myths of other cultures. What do they say about how they see themselves?

Chapter 3: lūdī

Circus Maximus

1   Sabīna per urbem festīnat.

2   puella Sabīnam salūtat.
puella est Iūlia.

3   puellae ad Circum festīnant.

4   maxima turba est in Circō.

5 amīcus Sabīnam salūtat.

6 amīcī Iūliam salūtant.

7 iuvenis vīnum bibit. fūr labōrat.

8 iuvenēs vīnum bibunt. fūrēs labōrant.

9 subitō senātor plaudit.

10 senātōrēs plaudunt. imperātor adest.

11   Nerō sedet. senātōrēs quoque sedent.

12   magnus clāmor est in Circō. quadrīga Circum intrat.

13   quadrīgae Circum intrant.

14   Sabīna Lūcīlium videt.   Lūcīlius rīdet.

15   Sabīna patrem et amīcum videt.
Faustus et amīcus spōnsiōnem faciunt.

16   fīlia est ānxia.

17

quid tū facis?

mātrōna clāmat.

18 mātrōnae clāmant.

īnfēlīx!

19 prasinus vincit. Lūcīlius est laetus.

fēlīx!

20 Faustus et amīcus nōn sunt laetī.

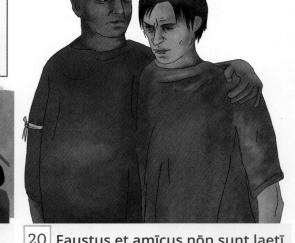

mē miserum!

LANGUAGE NOTE 1: NOMINATIVE PLURAL AND PLURAL VERBS

1. Look at the following pairs of sentences:

puella ad Circum festīnat.
The girl hurries to the Circus.

puellae ad Circum festīnant.
The girls hurry to the Circus.

amīcus Sabīnam salūtat.
A friend greets Sabina.

amīcī Iūliam salūtant.
The friends greet Julia.

fūr labōrat.
A thief is working.

fūrēs labōrant.
The thieves are working.

2. In Latin, the endings of both the nominative noun and the verb indicate whether one person or more than one person is carrying out an action.

3. If one person is doing something, Latin uses the nominative singular (**puella, amīcus, fūr**). If more than one person is doing something, Latin uses the nominative plural (**puellae, amīcī, fūrēs**).

Compare the nominative singular and plural forms of each declension:

SINGULAR	1st decl.	2nd decl.	3rd decl.
nominative	**puella**	**amīcus**	**fūr**

PLURAL			
nominative	**puellae**	**amīcī**	**fūrēs**

4. Notice that the **-nt** ending of the verb also indicates that more than one person is carrying out the action:

puellae festīnant.   *The girls are hurrying.*
iuvenēs clāmant.   *The young people are shouting.*
frātrēs bibunt.   *The brothers are drinking.*

5. Note the use of **sunt** in the following sentences:

amīcī nōn sunt laetī.   *The friends are not happy.*
senēs sunt in popīnā.   *The old men are in the bar.*

Public festivals

Romans did not have days off work each week, as we do now. But throughout the year they celebrated a number of religious festivals, and these days were public holidays: the *diēs fēstī* (festival days). On festival days all business was suspended and even some slaves were allowed time off. Anyone caught conducting public business could be fined. The number of festival days increased over time, and under Nero people probably had more than eighty days off a year.

The celebrations included religious rites such as processions, prayers, and offerings to the gods. Often there were also public entertainments called *lūdī* (games). Most ludi were held annually, but some were held every four years, and the *lūdī saeculārēs* were meant to be held every 100 years (although the Romans appeared to have lost count quite often). Two types of entertainment associated with festivals were chariot-racing and theatrical performances.

Free to attend

The ludi were free to attend for all spectators, and were mostly paid for by the state. Money came from taxes, or sometimes fines from lawbreakers. However, the games were also referred to as *mūnera*, literally 'gifts', as they were often paid for by wealthy citizens and the emperor as gifts to the people of the city. New festivals were added frequently. In AD 59, when Nero first shaved his beard, he celebrated his passage into adulthood with a new festival, the Juvenalia. This festival was then repeated annually.

A festival for everything

Festivals were held in honor of a wide range of gods and occasions, and each had its own rituals and traditions.

Florales April–May	• In honor of the goddess Flora, celebrating the fertility of spring. • In AD 68 the emperor presented a tightrope-walking elephant at the games.
Apollinares July	• In honor of Apollo. • First celebrated to secure the aid of the god Apollo in the war against Hannibal.
ludi Romani September	• In honor of Jupiter. • The chief festival and one of the oldest. • The first festival to include drama.
Plebeii November	• Instituted to celebrate and entertain the common people of Rome (the plebeians). • Mainly featuring chariot races, it also included a cavalry parade.

RESEARCH

Find out about the entertainments and traditions associated with one festival. Choose either a festival from the table above, or one of the following: Augustales, Victoriae Caesaris, Ceriales, Saeculares, Taurii.

We have several surviving examples of Roman calendars, called **fāstī**, *on which the year's business days, political events, and festival days were shown. Some festival days were on the same date each year, others were held on different dates, while some events were held only once.*

This fragment of a calendar is inscribed on stone. The left-hand letters and numbers indicate the date. The letters NP in the second row indicate the day was a public holiday and its note explains that the ludi Florae, the games of Flora, were held.

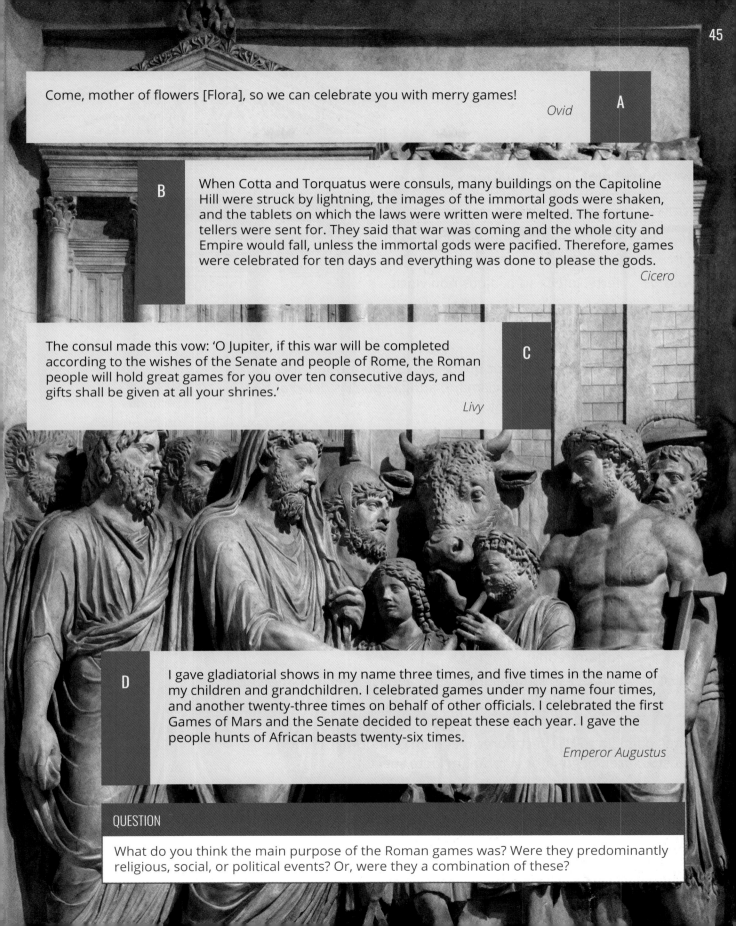

> Come, mother of flowers [Flora], so we can celebrate you with merry games!
>
> *Ovid*

A

B

> When Cotta and Torquatus were consuls, many buildings on the Capitoline Hill were struck by lightning, the images of the immortal gods were shaken, and the tablets on which the laws were written were melted. The fortune-tellers were sent for. They said that war was coming and the whole city and Empire would fall, unless the immortal gods were pacified. Therefore, games were celebrated for ten days and everything was done to please the gods.
>
> *Cicero*

> The consul made this vow: 'O Jupiter, if this war will be completed according to the wishes of the Senate and people of Rome, the Roman people will hold great games for you over ten consecutive days, and gifts shall be given at all your shrines.'
>
> *Livy*

C

D

> I gave gladiatorial shows in my name three times, and five times in the name of my children and grandchildren. I celebrated games under my name four times, and another twenty-three times on behalf of other officials. I celebrated the first Games of Mars and the Senate decided to repeat these each year. I gave the people hunts of African beasts twenty-six times.
>
> *Emperor Augustus*

QUESTION

What do you think the main purpose of the Roman games was? Were they predominantly religious, social, or political events? Or, were they a combination of these?

palma

Faustus est in Circō. Giscō quoque est spectātor in Circō. veterānus
Faustum salūtat. turba clāmōsa est.

Giscō	tū pecūniam āmittis?
Faustus	vah! ego spōnsiōnēs faciō et ego magnam pecūniam āmittō.
Giscō	īnfēlīx es. 5
Faustus	certē, īnfēlīx sum. albus nōn vincit.
Giscō	russeus quoque est īnfēlīx. aurīga est mortuus.
Faustus	lūdī sunt perīculōsī!

cursus secundus est. quattuor quadrīgae Circum intrant. spectātōrēs
quadrīgās vident et maximē clāmant. aurīgae puellās dēlectant.   10
puellae aurīgās laetē spectant.

Faustus	spōnsiōnem facis?
Giscō	ita vērō. albus est optimus.
Faustus	quid dīcis?
Giscō	equī sunt magnificī. 15

Faustus spōnsiōnem iterum facit. spectātōrēs tacent. mappa cadit.
aurīgae equōs agitant.

Faustus	vah! albus est nimium lentus.
Giscō	mēta est. albus trēs equōs maximē agitat, sed ūnum equum retinet. 20
Faustus	hercle! est naufragium! trēs quadrīgae sunt in naufragiō!
Giscō	albus vincit!

albus palmam tollit. spectātōrēs magnum clāmōrem tollunt.
Faustus tacet. negōtiātor veterānum laetē spectat.

---

palma *palm; victory*

spectātor *spectator*

āmittō *I lose*

albus *white; white team*
russeus *red; red team*
aurīga *charioteer*
mortuus *dead*
lūdī *games, races*
cursus *race*
secundus *second*
quattuor *four*
maximē *very much, a lot*
dēlectō *I please, delight*
laetē *happily, gladly*
ita vērō *yes, absolutely*

iterum *again*
taceō *I am silent, I am quiet*
mappa *cloth, flag*
agitō *I drive, drive on*
lentus *slow*
mēta *turning post*
trēs *three*
ūnus *one*
retineō *I hold back, restrain*
naufragium *crash, wreck*
tollō *I raise, hold up*

LANGUAGE PRACTICE

1. Complete each sentence using the correct form of the nominative noun, then translate.

   a. quattuor .... in Circō sedent. (senātor, senātōrēs)
   b. .... pecūniam habent. (mātrōna, mātrōnae)
   c. .... vīnum bibit. (senex, senēs)
   d. .... per urbem ānxiē ambulant. (ancilla, ancillae)
   e. .... in viā lātrat. (canis, canēs)
   f. .... cibum in forō quaerunt. (puella, puellae)

2. Complete each sentence using the correct form of the verb, then translate.

   a. puellae quadrīgam in Circō .... (spectat, spectant)
   b. Currāx canem in viā .... (audit, audiunt)
   c. dominus meus cellam .... (habet, habent)
   d. in forō .... multī mercātōrēs. (est, sunt)
   e. fīlia Lūcriōnem in īnsulā .... (videt, vident)
   f. frātrēs vīnum in popīnā .... (bibit, bibunt)

Mosaic from Lugdunum (Lyon in modern France), showing a chariot race in a circus. Eight quadrigae are competing, two from each team. The central barrier is a **eurīpus** *(channel filled with water), divided into two parts.*

Chariot-racing

Chariot-racing was the most popular form of public entertainment in ancient Rome, and attracted huge crowds. Races were held in a circus, an oval-shaped open-air stadium, like a modern athletic track. The Circus Maximus was the largest man-made structure in the Roman Empire and could hold 150,000 spectators.

> One of the finest and most wonderful structures in Rome.
>
> *Dionysius of Halicarnassus*

> The vast facade of the Circus rivals the beauty of the temples. It is a suitable place for a nation which has conquered the world, a sight worth seeing for its own sake as well as for the spectacles presented there ... The emperor, as a spectator, shares the public seats as much as he does the spectacle. In this way, Trajan, your subjects can look on you in their turn; they will be able to see not just the imperial box, but the emperor himself, seated amongst his people.
>
> *Pliny*

In this extract from a speech, Pliny praises Emperor Trajan for adding more seats to the Circus Maximus.

QUESTIONS

1. Why do you think Trajan and other emperors provided buildings like the Circus Maximus?

2. Why was it important for the emperor to attend the chariot races?

Box for presiding magistrate

The presiding magistrate sat in a box above the starting gates. He dropped a white cloth (*mappa*) onto the track as a sign that the race was about to start. This was probably followed by a trumpet signal.

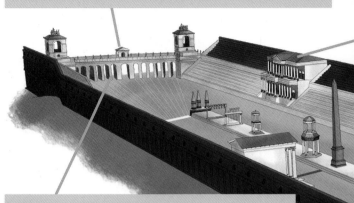

carcerēs

At one end of the track were twelve **carcerēs** (starting gates), the stalls where the chariots and horses lined up before the race. Each carcer had a gate. At the start of the race, an attendant pulled a lever which activated a spring mechanism. This pulled out the latches of each gate so that they flew open, all at the same time. Near the carceres were temples, a reminder of the religious associations of the sport.

eurīpus

The area within the center of the track, called the **eurīpus** (channel), acted as a crash barrier. This is also sometimes known as the **spīna**. It was decorated with statues of the gods; there was also an obelisk, which had been brought from Egypt by Emperor Augustus. At one end were seven wooden eggs and seven bronze dolphins. These were moved to show the spectators which of the seven laps was now in progress.

shops

On the outside of the Circus there was a colonnade with shops and bars.

pulvinar

The emperor had his own box, the *pulvinar*, on the Palatine side of the Circus Maximus. At the end of the procession which preceded the start of the day's events, the images of the gods were taken to the pulvinar, and from there they presided over the games, along with the emperor. This was an opportunity for the emperor to show himself to his subjects and to display his generosity in hosting the games and providing the amenities. In return, people had the opportunity to ask the emperor for favors.

Altar of Consus

Near the *mētae* was an underground altar of the god Consus. This was uncovered only on the days of his festival, the Consualia. Consus was a god of fertility and of horses.

mētae

At either end of the track there were three tall, conical pillars made of gilded bronze. These were the turning posts. The charioteers drove as close as possible to the *mētae* to take the corner and reduce the distance covered, but this was a dangerous tactic. Crashes often occurred at the metae. A crash was called a *naufragium* (shipwreck).

cavea

The spectators were accommodated in three tiers facing each other. The first tier was stone, the second wood. The third tier was probably standing room only. There was a wall separating the track from the front row to protect spectators.

A day at the Circus

The day began with a procession through the streets of Rome. Leading the procession were statues of the gods. Next came magistrates, young noblemen, charioteers, dancers, musicians, incense burners, and temple attendants. After entering the Circus Maximus, the procession circled the track and the statues of the gods were taken to the pulvinar.

When the signal was given, the horses and chariots burst out of the starting gates. Up to twelve chariots, each usually with a team of four horses, driven by a charioteer, charged down the lanes in parallel, going counterclockwise round the track. At a certain marker, they were allowed to cross lanes.

The charioteer would now try to drive his horses as close as possible to the euripus, to shorten his path. Then, at the metae he had to slow down the horses to negotiate the turn.

The charioteer wrapped the reins tightly around his body and used his weight to help him steer. If the chariot crashed, he would be dragged along by the horses and risked death or serious injury, so he carried a knife tucked into his belt to cut himself free from the reins. After seven laps, the trumpet sounded to announce that the winner had crossed the finishing line. He then went up to the judges' box to receive his prize – a palm branch, a wreath, and money – before doing a victory lap.

post lūdōs

spectātōrēs per urbem discēdunt. tōta urbs est clāmōsa. omnēs
viae sunt plēnae. multī spectātōrēs in viā ambulant. lectīcae lentē
prōcēdunt. mendīcī senātōrēs salūtant. servī mendīcōs et spectātōrēs
vituperant. omnēs tabernae sunt plēnae. mercātōrēs mātrōnās
salūtant. mātrōnae mercātōrēs audiunt et tabernās intrant.   5

omnēs popīnae sunt plēnae. amīcī popīnās intrant. ancillae vīnum
portant. amīcī bibunt. fūrēs labōrant. sed Rūfīna et Quārtilla sunt
ānxiae. lūdī Rūfīnam et Quārtillam nōn dēlectant. duo aurīgae ad
popīnam ambulant.

Rūfīna   mē miseram!   10

aurīgae popīnam intrant.

aurīga   ohē, popīnāria! ancilla tua est pulchra!
prīmus

aurīga secundus ancillam capit. aurīgae maximē rīdent.

aurīga   ecce, popīnāria! ego ancillam tuam habeō!
secundus

Catia aurīgam secundum audit. Catia ex īnsulā currit. Catia   15
gladium tenet.

Catia   quid dīcis?

aurīgae gladium vident. aurīgae sunt perterritī et
ē popīnā currunt. Quārtilla et Rūfīna attonitae sunt.

Catia   vah! in Britanniā multae fēminae gladiōs habent.   20

post *after*

discēdō *I leave, depart*
tōtus *whole*
omnis *all, every*
plēnus *full*
lentē *slowly*
taberna *shop, inn*
audiō *I hear, listen*

duo *two*

ohē! *hey!*
popīnāria *barkeeper*
tuus *your*
pulcher *beautiful, handsome*
capiō *I take, grab*

ex *out of*
gladius *sword*

attonitus *astonished, shocked*
Britannia *Britannia, Britain*
fēmina *woman*

LANGUAGE NOTE 2: ACCUSATIVE PLURAL

1. Compare the accusative singular forms of the first, second, and third declensions:

   veterānus cellam quaerit.
   The veteran is looking for a room.

   ego cibum vēndō.
   I'm selling food.

   tū imperātōrem vidēs?
   Do you see the emperor?

2. In this chapter we have met examples of the accusative plural:

   amīcī popīnās intrant.
   Friends are entering bars.

   in Britanniā multae fēminae gladiōs habent.
   In Britain many women have swords.

   mendīcī senātōrēs salūtant.
   The beggars are greeting the senators.

3. Compare the forms you have now met of the three declensions:

SINGULAR	1st decl.	2nd decl.	3rd decl.
nominative	**puella**	**amīcus**	**fūr**
accusative	**puellam**	**amīcum**	**fūrem**

PLURAL			
nominative	**puellae**	**amīcī**	**fūrēs**
accusative	**puellās**	**amīcōs**	**fūrēs**

4. You may have noticed that, in the third declension, the -**ēs** ending is used for both the nominative and the accusative plural. Look at the following sentence:

   mercātōrēs canēs spectant.

   How do we know whether the merchants are watching the dogs, or the dogs are watching the merchants? Unless there's a strong reason to think otherwise, assume the nominative is first. So this sentence means *The merchants are watching the dogs.*

Charioteers

This mosaic shows four charioteers, one from each of the four teams or factions (*factiōnēs*). They wear tunics in the color of the team they represent, just like a modern football jersey or a jockey's shirt. Their chests are bound with leather straps for protection and they wear helmets, possibly of leather, in their team colors. Each charioteer is holding a whip. Four teams of charioteers competed regularly in Rome: green, blue, red, and white. Each team had its fans. The green team was the most popular with the common people. Juvenal says that some people even clothed their children in green shirts.

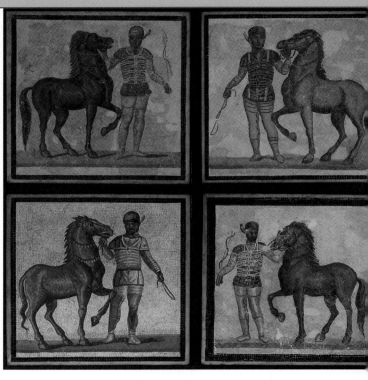

Status and fame

Most charioteers were slaves or former slaves. Although they belonged to the lowest class of Roman society, they could win fame and fortune if they were lucky and skillful enough to survive – they were the pop stars and celebrities of their day. A charioteer who started out as a slave could even win enough money to buy his freedom.

> **QUESTION**
>
> Study these sources. What can we learn from them about charioteers and their place in Roman society?

Source 1

From Suetonius' biography of Emperor Caligula:

> He was so devoted and dedicated to the Green team that he often dined in the stable and stayed there. At a party he gave a charioteer called Eutychus a gift of two million sesterces.

Source 2

Pliny the Elder recorded a story he had read about in the 'Daily Records':

> At the funeral of Felix, the charioteer of the Reds, one of his supporters threw himself on the pyre.

Source 3

An inscription from the tomb of a charioteer called Polynices:

> M. Aurelius Polynices, a home-born slave, lived 29 years, 9 months, and 5 days. He won 739 races, receiving the palm of victory. Of these victories, 655 came with the Red team, 55 with the Green, 12 with the Blue, and 17 with the White. He won 40,000 sesterces 3 times, he won 30,000 sesterces 26 times, and 11 times he won a race with no prize. He raced in an eight-horse chariot 8 times, in a ten-horse chariot 9 times, and in a six-horse chariot 3 times.

Source 4

Martial wrote this poem about the charioteer Scorpus, who had died. Scorpus is speaking:

> **ego sum Scorpus, clāmōsī glōria Circī**
>
> I am Scorpus, the glory of the noisy Circus, your much-applauded, short-lived darling, Rome. Envious Fate snatched me away when I was not yet twenty-seven years old. She counted my victories and thought I was an old man.

LANGUAGE PRACTICE

3.   Add the missing endings to the nouns to match the English translations.

a. Giscō fūr… in īnsulā videt.
Gisco sees a thief in the apartment building.

b. Currāx mendīc… in viā audit.
Currax hears the beggars in the street.

c. ego mātrōn… prō templō salūtō.
I greet the ladies in front of the temple.

d. tū cib… in popīnā habēs?
Do you have food in the bar?

e. Rūfīn… Cati… et fīli… salūtat.
Rufina greets Catia and her son.

f. sen… serv… et mercātōr… in Circō spectant.
The old men watch the slaves and the merchants in the Circus.

A terracotta plaque showing a four-horse chariot approaching the metae (the turning posts). The charioteer is wearing leggings, a cap, and a short tunic, with leather straps wrapped round his body for protection. The reins are tied tightly round his waist. A fallen charioteer can be seen at the base of the meta.

Three phases of ruling

The Romans claimed that a Trojan prince, Aeneas, left Troy and settled in Italy. There, his son created a new town, Alba Longa, which his descendants ruled for hundreds of years. One of the kings of Alba Longa had a grandson called Romulus.

CLUSIUM •

ETRUSCANS

SABINES

RIVER ALLIA

• ROME

RIVER TIBER

OSTIA

Monarchy (753–509 BC)

Romulus founded Rome and was its first king. Six kings succeeded him, until the monarchy came to an end with Tarquinius Superbus (Tarquin the Proud). The seven kings of Rome were Romulus, Numa Pompilius, Tullus Hostilius, Ancus Marcius, Tarquin the Elder, Servius Tullius, and Tarquin the Proud.

The birthplaces of the kings reflect the development of Rome: as the Romans brought nearby Sabine women to be their wives, the early kings alternated between true Romans (Romulus and Tullus Hostilius) and Sabines (Numa Pompilius and Ancus Marcius). Finally, Tarquin the Elder came from Etruria, north of Rome, reflecting Etruscan influence in Rome.

Republic (509–31 BC)

Angry at the behavior of Tarquin the Elder's son, Tarquin the Proud, a group of wealthy Romans, led by Marcus Junius Brutus, overthrew the monarchy and created a new political system that they called *Rēs Pūblica*, which means 'that which the people control': hence our modern name for it, the Roman Republic. In the new system Rome was governed by both a Senate and the People of Rome.

The Senate was composed of senior, wealthy Roman men, many of whom had been politicians, and they made the political decisions in Rome. The People, in fact, meant only Roman-born male citizens – not women, slaves, or non-citizens.

The People voted for or against laws proposed by the Senate, and each year they elected politicians to run the day-to-day life of the city. The two chief magistrates were the consuls. The politicians belonged to the aristocracy. To prevent the return of one-man rule, the politicians were elected to work in pairs or groups, and there were strict rules to avoid individuals being regularly re-elected to public office.

The system clearly gave more power to the aristocracy than to everyone else, but for centuries it created a very stable form of government. Under the Republic, Rome gradually developed a huge empire.

Empire (31 BC–AD 476)

During the first century BC a weakness in the Republic became apparent. The huge size of the Empire required large armies commanded by powerful generals, and those generals started to want more power. A series of bitter civil wars among its generals plunged Rome into crisis.

The civil wars ended only when one general, Octavian (later called Augustus), was victorious. He changed the Republican system back into rule by one man, becoming Rome's first emperor. As the Romans traditionally did not approve of rule by a single individual, Augustus maintained all the institutions of the Republic (the Senate, the politicians, and the elections). However, he kept for himself the most important positions of power: he was Commander-in-Chief of the army (*imperātor*), Chief Priest (*pontifex maximus*), and had continuous consular power (chief magistrate for life), among other things. By the time he died, the Romans had become used to this new form of government, and they continued to be ruled by emperors until the collapse of the Empire in the fifth century AD.

*A drain cover from modern Rome. Rome still celebrates the Republic. SPQR stands for **Senātus PopulusQue Rōmānus** – the Senate and the People of Rome.*

Chapter 4: deī

The number of divine beings living in the city can be thought of as larger than that of humans.

Pliny the Elder

saxum

		saxum *rock, stone*

Mānius īnsulam intrat. Christiānī sunt in īnsulā. Christiānī mendīcum accipiunt. mendīcus Rūfīnam et Quārtillam videt. domina et ancilla Christum adōrant.

Christiānus Christian
accipiō I accept, take in, receive
Christus Christ
adōrō I worship
fenestra window
verbum word

subitō saxum per fenestram volitat. Quārtilla saxum tollit.

Quārtilla   est verbum in saxō!   5

Rūfīna verbum legit: 'cavē!'

periculum danger

Mānius   magnum perīculum est, Rūfīna!
Rūfīna   multa perīcula sunt in Subūrā, sed perīcula nōn timeō. Christus est rēx.
Mānius   quid? rēgem nōn habent Rōmānī!   10
Rūfīna   ego Christum sōlum adōrō. Christus caelum regit. rēgnum exspectō. rēgnum advenit.
Mānius   sed deōs Rōmānōs nōn adōrās. perterrita nōn es?
Rūfīna   ego perterrita nōn sum, quod praemium meum est in caelō. Christus multa gaudia nūntiat. gaudium meum est plēnum.   15

timeō I fear
rēx king
sōlus only, alone
caelum sky, heaven
regō I rule
rēgnum kingdom
exspectō I wait for, expect
adveniō I arrive
deus god
quod because
praemium reward
gaudium joy, pleasure
nūntiō I announce
fax torch
ei! ai!
incendium fire

subitō fax per fenestram volitat. mendīcus est perterritus.

Mānius   ei! incendium advenit!
Quārtilla   saxa et incendia nōn timeō. Christus est saxum meum.   20

exstinguō I put out

ancilla facem exstinguit. omnēs Christiānī ancillam laudant.

Christianity

Rufina and Quartilla were Christians. Christianity was a new religion which had originated in the Roman province of Judaea. The earliest followers of Jesus Christ were Jews, but soon Christianity attracted non-Jewish believers and spread outside Judaea. Some of the first Christians, such as Peter and Paul, were in Rome during the reign of Nero, preaching and converting others to Christianity. Their message was that anyone who worshiped Jesus Christ and led a good life would be rewarded with a blessed afterlife. For this reason Christianity appealed to the poor and slaves.

Christians believed that there was only one god: Christianity was a monotheistic religion. Because they did not acknowledge any other gods, Christians refused to participate in the public worship of the Roman state gods. This might explain why the Romans were less tolerant of Christianity, though they generally accepted other religions and embraced new practices.

> the Christians ... a group of individuals given over to a new and harmful set of superstitions.
>
> *Suetonius*

This Christian funerary monument from AD 313 is decorated with portraits of the early Christians Peter and Paul, who lived in the first century AD.

The common people called them Christians, and they were hated for their vices. Christus, who gave them their name, had been executed in the reign of Emperor Tiberius, on the order of the procurator Pontius Pilate. The deadly superstition had been suppressed for a while, but was starting to break out again, not only in Judaea, where the evil had originated, but even in Rome itself, to where everything in the world that is foul and shameful flows and becomes popular.

Tacitus

Minucius, a Christian living in the third century AD, lists some of the worst accusations against the Christians (he later refutes all the charges):

> The Christians attract women (since women are weak and gullible) and ignorant men, the dregs of society. They despise the temples and reject the gods, they mock our ceremonies, pity our priests. Why do they make such an effort to hide what they worship? Why do they never speak in public? Why do they never assemble freely, unless they are secretly worshiping something which is either illegal or shameful? They can neither show nor see that god of theirs. Yet they believe that he is present everywhere, and that he looks closely into everyone's character, everyone's actions, their words, even their hidden thoughts.
>
> *Minucius*

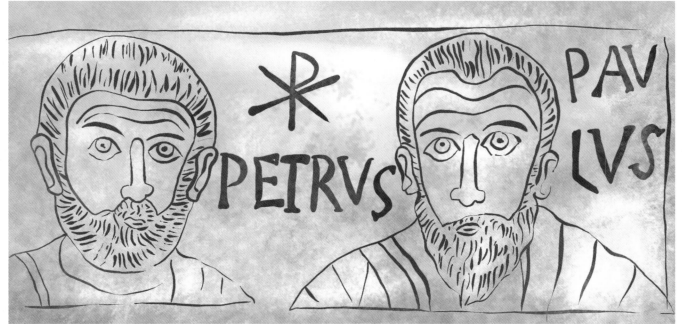

PETRVS   PAVLVS

LANGUAGE NOTE 1: 2ND DECLENSION NEUTER NOUNS

1. Most second declension nouns, such as **lūdus** (*game*) and **mendīcus** (*beggar*), are masculine. You have already met their nominative and accusative endings in Chapters 2 and 3.

2. Some second declension nouns, such as **perīculum** (*danger*) and **vīnum** (*wine*), are neuter. Their endings are different from those of the masculine nouns. Study the following sentences:

vīnum est cārum.	**Faustus vīnum bibit.**
The wine is expensive.	*Faustus is drinking wine.*

    In the singular, both the nominative case and the accusative case end -**um**.

multa perīcula sunt in Subūrā.	**ego perīcula nōn timeō.**
There are many dangers in the Subura.	*I don't fear the dangers.*

    In the plural, both the nominative case and the accusative case end -**a**.

3. Compare the endings of masculine and neuter nouns in the second declension:

SINGULAR	game (m.)	beggar (m.)	danger (n.)	wine (n.)
nominative	**lūdus**	**mendīcus**	**perīculum**	**vīnum**
accusative	**lūdum**	**mendīcum**	**perīculum**	**vīnum**

PLURAL				
nominative	**lūdī**	**mendīcī**	**perīcula**	**vīna**
accusative	**lūdōs**	**mendīcōs**	**perīcula**	**vīna**

Vesta

The goddess Vesta had a shrine in the heart of the city, in the Forum Romanum, where the fire of Vesta was kept burning at all times. If it was ever allowed to go out, it would jeopardize the safety of the entire state. The Romans held a festival in honor of Vesta every June: the Vestalia.

The Vestal Virgins, the priestesses who looked after the fire, were thought to be essential to the prosperity and security of the city. When she became a priestess, a Vestal Virgin took a vow of chastity for thirty years. The Vestals lived in the House of the Vestals, at the foot of the Palatine Hill, and held a special position in Roman society: they were given a place of honor at public games, were considered incorruptible and therefore did not have to take an oath to give evidence in court, and their person was sacrosanct, meaning that anyone who injured them would be condemned to death. However, if a Vestal ever neglected her duty she was beaten, and if she was caught breaking her vow of chastity, she would be punished by being buried alive.

State religion

The Roman state religion was a complex system of religious observances that affected all aspects of public and private life in Rome. At the heart of Roman religion was the need to keep *pāx deōrum*, 'peace with the gods'. This was done by worshiping the many gods that looked after Rome with sacrifices, festivals, rituals at temples, and processions. The most important ceremonies were held publicly, and a large portion of the population would attend. If people did not take part in sufficient numbers, the deity might be offended, and this would disrupt the pax deorum.

The Romans honored many gods; this kind of religion is called polytheistic. The main gods the Romans worshiped corresponded roughly to the Greek Olympian gods, a group of twelve gods whose statues stood in the Forum Romanum. Their temples survive all over the Empire.

SOURCE 1 Firstly, when determining the nature of the gods, the question presents itself whether they exist or not. 'It's difficult to deny.' Well, I think it is difficult to deny, when speaking publicly, but in a conversation with friends, it would be easy. I myself, as a priest, believe that the ceremonies and public rites should be observed most piously. I should like to be persuaded that the gods exist not only as a matter of opinion, but also as a proven truth.

Cicero

1. What are the reasons for worshiping the gods according to this list? Do people worship gods only in order to get something from them?

SOURCE 2 There are different forms of address to the gods, one form for making requests, another form for averting evil, and another for securing help.[1] We see how our highest officials[2] use certain words for their prayers. So that not a single word should be omitted or said at the wrong time, it is the duty of one person to precede the official by reading the words before him from a written copy[3] and of another person to keep watch on every word, and of a third to see that silence is not broken, which would be a bad omen. Meanwhile a musician plays the flute to prevent anything else being heard.[4] Indeed, there are memorable instances recorded of cases where either the sacrifice has been interrupted and ruined, or a mistake has been made in reading out the prayer.[5]

Pliny the Elder

2. The highest officials (politicians and the emperor) were in charge of the prayers.

3. A priest would read the prayers from a book phrase by phrase, and the official would repeat them.

4. Many prayers would be spoken as part of public ceremonies, so there could be plenty of potential interruptions and noises.

5. If a ritual was performed in any way incorrectly, the officials would start all over again from the beginning.

SOURCE 3 This statue shows Emperor Augustus in his ceremonial robes as the Chief Priest (*pontifex maximus*). From Augustus' time onwards, the emperor took on the role of Pontifex Maximus, putting him in charge of all religious worship in the Empire.

QUESTIONS

1. Why did the Romans participate in the state religion?

2. The Romans did not separate religion from politics. What do you think are the consequences of having no separation between religion and politics?

Vestālia

1 diēs fēstus est. Forum Rōmānum est clāmōsum. mātrōnae Rōmānae Vestālia celebrant.

2

tībīcinēs per forum prōcēdunt.

3

tībīcinēs vestīmenta pulchra gerunt. cūr vōs vestīmenta sordida geritis?

nōs vestīmenta sordida gerimus, quod nōs Vestālia celebrāmus. dea Vesta familiās cūrat.

4

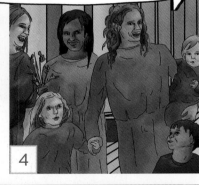

5

multa templa sunt in forō.
ūnum templum est rotundum.

6

mātrōnae templum intrant.
virginēs Vestālēs ignem sacrum cūrant.

7

nōs sumus in Forō Rōmānō.
nōs ad templum prōcēdimus.

8

nōs dōnum portāmus.
omnēs mātrōnae dōna portant.

9

vōs estis in forō.
vōs ad templum venītis?

certē, nōs ad templum venīmus, Cornēlia!
nōs Vestālia spectāmus.

10

ecce! asinī sunt in viā!
vōs asinōs pulchrōs vidētis?

11

stercus quoque est in viā!
cavē stercus, Cornēlia!

LANGUAGE NOTE 2: 'WE' AND 'YOU'

1.   Look at these sentences:

nōs ad templum prōcēdimus.
We are heading to the temple.

nōs dōnum portāmus.
We are carrying a gift.

vōs vestīmenta sordida geritis.
You are wearing dirty clothes.

vōs ad templum venītis?
Are you coming to the temple?

2.   The -**mus** ending of the verb indicates **we** are carrying out the action, and the -**tis** ending shows **you** (plural) are carrying out the action.

3.   You have now met the following endings of the verb:

-ō	e.g. **labōrō**	*I work, am working*
-s	e.g. **vidēs**	*you (singular) see, are seeing*
-t	e.g. **dormit**	*he/she/it sleeps, is sleeping*
-mus	e.g. **spectāmus**	*we watch, are watching*
-tis	e.g. **venītis**	*you (plural) come, are coming*
-nt	e.g. **portant**	*they carry, are carrying*

For example, the endings of the verb **vocō** (*I call*) change as follows:

vocō	*I call, am calling*
vocās	*you (singular) call, are calling*
vocat	*he/she/it calls, is calling*
vocāmus	*we call, are calling*
vocātis	*you (plural) call, are calling*
vocant	*they call, are calling*

4.   You have now also met all the forms of **sum** (*I am*):

sum	*I am*
es	*you (singular) are*
est	*he/she is, it is, there is*
sumus	*we are*
estis	*you (plural) are*
sunt	*they are*

Homes of the gods

Temples were considered to be the homes of the gods, their physical residences among men. Inside each temple was a statue of the god, which could be seen from outside when the doors were open. However, the temples were closed most of the time; usually people could not go into them as they were considered sacred spaces. Instead, in front of the temples there were altars for sacrifices and offerings. All kinds of people would bring gifts to the gods at their temples: ordinary people, politicians, wealthy individuals, and heads of foreign states.

The grander and more beautiful a temple was, the more it honored the god to whom it was dedicated. The interiors were lavishly decorated, even though only priests, temple attendants, and the gods themselves would see them. As well as honoring the gods, the temples fulfilled other functions: the Temple of Saturn held the state treasury; the Temple of Vesta held wills and testaments and documents of state such as treaties; some temples even kept money and valuables safe for private citizens. Sometimes the temples were robbed for the gold and valuables they housed.

Remains of a Roman temple in Nîmes, France. You can see clearly where the inner part of the temple would be closed off. The Romans believed emperors became gods after they died, and they were worshiped along with other gods. This temple was dedicated to the imperial family.

LANGUAGE PRACTICE

1. Complete each Latin sentence with the correct ending from the box below to match the English translation. Use each ending once.

-ō	-s	-t	-mus	-tis	-nt

   a. vōs ignem sacrum in templō cūrā... .
     You look after the sacred fire in the temple.

   b. vestīmenta sordida ger... .
     I'm wearing dirty clothes.

   c. Christiānī deōs Rōmānōs nōn adōra... .
     The Christians don't worship the Roman gods.

   d. ad templum ambulā... .
     We are walking to the temple.

   e. tū sorōrem in forō audī... .
     You hear your sister in the forum.

   f. Sabīna vōs in īnsulā vide... .
     Sabina sees you in the apartment building.

ōmina

pompa Capitōlium ascendit. Lūcīlius est in pompā. magna turba
pompam spectat, quod imperātor adest. servī animālia dūcunt.
animālia mūgiunt et bālant.

pompa ad templum venit. templum est maximum et optimum.
Nerō ē lectīcā dēscendit. turba magnum clāmōrem tollit.   5

turba   iō, Nerō! iō, iō, Nerō! nōs tē amāmus.

prō templō, sacerdōs ūnum animal ad āram dūcit. animal est taurus.
taurus caput inclīnat. servus caput percutit. sacerdōs cultrum capit
et taurum necat. multus sanguis imperātōrem spargit. sacerdōs exta
īnspicit. turba est laeta, quod ōmina sunt optima.   10

Nerō templum intrat et simulācrum adōrat. simulācrum est Iuppiter.

Nerō   ō pater! ō rēx Iuppiter!

Nerō ē templō exit.

turba   nōs sumus fēlīcēs! nōs nūmen vidēmus!

imperātor rīdet.   15

Nerō   vōs estis cīvēs optimī! sed vōs nūmen nōn vidētis.
                   ego nōndum sum deus.
Lūcīlius   vōs estis īnfēlīcēs. vōs deum nōn vidētis, sed hominem
(susurrāns)   perīculōsum.

ōmen *omen, sign*

pompa *procession*
Capitōlium *the Capitoline Hill*
ascendō *I climb*
animal *animal*
mūgiō *I bellow, moo*
bālō *I bleat*
dēscendō *I climb down*
iō! *ho! hurray!*
amō *I love*
sacerdōs *priest*
āra *altar*
taurus *bull*
caput *head*
inclīnō *I lower*
percutiō *I strike*
culter *knife*
necō *I kill*
sanguis *blood*
spargō *I shower, spray*
exta *entrails*
īnspiciō *I inspect*
simulācrum *statue, image*
Iuppiter *Jupiter*
nūmen *deity*
cīvis *citizen*
nōndum *not yet*
susurrāns *whispering*
homō *man, person*

Sacrifice

One of the most important ways Romans honored their gods was by making sacrifices to them. Sacrifices ranged from small offerings of food or wine at a shrine in the home to great public ceremonies where dozens of sacrificial animals were slaughtered at the altars of the temples. Sacrifices made by people in their homes included cakes, grapes, little wreaths, or some incense, accompanied by prayers (often asking for specific favors from the gods). Public sacrifices were held on days of significance in the calendar, or when the help of a particular god was desired. These nearly always involved the slaughter of animals, usually cattle, sheep, and pigs. Gods often had a preference for a particular animal: Jupiter, for instance, usually received a white ox, and Juno a white heifer. Extraordinary circumstances could dictate special sacrifices. During the wars against Hannibal, for instance, the Romans promised Jupiter every single animal born that spring, if he gave them protection for five years. If the gods didn't keep their side of the bargain, the sacrifices were not carried out.

Roman relief showing a bull being sacrificed.

The remains of the Temple of Apollo in Pompeii. At the bottom of the steps leading up to the temple there is an altar, where sacrifices were made.

Animal sacrifices

The same steps were followed meticulously for each sacrifice. If the correct procedure was not followed exactly, the sacrifice could be declared invalid, and the whole ceremony had to be restarted.

1. The animal was consecrated (made holy): to do this the priest in charge sprinkled *mola salsa* (a special mixture of flour and salt prepared by the Vestal Virgins) on the animal's back and wine on its forehead, and passed the sacrificial knife along its back.

2. The animal was slaughtered. A butcher might do this job, or the priest if there was no special butcher available. The animal should consent by lowering its head and showing no panic. For this reason bigger animals like cows would be stunned by a blow to the head first.

3. The animal was laid on its back and its entrails (*exta*) were exposed to the gods, and checked. If no irregularities were found, the sacrifice was deemed successful. However, if there were any abnormalities the sacrifice was aborted and had to restart with a new animal. Sometimes the entrails, especially the liver, were also examined by a soothsayer (*haruspex*). His job was to interpret any omens (messages from the gods).

4. The entrails were then sprinkled with mola salsa and burned on the altar for the gods to receive.

5. The rest of the meat was cooked and eaten in a banquet by the people attending the sacrifice.

LANGUAGE NOTE 3: 3RD DECLENSION NEUTER NOUNS

1. Most third declension nouns are either masculine or feminine. For example, **senātor** (*senator*) is a masculine noun and **nox** (*night*) is feminine. You met the endings of masculine and feminine nouns in Chapters 2 and 3.

2. Some third declension nouns, such as **caput** (*head*) and **animal** (*animal*) are neuter. Their endings are different from those of masculine and feminine nouns. Study the following sentences:

   caput est magnum.   **servus caput percutit.**
   Its head is large.   *The slave strikes its head.*

   In the singular, both the nominative case and the accusative case have the same form.

   animālia sunt in viā.   **servī animālia dūcunt.**
   The animals are in the road. *Slaves are leading the animals.*

   In the plural, both the nominative case and the accusative case end -**a**.

3. Compare the endings of masculine and feminine nouns with neuter nouns in the third declension:

SINGULAR	senator (m.)	night (f.)	head (n.)	animal (n.)
nominative	**senātor**	**nox**	**caput**	**animal**
accusative	**senātōrem**	**noctem**	**caput**	**animal**

PLURAL				
nominative	**senātōrēs**	**noctēs**	**capita**	**animālia**
accusative	**senātōrēs**	**noctēs**	**capita**	**animālia**

A religious procession from the Ara Pacis.

LANGUAGE PRACTICE

2. Select the correct form of the neuter noun to complete the sentence, then translate.

    a. multa .... in urbe vidēmus.   (forum, fora)

    b. ūnum .... est rotundum.   (templa, templum)

    c. in Subūrā sunt multa ....   (perīcula, perīculum)

    d. quattuor .... ad templum portātis.   (dōnum, dōna)

    e. .... magnum clāmōrem in viā faciunt.   (animālia, animal)

    f. nōs .... tollimus et caelum spectāmus.   (caput, capita)

3. Translate each sentence into Latin by choosing the correct word or phrase from each pair.

    a. *Catia has a sword and hurries to the bar.*

    | Catia | gladium | habēs | sed | ad popīnam | festīnās. |
    | Catiam | gladiōs | habet | et | ad popīnās | festīnat. |

    b. *We are holding gifts and walking to the temple.*

    | vōs | dōnum | tenētis | sed | ad templa | ambulātis. |
    | nōs | dōna | tenēmus | et | ad templum | ambulāmus. |

    c. *You are also coming to the apartment building, because you're looking for a room.*

    | semper | ad īnsulās | vidētis, | quod | cellam | quaerunt. |
    | quoque | ad īnsulam | venītis, | et | cella | quaeritis. |

    d. *The little girls are suddenly running through the city.*

    | parva puella | per urbēs | subitō | currunt. |
    | parvae puellae | per urbem | semper | currit. |

    e. *Nero is present. The crowd is happily praising the emperor.*

    | Nerōnem | adest. | turba | imperātor | lentē | laudāmus. |
    | Nerō | ades. | turbam | imperātōrem | laetē | laudat. |

Private worship

May god make Felix Aufidius lucky.

Graffito from Pompeii.

At a Roman dinner, after the first course, people used to stay silent until the bit of food that was set aside as an offering was carried to the hearth and put into the fire, and a child had announced that the gods were favorably disposed.

Servius

It is the custom of pious travelers, when they pass by a grove or a holy place by the roadside, to say a prayer, to put down an apple as an offering, and to stop for a moment.

Apuleius

*A statuette of a household god (**Lar**) made from bronze, about 8 inches high.*

Votive offering of a pregnant woman. Votive offerings were given to the gods in the hope of help (often to cure an illness) or as thanks for a service rendered. This pregnant female terracotta figure suggests that a woman might have made the offering to pray for the safe delivery of her baby.

What is more holy, what is more protected by sanctity, than the house of each individual citizen? This is where his altars (*ārae*) are, his hearth fires (*focī*), his household gods, here his sacred rites and ceremonies are held.

Cicero

QUESTION

How do these examples of worship differ from the public rituals of the state religion?

dōna

hōra nōna est. Faustus et fīlia ad īnsulam ambulant. puella servōs vocat.

Sabīna	Lūcriō! Currāx! nōs omnēs ad focum iam convenīmus. vōs dōna habētis?
Lūcriō	certē, nōs dōna habēmus, Sabīna. ecce! dōna sunt tūs et fār et vīnum.

5

familia ad focum convenit. parva simulācra sunt in focō. simulācra sunt Larēs, quod Larēs familiam cūrant. parva lucerna quoque est in focō. Sabīna prope lucernam stat. silentium est. pater vōta facit.

Faustus	vōs Larēs familiam nostram cūrātis. nōs tūs incendimus. nōs fār damus. nōs quoque vīnum ...

10

subitō Sabīna clāmat, quod perterrita est.

Sabīna	ei! vestīmenta mea! est incendium!

magnum perīculum est. Lūcriō vīnum iacit et incendium exstinguit. dominus eum laudat, sed ānxius est. ōmina nōn sunt bona.

Faustus	vōta nostra sunt inūtilia. Larēs sunt īrātī.

15

nōnus *ninth*

ad *at*
focus *hearth*
iam *now, already*
conveniō *I meet*
tūs *frankincense*
fār *grain*
familia *household*
Lar *household god*
lucerna *lamp*
prope *near*
silentium *silence*
vōtum *prayer*
noster *our*
incendō *I burn*
iaciō *I throw*
eum *him*
bonus *good*
inūtilis *useless*
īrātus *angry*

SOURCE 7

*A shrine to the household gods (**larārium**) from a house in Pompeii. A Roman household would have its own lararium.*

Deucalion and Pyrrha

In the earliest times of men, Jupiter, the king of the gods, traveled the earth and saw the impious acts and violent crimes of the human race. In anger he threw down his thunderbolts and released a flood which covered the earth, merging sea and land. Only two people survived, who would recreate the whole human race: Deucalion and his wife, Pyrrha.

- Read or listen to the myth of Deucalion and Pyrrha.

God and man

Ovid was a Roman poet who wrote *The Metamorphoses*, a collection of stories from mythology linked by the theme of transformation. In Ovid's version of the myth of Deucalion and Pyrrha, when Jupiter tells the other gods that he plans to destroy mankind, they are sad. They wonder who will honor their altars with incense. Roman religion was based on the reciprocal relationship between gods and men. Humans offered prayers and sacrifices to the gods, and in return received good fortune from the gods. A lack of offerings and piety would result in punishment.

- Think about other religions. Is there the same reciprocal relationship between gods and men?
- Do you think it is surprising that the gods rely on the offerings of mankind?

Flood myths

Flood myths are common in many cultures around the world. In almost all forms of the myth, the flood is sent by a god or gods as a punishment for mankind. In most versions, after the purge, there is at least one survivor to populate the earth, often after a sacrifice.

- Why do you think the narrative of a flood myth is so common?

Look at Source 1. Matsya is one representation of the Hindu god Vishnu. He takes the form of a giant fish with a horn on his head, or he is half-man, half-fish. In the flood myth, he saves Manu by pulling his boat to safety on the top of a mountain.

SOURCE 2

Look at Source 2. In this illustration of the flood myth from the Christian Bible, God watches from above as the flood engulfs mankind.

- How do the depictions of the relationship between god and man differ in the two images?
- How do they compare to the myth of Deucalion and Pyrrha?

Born again

Once Deucalion and Pyrrha had reached safety and thanked the gods with sacrifice, they sought a way to repopulate the earth. They were told they must scatter the bones of their great mother behind them. They understood their great mother was Mother Earth, and threw stones from the ground behind them, from which sprang a new race of men.

SOURCE 3

From here we are a tough race, able to endure hard labor, and so we give proof of the source from which we are sprung.

Ovid

- Look at Source 3. Why do you think the Romans would like the idea that their ancestors were born from stones?

RESEARCH

Find out about:
- Flood myths from other cultures.
- The story of Jupiter and Lycaon.
- The origins of sacrifice.

SOURCE 1

Chapter 5: aqua

mēns sāna in corpore sānō.
A healthy mind in a healthy body.
Juvenal

febris

nox est calida. nēmō dormit. multī Subūrānī popīnam intrant, ubi
Rūfīna et Quārtilla labōrant. popīna est clāmōsa, quod Subūrānī
bibunt et lūdunt. Subūrānī per diem labōrāre solent, sed per noctem
bibere et lūdere cupiunt. popīnāria et ancilla dormīre cupiunt.
subitō Sabīna appropinquat.   5

'Mānius est aeger, amita!' clāmat Sabīna. 'nōn surgit!'

'quid?' rogat popīnāria. 'ubi est?'

'prope fontem iacet,' respondet puella. 'calidissimus est mendīcus!'

Rūfīna ad fontem venit, ubi Mānius iacet. mendīcus surgere nōn
temptat, quod nimium aeger est. aqua per rīmam fluit et canēs in   10
viā aquam lambunt. Mānius aquam quoque bibere temptat.

nēmō appropinquāre audet, quod mendīcus febrem habet. sed
popīnāria ad Mānium venīre nōn timet. Mānius eam videt et
rīdet. Rūfīna rīdēre cupit, sed lacrimat. lacrimae in mendīcum
cadunt.   15

'valē, Rūfīna,' susurrat Mānius. 'fīnis est.'

mendīcum tollere incipit popīnāria, sed Mānius iam mortuus est.

febris	*fever*
calidus	*hot*
nēmō	*no one, nobody*
Subūrānus	*inhabitant of the Subura*
lūdō	*I play, am at leisure*
soleō	*I am accustomed, am used*
cupiō	*I want*
appropinquō	*I approach*
aeger	*sick, ill*
surgō	*I get up*
rogō	*I ask*
fōns	*fountain*
iaceō	*I lie down*
respondeō	*I reply*
calidissimus	*very hot*
temptō	*I try*
aqua	*water*
fluō	*I flow*
lambō	*I lick, lap*
audeō	*I dare*
eam	*her*
lacrimō	*I weep, cry*
lacrima	*tear*
in (+ acc.)	*onto*
valē	*goodbye, farewell*
susurrō	*I whisper*
fīnis	*end*
incipiō	*I begin, start*

A public water fountain in Pompeii.

LANGUAGE NOTE 1: 'TO DO' SOMETHING

1. Study the following sentences:

ego labōrāre temptō.
I am trying to work.

Mānius aquam bibere temptat.
Manius tries to drink the water.

Rūfīna rīdēre cupit.
Rufina wants to smile.

ancilla dormīre cupit.
The female slave wants to sleep.

2. In each of the Latin sentences above, the verb ending **-re** means '*to do*' something. This form of the verb is known as the **infinitive**.

3. The infinitive form of the verb is often found with verbs such as **cupiō** (*I want, desire*), **soleō** (*I am accustomed, used*), **temptō** (*I try*), **audeō** (*I dare*), and **incipiō** (*I begin*).

LANGUAGE PRACTICE

1. Choose the correct form of the verb to complete the sentence, then translate.

a. Rōmānī rēgem .... nōn solent.   (adōrant, adōrāre, adōrāmus)

b. vīnum in popīnā .... cupiō.   (bibō, bibunt, bibere)

c. in Subūrā .... nōn audēs.   (habitāre, habitās, habitāmus)

d. iuvenēs imperātōrem in forō .... temptant.   (audiunt, audiō, audīre)

e. prīma hōra est, et Sabīna in cellā .... cupit.   (legitis, legere, legit)

f. mendīcī semper in viā .... solent.   (dormiunt, dormīs, dormīre)

g. nēmō senātōrem īrātum .... audet.   (vituperat, vituperāre, vituperō)

h. nōs āram prō templō .... temptāmus.   (vidēre, vidēmus, vident)

thermae Nerōniānae

Lūcīlius apodȳtērium intrat. hōra octāva est.

Lūcīlius in apodȳtēriō vestīmenta dēpōnit.

iuvenis palaestram intrat, ubi amīcōs quaerit.

palaestra est plēna, sed Lūcīlius amīcōs vidēre nōn potest.

duo puerī pugnant. Lūcīlius puerōs intentē spectat.

4 ōh! nimium parvus sum.
ego pugnāre nōn possum.

5 vah! parvus es, sed
Rōmānus. tū vincere potes.

6 Lūcīlius ē palaestrā exit et ad piscīnam ambulat.
   piscīna quoque est plēna.

7 Lūcīlius est laetus,
   quod amīcōs audīre potest.

8 amīcī sunt in piscīnā, sed Lūcīlium vidēre nōn possunt.
   Lūcīlius amīcōs vocat.

9 quid? est Lūcīlius?

   in aquā sumus!

   nōs tē vidēre nōn possumus!

10 iuvenis currit ...

   ... et in piscīnam salit.

11 ecce! estis laetī?
    nunc vōs mē vidēre potestis!

   amīcī maximē rīdent.

12   thermae Nerōniānae sunt magnificae.

13   Nerō magnificam domum quoque aedificāre cupit.

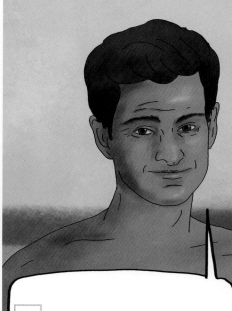

imperātor novam domum aedificāre nōn potest.

quid dīcis?!

urbs iam est plēna!

14

15   Nerō omnia facere potest.

LANGUAGE NOTE 2: POSSUM

1. In the picture story **thermae Nerōniānae**, you met all the forms of **possum**
(*I am able, I can*). For example:

> **ego pugnāre nōn possum.**   *I am not able to fight.*
> **Lūcīlius amīcōs audīre potest.**   *Lucilius is able to hear his friends.*
> **vōs mē vidēre potestis.**   *You are able to see me.*

Notice that **possum** is often used with an infinitive.

2. **possum** is made up of the verb **sum** (*I am*) and the adjective **potis** (*able*). Compare
the forms of **sum** and **possum**:

sum	*I am*	**possum**	*I am able*
es	*you* (singular) *are*	**potes**	*you* (singular) *are able*
est	*he/she/it is*	**potest**	*he/she/it is able*
sumus	*we are*	**possumus**	*we are able*
estis	*you* (plural) *are*	**potestis**	*you* (plural) *are able*
sunt	*they are*	**possunt**	*they are able*

3. Note that **possum** can be translated as *I am able* or *I can*. For example:

> **tū vincere potes.**   *You are able to win.*
> or   *You can win.*

A bronze statue of a boxer. Note the leather boxing gloves on his hands and the realistic portrayal of his battered face after numerous brutal fights.

The baths

A visit to the baths

Romans believed that regular exercise and bathing were good for health, preventing illness and sometimes providing a cure. A few very wealthy Romans had their own baths at home. But even rich people went to the public baths, because a visit to the baths involved much more than washing. The large *thermae*, such as the Baths of Nero and the Baths of Agrippa, had facilities for sport and leisure activities, including concerts, poetry readings, and lectures. And the baths were a social center, where you would meet your friends. For many Romans, at least those who had enough free time, a visit to the baths was part of their daily routine.

The working day usually ended at about noon and the main meal was in the late afternoon or early evening. Between midday and evening was the time for visiting the baths. All baths had an *apodȳtērium* (changing room), *frīgidārium* (cold room), *tepidārium* (warm room), and *caldārium* (hot room). Some also had a *palaestra* (exercise ground), a *piscīna* (swimming pool), or a *Lacōnicum* (sauna). There was no set pattern for a visit. Generally, a bather would spend some time in the tepidarium, then go to the caldarium. However, which rooms you went to and which facilities you used would depend on how much time you had, your personal preferences, and, to some extent, how much you could afford. Although entrance to the baths cost very little (and sometimes was even free), some treatments such as massages would be extra.

If you visit Rome, you can see the remains of the huge, elaborate thermae built by the emperors Caracalla and Diocletian in the third and early fourth century AD. Very little now is left of the thermae built by Nero, which Lucilius visits in the story. They opened in AD 62 and were famous for their luxury. The Baths of Nero were on the Campus Martius, near the Baths of Agrippa (named after the friend and adviser of Emperor Augustus); these establishments were open to the public. As well as these large public thermae, there were lots of privately-owned baths all over the city, ranging from the grand and luxurious to the small and grubby, some of them on the first floor of insulae. This illustration shows a typical bathing complex decorated in the luxurious imperial style.

Who went to the baths?

Most wealthy men would have visited the baths every day. But what about women, the poor, and slaves? Women certainly went to the baths. In the first century AD, men and women could sometimes bathe together unclothed, but it is hard to know how widespread this practice was. There were probably some baths or parts of baths for the use of men or women exclusively, and certain times may have been set aside for women. Some slaves also went to the baths, either to attend their masters or to bathe. As for the poor, they may have bathed less frequently or gone to the baths which had cheaper entrance fees.

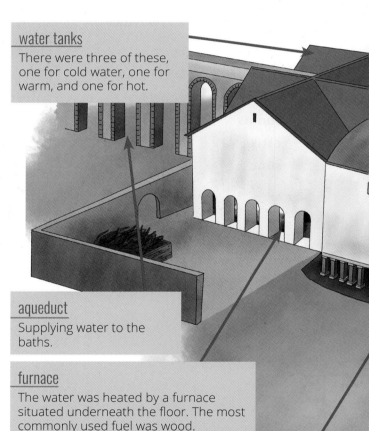

water tanks
There were three of these, one for cold water, one for warm, and one for hot.

aqueduct
Supplying water to the baths.

furnace
The water was heated by a furnace situated underneath the floor. The most commonly used fuel was wood.

Laconicum
A Laconian (Spartan) bath was a hot, dry room, like a sauna, where people would sweat. It had a domed roof, and an opening was left in the center of the dome. A bronze shield was hung from the top of the dome by chains; this could be lowered and raised to regulate the temperature in the room. The grooves in the ceiling allowed condensation to be channeled down the walls.

caldarium

Hot room, with a large, rectangular marble bath, filled with hot water. After sitting and soaking in the hot water, the bather would lie down on a marble slab, either in the caldarium or in an adjoining room. A slave rubbed olive oil into his skin, then scraped off the oil and dirt with a metal instrument called a strigil (*right*). This was followed by a massage. The bather then rinsed himself with water from a stone basin. Finally, if the bather could afford it, he would be anointed with perfume.

apodyterium

Changing room. People undressed here, then gave their clothes to slaves who put them on shelves arranged along the walls. Some people brought a slave to guard their belongings.

piscina

A swimming pool.

latrina

Communal toilet.

frigidarium

The cold room had a circular plunge pool filled with unheated water. Some people finished off their visit to the baths with a dip in the cold pool; others preferred a refreshing cold bath after exercise.

shops and popinae

Visitors to the baths could buy food and drink, and other things they might need for their visit, such as perfume, perfume bottles, and strigils.

tepidarium

Warm room. There were benches around the walls where people could sit and chat while enjoying the warm, steamy atmosphere. Windows high in the walls admitted light and sun.

palaestra

An open space surrounded by a covered walkway. People would go here to exercise before bathing. Exercises included ball games, wrestling, and weightlifting.

peristylium

A covered walkway surrounding the palaestra.

hypocaust

Underfloor heating system. The floor of the baths was suspended on piles of bricks, so that hot air could circulate and provide underfloor heating to the rooms above. Hollow channels in the walls allowed warm air to be drawn up and heat the walls. The Laconicum and the caldarium were nearest to the furnace. The floors of these rooms were so hot that bathers had to wear wooden shoes.

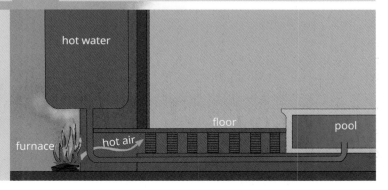

in lātrīnā

Faustus et Giscō lātrīnam vīsitāre cupiunt. Faustus et Giscō lātrīnam intrāre volunt, sed nōn possunt. in lātrīnā mercātōrēs adsunt et negōtium agunt. Subūrānī amīcōs salūtant.

Faustus	ego intrāre volō. in viā manēre nōlō!
Giscō	certē tū manēre nōn vīs, sed lātrīna est plēna. 5

tandem Giscō et Faustus lātrīnam intrāre possunt. Celer in viā manet.

Faustus	ēn, lātrīna est optima. Rōma multās luxuriās habet. tū Rōmae manēre vīs, Giscō?
Giscō	vah, Rōma certē est splendida, sed in urbe manēre nōlō. nōs in īnsulā habitāre nōlumus. in fundō rūsticō 10 habitāre volumus.
Faustus	vērum? Catia Rōmae manēre nōn vult? vōs in Subūrā habitāre nōn vultis, in īnsulā optimā, cum amīcīs optimīs?
Giscō	vōs amīcī optimī estis, sed Subūra est perīculōsa. vītam sēcūram volumus. fīlium habēmus ... 15
Faustus	ego fīliam habeō. Sabīnam prōtegere volō, sed difficile est ...
Giscō	Sabīna in perīculō est?
Faustus	ēheu! senātor aut pecūniam aut fīliam habēre vult ...
senex	heus! vōs tacēre nōn potestis? 20 compressus sum et nunc quoque ānxius sum!

Faustus et Giscō ē lātrīnā exeunt. Celer in viā mingit.

---

lātrīna *toilet*

vīsitō *I visit*
volō *I want*
negōtium agō *I do business*
maneō *I remain, stay*
nōlō *I don't want*

tandem *at last*

ēn *see!*
luxuria *luxury*
Rōmae *in/at Rome*
splendidus *splendid, sumptuous*
fundus *farm*
rūsticus *rural*
vērum? *really?*

vīta *life*
sēcūrus *safe*
prōtegō *I protect*
difficilis *difficult*

ēheu! *oh no! (in despair)*
aut ... aut ... *either ... or ...*
heus! *hey!*
compressus *constipated*

mingō *I urinate*

*Left: a replica **xylospongium**, sponge on a stick. It's not known whether the Romans used it instead of toilet paper, or to clean the toilet itself.*

What can we learn from this source about the various activities that took place in the baths and the reasons people would visit the baths?

In a letter to a friend, the philosopher Seneca describes the noise from the baths above which he lives:

I'm surrounded by noise. I live above a set of baths. Imagine the din which makes my ears ache. When the strong lads are working out – or just pretending to work out – I hear their groans as they lift the heavy lead weights, I hear their hissings and harsh gasps as they expel the breath they have been holding in. When my attention turns to an inactive fellow, content with an ordinary, cheap massage, I hear the slap of a hand striking his shoulders. If a ballplayer comes along and begins to count the score, that's it! Add to this, someone starting a fight, and a thief being caught, and someone who likes the sound of his own voice in the bath. Add now, people jumping into the pool with a loud splash. Imagine the shrill cry of the hair-plucker advertising his services by shouting out, and never silent unless he is plucking armpits and making someone else scream for him. Now there's the yelling of the sausage-sellers and cake-sellers and all the bar owners selling their wares, each with his own distinct cry.

Public toilets

Although wealthy Romans had a private toilet in their houses, and some apartment buildings probably had toilets on the first or second floor, most of Rome's population had no access to private facilities; most people had a bucket or pot at home. There were also some public toilets. These had no privacy. People sat next to each other on stone benches arranged in a rectangle or semicircle. Water flowed round their feet in a channel and waste was carried into the sewer.

The public toilets were social spaces where people could chat and issue dinner invitations. We do not know who managed the toilets and cleaned them, and there is no evidence about whether people had to pay to use them.

Instead of toilet paper, Romans may have used a sponge on a stick; after using the sponge they put it into a bucket filled with vinegar or salt water as an antiseptic, ready for the next person to use. Other options would have been dry leaves, scraps of cloth, and even pine cones!

Water supply

> If we consider the distances traveled by the water before it arrives, the raising of arches, the tunneling of mountains, and the building of level routes across deep valleys, we shall readily admit that there has never been anything more remarkable in the whole world.
>
> *Pliny the Elder*

In the early days of Rome, people mostly used water from rivers, streams, springs, and wells. Some also collected rainwater from the roofs of buildings in storage jars or tanks under the house.

As the city grew, the Romans constructed aqueducts to bring water from outside sources and springs into the city. The water supplied public baths, fountains, toilets, and some private houses. The aqueducts were an outstanding feat of engineering. They traveled miles, moving the water by gravity alone and maintaining a constant downward gradient. Most of the channels were underground and the Romans used the natural slope of the land as much as possible, sometimes making detours around mountains or valleys to reduce expensive engineering work. Occasionally, however, they tunneled a direct route through a mountain or crossed huge valleys with multi-arched aqueducts, some of which are still visible today.

Growing demand

By Nero's time Rome was supplied by nine aqueducts which brought into the city an impressive 150,000,000 gallons of water every day. This huge volume of water was needed to meet the demand of the hundreds of public fountains and the extravagant public baths which had become a fundamental part of Roman life. The availability of fresh water was abundant even by modern standards. The fresh water gushing day and night from public fountains fulfilled a basic human need and raised the level of hygiene for the entire populace. It also displayed the supremacy of the Romans and their power to control natural resources.

Distribution

When the water reached the city it went straight to water tanks. From here smaller branches of the aqueduct or pipes distributed the water to various public amenities or private houses. Most of the water went to the multitude of public fountains and baths, but individuals could pay to have fresh water piped to their houses. These individuals had to be registered, and paid a fee based on the circumference of the pipe that serviced their property (a fairly inaccurate measure). Tampering and fraud were common, with people illegally tapping the aqueducts or widening their private pipes.

These pipes were often made of lead and some people think that the Romans were affected by lead poisoning. However, because the water flowed constantly and was not still, there was not much build-up of lead in the water. Some pipes would gain a lining of minerals from the water, and therefore were safe from contamination from the lead.

Having water plumbed straight into your house was a luxury few could afford and it was common to find the owner's name cast into the pipe. This inscription translates as 'The most notable lady Valeria Messalina.'

No waste

Any excess from the huge volume of water brought into the city overflowed into Rome's main sewer, the Cloaca Maxima, and into the River Tiber, flushing the city clean of waste.

The remains of the Aqua Claudia, which brought water to Rome. It was completed by Emperor Claudius in AD 52. Its total length was about 43 miles.

LANGUAGE NOTE 3: VOLŌ AND NŌLŌ

1. In the story **in lātrīnā**, you met all the forms of the verb **volō** (*I want, I am willing*). For example:

   ego intrāre volō.
   I want to enter.

   nōs vītam sēcūram volumus.
   We want a safe life.

2. You also saw forms of the verb **nōlō** (*I don't want, I am unwilling*), which is the negative of **volō**. For example:

   ego in urbe manēre nōlō.
   I don't want to stay in the city.

   nōs in īnsulā habitāre nōlumus.
   We don't want to live in an apartment building.

3. Compare the forms of **volō** and **nōlō**. What do you notice about the way **volō** forms its negative?

volō	*I want*	**nōlō**	*I don't want*
vīs	*you* (singular) *want*	**nōn vī**s	*you* (singular) *don't want*
vult	*he/she/it wants*	**nōn vul**t	*he/she/it doesn't want*
volumus	*we want*	**nōlu**mus	*we don't want*
vultis	*you* (plural) *want*	**nōn vul**tis	*you* (plural) *don't want*
volunt	*they want*	**nōlu**nt	*they don't want*

   Note that the person endings of **volō** and **nōlō** fit the pattern you met on page 62.

LANGUAGE PRACTICE

2. Complete each sentence by choosing the correct form of the verb, then translate.

a. pauper sum. multa dōna dare nōn .... (possum, possumus).

b. Faustus et Lūcriō in īnsulā per diem labōrāre .... (nōn vult, nōlunt).

c. nēmō sanguinem in viā vidēre .... (vult, volunt).

d. equum tuum vēndere .... (vīs, vultis), Giscō?

e. Catia familiam et amīcōs cūrāre .... (potest, possunt).

f. nōs in viā stāre .... (nōlō, nōlumus). thermās intrāre et negōtium agere .... (volō, volumus).

Sanitation

The Romans went to great lengths to maintain the purity of the water brought into the city. The channels in the aqueducts were covered to prevent contamination from dirt and to keep the water cool. The water was also filtered using settling tanks. However, the quality of water from the nine different aqueducts varied greatly.

When judging the quality of the water, the Romans examined taste, temperature, smell, and appearance. The worst, most dirty water was used for gardens, artificial lakes, and agriculture. The best and purest was used for drinking.

Frontinus was appointed the supervisor of the aqueducts (*cūrātor aquārum*) shortly after the time of our stories. He wrote:

> The job of the curator aquarum is to look after not merely the water supply but also the health and even the safety of the city.

You might assume that, with the aqueducts constantly bringing in fresh water and the Cloaca Maxima flushing away the city's waste, Rome would have been very clean. However, there are records of people on the street being hit by waste thrown from upstairs windows. There is also an inscription from Herculaneum warning that any man caught dumping excrement would be punished.

The Romans also had many practical uses for urine. Far from flushing it away, people were encouraged to relieve themselves or empty their urine into giant clay pots on the street. The collected urine was then put to use in various ways: for cleaning clothes, tanning leather, preparing wool, and even cleaning your teeth! Urine contains ammonia and would actually have worked very well as a cleaning agent.

Eventually, urine became so important as a commodity that Emperor Nero put a tax on the buyers of urine. The phrase *pecūnia nōn olet* (money does not stink), comes from this idea.

A Roman wall painting showing workers in a laundry, hanging clothes to dry.

fuga: pars prīma

multī servī sub thermīs labōrant. calidum et obscūrum est. servī ligna ad fornācēs portant. duo servī susurrant.

'ligna portāre temptō, sed difficile est,' inquit Thellus. 'ligna sunt gravia. mē adiuvāre potes?'

'tē adiuvāre possum,' respondet Galliō. 'et tū mē adiuvāre potes. effugere volō.'   5

'quid? effugere vīs? īnsānus es!' exclāmat Thellus.

'st! custōs tē audīre potest,' Galliō susurrat.

'vah! custōs mē audīre nōn potest. longē abest, et dormīre vult. quōmodo effugere vīs?' rogat Thellus.   10

'per cloācam in aquā sordidā effugere volō,' inquit Galliō. 'sed cloāca portam habet. portam aperīre nōn possum. ūnā tamen eam aperīre possumus.'

'per cloācam effugere nōn potes,' respondet Thellus. 'nimium perīculōsum est. et poenās dare nōlō.'   15

'nēmō tē vidēre potest! obscūrum est! tē ōrō!' susurrat Galliō.

servī portam aperiunt et in cloācam saliunt. custōs sonōrem audit et canēs vocat. canēs vehementer lātrant et servōs per cloācam agitant. Thellus et Galliō canēs audiunt et per tenebrās celeriter currunt.

fuga	*escape*
pars	*part*
sub	*below*
lignum	*log, wood*
fornāx	*furnace*
inquit	*says*
gravis	*heavy*
adiuvō	*I help*
effugiō	*I flee, escape*
īnsānus	*mad, insane*
exclāmō	*I exclaim*
custōs	*guard*
longē	*far off*
absum	*I am away*
quōmodo?	*how?*
cloāca	*sewer*
porta	*gate, grate*
aperiō	*I open*
ūnā	*together*
tamen	*however*
eam	*it*
poenās dō	*I pay the penalty, I am punished*
ōrō	*I beg*
sonor	*noise*
vehementer	*loudly*
tenebrae	*darkness*
celeriter	*quickly*

A Roman hypocaust (underfloor heating system). On the left you can see where the hot air would have flowed through from the furnace.

Rome under attack!

Was Rome always mighty?

For most of its history Rome was at the heart of a vast empire, which kept peace within its borders and successfully defeated external enemies. However, there were moments at which the city of Rome was in danger of disappearing: what made Rome vulnerable?

Marauding Gauls

In 387 BC the Senones, a band of Gauls from northern Italy, defeated the Roman army near Rome, leaving the city almost entirely unprotected. The Romans decided to save what they could of the city: men of fighting age, women, and children took a last stand on the Capitoline Hill. The rest either fled to surrounding villages or, if they were too infirm to move, were left undefended to meet their death.

When the Gauls entered the city, it was quiet and almost empty. They burned and looted what was at hand and killed many of the people still in the city. Then they laid siege to the Capitol. Eventually the Romans were starving and unable to resist any longer. The Gauls and Romans came to an agreement: the Romans would pay 1,000 pounds in weight of gold and the Gauls would go home. The humiliation inflicted by the Gauls was never totally forgotten.

Rome moved on to be the mighty empire we all know, and the city was never attacked again, until ...

The Visigoths

AD 408. The Roman Empire was now in decline. The city of Rome was no longer the capital of the Empire. There were two emperors ruling two halves of the Empire: Emperor Honorius, based in Ravenna (in Italy), was in charge of the West, and his brother Arcadius ruled the East from Constantinople (in modern Turkey).

Groups of Germanic tribes had been slowly infiltrating the Roman Empire. One group, the Visigoths, led by Alaric, crossed into Italy without any difficulties and laid siege to Rome itself. Starving, the people of Rome decided to negotiate for peace. Alaric was not merciful: according to the historian Zosimus, he asked for 'all the gold and silver in the city, all the household goods, and the foreign slaves.' When asked what would be left for the citizens, he replied 'their lives.'

The final payment to liberate Rome was 5,000 pounds of gold and 30,000 of silver, 4,000 silk robes, 3,000 scarlet fleeces, 3,000 pounds of pepper, and some hostages. To pay the sum, individuals had to hand over most of their possessions, but that was still not enough. So the Romans took many of the robes and decorations from the old statues of the gods and even melted some of them down. The siege was lifted, although the peace was not concluded, as the hostages had not been sent to Alaric. He ransacked many of Rome's monuments and enslaved many of its citizens, including the emperor's sister, Galla Placidia.

Rome was sacked again by another foreign people, the Vandals, in AD 455. The Western Empire finally collapsed when Odoacer, an Ostrogoth, removed the last emperor of Rome, Romulus Augustulus, and declared himself King of Italy in 476.

Brennus, the leader of the Gauls, weighs out the spoils.

Chapter 6: servitium

dē cellā

mediā nocte familia dē cellā dēscendit.
marītus sarcinās portat et uxor līberōs dūcit.
omnēs tacitē prōcēdere temptant.

mediā *middle,*
  middle of
dē *from, down from*
sarcina *bag*
līberī *children*
tacitē *quietly, silently*

BAU AU
BAU AU AU

sed Celer familiam audit et lātrat. Faustus surgit, et
marītum cum sarcinīs et uxōrem cum līberīs videt.   5
'ohē!' clāmat Faustus. 'quō festīnātis?'
'in cellā obscūrā et sordidā manēre nōn possumus,'
respondet marītus.
'columbae per rīmam volitant et mūrēs per iānuam
currunt.'   10
'cum columbīs et mūribus habitāre nōlumus,' inquit uxor.
'sed pēnsiōnem dēbētis!' clāmat Faustus.
marītus et uxor nihil dīcunt, sed celeriter discēdunt.

quō? *where ... to?*
nihil *nothing*

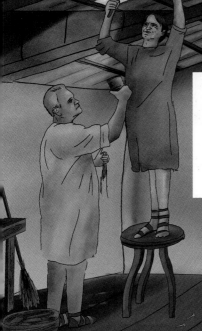

hōrā prīmā Faustus cum Lūcriōne ad cellam
ascendit. Lūcriō īnstrūmenta portat.
negōtiātor et servus tēctum reficere
temptant. Celer quoque in cellā labōrat.
canis mūrēs capere temptat.

15

īnstrūmentum
instrument, tool
tēctum *roof*
reficiō *I repair*

---

hōrā quīntā Faustus clāmōrem in viā audit.
magnus servus prō popīnā stat, ubi Sabīna cum ancillā labōrat.

20

quīntus *fifth*

ubi est pater tuus?

dominus meus pēnsiōnem
annuam exspectat.

annuus *yearly,
annual*

Sabīna nōn respondet.

servus circumspectat, sed Faustum vidēre nōn potest.

'negōtiātor!' clāmat servus. 'tribus diēbus pecūniam
exspectō!'

servus īrātus Sabīnam intentē spectat.

'pater tuus magnam pecūniam dēbet,' inquit servus.

'es in magnō perīculō!'

25

circumspectō *I look
around*

LANGUAGE NOTE 1: THE ABLATIVE CASE

1.   Since Chapter 1 you have been reading sentences like these:

> **ego in viā ambulō.**
> *I am walking in the street.*

> **Sabīna ē forō currit.**
> *Sabina runs out of the forum.*

> **Faustus cum Lūcriōne exit.**
> *Faustus leaves with Lucrio.*

In this chapter, you have met sentences such as these:

> **uxor cum līberīs discēdit.**
> *The wife is leaving with her children.*

> **cum columbīs et mūribus habitāre nōlumus.**
> *We don't want to live with doves and rats.*

2.   The words in red above are in the **ablative** case. The ablative case is used in a variety of situations. For example, it can be used to mark the place of departure, e.g. **ē forō** (*out of the forum*) or to mark the objects or people with which something happens e.g. **cum līberīs** (*with her children*). The ablative can often be represented in English as *from*, *with*, or *by*.

3.   You have now met the following noun endings:

SINGULAR	1st decl.	2nd decl.		3rd decl.	
nominative	**puella**	**amīcus**	**dōnum**	**fūr**	**caput**
accusative	**puellam**	**amīcum**	**dōnum**	**fūrem**	**caput**
ablative	**puellā**	**amīcō**	**dōnō**	**fūre**	**capite**

PLURAL					
nominative	**puellae**	**amīcī**	**dōna**	**fūrēs**	**capita**
accusative	**puellās**	**amīcōs**	**dōna**	**fūrēs**	**capita**
ablative	**puellīs**	**amīcīs**	**dōnīs**	**fūribus**	**capitibus**

Currāx et Quārtilla

hōrā septimā Currāx et Celer prope popīnam sedent. hodiē Currāx
est trīstis et canem mulcet. canis puerum lambit.

Quārtilla Currācem videt et eum ānxiē vocat.

'cūr trīstis es, Currāx?' rogat Quārtilla.

'Giscō et Catia mox ex urbe discēdere volunt,' respondet puer. 'trīstis   5
sum, quod Celer discēdit. Celer amīcus meus est.'

'tū multōs amīcōs habēs. ego, māter tua, tē amō, et Faustus ... apud
Faustum sēcūrus es,' inquit ancilla.

'māter mea es, sed in popīnā tōtum diem labōrās,' clāmat Currāx. 'in
viīs tōtum diem labōrō. nōn sumus hominēs, sed īnstrūmenta.'   10

'st!' susurrat Quārtilla. 'Faustus familiam optimē cūrat et cum
Lūcriōne strēnuē labōrat. Sabīna et Rūfīna multās hōrās quoque
labōrant. dūra sunt tempora. nōs omnēs diem et noctem labōrāmus.'

'ego nōn sum asinus, māter. Faustus nōn nōs cūrat. Faustus nōs
tenet. Rūfīna tē pulsat. ego effugere volō. ego lībertātem volō.'   15

'minimē! perīculōsum est effugere. sī servus effugere temptat ...

subitō vir ad popīnam advenit et Quārtillam intentē spectat. vir,
Septimus nōmine, clāmat,

'Rūfīna, vīsne ancillam tuam vēndere?'

septimus	*seventh*
hodiē	*today*
trīstis	*sad*
mox	*soon*
māter	*mother*
apud	*at the house of*
optimē	*very well*
strēnuē	*strenuously, hard*
dūrus	*hard, harsh*
tempus	*time*
pulsō	*I beat, hit*
lībertās	*freedom*
sī	*if*
vir	*man*
nōmen	*name*

Slavery in the Roman world

A slave was the property of his or her enslaver, regarded as a commodity that could be bought or sold like a cow or a donkey. Enslaved people had no liberty and no rights. They could not leave their employment and they could not choose what to do, but had to obey the orders of their master. Slave owners had complete control over their slaves, even the power of life and death.

Enslaved people had no right to a family life, were not allowed to marry, and could not own property. They did not even keep their own name; the enslaver would choose a new name for them. In this way, the enslaved person suffered a total lack of freedom and loss of identity.

Enslaved people had many different ethnic backgrounds and were born in various places, including the countries and regions we now call Italy, France, Britain, Spain, Germany, Greece, Egypt, North Africa, and Turkey. They weren't distinguished from free people by skin color or race, or even by dress or occupation. Slaves and free people often worked alongside each other.

Although the living conditions of slaves varied, what did not vary was the acceptance of slavery. The Romans, and other people who lived around the Mediterranean, regarded slavery as a normal part of life, and there was no movement to abolish it. Even some former slaves would, once they became free, buy slaves of their own.

Slave or servant?

Many enslaved people, like Currax, Quartilla, and Lucrio, were part of a *familia*. This was not the same as a modern family. The Latin word, familia, means household, i.e. all who live in the house. Household slaves lived in their enslaver's house and did the work of domestic servants: cooking, cleaning, attending to the owners of the house, and looking after children. Some worked in a trade or business for or alongside their enslaver.

How were people enslaved?

1. Prisoners of war

The Romans believed that they had the right to enslave people they captured in war. In the second and first centuries BC, Rome was expanding its territory and acquiring an empire. Roman armies captured vast numbers of people in war and took them to Rome to be sold as slaves. The geographer Strabo records one such event from 167 BC:

> Aemilius Paullus [a Roman general] captured seventy cities in Epirus [in Greece] and enslaved 150,000 human beings.

Prisoners of war continued to be a source of slaves, although not in such large numbers. In the first century AD Rome was still conquering territory overseas and enslaving the conquered peoples. After the sack of Jerusalem in AD 70, the victorious Roman army captured thousands of Jews, enslaved them, and brought them to Rome.

Rome

2. Pirates and kidnappers

Some people were enslaved as a result of being captured by pirates or bandits. Pirates took their victims to slave markets, such as one on the island of Delos in the eastern Mediterranean. Slave traders then brought the slaves to Rome and other parts of the Empire. Slave traders also brought slaves from outside the Roman world, for example from sub-Saharan Africa and the region which is now Russia, but these would have formed only a small proportion of the slaves in Rome.

Strabo wrote:

> The slave trade was very profitable, because it was easy to capture slaves. Delos was a large and very rich market, with the capacity to receive and export thousands of slaves in a single day. The reason for this growth in the slave trade is that the Romans had become rich after the destruction of Carthage and Corinth, and began to use large numbers of slaves. The pirates saw how easy it was to make money in this way, so they sprang up all over the place, making raids and trading in slaves.

3. Born a slave

Children of female slaves automatically became slaves themselves. These home-born slaves were known as *vernae*. The Romans regarded vernae as the property of the enslaver. The mother of the child had no rights. The enslaver could decide to sell the mother or the child and thus separate them from each other.

4. Abandoned children

Parents who couldn't afford or didn't want to bring up their children sometimes abandoned babies in rubbish heaps, at crossroads, or in other public places. Anyone could take the infant to bring up as a slave. Even after many years as a slave, a freeborn Roman could legally claim freedom. This would be difficult to prove, but there is some evidence that it did happen.

5. Choosing slavery

Some desperate people even sold themselves into slavery because of extreme poverty or debt. There was no welfare system in the Roman world and for some people life as a slave might have seemed preferable to being a homeless beggar.

Epirus

GREECE

ASIA MINOR

Delos

The slave market

When a Roman wanted to buy a new slave he might go to the slave market. Every town would have a slave market. There were two in Rome. One was in the Forum Romanum, behind the Senate House. The other was in the Campus Martius. The poet Horace gives an idea of what a slave market might have been like. He imagines a slave dealer speaking to a potential buyer:

> This boy is fair and handsome from head to toe. He can be yours for 8,000 sesterces. A home-born slave, obedient to his master. He has some knowledge of Greek – he's equipped for any art. With moist clay like this you can mold anything! What's more, he will sing – his voice is untrained but it will be a pleasant accompaniment when you are drinking ... None of the slave dealers would do this deal for you. And I wouldn't do this favor for everyone.

QUESTIONS

1. What good qualities of the boy does the slave dealer point out?

2. What does this passage tell us about the way Romans regarded the people they enslaved?

Jerusalem

LANGUAGE NOTE 2: PREPOSITIONS

1.   Study the following sentences:

Sabīna per urbem festīnat.
Sabina hurries through the city.

Rūfīna ē popīnā currit.
Rufina runs out of the bar.

Mānius est prope fontem.
Manius is near the fountain.

familia dē cellā dēscendit.
The family comes down from their room.

Words such as **per** (*through*), **prope** (*near*), **ē** (*from, out of*), and **dē** (*from, down from*) are known as **prepositions**.

2.   Some prepositions, such as **per** and **prope**, are followed by the accusative case; others, such as **dē** and **ē**, are followed by the ablative case.

3.   You have already met the following prepositions:

Prepositions + accusative		Prepositions + ablative	
ad	*to, towards*	**ā, ab**	*by, from*
apud	*at the house of, among*	**cum**	*with*
in	*into, onto*	**dē**	*from, down from*
per	*through*	**ē, ex**	*from, out of*
post	*after, behind*	**in**	*in, on*
prope	*near*	**prō**	*in front of*

4.   Note that the meaning of **in** depends on whether it is followed by the accusative or the ablative case:

Faustus **in viam** ambulat.
Faustus walks into the street.

Faustus **in viā** ambulat.
Faustus walks in the street.

Mosaic from Dougga, Tunisia, showing slaves serving food and drink at a Roman feast.

The life of a slave

It is difficult to imagine what life was like for an enslaved person in the Roman world. Almost all the evidence we have is written by enslavers and shows their point of view. The lives of slaves and the extent of the physical suffering they had to endure varied depending on their masters and the type of work the slaves did. Not all enslaved people worked in a household as Currax, Quartilla, and Lucrio did. In the city, some worked in industry or were public slaves. For example, crews of slaves owned by the state looked after the aqueducts and the water supply or worked in public buildings such as temples. In the countryside, many slaves were agricultural laborers. And in provinces such as Spain and Britain, slaves worked in the mines.

On the farms

Wealthy Romans often had huge estates in the countryside outside Rome and in the provinces. Enslaved people managed and farmed these estates. Columella, in a handbook on agriculture, advised how to treat slaves on an estate:

> All careful masters inspect the slaves in the farm prison, to check whether they are properly chained and whether the building is secure. I reward slaves who are hardworking and obedient. To female slaves who have had children I have given time off from work, and sometimes even freedom after they raised several children.

An educated slave

The Romans admired the cultures of some of the nations they had conquered, especially the Greeks. Enslaved Greeks were often skilled workers, such as teachers, doctors, and librarians. In this letter, Pliny praises a slave and worries about his health:

> Encolpius, my reader and a favorite of mine, is sick. How grim it will be for him and what a bitter blow to me if he is unable to study, since studying is his chief accomplishment. Who will read my books and take such pleasure in them as he does?

Domestic slaves

Slaves working in a household were often the victims of brutality, as Romans believed they had the right to punish their slaves with violence. Some Romans were extremely cruel towards their slaves. Seneca records that Emperor Augustus was having dinner with Vedius Pollio when one of Vedius' slaves broke a crystal cup:

> Vedius ordered the slave to be seized and executed in a particularly bizarre way, by being thrown as food to lampreys – he kept some huge ones in his fish pond. Why did he do this? Just to show off his wealth? It was an act of savagery.

At the other extreme, some Romans felt affection for their slaves. Martial wrote this poem expressing his grief for the death of the home-born slave (*vernula*, little verna) he called Erotion:

> Erotion is still warm on her funeral pyre. The cruel law of the Fates has carried her off, my love, my joy, my delight, with her sixth year not yet complete.

In the mines

The worst conditions for enslaved people were in provinces such as Spain and Britain where they worked in the mines. The historian Diodorus Siculus described the terrible sufferings of the people working in the mines in Spain:

> These men exhaust their bodies by working underground day and night, and the mortality rate is high because of the terrible conditions. They are not allowed to pause or rest – the supervisors beat them to force them to continue working. They throw away their lives as a result of these terrible hardships. Some of them survive because of their physical stamina or willpower, and endure their misery for a long time but, because of the extent of their suffering, they prefer death to life.

QUESTION

Although the conditions of their lives varied, what did all enslaved people have in common?

epistula

in Siciliā, Kalendīs Iūliīs, C. Liciniō C. Laecāniō cōnsulibus.   1

Lūcīlius fīlium Lūcīlium salūtat.

in Siciliā maneō, et prōvinciam administrō. Sicilia nōn est
prōvincia magna, et multōs diēs librōs scrībere possum. multās
hōrās philosophiam, historiam, et epistulās ab amīcīs legō.   5

sed epistulae ab urbe mē ānxium faciunt.

amīcōs habēmus et in urbe et in prōvinciīs. multī mē monent.
quid facit imperātor, et quid vult facere? Nerō aedificāre cupit sed
urbs est plēna. domus nostra est sēcūra?

in temporibus dūrīs vīvimus. imperātor est perīculōsus,   10
perīculōsa est urbs.

lēgātus in Lūsitāniā, nōmine Othō, tribūnum quaerit. tū es iuvenis
sapiēns, et tribūnus optimus esse potes. tē iubeō ab urbe statim
discēdere, et in Lūsitāniam iter facere. Othō Īdibus Augustīs tēcum
convenīre vult.   15

servī et lībertī fidēlēs domum nostram in urbe administrāre
possunt.

valē.

epistula *letter*	ab *from*	iubeō *I order*
cōnsul *consul (leading politician)*	et ... et ... *both ... and ...*	statim *immediately*
prōvincia *province*	moneō *I advise, warn*	iter *journey*
administrō *I manage, administer*	vīvō *I live*	tēcum = cum tē
liber *book*	lēgātus *governor*	lībertus *former slave, freedman*
scrībō *I write*	tribūnus *tribune (officer in the army)*	fidēlis *faithful*
philosophia *philosophy*	sapiēns *wise*	
historia *history*	esse *to be*	

Dates

Kalends: *1st day of the month.*
Ides: *13th or 15th day of the month, depending on the month. In August the Ides were the 13th.*

Romans referred to the year by the names of the two men who were consuls at the time. The consuls held this office for just one year. **Gaius Licinius** and **Gaius Laecanius** were consuls in AD 64.

Lucilius senior

We know about the existence of the older Lucilius through his correspondence with Seneca, the philosopher and adviser to Nero. Their letters are largely about philosophy. In AD 64 Lucilius was governor of the province of Sicily. Lucilius was originally from the Bay of Naples, and he may have written a book on volcanic activity in Sicily called *The Aetna*.

Otho (*below*)

Otho had been a friend of Nero's but the two had fallen out over Nero's desire to marry Otho's wife, Poppaea. After Poppaea and Otho's divorce, Otho was sent to Lusitania to govern the province, and Poppaea became the new empress of Rome.

Roman letters: epistulae

Romans did not have paper. They usually wrote their letters on papyrus, a material made from reeds grown in Egypt. A well-off man like Lucilius senior probably dictated his letters to a slave. Once the letter was written the papyrus was rolled into a scroll and sealed with wax. Then a slave or freedman took his letters to their recipients across the Empire, to ensure their safe arrival.

Most Latin letters had the same format as modern letters:

1. **date of writing**
   Particularly relevant as post could take a long time to arrive.

2. **a greeting**
   More or less formal, depending on whom one wrote to. What might seem unusual to us is that the greeting might be written in the third person: 'Lucilius greets his son,' rather than 'Dear Lucilius.'

   Other examples:

   ◊ **Sabīna salūtem plūrimam dīcit.**
   Sabina sends many greetings.

   ◊ **sī valēs bene est. ego valeō.**
   (can be abbreviated to: *SVBEEV*)
   If you are well, it is good. I am well.

3. **a farewell**
   There were a number of standard phrases to end a letter, and they could be formal or affectionate.

   Commonly used were:

   ◊ **valē**   *goodbye, be well*
   ◊ **optimē valē**   *be very well*
   ◊ **cūrā ut valeās**   *take care that you are well*

QUESTIONS

1. On which day was the letter written? (line 1)
2. a. Who is writing the letter?
   b. Where is he sending it from?
   c. Who is he writing to?
3. What does Lucilius senior's life seem like, according to the first paragraph of his letter? (lines 3–5)
4. What concerns does Lucilius senior have? (lines 6–11)
5. What is meant to happen on the Ides of August? (lines 14–15)

EXTENSION ACTIVITY

6. Investigate the speed at which letters and people could travel in the Roman world.

fuga: pars secunda

Thellus et Galliō per cloācam currunt. subitō Galliō cadit. servus surgere nōn potest. capiunt eum canēs. Galliō frūstrā pugnāre temptat. fīnis est. servus effugere nōn potest.

procul Thellus comitem vocat. nēmō respondet. servus ē cloācā festīnat et in flūmen salit.

in carcere, custōdēs servum torquent.

'ubi est Thellus?' postulat custōs.

'Thellus est mortuus,' Galliō susurrat.

'Thellus nōn est mortuus. ubi est?' custōs iterum postulat.

'mortuus est,' inquit Galliō. 'corpus in flūmine est.'

'mendāx es,' respondet custōs.

custōdēs servum duās hōrās torquent. tertiā hōrā, custōdēs cautērium ē fornāce extrahunt. cautērium ad Galliōnem portant et caput notant. dolor est intolerābilis. in capite sunt trēs litterae.

trēs diēs et trēs noctēs, Thellus fugit. quārtō diē servus in agrō dormit. hōrā prīmā, duo agricolae eum vident. agricolae Thellum capiunt et eum ad custōdēs dūcunt. custōdēs rīdent. Thellus perterritus est.

frūstrā *in vain, without success*	
procul *far off*	
comes *companion, comrade*	5
in (+ acc.) *into*	
flūmen *river*	
carcer *prison*	
torqueō *I torture*	
postulō *I demand*	
corpus *body*	10
tertius *third*	
cautērium *branding iron*	
extrahō *I pull out*	
notō *I mark*	
dolor *pain*	15
intolerābilis *unbearable*	
littera *letter*	
fugiō *I flee*	
quārtus *fourth*	
ager *field*	
agricola *farmer*	

Marble relief from Smyrna, in modern Turkey. The two men on the right have been enslaved. They are in chains connected by neck collars.

Seeking freedom

You have as many enemies as you have slaves.

This Roman proverb is quoted by Seneca. He tells us that the Senate discussed whether all slaves should be dressed in the same way. The senators rejected the proposal, because they feared what would happen if slaves recognized how great their numbers were.

Slave revolts

Large-scale slave rebellions were rare, but when they occurred they could be serious. There were three major slave revolts in the second and first centuries BC. These revolts occurred not in Rome itself, but in Sicily and southern Italy. The most famous was one led by Spartacus, which lasted two years, from 73 to 71 BC. Spartacus and some of his fellow slaves escaped from a gladiator school in Capua, where they were being trained to fight as gladiators (men who fought to entertain an audience), and were then joined by slaves from the large farms in the region. The slaves were eventually defeated by forces from the Roman army.

> The slaves continued to resist until all of them were killed, except for 6,000 who were captured and crucified along the road from Capua to Rome. *Appian*

There is no evidence that any of these slave revolts had the aim of abolishing slavery. The aim of the slaves who rebelled may have been to gain freedom for themselves. However, we have no access to the thoughts and motives of Spartacus and his fellow freedom seekers. The only evidence is the writings of the enslavers.

Running away and resistance

On a much smaller scale, slaves put up resistance in their daily lives by working inefficiently, stealing, or other forms of disruption – if they could do so undetected. Many slaves sought freedom by running away. Some slave owners employed professionals to look for slaves who had sought their freedom, or offered rewards for their return. Others relied on religion or friends:

> Nowadays we believe that our Vestal Virgins have the power by their prayers to make runaway slaves stay where they are as long as they have not gone outside the city. *Pliny the Elder*

In one of his letters, Cicero wrote to a friend asking for help in returning a slave who had sought freedom:

> Dionysius, my slave who looked after my very valuable library, has stolen a large number of books. He thought that he would be punished, so he has run away. He is in your province. My friend Marcus Bolanus and many others have seen him at Narona; but he said that he had been freed by me, and they believed him. If you would arrange for this man to be brought back to me, I can't tell you how grateful I shall be to you. It is an unimportant matter in itself; yet my annoyance is serious.

If they were caught, slaves who had tried to gain their freedom by running away risked harsh punishment: branding on the face, wearing a collar, even death, as Tacitus describes:

> The man was asked his identity. As his statement did not ring true and he was recognized by his master as a runaway slave called Geta, he was crucified, the usual manner of execution for slaves.

Some enslaved people were forced to wear metal collars such as this one. The inscription on the tag says:

> *I have run away. Keep me. When you bring me back to my master Zoninus, you will receive a gold coin.*

LANGUAGE NOTE 3: TIME

1.   Study the following sentences. What is the effect of expressing time in the accusative case?

   Sabīna multās hōrās labōrat.
   Sabina works for many hours.

   trēs diēs et trēs noctēs, Thellus fugit.
   For three days and three nights Thellus flees.

   tōtam noctem dormīs.
   You sleep all night.

   When time is given in the accusative case, it tells us **how long** something lasts for.

2.   Now look at these sentences. How does the meaning change when time is expressed in the ablative case?

   mediā nocte familia discēdit.
   The family leaves in the middle of the night.

   hōrā quīntā Faustus clāmōrem audit.
   At the fifth hour Faustus hears a shout.

   tribus diēbus pecūniam exspectō!
   I expect the money in three days.

   When time is given in the ablative case, it tells us **when** something is happening.

LANGUAGE PRACTICE

1.   Change the nouns in bold type from singular to plural, or plural to singular, then translate the new sentence.

   a.   frāter meus semper ad templum sacrum cum **dōnō** advenit.

   b.   fēmina misera cibum in **viā** cum **fīliā** exspectat.

   c.   senātor vīnum cārum cum **sorōribus** bibit.

   d.   cīvēs īrātī ē **forō** fūrēs agitant.

   e.   nēmō rēgēs in **urbibus** vidēre vult.

2.   Translate each sentence into Latin by choosing the correct word or phrase from each pair.

a.   *For three hours you worship the goddess in the forum.*

hōrā tertiā	deam	in forum	nōs	adōrātis.
trēs hōrās	deās	in forō	vōs	adōrāmus.

b.   *On the fourth day my mistress walks slowly down from the Capitoline Hill.*

quattuor diēs	dominus	lentē	prō Capitōliō	ambulat.
diē quārtō	domina	laetē	dē Capitōliō	ambulās.

c.   *The old man sleeps behind the shop for one hour.*

senex	prope tabernam	hōrā prīmā	dormiunt.
senēs	post tabernam	ūnam hōram	dormit.

d.   *We don't want to walk into the bar at the second hour.*

in popīnam	duās hōrās	laudāre	nōlumus.
in popīnā	hōrā secundā	ambulāre	nōn vultis.

e.   *For three days I am staying happily among the Suburani.*

trēs diēs	ā Subūrānīs	laetē	manēs.
diē tertiō	apud Subūrānōs	frūstrā	maneō.

Manumission

If you were a slave you might not have to remain enslaved for life. If you were a hardworking slave in a wealthy household you might have been able to earn or buy your freedom. Manumission was a common practice in ancient Rome. The Latin word *manūmissiō* is formed from *manus* (hand) and *missus* (sent). The literal meaning is 'sending from the hand', i.e. 'setting free from control.'

Often slaves were freed after the death of their owner, if he had put this in his will. Some Roman slaves received a small wage or gifts from their owner and they were able to save up this money and use it to buy their freedom. The owner could then use this money to buy a new slave. After being freed, the former slave became a *lībertus* (freedman) or *līberta* (freedwoman).

Some Romans wrote about giving freedom to their slaves as a reward, and describe the friendly relationships they had with their slaves and freedmen. For example, Cicero received this letter from his brother:

My dear Marcus, I am delighted about Tiro. He was much too good for his position and I am very pleased that you preferred that he should be our friend rather than our slave.

It is important to bear in mind, however, that we have no evidence for what Tiro thought about Cicero and their relationship.

It could be in the owner's interest to free his slaves. The Romans used manumission as an incentive to keep slaves working industriously and obediently. Moreover, often slaves were freed once they had reached an age at which they were less productive or had become sick, so owners no longer had the obligation to provide for them.

Laws were introduced to limit the number of slaves who could be granted their freedom. Romans were allowed to free only a proportion of their slaves, and never more than 100, however many slaves they might own.

Most slaves, however, probably never became free. Those working on the large agricultural estates or in the mines had little chance of manumission.

Theseus and the Minotaur

The ancient Greeks told a story about a mythical king, King Minos, who ruled the Mediterranean island of Crete. His wife gave birth to a son who was part-man, part-bull – the Minotaur.

- Find Crete and Athens on the map on pages 2–3.
- Then read or listen to the myth of Theseus and the Minotaur.

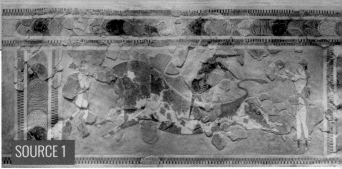

SOURCE 1

An image of a man leaping over a bull, from the palace of Knossos in Crete.

SOURCE 2

A floor plan of the palace of Knossos.

The location

What do Sources 1 and 2 tell us about the palace of Knossos on Crete? Why might a story set at the palace, involving a bull and a labyrinth, have developed?

The Minotaur

Look at Source 3. The Minotaur was part-man, part-bull. Research other creatures from Greek and Roman mythology, and the mythologies of other cultures, which are part-human, part-animal. Why do you think such creatures hold so much interest for us?

SOURCE 3

Roman statue of the Minotaur.

Minoan civilization

Although King Minos was a mythical king, a complex and advanced civilization existed on the island of Crete from about 2700 BC to about 1450 BC. It has been named the 'Minoan civilization' after the mythical king. What can you find out about the civilization? Is it possible that the Minoans really did force Athens, and perhaps other cities, to send hostages every year? Why might the Minoans have required hostages?

Theseus

Look at Source 4. Theseus was the mythical founder of the Greek city of Athens. Why might the Athenians have liked a story about Theseus killing the Minotaur? For the Athenians, what might the Minotaur have symbolized? What else can you discover about Theseus?

Daedalus

Look at Source 5. How is Daedalus connected with the myth of Theseus and the Minotaur? Why did Minos not want to let him go?

SOURCE 4

This Ancient Athenian vase painting shows Theseus killing the Minotaur.

SOURCE 5

Daedalus creates countless winding corridors and is himself hardly able to return to the entrance, so great is the building's deception.

Ovid

RESEARCH

Find out about:
- the mythical King Minos.
- Ariadne (Minos' daughter).
- the role of bulls in sport and culture.
- labyrinths, ancient and modern.

Chapter 7: Londīnium

amīcī

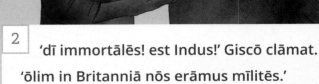

1 Faustus, Giscō et Celer sunt in Forō Boāriō.
subitō Celer lātrat.
Giscō circumspectat et amīcum cōnspicit.

2 'dī immortālēs! est Indus!' Giscō clāmat.
'ōlim in Britanniā nōs erāmus mīlitēs.'

3 Giscō! salvē!
quid tū in urbe agis?

cum Catiā et Celere
in Subūrā habitō.

4 hic est Faustus.
Faustus īnsulam in Subūrā cūrat.

dē Britanniā

1 amīcī in popīnā sedent.
Catia dē Britanniā rem nārrat.

2 ego prope Londīnium cum parentibus habitābam.

3 pater meus erat ferrārius optimus.

5 parentēs gladiōs pulchrōs faciēbant.

4 māter mea erat artifex mīrābilis.

6 cōtīdiē ego trāns pontem ambulābam.
cōtīdiē ego gladiōs in forō vēndēbam.

7 ōlim mīles pontem custōdiēbat.
mīles negōtiātōrēs spectābat.
mīles erat Giscō.

8 frīgidum erat.
tū laenam viridem gerēbās.

9 minimē! calidum erat.
ego stolam russeam gerēbam!!

10 ego cum sorōre ambulābam.

11 minimē!
tū cum patre ambulābās.

Londinium

Soon after the successful invasion of Britannia by the Roman Emperor Claudius in AD 43, the town of Londinium was established. Before the arrival of the Romans there was no settlement there. The area was predominantly pasture and farmland, surrounded by large oak forests, but Londinium was to become the largest city in the new province of Britannia.

Why here?

When Roman troops landed on the south coast, they crossed the River Thames at a narrow point close to the estuary. This became an important gateway to the rest of Britannia. Later a new crossing point was made slightly east, downriver, at a place where ships could dock at high tide to unload. The area, particularly on the south bank of the river, was marshy and liable to flooding; however the two hills on the north bank, Ludgate and Cornhill, were ideal points for building. There was also an abundance of fresh water from the Thames tributaries, such as the Walbrook stream.

Trade

Before the invasion in AD 43, the Britons were already exporting metal, livestock, wool, and cloth to the Roman Empire, and importing food and wine from Gaul. (Gaul is the modern name used for the four provinces of Gallia: Belgica, Lugdunensis, Aquitanica, and Narbonensis.) The Britons lived in tribes, each controlling its own area, and any increase in trading was hampered by the absence of a proper road system, different currencies, and lack of cooperation between the tribes. After the Romans conquered Britannia, they built an impressive network of roads and united the British tribes under a single currency. Importing and exporting increased greatly.

Londinium was originally established around AD 50 as a trading base rather than an adminstrative or military center. The new network of roads connected it to other parts of Britannia. Here the River Thames was deep enough for large ships to sail up from the sea at high tide. This was a cheaper and more efficient way of transporting goods than by land. From Londinium, the goods could then be distributed by road to the rest of Britannia. Native Britons, along with traders and businessmen from across the Empire, moved to Londinium, drawn by the opportunities in the new trading center.

The map on the right shows some features of Londinium in about AD 59, superimposed on a map of modern London.

Bloomberg tablets

About 400 writing tablets (pieces of wood which the Romans wrote on) have been found here, preserved by the waterlogged ground around the Walbrook stream. The tablets are named after the company Bloomberg because they were discovered by archaeologists excavating the site of the company's new building. They tell us about the daily life and trades of the earliest Londoners.

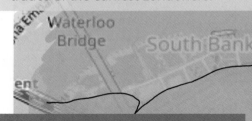

The River Thames was much wider than it is today. At low tide it was about 1,000 feet wide, 3,000 feet at high tide. It is about 300 feet today at low tide.

North and South

The south bank of the river was a marshy swamp that would be partly underwater at high tide. Roman Londinium was built mostly on the northern bank, but there were some smaller settlements on the south, possibly occupied by local Britons.

Buildings

Native Britons lived in round huts, built using a technique called wattle and daub. This involved constructing wooden frames and filling in the walls with earth and clay. The roofs were thatched with dried grass or reeds.

The first buildings in Roman Londinium were rectangular in shape. There was no local stone so they were built using the same materials as native British huts. They were made quickly, as the town expanded rapidly. The remains of a group of round and rectangular buildings have been found near the Walbrook stream, at Gresham Street.

Temporary fort

Although Londinium was not a military base, there was probably a small garrison of Roman troops in a temporary wooden fort on Cornhill.

The bridge

It is not known when the first bridge was built across the Thames. Evidence for a wooden bridge has been found by archaeologists on the north bank of the river, near modern-day London Bridge, and has been dated to around AD 85–90. Since Londinium grew rapidly as a trading settlement after the invasion of AD 43, it is likely that there was an earlier wooden bridge in a similar location.

Timeline

AD

43 Successful invasion of Britannia by Emperor Claudius.

60 Londinium destroyed by fire and rebuilt as a planned town, north and south of river.

70 Large stone forum, basilica, and amphitheater constructed.

100 Londinium replaces Camulodunum as capital of Britannia.

120 The great second forum built.

122 Emperor Hadrian visits Londinium.

190 The Romans construct a defensive wall around Londinium.

Surviving section of the city of London Roman wall.

Made in Londinium

The population of the newly established town of Londinium was mixed. The largest group would have been the local native Britons, but there were also the Roman soldiers stationed in the town and an influx of traders and craftsmen attracted by the new opportunities. It is likely that many were from Gaul, but merchants could have come from further away. Within a few decades Londinium had become a cosmopolitan city, the home of skilled craftsmen and a center of trade and exchange.

Glass

Excavations at a house on Gresham Street recovered a workshop which made glass beads. These were made by melting recycled Roman glass, but using traditional British methods, and their color and design are typical of beads produced in Britannia before the Roman conquest.

dābes lūniō cupariō contrā Catullu

You will give [this] to Junius the cooper, opposite [the house of] Catullus.

This is one of the Bloomberg tablets. It gives us an insight into the sorts of job early Londoners might have had. A cooper made wooden barrels which were used instead of amphorae to transport wine and other liquids.

Wool and clothes

After the Roman conquest, wool processing took place on a much larger scale. Spinning and weaving were probably still done at home or in small workshops. Woolen cloth was a British speciality and was dyed using locally available plants such as madder (red), whortleberry or blueberry (blue/purple), woad (blue), or elderberry (gray/purple).

Metalwork and jewelry

Britannia was a rich source of raw metals – gold, silver, iron, lead, and tin – all of which were in high demand across the Roman Empire. Britons were already exporting these materials before the Roman invasion, but the Romans greatly increased the scale of mining.

*This iron stamp was used to mark ingots of metal. It is engraved with the letters MPBR, which is thought to stand for **Metalla Prōvinciae Britanniae**: 'the mines of the province of Britannia.' It shows how the Romans exploited Britannia's raw resources on an industrial scale, to be exported to other parts of the Empire.*

The native Britons were skilled in metalwork before the arrival of the Romans. In Londinium some jewelry was still made in a traditional British style, like the brooch in the shape of a hunting dog on the facing page. This intaglio (*below*), an engraved stone for a ring, shows the winged horse Pegasus. It was probably made by a skilled immigrant jeweler.

- Who do you think this jewelry was made for?

Leather

Evidence for leatherworking has survived well in the waterlogged ground in the Walbrook area of Londinium. Archaeologists have found not only intricately-cut leather shoes (*below*), but also scraps of cut leather and leatherworking tools. It is likely that leatherworking was originally practiced in Londonium by skilled immigrant craftsmen.

LANGUAGE NOTE 1: IMPERFECT TENSE

1. Can you spot the difference between these pairs of sentences?

    Catia gladium portat.
    Catia is carrying a sword.

    Catia gladium portābat.
    Catia was carrying a sword.

    And again in these examples?

    nōs prope Londīnium habitāmus.
    We live near London.

    nōs prope Londīnium habitābāmus.
    We used to live near London.

    What is the difference in the form of the Latin verbs? How does that difference affect the meaning of the verbs?

2. The **-ba-** in the ending of the Latin verb indicates that the action was taking place in the past, and was happening for some time. This form of the verb is known as the **imperfect tense**.

3. Look at the imperfect tense of the Latin verb **vocō** (*I call*):

vocābam	*I was calling, used to call*
vocābās	*you* (singular) *were calling, used to call*
vocābat	*he/she/it was calling, used to call*
vocābāmus	*we were calling, used to call*
vocābātis	*you* (plural) *were calling, used to call*
vocābant	*they were calling, used to call*

    Note that the very end of the verb (**-m**, **-s**, **-t**, **-mus**, **-tis**, **-nt**) tells us *who* was carrying out the action and the **-ba-** tells us *when* they were doing it.

4. Now compare these two sentences:

    māter mea est artifex.
    My mother is an artist.

    māter mea erat artifex.
    My mother was an artist.

5. The imperfect tense of **sum** (*I am*) is as follows:

eram	*I was, used to be*
erās	*you* (singular) *were, used to be*
erat	*he/she/it was, used to be*
erāmus	*we were, used to be*
erātis	*you* (plural) *were, used to be*
erant	*they were, used to be*

Brooch in the shape of a hunting dog. You can still see traces of colored enamel.

Celer

in popīnā Celer prope Giscōnem sedēbat. canis cicātrīcem lambēbat.

'cūr Celer cicātrīcem habet, Giscō?' rogāvit Currāx. 'cicātrix ē vulnere est?'

Giscō rem nārrāvit: 5

'ingēns aper in silvīs prope Londīnium habitābat. agricolae Britannicī dē aprō erant ānxiī, quod aper in agrīs currēbat et frūgēs dēlēbat. aper vīcōs quoque intrābat et animālia petēbat. Britannī aprum necāre cupiēbant.

'tum agricolae mē ad vēnātiōnem invītāvērunt. Indus quoque   10
aderat. nōs duo equitābāmus et vēnābula portābāmus. Britannī ad vēnātiōnem ambulābant et canēs dūcēbant. ūnus ē canibus erat Celer. mox silvās intrāvimus, ubi aper habitābat. agricolae magnum clāmōrem tollēbant et canēs vehementer lātrābant.

'subitō fragōrem audīvimus. aper aderat et ad Britannōs   15
currēbat. Indus vēnābulum in aprum iactāvit, sed aper vēnābulum vītāvit. equus meus erat perterritus et calcitrābat. ego ad terram praecipitāvī. dē vītā dēspērāvī. ingēns aper nunc mē petēbat.

'sed canēs Britannicī sunt fortēs. ad aprum currēbant. dux erat   20
Celer. postquam Celer aprum petīvit, aper eum vulnerāvit. tum canēs aprum superāvērunt. Celer mē servāvit.'

cicātrīx *scar*

vulnus *wound*

ingēns *huge*
aper *boar*
frūx *crop*
dēleō *I destroy*
vīcus *settlement*
petō *I attack*
tum *then*
vēnātiō *hunt*
invītō *I invite*
equitō *I ride*
vēnābulum *hunting spear*
Britannī *Britons*
fragor *crash, noise*
iactō *I throw*
vītō *I avoid*
calcitrō *I kick out*
terra *ground*
praecipitō *I fall*
dēspērō *I despair*
fortis *brave*
dux *leader*
postquam *after*
vulnerō *I wound*
superō *I overpower*
servō *I save*

Section from the Little Hunt mosaic, in Sicily.

frūctus mīrābilis

Catia rem nārrat.

ōlim in oppidō cum sorōre, nōmine Aucissā, ambulābam. in forō erāmus quod cibum quaerēbāmus. multī īnstitōrēs cibum mīrābilem vēndēbant. ūnus īnstitor appropinquāvit.

'ecce menta et cucumerēs!' īnstitor clāmābat. 'ecce prūna et māla! vōs puellae cunīculōs anteā spectāvistis?'   5

'certē, īnstitor!' Aucissa clāmāvit. 'sed mālum nōn gustāvī.'

'quid?' īnstitor rogāvit. 'tū mālum nōn gustāvistī? mālum est frūctus dulcissimus!'

tandem ē forō ambulāvimus. Aucissa mentam et multa māla in sportā portābat. prope pontem popīna sordida erat, ubi nautae tōtum diem lūdēbant et bibēbant. mīles pontem custōdiēbat, et prope popīnam stābat. mīles erat Giscō. ingēns nauta Hispānus, postquam Aucissam spectāvit, vehementer clāmāvit, 'ohē, puella! quid in sportā portās?' omnēs nautae rīdēbant.   10 ... 15

'vidēre vīs?' ego clāmāvī. tum ego mālum in nautam vehementer iactāvī, sed nauta mālum vītāvit. Giscō mālum nōn vītāvit. mālum mīlitem vulnerāvit. sanguis ē nāsō effluēbat.

ego valdē timēbam, quod mīlitem Rōmānum vulnerāvī. sed mīles rīdēbat. 'cavē, puella! mālum est frūctus perīculōsus!'   20

Aucissa quoque rīdēbat, et 'cavē, mīles, soror mea est perīculōsa!' clāmāvit.

frūctus	*fruit*
oppidum	*town*
īnstitor	*vendor, peddler*
menta	*mint*
cucumis	*cucumber*
prūnum	*plum*
mālum	*apple*
cunīculus	*rabbit*
anteā	*before*
gustō	*I taste*
dulcissimus	*very sweet*
sporta	*basket*
nauta	*sailor*
Hispānus	*Spanish*
nāsus	*nose*
effluō	*I flow*
valdē	*very*

Heavy goods and liquids, including wine and olive oil, were transported in amphorae. These were large pottery containers with two handles, a narrow neck, and a bottom tapering to a point. The spike on the bottom was useful as a third handle for lifting or pouring. A cork or stopper made of fired clay was used to plug the mouth; this was then sealed with mortar. Many of these amphorae were stamped with names or symbols which identify the pottery workshop or its owner. Sometimes the mortar seal was stamped with the name of the merchant. Details of the contents were sometimes painted on the amphora. Many shipwrecks carrying amphorae have been found by archaeologists.

Food

The Romans brought to Britannia new foods and new methods of cooking and farming. Some of the foodstuffs taken for granted in Britain today were introduced by the Romans.

Pre-Roman diet

Native Britons had a simple diet, consisting mainly of bread, a kind of porridge made from grains, vegetables, wild native fruits, and some dairy products. This was supplemented by a little meat and, in some areas, fish. Cattle, sheep, goats, pigs, geese, and hens were kept on farms and the main crops grown were wheat, oats, barley, and rye. Barley was used for brewing beer. Pliny the Elder said that roast goose was 'the richest dish known to the Britons.' Cattle also provided dairy products – milk, cheese, and butter. Romans did not eat butter: they used olive oil for cooking. Honey was used as a sweetener.

Hunting was a popular sport, so the diet included meat such as wild boar, venison, and possibly hare. British hunting dogs were valued so much that they were exported to Rome.

Terracotta cup showing a hunting scene with a stag.

Roman food and drink

For the majority of Britons, especially those outside the towns, there was little change in this simple diet. However, even the lower classes would have benefited from the introduction of a wide range of vegetables and fruits. The upper classes were more influenced by the Roman way of life, and they could afford to eat and drink imported foods.

Even before the invasion, Britons had been importing goods from the nearest parts of the Roman Empire, including wine from Gaul and Italy. After AD 43 trade with the rest of the Roman Empire increased. There was a demand for imported food from Romans who had settled in Britannia, and from the British elite who wanted to show off their status by adopting a Roman way of life.

Introduced by the Romans

Some of the most common fruits and vegetables eaten today in Britain were introduced by the Romans, including onions, turnips, leeks, cabbages, lettuce, peas, and lentils. The only apple growing in Britannia before the conquest was the crab apple. The Romans introduced varieties of eating apple, as well as other fruit and nut trees, including cherry, walnut, and sweet chestnut. Romans were very fond of flavoring their food with herbs, and they brought to Britannia parsley, mint, thyme, garlic, rosemary, sage, and many other herbs.

Animals brought to Britannia by the Romans include pheasant, peacock, guinea fowl, a new breed of sheep, and perhaps even rabbits. Archaeologists have found a rabbit bone at Fishbourne palace on the south coast of Britain, which has been carbon dated to the first century AD.

Documents written in ink on thin sheets of alder wood, dating from about AD 100, have been found at Vindolanda, a military camp near Hadrian's Wall in northern England. They include lists of supplies and requests for food, like this shopping list:

… 20 liters of beans, 20 chickens, 100 apples (if you can find any nice ones), 100 or 200 eggs (if they are a good price), 5 liters of fish sauce, 10 liters of olives.

There are also letters mentioning goat's milk, salt, young pig, ham, corn, venison, flour, and pepper. A record of food supplies issued to soldiers includes barley, beer, wine, vinegar, olive oil, and lard.

Oysters

One favorite food the Romans did not have to import was shellfish, especially oysters. Oysters from the British coast were famous. They were so popular that they may have been transported inland live in tanks. Archaeologists have found large quantities of oyster shells on Roman sites.

Trade routes

Heavy goods were transported, as far as possible, by ship. However, sea voyages were dangerous and ships hugged the coast, avoiding the open sea. In the western Empire, navigable rivers such as the Rhône in France were used to take goods from southern France, Italy, or Spain to Britain. The alternative route from Spain around the west coast was longer and more dangerous, and usable only in summer.

The River Rhine was directly opposite the Thames estuary, so it was a good route for carrying goods between Britain and Gaul and Germany.

Olives and olive oil

Olives and olive oil were imported from the Mediterranean, especially southern Spain and North Africa. Broken amphorae have been found at Canterbury.

Fish sauce

Fish sauce (*garum*) was an essential ingredient in lots of Roman dishes. It was similar to the fish sauce used in Vietnamese and Thai cooking today (*nam pla*). Garum was so important that it was made on an industrial scale in many towns in the Empire. Archaeologists have found amphorae for bottling garum near the Roman docks in Londinium, along with traces of the sprats and herring from which it was made.

Recipe: *Put fish guts or small whole fish in a pot and mix with salt. Leave the pot in the sun to ferment for up to two months, shaking it frequently. Strain off the resulting liquid, store it in an amphora, and seal.*

Spices

Some exotic spices were imported from outside the Empire. Pepper came from India, cinnamon from East Africa, and ginger from Southeast Asia.

Dates

Dates were imported from the eastern Empire. Remains of charred dates have been found at St Albans.

Wine

vīta vīnum est   Life is wine.   *Petronius*

Wine was an important part of Roman culture, and the Britons adopted the Roman love of wine. The wine trade predated the Roman invasion. Archaeologists have found evidence of wine across Britain. Wine was imported from Italy, Spain, and southern France.

QUESTION

What different types of evidence do historians use to find out about life in Roman Britain?

LANGUAGE NOTE 2: PERFECT TENSE

1. Earlier in the chapter we met sentences like these, where the verb is in the imperfect tense:

    ego cum sorōre ambulābam.
    I was walking with my sister.

    mīles pontem custōdiēbat.
    The soldier was guarding the bridge.

2. We have now met sentences such as these:

    ego mīlitem Rōmānum vulnerāvī.
    I wounded a Roman soldier.

    nauta vehementer clāmāvit.
    The sailor shouted loudly.

    subitō nōs fragōrem audīvimus.
    Suddenly we heard a crash.

    The verbs in these sentences are in the **perfect tense**, which is often indicated by **-v-** in the ending.

3. Both the imperfect tense and the perfect tense indicate that the action took place in the past. How would you describe the difference between the meaning of the two tenses?

4. Look at the way the perfect tense of **vocō** (*I call*) is formed:

vocāvī	*I called, have called*
vocāvistī	*you* (singular) *called, have called*
vocāvit	*he/she/it called, has called*
vocāvimus	*we called, have called*
vocāvistis	*you* (plural) *called, have called*
vocāvērunt	*they called, have called*

5. Finally, compare the forms of **vocō** in the following sentences:

Present	**Catia Giscōnem vocat.**	*Catia calls Gisco.*
Imperfect	**Catia Giscōnem vocābat.**	*Catia was calling Gisco.*
Perfect	**Catia Giscōnem vocāvit**.	*Catia called Gisco.*

The Iron Age Britons kept sheep similar to this one, a Soay sheep from the island of Soay off the west coast of Scotland. The Romans introduced a new breed of sheep which was hornless, white-faced, and with short wool.

LANGUAGE PRACTICE

1.   Fill each gap using a verb from the box. Then translate each sentence.

bibēbam	accipiēbant	portābāmus	audiēbātis
tenēbās	vēndēbat	adōrābant	gerēbat

   a. cōtīdiē nōs dōna ad templa pulchra ....

   b. vōs maximam turbam in urbe Londīniō ....

   c. soror vestīmenta nova .... et gladiōs in forō ....

   d. tū multum cibum .... , et ego vīnum cārum ....

   e. cīvēs fidēlēs magna praemia .... , quod deōs Rōmānōs ....

2.   Add the missing endings to the verbs to match the English translations.

   a. Catia rem mīrābilem dē vītā in Britanniā nārrāv... .
   Catia told an amazing story about life in Britannia.

   b. postquam nōs clāmōrēs audīv... , in viam ambulāv... .
   After we heard the shouts, we walked into the street.

   c. cūr tū frātrēs tuōs hodiē vituperāv... ?
   Why did you criticize your brothers today?

   d. parvae ancillae fūrem īnfēlīcem celeriter superāv... .
   The small slaves quickly overpowered the unfortunate thief.

   e. ego lentē appropinquāv... et equōs in agrō spectāv... .
   I approached slowly and looked at the horses in the field.

   f. cūr vōs per iānuam nōn festīnāv... , postquam fūrem audīv... ?
   Why didn't you hurry through the door, after you heard the thief?

Section of a mosaic from Conimbriga, Portugal.

Romans invading

The Roman Empire was made up of a political center, Italy, and a periphery of territories called provinces. These provinces had been acquired by Rome over the centuries, some by peaceful means, but the majority by military conquest.

Romans invaded other lands for a range of reasons. For individual commanders or emperors, military victories brought great glory, and often vast personal wealth, as they stole others' possessions for themselves. For the Roman state, conquering territory meant it took control of the people, property, and resources of the area. Many of the people who suffered invasion were then enslaved and sold; those who weren't enslaved were required to pay tax to the Romans. The mineral resources of the invaded territory often included metals, such as gold, silver, iron, and tin, which were both useful and valuable. All of this, combined with other resources such as crops, animals, and timber, amounted to a huge source of income and benefit for Rome.

Background to the invasion of Britain

Claudius was not the first Roman to consider invading Britain. Almost 100 years earlier, Julius Caesar had twice invaded the island (in 55 and 54 BC). However, he and his troops did not stay. Instead, after a series of battles, and having become the first Roman general to lead troops to the largely unknown and mysterious island, he established peace treaties with tribes in the south, and returned to Gaul. Emperor Augustus planned invasions on three separate occasions, but twice events elsewhere in the Empire took precedence, and on the other occasion the Britons appeared ready to make peace. Caligula, too, had made preparations for an invasion, but did not see them through.

Why were the Romans so ambivalent about invading Britain? The ancient historian Strabo, writing at least twenty years before Claudius' invasion, may provide part of the answer. He states that the Britons paid so much money to trade with the Roman Empire, and submitted to Roman influence so easily, that there was little point invading and securing the island: 'some of the British chieftains have made the whole island almost Roman property and the cost of funding our army would outweigh the money that would be gained.' Strabo also noted that violent opposition might be created if the Romans used military force.

So why did Claudius decide to invade? The first two emperors, Augustus and Tiberius, had been proficient military commanders and expanded the Empire significantly. The third emperor, the short-lived Caligula, had been brought up in a military camp. So when Claudius (the fourth emperor) came to power, he knew that a military conquest would be a vital way of displaying his own power.

We know that the British tribes sometimes cooperated with one another, and sometimes fought each other to obtain land, wealth, slaves, and political power. In times of conflict they would ask their neighbors, including the Romans, for help. It so happened that Verica, the leader of a British tribe, was expelled from Britain during an uprising. He appealed to Rome for support. This presented Claudius with a perfect excuse to invade.

The invasion of Britain

In AD 43, two years after becoming emperor, Claudius sent an invading force to Britain, consisting of four legions, under the supreme command of Aulus Plautius. A commander called Vespasian (who years later himself became emperor) was in charge of the Second Legion. The invading Roman army was organized into three sections, landing in different parts of southern Britain in order to divide the British defense.

It took the Romans some time to bring the enemy to battle: the Britons took refuge in swamps, hoping the Romans would run out of provisions and leave. However, Plautius persevered and, with the arrival of Claudius in the final days of the conflict, eventually defeated the Britons in a series of battles. Before the end of the year, the Romans captured the capital of the Catuvellauni, Camulodunum, which they then used as their first capital of Britain. With Camulodunum in Roman hands and south-east Britain secured, Claudius could claim his victory. This first phase of the conquest consolidated Roman power over the southern corner of Britain. However, it would take the Romans a lifetime to extend their control across the island, and work on Hadrian's Wall would not be started for almost eighty years.

vēnī vīdī vīcī – I came, I saw, I conquered. The Roman general Julius Caesar said this after his victory in Pontus (in modern Turkey).

Chapter 8: Britannia

Some British tribes lived in hill forts, settlements of round huts surrounded by ditches and high banks, like this one at Maiden Castle in Dorset, in southern England.

gladius

ēheu!

1 ōlim cum patre labōrābam.
pater gladium faciēbat. māter intrāvit.

2 gladius optimus abest, Catia! tū gladium vīdistī?

3 cūr soror tua discessit?

4 ego attonita eram.

ego ē vīcō cucurrī et sorōrem quaesīvī.

5 tandem Aucissam prope flūmen invēnī.

6 soror lacrimābat.

14 dēsiste!

13 tum tōtam rem intellēxī.

sed Luccus nōn dēstitit.

15 cum Luccō pugnāvī et gladium capere temptāvī.

16 sed Luccus ad amīcōs gladium iactāvit.

17

18 Luccum superāvī et sine gladiō ad parentēs dūxī.

duo amīcī nunc gladium habuērunt.
cum gladiō trāns pontem cucurrērunt.

LANGUAGE NOTE 1: PERFECT TENSE (CONTINUED)

1. In the last chapter, you saw that the perfect tense is often indicated by -**v**- in the ending of the verb. For example:

Present tense	Perfect tense
ego sorōrem quaerō.	**ego sorōrem quaesīvī.**
I am looking for my sister.	*I looked for my sister.*
māter intrat.	**māter intrāvit.**
My mother comes in.	*My mother came in.*
iuvenēs Aucissam salūtant.	**iuvenēs Aucissam salūtāvērunt.**
The young men are greeting Aucissa.	*The young men greeted Aucissa.*

2. Now study these sentences:

Present tense	Perfect tense
ego ē vīcō currō.	**ego ē vīcō cucurrī.**
I am running out of the settlement.	*I ran out of the settlement.*
soror tua discēdit.	**soror tua discessit.**
Your sister is leaving.	*Your sister has left.*
amīcī gladium habent.	**amīcī gladium habuērunt.**
The friends have a sword.	*The friends had a sword.*
māter et pater gladium faciunt.	**māter et pater gladium fēcērunt.**
Mother and father are making a sword.	*Mother and father made a sword.*

3. While some Latin verbs use -**v**- to form their perfect tense, some use -**u**- and others form their perfect tense by changing in different ways.

4. When you look up a verb in the dictionary, you are given three parts. For example:

   vocō, vocāre, vocāvī   *call*
   discēdō, discēdere, discessī *leave*

   The first part is the present tense (*I do something*), the second part is the infinitive (*to do something*) and the third part is the perfect tense (*I did something*).

   If you are not sure whether the form of a verb is present or perfect, look up the verb in the dictionary to check.

This Iron Age sword and scabbard were found in the River Thames. The sword is made of iron and the scabbard of bronze. Most British warriors would not have been able to afford a sword.

Britannia

Britain in the Late Iron Age
(800 BC–AD 43)

Archaeologists call the period before the Romans conquered Britain the Iron Age, because tools and weapons made of iron were used. In Iron Age Britain people lived in tribes, each tribe having its own land. At the head of most tribes there was a king or queen. Below them were chieftains, who controlled smaller areas within the tribal region. Some tribes lived in family groups in villages and farms scattered about the countryside. Others had settlements known as hill forts: a hill fort was a collection of round huts on top of a hill, surrounded by ditches and high banks.

By the time of the Roman invasion in AD 43, some tribes in the south and south-east had formed sprawling settlements as centers for commerce and industry, such as minting coins, metalworking, and pottery manufacture. But these were not towns in the Roman or the modern sense. There were no permanent stone structures, no public and administrative areas and buildings. Soon after the invasion, the Romans began to unify Britain by building towns linked by a network of roads. As you have seen in Chapter 7, Londinium grew quickly into a commercial center on a site that had not been an Iron Age settlement. Some other towns were developed in a more organized way. The Romans divided the province of Britain into areas (*cīvitātēs*), so that they could administer it more efficiently. These areas were based on tribal districts. Each *cīvitās* had a capital town, which was the center of the regional government. These towns were often on, or near, the sites of Iron Age tribal centers or settlements. Other towns grew up around the sites of Roman forts, and a few were built as settlements for retired Roman soldiers (veterans); these were called colonies (*colōniae*).

Celts

The people living in Iron Age Britain before the Roman conquest are sometimes now called Celts. The term 'Celtic' is used also of other peoples of northern Europe and their culture. The main thing these societies had in common is that they spoke a Celtic language. They also shared some cultural and religious practices, and they had a distinctive artistic style. Celtic art used curved and spiral patterns, and stylized depictions of animals were common. You can see some examples of art in the Celtic style on pages 110 and 111.

What was a legion?

The Roman army was divided into units called legions. Under the Empire, there were between twenty-five and thirty-five legions (the number varied), with about 5,000 infantry in each, and 120 cavalry. Each legion was commanded by a legate (*lēgātus*). Below him were six officers called military tribunes (*tribūnī mīlitum*).

Road network

The Roman army successfully defeated a British force at Camulodunum. Then the army divided: Legion II went south-west; Legion IX went north towards Lindum; Legion XIV and part of XX went north-west; the rest of Legion XX remained in base at Camulodunum.

As the invading legions progressed, they built straight, paved roads. These roads allowed the troops to move quickly. The road network joined major ports on the coast with army camps and Roman towns inland, so that it was easy to bring supplies.

Mona
(Anglesey)

DEMETAE

DUMNONII

Ictis

The British tribes and Rome

Even before the Roman invasion, life in the different British tribes varied greatly. Some lived in remote hill forts in the mountains. Others, like the Catuvellauni, Trinovantes, and Cantiaci, had close contact with Gaul and were influenced by the Roman world. Unlike most of the people of Iron Age Britain, these tribes cremated their dead, drank wine, and used coins. After initial resistance to the Roman invasion, some tribes, particularly in the south-east, quickly accepted Roman rule and began to adopt a Roman lifestyle, building large towns on the Roman model.

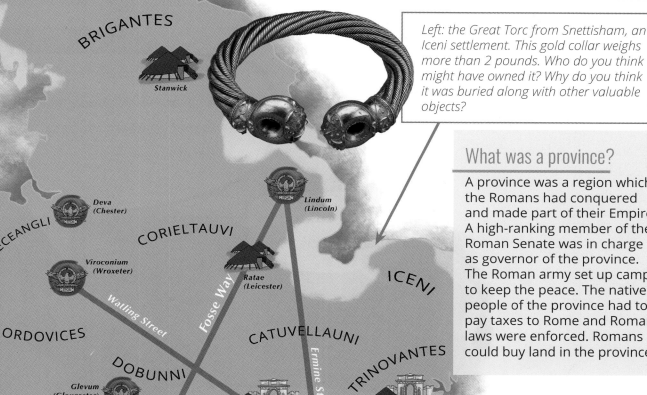

Left: the Great Torc from Snettisham, an Iceni settlement. This gold collar weighs more than 2 pounds. Who do you think might have owned it? Why do you think it was buried along with other valuable objects?

What was a province?

A province was a region which the Romans had conquered and made part of their Empire. A high-ranking member of the Roman Senate was in charge as governor of the province. The Roman army set up camps to keep the peace. The native people of the province had to pay taxes to Rome and Roman laws were enforced. Romans could buy land in the provinces.

Key

Iron Age settlement

Iron Age hill fort settlement

Settlement that developed into a Roman town

New Roman town

Roman fort

This map shows some of the main features of the province of Britannia in AD 60.

Luccus I

simulatque ad vīcum vēnimus, parentēs vocāvī et tōtam rem nārrāvī. postquam parentēs rem audīvērunt, attonitī erant. tum māter Luccum dē gladiō rogāvit. prīmō Luccus nihil dīxit, sed tandem respondit.

simulatque *as soon as*

5   prīmō *at first*

1   ad casam vēnī, quod gladiōs vidēre cupiēbam. Aucissa aderat ...

2   quid? tū aderās, Aucissa?

3   ita vērō, māter. aderam. sed gladium trādere nōlēbam. eum cēpit Luccus.

4   quid respondēs, iuvenis?

5   pater meus gladium cupīvit. veterānum Rōmānum occīdere vult.

casa *cottage*
occīdō *I kill*

II

postquam nōs omnēs eum audīvimus, maximē timēbāmus.

pater   hercle! pater tuus est īnsānus!

Luccus   minimē, senex. pater erat agricola prope Camulodūnum. cum
meīs frātribus patrem in agrīs adiuvābam. tum veterānī ad
vīcum nostrum vēnērunt. animālia ex agrīs trāxērunt et casās   5
incendērunt. tōtum vīcum dēlēvērunt, quod colōniam aedificāre
volēbant. frāter minor erat fortissimus et veterānōs petīvit. sed
ūnus ē veterānīs frātrem occīdit.

trahō	*I pull, drag*
colōnia	*colony*
minor	*younger*

ibi	*there*
opprimō	*I crush,*
	overwhelm
paucī	*few*

māter   ēheu! certē Rōmānī Britannōs ibi maximē opprimēbant. sed in
oppidō Londīniō sunt paucī mīlitēs Rōmānī.   10

pater   cum Rōmānīs nōs Britannī multum negōtium agimus.

Luccus   quam stultī estis! Camulodūnum vīdistis? Rōmānī arcum in
colōniā aedificāvērunt. in summō arcū est statua. statua est
Claudius imperātor. ingēns templum in mediā colōniā aedificant.
in templō est alia statua. quoque est Claudius. gentēs Britannicās   15
opprimunt Rōmānī! Britannōs līberāre volō!

quam!	*how!*
stultus	*stupid*
summus	*top (of)*
statua	*statue*
alius	*another*
gēns	*people, race*
līberō	*I free, set free*

Luccus ē vīcō ad pontem cucurrit. perterritissima eram.

Camulodunum: Britain's first city

When Emperor Claudius invaded Britain in AD 43, the Roman army pushed back the opposing forces of King Caratacus to his stronghold at Camulodunum. There the Britons were decisively defeated. Then Claudius himself arrived in triumph, leading a force that included elephants. The Romans destroyed the Iron Age fortification and made Camulodunum the capital of their new province.

Army camp to colonia

A large fortress was built immediately. This housed the Twentieth Legion for the first years after the invasion. As the years went on, the legion left, and the fortress was transformed into a town with Roman-style buildings. This was the first time brick buildings were constructed in Britain. The town became a *colōnia*, a settlement for veteran soldiers. The veterans were given land at the end of their service in the Roman legions. The Roman historian Tacitus wrote:

> A colony with a large unit of veterans was established at Camulodunum on territory which had been conquered. This would act as a defense against rebellion and would be a way of making the allies respect our laws.

Some local people were forced off their land to make room for the arrival of large numbers of ex-soldiers. Others, however, found employment in the Roman town and lived in settlements in the surrounding area.

Triumphal architecture

At one end of the town, a large triumphal arch was constructed to commemorate Claudius' victory over the Britons. It was probably similar to the arch Catia and Gisco passed through when they arrived in Rome; this arch commemorated the same victory (see Chapter 2). At the top of the arch in Camulodunum stood a statue of Emperor Claudius. After his death, construction began on a large temple to the Divine Claudius, with a bronze statue of him inside. The local British people financed most of these building projects through the taxes they had to pay to Rome.

Source 1

This tombstone, from Camulodunum, commemorates a Roman cavalry officer called Longinus Sdapeze, who was originally from Bulgaria. It shows the soldier's horse trampling a naked enemy, who is crouching over his shield. Sdapeze would have held a metal weapon (now lost) in his hand.

Source 2

The historian Tacitus wrote this about the Britons' attitude towards the Roman veterans:

> The Britons most bitterly hated the veterans, who had arrived recently in the colony of Camulodunum. For these men were driving people out of their houses, throwing them off their land, and calling them prisoners and slaves. And the violent behavior of the veterans was encouraged by the serving soldiers, who hoped to behave in a similar way themselves once they retired. A temple to the Divine Claudius had been built and was forever before the eyes of the Britons, as if a stronghold of everlasting tyranny.

QUESTION

How do you think (a) the Romans and (b) the local Britons felt about Camulodunum?

Resist or accept?

Look at these three profiles of British tribal leaders:

1. Togidubnus

Togidubnus was king of the Regni. The Regni was a new tribe created by the Romans to control some of the territory of the Atrebates. Togidubnus was a strong supporter of the Romans. In return for his loyalty to Rome, they made him a client king. This meant that he ruled semi-independently and had the protection of the Roman army. It also secured for the Romans a strategic base for the conquest of south-west Britain.

Togidubnus fully adopted a Roman lifestyle, changing his name to Tiberius Claudius Togidubnus. He built a temple to the Roman gods Neptune and Minerva, and may have built a grand villa near Noviomagus on the south coast. The remains of this villa were found in modern Fishbourne.

2. Cartimandua

Cartimandua, the queen and leader of the Brigantes, was friendly towards the Romans. In exchange for her loyalty, the Romans allowed her to keep her independence and territory. Instead of advancing north, the Roman army concentrated their efforts on the resistance from the west. After she divorced her husband, Venutius, he stirred up unrest within the Brigantes and gathered a force to attack her. The Romans came to her aid and rescued her, but she lost the throne. Venutius became leader of the Brigantes and led the resistance against the Romans.

3. Caratacus

Caratacus, chief of the Catuvellauni, was the leader of the resistance to the Roman invasion. After he was defeated at Camulodunum, he fled west. He stirred up the Silures and the Ordovices to oppose the Roman advance, but was finally defeated. He escaped and sought protection from the Brigantes. Queen Cartimandua, far from helping him, turned him over to the Romans. He was taken to Rome as a captive, along with his wife, daughter, and brothers. There, they were paraded before the Roman people. Instead of pleading for mercy, Caratacus made a proud speech. Tacitus reports these words: 'If you want to be masters of the world, does it follow that the world should welcome slavery?' Impressed by his courage, Emperor Claudius freed him, along with his family.

What did the Britons think of the Roman Empire?

Few people in Iron Age Britain could read and write, so we have only Roman accounts of what the Britons thought of their conquerors. Tacitus reported a speech of the British chief Calgacus, who was defeated by the Roman general Agricola at the Battle of Mons Graupius in Scotland in AD 83. Calgacus addressed his men before the battle:

> The Romans rob, they slaughter, they ravage, and they falsely call this empire. They make a desert and they call it peace. Every day Britain feeds its own servitude.

QUESTIONS

1. What were the benefits of accepting Roman rule?

2. In Tacitus' account, Caratacus says:

   habuī equōs, virōs, arma, opēs.
   I had horses, men, weapons, and wealth.

   The Romans often believed that they were bringing a better way of life to the people they conquered. How does Caratacus reject this idea?

3. If you were a leader of a British tribe, what do you think you would have done?

Druidēs

postquam Catia rem cōnfēcit, Sabīna dīxit, 'Luccus erat iuvenis stultus. in Britanniā omnēs iuvenēs contrā Rōmānōs pugnāre volēbant?'

'minimē, Sabīna,' respondit Giscō. 'multī prīncipēs Britannicī pugnāre nōlēbant, quod pācem cupiēbant.'

'sed Druidēs ad bellum iuvenēs Britannicōs saepe incitābant,' dīxit Indus.　　5

'Druidēs vīdistī?' rogāvit Sabīna.

'ubi in Batāviā habitābam, Druidēs nōn vīdī,' respondit Indus. 'sed in Britanniā, sīcut in Galliā, multī Druidēs aderant.'

'dē contrōversiīs inter hominēs et gentēs cōnstituēbant,' inquit Catia.

'Druidēs quoque erant sacerdōtēs,' inquit Giscō. 'in silvīs sacrīs ingēns　　10
simulācrum vīmineum faciēbant, et in simulācrum captīvōs pellēbant.'

'postquam simulācrum hominibus vīvīs plēnum erat, Druidēs simulācrum incendēbant,' inquit Indus. 'captīvī vehementer clāmābant, sed effugere nōn poterant.'

'quid accidit?' rogāvit Rūfīna attonita.　　15

'mox omnēs captīvī in simulācrō vīmineō periērunt,' susurrāvit Giscō.

'rem mīrābilem nārrāvistis, amīcī,' inquit Faustus.

sed Catia, postquam marītum audīvit, clāmāvit, 'fābulae! Druidēs nōn erant crūdēlēs!' tum Giscō et uxor in popīnā contrōversiam habēbant.

'contrōversia est!' clāmāvit Indus. 'ubi sunt Druidēs?'　　20

Druidēs *Druids*

cōnficiō *I finish*

prīnceps *chief, leader*
pāx *peace*

bellum *war*
incitō *I incite, stir up*

ubi *when*
Batāvia *Batavia (in Germania Inferior)*
sīcut *just as, like*
contrōversia *argument, dispute*
inter *among, between*
cōnstituō *I decide*
vīmineus *made of wicker*
captīvus *captive, prisoner*
pellō *I drive, push*
vīvus *alive, living*
pereō *I die, perish*
crūdēlis *cruel*

The Druids

The Druids were a powerful and influential group of people in Iron Age Britain and Gaul. They belonged to the highest rank of society and acted as judges and teachers as well as priests. When the Romans visited and conquered Gaul and Britain, they came into contact with the Druids, and several Romans wrote about their beliefs and practices.

The Druids did not take part in fighting. But their position of authority gave them the ability to organize opposition to the Romans. After the Roman conquest, some Britons, including Druids, fled westwards to the island of Anglesey (the Romans called it Mona), off the west coast. In AD 60 or 61 Suetonius Paulinus, the Roman governor of Britain, attacked this outpost of resistance to Roman rule. The historian Tacitus describes the force that was waiting for the Romans:

> Standing on the shore was the enemy line, thick with weapons and men. Women were running about like Furies, wearing dark clothing, their hair disheveled, carrying firebrands. And around them were the Druids, pouring out terrible prayers, their hands raised to heaven. They were such a strange sight that the Romans at first, as if their limbs were paralyzed, didn't move and offered their bodies to be wounded.

The Romans recovered from their initial shock and defeated the British force. Tacitus continues:

> Then the groves dedicated to barbaric superstitions were cut down; for the Britons thought it was right to stain their altars with the blood of their captives and to find out the will of the gods by examining human entrails.

Tacitus wasn't the only writer to claim that the Druids practiced human sacrifice; the belief was widespread among the Romans and was also recorded by Julius Caesar. In contrast to this presentation of the Druids as barbaric, Caesar also described their education system and teachings in a way that shows them in a very different light. They believed that 'souls do not perish, but instead pass from one body to another after death' and they were interested in 'the stars and their movements, the extent of the universe and the earth, the nature of things, and the power of the immortal gods.' Sometimes their training lasted for twenty years. They learned everything by heart, so no written account of Druidic teachings has survived.

Emperor Claudius banned the Druids on the grounds that human sacrifice was magic and superstition. However, there is no firm evidence to support the claim that the Druids practiced human sacrifice: the accusation could have been Roman propaganda.

QUESTION

3. Generally the Romans were tolerant of other religious beliefs and practices. Why do you think that they persecuted the Druids?

This headdress or crown made of bronze was found on the skull of a man in an Iron Age grave. He was buried with his sword and shield. Some priests in Roman Britain more than two hundred years later wore similar crowns. This has given rise to the theory that the man may have been a Druid priest.

QUESTIONS

1. Tacitus gives two examples of 'barbaric superstitions'. In what ways are they (a) similar to and (b) different from Roman religious rites?

2. How do you think a Roman reader would have reacted to this account of the British resistance?

hērōs

ubi ego et Aucissa erāmus minōrēs, hiems frīgidissima erat. Aucissa
cum amīcā ad flūmen congelātum cucurrit. Aucissa dīxit, 'ecce, super
flūmen ambulāre possum!' longē super glaciem prōcessit. subitō
fragōrem audīvērunt. in glaciē erat rīma, et Aucissa repente in
aquam frīgidam cecidit. amīca et Aucissa perterritae exclāmābant.   5

mīles Rōmānus puellās audīvit et ad flūmen cucurrit. Aucissam in
aquā cōnspexit. statim arma dēposuit. amīca et mīles super glaciem
lentē prōcessērunt. 'adsum, puella!' mīles clāmāvit. ad Aucissam
veniēbat, sed Aucissa natāre nōn poterat, et sub glaciem ēvānuit.
mīles in aquam saluit et quoque ēvānuit. silentium erat. tandem   10
Aucissa et mīles appāruērunt. mīles eam ex aquā in glaciem pepulit.
nunc Aucissa in glaciē iacēbat et amīca mīlitem ex aquā trahere
temptābat. sed mīles erat nimium gravis, puella nōn valida, glaciēs
nōn firma.

hērōs	hero
hiems	winter
congelātus	frozen
super	over
glaciēs	ice
repente	suddenly
arma	arms, weapons
amīca	friend (female)
natō	I swim
ēvānēscō	I disappear
appāreō	I appear
validus	strong
firmus	firm

LANGUAGE NOTE 2: SUPERLATIVES

1. Study the following sentences:

   Subūra nōn est quiēta, sed cella est quiētissima.
   The Subura isn't quiet, but the room is very quiet.

   māter erat fortis et frāter erat fortissimus.
   My mother was brave and my brother was very brave.

   hiems frīgidissima erat.
   The winter was very cold.

   quiētissima, **fortissimus**, and **frīgidissima** are known as **superlatives**.

2. Superlatives can be translated into English using *very* or *most*, or by adding *-est* to
   the English word. For example, **cella est quiētissima** can be translated as *the room
   is very quiet* or *it is the quietest room*.

3. Most superlatives are formed by using -**issim**-, but some are formed differently:

   iter meum erat difficile, sed iter tuum erat difficillimum.
   My journey was difficult, but your journey was very difficult.

   māter gladiōs pulcherrimōs facit.
   My mother makes the most beautiful swords.

LANGUAGE PRACTICE

1. Complete the sentence with the correct verb, then translate.

    a. hōrā quārtā, ad urbem trāns pontem cum amīcīs ....
        (respondī, accidī, cucurrī)

    b. heri Rōmānī frātrem meum .... , quod agrōs nostrōs cupiēbant.
        (dīxērunt, occīdērunt, vēnērunt)

    c. taurum ad forum .... , quod eum vēndere cupiēbātis.
        (vīxistis, fūgistis, dūxistis)

    d. postquam Luccum superāvimus, eum ad parentēs meōs statim ....
        (invēnimus, trāximus, dīximus)

    e. post paucās hōrās, Catia Aucissam sōlam prope flūmen ....
        (invēnit, respondit, accidit)

    f. cūr ā vīcō cum gladiō nostrō subitō .... ?
        (dūxistī, discessistī, vīdistī)

2. Translate these sentences into English.

    a. parentēs īrātissimī erant, quod Luccus gladium cārissimum cēpit.

    b. Aucissa erat trīstissima, sed prīmō nihil dīxit.

    c. frātrēs Britannī erant laetissimī, quod Druidēs contrōversiam difficillimam cōnstituērunt.

    d. amīca mea mīlitem Rōmānum dē aquā frīgidissimā trahere nōn poterat.

    e. multōs diēs comes miserrimus in agrīs habitābat.

    f. fēmina, postquam iter longissimum fēcit, ad urbem pulcherrimam advēnit.

For several years the Fosse Way marked the limit of the Roman advance. But gradually the Roman army marched north into Caledonia (Scotland). Although the Romans defeated the Caledonian tribes at the Battle of Mons Graupius in AD 83, they withdrew without securing their victory.

Forty years later, in AD 122, Emperor Hadrian decided to put an end to the expansion of the Empire and to consolidate its frontiers. He ordered the construction of a wall. Parts of Hadrian's Wall can still be seen, stretching 74 miles across the north of England (*pictured here*).

Although there is evidence that the Romans visited Ireland, which they called Hibernia, it never became part of the Empire.

The Amazons

In ancient mythology the Amazons are a tribe of female warriors. They lived without men and beyond what the ancient Greeks considered the civilized world. It was commonly said that they lived in the East, between modern-day Ukraine and Mongolia. The Amazons fascinated Greek writers and audiences, because they were seen as strange and dangerous, and completely different.

Amazons in stories and art

The Amazons were skilled in battle. Usually they fought on horseback, armed with bow and arrow, and a double-edged axe. They are mentioned in Homer's *Iliad*, an ancient Greek poem about the war between the Greeks and the Trojans. Homer describes them as 'equals of men'. They fight alongside the Trojans, although they do not join the battle until after the end of the poem. Ancient Greek men were both fascinated and appalled by this race of independent fighting women – so different from their mothers, sisters, and wives.

Scenes with Amazons fighting Greeks were common in art, always with the Greeks winning. These mythical battles often represented the Greek wars against the Persians in the fifth century BC. They were a symbol of Greek victory over a foreign invader.

SOURCE 1

Look at Source 1. The Greek hero Hercules, recognizable from his lionskin cape, overpowers three Amazons. The Amazon on the left wears the tunic and leather cap associated with Persian dress.

Amazons in love

Although the Amazons lived apart from men, a particularly popular narrative in mythology was of Amazons falling in love with men. In these stories, the women are depicted as powerful and dangerous, but in the end they always fall in love with a Greek hero.

SOURCE 2

Statue of Achilles and the Amazon Penthesilea, by Bertel Thorvaldsen, 1801.

- Read or listen to one of these stories:
  - ◊ Achilles and Penthesilea.
  - ◊ Hercules and Hippolyta.
  - ◊ Theseus and Antiope.

Men overcoming and dominating women – in love or in war – is a common theme in myths about the Amazons.

- Why do you think this was such a popular theme?

Myth and reality

For a long time it was thought that the Amazons were imaginary. However, archaeologists have found evidence of female warriors among the nomadic tribes who ranged across vast distances from the Black Sea all the way to Mongolia, traveling on horses. These women were buried with bows, arrows, spears, and horses. Some of them appear to have been wounded in battle.

- Research the Siberian Ice Maiden.
- Do you think the mythological Amazons could have been based on someone like this?

QUESTIONS

1. Do you think ancient Greek women would have shared the male view of the Amazons?
2. What do you think about the idea that strong females always give in to love?
3. Can you think of modern-day Amazons in films, books, or reality?

Chapter 9: rebelliō

Camulodūnum I

1 *mediā nocte. in colōniā Camulodūnō.*

veterānī nūntium vocāvērunt.

2

veterānī nūntiō epistulam trādidērunt.

3 *prīmā lūce. in oppidō Londīniō.*

nūntius ad prōcūrātōrem festīnābat.

4

nūntius prōcūrātōrī epistulam trādidit.

5 *apud Icēnōs et Trinobantēs.*

mīlitēs Rōmānī mē et fīliās violāvērunt!

cōpiae Britannicae rēgīnam Boudicam audiēbant.
Boudica cōpiīs rem gravissimam nūntiābat.

6

iō, Boudica!
iō, iō Boudica!

Britannī Boudicae magnum clāmōrem
tollēbant.

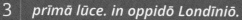

II

amīcī in popīnā intentē audiēbant. Indus amīcīs rem nārrābat.

'nūntius veterānīs auxilium petēbat,' inquit, 'quod cōpiae Britannicae ad colōniam Camulodūnum celeriter prōcēdēbant. Boudica caedem gravissimam parābat.

'centuriō prope prōcūrātōrem stābat. prōcūrātor centuriōnī epistulam   5
ostendit. tum centuriō prōcūrātōrī cōnsilium dedit: "nōs veterānīs auxilium dare dēbēmus." statim prōcūrātor ducentōs mīlitēs ad colōniam mīsit, sed mīlitibus arma iūsta nōn dedit.'

'quam gravis erat caedēs!' clāmāvit Giscō. 'Britannī erant multī, Rōmānī paucī. postquam cōpiae Britannicae Camulodūnum advēnērunt,   10
Boudica cōpiīs signum dedit. Icēnī et Trinobantēs erant crūdēlēs. virōs, fēminās, līberōs in viīs et domibus occīdērunt. veterānī in templum fūgērunt.

'duōs diēs in templō resistēbant. sed nūlla spēs veterānīs erat. tertiō diē Britannī templum incendērunt. Boudica omnibus Rōmānīs mortem   15
tulit.'

Giscō dīxit, 'tum ad oppidum Londīnium prōcessit Boudica.'

auxilium	*help*
petō	*I beg for*
caedēs	*killing, slaughter*
parō	*I prepare*
centuriō	*centurion (officer in the army)*
ostendō	*I show*
cōnsilium	*advice, plan*
dēbeō	*I ought*
ducentī	*two hundred*
mittō	*I send*
iūstus	*suitable*
resistō	*I resist*
nūllus	*no*
spēs	*hope*
mors	*death*
tulī	*I brought*

LANGUAGE NOTE 1: THE DATIVE CASE

1.   Look at the following sentences. What do you notice about the meaning of the words in red?

>   **Britannī Boudicae clāmōrem tollēbant.**
>   *The Britons were raising a shout for Boudica.*

>   **veterānī nūntiō epistulam trādidērunt.**
>   *The veterans handed over a letter to the messenger.*

>   **nūntius prōcūrātōrī epistulam trādidit.**
>   *The messenger gave the letter to the procurator.*

2.   The words in red are all translated in English as *to* or *for*. They are in the **dative case**. The dative case is used primarily to indicate the person for whom an action is carried out.

3.   Now look at the order of the words in the Latin sentences above. Can you spot a pattern? The dative noun is often placed between the nominative and the accusative nouns.

LANGUAGE PRACTICE

1.   Give the meanings of the following nouns, which are all dative singular.

For example: marītō   *to/for the husband*

a.	fēminae	**e.**	fīliō	**i.**	mātrī
b.	fīliae	**f.**	deō	**j.**	senī
c.	turbae	**g.**	custōdī		
d.	nūntiō	**h.**	hostī		

Chain of command

The emperor had overall responsibility for the government of Britannia, but he appointed men to govern the province in his name. The governor would have had experience in politics and a record of military success. In AD 60 the province of Britannia was governed by:

1. The governor: Suetonius Paulinus

The governor's role was primarily military, holding general command over the entire force stationed in the province. He also had other responsibilities, such as maintaining relationships with local chiefs, building roads, conducting religious affairs, and acting as a judge in important legal cases.

2. The procurator: Catus Decianus

The procurator was in charge of the province's financial affairs and reported directly to the emperor. His main duties were collecting taxes and arranging payment for the wages of the soldiers.

3. The legionary commanders

In AD 61 there were four legions stationed in Britannia. Each of these had a commander who answered to the governor.

Representing Rome

Provincial governors reported to the emperor, but were usually left to rule independently, particularly in peaceful provinces. Pliny, the governor of Bithynia and Pontus, wrote to Emperor Trajan on many occasions asking for advice and guidance on matters of seemingly little importance. In one of his replies, Trajan wrote:

> I chose you so that, in your wisdom, you might exercise a moderating influence on the customs of that province, and that you might put in place everything that is necessary for the peaceful future of the province.

Heavy hands

Many governors and procurators used their command as an opportunity to exploit the province with high taxes and increase their personal wealth. When Prasutagus, king of the Iceni, died he left half his kingdom to his wife Boudica and half to Emperor Nero. He hoped this generous gesture would satisfy the Romans and secure peace for his people. Instead Catus Decianus took the whole kingdom, and ordered Boudica to be flogged and her daughters to be violated.

The humiliated Iceni rose up under the command of Boudica, and were joined by other tribes who had also suffered at the hands of the greedy Romans. When Suetonius finally faced Boudica's army, he massacred them savagely and inflicted violence in retribution, as Tacitus recorded:

> Although he was outstanding in other respects, his behavior towards the conquered was arrogant and cruel, as if he were avenging a personal injury.

Catus Decianus, whose greed had initiated the uprising, had already fled to Gaul and was replaced by Gaius Julius Alpinus Classicanus, a Gaul. Subsequently, Suetonius was replaced by Publius Petronius Turpilianus, a less aggressive and more forgiving governor. Under the leadership of Classicanus and Turpilianus, Britannia was pacified without additional punishment: wounded relationships were repaired and towns were rebuilt.

QUESTIONS

1. Why do you think the Romans chose a man like Turpilianus to replace Suetonius?

2. How do you think the Britons would react to his style of governing?

Septimus revenit

Quārtilla in popīnā dīligenter labōrābat. ancilla erat fessa, quod multīs Subūrānīs cibum offerēbat. Faustus 'vīnum!' clāmāvit. Quārtilla Faustō vīnum trādidit. 'vah!' dīxit Faustus. 'ego bibere volō, sed tū es lenta!'

Quārtilla nihil dīxit. Rūfīna īrāta 'Quārtilla! festīnā!' clāmāvit. cibum ancillae lentae dare nōlō.'   5

Quārtilla nihil dīxit. ancilla ē popīnā quiētē ambulāvit, et in viā sēdit. Currāx mātrem invēnit. 'cūr tū lacrimās?' puer Quārtillae dīxit. 'vīta est dūra,' Quārtilla fīliō respondit. 'quamquam tōtum diem labōrō, Rūfīna mihi cibum dare nōn vult.'

subitō Septimum in viā cōnspexērunt. vir popīnam intrāvit. 'Septimus   10
est,' inquit Currāx. 'nūper tē emere temptābat. Rūfīnae magnam pecūniam offerēbat, sed domina tē nōn vēndidit. cūr iterum adest?' Quārtilla nihil dīxit.

brevī tempore Septimus īrātissimus ē popīnā exiit. 'domina tua est stultissima,' clāmāvit. 'Rūfīnae plūrimōs dēnāriōs offerēbam, sed tē   15
vēndere nōlēbat. valē.' Quārtilla nihil dīxit, sed rīdēbat.

'cūr rīdēs, māter?' inquit Currāx. 'vītam novam nōbīs offerēbat Septimus!'

'nōn nōs sed mē sōlam emere volēbat. vīta in Subūrā est dūra, sed hīc tēcum vīvere possum. nōta domina est Rūfīna, Septimus est dominus   20
ignōtus. melius est mihi in popīnā manēre.'

Quārtilla surrēxit et in popīnam festīnāvit. Currāx mātrī nihil dīxit. puer in viā mānsit.

---

reveniō *I return*

dīligenter *carefully*
fessus *tired*
offerō *I offer*

quiētē *quietly*

quamquam *although*

nūper *recently*
emō *I buy*

brevis *short*
plūrimī *very many*
dēnārius *denarius*
   (silver coin)

hīc *here*
nōtus *known, familiar*
ignōtus *unknown*
melius est *it is better*

LANGUAGE NOTE 2: THE DATIVE PLURAL

1. The sentences below contain examples of the dative plural:

   Boudica cōpiīs signum dedit.
   Boudica gave a signal to her troops.

   nūntius veterānīs auxilium petēbat.
   The messenger was seeking help for the veterans.

   prōcūrātor mīlitibus arma iūsta nōn dedit.
   The procurator didn't give the right weapons to the soldiers.

2. Compare the forms of the dative case with the nominative singular in each declension:

SINGULAR	1st decl.	2nd decl.		3rd decl.	
nominative	puella	amīcus	dōnum	fūr	caput
dative	puellae	amīcō	dōnō	fūrī	capitī

PLURAL					
dative	puellīs	amīcīs	dōnīs	fūribus	capitibus

3. Notice that the forms of the dative are often the same as the ablative:

SINGULAR	1st decl.	2nd decl.		3rd decl.	
ablative	puellā	amīcō	dōnō	fūre	capite

PLURAL					
ablative	puellīs	amīcīs	dōnīs	fūribus	capitibus

LANGUAGE PRACTICE

2. Complete each sentence with the correct form of the noun in brackets, then translate.

   a. ego .... praemium dedī, quod mē adiuvābant.   (comitēs, comitibus)

   b. postquam ad āram advēnimus, dominus noster .... dōna obtulit.   (deae, dea)

   c. nōs .... gladiōs pulcherrimōs in tabernīs ostendēbāmus.   (lībertōs, lībertīs)

   d. tū .... arma gravissima trādidistī, sed contrā Britannōs inūtilia erant.   (mīlitī, mīles, mīlitēs)

   e. quod Boudica est dux fortis, nōs .... mortem tulimus.   (hostēs, hostibus)

   f. puerī .... cibum parāvērunt, quod iter longum faciēbat.   (amīcum, amīcō, amīcus)

The forces

Roman legionary

- Iron helmet
- Body armor: several iron plates with leather straps
- Loose, knee-length tunic, made of wool
- Woolen cloak
- Leather sandals, with nails on the soles
- Socks may have been worn
- Some wore metal leg guards – sometimes only on one leg
- Short, straight-edged stabbing sword (*gladius*), kept inside a scabbard
- Javelin (*pīlum*): wooden shaft with iron tip
- Shield (*scūtum*), made of strips of wood glued together, covered with leather or felt

British warrior

- Woolen cloak
- Woolen tunic
- Trousers
- No breastplate or body armor
- Iron-tipped spear
- Some had a long slashing sword kept inside a scabbard
- Tall oval or rectangular shield, made of wood covered with leather
- Leather sling, for throwing stones
- Blue body paint

All the Britons dye themselves with woad because it produces a blue color and this makes them appear more terrifying in battle.   *Julius Caesar*

Romans	Britons
Highly trained professional army.	Warrior culture; warfare between tribes common before Roman invasion; but no standing army.
From all parts of the Roman Empire.	All native Britons.
Fought as a team; trained in maneuvers such as standing in line and resisting a charge with their shields, and the tortoise formation.	Fought as individuals. The Romans admired the bravery of the British warriors, but thought they lacked discipline.
Loyalty to legion and comrades. Only men served in the army.	Loyalty to family and tribe. Occasionally some British tribes joined together but in general did not unite against the Romans. Wives and children watched the battle; sometimes women may have led the offensive.
Preferred pitched battle on open ground.

Traveled by marching along roads. | Preferred fighting on treacherous terrain – mountains, woods, marshes; guerrilla warfare; raiding parties; attacking marching column from concealed positions. |

Why was the Roman army so successful?

In pitched battles on open ground the Roman army was extremely difficult to beat, even when greatly outnumbered. Tacitus says that in the final battle against Boudica almost 80,000 Britons died and about 400 Romans. However, on difficult terrain such as mountains, woods, and marshes the Romans were vulnerable, and the Britons had several successes.

What made the Roman army so successful? First of all, it was a professional army, so soldiers trained and prepared full-time (although they did many other jobs besides fighting). The physical training and weapons practice was strict and rigorous. Soldiers had to go on exercise marches three times a month, wearing armor and carrying heavy packs: their full equipment weighed almost 70 pounds. They were expected to cover 20 miles in five hours.

Preparing for battle

Suetonius, the governor, chose a site for the battle where there was a narrow pass and he had woods to his rear for cover. He had made certain that the enemy was only on the open plain in front of him, so he had no fear of ambush. The legionaries stood close together in lines, with the auxiliary light infantry around them and the cavalry on the wings. In contrast, the Britons, huge numbers of them, darted about in groups all over the field.

Tacitus

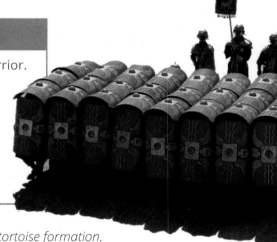

QUESTIONS

1. Look at the images of the Roman legionary and the British warrior. Compare their armor and equipment. What advantages and disadvantages did each have?
2. What type of fighting would favor (a) the Britons and (b) the Romans?
3. What other advantages did the British forces have?
4. What other reasons can you think of for the success of the Roman army?

A modern re-enactment of a tortoise formation.

Women and war

Roman authors record how Boudica led the Iceni against the Romans. Cassius Dio describes her delivering a speech to her troops:

> She was very tall, fierce in appearance, with piercing eyes. Her voice was rough and her thick golden hair fell to her hips. She had a great gold necklace and wore a multicolored tunic and a thick cloak. Grasping her spear, so as to terrify everyone, she spoke.

According to Tacitus, Boudica said that it was normal for Britons to fight under a woman's command. In his description of the final battle between the Romans and the British forces led by Boudica, Tacitus also mentions other British women present at the battle:

> The British forces were so fierce in spirit that they brought their wives to witness their victory; they put them on wagons which they had drawn up on the extreme edge of the plain.

Roman male writers found these fighting women fascinating and glamorous because they were so different from Roman women who did not have such independence.

umbra

in popīnā, amīcī intentē audiunt.

Catia	mox Boudica et cōpiae ad oppidum Londīnium advēnērunt. ubīque erant hostēs. nūlla spēs erat cīvibus. Aucissa erat in oppidō, quod gladiōs in forō vēndēbat. ego cum parentibus ad oppidum festīnāvī. in ponte Giscōnem et Indum invēnimus. 5
Giscō	trāns pontem hostēs oppidum iam incendēbant. ignēs et flammae tōtum oppidum implēbant. Catia oppidum intrāre voluit. eam retinēre temptāvī. omnēs cīvēs effugiēbant. sed Catiae nōn persuāsī.
Catia	necesse erat nōbīs Aucissae subvenīre. ego cum Giscōne ad 10 forum festīnāvī, et parentēs Aucissam per viās quaerēbant. tandem in forum equitāvimus, ubi Aucissam invēnimus. sanguis ē pectore effluēbat. vehementer lacrimāvī et 'soror, cūr nōn effūgistī?' clāmāvī. 'Boudicam cōnspicere voluī. Luccus ...' sed plūs dīcere nōn poterat. 'quid? quid dīcis, 15 soror?' exclāmāvī. sed Aucissa nōn respondit. soror in bracchiīs meīs periit. nōn potuī ...
Giscō	per flammās et turbās perterritās equitābāmus et parentēs quaerēbāmus. clāmōre viās implēvimus. parentēs iterumque iterumque frūstrā vocāvimus. subitō ante oculōs umbra 20 appāruit.
Catia	māter erat. perterritī erāmus. 'necesse est vōbīs discēdere, columba mea,' dīxit māter. 'valē, mea cārissima.' tum umbra ēvānuit.
Giscō	difficile est nōbīs rem intellegere. sed nūmen aut umbra nōs 25 servāvit.

umbra *shade, ghost*

ubīque *everywhere*

hostis *enemy*
flamma *flame*

persuādeō *I persuade*

necesse *necessary*
subveniō *I help*

pectus *chest*

plūs *more*

bracchium *arm*

impleō *I fill*
iterumque iterumque *again and again*
ante *before, in front of*
oculus *eye*

fuga ex oppidō Londīniō

in popīnā silentium erat. Subūrānī attonitī erant. tandem Rūfīna rogāvit, 'quōmodo ab oppidō effūgistis?'

Rūfīnae respondit Indus, 'pontem contrā hostēs dēfendēbam. nūllum auxilium mihi erat. mox cōpiae Britannicae pontem incendēbant. subitō Catiam et Giscōnem in rīpā cōnspexī.'   5

'pontem et Indum per turbam vix vidēre poterāmus,' inquit Catia. 'frūstrā pontī appropinquāre temptābāmus. multī hostēs nōs in rīpā opprimēbant. tandem in flūmen saluimus. deinde ingentem fragōrem audīvimus. pōns dēcidit.'

omnēs amīcī Indum spectābant.   10

'in flūmen saluī,' inquit Indus. 'arma gerēbam. vix ad rīpam ulteriōrem natāre poteram. hostēs tēla in mē iaciēbant. tēla tamen vītāvī, quod sub aquā natābam.'

posteā difficile erat nōbīs iter facere, quod hostēs ubīque erant. per diem dormiēbāmus, per noctem iter faciēbāmus. tandem ad   15
exercitum Rōmānum advēnimus.

dēfendō *I defend*

rīpa *bank (of a river)*

vix *scarcely, hardly*

deinde *then*
dēcidō *I fall down*

ulterior *further, opposite*
tēlum *weapon*

posteā *afterwards*

exercitus *army*

Fenwick Treasure

The Fenwick Treasure (*right*) was found in Colchester (Roman Camulodunum) in 2014 by archaeologists excavating the site of Fenwick's department store. This hoard of gold and silver jewelry and Roman coins was under the floor of a house which had been destroyed by fire. The dating and the absence of any bodily remains suggest that the jewelry and coins were deliberately buried around the time of the Boudican revolt. Among the items are gold earrings, a gold bracelet, and five gold rings. The earrings are hollow gold balls, similar to some which have been found in Pompeii. There is also a silver **armilla**, an award which was given to a retired soldier.

QUESTIONS

1. Who might this treasure have belonged to?

2. Why do you think it was buried?

LANGUAGE NOTE 3: VERBS WITH THE DATIVE CASE

1. Some Latin verbs, because of their meaning, are accompanied by a noun in the dative case. Look at the Latin sentences below. Can their English translations be simplified?

    Catiae nōn persuāsī.
    I was not persuasive to Catia.

    multī Britannī Rōmānīs favēbant.
    Many Britons were giving support to the Romans.

    pontī appropinquāre temptābāmus.
    We were trying to draw near to the bridge.

    Rōmānī Boudicae resistere nōn poterant.
    The Romans weren't able to offer resistance to Boudica.

2. The sentences might more naturally be translated as follows:

    Catiae nōn persuāsī.
    I did not persuade Catia.

    multī Britannī Rōmānīs favēbant.
    Many Britons were supporting the Romans.

    pontī appropinquāre temptābāmus.
    We were trying to approach the bridge.

    Rōmānī Boudicae resistere nōn poterant.
    The Romans weren't able to stop Boudica.

3. Other verbs which are accompanied by the dative case include **imperō** (*order, give an order to*), **parcō** (*spare, give mercy to*), **crēdō** (*trust, give one's trust to*), **placeō** (*please, be pleasing to*), **subveniō** (*help, bring help to*), and **nūbō** (*marry, marry oneself to*).

LANGUAGE PRACTICE

3.   Add the missing endings to the nouns to match the English translations.

   a.   nōs mendīc... cibum dedimus.
        We gave food to the beggar.

   b.   tū sorōr... pecūniam obtulistī.
        You offered money to your sisters.

   c.   ego fīli... templum ostendī.
        I showed the temple to my daughter.

   d.   rēx imperātōr... captīvōs trādidit.
        The king handed over prisoners to the emperor.

   e.   mātrōn... dōna quaerēbātis.
        You were looking for gifts for the ladies.

   f.   Britannī cōpi... arma dābant.
        The Britons were giving weapons to their forces.

Why join the army?

There was not often compulsory military service in the Roman Empire: men who served as soldiers were usually volunteers. Being a soldier was considered a prestigious job, and it came with many rewards. Soldiers earned a good wage compared with other professions and were housed and well fed. In addition, the emperors often gave the legions gifts of money to be distributed among the men. While there were dangers associated with warfare, many soldiers saw very little combat, depending on where they were stationed. Instead they spent much of their time constructing roads and buildings, or on administration. Some trained in one of the many trades needed to support an army camp, as, for example, blacksmiths, shoemakers, or butchers. All soldiers were expected to be able to read basic documents, and a discharged soldier had learned valuable skills during his years of service.

Enlisting

Young men from the age of 16 could sign up for the army. Those wishing to join were vetted to ensure they were healthy, of good character, and freeborn citizens. Preference was given to men who had a trade that would be useful, such as carpenters or smiths. The recruits were given official documentation stating their date of joining; this was important, as the date of their discharge would be calculated from this time. They received their equipment, which included clothing and armor, and completed a rigorous training program before traveling to join a legion.

Legionary and auxiliary soldiers

Men who were freeborn and citizens of the Roman Empire could join one of the legions. Legionaries usually signed up for a period of twenty-five or thirty years' service. On retirement they received a pension and sometimes some land, often in the province where they had been stationed. Auxiliary soldiers, on the other hand, came from one of the provinces of the Empire where the inhabitants were not automatically citizens. They formed their own smaller divisions, comprised of men from the same province. Auxiliary cohorts often had a specialist skill; they were, for example, archers, cavalry, scouts, or camel riders. Auxiliaries served for twenty-five years before being discharged. They were paid less than legionaries and did not receive a pension or land. However, on retirement they were granted full citizenship, which brought tax exemptions and legal benefits.

QUESTIONS

1. Why do you think it was appealing for young men to join the army?

2. In the stories, Indus is an auxiliary soldier in a *cohors Batāvōrum* (a regiment from Batavia), while Gisco is a legionary. What difference would this make to their status and experience, do you think?

Every auxiliary soldier received a military diploma granting him citizenship upon completing twenty-five years of service in the Roman army. This diploma belonged to a soldier named Dasmenus Azalus, who was discharged in AD 149. It is made of bronze and measures about 5 x 4 inches.

proelium

1 imperātor proeliō optimum locum lēgit.

3 hodiē victōria est nōbīs!

2 Britannī clāmōrem ingentem tollēbant.
Boudica prīncipēs et gentēs incitābat.

4 vae Rōmānīs!

imperātor *general*
proelium *battle*
locus *place*
victōria *victory*
vae! *woe!*
virtūs *courage, virtue*

5 hostēs sunt multī, nōs paucī!
necesse est nōbīs cum
magnā virtūte pugnāre!

6 imperātor proeliō exercitum parābat. tōtus exercitus imperātōrī magnum clāmōrem sustulit.

7 cōpiae Britannicae ad exercitum Rōmānum fortiter currēbant.

fortiter *bravely*

imperātor signum dedit. 8

9   prīmō mīlitēs in Britannōs pīla iēcērunt.

10   deinde equitēs hastīs Britannōs occīdērunt.

pīlum *javelin*
eques *horseman;*
pl. = cavalry
hasta *spear*

11

tum et mīlitēs et auxiliārēs
gladiīs hostēs oppugnāvērunt.

12   mox exercitus Rōmānus Britannicās cōpiās dēlēvit.

auxiliāris *auxiliary soldier*
oppugnō *I attack*

Giscō   in mediā caede ego Luccum
cōnspexī. iuvenī īnfēlīcī parcere
prīmō volēbam. tum gladium
cōnspexī. īrātissimus eram.
'sceleste!' clāmāvī.
iuvenem occīdī.

parcō *I spare*
scelestus *wicked*

Resistance

Boudica was not the only leader to resist Roman invasion. Across Europe, North Africa, and the Middle East, people fought for their freedom.

Caesar in Gaul

In 59 BC, there were two Roman Gallic provinces: Gallia Cisalpina and Gallia Transalpina. The rest of Gaul was home to free, independent peoples. They were not, however, a cohesive country, but a collection of tribes (with leaders elected for their military prowess).

In 58 BC Julius Caesar became the governor of the two provinces, and traveled there with four legions. Once there, he levied two more legions, so had about 30,000 legionaries and 4,000 auxiliary troops. Caesar began by supporting some Gallic tribes against threats from their enemies (for instance, from Germanic tribes across the Rhine, or from other Gallic tribes). He led a number of summer campaigns that allowed his legions to move north into the Gauls' territory. He increased his power by demanding taxes, food, and hostages.

Vercingetorix

However, in 52 BC resentment among the Gauls grew. They felt that they were paying far too high a price for Roman help. Gathered under a new leader, Vercingetorix, they rebelled against the Romans.

Vercingetorix tried to overcome some of the traditional problems of large Gallic armies: disorganization, lack of cohesion and discipline, and poor supplies. He started the rebellion in winter, while Caesar was away in Cisalpine Gaul and his legions were dispersed in their winter quarters. However, Caesar reacted quickly, and rapidly reassembled his army. After several defeats for the Gauls, and one at Gergovia for the Romans, Caesar's army was closing in on the Gauls.

This statue of Vercingetorix was set up in 1865 at the presumed site of Alesia.

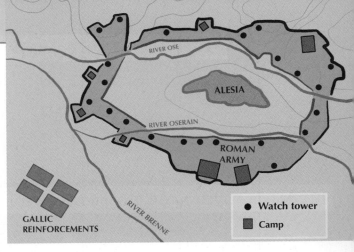

The battle of Alesia

Vercingetorix and his 80,000 men decided to withdraw to the well-fortified hilltop town of Alesia. Caesar, calculating that a force of so many soldiers, together with the local population, would soon run out of food, decided to lay siege to Alesia. Noticing what was happening, Vercingetorix dispatched his cavalry to seek reinforcements across Gaul.

Caesar ordered three sets of ditches to be dug, completely encircling the town of Alesia, and beyond these he constructed a rampart and wall 11.5 feet high, with defensive turrets at regular intervals. The siege works were vast, stretching for 10 miles.

Then, in order to defend his troops against the reinforcements Vercingetorix had called for, Caesar ordered a second set of defensive works to be built, facing the opposite direction. These fortifications ran for 13 miles. The Romans had provisions to last about a month. They positioned themselves in between the two sets of fortifications, and waited.

One episode shows the utter cruelty of the siege: as provisions were decreasing in the town, Vercingetorix ordered all the inhabitants who couldn't fight (children, women, old people, and the sick and injured) to leave the walled town. Caesar refused to allow them through the Roman fortified area, either for fear of an attack or to demonstrate his power. Whatever the reason, they were left to starve in no-man's land.

Finally, the Gallic relief force arrived, and the main battle began. The Romans were significantly inferior in number, and the battle was harshly fought, but the Romans' military training and experience prevailed. Vercingetorix was taken prisoner and, five years later, was paraded through the streets of Rome in Caesar's triumphal procession, before being publicly executed. After the fall of Alesia, Gallic resistance to Caesar was broken. The conquest of Gaul was completed the following year.

Chapter 10: Aquae Sūlis

pāx Rōmāna

sōl lūcēbat.
in valle erat nebula. nebula dēnsa dē palūde surgēbat.
in palūde erant aquae. aquae calidae dē terrā surgēbant.

vir ad palūdem stābat et dēnārium novum tenēbat.

vir, nōmine Antigonus, dēnārium novum
per nebulam dēnsam iēcit.

5

dēnārius in aquās calidās cecidit.

Giscō rem nārrat.

Antigonus, postquam dēnārium in aquās calidās iēcit, mihi
appropinquāvit. locum intentē spectābat, ubi labōrābam.   10
deinde 'locus est bonus, Giscō,' inquit. 'thermīs locum bonum
lēgistis.' 'certē, sumus fēlīcēs,' Antigonō respondī. 'aquae sunt
bonae. saxum est bonum. lignum bonum ē silvīs proximīs
ferimus. et Britannī et Rōmānī bene labōrant.'

'vōs mīlitēs estis amīcī bonī Britannīs,' inquit Antigonus. 'ubi ego   15
mīles eram, multae gentēs Britannicae erant hostēs Rōmānīs.'

'multōs annōs contrā gentēs Britannicās bellum gerēbāmus,'
dīxī. 'nunc decōrum est nōbīs pācem in Britanniā habēre.'

tum tubam audīvimus. nōs omnēs – et operāriī et mīlitēs –
statim tacuimus et ad āram parvam convēnimus. sacerdōtēs   20
ad āram parvam prōcessērunt et sacrificium deae Sūlī
Minervae fēcērunt. tum tōta turba – et Britannī et Rōmānī –
vōtum deae Sūlī Minervae fēcit.

proximus	*nearest, next to*
ferō	*I carry, bring*
bene	*well*
annus	*year*
bellum gerō	*I wage war*
decōrum	*proper, right*
tuba	*trumpet*
operārius	*workman*
sacrificium	*sacrifice, offering*
Sūlis	*Sulis (local Celtic goddess)*
Minerva	*Minerva (Roman goddess)*

magnum perīculum

Indus rem nārrat.

thermae, ubi Giscō labōrābat, erant novae. templum prope thermās
novās simul aedificāre coepimus. decōrum erat nōbīs templum
magnificum aedificāre, quod aquae calidae erant sacrae. fabrī erant
Gallī, operāriī erant Britannī et servī erant captīvī ē gentibus Britannicīs.   5

cōtīdiē viae novae erant plēnae. multa plaustra ad locum, ubi strēnuē et
dīligenter labōrābāmus, veniēbant. alia saxum portābant, alia lignum.
puerī saepe ad plaustra conveniēbant, quod prō praemiō operāriōs
adiuvāre volēbant. ūnum ē puerīs bene meminī.

parvus puer nōs semper adiuvābat. īnstrūmenta portābat et cibum   10
ferēbat. ōlim, ubi mūrōs exstruēbāmus, cāsus dīrus erat. plaustrum
saxa ingentia portābat; puer prope plaustrum labōrābat. subitō
magnum fragōrem audīvimus. ūnum ē saxīs dē plaustrō cecidit et
puerum percussit.

'ei mihi!' exclāmāvit puer miser. in perīculō dīrō erat. in magnō dolōre   15
sub saxō ingentī iacēbat.

'Giscō! Inde!' clāmāvit Antigonus. 'necesse est vōbīs puerum adiuvāre!'

ego et Giscō ad puerum miserum cucurrimus, sed saxum tollere nōn
poterāmus. Celer vehementer lātrābat. tum ūnus ē captīvīs Britannicīs
ad nōs festīnāvit. captīvus erat ingēns et validus. ingēns captīvus saxum   20
cum summā difficultāte sustulit et puerum līberāvit.

ingentī captīvō dīxit Giscō, 'tibi grātiās agō. puerum servāvistī. tibi
lībertātem prōmittō.'

simul	*at the same time*
coepī	*I began*
faber	*craftsman*
Gallus	*a Gaul*
plaustrum	*cart*
alia … alia …	*some … others …*
prō	*for, in return for*
meminī	*I remember*
mūrus	*wall*
exstruō	*I build*
cāsus	*accident*
dīrus	*dreadful*
ei mihi!	*argh!*
difficultās	*difficulty*
grātiās agō	*I give thanks*
prōmittō	*I promise*

Aquae Sulis

The hot spring

Aquae Sulis (modern Bath) lies where the Fosse Way crosses the River Avon. It grew into an important town in the Roman Empire because of its sacred springs. Still today 309,000 gallons of hot water (115°F), rich in minerals, rise up out of the ground, as they have done for thousands of years. It is likely that, for a long time before the Romans came, the Britons living nearby had regarded the spring as a holy place whose waters had healing properties.

Winning hearts and minds

Soon after the invasion of Britain in AD 43, the Roman army was campaigning against the Silures. It is possible that soldiers injured in the fighting came to recuperate in the healing waters of the spring. As you learned in the previous chapter, after the suppression of Boudica's revolt, the new governor and procurator took a gentler approach to governing Britain. They wanted to win over the native Britons and encourage them to adopt a Roman way of life. One way they did this was by building Roman-style towns and amenities in the territory they had already conquered.

At Aquae Sulis they began to construct a religious, health, and leisure complex on the site of the sacred spring. In our stories Gisco and Indus are working on the first stages of this building project in AD 62; it was completed by AD 76.

The temple

The hot spring was at the center of the complex. The Romans, like the Britons, thought the spring was a holy place. On one side they built a temple to Sulis Minerva. Sulis was a local British goddess and Minerva was the Roman goddess of healing. By joining the names together, the Romans encouraged the Britons to associate Sulis with the Roman goddess. The area around the temple and spring was the sacred courtyard. In the middle of the courtyard was an altar, where sacrifices were made.

The baths

On the other side of the spring, a huge set of public baths was constructed. There were three warm baths, using water from the naturally hot spring.

Later another set of baths was added, heated by a hypocaust; here there was a caldarium, a tepidarium, and a frigidarium.

The spring overflow

Roman engineers designed a plumbing and drainage system which can still be seen today. Hot water from the spring was carried to the baths in lead pipes, using the flow of gravity. The original Roman drain carries surplus water from the spring, which then flows into the River Avon. Archaeologists have made some important discoveries in the drain, including thirty-four gemstones and a tin mask.

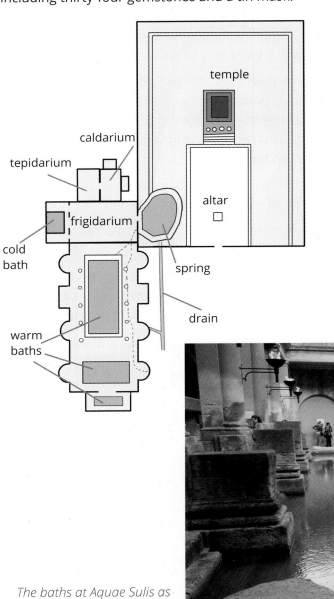

The baths at Aquae Sulis as they look now.

Visitors and their offerings

Aquae Sulis grew into an important religious center. People traveled there to worship the goddess, to visit the spring and the baths, and to seek a cure for their ailments. They made sacrifices to Sulis Minerva (sometimes just called Sulis), dedicated altars to her, and threw offerings into the sacred spring. Romans offered presents to the gods in the hope of receiving an answer to a prayer, or thanking them for a prayer which had been granted.

Part of the handle of a metal dish which might have been used for offering holy water. Archaeologists have found many dishes like this in the spring. They have the letters **DSM** *on them, which is short for* **deae Suli Minervae.** *What do you think the words mean?*

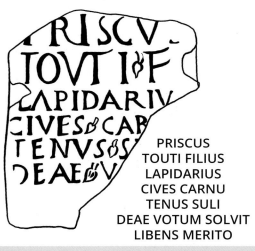

PRISCUS
TOUTI FILIUS
LAPIDARIUS
CIVES CARNU
TENUS SULI
DEAE VOTUM SOLVIT
LIBENS MERITO

Priscus, son of Toutius, stonemason, from the Carnutes tribe, willingly and deservedly fulfills his vow to the goddess Sulis.

Dedication to the goddess Sulis by a stonemason from Gaul.

DEAE
SVLIMI
NERVAE
SVLINVS
MATV
RI FIL
V S L M

To the goddess Sulis Minerva, Sulinus son of Maturus willingly and deservedly kept the promise he made.

The abbreviation VSLM = *votum solvit libenter merito*

◊ Find a letter written backwards.
◊ Find an 'i' written above another letter.
◊ Find some letters that are joined together.

Sulinus set up this altar to Sulis Minerva. He had made a promise and kept it. We don't know what the promise was. Perhaps he had promised to set up the altar if his prayer was granted.

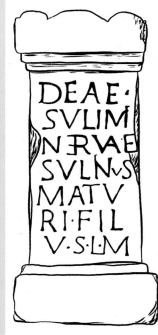

QUESTION

Why did people come to Aquae Sulis?

Think of as many reasons as you can.

Different gods

The Roman state religion was polytheistic. The Romans worshiped many gods and had no problem with adding more. As the Roman Empire expanded, the Romans merged local gods and goddesses with their own. In doing so, they encouraged the conquered peoples to identify with Roman customs and peacefully accept a Roman way of life.

nōmina alia aliīs gentibus

'Different names to different peoples.' This is how Pliny the Elder expressed the idea that different peoples worshiped the same gods, but gave them different names. Often the gods that were merged shared characteristics, but they did not have to match perfectly.

Sulis Minerva

Sulis: The local goddess of the thermal springs. Her name probably derived from a Celtic word for 'sun'.

Minerva: The Roman goddess of wisdom, medicine, and crafts.

The natural springs were a sacred place for the native Iron Age Britons. They associated the hot spring, with its bubbling and mineral-rich waters, with the goddess Sulis.

Although there is no evidence of any shrine or settlement, coins from the late Iron Age have been found in the spring. This suggests that people in the Iron Age probably worshiped Sulis, the goddess of the spring. The name the Romans gave the town, Aquae Sulis, means Waters of Sulis.

The grand temple and bathing complex were constructed in honor of Sulis Minerva, the fusion of the British and Roman goddesses. This was a powerful strategic decision by the occupying Roman force. The native Britons would continue to worship Sulis, assimilated with the Roman Minerva, and therefore would be likely to accept and respect the Roman-style complex.

Bronze head of Sulis Minerva, probably from the statue inside the temple at Aquae Sulis.

Hadad and Jupiter

Hadad was the god of storm and rain in the ancient Semitic and Mesopotamian religions. He was depicted as a bearded man, often holding a club and a thunderbolt.

When the Romans conquered Damascus, in Syria, in 64 BC, they assimilated Hadad with Jupiter, the Roman god of thunder and the king of the gods. They commissioned the local architect Apollodorus to design a new temple for Hadad-Jupiter. He copied the symmetry and scale of Roman temples, but kept much of the original Semitic design.

Isis

Isis was the Egyptian mother goddess and had been worshiped from around 3000 BC. Private shrines to Isis were set up in Rome from about the first century BC, and her cult was gradually accepted into Roman religion.

As her popularity grew, Isis was given new titles. She was sometimes referred to as 'having 10,000 names.' In a novel by Apuleius, the main character, Lucius, is visited by Isis, who says:

> The whole world worships my single divinity, in many forms and various rituals, and under different names. The Phrygians call me the Pessinuntican mother of the gods, the Athenians call me Minerva, the Cypriots Venus, the Cretans Diana, the Sicilians Stygian Proserpina, the Eleusinians Ceres. Some call me Juno, others Bellona, and others Hecate. The Ethiopians and the Egyptians call me by my true name, Queen Isis.

QUESTION

Do you agree with Pliny that people worship the same gods but under different names?

LANGUAGE NOTE 1: 1ST AND 2ND DECLENSION ADJECTIVES

1.   Study the following sentence:

> **subitō fragōrem audīvimus.**
> *Suddenly we heard a crash.*

Look at the word **fragōrem**.

    i.   What case (nominative, accusative, dative, ablative) is it?
    ii. Is it singular or plural?
    iii. Look up **fragor** in the dictionary: is it masculine, feminine, or neuter?

2.   Now look at this sentence:

> **subitō magnum fragōrem audīvimus.**
> *Suddenly we heard a big crash.*

magnum (*big*) is an **adjective** and describes **fragōrem**. Look at the ending of **magnum**. **fragōrem** is accusative, singular, and masculine, so **magnum** is also accusative, singular, and masculine.

3.   Finally study this sentence:

> **nōs viās bonās aedificābāmus.**
> *We were building good roads.*

viās is accusative, plural, and feminine. **bonās** describes **viās**, so **bonās** is also accusative, plural, and feminine.

4.   Latin adjectives change their endings to match the noun they describe in **case**, **number** (singular or plural), and **gender**.

5.   Adjectives like **magnus** and **bonus** can change their endings as follows:

SINGULAR	*masculine*	*feminine*	*neuter*
nominative	**bonus**	**bona**	**bonum**
dative	**bonō**	**bonae**	**bonō**
accusative	**bonum**	**bonam**	**bonum**
ablative	**bonō**	**bonā**	**bonō**

PLURAL			
nominative	**bonī**	**bonae**	**bona**
dative	**bonīs**	**bonīs**	**bonīs**
accusative	**bonōs**	**bonās**	**bona**
ablative	**bonīs**	**bonīs**	**bonīs**

Because the masculine changes like **amīcus**, the feminine like **puella**, and the neuter like **dōnum**, adjectives such as **magnus** and **bonus** are known as **1st and 2nd declension adjectives**.

senex ignōtus

Catia rem nārrat.

Giscō et Indus, ubi oppidum pulchrum cum Britannīs aedificābant,
laetī erant, quamquam labor erat dūrus. duōs annōs ibi
habitābāmus. annō prīmō ē Giscōne concēpī. laetissima eram.

simulatque Giscōnī rem fēlīcem nūntiāvī, vir laetus   5

'ō mea pulchra Catia!' clāmāvit. 'quam fēlīx sum! laeta es, mea
columba?'

'certē,' respondī, 'laetissima sum.'

tum Giscōnī ōsculum dedī. Celer lātrābat. dominus rīsit et

'ōsculum quoque cupis, Celer?' rogāvit. 'hahae! quam fidēlis es!'   10

Giscō, postquam canem fidēlem mulsit, ad labōrem laetē rediit.
intereā ego ad fontem sacrum ambulāvī, quod Mātribus Sūleviīs
vōtum facere volēbam. Celer fidēlis mēcum ambulābat.

ubi ad fontem stābam, senem ignōtum cōnspexī. senex
vestīmenta sordida gerēbat et tabulam parvam tenēbat. fūrtim   15
circumspectābat. Celer senem miserum intentē spectābat, et
vehementer lātrāvit. senex, postquam canem ferōcem audīvit,
perterritus ā fonte cucurrit. tabula parva dē manū cecidit.

tabulam sustulī. perterrita vōtum malum lēgī:

labor *work*	
concipiō *I conceive,*	
become pregnant	
ōsculum *kiss*	
hahae! *ha ha!*	
redeō *I go back, return*	
intereā *meanwhile*	
Sūleviae *Suleviae (Celtic*	
goddesses)	
mēcum = cum mē	
tabula *curse tablet*	
fūrtim *secretly, like a thief*	
ferōx *fierce*	
ā = ab	
manus *hand*	
malus *bad, evil*	
eques *horseman*	
Numidicus *Numidian*	
dēvoveō *I curse*	

Sūlī equitem Numidicum dēvoveō

eques Numidicus fīlium meum necāvit   20

*A Roman curse tablet (Source 1
on the facing page).*

Curses

A curse tablet is a small piece of lead or pewter, flattened into a thin flexible sheet, with a smooth surface. You would scratch your curse on the sheet with a metal stylus, then roll it up and throw it into the spring. The lettering is sometimes of very poor quality, suggesting that an illiterate person was copying letters. Some of the inscriptions are just scratches imitating letters. It is likely that there were people who made a living from inscribing curses on tablets and selling them.

One hundred and thirty curse tablets have been found in the spring at Aquae Sulis. Similar curse tablets have been found in other parts of Britain and all over the Roman Empire. Often they use formulae which we would think of as magic: writing the words backwards or using nonsense words such as *bescu*, *berebescu*, and *bazagra*. Some uses of magic were outlawed in the Roman world. In Chapter 8 you read that Emperor Claudius banned the Druids on the grounds that human sacrifice was magic. The presence of these curse tablets in a sacred place shows that the distinction between religion and magic was not always clear-cut.

SOURCE 1

QU[I] MIHI
VILBIAM IN[V]
OLAVIT SIC
LIQUAT COM[O]
AQUA ..... EL[LA]
M[U]TA QUI EAM
[INVOL] AVIT
... VELVINNA
EX[S]UPEREUS
VERIANUS
SEVERINUS
AUGUSTALIS
COMITIANUS MINIANUS CATUS
GERMANILL[A] IOVINA

May he who stole vilbia (?) from me become liquid as water. May she who stole [or devoured] her become dumb ... Velvinna Exsupereus ... (a list of names follows)

Some people think that Vilbia is a woman's name. Others think that the word refers to an object which has been stolen.

◊ The words are in the correct order, but each word is written backwards. Can you see MIHI and VILBIAM in the first line?

SOURCE 2

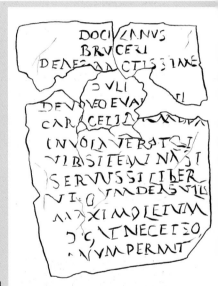

DOCILIANUS BRUCERI
DEAE SANCTISSIMAE
SULI
DEVOVEO EUM QUI
CARACALLAM MEUM
INVOLAVERIT SI VIR SI
FEMINA SI SERVUS SI
LIBER ...

Docilianus son of Brucerus to the most holy goddess Sulis. I curse whoever stole my hooded cloak – whether man or woman, slave or free. May the goddess Sulis inflict death on him and not allow him to sleep or have children now or in the future until he has brought my cloak back to her temple.

SOURCE 3
Docimedis has lost two gloves. He asks that the thief should lose his mind and eyes in the goddess' temple.

QUESTIONS

These sources are examples of the curse tablets from the spring at Aquae Sulis.

1. What do the curses have in common?

2. Does it seem strange to you that religion is used to bring harm to people?

LANGUAGE NOTE 2: 3RD DECLENSION ADJECTIVES

1.   Study the following sentences:

> **Quārtilla fēminās trīstēs spectābat.**
> *Quartilla was watching the unhappy women.*

> **senex canem ferōcem audīvit.**
> *The old man heard the fierce dog.*

In the first sentence, **fēminās** is accusative, plural, and feminine. **trīstēs** describes **fēminās**, so **trīstēs** is also accusative, plural, and feminine.

In the second sentence, **canem** is accusative, singular, and masculine. **ferōcem** describes **canem**, so **ferōcem** is also accusative, singular, and masculine.

2.   Adjectives such as **trīstis** and **ferōx** change their endings as follows:

SINGULAR	masculine/ feminine	neuter	masculine/ feminine	neuter
nominative	**trīstis**	**trīste**	**ferōx**	
dative	**trīstī**		**ferōcī**	
accusative	**trīstem**	**trīste**	**ferōcem**	**ferōx**
ablative	**trīstī**		**ferōcī**	

PLURAL				
nominative	**trīstēs**	**trīstia**	**ferōcēs**	**ferōcia**
dative	**trīstibus**		**ferōcibus**	
accusative	**trīstēs**	**trīstia**	**ferōcēs**	**ferōcia**
ablative	**trīstibus**		**ferōcibus**	

Because the masculine and feminine change like **fūr**, and the neuter like **caput**, adjectives such as **trīstis** and **ferōx** are known as **3rd declension adjectives**.

3.   Adjectives can come either before or after the noun they describe, although adjectives of size and quantity (such as **magnus** and **omnis**) are more likely to come before their noun.

votum malum diu cogitabam. nocte dormire non poteram. nonnullas
hōrās in lectō iacēbam. Giscō dormiēbat. tum surrēxī. summum
perīculum sēnsī. domum circumspectāvī, sed nihil vīdī. vīcus erat
quiētus. Celer dormiēbat. itaque ad lectum redībam.

subitō manus mē tenuit. tum pugiōnem cōnspexī. dē pugiōne   5
    cadēbat sanguis. 'custōdem Rōmānum iam necāvī,'
      susurrāvit vōx crūdēlis. 'canem saevum tuum sopōrāvī.
        nunc equitem Numidicum scelestum petō.'
        Giscōnem ē somnō excitāre volēbam, sed
        exclāmāre nōn audēbam.   10

        deinde rēs mīrābilis accidit. dē manū
        cecidit pugiō sanguineus. cum magnō
        clāmōre vir ignōtus periit. tum vōcem
        nōtam audīvī: 'es tūta, Catia.' Indus
        prope senem mortuum stābat.   15
        gladium magnificum tenēbat.

diu *for a long time*
cōgitō *I think, consider*
nōnnūllī *some, several*
lectus *bed*
sentiō *I feel, notice*
itaque *and so, therefore*
pugiō *dagger*
vōx *voice*
saevus *savage*
sopōrō *I drug*
somnus *sleep*
excitō *I wake up*
sanguineus *bloody*

tūtus *safe*

LANGUAGE PRACTICE

1. Translate the following sentences, taking care to pair the adjectives with the appropriate nouns.

    a. multōs annōs mīlitēs nostrās thermās aedificābant.
    b. Rōmānī bonam pācem habēre cupiēbant.
    c. contrā hostēs crūdēlēs Luccus vīcum dēfendēbat.
    d. dē plaustrō grave saxum subitō cecidit.
    e. captīvus īnfēlīcem puerum servāvit.
    f. tandem senex saevus custōdem vīdit.

2. Select the correct form of the adjective to fill the gap, then translate the sentence.

    a. Giscō et Indus in .... popīnā sedēbant.   (parvō, parvā, parvīs)
    b. Druidēs dē contrōversiīs .... cōnstituērunt.   (difficilibus, difficilēs, difficilis)
    c. .... līberī deae vōta dedērunt.   (omnēs, omnī, omnibus)
    d. ego Lūcīliō epistulam .... mīsī.   (brevis, breve, brevem)
    e. praemia amīcīs .... dabāmus.   (fidēlis, fidēlēs, fidēlibus)
    f. cōtīdiē tū cum .... frātribus labōrābās.   (laetus, laetīs, laetōs)

Military life

Roman camp at Aquae Sulis

In about AD 44 the Roman force arrived in the area which was to become the town of Aquae Sulis. They met no resistance from the local British tribe. The Dobunni had been trading with the Roman Empire for decades and accepted the Romans peacefully. The Romans built a wooden fort there to protect the strategically important crossing point of the River Avon, about 800 meters away from the spring. It was an important location, on the Fosse Way, ready to protect the Roman terrritory to the east and continue the assault against the Silures to the west.

The vicus

The arrival and construction of a Roman camp attracted craftsmen and traders. Settlements grew organically next to Roman camps. Here native Britons, foreign merchants, and Roman veterans lived and interacted with the soldiers in the camp. In this way early Roman Aquae Sulis was shaped by military needs.

We can see the Latin word **vīcus** *in many place names in Britain. It was adapted in Old English to become wic, wick, wich, or wych. Some examples of places which grew from Roman settlements are Hackney Wick, Gatwick, Aldwych, Dulwich, Norwich, and Ipswich.*

Vindolanda

The fort at Vindolanda was on the northern frontier of the Roman Empire in Britannia. When it was first built in the 80s AD it was a wooden structure, but it was later rebuilt in stone. Just outside the walls of the military fort was a vicus which also contained a bathhouse.

What makes the site of Vindolanda special is the discovery of over four hundred wooden tablets, preserved in the waterlogged ground of a rubbish heap in the corner of the commander's house. Most of these are from AD 97–103. Although they were written a few decades after our stories are set, the picture they paint of daily life in a Roman camp would not have changed significantly.

The tablets are made of thin slivers of wood approximately 1/10 inch thick, about the size of a postcard. They give us an insight into the lives of ordinary soldiers, usually not mentioned in historical texts. From the tablets we can also see how the soldiers interacted with the local people.

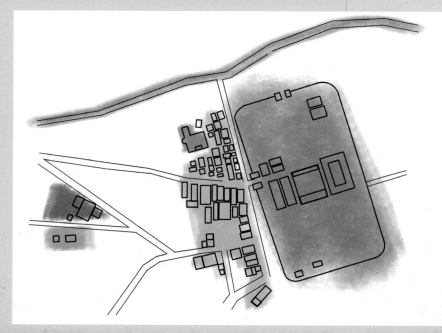

Key

red: army camp

yellow: vicus

blue: bathhouse

purple: temples

orange: industrial area

green: road

Work duties

One tablet from Vindolanda records the duties of the soldiers at the camp:

> Of 343 men present, twelve were making shoes, eighteen were building the bathhouse, some were out collecting lead, clay, and rubble. Others were assigned to the wagons, the kilns, the hospital, and to plastering duty.

QUESTION

Look at these images from Trajan's column. What are the soldiers doing?

Trajan's column

Trajan's column is a huge monument in Rome, built to commemorate Emperor Trajan's defeat of the Dacians (in modern Romania). The continuous image carved on stone winds twenty-three times round the column from the base to the top and depicts scenes from the conquest.

Although it depicts a military campaign, there are relatively few scenes of battle. Instead we can see tasks carried out by the soldiers.

Everyday life

The Vindolanda tablets and other artefacts found at the site allow us to see the more intimate relationships within the camp and the preoccupations of the people who lived there.

Flavius Cerialis

Flavius Cerialis was the commander of the camp from about AD 97. His family was allowed to live within the camp. Archaeologists have found a party invitation to his wife Lepidina from her friend at a nearby camp:

> Greetings from Claudia Severa to Lepidina. On September 11, sister, for my birthday, I ask you to come and visit us, to make the day more enjoyable for me, if you are free.

Other soldiers would also have had contact with their families. This lucky soldier received a package containing some essentials and a note from his family:

> I have sent you ... pairs of socks from Sattua, two pairs of sandals and two pairs of underpants. Greet all your messmates with whom I pray that you live in the greatest good fortune.

Games and passing the time

Life in an army camp was not all about battles and training. Many soldiers saw little military combat. Instead they built roads and infrastructure for the conquered territory. In their free time, soldiers played games and gambled with dice. These dice are made of ivory and glass.

The people of Roman Britain

D[IS] M[ANIBUS] REGINA LIBERTA ET CONIUGE BARATES PALMYRENUS NATIONE CATVALLAVNA AN XXX

To the spirits of the dead, for Regina his freedwoman and wife, of the Catuvellaunian tribe, aged 30, Barates, a Palmyran by birth [set this up]
Regina the freedwoman of Barates, alas.

Most of the inscription is in Latin; the last line is in Palmyrene (Aramaic). Barates was from Palmyra in Syria.

This tombstone was found at Arbeia, a fort near the eastern end of Hadrian's Wall. In the late second century AD Arbeia was a busy port and supply base for the troops stationed on Hadrian's Wall. Near to the fort there would have been a small civilian settlement occupied by traders and workmen who supplied the needs of the soldiers, veterans who had settled there rather than returning to their native lands, and the families of the soldiers. Officially, Roman soldiers were not allowed to marry, but they often formed relationships with local women, as Gisco did with Catia. After discharge a soldier could marry, and any children he already had would become Roman citizens.

A multilingual society

The Iron Age Britons spoke a language (more precisely, several variants of a language) which historians call Brittonic. The Roman conquest introduced to Britain not just the Latin language, but also the languages of the Empire. People came to Britain from all over the Empire, as soldiers, traders, slaves, and administrators, and they brought with them their languages, such as Greek, the languages of the Gallic and Germanic tribes, and the languages of the Near East. For these people Latin was their common language.

The curses from Aquae Sulis are almost all written in Latin. The curse on this tablet (*right*) is intriguing because it is in a language which isn't Latin. It could be a British language.

QUESTIONS

Look at the maps of the Empire (pages 2–3) and Britannia (page 125). Find Syria, and the territory of the Catuvellauni.

1. Both Regina and Barates were far from home. How might they have felt about living in Arbeia? How might they have come to live so far from their places of birth?

2. What can we learn from this tombstone about the people who were living in Britain in the second century AD?

Chapter 10: Aquae Sūlis 165

valē

Catia	annō secundō nūntium fēlīcem accēpimus. praefectus ab exercitū Giscōnem dīmīsit. itaque nōs ā Britanniā discēdere cōnstituimus.
Giscō	nūntium trīstem simul accēpimus. Antigonus ā morbō ignōtō periit.
Sabīna	quōmodo tū ad urbem Rōmam advēnistī, Inde?

praefectus *commander*
dīmittō *I release, discharge*

nūntius *message, news*
5 morbus *illness*

Indus respondēre coepit, sed subitō Lūcriō popīnam intrāvit et Faustō appropinquāvit. dominō susurrāvit servus, 'omnia parāvī.'

Faustus	necesse est tibi ab urbe discēdere, fīlia mea.

The pediment of the temple at Aquae Sulis, with its original colors shown. The carved head is thought to be based on the Gorgon's head, a symbol of the goddess Minerva.

QUESTION

As you learned in the previous chapter, the Britons burned the temple of Claudius at Camulodunum, yet they accepted the temple at Aquae Sulis. Why do you think the reactions were so different?

The Gorgons

The Gorgons were three sisters in Greek mythology. They were such terrifying monsters that anyone who looked at their faces was turned to stone. Often they were portrayed with glaring eyes and protruding tongues, snakes in their hair, beards, tusks, and golden wings.

SOURCE 3

A fifth-century BC Greek painting from a vase.

The inside of a Greek drinking cup from the sixth century BC, decorated with a Gorgon's face.

SOURCE 1

- Look at Source 1. What features of a Gorgon does this painting have? Why might the painter have chosen to decorate a drinking cup in this way?
- Similar images were often used by the Greeks on armor such as shields and breastplates. Why was that appropriate?

Medusa and Perseus

The most famous of the Gorgons was Medusa. She is often depicted with snakes in her hair, but with the face and body of a young girl. King Polydectes ordered Perseus to bring him the head of Medusa. With the help of the gods, Perseus was able to decapitate Medusa with his sword while she was asleep. But even after death Medusa's gaze retained its power, so Perseus put the head in a bag and eventually gave it to Minerva.

- Read or listen to the story of Perseus and Medusa.
- How was Perseus helped by the gods? What did they give him?
- How are Perseus and Medusa presented in this statue?

A nineteenth-century sculpture, showing Perseus with the head of Medusa.

SOURCE 2

- What parts of the story of Perseus and Medusa are being depicted in Source 3?

Study Sources 1, 2, and 3.

- Compare the way Gorgons are depicted in these three images.

Minerva and the Gorgon

Minerva (called Athena by the Greeks) was the goddess of war. She was often shown wearing a helmet and a breastplate, which was sometimes decorated with the image of a Gorgon's head.

- Look at the pediment of the temple at Aquae Sulis on page 165. Why do you think that some people think the figure in the middle is a Gorgon?

Petrification

If you are petrified, you are, literally, turned to stone. Petrification ('turning into stone') comes from the Latin words *petra* (rock) and *faciō* (make).

- Petrification is a punishment in myths and stories from many cultures. Why do you think it is such a common theme?
- Imagine what it would mean to be turned to stone. How might it be different from being dead?
- Why is it such a frightening and terrible punishment?

RESEARCH

Find out about:
- the winged horse Pegasus.
- Perseus and Andromeda.
- other female monsters in mythology, e.g. Scylla, the Sirens, the Sphinx, the Harpies.
- people being turned to stone in other myths.

Chapter 11: mare

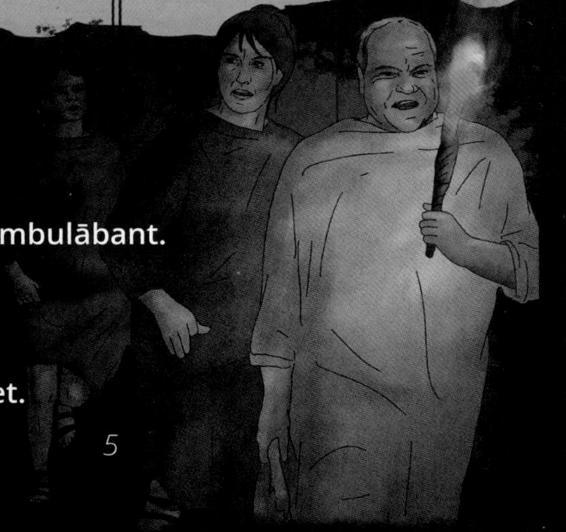

Ostia

nox erat. urbs erat quiēta. paucī hominēs per urbem ambulābant.

nōs per viās urbis celeriter prōcēdēbāmus.

Sabīna	cūr festīnāmus?
Lūcriō	pater tuus senātōrī magnam pecūniam dēbet.
Rūfīna	Faustus senātōrem maximē timet. servus 5
	senātōris tē quaerit.

ROMA

OSTIA

postquam Lūcriō mē ad Forum Boārium
dūxit, flūmen per tenebrās vīdī.
tum scapham ascendimus.

trēs hōrās per flūmen nāvigābāmus,   10
tum ad portum vēnimus. portus Rōmae,
nōmine Ostia, iam erat clāmōsus.
multī operāriī ibi labōrābant.

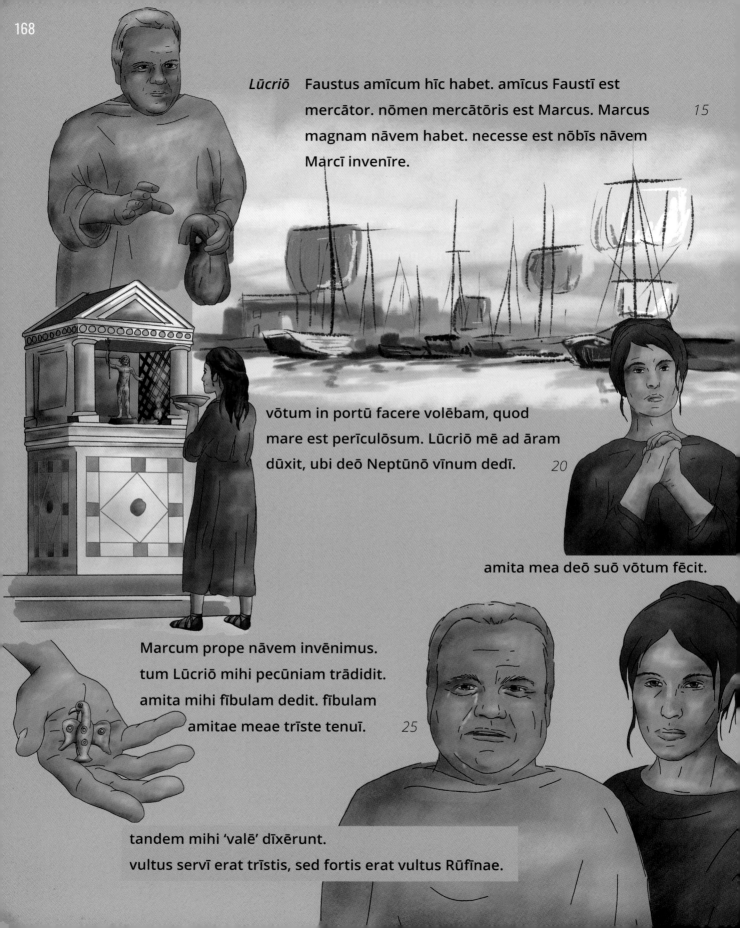

Lūcriō   Faustus amīcum hīc habet. amīcus Faustī est
mercātor. nōmen mercātōris est Marcus. Marcus   15
magnam nāvem habet. necesse est nōbīs nāvem
Marcī invenīre.

vōtum in portū facere volēbam, quod
mare est perīculōsum. Lūcriō mē ad āram
dūxit, ubi deō Neptūnō vīnum dedī.   20

amita mea deō suō vōtum fēcit.

Marcum prope nāvem invēnimus.
tum Lūcriō mihi pecūniam trādidit.
amita mihi fībulam dedit. fībulam
amitae meae trīste tenuī.   25

tandem mihi 'valē' dīxērunt.
vultus servī erat trīstis, sed fortis erat vultus Rūfīnae.

Romans and the sea

If you look at the map on pages 2–3 you will see that the Roman Empire hugs the coast of the Mediterranean Sea, from Lusitania and Mauretania in the west to Syria in the east, with the city of Rome at the center. The Romans called the Mediterranean *Mare Nostrum* (Our Sea) as well as *Mare Internum* (Internal Sea).

Oceanus and the gods of the sea

Romans believed that the Mare Internum, along with all the rivers, flowed into a great sea that surrounded the world, which they called Oceanus. Britannia was beyond Oceanus, which added to its mystery and strangeness in the eyes of Romans, especially before the conquest.

The poet Horace wrote this in 13 BC:

> **bēluōsus quī remōtīs**
> **obstrepit Ōceanus Britannīs**
> monster-filled Oceanus
> who roars round the far-off Britons

Oceanus was worshiped as a god. In this mosaic (*below*) he has lobster claws sprouting from his head, while dolphins and other fish are swimming out of his beard. The mosaic was made to decorate the floor of a grand villa in Cordoba, in Spain.

Neptune (the equivalent of the Greek Poseidon) was the main sea god worshiped by the Romans. His festival, the Neptunalia, was celebrated on July 23 and he had a temple on the Campus Martius in Rome. There were temples and statues of Neptune all over the Empire. For example, this inscription is from a temple in Chichester (Noviomagus) in Britain.

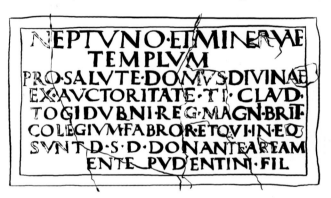

NEPTVNO·ET·MINERVAE
TEMPLVM
PRO·SALVTE·DOMVS·DIVINAE
EX·AVCTORITATE·TI·CLAVD·
TOGIDVBNI·REG·MAGN·BRIT·
COLEGIVM·FABROR·ET·QVI·IN·EO
SVNT·D·S·D·DONANTE·AREAM
·ENTE·PVDENTINI·FIL

QUESTIONS
1. Which two gods is the temple dedicated to?
2. Why might these two gods have been chosen?

Before setting out on a voyage travelers gave offerings and prayers to Neptune, asking for a safe journey. And again, when they arrived safely at their destination, they would make more offerings and prayers of thanksgiving. Read these two excerpts from plays by Plautus. Why have the speakers been to sea?

> I give thanks to Neptune, my patron, who lives in the fish-teeming salt sea, for bringing me home from his dwelling, weighed down with my catch and with my boat safe.

> I give thanks to Neptune and to the Tempests because I am returning home safe, my business successful. And also to Mercury, who has helped me in my business affairs and quadrupled my fortune with profits.

Right: underwater archaeologists found this statue of Neptune in the River Rhône at Arles (Arelate) in the south of France.

ad Galliam

nōnnūllōs diēs nāvigābam. nāvis animālia ad amphitheātra Galliae ferēbat. Marcus erat benignus, sed sōla eram. mox artificem iuvenem cognōscēbam. nōmen artificis erat Alexander. Alexander quoque erat sōlus. familia Alexandrī in Lūsitāniā habitābat.

Sabīna	ecce, terra! estne Gallia?	5
Alexander	minimē, Sabīna. est īnsula Corsica.	
Sabīna	quālis īnsula est Corsica?	
Alexander	īnsula magna et perīculōsa est, ubi latrōnēs saevī in montibus habitant.	

amphitheātrum	*amphitheater*	-ne	*(marks a question)*
benignus	*kind*	quālis?	*what sort of?*
sōlus	*lonely*	latrō	*robber*
cognōscō	*I get to know*	mōns	*mountain*

tum nauta vetus nōbīs appropinquāvit. barba nautae erat longa, vultus rūgōsus.   10

nauta	hodiē mare est quiētum. mihi placet. placetne tibi, puella?
Sabīna	certē, mihi placet. mare est pulchrum. sed ānxia sum. vīdistīne mōnstra in marī? vīdistīne pīrātās?
nauta	multās fābulās nautārum dē mōnstrīs audīvī, 15 sed mōnstra numquam vīdī – nisi elephantōs et crocodīlōs et hippopotamōs! hahae! fābulīs dē mōnstrīs nōn crēdō. sed ōlim manus pīrātārum nāvem meam petīvit. 20

quid? pīrātaene tē petīvērunt? ubi accidit?

vetus	*old*	nisi	*except*
barba	*beard*	elephantus	*elephant*
longus	*long*	crocodīlus	*crocodile*
rūgōsus	*full of wrinkles*	hippopotamus	*hippopotamus*
placet	*it is pleasing, it pleases*	crēdō	*I believe*
pīrāta	*pirate*	manus	*gang*
numquam	*·never*		

LANGUAGE NOTE 1: THE GENITIVE CASE

1.   Look at the way the words **nauta**, **amīcus**, and **urbs** change in these sentences:

   nauta nōbīs appropinquāvit. barba nautae erat longa.
   A sailor approached us. The beard of the sailor was long.

   amīcus nāvem habet. nōmen amīcī est Marcus.
   A friend has a boat. The name of the friend is Marcus.

   urbs erat quiēta. per viās urbis prōcēdēbāmus.
   The city was quiet. We were going through the streets of the city.

   The words **nautae** (*of the sailor*), **amīcī** (*of the friend*), and **urbis** (*of the city*) are all examples of the **genitive case**.

2.   The genitive case can be represented in English in two ways. For example:

   barba nautae erat longa.   *The beard of the sailor was long.*
                                or   *The sailor's beard was long.*

3.   Think of two different ways to translate the words in bold below:

   nōmen īnsulae est Corsica.

   nōs **nāvem Marcī** quaerēbāmus.

   tū **pecūniam fūris** invēnistī.

The first sailors

These extracts from two Latin poems tell us about how some Romans felt about the sea and sailing.

1. Ovid is speaking about his girlfriend, who is preparing to go on a voyage:

   If only the first ship, the Argo, had sunk
   and no more seagoing ships were ever made ...
   Look, Corinna is leaving her familiar bed and
      household gods
   and is preparing to go on treacherous paths.

2. Horace expresses amazement at the daring of the first person who ever set sail, braving the dangers of the sea. The poem continues:

   God, in his wisdom, separated
   the land from the sea – they are not compatible.
   But he wasn't successful; unholy boats
   still cross the waters they shouldn't touch.
   Humans are in a hurry to commit every
      forbidden sin.

The language of the sea

You have met the word *mare* for 'sea'. This isn't the only word the Romans had for the sea.

unda/undae *wave/waves*	**altum** *the deep*
frētum *narrow channel*	**sal** *salt*
vada *the shallows*	**marmor** *marble*
aequor *level surface of the sea*	
pontus *a Greek word for 'sea'*	

*   Why do you think the Romans had so many words for the sea?
*   How many words for 'sea' can you think of in English?

QUESTIONS

1.   What different attitudes to the sea and sailing are shown in these poems?

2.   Can you think of any things people do nowadays that the Romans would have regarded as impossible or unnatural?

Underwater archaeology

More than a thousand shipwreck sites have been found in the western Mediterranean, mostly off the French coast, dating between 100 BC and AD 100. Some of these ships were very large, able to carry heavy cargo.

A large merchant ship discovered off the coast near Toulon in southern France is one of the largest ancient ships ever found under the sea: it was about 130 feet long and 30 feet wide, with two masts. It was carrying a cargo of wine and pottery when it sank in about 75–60 BC. Archaeologists found amphorae stamped with the name of the potter, Publius Veveius Papus, who had a workshop in the wine-exporting area of Terracina in southern Italy, not far from Rome. After the excavation the ship was reburied in sand and left on the seabed.

In 2004 archaeologists found a river barge (*above*) in the mud at the bottom of the River Rhône at Arles in southern France. The boat had sunk with its cargo of building stones from a quarry less than 10 miles north of the town. The mud in the river had protected the boat from decay, but the water had damaged the wood. As a result, the whole boat was soft and spongy, held together only by the water of the river. It would disintegrate if the water evaporated. Conservationists found a solution. They soaked the wood for months in polyethylene glycol, then freeze-dried it. But the barge had to be cut into sections so that it would fit into the freeze-dryers. The whole process took two years.

Roman Arelate (modern Arles) was nearer the sea than it is nowadays, because the mouth of the River Rhône has silted up and moved the coastline out. It was one of three great harbors in southern Gaul: the others were Massalia (modern Marseille) and Narbo (modern Narbonne). Ships sailed upriver from the Mediterranean or via a canal which linked Arelate with Massilia. Goods were then unloaded and transported from Arelate up the Rhône on barges. This was the supply route for the north of the Empire, including the legions stationed in Britannia.

RESEARCH

Find out about other discoveries made by underwater archaeologists. What techniques do they use to preserve what they find?

Navigation and maps

The Romans did not have compasses or charts; instead, they navigated by careful observation of their surroundings. They learned astronomy from the Phoenicians, an ancient civilization which originated in modern-day Lebanon. They applied this knowledge to navigate the sea at night, using the stars to find which direction was north. They also used the position of the sun at midday and the direction of the winds.

> The helmsman keeps watch all night long and observes the movement of the stars.   *Petronius*

In general, the Romans sailed close to the coast to avoid straying off course. They also used landmarks on the mainland or the many islands of the Mediterranean to navigate their route. When sailing close to the coast, they used a device called a sounding line to avoid hitting rocks or sandbanks. A sounding line was a heavy bell-shaped mass, usually made of lead, attached to a rope. Sailors would hang it over the side of the ship and let it fall to the bottom of the sea to estimate the depth of the water.

The first sailing directions for coastal trips were written in Greek and described voyages within the Mediterranean. These directions listed landmarks that sailors could follow to stay on course and warned of dangers along the way. Later directions, in Latin or Greek, covered trips along the Atlantic coast of Africa and past the Persian Gulf to India and beyond.

Roman geography

Without planes or satellites to record the earth from above, creating a precise map was incredibly difficult. Generally, the Romans were more concerned with making their maps practical, rather than accurate – just like subway transit maps where stations are positioned relatively, but the distances between them are completely wrong. Roman maps are effective for following a route from point A to point B, but give no real sense of the distances between.

Strabo's *Geographica*

Strabo was a Roman geographer, who came originally from Greece. He wrote his *Geographica* between AD 14 and 37. His work, which included maps, was a history and description of the known world. It focused on people and cultures, as well as geographical features.

QUESTIONS

Compare this reconstruction of Strabo's map to a modern map of the world.

1. How accurate is it?
2. What is missing?

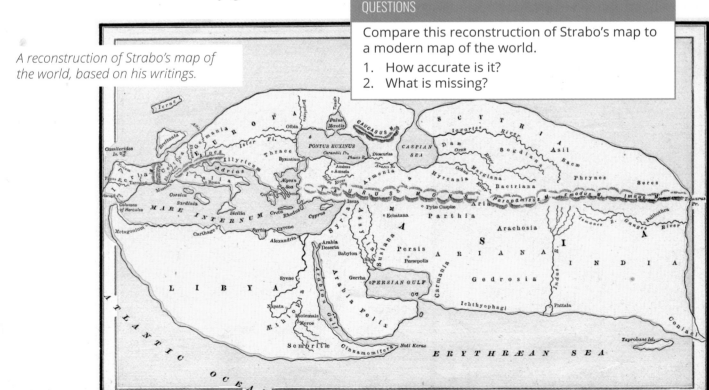

A reconstruction of Strabo's map of the world, based on his writings.

pīrātae

tum nauta fābulam mīrābilem dē pīrātīs nārrāvit.

'rem bene meminī. cum patre meō iter longum faciēbam. multae amphorae erant in nāve – vīnum ad Āfricam ferēbāmus – et inter nautās erant nōnnūllī senēs iuvenēsque. prope īnsulam Siciliam, ubi multī pīrātae habitābant, nāvigābāmus. subitō pater exclāmāvit: "ecce nāvis! sunt pīrātae! sunt fūrēs!"   *5*

'mox manus fūrum saevōrum nāvem nostram oppugnāvit et superāvit. nōs omnēs perterritī erāmus. aliī pīrātīs frūstrā resistēbant, aliī ā pīrātīs fugere temptābant. clāmōrēs senum et iuvenum perterritōrum nāvem implēbant. pater meus sub multitūdine amphorārum mē cēlāvit.   *10*

'dux pīrātārum nautīs duōbus appropinquāvit et exclāmāvit, "nunc vōs estis captīvī nostrī. quantam pecūniam in nāve habētis?"

'nautae respondēre nōlēbant. itaque dux scelestus eōs statim occīdit. tum corpora duōrum nautārum in mare iēcit. pīrātae pecūniam per tōtam nāvem quaerere coepērunt. ūnus pīrāta amphorīs appropinquāvit. perterritus cucurrī. tum ante oculōs pīrātārum et captīvōrum in mare dēsiluī. patrem nōn iterum vīdī.'   *15*

mihi attonitae susurrāvit Alexander, 'nautae perīcula nārrāre gaudent.'

amphora *amphora, jar*
Āfrica *Africa (Roman province in what is now North Africa)*
-que *and*

aliī ... aliī ... *some ... others ...*
multitūdō *large number, crowd*
cēlō *I hide*
duo *two*
quantus? *how big? how much?*
eōs *them*

dēsiliō *I jump*
gaudeō *I rejoice*

Dangers at sea

Piracy was a big problem in the Mediterranean in the first century BC, but by the time of our stories it was under control. Emperor Augustus established a navy, with fleets based at several points on the coasts of Italy, Gaul, and Egypt. One of the duties of these fleets was to suppress piracy.

Pirates still operated in the Red Sea. The *Travelers' Guide to the Red Sea*, an ancient handbook for merchants and sailors, advises ships to sail down the middle of the Red Sea, avoiding coming close to shore, to escape being detected by pirates.

Pirates would seize the cargo of a ship and kill the crew and passengers, or sell them into slavery. If the passengers were wealthy or important, the pirates would ransom them.

SOURCE 1 In this extract from Vergil's *Aeneid*, the hero of the poem, Aeneas, is sailing from Sicily to Italy when the goddess Juno sends a storm to destroy his fleet:

Suddenly the clouds snatch away both sky and daylight
from the Trojans' eyes; black night lies over the sea.
The poles thunder and the sky flashes with repeated lightning,
and everything threatens the crew with immediate death.
As Aeneas is praying, a screeching blast from the North Wind
strikes the sail head-on, and lifts the waves up to the stars.
The oars shatter. Then the prow turns and offers its side
to the waves. A sheer mountain of water presses against it in a mass.
Some men are dangling on the crest of a wave; for others, the water gapes open
and reveals the seabed between the waves; the water seethes with sand.
The South Wind snatches up three ships and hurls them onto hidden rocks.
The East Wind drives three ships from the deep sea
onto the shallow sandbanks, a pitiful sight,
smashes them into the shallow water, and surrounds them with a pile of sand.

SOURCE 2 Propertius is lamenting the death of Paetus, a young merchant who drowned at sea:

Money, it's you who are the cause of life's stress;
because of you we set out early on the road that leads to death.
When Paetus spread his sails for Alexandria,
it was you who overwhelmed him – three, four times – in a furious sea.
For, in pursuit of you, the poor boy lost his life at a young age,
and now floats as unfamiliar food for far-off fish.
Paetus, your mother is unable to give you the proper rites of a loving burial,
or put you in the tomb with your family ashes.
But now the sea birds stand over your bones,
now for you the whole Carpathian Sea is your tomb.

QUESTIONS

Look at Source 1.
1. Does reading this passage help you imagine what it feels like to be caught in a storm at sea?
2. How does Vergil use detail and images to make the storm seem exciting and frightening? Pick out some examples to support your ideas.

Look at Source 2.
3. Why do you think the Romans considered dying at sea to be a terrible fate?

LANGUAGE NOTE 2: THE GENITIVE PLURAL

1. The sentences below contain examples of the genitive plural:

   dux pīrātārum nōbīs appropinquāvit.
   The leader of the pirates approached us.

   ante oculōs captīvōrum in mare dēsiluī.
   Before the eyes of the prisoners I jumped into the sea.

   clāmōrēs senum nāvem implēbant.
   The shouts of the old men were filling the ship.

2. Compare the forms of the genitive case with the nominative singular in each declension:

SINGULAR	1st decl.	2nd decl.		3rd decl.	
nominative	**puella**	**amīcus**	**dōnum**	**fūr**	**caput**
genitive	**puellae**	**amīcī**	**dōnī**	**fūris**	**capitis**

PLURAL					
genitive	**puellārum**	**amīcōrum**	**dōnōrum**	**fūrum**	**capitum**

3. There is a chart of all the noun endings you have met on page 272.

This mosaic from Sicily is called The Great Hunt. It shows wild African animals being hunted and put onto ships to be taken to Rome.

tempestās I

1 mare erat quiētum. lūna surgēbat.
sed vultus Sabīnae erat gravis.

2 esne ānxia, Sabīna?

3 ego sum sōla, Alexander.

4 nōnne familia tua in Galliā tē exspectat?

5 minimē. Marcus mē ad Galliam dūcit, ubi familia eius mē exspectat. familia mea in Subūrā habitat, et dē salūte patris meī timeō.

tempestās *storm*   eius *his, her, its*
lūna *moon*   salūs *safety*
nōnne? *surely?*

II

mediā nocte vōx Alexandrī Sabīnam ē somnō excitāvit:

'tempestās appropinquat, Sabīna!'

puella fessa surrēxit et circumspectāvit.
ventus iam erat validus.

mox multum pluēbat.   *5*

deinde fulgēbat
et   *vehementer*
tonābat.

Sabīna mare ānxiē spectāvit.
nunc undae altae ubīque erant.   *10*
fragor undārum altārum eam terruit.

tum undae altissimae nāvem percutere
coepērunt. omnēs in nāve erant perterritī. aliī
deum Iovem ōrābant, aliī deum Neptūnum.
nautae valdē timēbant, et clāmōrēs   *15*
animālium – leōnum elephantōrumque –

ventus *wind*	tonābat *it was*
multum *much*	*thundering*
pluēbat *it was raining*	undae *waves*

subitō ingēns unda nāvem percussit.

ei mihi!

omnis spēs salūtis aberat.   20

Alexander manum puellae vix
tenēre potuit.

haereō   *I cling*
vīs   *force*
sēdō   *I settle, calm down*
Arelātē   *Arles (town in southern France)*

ūnā ad nāvem diū haerēbant.
nōnnūllās hōrās ventus erat validissimus.
sed tandem vīs ventī sēdāvit. nāvis ad portum   25
Galliae, nōmine Arelātē, lentē advēnit.

LANGUAGE NOTE 3:-NE AND -QUE

1. In this chapter, you have met **-ne**. Can you explain what it does? Why do you think the Romans added it to the first word in the sentence?

est Gallia.
It's Gaul.

estne Gallia?
Is it Gaul?

pīrātae tē petīvērunt.
Pirates attacked you.

pīrātaene tē petīvērunt?
Did pirates attack you?

2. You have also met **-que**, which is an alternative to **et** (*and*). Can you explain where it is placed?

cibum et vīnum cupiēbant.
cibum vīnumque cupiēbant.

They wanted food and wine.

leōnēs audīvī et elephantōs ingentēs vīdī.
leōnēs audīvī elephantōsque ingentēs vīdī.

I heard lions and saw huge elephants.

Traveling by sea

In the Roman world people often traveled long distances, despite the discomfort, dangers, and time which this involved. Soldiers, traders, skilled craftsmen and artists, students and teachers, and government officials (sometimes with their wives and households) undertook long journeys all over the Roman Empire. Sabina's journey from Ostia to Arelate would have taken about nine days in July.

When deciding whether to go by road or sea, travelers had to weigh several factors: cost, time, weather, the season of the year, and comfort. A sea voyage was generally preferred to an overland journey because it was cheaper and took less time, even if the distance was greater. The Mediterranean Sea is relatively calm for part of the year, but in winter sailing is dangerous, and rocky outcrops around islands are always a risk. There was a sailing season, from March to October. Outside these months sailing was less frequent, although it was still possible.

There were no passenger ships. Instead, people traveled on merchant ships. Either they slept on deck or the ships put into shore and the passengers slept in tents or inns.

Pliny traveled from Rome to Bithynia, on the south coast of the Black Sea (which Romans called Pontus Euxinus), in AD 110, to take up the post of governor of the province. He wrote to Emperor Trajan to update him on his journey:

I am reporting to you that I am at Ephesus with all my staff, having sailed round Cape Malea* despite being held back by opposing winds. Now I intend to make for my province, partly by coastal ships and partly by carriage. For, while the intense heat discourages overland travel, the continual winds are a deterrent to going by sea.

* *Cape Malea, at the south-eastern tip of Greece, was notoriously dangerous for ships.*

QUESTIONS

1. Find Bithynia and Ephesus on the map of the Roman Empire (pages 2–3).

2. What difficulties and dangers of travel does Pliny mention, (a) by land and (b) by sea?

LANGUAGE PRACTICE

1. Choose the genitive form of the noun to complete each sentence, then translate.

    a. Boudica erat dux et rēgīna ....   (Britannōs, Britannōrum, Britannīs)
    b. pater .... Giscōnem occīdere temptāvit.   (Luccō, Luccī, Luccus)
    c. nēmō pecūniam .... invenīre potuit.   (puella, puellam, puellae)
    d. manus .... nōs ē vīcō discēdere iussit.   (mīlitēs, mīlitibus, mīlitum)
    e. turba .... prope templum conveniēbat.   (fēminārum, fēminās, fēminīs)
    f. pācem et spem .... petīvimus.   (pāx, pācis, pācem)

2. Rewrite the following sentences using -**que** instead of **et**, then translate.

    For example: Rūfīna et Lūcriō ad portum Sabīnam dūxērunt.
                    Rūfīna Lūcriōque ad portum Sabīnam dūxērunt.
                    Rufina and Lucrio took Sabina to the port.

    a. Lūcriō pecūniam et cibum ferēbat.
    b. ego ad portum vēnī et nāvem invēnī.
    c. altōs montēs et flūmina magna in Corsicā vīdimus.
    d. Sabīna cum nautā veterī et iuvenī artifice nāvigābat.

3. Use -**ne** to change each statement into a question, then translate the question.

    For example: pīrātae crūdēlēs sunt.
                    pīrātaene crūdēlēs sunt?
                    Are the pirates cruel?

    a. Rūfīna in popīnā labōrat.
    b. tū in urbe habitāre vīs.
    c. līberī silvam sine patre intrāvērunt.
    d. animālia tempestātem timent.

In this mosaic you can see two merchant ships, sea creatures, including a whale and a dolphin, and shells.

Pirates in the Mediterranean Sea

Pirates in the Mediterranean Sea

Pirates, robbers of the sea, had long been a problem in the ancient Mediterranean. It was only when the Roman Empire became strong enough to control the whole Mediterranean that being a pirate became so dangerous that it was no longer an attractive means of making money. Before that, in the first century BC, piracy was such a serious nuisance for the Romans, and interfered so regularly with traffic across the sea, that it endangered trade and vital food supplies to Rome. The pirates mostly operated from bases on the wild and rugged coast of Cilicia.

Caesar captured by pirates

In 75 BC, at just 25 years old, Julius Caesar was captured by a crew of pirates. When they demanded a ransom to release him, Caesar laughed at them. They clearly had no idea who he was. Feeling that the ransom demand was too low for someone of his status, Caesar replied that he would pay more than twice the amount they had asked for. While his men went to gather the money for the ransom, he spent about forty days in the hands of the pirates. He exercised with them, told them to be quiet when he wanted to sleep, and read his own poetry to them, to show how unconcerned he was about being captured. He also jokingly promised the pirates that, once he was freed, he would find them, capture them, and crucify them. And that is exactly what he did. Once he regained his freedom, he quickly put together a fleet, captured the pirates when they were anchored, and crucified them all.

Stone portrait of Pompey, 50 BC.

This marble bust of Julius Caesar was made in 1514.

Pompey and the pirates

According to the ancient biographer Plutarch, the power of the pirates increased when civil wars between the Romans in the first century BC left the seas unguarded. The number of pirate ships grew to over a thousand, and they felt so secure in their power that they attacked not only ships, but also coastal cities and islands, demanding huge ransoms for their release. In 68 BC pirates even attacked Ostia, 15 miles from Rome, burning the military fleet stationed there. The impact on trade was so bad that the Romans were faced with famine.

The Romans then voted to give a special command to one of their best generals (Pompey the Great) to rid the sea of pirates. Pompey was granted enormous power: 500 ships, 120,000 troops, 5,000 cavalry, and as much money as he needed. He was also given complete *imperium* (power) over all Roman territory within 50 miles of the coast, for a period of three years.

Pompey accomplished the task in one single campaign in 67 BC, or at least so it was presented in ancient times. Modern scholars think that he may just have reduced the threat to a manageable size. Starting in the west, he is said to have cleared the Mediterranean as far as Sicily within forty days, and to have finished the job within three months. Trade across the Mediterranean increased immediately and so the price of food dropped, making Pompey extremely popular with the people of Rome.

This Roman coin, decorated with the prow of a ship, commemorates the achievements of Pompey the Great.

Chapter 12: incendium
fūmus

1 Lūcriō et Rūfīna nāvem Marcī diū spectābant.

2 tum scapham ascendērunt et ad urbem Rōmam trīste redīre coepērunt.

3 lacrimāsne, domina?

4 minimē! aliquid in oculō habeō. nihil est.

5 scapha lentē prōcēdēbat. mox in caelō fūmum dēnsum cōnspexērunt.

fūmus *smoke*
aliquid *something*

6 Rōmam spectā, domina! caelum spectā!

8 *Lūcriō*
spectā intentē et audī, domina! magnum est incendium. multae avēs ab urbe volitant.

7 pff. nōlī timēre, Lūcriō! saepe in urbe sunt incendia.

flammae

postquam ad Forum Boārium advēnimus, ego et Rūfīna ad Subūram
statim festīnāvimus. in aliīs partibus urbis nūllum incendium erat,
sed in aliīs partibus, fūmus dēnsissimus viās implēbat. flammae
maximae multās domōs dēlēbant. violentia ventī et inertia hominum
incendia augēbant. aestus flammārum in viīs angustīs erat   5
intolerābilis.

tandem ad Forum Rōmānum advēnimus, fessī et ānxiī. tum rem
terribilem audīvī et vīdī: templum et domus virginum Vestālium
ardēbant. nōnnūllae virginēs Vestālēs etiam nunc in domō erant.
vigilēs, cīvēs, servī servāre temptābant virginēs. equī sīphōnēs   10
ad incendium trahēbant. ubīque clāmōrēs hominum et equōrum
hinnītus aurēs nostrās implēbant.

'currite, servī!' clāmābant vigilēs. 'plūs aquae portāte! domum,
templum, virginēs Vestālēs prōtegite! deōs prōtegite! nōlīte timēre!'

'Lūcriō, vigilēs adiuvā! virginēs servā!' inquit Rūfīna. 'ego ad Subūram   15
eō. Faustum quaerere volō.'

statim vigil 'ohē, tū!' clāmāvit. 'aquam in domum fer! virginēs Vestālēs
quaere!' perterritus et immōtus stetī. 'nōlī timēre, serve! deī tē
exspectant! fortēs Fortūna adiuvat!'

vigil mē verberāvit. exclāmāvī. iterum vigil mē verberāvit. ad terram   20
dēcidī. dolor per tōtum corpus ruēbat. surrēxī, aquam tulī, et in
domum quam celerrimē ruī. sed fervor, flammae, fūmus mē statim
superāvērunt. vix spīrāre poteram. iterum dēcidī. nōn surrēxī.

violentia	*violence*
inertia	*inaction*
augeō	*I increase*
aestus	*heat*
angustus	*narrow*
terribilis	*terrible*
ardeō	*I burn*
etiam	*even*
vigil	*fireman*
sīphō	*fire engine, pump*
hinnītus	*neighing*
auris	*ear*
eō	*I go*
immōtus	*motionless*
Fortūna	*Fortune (goddess)*
ruō	*I rush*
quam celerrimē	*as quickly as possible*
fervor	*heat*
spīrō	*I breathe*

Fighting the fire

On the night of July 18 AD 64 a fire broke out in Rome. It spread rapidly throughout the city, moving easily between the tightly packed buildings, many of which were made of wood. The fire burned for nine days almost continuously, and when the ashes cooled only four of the fourteen regions of the city were left unscathed.

Rome had a permanent fire brigade, which had been created by Emperor Augustus in AD 6. Their official name was *vigilēs urbānī* (watchmen of the city), but they were commonly known by their nickname, *sparteolī* (little bucket-carriers). In AD 64 the brigade numbered about 4,000 men, who were freedmen; two hundred years later there were 7,000 vigiles. They lived in barracks which were distributed around the city and they stored their equipment in depots.

The vigiles patrolled the city, especially at night, on the lookout for fires. They may also have been responsible for maintaining law and order, but this always came second to prevention and control of fires. They carried buckets and axes. Other equipment included ladders, hooks, poles, and blankets soaked in water or vinegar. The vigiles would rush to the site of a blaze, then form a line to the nearest source of water, a fountain or tank, and pass buckets of water from hand to hand. Often they could not extinguish the flames directly, so they tried to control the spread of the fire by demolishing the building:

> The firemen broke down the door suddenly and began to create uproar with their water and axes.
>
> *Petronius*

When Pliny was governor of Bithynia, there was a fire in the city of Nicomedia. He wrote to Emperor Trajan about the lack of firefighting equipment:

> There was no publicly provided pump, no bucket, in short no equipment for putting out fires. I have given orders that these things shall be provided in the future.

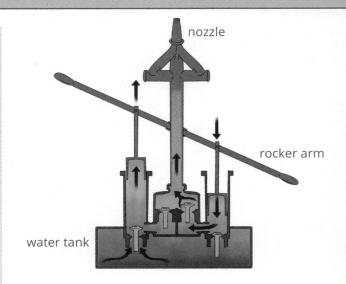

A diagram of a Roman water pump.

The first fire engine?

Ctesibius was a Greek who lived in Alexandria in Egypt in the third century BC. He discovered that compressed air could be used as a source of power and invented the water pump (*sīphō*) to raise water to a height. Three hundred years later another Alexandrian, Hero, developed this idea to invent the first fire engine. The pump was worked by two men, pushing down each side of a rocker arm alternately, like a seesaw. The nozzle could be adjusted so that you could aim the stream of water at a particular spot. The water pump could have been mounted on wheels and pulled by horses.

Some of Hero's inventions remained at the stage of theory and were never manufactured. Archaeologists have found remains of pumps, although they can't tell whether they were used for putting out fires or for other purposes such as drawing water up from a well.

QUESTIONS

1. What can you deduce from Pliny's letter about the equipment used in Rome for fighting fires?

2. What equipment do modern firefighters have which Romans lacked?

3. How might a pump have been used to control a fire? Would it have been more effective than buckets of water?

LANGUAGE NOTE 1: GIVING ORDERS

1. In the sentences below, the Latin words for *look!*, *move!*, *send!*, and *listen!* each have two forms. Can you explain why?

Rūfīna, caelum spectā!	**amīcī, incendium spectāte!**
Rufina, look at the sky!	*Friends, look at the fire!*
ohē, nauta! scapham movē!	**nautae! nāvem movēte!**
Hey, sailor! Move your rowboat!	*Sailors! Move your boat!*
serve, nūntium ad marītum mitte!	**servī, nūntium ad portum Ostiae mittite!**
Slave, send a message to my husband!	*Slaves, send a message to the port of Ostia.*
audī, domina!	**audīte intentē, nautae!**
Listen, mistress!	*Listen carefully, sailors!*

2. The form of the Latin verb used for giving orders is called the **imperative**. It changes depending on whether one person or more than one person is being told to do something.

3. In the singular the imperative ends in a single vowel (the infinitive without -**re**) and in the plural it ends -**āte**, -**ēte**, -**ite**, or -**īte**.

4. Now look at the following sentences:

nōlī timēre, Lūcriō!	**nōlīte currere, līberī!**
Don't be afraid, Lucrio!	*Don't run, children!*

Orders not to do something use **nōlī** or **nōlīte** followed by the infinitive. **nōlī** and **nōlīte** are the imperatives of **nōlō**, so mean *be unwilling* (to do something).

Vesta and Vulcan

For the Romans fire was a divine power which could be both protective and destructive. You have read about Vesta, the goddess associated with the sacred flame of Rome, on page 58. She represented the fire of the hearth and home. Vulcan, on the other hand, was the god of fire as a violent, and sometimes destructive, force. He had an annual festival on August 23, the Vulcanalia, and people offered prayers and sacrifices to him to ward off fires. Vitruvius, who wrote about architecture, said that Vulcan's temples should be built outside the city, to draw the god of fire away.

Vulcan was also the god of volcanoes and blacksmiths. The word 'volcano' comes from his name.

A marble relief of the god Vulcan, from Herculaneum.

incendium in Subūrā

in urbe

incendium per viās tōtīus urbis nunc ruēbat. flammae tabernās, popīnās, īnsulās violenter cōnsūmēbant. Subūrānī per viās fūmōsās ruēbant. mātrōnae līberīs haerēbant. dominī servōs vocābant. omnēs effugere temptābant.

violenter *violently*
fūmōsus *smoky*

prō popīnā

Catia ad popīnam festīnābat. Quārtillam prō popīnā cōnspexit.   *5*

'ubi est īnfāns?' ancilla perterrita rogāvit.

'nōnne tū eum cūrās?' exclāmāvit Catia.

Currāx perterritus fēminās spectāvit. 'īnfāns in īnsulā dormiēbat ...', puer susurrāvit.

Catia ferōciter exclāmāvit, et ad iānuam īnsulae cucurrit.   *10*   **ferōciter** *fiercely*

'tēcum veniō, īnsula est perīculōsa!' ancilla exclāmāvit. 'hīc manē, mī fīlī.'

in īnsulā

mātrōna et ancilla īnsulam intrāvērunt et per fūmum ascendēbant.
īnsula obscūra erat et fēminae mūrōs cellārum vix vidēre poterant.
lentē prōcēdēbant. in tabulātō secundō prōcēdere nōn potuērunt, quod
trabs conlāpsa erat. flammae nunc ubīque erant. Catia dēspērābat,   15
sed Quārtilla trabem cum magnā difficultāte sustulit. 'festīnā!' Quārtilla
exclāmāvit. Catia breviter dubitāvit, sed clāmōrem īnfantis audīvit, et
'nōlī timēre, Quārtilla!' dīxit, 'reveniō!' Catia sub trabem rēpsit, et in
tabulātum tertium festīnāvit. subitō ingēns fragor resonāvit.

tabulātum	*floor, story*
trabs	*beam*
conlāpsus	*collapsed*
breviter	*briefly*
dubitō	*I hesitate*
rēpō	*I crawl*
resonō	*I resound*

in viā

in viā Currāx īnsulam ānxiē spectābat. subitō Giscō advēnit et 'dīc mihi,   20
ubi est uxor? ubi est fīlius?' rogāvit.

'in īnsulā sunt, domine. īnfāns ...', servus dīcere coepit. tum Currāx et
Giscō ingentem fragōrem audīvērunt. Giscō puerum rapuit et celeriter
cucurrit. tōta īnsula in viam cecidit.

rapiō	*I grab*

LANGUAGE NOTE 2: VOCATIVE CASE

1.   Look at the words in red in the following sentences:

ubi es, puella?
Where are you, girl?

ubi estis, puellae?
Where are you, girls?

amīce, spectā caelum!
Friend, look at the sky!

amīcī, spectāte caelum!
Friends, look at the sky!

labōrāsne, fūr?
Are you working, thief?

labōrātisne, fūrēs!
Are you working, thieves?

2.   Latin uses the **vocative** case for someone who is being spoken to.

3.   The vocative case has exactly the same form as the nominative case, except in the singular of the second declension, where -**us** becomes -**e** and -**ius** becomes -**ī**:

Faustus est in popīnā.
Faustus is in the bar.

Fauste, quid tū in popīnā facis?
Faustus, what are you doing in the bar?

fīlius Quārtillae in viā currit.
Quartilla's son is running in the street.

hīc manē, fīlī!
Stay here, son!

Lucius Secundus Octavius

This tombstone is from Trier in Gaul. It was set up by a group of friends in memory of Lucius Secundus Octavius, who died in a fire. The inscription reads:

To the Gods of the Dead, and to the eternal memory of Lucius Secundus Octavius of Trier, who has suffered a most cruel death. He escaped half-naked from a fire, then, putting aside concern for his own safety, he was trying to save something from the flames when he was crushed by a falling wall and returned his friendly spirit and his body to the earth. Affected more greatly by his death than by the loss of their property, Romanius, Sollemnis, Januarius, and Antiochus, Secundus' fellow freedmen, have memorialized on the inscription of this tomb his most noble qualities, which he displayed towards them with all kinds of proof.

DISCUSSION

Think about what this inscription tells us about Lucius Secundus Octavius and the friends who set up his tombstone.

Fuel and fire

> We cannot help but marvel that almost nothing is made without using fire. Fire takes some sand and, depending on the place, turns out glass or silver, cinnabar or lead, paint pigments or medicines. It is fire that melts stones into copper, fire that produces iron and molds it, fire that purifies gold, fire that hardens the stones that hold our houses up.
>
> *Pliny the Elder*

All technology relies on energy. As the Empire grew and cities evolved, more and more energy was required to provide and maintain the luxuries of a civilized Roman lifestyle on a large scale. The Romans relied heavily on fire in most technological processes and imported large amounts of wood and coal. Just as they tamed water (see Chapter 5), the Romans harnessed the destructive nature of fire and used its power to fuel their Empire.

WOOD – Wood was the primary source of fuel. By AD 64 Italy was almost completely stripped of its forests. For this reason Rome had to import timber from the northern parts of its Empire. Archaeological evidence indicates that the more energy-packed charcoal (the black residue left after burning wood) was used in the manufacturing of glass and metals. Charcoal provides about twice as much energy as raw wood and burns evenly with little smoke.

COAL – The use of coal was confined to areas where it was available locally. Archaeological remains have shown coal being used in settlements and forts in Britain and around the River Rhine. Burning coal could produce very high temperatures so it was often used in iron workshops.

VEGETABLE WASTE – Olive pits, acorns, seeds, small branches, and straw were also used as fuel. They would have been used locally on country estates, where the residues of crop processing and food production were used to heat the villa and baths.

PETROLEUM – The word 'petroleum' comes from the Latin words *petra* (rock) and *oleum* (oil). The Roman geographer Strabo writes about naphtha, a black oil which was found in Babylon:

> If naphtha is brought near a flame it catches fire; if you smear it on something and bring it near a fire, then it too bursts into flames; and it is impossible to put these flames out with water (for they burn even more violently), unless a great amount is used.

Industry

Producing pottery, glass, and iron requires high temperatures of up to 2,000°F in furnaces or kilns. To reach these temperatures large amounts of charcoal or coal were needed, so the centers of these industries were often located close to sources of fuel. In the time of the Roman Empire, demand for these products increased and small, local industries expanded. Items began to be mass-produced and fine pottery, ironware, and glassware were exported across the Empire.

Left to right: a glass jug; a glass drinking cup made using a mold-blowing technique – the cup is signed in Greek 'by Ennion'; a green glass bowl; a terracotta beaker.

Solar power

One sign of luxury was a really hot bath. Seneca commented on the excessive temperatures of the imperial baths in Rome:

> The baths used to be heated to a temperature suitable for use and for health, not the heat that has recently become fashionable, like a real fire!

A huge amount of wood was required to reach these high temperatures. One estimate calculates that heating the caldarium of a single bath consumed over 100 tons of wood per year. Local resources were running out and prices were increasing, so instead the Romans turned to solar energy to heat their baths. They built bath complexes with huge glass windows and glazed the outside of the walls to trap the sun's rays, orientating the baths to face south-west.

After the fire

Rebuilding the city

Tacitus generally paints a very hostile picture of Nero. However, in his account of the immediate aftermath of the fire he reports that the Emperor introduced measures to relieve the plight of the homeless and destitute. He erected temporary shelters in the Campus Martius and his own gardens. He ensured supplies of food were shipped from Ostia and neighboring towns, and reduced the price of grain. Later, Nero saw to the rebuilding of Rome. The narrow, winding, haphazard alleys were replaced with a more organized, open layout of streets. Nero contributed to the construction of insulae from his own money. New regulations were introduced aimed at reducing the risk of fire. Height limits were placed on buildings and there had to be open areas between them to stop the spread of fire. Everyone had to keep equipment in their homes for putting out fire. Nero also made sure more watchmen were employed to safeguard the water supply, because people had been siphoning off water to their own homes.

Compensation

There was no property insurance in Rome. Instead, people who had lost property relied on the generosity of the emperor or friends for compensation. After the fire of AD 64, Nero gave owners grants to rebuild insulae and houses. Emperor Tiberius had compensated the owners of insulae after fires in AD 27 and 36. More informally, sometimes houseowners relied on contributions from friends. This system could be abused, as Martial indicates in this poem:

> You bought a house, Tongilianus,
> for 200,000;* a disaster that is only too frequent
> in this city took it from you.
> Gifts poured in, amounting to a million sesterces.
> Might you be suspected of having set fire to your
> own house, Tongilianus?

This was very cheap for a house in Rome.

QUESTIONS

1. Why were fires so frequent and so destructive in Rome? Think of as many reasons as you can.

2. What did some of the emperors do to prevent the outbreak of fires and to help the victims? What do you think their motives were?

Finding a scapegoat

There was a rumor that Nero was responsible for the fire, despite his aid to the victims and his plans for rebuilding the city. In order to shift suspicion from himself, Nero needed to find a scapegoat (someone to blame). He blamed the Christians. The Christians were already unpopular because they refused to join in with Roman religious ceremonies and worship Roman gods, so they were a minority who could easily be picked on. Christians in Rome were rounded up and punished in abominable ways: torn to pieces by dogs, or put on crosses and set on fire as human torches.

There may have been no evidence at all that some Christians were guilty of arson. On the other hand, there was a Christian prophecy that Christ would come to earth again and this event would be marked by fire. It is possible that some Christians, believing that this prediction was coming true, lit fires to add to the blaze.

Domus Aurea

Nero used the fire as an opportunity to build an extravagant new palace: the *Domus Aurea* (Golden House). It covered the Palatine and the Esquiline Hills, as well as the area in between them. In addition, he commissioned the Colossus, a huge bronze statue of himself, over 100 feet high.

The walls of the palace were painted with intricate frescoes, and the floors and even the ceilings were covered with mosaics of precious stones and ivory. To top it all, it had a golden roof. There were 300 large rooms, and it seems that the entire building was dedicated to entertainment and receiving guests. The domed ceilings, made from concrete, had never been seen before. Overall, the palace was an extraordinary feat of architecture and engineering.

There is evidence that the common people were invited into the extensive gardens of the palace. There are no archaeological remains of walls or fences around the grounds at all. Indeed two temples that had been destroyed in the fire were rebuilt within its grounds.

> The palace was so large that it had a triple colonnade a mile long. There was also a lake, like a sea, surrounded by buildings that represented cities. In addition to this, there was vast countryside, plowed fields, vineyards, pastures, and woods, with many wild and tame animals. In the rest of the house, everything was completely covered with gold leaf and decorated with jewels and mother-of-pearl. There were dining rooms with ceilings made from panels of ivory, which could rotate and scatter flowers down onto the guests. There were also pipes to sprinkle the guests with perfumes from above.
>
> *Suetonius*

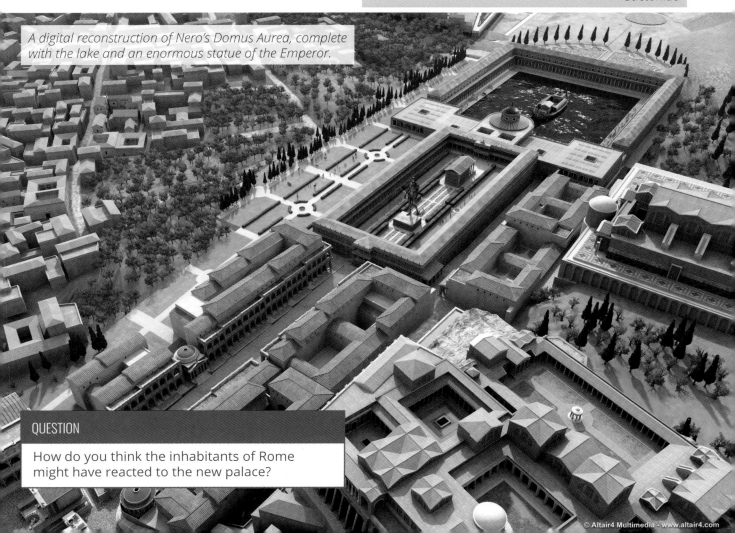

A digital reconstruction of Nero's Domus Aurea, complete with the lake and an enormous statue of the Emperor.

QUESTION

How do you think the inhabitants of Rome might have reacted to the new palace?

fūrēs

Chīlō ad fontem festīnābat. aqua nōn aderat in fonte, sed via prope fontem plēna Subūrānōrum perterritōrum erat. aliī aquam quaerēbant, aliī familiam vocābant. via erat fūmōsa et vōcēs Subūrānōrum raucae erant.

raucus *hoarse*

Chīlō	heus, Procle! hīc sum!	5
Proclus	Chīlō! tūtus es, amīce?	
Chīlō	certē sum tūtus. et tū?	
Proclus	omnia āmīsī, Chīlō. incendium cellam meam dēlēvit. necesse est nōbīs quam celerrimē effugere.	
Chīlō	vah! ego nihil āmīsī, quod nihil habuī! audī, amīce. effugere nōn dēbēmus. ecce, omnēs sunt perterritī. omnēs effugiunt. mercātōrēs tabernās nōn dēfendunt. quid dīcis?	10
Proclus	mercātōrēs nōn adsunt ...	
Chīlō	venī, mī amīce!	15

mī *vocative of* meus

amīcī per viās festīnābant, et tabernās intrābant. pecūniam, bona, statuās abstulērunt. nēmō eīs obstitit. in ūnā tabernā lībertus aderat. simulatque fūrēs cōnspexit ē tabernā cucurrit. in aliā tabernā duae ancillae aderant, sed fūrēs eās terruērunt et fēminae effūgērunt. in ūnā popīnā amīcī vīnum et cibum invēnērunt. fūrēs vīnum ex amphorīs bibēbant. subitō vōcem īrātam audīvērunt.

bona *goods*
auferō *I steal*

20

vir	heus, vōs! quid facitis? dēsistite!	
Chīlō	abī, stulte. fuge!	

abeō *I go away*

sed vir nōn effūgit. Chīlōnem petīvit et amphoram ē manū rapere temptāvit. Chīlō amphoram in virum iēcit. amphora caput virī percussit. vir in pavīmentum dēcidit. fūrēs ē popīnā exiērunt. vir immōtus in pavīmentō popīnae iacēbat. multus sanguis ē capite fluēbat. periit Faustus.

25

pavīmentum *floor*

LANGUAGE PRACTICE

1.   Translate each sentence into Latin by choosing the correct word or phrase from each pair.

a. *Brothers, carry water to the forum!*

frāter,	aquam	ad forum	portā!
frātrēs,	aqua	ā forō	portāte!

b. *My friend, praise the words of the king!*

mī amīce,	laudā	verbum	rēgum!
meus amīcus,	laudāte	verba	rēgis!

c. *Fireman, order the slaves to enter the apartment buildings!*

vigil,	servum	īnsulīs	intrāre	iubēte!
vigilēs,	servōs	īnsulās	intrāte	iubē!

d. *Show the book to your companions, sister!*

librum	comitī	ostendite,	sorōrēs!
librōs	comitibus	ostende,	soror!

e. *Find the enemy and kill them, soldiers!*

invenī	hostēs	et eōs	interfice,	mīles!
invenīte	hostium	et eum	interficite,	mīlitēs!

f. *Write a letter to your mother and send a gift, my son!*

epistulās	ad mātrēs	scrībite	dōnumque	mittite,	mī fīlī!
epistulam	ad mātrem	scrībe	dōnaque	mitte,	meus fīlius!

2.   Rewrite the sentences below, changing the words in bold type from dative singular to dative plural, or vice versa. Then translate the new sentence. For example:

veterānī **nūntiō** epistulam trādidērunt.
veterānī **nūntiīs** epistulam trādidērunt.
The veterans handed over a letter to the messengers.

a. heri prīncipēs **rēgī** arma pulchra obtulērunt.

b. proelium incipere volēbāmus, sed **cōnsulibus** persuādēre nōn poterāmus.

c. prīmō īnfēlīx rēgīna **cōnsiliō** cōpiārum nōn crēdidit.

d. **Rōmānīs mīlitibus** saepe resistēbās, posteā tamen poenās dedistī.

e. prīmā lūce pugnāvistis et **mātrōnae fīliae**que auxilium tulistis.

What caused the Great Fire of Rome?

In the wake of the disaster, people tried to find someone to blame. Even now, almost 2,000 years later, the cause of the fire is hotly debated.

Arson or accident? What do you think?

1. The ancient sources

Source 1: Suetonius

AD 69 – 122

As if he were offended by the ugliness of the old buildings and the narrow, crooked streets, Nero set fire to the city. He did this so openly that some ex-consuls did not stop his slaves, even though they caught them on their property with torches. There were some granaries near the Golden House. Nero particularly wanted the land they occupied, so they were first demolished by military machines before being set on fire, because their walls were made of stone. For six days and seven nights the destruction raged, and people were forced to look for shelter in monuments and tombs.

Source 2: Cassius Dio

AD 155 – 235

Nero decided to bring about what, no doubt, he had always wanted – to destroy the whole city during his lifetime. Therefore, he secretly sent out men who pretended to be drunk, with instructions to set fire, at first, to one or two or even a few buildings in different parts of the city. People were desperate; they couldn't find the source of the fires or put them out, though they were constantly aware of many strange sights and sounds.

Many houses were destroyed because there was nobody to help save them. Many others were set on fire by the men who came to help; for the vigiles, who were more interested in looting than in putting out fires, lit new ones.

Source 3: Tacitus

AD 56 – 120

Disaster followed – whether accidental or by the Emperor's treachery was uncertain (writers have recorded both explanations). It was more serious and more frightening than all the disasters which have happened to this city through the violence of fires. The fire started in the part of the Circus Maximus next to the Palatine and Caelian Hills, where there are shops containing flammable merchandise. Instantly it became fierce. Fanned by the wind, it whipped through the length of the Circus. For here there were no houses or temples surrounded by solid walls; no other obstacle lay in its path. The furious blaze ran first over level ground, then rose up to the hills, before again devastating the area below. It outstripped all attempts to stop it, because of the speed of its destructive advance and because the city was vulnerable, owing to the narrow, twisting lanes and irregular blocks which characterized old Rome.

Nobody dared fight the fire. Many people were opposing efforts to put out the flames, repeatedly shouting out threats. Others were openly throwing in torches and yelling that 'they had their orders.' Either they wanted more freedom to loot or else they were under orders.

QUESTION

Tacitus reports that some people deliberately tried to make the fire spread and prevent it being controlled.

What **two** possible motives does he suggest that these people had?

2. The modern experts

Expert A - Gerhard Baudy
Professor

(In Rome, Christians were circulating prophecies.) 'In all of these oracles, the destruction of Rome by fire is prophesied, that is the constant theme: Rome must burn. This was the long-desired objective of all the people who felt subjugated by Rome.'

Expert B - Andrea Carandini
Archaeologist

'For instance, there are serious scholars who now say that the fire was not Nero's fault. But how could he build the Domus Aurea without the fire? Explain that to me. Whether or not he started the fire, he certainly profited from it.'

Expert C - Eric Varner
Art historian

'It seems unlikely that Nero would have started the Great Fire of AD 64, because it destroyed his palace, the Domus Transitoria, a huge, villa-like complex that stretched from the Palatine to the Esquiline.'

3. The suspects

Nero

Nero was known for his cruelty and eccentricities. Could he have been driven by a mad rush of power and a desire to see his city burn? Or was it a means to clear land for his new palace, the Domus Aurea?

The Christians

They didn't join in with the Roman state religion. Perhaps they had even heard the prophecy that Rome would burn? Or were they just an easy target as a hated minority?

An accident

Fires in Rome were common. Buildings were made of flammable materials and stood too close together. Could an innocent oil lamp or brazier have started the blaze, which then spread with a breeze and the summer heat?

Arson

Could the fire have been started or spread by someone looking to profit from it?

Your decision

Consider everything you have read about the fire in this chapter and what you know about the city of Rome.

Prometheus

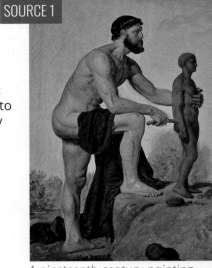

SOURCE 1

Life. And the four priorities for life: shelter, water, fire, and food. The ancient Greeks told a story about how humans first came into being, and first came to have fire. Prometheus, a Titan, created people out of nothing more than clay from the ground. He loved his new creations so much that he stole precious fire from Zeus to help them keep warm.

- Listen to or read the myth of Prometheus.
- Look at Source 1. In what ways is this similar to, and different from, how you imagined Prometheus with one of his creations? What do, and don't, you like about the painting? How similar to Prometheus is his creation?

A nineteenth-century painting showing Prometheus molding one of his creations.

SOURCE 2

Roman third-century AD stone carving.

A drawing of an ancient Greek bowl showing an eagle pecking out Prometheus' liver.

SOURCE 4

- Look at Source 2. Describe what you see in the image.

The creation of humans

Almost all cultures tell stories about how humans came to exist. Which can you think of? How similar and different are they to each other? What, if anything, do they have in common with the way Prometheus created humans? How do you explain the existence of humans?

SOURCE 3　God created mankind in his own image, in the image of God he created them; male and female he created them. God blessed them and said to them, 'Be fruitful and increase in number.'

The Bible

- Study Source 3. Do you think God/the gods created people to look like Him/them, or do we create gods to look like us?

Fire

Humans are the only creatures with the ability to control fire, and doing so allows us to stay warm, cook, ward off predators, be active in the dark, work metal, build machines, and run engines. Find out how long archaeologists think humans have been able to control fire, and how we first obtained it. What would life be like without it?

Defying the gods

Prometheus was willing to suffer perpetual torture to help humanity. Was he fighting for human rights against an oppressive ruler? A thief defying a direct instruction? How do you see Prometheus? Look at Source 4. Besides Prometheus, who else is being punished in the image?

RESEARCH

Find out more about:
- Pandora.
- other myths where characters are punished for their actions.
- the ancients' view of the liver.

Chapter 13: Arelātē
prīmā lūce

1 puella ad āram stat.

2 puella, quae ad āram stat, est Sabīna.

quī, quae, quod *who, which*

3 Sabīna per viās colōniae ambulat.

4 līberōs canēsque videt.

5 līberī, quī in viā lūdunt, sunt clāmōsī.
canēs, quī in viā iacent, dormiunt.

6 in colōniā est theātrum.

7 theātrum, quod est in colōniā, est pulchrum.

theātrum *theater*

8 in viā sunt cīvēs et servī. servus, quī pānem portat, Sabīnam salūtat.

9 tandem Sabīna ad pistrīnum venit.

pānis *bread*
pistrīnum *bakery*

minimē, Sabīna!
hōra prīma est.

vōs dormītis?

nōs labōrāmus!

How to build a Roman town
10 EASY STEPS

Follow these steps to build your own Roman-style town.

STEP 1: CHOOSE A LOCATION

When building a city, the first thing to do is choose a healthy location. It should be on high ground, not affected by fog or frost; its climate should be neither too hot nor too cold, but moderate.   *Vitruvius*

Sometimes the Romans built upon existing settlements in the territory they conquered, as at Arelate and Camulodunum; at other times they built new towns from scratch, as at Londinium. The advantage of a previously uninhabited location was that there was less risk of opposition from the local population who might not like the changes. For example, as you learned in Chapters 8 and 9, in Camulodunum some of the local people resented the arrival of the Romans. However, often the best sites had already been used by the native peoples.

STEP 3: ROADS

Roman towns built from scratch were constructed on a grid plan so all roads intersected at right angles. For Romans, the straighter the road the better. Consider how you can connect your new town to the road system of the Empire so that trade is easier and communications are faster. And within your town you'll want to build new roads or improve existing ones. You'll have to use the materials available to you locally to build your road. Efficient drainage and a level surface are key.

STEP 4: WALLS AND GATES

The walls around your city should have wide foundations and towers at regular intervals. At the top, the wall should be wide enough for two armed men to pass each other and the distance between the towers should not be further than you can shoot an arrow in case you are attacked. The towers should be round, not square, so they are stronger.

Public buildings have three purposes: defense, religion, community. Buildings for defense are walls, towers, and gates, designed to protect the town's inhabitants against enemy attacks. Religious buildings are the shrines and temples of the immortal gods. Buildings for communal use are gates, fora and marketplaces, baths, theaters, colonnades, and similar. Since they are for public use, they should be located centrally.   *Vitruvius*

STEP 2: WATER SUPPLY

Water is essential. Roman engineering enabled water to be carried for miles in aqueducts. However, find a spot with fresh water nearby and you save yourself time and money in construction and maintenance. Open streams, rivers, and lakes are the obvious sources of fresh water, but other sources can be found under the ground. Look for willows and rushes to indicate an underground source nearby.

What goes in must come out, so think about a way to remove waste from the city. Roman towns often had underground sewers, and cities close to large rivers used them to dispose of most of their waste directly.

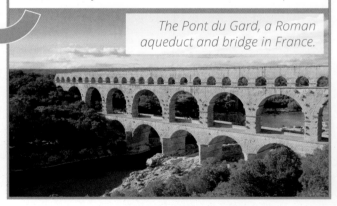

The Pont du Gard, a Roman aqueduct and bridge in France.

STEP 5: CIVIC BUILDINGS

Start with the focal point of the city, the forum. Build the forum in the center of the town and with it a basilica and the other buildings which make up the civic center.

STEP 8: ENTERTAINMENT

All good Roman towns had a large theater. Build a circus and an amphitheater as well, for greater impact and to provide more opportunities for entertainment.

The amphitheater at El Djem, Tunisia.

STEP 9: HOUSES AND SHOPS

You have the key features of your Roman town. Now fill in the space with houses, shops, and workshops – grand houses for the rich and small apartments for the poor.

STEP 10: GIVE IT A NAME

Roman towns were often named after their founders or benefactors. This was commonly an emperor, so many colonies carried the name of the emperor or a member of his family. These were commonly used:

- Colonia Iulia
- Colonia Claudia
- Colonia Augusta

Finally, choose a name for your Roman town.

STEP 7: SANITATION

You've got fresh flowing water, so add some pipes to reach the wealthier houses. Don't forget to build enough fountains at street corners, and public toilets for the ordinary people. Personal hygiene was important to the Romans and wealthier people bathed once a day. Build bath complexes and a palaestra to keep your inhabitants in good condition.

QUESTIONS

1. What features does a Roman town have which a modern town lacks?
2. What features does a modern town have which you wouldn't find in a Roman town?

STEP 6: PLEASE THE GODS
(PERHAPS THE MOST IMPORTANT)

Now you have the beginnings of a town, it is vital to please the gods. Place temples to the gods who protect the city somewhere with a high vantage point. Keep Mercury in the forum to help business, Apollo near the theater, and put Vulcan's temple far outside the city walls to draw away the risk of fire.

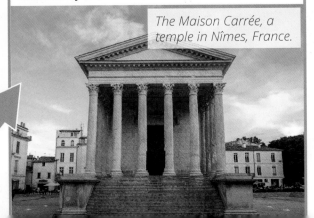

The Maison Carrée, a temple in Nîmes, France.

Arelate

Arelate (modern Arles) was on the River Rhône, in the Roman province of Gallia Narbonensis. The modern city is about 25 miles from the sea, but in Roman times it was a few miles nearer. The town was built at the lowest point at which the river could be crossed. You have already read a little about Arelate in Chapter 11 (page 172).

Arelate was originally a Greek town. When Julius Caesar was fighting in Gaul in 49 BC he used Arelate as a base for building warships to use against Massilia (modern Marseille). Three years later Arelate became a colonia, when Caesar settled veterans of the Sixth Legion there, taking some of the territory that had been occupied by Massilia. In return for their military support against Massilia, Caesar gave the people of Arelate Roman citizenship.

LANGUAGE NOTE 1: RELATIVE CLAUSES

1. In the sentences below, look at the clauses in red. Who or what do the clauses refer to?

    puella, *quae ad āram stat***, est Sabīna.**
    The girl, who is standing at the altar, is Sabina.

    servus, *quī pānem portat***, Sabīnam salūtat.**
    The slave, who is carrying bread, greets Sabina.

    theātrum, *quod est in colōniā***, est pulchrum.**
    The theater, which is in the colony, is beautiful.

2. In the first sentence **quae ad āram stat** relates to **puella** (*the girl*).
    In the second sentence **quī pānem portat** relates to **servus** (*the slave*).
    In the third sentence **quod est in colōniā** relates to **theātrum** (*the theater*).

3. The clauses are known as relative clauses, because they relate to someone or something.

4. Identify the relative clauses in the following sentences. To which Latin word does each relative clause refer?

    Marcus, quī magnam nāvem habēbat, Sabīnam laetē salūtāvit.

    in viā est plaustrum, quod ligna et saxa portat.

    colōnia, quae est in Galliā, templa pulchra habet.

    Sabīna Neptūnō, quī est deus maris, vīnum dedit.

The remains of a large bakery from Pompeii. You can see the millstones where the corn was ground. The oven is on the left.

in pistrīnō

Sabīna pistrīnum intrāvit et clāmāvit, 'salvēte! Poppille! Letta! adsum!'

in pistrīnō Poppillus, quī erat pistor et senex, pānem parābat. uxor rūgōsa, quae erat Letta, eum adiuvābat. Sabīnam simul vocāvērunt: 'venī ad nōs, cāra puella!'

Poppillō et Lettae appropinquāvit Sabīna. eīs ōsculum dedit.   5

ānser quoque erat in pistrīnō. animal ferōx, quod magnum clāmōrem tollēbat, puellam intentē spectābat.

'salvē, Manlī!' Sabīna ānserī dīxit. 'tūne domum nostram dīligenter custōdīs?'

Manlius tamen immōtus stetit.   10

tum exiit ānser. deinde Poppillus pānem calidum ad mēnsam tulit, Letta frīgidam aquam. quamquam Sabīna in pistrīnō labōrāre incipiēbat,

'sedē nōbīscum, Sabīna,' eī simul dīxērunt. 'cōnsūme et bibe.'

'vōbīs grātiās agō,' eīs respondit Sabīna. 'semper benignissimī estis. trēs mēnsēs mē iam cūrāvistis.'   15

'tē cūrāre gaudēmus,' dīxit Letta. 'diū sōlī habitāvimus. nec līberī nec servī nōbīs sunt, nisi ille ānser.'

subitō clangōrem ānseris in viā audīvērunt, tum magnum clāmōrem iuvenis.   20

'ohē, pistor! ubi es? ānser saevus tuus mē petit!'

Alexander in pistrīnum cucurrit. artifex, quī erat perterritus, vix spīrābat. omnēs trēs, quī ad mēnsam sedēbant, statim surrēxērunt.

Sabīna, quae paene rīdēbat, clāmāvit, 'salvē, Alexander! nōlī timēre! vīsne pānem emere?'   25

intereā Letta marītō suō susurrābat, 'puellam vidēre sōlum vult.'

'minimē!' respondit Alexander, quī multum ērubēscēbat. 'vōs omnēs invītāre ad theātrum volō.'

pistor	baker
ānser	goose
mēnsa	table
mēnsis	month
nec … nec …	neither … nor …
ille	that
clangor	honking
paene	almost
emō	I buy
sōlum	only

in theātrō

ingēns turba erat in theātrō, quod diēs fēstus erat. Alexander Sabīnaque ad summum gradum ascendērunt. Poppillus Lettaque, postquam ad duōs iuvenēs tandem pervēnērunt, inter eōs sēdērunt.

mē miserum! Sabīnam aut vidēre aut audīre vix possum! 5

gradus *step, row*
perveniō *I arrive, reach*

Poppillus	(*fessus*) ōh mihi! hic gradus est altus! senēs, quī in prīmō gradū sedent, sunt fēlīcēs!
Sabīna	sed aspectus est magnificus! ecce, scaenae frōns!
Alexander	nōnne emblēmata, quae sunt in scaenae fronte, vidētis?
Sabīna	ita vērō. 10
Poppillus	minimē, iuvenis! oculī meī nōn sunt validī.
Alexander	ūnum ex emblēmatibus, quae Sabīna vidēre potest, ego fēcī.
Sabīna	ōh! est pulcherrimum!
Poppillus	emblēma, quod indicās, vidēre nōn possum.
Letta	st, vōs trēs! tubae signum dant! 15

scaenae frōns *stage building*
emblēma *mosaic*
indicō *I point out*

chorus et pantomīmus, quōs multī spectātōrēs ardenter exspectābant,
scaenam intrāvērunt. fābula, quam chorus nārrābat, erat dē Pȳramō et
Thisbā. prīma persōna, quam pantomīmus agēbat, erat Pȳramus. deinde
pantomīmus persōnam Thisbae ēgit.

Poppillus	chorum audīre nōn possum. aurēs meae nōn sunt validae. 20
Letta	nihil est, mī lepus. fābulam bene nōvistī. spectā pantomīmum! prīmō Pȳramus, quem Thisba amat, ad mūrum stat. deinde Thisbam per rīmam vocat.
Alexander	pst! Sabīna!
Letta	nunc Thisba Pȳramō respondet. 25
Sabīna	quid est, Alexander?
Letta	Pȳramus Thisbaque iam cōnsilium capiunt ...
Alexander	mūrus, quī nōbīs obstābat, abest!

chorus *chorus*
pantomīmus *mime performer*
ardenter *eagerly*
Pȳramus et Thisba *Pyramus and Thisbe (star-crossed lovers)*
persōna *character*
agō *I act*
lepus *hare; darling*
nōvī *I know*

cōnsilium capiō *I make a plan*

amor *love*

amor semper vincit.

The theater

In Chapter 3 you learned that theatrical performances were part of the entertainment at some religious festivals. These performances took place in open-air theaters, which are some of the largest and most impressive Roman buildings. There was a large theater at Arelate, probably built in the time of Augustus. Some towns, for example Rome and Pompeii, also had smaller, roofed theaters.

The theaters in Gaul, and in other provinces of the Roman Empire, were modeled on those in Rome. But the government in Rome did not pay for them. Community buildings such as theaters were paid for by wealthy local people at their own expense.

The entertainment started early in the morning and lasted all day, with several plays being performed. As these were festival days, shops were closed and no business was done in the forum, so people were free to spend the day at the theater. Everyone could go – men, women, and children; free people and slaves; freedmen and freedwomen. A patron (*patrōnus*), who was a wealthy citizen, paid the expenses (actors, musicians, dancers, scenery, costumes), and admission was free.

> ## QUESTION
>
> Why do you think rich people would pay for theaters to be built and plays to be performed?

Plays and performers

The audiences enjoyed comedies, tragedies, and pantomimes. Sabina and her friends are watching a pantomime, which was a particularly popular kind of performance. Despite the name, this was nothing like the pantomimes performed nowadays. The Roman pantomime was a mixture of opera and ballet, performed by a single actor, a *pantomīmus*. The word 'pantomimus' is derived from two Greek words, and means 'acting everything'. The plots of pantomime were taken from myths and legends, such as the story of Pyramus and Thisbe. The pantomimus played all the parts; he or she would silently mime and dance. The pantomimus was accompanied by musicians and a chorus, who sang the words of the story.

Troupes of performers traveled from town to town. Most of the actors were men. They were often Greeks, either enslaved people or freedmen. The actors wore masks, probably made of linen, covered with plaster, and painted. Wearing a mask enabled the actor to play more than one character; he would show a change of character by changing his mask. Another advantage was that the features on the masks were exaggerated, so that members of the audience at the back of the theater would find it easier to identify the characters.

orchēstra

The *orchēstra* was a semicircular paved space in front of the stage. 'Orchestra' is a Greek word which means 'dancing-place'; in a Greek theater, the chorus danced and sang in the orchestra. In a Roman theater, there were two or three rows of wooden seats for leading citizens such as local magistrates.

cavea

The seating area was arranged in a semicircle around the orchestra, with stone seats rising in tiers. The best seats at the front were reserved for the richer, more important citizens. The theaters at Arelate and the nearby town of Arausio (modern Orange) had thirty-three rows and could hold about 6,000 to 8,000 people. The cavea was uncovered, but awnings (*vēla*) could be drawn over on ropes and pulleys to protect the audience from rain or sun.

scaenae frōns

The stage building behind the stage was as high as the auditorium. There were three or five doors, which served as entrances and exits to and from the stage. The *scaenae frōns* was elaborately decorated with columns, marble, mosaic, carvings, and niches holding statues of gods, goddesses, and emperors. Statues of Emperor Augustus and Venus, the goddess of love, decorated the theater at Arelate. The theater at Arausio had a statue, possibly of Augustus, in a niche above the center of the stage, and above the central door there was a carving of centaurs, mythical creatures which are half-man and half-horse.

altars

Plays often had scenes set at an altar. The theater at Arelate had two altars to Apollo, the god of music. One was on the stage and the other was in the orchestra.

scaena

The stage was a high, wide platform, covered with a roof.

The theater at Orange is one of the best preserved Roman theaters. In this illustration, a photograph of the theater as it is now is overlaid with a drawn reconstruction of the theater in Roman times.

sub vesperum

sub vesperum *towards evening*

sub vesperum spectātōrēs in theātrō stābant, gaudēbant, vehementer plaudēbant. post scaenam tamen āctōrēs, fessī et calidissimī, sedēbant aquamque frīgidam bibēbant. inter āctōrēs erat senex, nōmine Gabrus, quem cēterī valdē amābant. lentē surgere temptāvit, sed statim ad pavīmentum dēcidit. cēterī ad eum festīnāvērunt.   5

āctor *actor*

cēterī *the others*

| Darius | labor āctōris est dūrus, Gabre, et diēs sunt longī. quamquam optimus āctor erās, nunc nimium vetus es. nōbīs inūtilis es. manēre apud nōs diūtius nōn potes. |

diūtius *longer*

| Gabrus | ita vērō, Darī. quamquam difficile est mihi nūntium, quem tū fers, audīre, stultus tamen nōn sum – rem   10 intellegō. senex sum. sed nūllōs familiārēs habeō. nēmō mē cūrat. amīcī meī, quōs valdē amō, vērum mihi dīcite. quōmodo nunc vīvere possum? |

familiāris *relative*
vērum *truth*

| āctor prīmus | senex es, Gabre, et labōrāre nōn potes. necesse est tibi in viīs prope tabernās mendīcāre.   15 |

mendīcō *I beg*

| āctor secundus | minimē! in oppidō proximō sunt multae popīnae, in quibus fābulās mīrābilēs nārrāre potes. |

| Darius | ecce, Gabre! praemium, quod hodiē patrōnus nōbīs dedit, accipe! paucōs diēs bene vīvere potes! |

patrōnus *patron (who pays for the show)*

| omnēs | vīve ac valē, amīce!   20 |

ac *and*

| Gabrus | bene vīvite ac valēte, amīcī. |

eā nocte Gabrus sub aquaeductū sōlus dormiēbat.

eā nocte *that night*
aquaeductus *aqueduct*

QUESTIONS

What do you think happens to Gabrus next? Read these two options and discuss which you think is more likely. Alternatively, write your own ending.

a. fūrēs duo Gabrum et pecūniam eius cōnspexērunt. māne senex, quī frīgidus et ānxius erat, quoque pauper erat.

b. māne tamen duo frātrēs eum invēnērunt. 'tūne Gabrus es? sī tibi placet, nōbīscum venī. multōs annōs tū omnibus multum gaudium tulistī. nunc familiae nostrae placet tē cūrāre.'

māne *in the morning*

LANGUAGE NOTE 2: RELATIVE PRONOUNS

1. Look at **quae** and **quī**, the words for *who*, in the following sentences. Why do you think they have different forms?

    puella, quae ad āram stat, est Sabīna.
    The girl, who is standing at the altar, is Sabina.

    servus, quī pānem portat, Sabīnam salūtat.
    The slave, who is carrying bread, greets Sabina.

    quae and **quī** are both forms of the **relative pronoun**. **quae** is feminine because it relates to **puella** *(the girl)*. **quī** is masculine because it relates to **servus** *(the slave)*.

2. Now compare **quae** and **quam** in the following sentences.

    puella, quae ad āram stat, est Sabīna.
    The girl, who is standing at the altar, is Sabina.

    puella, quam Alexander videt, est Sabīna.
    The girl, whom Alexander sees, is Sabina.

    quae and **quam** both relate to **puella** *(the girl)*. In the first sentence, **quae** is nominative, because the girl is standing at the altar. In the second sentence, **quam** is accusative, because Alexander sees her.

3. The most common forms of the relative pronoun are given below. A chart of all the forms is on page 275.

SINGULAR	*masculine*	*feminine*	*neuter*
nominative	**quī**	**quae**	**quod**
accusative	**quem**	**quam**	**quod**

PLURAL			
nominative	**quī**	**quae**	**quae**
accusative	**quōs**	**quās**	**quae**

An incense burner in the shape of a comic actor sitting on an altar. The actor is wearing a comic mask.

Making bread

Bread was consumed in huge quantities throughout the Roman Empire. For the majority of the population, bread was an essential part of the diet. Grain and flour production were enormous industries, and bakeries were thriving businesses.

Grain was grown across the Empire, and particularly in those regions where the soil and climate were favorable. Most of the grain consumed in the city of Rome was grown in North Africa, then shipped across the Mediterranean. The grain was then ground into flour in mills. Some houses had their own hand-powered mills, and sizable towns had several larger mills, often driven by donkeys. The animals were harnessed to the mill, and walked round in circles to turn the rotating stones that ground the grain. Some mills produced finer flour than others, and the quality of the bread varied greatly.

Bakers (*pistōrēs*) used the flour to make loaves of bread that they baked in ovens. Towns had many bakeries of various sizes. Archaeologists have found thirty-one bakeries in Pompeii, a medium-sized town in southern Italy. Some bakeries had their own shops; others sold their bread to other shops or market vendors. A few bakers ran very big businesses and could make a fortune, such as the freedman Eurysaces, whose tomb survives in Rome.

The tomb of Eurysaces the baker, in Rome (first century BC). The circular holes perhaps represent grain-measuring vessels or kneading basins.

Industrial milling: Barbegal

A huge water-powered mill complex has been found at Barbegal, about five miles from Arelate. Sixteen waterwheels were set in two parallel rows on a steep hillside. A nearby aqueduct supplied them with water from above. The wheels powered grain mills that had the capacity to produce enough flour to feed about 10,000 people daily (approximately a third of the total population of Arelate). It's not certain whether the flour produced by these mills was used by local people to make bread, or whether it had another purpose. One theory is that the mill may have supplied flour to make *pānis nauticus*, a dry bread that could be stored for a long time and was used to feed sailors on ships traveling long distances. The Barbegal mill is the largest Roman watermill so far discovered, and one of the most impressive mechanical constructions from the ancient world.

Above: a reconstruction of the Barbegal mill.

LANGUAGE PRACTICE

1. Change the forms of **sum** from present tense to imperfect tense, then translate the new sentence. You may wish to use the chart on page 278 to help you.

    a. Sabīna **est** trīstissima, quod sōla **est**.

    b. quamquam **sum** iuvenis, fortissima tamen **sum**.

    c. in theātrō āctōrēs ad**sunt**. itaque in pistrīnō nōn **sumus**.

    d. quamquam crūdēlissimī **estis**, amīcī **sunt** fidēlēs.

    e. Poppillus et Letta per tōtum diem ab**sunt**. laetissimī **sunt**.

    f. chorum audīre nōn pot**es**, quod senex **es**.

2. Choose the correct form of the relative pronoun to complete each sentence, then translate.

    a. animālia, ... Alexander audīre poterat, erant ānserēs.
        (quae, quem, quod)

    b. caelum, ... fūmōsum est, intentē spectā!
        (quās, quod, quōs)

    c. taberna, ... frāter noster intrāvit, vestīmenta nova vēndēbat.
        (quōs, quam, quī)

    d. deinde artificem, ... emblēma cōnficiēbat, cōnspeximus.
        (quem, quae, quod)

    e. statuās pulcherrimās, ... fabrī in theātrum portābant, spectāre volumus.
        (quem, quōs, quās)

    f. quōmodo imperātōris equōs, ... in montibus altīs āmīsī, invēnistis?
        (quae, quōs, quam)

Mosaic of a theatrical tragic mask from the House of the Faun in Pompeii.

Pyramus and Thisbe

Pyramus and Thisbe were a young couple who lived next door to each other in the ancient city of Babylon. Although they were in love, their families did not approve of their relationship and would not allow them to marry. Pyramus and Thisbe would talk to each other through a crack in the wall between their two houses. They decided to meet and run away together secretly, but their plan ended in tragedy.

- Read or listen to the story of Pyramus and Thisbe.

Etiological stories

Etiological myths and stories are used to explain the origins and causes of natural phenomena which are not understood. Read Source 1:

> SOURCE 1   And tree, you who now cover the poor body of one man with your branches, and soon will shade two, keep the signs of our death and always bear fruit that is dark in color as is fitting for this grief, a memorial of our double death.
>
> *Ovid*

In Ovid's account of the story of Pyramus and Thisbe, he explains that the mulberry tree, under which Pyramus and Thisbe died, has red berries because of their blood.

- Why do you think humans make up stories that explain things in the world that they do not understand?

A sculpture of Pyramus and Thisbe, made in 1775.

SOURCE 2

'Star-cross'd lovers'

The story of Pyramus and Thisbe has inspired many other stories that are still well known today. The most famous is probably Shakespeare's *Romeo and Juliet*. Source 3 is an extract from this play.

> SOURCE 3   Two households, both alike in dignity
> In fair Verona, where we lay our scene
> From ancient grudge break to new mutiny
> Where civil blood makes civil hands unclean.
> From forth the fatal loins of these two foes
> A pair of star-cross'd lovers take their life
> Whose misadventured piteous overthrows
> Do with their death bury their parents' strife.
>
> *Shakespeare*

Look at Sources 2 and 3.

- What do you think the phrase 'star-cross'd lovers' means?

- Why do you think the tragedy of the star-cross'd lovers is so popular in literature, art, and drama?

Forbidden love

The parents of Pyramus and Thisbe forbade their relationship because of a family feud. Modern reworkings of the story give many other reasons why the couple can't be together.

- Think of examples of forbidden love from modern literature, drama, and film.

- Why do you think forbidden and secret love is often seen as more romantic?

RESEARCH

1. Find other stories from mythology or more modern sources that are etiological.

2. Shakespeare also told the story of Pyramus and Thisbe in *A Midsummer Night's Dream*. Read this version of the story.

Chapter 14: artifex

in officīnā fabrōrum

1 Sabīna in viā ambulābat, ubi officīnae fabrōrum erant. in ūnā ex officīnīs Alexander cum servīs labōrābat. Sabīna erat laeta, quod artificem cōnspexit.

2 salvē, Alexander!

3 salvē, Sabīna! intrā officīnam! opus novum meum tibi ostendere cupiō.

officīna *workshop*
opus *work*

4 Alexander laetus eī respondit.

5 vōsne emblēmata, quae sunt in forō, iam cōnfēcistis?

6 ita vērō, in forō diū labōrāvimus. heri pavīmentum prope basilicam, quae est in forō, cōnfēcimus. hodiē in officīnā labōrāmus, quod opus novum parāmus. crās in thermīs labōrābimus.

heri *yesterday*
crās *tomorrow*

7 artifex Sabīnae opus ostendit.

8 *Alexander* in mediō pavīmentō erit imāgō pulchra. in imāgine erunt fōrmae, partēs hominēs partēs piscēs, et alia animālia maris.

> imāgō *picture*
> piscis *fish*

9 *Sabīna* opus est optimum!
nautaene et Sīrēnēs in imāgine erunt?

> Sīrēn *Siren (a mythical creature: part-bird, part-woman)*

10 hahae! tūne nōs adiuvāre vīs?

11 ita vērō. hodiē Poppillum Lettamque adiuvō. sed crās vōs adiuvābō. tūne mē docēbis?

12 certē, crās tē docēbō. nōn difficile erit tē docēre. mīrābilis artifex eris.

> doceō *I teach*

LANGUAGE NOTE 1: THE FUTURE TENSE

1. Can you spot the difference in the verbs in these pairs of sentences?

   in thermīs labōrāmus.
   We are working in the baths.

   in thermīs labōrābimus.
   We shall work in the baths.

   And again in these sentences?

   ego amīcum doceō.
   I am teaching my friend.

   ego amīcum docēbō.
   I shall teach my friend.

   What is the difference in the form of the Latin verbs? How does that difference affect the meaning of the verbs?

2. The **-bō** and **-bi-** in the ending of the Latin verbs indicate that the action will take place in the future. This form of the verb is known as the **future tense**.

3. Look at the future tense of **vocō** (*I call*):

vocābō	*I shall call*
vocābis	*you* (singular) *will call*
vocābit	*he/she/it will call*
vocābimus	*we shall call*
vocābitis	*you* (plural) *will call*
vocābunt	*they will call*

   Note that the very end of the verb (**-ō**, **-s**, **-t**, **-mus**, **-tis**, **-nt**) tells us *who* will carry out the action and the **-b-**, **-bi-**, or **-bu-** tell us *when* they will do it.

4. Now compare these two sentences:

   imāgō pulchra est in pavīmentō.
   A beautiful image is in the floor.

   imāgō pulchra erit in pavīmentō.
   A beautiful image will be in the floor.

5. The future tense of **sum** (*I am*) is as follows:

erō	*I shall be*
eris	*you* (singular) *will be*
erit	*he/she/it will be*
erimus	*we shall be*
eritis	*you* (plural) *will be*
erunt	*they will be*

Creating mosaics

Mosaics covered floors, walls, and arches in public and private buildings in the Roman world. They were particularly suitable for decorating floors because they were strong and hard-wearing.

Above: pattern from a mosaic floor in Conimbriga, in Portugal.

Right: mosaic of Neptune and his wife Amphitrite, from a house in Herculaneum.

Preparing the floor

The Roman architect Vitruvius gives a description of how to lay mosaic floors well. He recommends starting with a timber base, then a two-level concrete floor (one rough layer and one smooth layer), which should be 'laid to rule and level.' Mosaics were made of small stones called *tesserae*. These stones were pressed into the concrete, then polished to smooth them down further, as Vitruvius instructs: 'the edges of the tesserae should be completely smoothed off, or the work will not be properly finished.' The cracks between the tesserae were filled with grout made of lime and sand.

> ### QUESTION
>
> Which materials do you think were used for the tesserae of the mosaics on this page?

Laying the mosaic

Simple mosaic floors could be laid directly with pegged lines or with guidelines scored into the concrete. Some examples of these guidelines have survived. Complicated designs, however, were probably pre-prepared in panels; the whole panel was then laid in place. The panels were made by gluing the tesserae onto a piece of fabric in a wooden frame, on which the design had been drawn in reverse image. These whole panels were then put in place on the prepared floor. Some mosaics show obvious errors where pre-prepared panels were fitted into the rest of a mosaic.

tesserae

Most tesserae were made from local natural stone, cut bricks, tiles, or pottery, which were cut to the right size. These tesserae were therefore predominantly in natural colors such as white, black, brown, and orange. The contrast between the different-colored tesserae could bring out patterns well. Some more exotic materials such as marble, glass, precious stones, and even gold were used as well for their brighter colors. The smaller the tesserae were cut, the more detailed the mosaics could be. As there was no paint involved, Roman mosaics look as bright now as when they were made.

Quality & fashion

Not all mosaics were made to the same standard of workmanship. Some were small and simple, made out of one or two colors only, with straightforward borders. Others included intricate geometric patterns, small details, vivid colors, and artistic use of shading and composition. The cost of a mosaic varied wildly as a result, and skilled mosaicists made a very good living and were in high demand. Certain mosaic designs appear to have gone in and out of fashion, too: in France and Italy in the first century AD, for instance, black and white mosaics became widespread. It is unlikely that this was to do with reducing cost (though the tesserae used were easier to source), since these mosaics are found in very large houses, including the villa of Emperor Hadrian. Instead, this was probably the current fashion.

Mosaic of the Minotaur in the labyrinth, from Conimbriga in Portugal.

Subject matter

Mosaics had a wide range of subject matter. Mythological scenes were popular, inspired by the Greek tradition. Imagery from nature, hunting scenes, abstract patterns, exotic or common animals, foods, and gods were all found. The location of a mosaic could influence its subject (sea gods in bathhouses, foodstuffs in dining rooms), but did not need to.

Mosaic makers

Very little is known about the people who made the beautiful mosaics we see today. Most ancient writers were not interested in craftsmen and have left us almost no record of their lives. Sometimes the art or work itself is praised, but the creator remains anonymous. Ancient writers, such as Pliny, praised famous artists and sculptors, but the trade of mosaic making was seen as a practical craft, tied to the construction of the building itself, rather than a true art form.

A whole team of craftsmen worked together to create a mosaic. The lead craftsman would draft the design and do the most intricate work, such as the faces, while less skilled craftsmen and apprentices would work on the borders.

Some mosaic makers left their signature within the design itself by including their name or a trademark symbol, such as a bird, in all their designs. One gravestone of a mosaic maker, set up by his son, reads:

> In many cities I exceeded all others in my skill, which I got from the gifts of Athena.

His son Proklos, who set up the gravestone, is described as being equally skilled. This is a rare insight into the lives of these craftsmen, who traveled around from city to city, perhaps gaining recognition for their work and passing the trade to their children and apprentices.

When archaeologists excavate a site they often lift mosaics and take them to museums. Sometimes they find markings in the cement underneath where the craftsmen sketched out the drawing in advance. At the Lod mosaic, in Israel, archaeologists have even found footprints of the ancient artists imprinted in the cement.

QUESTIONS

1. Look at the mosaics in this chapter. What do you think they can tell us about the tastes of the owners, and the space in which they were created?

2. Which aspects of life in the Roman world do these mosaics illuminate?

autumnus

autumnus erat. Sabīna etiam nunc in thermīs labōrābat. magnam imāginem delphīnī cum Philētō, quī erat ūnus ē servīs Alexandrī, faciēbat.

Sabīna	emblēmata paene cōnfēcimus, Philēte! laeta sum! omnēs cīvēs Arelātēnsēs nōs laudābunt.
Philētus	ego sum laetior quam tū! fortasse nunc Alexander mē nōn diūtius verberābit. heus, ubi est Alexander?
Sabīna	nesciō. heri epistulam ā parentibus, quī in Lūsitāniā habitant, accēpit. dē cōnsiliō parentum cognōvit.
Philētus	quid est cōnsilium eōrum?
Sabīna	nesciō. mihi nihil dē eō dīxit, sed Alexander est laetissimus.

illō tempore, Alexander advēnit et Sabīnam vīdit.

Alexander	(sibi susurrāns) Sabīna est tam pulchra! est pulchrior quam omnēs fēminae in Galliā! eam amō, eam semper amābō!
Sabīna	quid dīxistī? nōn tē audīre possum.
Alexander	Sabīna, imāgō est tam pulchra! imāgō est pulchrior quam omnēs imāginēs in Galliā! eam amō!
Sabīna	sōlum est imāgō delphīnī! nihilōminus, quid mē rogāre vīs?
Alexander	maximī mōmentī est.
Sabīna	Alexander, quid est?
Alexander	Sabīna, tūne eris mea … ? ōh, ānxius sum!
Sabīna	ānxior sum! quid est, Alexander?
Alexander	Sabīna, tūne eris mea … ministra?
Sabīna	quid?
Alexander	ei! mox in Lūsitāniā labōrābimus. tē mēcum venīre volō. tibi placet?

Line numbers: 5, 10, 15, 20, 25

Glossary:
autumnus *autumn*
delphīnus *dolphin*
Arelātēnsis *of Arles*
quam *than*
fortasse *perhaps*
nesciō *I don't know*
sibi *to himself*
tam *so*
nihilōminus *nevertheless*
mōmentum *importance*
ministra *employee, assistant*

Mosaic pattern books

Although the design and subject matter of mosaics vary widely, there are recognizable patterns and shared features across the Roman Empire. These similarities have led archaeologists to believe that there were standard pattern books which mosaic makers would work from. Clients could choose a particular scene or pattern that was fashionable at the time, just as one might now choose wallpaper or tiles.

Fishbourne Palace, England. About AD 160.

Conimbriga, Portugal. Second to third century AD.

Sanctuary of Artemis, Ephesus, Turkey. About AD 200.

Boutria (ancient Acholla), Tunisia. AD 150–170.

QUESTIONS

1. What similarities and differences can you see in these mosaics from across the Empire? Think about: color, subject matter, style, and layout.

2. How do you think these designs would have traveled and become popular?

manēre aut abīre

Poppillus ad Lūsitāniam cum Alexandrō iuvene nāvigābis, Sabīna?

Sabīna incerta sum. emblēmata facere gaudeō, sed vōs duōs relinquere nōlō. post mortem patris, vōs mē cūrāvistis. nunc vōs estis parentēs meī.

Poppillus pff! hīc in aeternum manēbis? sī tū ad Lūsitāniam ībis, tū   5
terrās mīrābilēs vidēbis. hīc senectūs ac mors tē exspectant.

Letta quid? nōn tacēbis, Poppille? Sabīnam terrēbis! mē audī, Sabīna. necesse est tibi verba mea dīligenter cōgitāre (nec stulta verba quae Poppillus murmurat). iūnior multō es quam nōs senēs. carpe diem! orbem terrārum trānsī! in ūnā colōniā tōtam vītam   10
ēgī. laeta eram, sed nunc laetior sum, quod tē cognōvī. et sī tū cum Alexandrō nāvigābis, laetissima erō.

Sabīna ille vult mē esse suam ...

Poppillus uxōrem?

Sabīna minimē. suam ministram.   15

Letta quid? nihil dē amōre dīxit?

Sabīna dē amōre nec ille nec ego dīcimus.

Letta numquam dē amōre dīcitis? numquam? sine dubiō tē amat et cūrābit, Sabīna. amāsne tamen eum?

Sabīna fortasse eum nunc amō. fortasse mē amat. sed eum semper   20
amābō? mē semper amābit?

Poppillus quandō Alexander ac servī abībunt?

Sabīna paucīs diēbus nāvigābunt.

subitō Sabīna surgit.

Letta quō īs?   25

Sabīna ad templum Minervae eō. necesse est mihi deam adōrāre ac verba vestra cōgitāre.

post paucās hōrās, Sabīna revēnit.

Poppillus salvē, puella. manēre aut abīre cōnstituistī?

---

incertus *uncertain*
relinquō *I leave*

in aeternum *forever*
senectūs *old age*

iūnior *younger*
murmurō *I mutter*
multō *much, by far*
carpō *I enjoy, use*
orbis terrārum *world*
trānseō *I cross*
agō *I spend (time)*

sine dubiō *without doubt*

quandō? *when?*

vester *your*

LANGUAGE NOTE 2: COMPARISON

1. Look at the following pairs of sentences. Can you see how the form of the adjective in the first sentence changes in the second sentence? How does its meaning change?

    laeta sum.
    I'm happy.

    ego sum laetior quam tū.
    I'm happier than you.

    ānxius sum.
    I'm worried.

    ānxior sum.
    I'm more worried.

    Sabīna est pulchra.
    Sabina is beautiful.

    Sabīna est pulchrior quam omnēs fēminae in Galliā!
    Sabina is more beautiful than all the women in Gaul!

    laetior, **ānxior**, and **pulchrior** are known as **comparative** adjectives.

2. Comparative adjectives are often translated using *more* or by adding *-er* to the English word. When **quam** is used with a comparative adjective, it means *than*.

3. Note that comparative adjectives change their endings in a similar way to third declension adjectives and nouns:

    spectātōrēs laetiōrēs erant quam āctōrēs.
    The spectators were happier than the actors.

    līberīs miseriōribus cibum dedimus.
    We gave food to the more unfortunate children.

4. You have now met both the comparative and the superlative forms of adjectives:

Positive	Comparative	Superlative
laetus (*happy*)	**laetior** (*happier*)	**laetissimus** (*happiest*)
trīstis (*sad*)	**trīstior** (*sadder*)	**trīstissimus** (*saddest*)
pulcher (*beautiful*)	**pulchrior** (*more beautiful*)	**pulcherrimus** (*most beautiful*)

5. A small number of adjectives have irregular comparative and superlative forms. For example:

Positive	Comparative	Superlative
bonus (*good*)	**melior** (*better*)	**optimus** (*best*)
magnus (*big*)	**maior** (*bigger*)	**maximus** (*biggest*)

    See page 274 for other irregular comparative and superlative adjectives.

Lūcīlius nunc est tribūnus mīlitum in Lūsitāniā. cum servō suō metallum in Tarracōnēnsī prōvinciā vīsitat. cūrātor metallī eōs per metallum dūcit.

cūrātor	metalla magna in Lūsitāniā administrās?
Lūcīlius	ita vērō. hoc tamen metallum maius est quam omnia in Lūsitāniā.
cūrātor	sine dubiō, hoc metallum est maximum! ecce, tibi omnia dēmōnstrābō.

5

metallum *mine*
Tarracōnēnsis
  of Tarraconensis
cūrātor *manager*
maior, maius *bigger*

dēmōnstrō *I show,*
  point out
cavō *I hollow out*

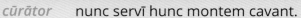

cūrātor   nunc servī hunc montem cavant.   mox servī trabēs verberābunt ...

anteā

posteā

... et sīc montem dēlēbunt. *10*

sīc *so, in this way*

ubi saxa dūriōra sunt, ignēs et aqua
ea dēlēre possunt.

hīc aqua, quae ex aquaeductibus effluit,
saxa aurō permixta ē monte fert.

aurum *gold*
permixtus *mixed*

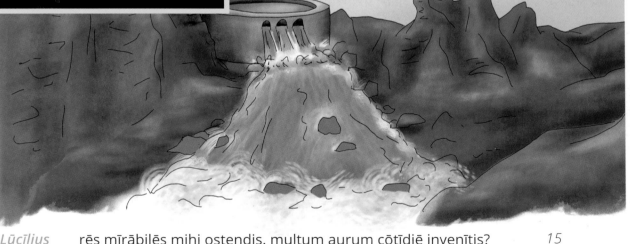

Lūcīlius	rēs mīrābilēs mihi ostendis. multum aurum cōtīdiē invenītis?	*15*
cūrātor	plūs aurī inveniēbāmus quam in hīs temporibus.	
Lūcīlius	cūr minus aurī nunc adest?	
cūrātor	nesciō, tribūne.	

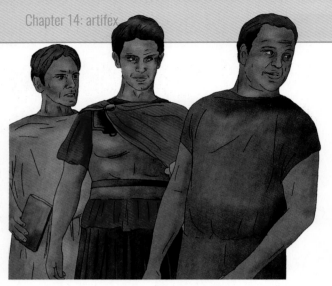

subitō servus sordidus exclāmāvit.

servus sordidus	bene scīs, sceleste! multum aurum invenīmus, sed aurum ēvānēscit! nōs servī diē et nocte labōrāmus sub monte. sub monte labor dīrus necābit nōs. coniūrātiō tamen est, tribūne! rogā cūrātōrem dē Cantabrō! rogā eum ubi plaustra ...

20

sciō *I know*

coniūrātiō *plot, conspiracy*
Cantaber *Cantaber*

tum custōdēs servum capiunt.

25

cūrātor	mendāx! servī quī dēspērant fābulās scelestās semper nārrant ...
Lūcīlius	certē, et eōs sevēriter pūnīre dēbēs. servī quī dominum timent sunt servī fidēlēs.
cūrātor	ita vērō, Lūcīlī. ēn, haec īnstrūmenta vidēs?

sevēriter *severely*
pūniō *I punish*

30

Tīrō, ī per metallum. servōs dē Cantabrō rogā. tōtam rem intellegere volō ...

LANGUAGE PRACTICE

1. Translate each sentence into Latin by choosing the correct word or phrase from each pair.

   a. *Tomorrow we will consider your leader's plan.*

heri	cōnsilium	ducem	tuum	cōgitābunt.
crās	cōnsiliō	ducis	tuī	cōgitābimus.

   b. *Soon our soldiers will terrify the enemy in battle.*

ita	nōs	mīles	hostēs	in proeliō	terrēbimus.
mox	nostrī	mīlitēs	hostium	in proelium	terrēbunt.

   c. *Will you sail across the sea for many days?*

tūne	trāns mare	multīs diēbus	nāvigābis?
egone	sub marī	multōs diēs	nāvigābō?

   d. *There will never be a girl more beautiful than Sabina.*

paene	puella	pulchrior	quoque	Sabīnae	erit.
numquam	puer	pulcher	quam	Sabīna	eris.

   e. *When will Alexander whisper the words which Sabina wants to hear?*

quandō	Alexandrum	verbum,	quae	Sabīnam	dīcere	volunt,	susurrābit?
cūr	Alexander	verba,	ubi	Sabīna	audīre	vult,	susurrābitis?

   f. *Will you hurry at first light to the city, or will you stay in the mountains?*

nōnne	prīmā lūce	ad urbem	festīnābit	nec	in montibus	manēbitis?
vōsne	prīma lūna	per urbem	festīnābitis	aut	in montēs	manēbit?

2. Translate the following sentences into English.

   a. saxa graviōra dūriōraque mox dēlēbimus.

   b. Alexander emblēmata, quae maiōra erunt quam cētera in oppidō, facit.

   c. nēmō est stultior quam imperātor quī audīre nōn vult.

   d. quamquam labor erit difficilior, maiōra erunt praemia.

   e. rēgīna, quae erat senior quam prīncipēs, quoque sapientior et fortior erat.

   f. vestrīne comitēs fidēliōrēs vōs adiuvābunt?

   g. spectātōrēs āctōrēs meliōrēs post fābulam laudābunt.

   h. equus tuus est minor quam meus, sed saepe celerior est.

Mining at Las Médulas

The Roman Empire depended heavily on metals. Iron, tin, copper, silver, and gold were mined throughout the Empire and used for construction, machinery, military equipment, coins, jewelry, and other purposes. Possibly the largest mining operation in the Empire was the gold mine at Las Médulas, in Spain.

The landscape at Las Médulas still shows the effects of Roman mining. One technique widely used there was known as *ruīna montium* (mountain collapsing): entire mountains were systematically collapsed to reach the gold deposits underground.

The power of water

The Romans developed a variety of mining techniques which used hydraulic power (the power of water). You have read about the watermill at Barbegal in Chapter 13. At Las Médulas, seven aqueducts were constructed to feed a series of basins and waterways.

Remains of a rock-cut aqueduct at Las Médulas.

Aerial view of the Las Médulas site, showing the effects of mountain collapsing.

Mining techniques

1. Prospecting with water

Aqueducts and rivers fed into reservoirs where water was stored. These reservoirs were then emptied to release an avalanche of water over a hillside. The water swept away the top layer of soil to reveal veins of gold for mining.

3. *ruina montium*: mountain collapsing

This technique was used at Las Médulas, where gold deposits were found deep underground, beneath hills that were at some points about 300 feet high. A network of tunnels was cut into the mountain. Workers then deliberately cut the beams supporting the tunnels, so that the tunnels caved in, causing the whole mountain to collapse (as in **in metallō**). A flood of water was then released from a reservoir above. The force of the water washed away all the debris, to expose the gold deposits below.

2. Sluicing

Where gold deposits were on the surface (mixed in with mud, silt, and rubble), water power was used to shift huge quantities of soil, and then sift them for gold. Aqueducts or rivers fed into a series of stepped basins that gradually filtered out gold from loose soil and debris. The basins were lined with rosemary, a spiky bush. The chunks of gold got caught in the bushes, while mud, silt, and sand passed through them. Workers could then collect the bushes and pick out the gold by hand.

4. Breaking up tougher rocks

Where the ground was too hard to mine with pickaxes, miners used fire and water to blow up the rocks. They lit fires at the base of the rock to heat the stone, then suddenly cooled the stone down by dousing it with water (or sometimes vinegar). The sudden drop in temperature caused the rock to crack or explode, as in the story **in metallō**.

5. Draining mines

As a result of the extensive use of water in the mines, as well as groundwater coming up from below, there was a constant need to drain the tunnels. Bailing out by hand with buckets was the simplest way to do this. However, more advanced techniques included the use of a series of water wheels to remove water from the mines, such as this one (*left*) found in the Rio Tinto copper mine in southern Spain.

Part of a wooden wheel used to drain a mine.

Working conditions in the mines

The men dig tunnels through the mountains, working by lamplight. For months the miners cannot see the sunlight, and the tunnels collapse suddenly, crushing the workmen.
Pliny the Elder

Thousands of people must have worked at the Las Médulas mine in various jobs: from low-skilled physical laborers to advanced engineers in charge of tunneling machinery and hydraulic systems. The vast majority of work in mines was done by slaves, though prisoners of war, convicts, and poor freeborn laborers also formed part of the workforce. For these men, working in the mines was extremely dangerous and they usually died young; the physical labor was exhausting, the poor air quality in the underground tunnels ruined their lungs, and accidents were very common.

Women

Roman historians wrote about many women, but they were typically women who, like the historians themselves, were from wealthy or aristocratic families. Their stories can tell us much about what Romans expected from such women, and in particular *mātrōnae* (married women).

Lucretia

Some wealthy young Romans were discussing their wives. As none could agree whose wife was best, they went home to check what their wives were up to. Most of the women were idly chatting and dining with their friends, but Lucretia was busy spinning wool and weaving. Not only was she properly occupied, but she immediately fulfilled her duties, producing food and wine for her husband and his friends. Her husband, Collatinus, was very proud of her, but Tarquinius, the king's arrogant son, fell in love with her.

One night, Tarquinius returned alone to visit Lucretia, with the intention of seducing her. At first she received him kindly as a guest, but when he tried to seduce her, she repeatedly refused. Finally, Tarquinius said he would kill her and a male slave, and place the slave naked next to her. He would then pretend he had found them committing adultery and had killed them. As Lucretia could not accept her reputation being insulted, she submitted to Tarquinius. Once he left, she sent for her husband and father. In front of them she explained what had happened, and then took her own life, ignoring the pleas of her family, who tried to reassure her that she had done nothing wrong.

Sempronia

The historian Sallust wrote about Sempronia, a wealthy lady who was involved in a conspiracy to kill the consuls of 63 BC and overturn the Republic. There were many positive things about Sempronia: she was from a good family, was well-married, and was a mother. She was also educated in Greek and Latin, played the lyre, danced well, wrote poetry, and had a witty way with words. However, her dancing was so good that it was better than was appropriate for a respectable woman! It seems that being too good at some activities was not acceptable: why should a proper Roman matrona dance and play so well? The implication is that Sempronia was performing the role of an entertainer rather than of a mother of the house. This is not the only criticism that Sallust levels at Sempronia: she was also lacking in modesty and chastity (she went after men more than they pursued her), she spent money extravagantly, often refused to pay her debts, broke her word, and was even involved in murder. We can't be sure that Sempronia actually did any of these things, but her story indicates what Romans thought was, and was not, acceptable behavior for aristocratic women.

Agrippina

Agrippina was sister, wife, and mother of emperors (Caligula, Claudius, and Nero respectively), and therefore probably the most powerful woman of her age. She lived during violent times when the first imperial family was establishing itself, and she had to navigate very dangerous waters. According to Roman historians she was beautiful, extremely ambitious, and ruthless. We are told that she had an incestuous relationship with her brother, who sent her into exile, and that she poisoned her third husband, Emperor Claudius, so that her son, Nero, could become emperor in AD 54. As Nero was only about 16, she exerted an enormous influence over her son, but he soon started to resent her power and ordered her execution in AD 59.

As a modern reader, one gets the impression that Roman historians believed Agrippina deserved what she got, and it is difficult to separate historical fact from obvious prejudice. Probably Agrippina's greatest failure in the eyes of Roman historians was that her ambition, in particular her manipulation of Claudius and Nero, moved her out of the sphere allotted to women into that of male power. However, when no other option was open, what else could a capable and ambitious woman do?

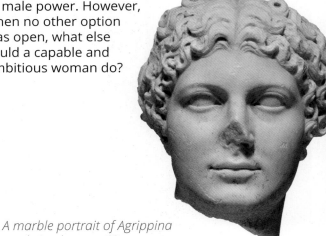

A marble portrait of Agrippina made in about AD 50.

Chapter 15: vīlla

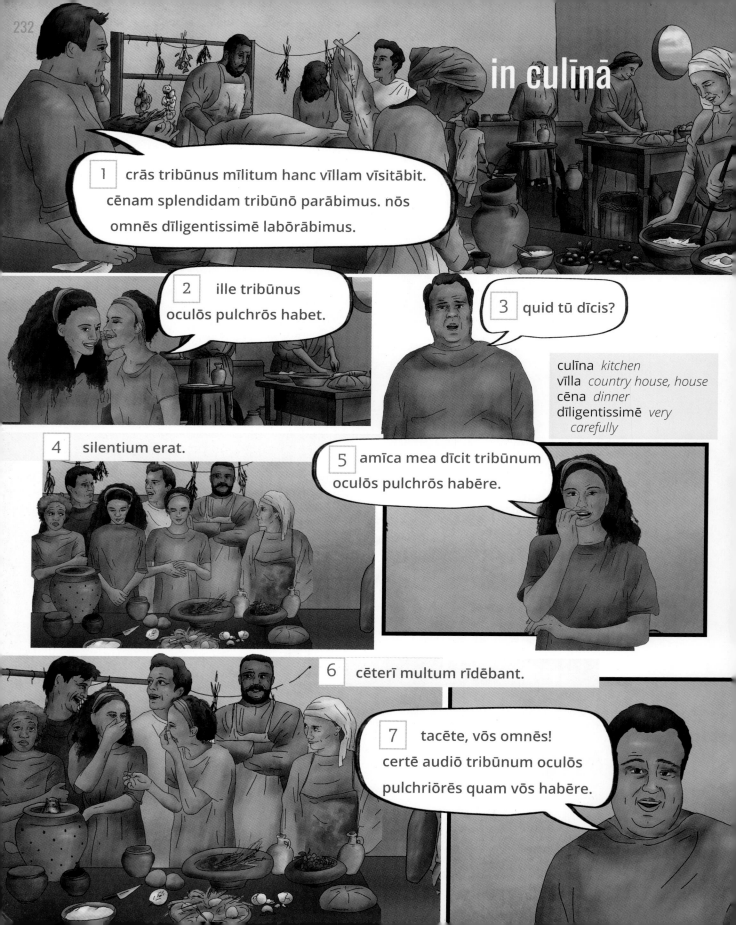

in culīnā

1 crās tribūnus mīlitum hanc vīllam vīsitābit. cēnam splendidam tribūnō parābimus. nōs omnēs dīligentissimē labōrābimus.

2 ille tribūnus oculōs pulchrōs habet.

3 quid tū dīcis?

culīna *kitchen*
vīlla *country house, house*
cēna *dinner*
dīligentissimē *very carefully*

4 silentium erat.

5 amīca mea dīcit tribūnum oculōs pulchrōs habēre.

6 cēterī multum rīdēbant.

7 tacēte, vōs omnēs! certē audiō tribūnum oculōs pulchriōrēs quam vōs habēre.

in hortō

hortus *garden*

8 servī ancillaeque nōn sōlum in culīnā vīllae sed etiam in hortō occupātī sunt.

9 ohē, comes! dā mihi auxilium! difficile est mihi hās amphorās in vīllam portāre.

10 tū stulte! numquam dīligenter labōrās! auxilium tibi dare nōn possum. necesse est mihi plūs cibī ab hortō ferre.

11 tūne dīcis mē neglegenter labōrāre?

12 tūne nōn intellegis mē occupātum esse?

13 ohē! bellumne geritis, vōs duo? dēsistite! dominus noster semper est īrātus ubi videt servōs nōn dīligenter labōrāre.

occupātus *busy*
neglegenter *carelessly*

Country estates

Cantaber owns a large house in Conimbriga and a country villa and estate about six miles outside the town. Wealthy men in Rome and the provinces often owned country houses, and some owned the surrounding farmland as well. Land was expensive, but it was a good investment for those who could afford it. Usually the owner did not maintain the farm himself. Some rented the land to tenant farmers who then had to pay the owner with a share of their produce. Often slaves worked the land; a freedman supervised them and kept everything running smoothly. Some landowners bought the adjoining farms, creating huge complexes known as *lātifundia*. Romans relied on the labor of enslaved people to farm these latifundia.

On a country estate there would be a main house for the owner and his family and guests. There would also be land for crops and animals, accommodation for slaves, a bathhouse, granary, and gardens.

An imagined reconstruction of the country estate known as the villa Rabaçal near Conimbriga in Portugal, based on the archaeological remains.

Idealization of the farmer

For peasants and tenant farmers, working the land was necessary for survival. Among wealthy Romans (who would never have to work the land themselves), the farmer's life was sometimes idealized. Cicero said:

> Of all the jobs from which we get some profit, none is better than agriculture, none more productive, none more pleasant, none more fitting for a free man.

Country living

Some country estates, like Cantaber's, were close to towns and their owners would visit for a few days, enjoying a brief relief from the bustling city. Others were further away, and wealthy Romans might stay there for the summer months to escape the heat of the city. For sophisticated Romans, having a country retreat was a necessary part of the good life. It was a place to enjoy leisure time in the fresh air: reading, horseback riding, walking, and hunting. However, they brought with them every amenity and comfort of the town and passed their time in the height of luxury.

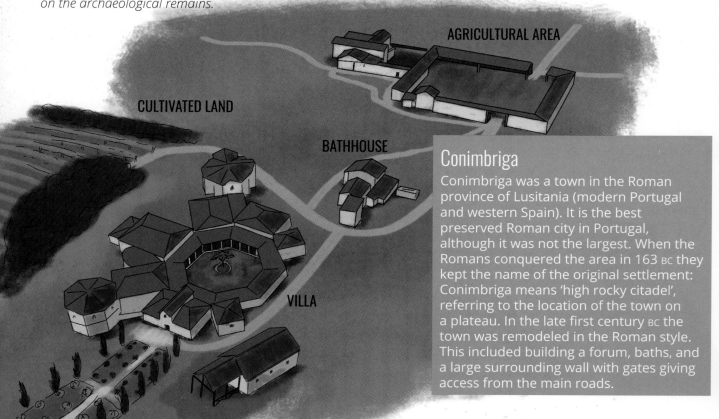

AGRICULTURAL AREA

CULTIVATED LAND

BATHHOUSE

VILLA

Conimbriga

Conimbriga was a town in the Roman province of Lusitania (modern Portugal and western Spain). It is the best preserved Roman city in Portugal, although it was not the largest. When the Romans conquered the area in 163 BC they kept the name of the original settlement: Conimbriga means 'high rocky citadel', referring to the location of the town on a plateau. In the late first century BC the town was remodeled in the Roman style. This included building a forum, baths, and a large surrounding wall with gates giving access from the main roads.

Honey bees

Although no beehives have survived from Roman times (they were made of biodegradable materials), many Roman authors wrote about beekeeping. The Romans did not have sugar; instead they used honey as a sweetener. The production of honey was not the only benefit of beekeeping. The wax was also used to make writing tablets and for medicinal purposes.

Snails

Snails were a special delicacy for the Romans. They were kept in pens in the garden and fattened on grain and aromatic herbs. The practice of farming snails is called heliculture, from the Greek word 'helix', which means spiral.

Fish ponds

Freshwater fish ponds in the gardens of country estates provided fish to eat, but they also housed luxury pet fish. Some Romans are reported to have become extremely attached to these expensive fish. Antonia (the mother of Emperor Claudius) is even said to have attached earrings to her favorite eel!

Gardens

Gardens were practical spaces. At any size, in the town or in the countryside, they were a source of fresh fruit, vegetables, and herbs for the household. In towns, people living in insulae might have had a window box for a few herbs; only wealthier houses had space for a garden. Outside the town, houses could have large gardens and grow a wide variety of produce. Some richer households even had greenhouses where they could grow more exotic fruit out of season.

Decorative gardens

By the time of our stories, wealthy Romans valued gardens more for decoration than for practicality. Gardens became an opportunity to display one's wealth with exotic plants, water features, and statues. The garden paradises Romans created were not only private spaces for the owner of the house to relax in; they were also designed to impress guests. They were often in the center of the house and could open onto a small garden room (*exedra*) which was used for entertaining guests. A skilled slave, called a *topiārius*, had the job of trimming the bushes and hedges into decorative shapes.

The garden at the Getty Villa in California is a reconstruction of a Roman garden.

Garden archaeology

Garden archaeology is still a new branch of study. Analysis of seeds, along with evidence from literature and art, helps determine which plants were grown in Roman gardens. Roses, lilies, and rosemary were some of the favorites. Other physical remains allow archaeologists to reimagine the layout of the gardens. For example, holes in the earth show where plants were planted, and sometimes remains of water systems, fences, and trellises survive. Archaeologists have also found flower pots in Roman gardens; these help them reconstruct the location of plants. They have even compared the DNA of Roman grape seeds to modern ones to find out more about ancient agricultural practices.

in vīllā Cantabrī

prope ātrium Lūcīlius et Tīrō susurrant. vultus tribūnī est gravis.

Lūcīlius	putō Cantabrum ab illō metallō aurum auferre.
Tīrō	(*attonitus*) sed, domine –
Lūcīlius	tacē, Tīrō! ī quam celerrimē per hanc vīllam. servōs dē Cantabrō rogā.

5

exit servus. Lūcīlius ātrium intrat, ubi duo artificēs emblēmata faciunt. prīmō tribūnus est ānxius: artificēsne eum Tīrōnemque audiēbant? deinde cōnspicit ūnam artificem vultum suum intentē spectāre.

Lūcīlius	hercle! tē agnōscō! salvē ... ?
Sabīna	... Sabīna. hic est Alexander, quī est meus ... magister.
Lūcīlius	Gāius Lūcīlius Iūnior, tribūnus mīlitum, sum. quid accidit, Sabīna? proximō annō Rōmae habitābās. nunc videō tē in Lūsitāniā habitāre.
Sabīna	in incendiō Rōmae exspīrāvit pater. dē vītā amitae meae, quae est Christiāna, dēspērō.
Lūcīlius	audiō Christiānōs esse in magnō perīculō.
Sabīna	certē, Lūcīlī. audī. tē iuvāre possum. servī dīcunt plaustra horreīs mediā nocte appropinquāre. servī quoque dīcunt hominēs plaustra horreaque custōdīre.
Lūcīlius	grātiās maximās tibi agō, Sabīna! necesse est mihi rem Cantabrī cognōscere.

10

15

20

Lūcīlius exit.

Alexander	(*īrātus*) esne īnsāna, Sabīna? Cantaber est vir magnī imperiī. et nōbīs et familiae meae multum nocēre potest.
Sabīna	tūtī erimus, Alexander. putō tribūnum esse virum magnae virtūtis.
Alexander	(*īrātior*) amāsne hunc tribūnum?
Sabīna	(*īrātissima*) quid? stultior quam asinus es, Alexander!

25

ātrium *reception room, entrance hall*
putō *I think*

agnōscō *I recognize*
magister *employer*

exspīrō *I die*

iuvō *I help, assist*
horreum *barn, granary, warehouse*

imperium *power*
noceō *I harm*

LANGUAGE NOTE 1: STATEMENTS, DIRECT AND INDIRECT

1. Since Chapter 1 you have seen statements like these:

> **Sabīna in Lūsitāniā habitat.**   *Sabina is living in Lusitania.*
>
> **senex dīligenter labōrat.**   *The old man is working carefully.*

These are known as **direct statements**: the author gives us information about Sabina and the old man directly.

2. In this chapter you have met sentences like these:

> **dīcit Sabīnam in Lūsitāniā habitāre.**   *He says Sabina to live in Lusitania.*
> = *He says that Sabina is living in Lusitania.*
>
> **putāmus senem dīligenter labōrāre.**   *We think the old man to work carefully.*
> = *We think that the old man works carefully.*

These are known as **indirect statements**: the author gives us information about Sabina and the old man indirectly, through what a character says or thinks.

3. Look at the sentences below. What case do **Lūcīlius** and **puella** become when they move from the direct to the indirect statements? What happens to **habet** and **mittit**?

Direct statement	*Indirect statement*
Lūcīlius oculōs pulchrōs habet. *Lucilius has lovely eyes.*	**dīcit Lūcīlium oculōs pulchrōs habēre.** *She says Lucilius to have lovely eyes.* = *She says that Lucilius has lovely eyes.*
puella nūntium mittit. *The girl is sending a message.*	**sciunt puellam nūntium mittere.** *They know the girl to be sending a message.* = *They know that the girl is sending a message.*

Indirect statements use an **accusative and infinitive** construction. The accusative usually comes immediately after the verb of saying, thinking, or perceiving. The infinitive often comes at the end of the sentence.

4. You may find indirect statements after verbs such as **dīcō** (*say*), **putō** (*think*), **audiō** (*hear*), **sentiō** (*notice*), **videō** (*see*), and **cognōscō** (*learn*).

5. When translating an indirect statement, it may be helpful to translate it first literally, then more naturally. It can also help to use *that* after the verb of saying, thinking, or perceiving, e.g. *They say that ... , I hear that ...* .

cēna

nōnā hōrā multī hospitēs magnificam cēnam in vīllā Cantabrī
cōnsūmēbant. Lūcīlius proximus Cantabrō recumbēbat. ūnus ex
hospitibus clāmāvit saltātrīcēs trīclīnium intrāre, deinde omnēs
exclāmābant plaudēbantque. Lūcīlius tamen ad Cantabrum sē vertit.

'ubi in prōvinciā Tarracōnēnsī iter faciēbam, metallum vīsitāvī,' inquit   5
Lūcīlius. 'cūrātor mihi nūntiāvit metallum esse maximum in prōvinciā.'

Cantaber, quī servum vīnum ferre iubēbat, clāmāvit, 'vah! num dē
metallīs cognōscere cupis, tribūne? cōnsūme glīrēs et plūs vīnī bibe!'

'quantum aurum dē metallō cōtīdiē trahis, Cantaber?' rogāvit Lūcīlius.
'sciō tē prō Nerōne illud metallum administrāre.'   10

'vērum? quid nescīs, tū callide?' Lūcīliō susurrāvit Cantaber, quī īram
suam vix cēlābat. 'nōnne scīs custōdēs meōs aurum in plaustrīs ad
monētam imperātōris rēctā dūcere? cognōvistīne tamen illa plaustra
esse paene inānia? etiam melius est mihi fundōs administrāre quam
metalla.'   15

Lūcīlius nihil respondit, quod crēdidit Cantabrum mendācem esse.

intereā Alexander et Sabīna in culīnā vīllae sedēbant. Alexander dulcis
'dīxī tē īnsānam esse, Sabīna,' inquit. 'sciō mē longē errāre. potesne
mihi ignōscere?'

'certē, tibi ignōscō, Alexander,' eī respondit Sabīna. 'īrāta eram, quod   20
putāvistī mē tribūnum amāre. intellegō tamen Cantabrum esse
perīculōsum. rēs est gravis. erō comes fidēlis nōn sōlum cōnsiliōrum
tuōrum sed etiam omnium perīculōrum.'

hospes	guest
recumbō	I recline, lie down
saltātrīx	dancer
trīclīnium	dining room
sē	himself
vertō	I turn
num?	surely ... not?
glīs	dormouse
callidus	clever
īra	anger
monēta	mint (coin factory)
rēctā	directly, straight
inānis	empty
dulcis	sweet, pleasant
errō	I make a mistake
ignōscō	I forgive

Dormice were a popular delicacy. One recipe was roasted
dormouse, glazed in honey and rolled in poppy seeds. The jar on
the right is a *glīrārium*, an earthenware vessel used for keeping
and fattening dormice. The side has been cut away to show the
interior. The wall is pierced with holes and inside there is a ledge
which spirals from the rim to the base. Varro wrote:

> Dormice are fattened in jars, which many people keep inside
> their villa. Potters make these in a very different form from
> other jars; they have ridges along the sides and a hollow for
> holding food. Acorns, walnuts, or chestnuts are put inside; a
> cover is placed on top and the dormice grow fat in the dark.

LANGUAGE NOTE 2: INDIRECT STATEMENTS – PERFECT MAIN VERBS

1. Study the following pairs of sentences:

    Present tense main verb

    dīcit Sabīnam in Lūsitāniā habitāre.
    He says Sabina to live in Lusitania.
    = *He says that Sabina is living in Lusitania.*

    putāmus senem dīligenter labōrāre.
    We think the old man to work carefully.
    = *We think that the old man is working carefully.*

    Perfect tense main verb

    dīxit Sabīnam in Lūsitāniā habitāre.
    He said Sabina to live in Lusitania.
    = *He said that Sabina was living in Lusitania.*

    putāvimus senem dīligenter labōrāre.
    We thought the old man to work carefully.
    = *We thought that the old man was working carefully.*

2. Notice how the translation of the indirect statement changes when it is introduced by a verb in the perfect tense.

LANGUAGE PRACTICE

1. Translate the following direct and indirect statements.

    a. Sabīna Lūcīlium amat.
    b. Alexander putat Sabīnam Lūcīlium amāre.

    c. Alexander stultus est.
    d. Sabīna dīcit Alexandrum stultum esse.

    e. comes cēnam magnificam cōnsūmit.
    f. lībertus cognōscit comitem cēnam magnificam cōnsūmere.

    g. hostēs ferōcēs bellum saepe gerunt.
    h. mīlitēs sciunt hostēs ferōcēs bellum saepe gerere.

    i. puerī plūs pecūniae quaerunt.
    j. nēmō sentit puerōs plūs pecūniae quaerere.

2. Translate the following direct and indirect statements.

    a. rēx hominēs līberat.
    b. ducēs audīvērunt rēgem hominēs līberāre.

    c. labor est dūrus.
    d. intellēximus labōrem esse dūrum.

    e. rēgīna in proeliō frūstrā pugnat.
    f. prīncipēs scīvērunt rēgīnam in proeliō frūstrā pugnāre.

    g. nōs auxilium ad amīcōs mittimus.
    h. nūntiāvimus nōs auxilium ad amīcōs mittere.

    i. puer ē vīllā festīnat.
    j. sēnsistis puerum ē vīllā festīnāre.

Dinner parties

surgite: iam vēndit puerīs ientācula pistor
Get up: now the baker is selling breakfast to boys.
Martial

Romans ate three meals a day:

ientāculum (breakfast), was bread, possibly with some cheese.

prandium (lunch) was eaten at about midday. It was just a snack, perhaps bread and cheese and some vegetables.

cēna (dinner) was the main meal of the day. Generally this was eaten in the late afternoon or early evening, while it was still daylight. For most people it was a simple meal, often a takeaway, as you learned in Chapter 1 (pages 18–19). Rich Romans sometimes gave dinner parties which started later, lit by lamplight, because they could afford lamps or torches. The word for dinner party or banquet is *convīvium* – literally a living together or get-together. The host and his guests often met in the baths beforehand, and some people went to the baths in the hope of receiving an invitation to dinner. Business associates, political contacts, and the host's freedmen would be invited, as well as friends and family.

Preparing and serving the meal

When the guests arrived, a slave would remove their shoes and wash their feet, then lead them to the dining room (*triclīnium*). Slaves cooked and served the food. They cut it up beforehand, then the guests served themselves from a central table, using their fingers or a spoon. Guests often brought their own napkins (*mappae*), and used them later as doggy bags for taking away leftovers. The food was served on expensive tableware made of silver, glass, and bronze.

Often the food was intended to impress the guests and provide a spectacle as well as being tasty. Exotic produce such as peacock and flamingo was served because of its rarity and high cost, and elaborate recipes were invented.

QUESTIONS

1. Look at Sources 1 and 2. Which menu is more elaborate and which is more simple?
2. What impression of their own tastes and lifestyle do you think the hosts want to give?

SOURCE 1   Listen to the menu; there's nothing bought in the market. From my farm at Tivoli, a plump little goat, the most tender of the herd, which has not yet tasted grass, with more milk than blood in its veins; wild asparagus which the farm manager's wife picks after she's finished her spinning; big, warm eggs, wrapped in straw – along with their mothers; grapes, preserved for half a year, but as fresh as they were on the vine; Syrian pears and fragrant apples.   *Juvenal*

SOURCE 2   A guest at a dinner party is describing some of the dishes that were served. He notes how the host explained in detail where the ingredients came from and how they were cooked. The dishes included:

- wild boar, served with spiced turnips, lettuce, radishes, water-parsnips, and pickled fish.
- oysters, fillets of plaice, turbot – all of these cooked in new ways.
- lamprey with prawns, and a dressing of olive oil from Venafrum from the first pressing, fish sauce made from Spanish mackerel, five-year-old wine (Italian not Greek), white pepper, vinegar made from fermented grapes from Lesbos, and rocket.
- crane's legs, goose liver (from a goose fed on figs), shoulder of hare, blackbird, and pigeon.   *Horace*

A blue, glass drinking cup and a bronze serving fork. Although the Romans did not use forks to eat, larger forks, like this one, were used to serve the food.

The dining room

One of the most important rooms in a town house or country villa was the triclinium, the dining room. This was where wealthy Romans entertained their guests with lavish dinner parties. The word 'triclinium' comes from the Greek for 'three couches'. The dining room was called the triclinium because the main items of furniture were three couches, arranged on three sides of one or several small tables. Rich Romans reclined on couches to eat at their dinner parties, lying on their left side and resting on cushions. Each couch had room for three people. The reclining arrangements reflected the importance of the guests. One of the couches was for the guests of honor, while another was for the least important. Some couches were permanent: they were made of stone, with sloping surfaces, and would be covered with mattresses and cushions. There were also wooden and bronze couches which could be moved around. Some grand houses had a separate open-air summer triclinium. These rooms were lavishly decorated with wall paintings and mosaic floors.

Entertainment

At some banquets there was music, played on the flute or lyre. Other entertainment included singing, dancing, acrobatic displays, or recitals of poetry.

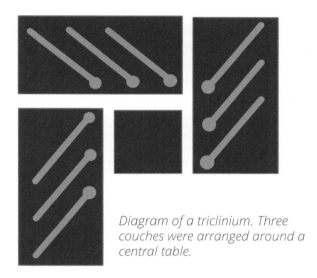

Diagram of a triclinium. Three couches were arranged around a central table.

Wall painting with a scene from a dinner party.

Menus

ab ōvō usque ad māla
from egg to apples

Horace

Dinner was usually three courses, and this saying was used to mean 'from start to finish'.

gustātiō: appetizers, e.g. eggs, olives, snails, cheese, vegetables.
mēnsae prīmae: first course, e.g. meat or fish dishes with various sauces.
mēnsae secundae: dessert, e.g. fruit, nuts, sweet things.

Wine, mixed with water, was drunk during the meal.

Recipes

Several authors wrote about the food at dinner parties. The most valuable source is a cookbook by Apicius, which was probably compiled in the fifth century AD. Cato, who lived about 200 BC, wrote a handbook on farming which includes some recipes.

gustātiō

Olive paste
Remove the stones from green, black, or mixed olives. Chop the olives. Add oil, vinegar, coriander, cumin, fennel, and mint. Put in a dish, cover with oil. Serve.

Cabbage or broccoli
Boil the cabbage or broccoli. Season with cumin, garum, wine, and oil. Add pine nuts and raisins.

mēnsae prīmae

Poached ostrich
First, make a stock. Put into a pot: pepper, mint, cumin seeds, leeks, celery seeds, dates, honey, vinegar, sweet wine, water or stock, a little olive oil. Bring to boil and add the ostrich pieces. Simmer until the meat is done. Remove the ostrich pieces and strain the broth. Thicken the broth with flour, pour over the pieces of cooked ostrich in a serving dish, and sprinkle with pepper. Add garlic during the cooking if you like.

Fish in a coriander crust
Put salt and coriander seeds in a mortar and crush finely. Roll the fish fillets in the mixture. Put them in a dish, cover, and cook in the oven. When cooked, remove the fish, sprinkle with vinegar, and serve.

mēnsae secundae

Stuffed dates
Remove the stones from the dates. Stuff with a nut or nuts and ground pepper. Sprinkle the outside with salt and cook in honey.

QUESTIONS

1. Compare these recipes with those in a modern cookery book or magazine. What similarities and differences do you notice?

2. Would it be possible for a modern cook to make these dishes? What difficulties would you have if you tried to make them at home?

LANGUAGE NOTE 3: INDIRECT STATEMENTS – SĒ OR EUM?

1. What do you think might be the difference in meaning in these two sentences?

    a. **Lūcīlius scit sē magnam pecūniam habēre.**
        Lucilius knows that he has a lot of money.

    b. **Lūcīlius scit eum magnam pecūniam habēre.**
        Lucilius knows that he has a lot of money.

2. **sē** refers to the subject of the main verb, i.e. Lucilius, whereas **eum** refers to someone else. So sentence **a.** means Lucilius knows that he himself has a lot of money, while sentence **b.** means Lucilius knows that someone else has a lot of money.

3. Latin always uses **sē** to refer to the subject of the main verb, whether it's a man, a woman, or a number of people. **eum**, **eam**, **eōs**, and **eās** are used as appropriate to refer to others.

LANGUAGE PRACTICE

3. Choose the correct pronoun to match the English meaning.

    a. Lūcīlius dīxit ..... ē vīllā discēdere.   (sē, eum)
        Lucilius said that he (himself) was leaving the villa.

    b. Alexander putat ..... Sabīnam amāre.   (sē, eum)
        Alexander thinks that he (someone else) loves Sabina.

    c. Sabīna scit ..... nūllam pecūniam habēre.   (sē, eam)
        Sabina knows that she (herself) has no money.

    d. Rōmānī cognōvērunt ..... arma parāre.   (sē, eōs)
        The Romans learned that they (others) were preparing their weapons.

A Roman wall painting showing two men preparing food.

post cēnam

mediā nocte Lūcīlius in lectō iacēbat, sed nōn dormiēbat. subitō vōcem Tīrōnis per fenestram audīvit.

'age, domine!' susurrāvit Tīrō, quī in hortō vīllae stābat. 'ancilla dīxit plaustra horreō appropinquāre.'

age! *come!*

Lūcīlius statim surrēxit et ad iānuam cubiculī festīnāvit. Tīrō tamen 'nōlī per vīllam īre, domine!' inquit. 'anteā cognōvī lībertōs cubiculum tuum custōdīre.'

5

cubiculum *bedroom*

itaque Lūcīlius dē fenestrā cubiculī in hortum tacitē dēscendit, et cum Tīrōne per hortum prōcēdēbat.

brevī tempore tribūnus servusque ad horreum advēnērunt et post   10
mūrum sē cēlāvērunt. prīmō vīdērunt servōs saccōs frūmentō plēnōs
ē plaustrīs trahere. lībertus ingēns et ferōx, quī hūc illūc ambulābat,
servōs saccōs in horreum portāre iubēbat. servī, postquam ad plaustra
rediērunt, gravēs arcās accēpērunt. arcās quoque in horreum cum
magnā difficultāte trahēbant. tum Lūcīlius et Tīrō duōs custōdēs, quī   15
inter sē susurrābant, audīvērunt.

prīmus custōs	quot arcae iam sunt in horreō?
secundus custōs	nesciō, comes. sed putō dominum esse laetum. amīcus meus dīxit eum arcās in horreō aperīre et ex arcīs multum aurī tollere. 20

subitō manus ignōta Lūcīlium rapuit. tribūnus servusque audīvērunt
vōcem lībertī ingentis. ille ferōciter dīxit, 'nōlīte resistere nōbīs, vōs duo.'
tum custōdēs ad Cantabrum eōs dūcere iussit.

---

saccus *sack, bag*
frūmentum *corn, grain*
hūc illūc *here and there*
arca *crate, strongbox*

quot? *how many?*

Civil War

Civil War in the Late Republic

As mentioned in Chapter 3, the Republic in the first century BC was plagued by vicious civil wars. As the Empire grew larger, keeping control of distant provinces required strong armies led by capable commanders. Two of those commanders were Marius and Sulla.

Marius (157–86 BC)

Marius championed the poor. He restructured the army, changing it from a part-time citizen force to a full-time professional one. All Roman citizens, including the poor, could find reliable employment and careers as legionary soldiers. When these professional soldiers retired, they received money from their commander, and a plot of land in a conquered region. That money was provided by the generals themselves (not by the state), and therefore close bonds developed between soldiers and their commanders. The power and influence of individual Roman generals, with loyal armies behind them, increased greatly.

In addition to reshaping the army, Marius was a very successful general. He was credited with the victory against the Numidian king Jugurtha and with stopping two German tribes from threatening the Roman provinces of southern Gaul (and perhaps Italy itself).

Marius' political career was also groundbreaking: he was the first man to be consul for five years in a row (104–99 BC), and in total he was elected consul seven times. This success may help to explain how he came to believe that he was the only man entitled to take the lead in Rome's battles and politics.

Sulla (c.138–78 BC)

Sulla was an aristocrat and one of Marius' quaestors (subordinate officers). In 88 BC he was himself elected consul, and was given command of a Roman army fighting in the East. However, Marius was jealous of Sulla's opportunity to prove himself. He convinced one of the tribunes to persuade the Popular Assembly to remove Sulla's command and give it to him. Sulla did not accept the Assembly's decision. He took his army and marched against Rome, as an external enemy would have done, and forced the Romans to give him back his command. He then returned to fight in the East.

While Sulla was away from Rome, Marius and his faction slaughtered a number of Sulla's supporters. In 86 BC Marius obtained the last of his seven consulships, together with a man called Cinna. Although Marius died at the beginning of the year, Cinna continued the violence against Sulla's supporters. Sulla returned from the East and marched on Rome for a second time. He was appointed dictator, executed Marius' and Cinna's supporters, and confiscated their property. Once he had achieved his revenge, he undid any laws created by Marius and his allies which undermined the aristocracy and the Senate. He then resigned his post and retired to live a private life.

Marius and Sulla therefore both broke the traditional constitution of Rome: Marius was consul repeatedly; Sulla led an army against his own city of Rome. Both headed factions which killed fellow Roman citizens. Powerful commanders who came after them now had an example to follow. Marius and Sulla had set precedents for continued consulships, marching on Rome with armies, and killing fellow citizens. These actions were all to be repeated in the decades to come.

Chapter 16: nūptiae

familia Alexandrī

1   haec fēmina est Hettia, māter Alexandrī.

2   hic vir est Maelō.
Maelō est pater Alexandrī.

3   hī virī sunt servī, quōs Maelō in forō ēmit. servī laterēs faciunt.

later   *brick*

4   hī sunt frātrēs Alexandrī, quī quoque laterēs faciunt.

5   hae fēminae, quae vestīmenta parant, sunt sorōrēs Alexandrī.

6 Maelō! Alexander adest!

7 Maelō tamen uxōrem suam vix audiēbat, quod officīna erat clāmōsa. servī fīliīque Maelōnis laterēs faciēbant et eōs ad plaustra portābant. Maelō laterēs dīligenter īnspiciēbat. tandem rogāvit ...

8 quid, mea columba? Alexander abest? quō iit?

9 'minimē, Maelō! Alexander nōn abiit,' eī respondit Hettia. 'revēnit, et dīcit sē nūntium magnī mōmentī habēre.'

10 'āh! ille artifex!' susurrāvit ūnus ē fīliīs. 'eum bene cognōvimus. num Alexander patrem plūs pecūniae ōrābit?'

āh! *ah!*

pater ānxius

prīmā lūce postrīdiē, ubi Alexander cum parentibus sedēbat, eīs multa
dē Sabīnā nūntiābat. māter Alexandrī multō laetior quam marītus suus
erat. illa gaudēbat, sed hic ānxiē

'quālis puella est illa Sabīna?' rogāvit. 'unde venit? quis est pater eius?'

eī Alexander trīste respondit patrem eius esse mortuum. tum dīxit   5
Sabīnam esse Subūrānam et multō fidēliōrem quam puellās in oppidō
Conimbrīgā.

'Sabīna dīligenter labōrat. lānam cōtīdiē facit. emblēmata eius sunt
magnifica. domum optimē servābit. Sabīnam in Galliā relinquere nōluī.
eam in mātrimōnium dūcere volō. tandem pecūniam habeō. nunc   10
līberōs et uxōrem habēre volō.'

tandem Maelō sēnsit fīlium uxōrem bonam legere.

'sed eam amās?' rogāvit māter.

'sine dubiō, māter. iam tibi dīxī,' eī respondit Alexander. 'et sub
vesperum eam rogābō.'   15

postrīdiē *on the
following day*

unde? *from where?*

Subūrānus *from the
Subura*
Conimbrīga
*Conimbriga (town in
Lusitania)*
lāna *wool*
in mātrimōnium dūcō
I marry

*Brickmaking was an important industry in Conimbriga.
This ceramic brick is inscribed with the words:* **AVE MAELO**
*(Greetings, Maelo). It is one of several which record Maelo
as the owner of a factory which made bricks.*

ānulus

Alexander per viās festīnāvit. tandem parvam officīnam fūmōsam
intrāvit, ubi ferrārius dīligenter labōrābat, et dē ānulō rogāvit. 'ecce,
ānulus est parātus,' eī respondit ferrārius, et Alexandrō eum trādidit.

ānulus *ring*
parātus *ready*

vestīmenta

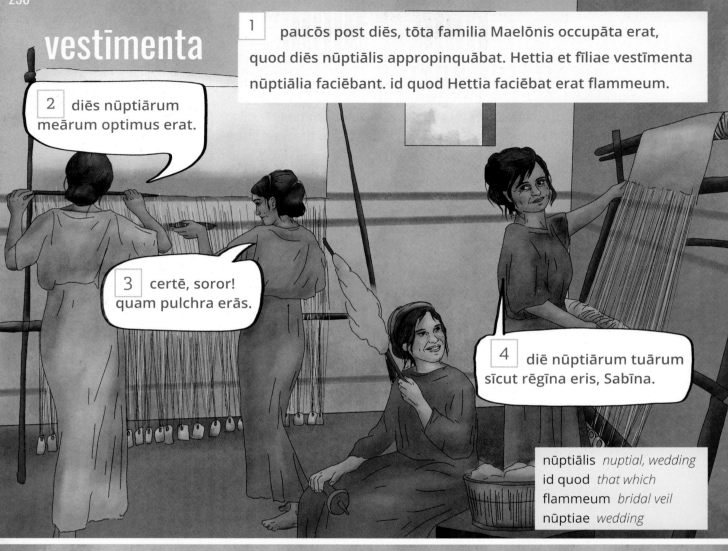

1 paucōs post diēs, tōta familia Maelōnis occupāta erat, quod diēs nūptiālis appropinquābat. Hettia et fīliae vestīmenta nūptiālia faciēbant. id quod Hettia faciēbat erat flammeum.

2 diēs nūptiārum meārum optimus erat.

3 certē, soror! quam pulchra erās.

4 diē nūptiārum tuārum sīcut rēgīna eris, Sabīna.

nūptiālis *nuptial, wedding*
id quod *that which*
flammeum *bridal veil*
nūptiae *wedding*

5 iō, rēgīna Sabīna!

6 omnēs quattuor laetē rīdēbant.

porcus fugitīvus

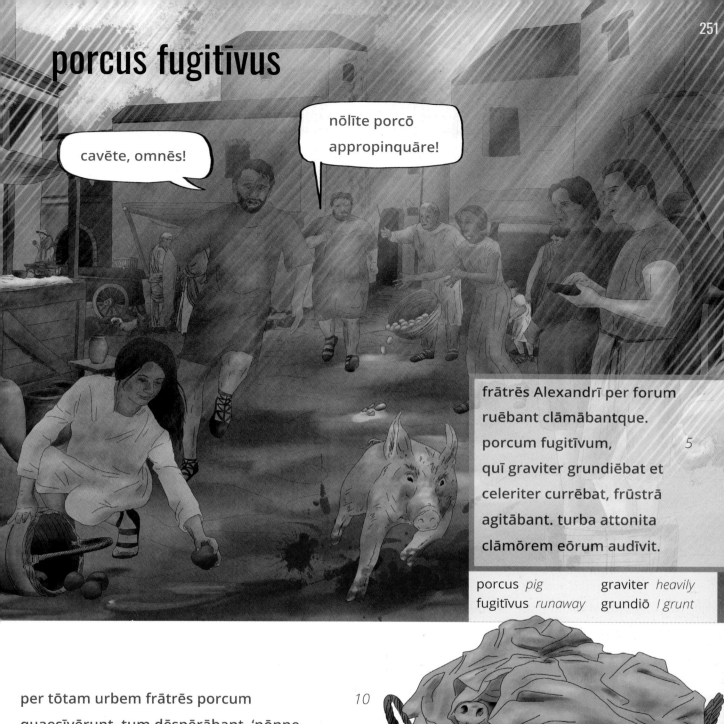

cavēte, omnēs!

nōlīte porcō appropinquāre!

frātrēs Alexandrī per forum
ruēbant clāmābantque.
porcum fugitīvum,   5
quī graviter grundiēbat et
celeriter currēbat, frūstrā
agitābant. turba attonita
clāmōrem eōrum audīvit.

porcus	*pig*	graviter	*heavily*
fugitīvus	*runaway*	grundiō	*I grunt*

per tōtam urbem frātrēs porcum   10
quaesīvērunt, tum dēspērābant. 'nōnne
aliquis eum abstulit?' sibi dīxērunt.
tandem invēnērunt animal īnfēlīx, quod in
vestīmentīs nūptiālibus sē cēlābat.

LANGUAGE NOTE 1: THIS AND THAT

1. In the sentences below, what do **hic**, **haec**, **hōs**, and **hās** all have in common?

    hic vir est Maelō.
    This man is Maelo.

    haec fēmina est Hettia.
    This woman is Hettia.

    hōs gladiōs vēndimus.
    We are selling these swords.

    hās amphorās movēre temptō.
    I'm trying to move these amphorae.

2. **hic**, **haec**, **hōs**, and **hās** are all forms of **hic**, meaning *this* (in the singular) and *these* (in the plural). Like other adjectives, **hic** changes its form to match the case, number, and gender of the noun described.

3. In these sentences, what do **ille**, **illa**, **illōs**, and **illās** all have in common?

    ille artifex pecūniam ōrābit.
    That artist will ask for money.

    quālis puella est illa Sabīna?
    What sort of girl is that Sabina?

    illōs virōs saepe sentiēbāmus.
    We often used to noticed those men.

    illās amphorās movēre nōn potes.
    You can't move those amphorae.

4. **ille**, **illa**, **illōs**, and **illās** are all forms of **ille**, meaning *that* (in the singular) and *those* (in the plural). Again, the form changes to match the case, number, and gender of the noun described.

5. Now look at these sentences:

    hic est Faustus.
    This (man) is Faustus.

    haec est Sabīna.
    This (girl) is Sabina.

    ille nihil dīxit.
    That man said nothing.
    or *He said nothing.*

    illam nōn amō.
    I don't like that woman.
    or *I don't like her.*

    Forms of **hic** and **ille** can be used on their own to refer to people or things.

6. There is a chart of all the forms of **hic** and **ille** on page 275.

The tomb of a wool merchant. The decoration shows different stages of wool production.

Wool and weaving

The majority of clothes were made from wool. However, wealthy Romans also had access to linen from Egypt and Syria, and even silk all the way from China. The production of woolen clothes was a long and time-consuming process.

1. Getting the fleece

The Romans kept many different breeds of sheep, which were valued for the color and quality of their fleece. The Roman author Varro even described sheep being given leather jackets to protect their wool! By the time of our stories, it was common to cut the fleece off the sheep using iron shears like these.

4. Weaving

The threads were then woven together on a loom. Most garments were simple in shape, either rectangular tunics or semicircular cloaks, but weaving an item of clothing of the right size required practice and skill.

Factory production

Originally all clothes were woven at home, but by the time of our story textiles were being produced in workshops. Even the poorer classes normally bought their clothing, which was produced locally. Wealthier Romans would buy luxury textiles from across the Empire and beyond.

The province of Asia was a center of the textile industry and, on its west coast, the city of Miletus was well known for its fine wool exports. Miletus' coastal position provided a direct trade route to Rome but also granted access to a precious purple dye, extracted from a particular type of sea snail, the murex. This dye was known as Tyrian purple because it was produced in Tyre, in modern Lebanon. It was used for the edging on the togas of the most senior senators. Laodicea, near Miletus, was a great exporter of clothes. Evidence of the wide-reaching textile trade is found on a gravestone from Lugdunum, in Gaul, which was set up to Iulius Verecundus, a *negōtiātor Laodicēnārius* – a trader in cloth goods from Laodicea.

2. Preparing the wool

The fleece from a sheep contains an oily substance called lanolin, as well as mud and dirt. Before the fleece could be spun into thread, it was washed to remove any impurities and combed to separate the fibers so that the spun thread would be even.

If the fleece was to be dyed, it was done at this stage. The Romans used various plants and shells to obtain a wide variety of colors. Saffron, a bright orange dye, was harvested from the crocus flower. It was used to dye a Roman bride's veil (*flammeum*). Pliny the Elder describes another plant, called radicula:

> It releases a juice often used when washing wool, and it is quite wonderful how much it adds to the whiteness and softness of wool.

3. Spinning the thread

The main tools for spinning wool into thread were the distaff and spindle. The bottom of the spindle was attached to a whorl, a heavier wheel which was spun around. The prepared wool was rolled into a ball and placed on the end of a distaff which was held in the left hand. The spinner drew fibers from the wool and twisted them in her right hand, winding them around the spindle, which hung down from the distaff. The weight of the whorl aided the spinner in drawing the fibers out and winding them round the spindle. The illustrations to the stories on pages 247 and 250 show Alexander's sisters spinning and weaving.

A bronze distaff and a decorated glass whorl.

Pallade plācātā lānām mollīre puellae discant et plēnās exonerāre colōs.

With the blessing of Pallas [Minerva], let girls learn to soften wool and unwind the full distaffs.

Ovid

cōnsilium

intereā Lūcīlius, quem mīlitēs custōdiēbant, in vīllā Cantabrī sedēbat.
duo virī prō eō stābant. alter erat Cantaber, quī īram cēlāre nōn
poterat, alter Othō, lēgātus prōvinciae Lūsitāniae. Othō tribūnum
intentē spectābat sed nihil dīcēbat. Cantaber tamen Lūcīlium
ferōciter 'cūr mediā nocte errābās per hortum meum cum illō servō,   5
iuvenis?' rogāvit.

'cūr necesse est tibi cēlāre tantum aurum tam dīligenter, Cantaber?'
rogāvit tribūnus. 'unde aurum abstulistī? quō id mittis? num tantam
pecūniam dēbēs?'

ubi Cantaber Lūcīlium vituperābat, Othō vīdit comitem īram   10
temperāre nōn posse. igitur Cantabrō 'dēsiste, mī amīce,' graviter
inquit. 'tempus est breve.' tum ad tribūnum sē vertit, et dulcis
'multum cognōvistī, mī Lūcīlī,' inquit. 'bene ēgistī et fēlīciter. audī
nunc meum cōnsilium, quod tibi libenter offerō.'

deinde lēgātus Lūcīliō dīxit imperium Rōmānum in maximō perīculō   15
esse, et 'Nerō nōn sīcut imperātor sed sīcut rēx agere cupit,' inquit.
'quālis prīnceps urbem suī populī et domōs suōrum cīvium incendit?
vīsne illī virō īnsānō crūdēlīque imperium relinquere?'

Othō, postquam sēnsit Lūcīlium dubitāre, rogāvit, 'nescīsne mortuum
esse Senecam, patris tuī amīcum cārum? hōc annō Nerō eum coēgit   20
suā manū perīre. itaque aurum, quod Cantaber in horreō cēlat, mihi
est. legiōnēs parāre iam coepī. cum hīs legiōnibus legiōnēs illius
mōnstrī oppugnābō. adiuvābisne mē? ingēns praemium tibi erit.'

---

alter ... alter ... *the one ... the other ...*

tantus *so much*
id *it*

temperō *I control, restrain*
igitur *therefore*
fēlīciter *successfully*
libenter *willingly, gladly*
imperium *empire*

prīnceps *emperor*
populus *people*

cōgō *I force, compel*
suā manū *by his own hand*
legiō *legion*

LANGUAGE NOTE 2: HIM, HER, IT, THEM

1. Study the use of the words in red in the following sentences:

    frāter meus clāmābat. vōs omnēs eum audīvistis.
    My brother was shouting. You all heard him.

    Sabīna est in vīllā. eam vocābō.
    Sabina is in the villa. I shall call her.

    imāgō est tam pulchra. eam emere volō.
    The image is so beautiful. I want to buy it.

    duae fēminae aderant, sed fūrēs eās terruērunt.
    Two women were present, but the thieves terrified them.

    postquam laterēs fēcērunt, nōs eōs ad plaustra portāvimus.
    After they made the bricks, we carried them to the carts.

    quis est pater eius?
    Who is her father? or *Who is his father?*

    unde aurum abstulistī? quō id mittis?
    Where did you steal the gold from? Where are you sending it to?

2. The words in red are all forms of the pronoun **is**, **ea**, **id**. Latin uses them to refer to someone or something that has previously been mentioned.

3. **is**, **ea**, **id** changes its form to match the gender and number of whatever it is referring to. Its case depends on its own role in the sentence.

4. There is a chart of all the forms of **is**, **ea**, **id** on page 275.

LANGUAGE PRACTICE

1. Use the chart of **is**, **ea**, **id** on page 275 to translate the words in bold into Latin.

    a. The boys often helped us. We liked **them** very much.

    b. You saw **her** yesterday in the forum.

    c. They led **him** towards the Subura.

    d. The sisters often met at our house. I knew **them** well.

    e. Give the food **to her**.

    f. The money belonged to the actors. We gave it back **to them**.

    g. My mother was an excellent artist. This is **her** sword.

    h. The brothers bought the pig in the market. It is **their** animal.

Marriage

For Romans there was no official legal or religious wedding ceremony. Simply by living together a couple declared their agreement to be husband and wife. However, people who wanted to celebrate their marriage could choose from various traditions and ceremonies. The main reason for getting married was to have legitimate children who would continue the family line and inherit the family property or business. Among the upper classes marriage was often for political reasons. Men made political alliances through marriage. But marriage was also viewed as a partnership between a couple who wanted to live together harmoniously, and some people married for love.

Most of our knowledge of Roman marriage refers to the upper classes. We know much less about marriage among ordinary people and the poor. There is also very little evidence from the wife's point of view, because most of the sources are written by men. The subject is also complicated by the fact that conventions, attitudes, and laws changed over the years.

Generally the youngest age for marriage was twelve for girls and fourteen for boys, although the average ages were higher. Young girls often married much older men who had been widowed. Although in upper-class families marriages were often arranged, a father could not force his son to marry a particular wife. By law a woman had to give her consent, but the only grounds she had for refusal were that the bridegroom was morally unfit.

There were two kinds of marriage. In marriage *cum manū* (with control) the woman passed from her father's family and guardianship to her husband's, and her property then belonged to her husband. By the first century AD marriage *sine manū* (without control) was the norm, except in some upper-class families. The woman stayed under the guardianship of her father and owned her own property.

Dowry

It was traditional for the woman's family to give a dowry to the husband, although this may not have applied to the poorest members of the population. The dowry was a payment in the form of money, property, or land. It was intended to be a contribution towards the cost of maintaining the new household. During the marriage the dowry and any income it generated were the property of the husband. When he died or the couple divorced, all or part of the dowry was returned to the wife's family. This was a way of protecting the woman financially, and made it easier for her to remarry.

A large dowry was an important factor in securing a desirable husband. Pliny wrote the following, in a letter to a friend whose daughter was about to get married:

> Since your daughter is about to marry that most successful man Nonius Celer, and since his position requires a certain amount of elegance, she must show respect for her husband's status by having clothes and an escort of slaves which make her look suitably distinguished. I am also aware that your resources are limited, so I am offering to contribute to your expenses. As though I were a second father to the girl, I am giving you 50,000 sesterces.

Pliny

Engagement

The marriage was often preceded by an engagement. This involved agreements between the two families about property and dowries. The man gave the woman a ring made of gold or iron, which she wore on what is now known as the ring finger of her left hand. There was a belief that a nerve ran directly from this finger to the heart.

> When the human body is cut open a very delicate nerve is found, which starts from the finger next to the smallest finger and runs to the heart. It is therefore appropriate that this finger, which is connected directly to the body's most vital organ, should be given the ring.

Aulus Gellius

A gold engagement ring from the third century AD. Its small size suggests that it was given to a young girl.

QUESTION

Why do you think the woman wore an engagement ring and the man did not?

LANGUAGE PRACTICE

2. Choose the correct word in the brackets to complete the sentence, then translate. You may wish to use the chart on page 275 for help.

a. nōs .... hominem in vīllā numquam vīdimus.   (hunc, hanc, hōs)

b. nōnne .... fēmina Alexandrō nūbere vult?   (hās, hic, haec)

c. vōsne .... montēs sine cibō et aquā ascendistis?   (illōs, illa, illius)

d. verba .... puellae intentē audīvimus.   (hic, huius, hōs)

e. frātrēs .... porcum per tōtam urbem Conimbrīgae quaesīvērunt.   (illō, illum, illās)

f. tandem Maelō cum .... virīs ad officīnam revēnit.   (hunc, hīs, hōs)

g. .... dīxit sē Alexandrum amāre.   (illōs, illās, illa)

h. mox .... cognōvī quod saepe in urbe clāmōrēs sustulērunt.   (illōs, illius, illō)

Divorce

Divorce was easy and frequent among the upper classes. (We don't have evidence for the lower classes.) A divorce could be by mutual agreement, or either the husband or the wife could make the decision.

Marriage laws

Emperor Augustus introduced laws to encourage marriage and having children, because the birth rate had fallen, especially in the wealthier classes. There were penalties for remaining single: for example, single people had to pay higher taxes and could not inherit property. There were also rewards for married couples who had three or more children. In addition, Augustus introduced laws to punish adultery as a crime.

Julia, daughter of Augustus

Julia, the daughter of Emperor Augustus, was married three times to men chosen for her by her father to promote his political interests. Augustus had no surviving male children. Therefore, he married Julia to men who would be suitable heirs. Julia's first marriage, when she was 14, was to Marcus Claudius Marcellus, her cousin, who was about 17. Three years later Marcellus died, and Julia was married to Agrippa, Augustus' friend and trusted general, the man Augustus saw as his successor. Julia was 18 and Agrippa was in his late forties. When Agrippa died, Augustus arranged for Julia to marry Tiberius, her stepbrother, Augustus' preferred heir. When Julia was accused of being unfaithful, Tiberius divorced her. She was banished by her father and spent the rest of her life in exile.

Marble bust of Julia.

Husbands and wives

Most of the evidence we have about the relationships between husbands and wives is from tombstones, letters, and literature. Almost all of this was written by men.

Look at Sources 1 and 2.

SOURCE 1

A funerary inscription set up by a wife for her husband:

> To the spirits of the dead
> for Quintus Sittius Flaccus
> centurion of the 1st cohort,
> tribune of the 10th praetorian cohort,
> Anicia Caecilia, daughter of Marcus,
> set up this monument
> for her most excellent husband.

SOURCE 2

A funerary inscription set up by a husband for his wife:

> Stranger, what I say is brief. Stop and read it. This is the unlovely tomb of a lovely woman. Her parents named her Claudia. She loved her husband with all her heart. She gave birth to two sons. One of them she leaves on earth, the other she placed beneath the earth. Her conversation was charming and her movements were graceful. She looked after the house. She made wool. I have spoken. Go.

QUESTIONS

1. For what achievements does Anicia Caecilia praise her husband?

2. For what qualities is Claudia remembered by her husband?

In praise of women

SOURCE 3

A funeral speech by a son for his mother:

> The eulogies of all good women are simple and almost the same since there's a limited number of ways to describe their natural goodness and self-control. It is enough that they have all done the same good deeds which merit a fine reputation. And because it is hard to find new ways to praise a woman since women's lives have little variation, it is necessary to remember the virtues they share so that none is omitted; for this might devalue the rest.

SOURCE 4

A funerary inscription set up by a man for his young wife:

> Here I lie, a married woman, Veturia, wife of Fortunatus and daughter of Veturius. I lived for just twenty-seven years, and I was married for sixteen years. I had only one lover and husband. I gave birth to six children, but only one survived. Titus Iulius Fortunatus, centurion of the Second Legion, set this up for his loyal and virtuous wife.

SOURCE 5

Part of a funerary inscription set up by a man in praise of his wife, Turia:

> Why should I list all your domestic virtues: your loyalty, obedience, friendliness, reasonableness, skill at working wool, religion without superstition, demure dress, modesty of appearance? Why dwell on your love for your relatives, your devotion to your family? You have shown the same care to my mother as you did to your own parents, and have taken care to secure an equally peaceful life for her as you did for your own family, and you have innumerable other merits in common with all married women who care for their good name.

QUESTIONS

3. How much do these sources tell us about the individuals who are commemorated?

4. How reliable do you think funerary inscriptions and speeches are as a source?

An ideal match

SOURCE 6

Part of a funerary inscription from Rome. Both Hermia and his wife were freed slaves.

Lucius Aurelius Hermia, freedman of Lucius, a butcher from the Viminal Hill.
This woman, who has gone before me by fate, pure in body, was my one and only wife, loving possessor of my heart. She lived as a faithful wife to a faithful husband, with equal devotion on both sides. She never deserted her duty because of greed.

SOURCE 7

An extract from an essay by Plutarch called *Advice to the Bride and Groom*:

A man should not choose a wife with his eyes or by counting how much money she has. Instead his decision should be based on how well they will live together as partners.

SOURCE 8

SOURCE 9

Pliny wrote this letter to a friend. His friend's niece was 14 years old and Minicius was in his early thirties:

You ask me to look out for a husband for your niece. Minicius Acilianus is available. He is very energetic and hard-working, but still extremely modest. He has a noble appearance, with a rosy complexion and a handsome build. He is a senator, and behaves in a way which is suited to his rank. I think that these qualities shouldn't be disregarded. I don't know whether I should add that his father is rich. Money has to be taken into account when making a marriage contract.

Left: Terentius Neo, the owner of a bakery, and his wife, in a wall painting from their house in Pompeii.

QUESTIONS

5. Look at Sources 6–8. What do they reveal about what Romans considered to be an ideal marriage?

6. Look at Source 9. What qualities does Pliny think should be looked for in a husband?

7. How honest do you think these attitudes to marriage are?

diēs nūptiālis

diēs nūptiārum erat. familia Alexandrī nūptiās celebrābat.

Sabīna tunicam albam flammeumque gerēbat. servī porcum ad parvam āram dūxērunt, ubi Maelō sacrificium nūptiāle fēcit. tum deae Iūnōnī precēs obtulit.

Maelō	vōbīs omnibus nūntiō hanc virginem esse uxōrem huius virī.	5

omnēs clāmābant, 'fēlīciter! fēlīciter!'

Alexander Sabīnae manum dextram tenēbat, et eī ōsculum dedit.

Sabīna   tantum gaudeō quod tū mē in mātrimōnium dūcere cupis, Alexander.

post nūptiās cēna splendida erat. posteā māter Alexandrī facēs sacrās deae Cererī incendit, et sorōrēs eās tulērunt. omnēs Sabīnam ad Alexandrum dūxērunt. Alexander prō iānuā stābat.   10

Alexander   quis es? unde vēnistī?

Sabīna   ubi tū es Gāius, ego sum Gāia.

frātrēs clāmābant rīdēbantque: 'Alexander, fēlīciter!'   15

tunica *tunic*

precēs *prayers*

virgō *girl, young woman*

dexter *right*

tantum *so much*

Cerēs *Ceres (goddess of agriculture)*

The ceremony

The Roman wedding was a mixture of religious and private rituals. There was no official legal ceremony or license required. Most important was the consent from both parties (although in some cases this could be from the bride's father rather than the bride). We have very little evidence for lower-class weddings, but it is likely they had similar but less elaborate festivities.

Preparations

The first task was to choose a lucky day for the ceremony. The *Kalendae* (first day of the month), *Nōnēs* (nine days before the Ides), and *Īdēs* (the fifteenth or thirteenth day) of each month, and the day following each of them, were unlucky. So was all of May and the first half of June. Festival days were also a bad choice, as it was likely that friends and family would be busy.

The night before her wedding, the bride dedicated objects from her childhood to her family Lares. These might be her toys or clothes, a symbol of what she was leaving behind.

On the day itself the bride was dressed by her mother or female relatives. She wore a simple, long, white or orange tunic, which was only worn once. The tunic was bound by a belt tied in a special knot, the knot of Hercules. Only her new husband was allowed to undo the knot. Hercules had fathered many children and this ritual was supposed to secure the fertility of the couple. The bride's hair was arranged into a special style. Using a bent iron spearhead, her hair was divided into six parts, and then twisted up into a cone and crowned with

flowers which she had picked herself. The origins of this ritual are not understood. The bride was then covered with the flame-colored veil (*flammeum*) which reached down to her feet. Sometimes she also wore orange shoes.

The marriage

There were variations on the Roman wedding ceremony. The most formal was presided over by the Pontifex Maximus, but this was reserved for only a few couples from the upper classes. Most ceremonies involved lighting a torch to the goddess Ceres, in hope of the couple's fertility. Pliny the Elder wrote that a torch made of wood from the may tree was best, because it bore many fruits. There was then a sacrifice – a pig was a common choice – and the bride and groom sometimes exchanged gifts. This was followed by a marriage feast at the bride's house.

Then came the most important part of the day. First the bride was snatched from her mother, with a show of force. This was called the *raptiō* and was a tradition which mimicked the earliest Roman weddings. According to legend, the early Romans stole the local Sabine women to become their brides. The poet Catullus describes the raptio, addressing Hesperus (the Evening Star) and Hymen, the god of marriage:

> Hesperus, you can tear the daughter from her
>   mother's arms,
> and give the virgin girl to the passionate youth.
> O Hymenaeus Hymen, O Hymen Hymenaeus!

The bride was then escorted to her new home, surrounded by a crowd of well-wishers singing crude wedding songs. This procession, the *dēductiō*, was a public act and was an important symbol of the bride's consent. Behind the bride were carried the spindle and distaff, tokens of her domestic life. The groom also scattered nuts on the ground, a sign that he was giving up his childish ways.

When they reached her new home, the groom lifted the bride across the threshold to prevent her tripping – a bad omen. She then made the vow:

ubi tū Gāius, ego Gāia.
Where you are Gaius, I am Gaia.

And the doors closed behind the newly-weds.

ad lūcem

puer aeger in lectō iacet. febrem gravem habet. prope lectum sedet
Rūfīna. pōculum tenet. lacrimae eius in puerum cadunt.

pōculum *cup*

Rūfīna   tolle caput, mī lepus! bibe!

LANGUAGE PRACTICE

3. Choose the correct word in the brackets to complete the sentence, then translate. You may wish
    to use the chart on page 275 for help.

    a. Lūcīlius et Tīrō aderant. custōs .... in hortō vīdit.   (eās, eōs, eum)

    b. postquam frātrēs Alexandrum vīdērunt, ... laetē salūtāvērunt.   (ea, eum, eam)

    c. simulatque Sabīna vīllam intrāvit, Hettia flammeum .... ostendit.   (eī, eōs, eās)

    d. est nūlla pecūnia in tabernā. ubi .... cēlāvistī?   (ea, eum, eam)

    e. Lūcīlius effugere voluit. custōs tamen bracchium .... rapuit.   (eīs, eius, eō)

    f. sorōrēs Alexandrī rīdēbant. Hettia clāmōrēs .... audīvit.   (eōrum, eārum, id)

    g. quamquam fīliae tuae nōn crēdō, verba .... cōgitābō.   (eius, eum, eam)

    h. mox amīcī revēnērunt. tum.......... dōna obtulī.   (eum, eās, eīs)

4. Translate each sentence into Latin by choosing the correct word or phrase from each pair.

    a. *We often said that the freedmen were working for a long time.*
        nōs   semper   dīcimus   lībertōs   diū   labōrābant.
        vōs   saepe   dīcēbāmus   lībertī   vix   labōrāre.

    b. *For three days the Romans resisted the fierce Britons in vain.*
        tribus diēbus   Rōmānī   Britannōs   ferōcibus   frūstrā   resistēbant.
        trēs diēs   Rōmānōs   Britannīs   ferōcēs   fortiter   resistēbāmus.

    c. *I decided to leave the city without food and to travel across the mountains.*
        ad urbem   sine cibum   discēdere   aut   trāns montēs   prōcēdere   convēnī.
        ab urbe   sine cibō   dūcere   ac   trāns montibus   prōmittere   cōnstituī.

    d. *However, the queen always kills her enemies if she can.*
        rēx   tamen   hostēs   saepe   necat,   sī poterat.
        rēgīna   tandem   hostibus   semper   necāvit,   sī potest.

    e. *Although they know life is short, they do not fear death.*
        quoque   scīvērunt   vītam   brevem   est,   mortem   nunc   timent.
        quamquam   sciunt   vīta   brevis   esse,   mortis   nōn   timēbunt.

    f. *'Where are you going?' 'We are going to the house which is near the wood.'*
        'quō   īmus?'   'ad   vīllās,   quās   prope   silvae   erit,   īmus.'
        'cūr   itis?'   'ā   vīllam,   quae   post   silvam   est,   itis.'

Arachne

Arachne, the daughter of a cloth-dyer, created more beautiful weaving work than any other woman. She claimed her skill was entirely her own, rather than due to the gods' gifts. When the goddess Athena heard of this, she paid Arachne a visit.

- Now read or listen to the story of Arachne.

Hubris

The ancient Greek word 'hubris' refers to the behavior of humans who defied the authority of the gods. Often acts of hubris involved people believing themselves to be equal to the gods. In the end, the overconfident mortal usually brought about their own downfall or was punished by a god for their arrogance.

- Look at Source 1. What do you think Arachne's hubris is precisely?
- And what is her punishment?

SOURCE 1   You could see she was taught by Athena. However, the girl herself denied this and she was offended at the idea of having such a teacher. 'Let Athena compete with me,' she said, 'and I won't at all deny it if she defeats me.'

Ovid

Look at Source 2.

- Which part of the story does this painting show?
- Why do you think the painter chose to represent this part?

Jealous gods

In many Greek myths, the gods display a human temperament, and they're just as prone to jealousy, anger, or pride as mortals. Do you think the Greek gods model good behavior, and are they fair and just in their dealings with mortals? What does the story of Arachne tell you about the relationship between gods and humans?

RESEARCH

1. Find other stories in Greek mythology that involve hubris (for instance: Niobe, Icarus, Oedipus).

2. Find out who the goddess Nemesis was, and what her connection was to hubris.

3. Can you think of stories from other times that involve hubris?

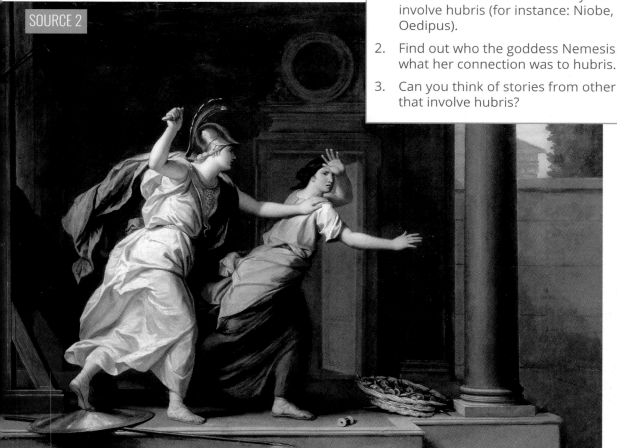

SOURCE 2

Reference

VOCABULARY FOR LEARNING

Chapter 1

dormiō	*I sleep*
ego	*I*
frāter	*brother*
hōra	*hour*
in	*in, on*
īnsula	*apartment building*
labōrō	*I work*
legō	*I read*
meus	*my*
nōn	*not*
pater	*father*
rīdeō	*I laugh, smile*
servus	*slave, enslaved person (male)*
tū	*you (singular)*
turba	*crowd*
ubi?	*where?*
via	*street, road, way*
sum	*I am*
es	*you (singular) are*
est	*(he/she/it) is*

Chapter 2

cadō	*I fall*
cibus, cibum, *m.*	*food*
dūcō	*I lead, take*
et	*and*
fīlia, fīliam, *f.*	*daughter*
fīlius, fīlium, *m.*	*son*
forum, forum, *n.*	*forum, marketplace*
habeō	*I have, hold*
habitō	*I live*
intrō	*I enter*
magnus	*big, large, great*
pecūnia, pecūniam, *f.*	*money, sum of money*
quaerō	*I search for, look for, ask*
quoque	*also, too*
salūtō	*I greet*
sed	*but*
spectō	*I look at, watch*
videō	*I see*
vīnum, vīnum, *n.*	*wine*
vocō	*I call*

Chapter 3

ambulō	*I walk*
amīcus, amīcum, *m.*	*friend*
ancilla, ancillam, *f.*	*slave, enslaved person (female)*
clāmō	*I shout*
clāmor, clāmōrem, *m.*	*shout, shouting, noise*
cum	*with*
currō	*I run*
dīcō	*I say, speak, tell*
equus, equum, *m.*	*horse*
festīnō	*I hurry*
gladius, gladium, *m.*	*sword*
īnfēlīx	*unlucky, unhappy*
laetus	*happy*
multus	*much, many*
omnis	*all, every*
per	*through, along*
prīmus	*first*
senātor, senātōrem, *m.*	*senator*
urbs, urbem, *f.*	*city*
vincō	*I conquer, win, am victorious*

Chapter 4

ad	*to, towards; at*
adsum	*I am here, I am present*
deus, deum, *m.*	*god*
dominus, dominum, *m.*	*master*
dōnum, dōnum, *n.*	*gift, present*
laudō	*I praise*
nōs	*we, us*
parvus	*small*
perīculum, perīculum, *n.*	*danger*
perterritus	*terrified*
puella, puellam, *f.*	*girl*
quod	*because*
rēx, rēgem, *m.*	*king*
Rōmānus	*Roman*
subitō	*suddenly*
templum, templum, *n.*	*temple*
teneō	*I hold, keep, possess*
tollō	*I raise, lift up, hold up*
veniō	*I come*
vōs	*you (plural)*

Chapter 5

aqua, aquam, *f.*	*water*
audiō, audīre	*hear, listen to*
cupiō, cupere	*want, desire*
custōs, custōdem, *m.f.*	*guard*
dēbeō, dēbēre	*owe*
dō, dare	*give*
effugiō, effugere	*escape*
iuvenis, iuvenem, *m.f.*	*young person*
maneō, manēre	*remain, stay*
nēmō, nēminem	*no one, nobody*
nōlō, nōlle	*don't want, refuse*
nox, noctem, *f.*	*night*
portō, portāre	*carry, bear, take*
possum, posse	*can, am able*
pulcher	*beautiful, handsome*
respondeō, respondēre	*reply*
taceō, tacēre	*am silent, am quiet*
timeō, timēre	*fear, am afraid*
vēndō, vēndere	*sell*
volō, velle	*want, wish, am willing*

Chapter 6

ā, ab + *abl.*	*from, away from*
capiō, capere	*take, catch, capture, adopt (a plan)*
diēs, diem, *m.*	*day*
discēdō, discēdere	*depart, leave*
ē, ex + *abl.*	*from, out of*
exspectō, exspectāre	*wait for, expect*
faciō, facere	*make, do*
iam	*now, already*
in + *acc.*	*into, onto*
inquit	*says*
marītus, marītum, *m.*	*husband*
māter, mātrem, *f.*	*mother*
prope + *acc.*	*near*
rogō, rogāre	*ask, ask for*
sedeō, sedēre	*sit*
stō, stāre	*stand*
tōtus	*whole*
trīstis	*sad*
tuus	*your (*singular*), yours*
uxor, uxōrem, *f.*	*wife*

Chapter 7

appropinquō, appropinquāre, appropinquāvī	*approach, come near to*
cūr?	*why?*
epistula, epistulam, *f.*	*letter*
homō, hominem, *m.*	*man, person*
ingēns	*huge*
īnsula, īnsulam, *f.*	*island; apartment building*
mīles, mīlitem, *m.*	*soldier*
minimē	*no*
nārrō, nārrāre, nārrāvī	*tell, relate*
nauta, nautam, *m.*	*sailor*
nunc	*now*
ōlim	*once, some time ago*
pars, partem, *f.*	*part*
puer, puerum, *m.*	*boy*
pugnō, pugnāre, pugnāvī	*fight*
rēs, rem, *f.*	*thing, story*
saepe	*often*
silva, silvam, *f.*	*wood, forest*
tum	*then*
vehementer	*loudly, violently, strongly*

Chapter 8

agō, agere, ēgī	*do*
bibō, bibere, bibī	*drink*
cōnspiciō, cōnspicere, cōnspexī	*catch sight of, notice*
dē + *abl.*	*from, down from; about*
domus, domum, *f.*	*house, home*
eam	*her; it*
eum	*him; it*
gerō, gerere, gessī	*wear*
iaceō, iacēre, iacuī	*lie down*
incendō, incendere, incendī	*burn, set on fire*
mox	*soon*
nihil	*nothing*
noster	*our*
porta, portam, *f.*	*gate*
postquam	*after*
prōcēdō, prōcēdere, prōcessī	*go along, proceed*
senex, senem, *m.f.*	*old person*
surgō, surgere, surrēxī	*get up*
tandem	*at last, finally*
trāns + *acc.*	*across*

Chapter 9

adveniō, advenīre, advēnī	*arrive*
cīvis, cīvem, *m.f.*	*citizen*
difficilis	*difficult*
domina, dominam, *f.*	*mistress, lady*
gravis	*heavy; serious*
hostis, hostem, *m.*	*enemy*
imperātor, imperātōrem, *m.*	*emperor, general*
īrātus	*angry*
iter, iter, *n.*	*journey, route, way*
lacrimō, lacrimāre, lacrimāvī	*cry, weep*
līberī, līberōs, *m. pl.*	*children*
medius	*middle, middle of*
nūntius, nūntium, *m.*	*messenger; message, news*
paucī, *pl.*	*few, a few*
petō, petere, petīvī	*attack; seek, beg, ask for*
sanguis, sanguinem, *m.*	*blood*
statim	*immediately, at once*
trādō, trādere, trādidī	*hand over, hand down*
vir, virum, *m.*	*man*
vīta, vītam, *f.*	*life*

Chapter 10

accipiō, accipere, accēpī	*accept, take in, receive*
alius, alia, aliud	*another, other*
annus, annum, *m.*	*year*
bonus, bona, bonum	*good*
contrā + *acc.*	*against*
dea, deam, *f.*	*goddess*
deinde	*then*
ferō, ferre, tulī	*bring, carry, bear*
fidēlis, fidēlis, fidēle	*loyal, faithful, trustworthy*
iaciō, iacere, iēcī	*throw*
locus, locum, *m.*	*place*
miser, misera, miserum	*poor, unfortunate*
novus, nova, novum	*new*
nūllus, nūlla, nūllum	*no, not any*
occīdō, occīdere, occīdī	*kill*
pāx, pācem, *f.*	*peace*
pereō, perīre, periī	*die, perish*
quam ... !	*how ... !*
sacer, sacra, sacrum	*sacred, holy*
sub + *acc.* or *abl.*	*under, below, beneath*

Chapter 11

absum, abesse, āfuī	*am out, absent, away*
accidō, accidere, accidī	*happen*
altus, alta, altum	*high, deep*
bene	*well*
dux, ducis, *m.*	*leader*
flūmen, flūminis, *n.*	*river*
fortis, fortis, forte	*brave*
frūstrā	*in vain, without success*
fugiō, fugere, fūgī	*run away, flee*
hodiē	*today*
ibi	*there*
inveniō, invenīre, invēnī	*find*
itaque	*and so, therefore*
mare, maris, *n.*	*sea*
nāvigō, nāvigāre, nāvigāvī	*sail*
nāvis, nāvis, *f.*	*ship*
prō + *abl.*	*in front of; for*
saevus, saeva, saevum	*savage, cruel*
sōlus, sōla, sōlum	*alone, only, lonely, on one's own*
ubi	*where? where, when*

Chapter 12

caelum, caelī, *n.*	*sky, heaven*
caput, capitis, *n.*	*head*
corpus, corporis, *n.*	*body*
crūdēlis, crūdēlis, crūdēle	*cruel*
dēleō, dēlēre, dēlēvī	*destroy*
diū	*for a long time*
iānua, iānuae, *f.*	*door, doorway*
iterum	*again*
mittō, mittere, mīsī	*send*
offerō, offerre, obtulī	*offer*
quis? quid?	*who? what?*
redeō, redīre, rediī	*go back, come back, return*
Rōma, Rōmae, *f.*	*Rome*
servō, servāre, servāvī	*save, protect, keep, look after*
stultus, stulta, stultum	*stupid, foolish*
superō, superāre, superāvī	*overcome, overpower*
taberna, tabernae, *f.*	*shop, inn*
terra, terrae, *f.*	*ground*
trahō, trahere, trāxī	*drag, draw, pull*
vōx, vōcis, *f.*	*voice, shout*

Chapter 13

coepī	*began*
cōnsūmō, cōnsūmere, cōnsūmpsī	*consume, eat*
intellegō, intellegere, intellēxī	*understand, realize*
inter + *acc.*	*among, between*
ita vērō	*yes, absolutely*
labor, labōris, *m.*	*work*
longus, longa, longum	*long*
mūrus, mūrī, *m.*	*wall*
nōmen, nōminis, *n.*	*name*
parō, parāre, parāvī	*prepare*
post + *acc.*	*after, behind*
praemium, praemiī, *n.*	*prize, reward, profit*
quamquam	*although*
quī, quae, quod	*who, which*
quōmodo?	*how? in what way?*
semper	*always*
summus, summa, summum	*highest, greatest, top (of)*
suus, sua, suum	*her, his, its, their (own)*
tamen	*however*
vīvō, vīvere, vīxī	*live, am alive*

Chapter 14

amō, amāre, amāvī	*love, like*
amor, amōris, *m.*	*love*
cōgitō, cōgitāre, cōgitāvī	*think, consider*
cōnficiō, cōnficere, cōnfēcī	*finish*
cōnsilium, cōnsiliī, *n.*	*plan, idea, advice*
cōnstituō, cōnstituere, cōnstituī	*decide*
dīrus, dīra, dīrum	*dreadful*
eōs	*them*
fēmina, fēminae, *f.*	*woman*
mōns, montis, *m.*	*mountain*
mors, mortis, *f.*	*death*
nec	*and not, nor, neither*
nec ... nec ...	*neither ... nor ...*
necō, necāre, necāvī	*kill*
nesciō, nescīre, nescīvī	*don't know*
numquam	*never*
ostendō, ostendere, ostendī	*show*
tempus, temporis, *n.*	*time*
terreō, terrēre, terruī	*frighten*
verbum, verbī, *n.*	*word*

Chapter 15

anteā	*before*
bellum, bellī, *n.*	*war*
cēna, cēnae, *f.*	*dinner, meal*
cēterī, cēterae, cētera, *pl.*	*the rest, the others*
cognōscō, cognōscere, cognōvī	*get to know, find out, learn*
comes, comitis, *m.f.*	*comrade, companion*
eō, īre, iī	*go*
etiam	*even, also*
ferōx, ferōx, ferōcis	*fierce, ferocious*
hortus, hortī, *m.*	*garden*
intereā	*meanwhile*
iubeō, iubēre, iussī	*order*
lībertus, lībertī, *m.*	*freedman, former slave*
multum	*much*
nōnne?	*surely?*
nūntiō, nūntiāre, nūntiāvī	*announce, report*
putō, putāre, putāvī	*think*
sē	*himself, herself, itself, themselves*
simulatque	*as soon as*
vīlla, vīllae, *f.*	*country house, house*

Chapter 16

ac	*and*
auferō, auferre, abstulī	*steal, carry off*
brevis, brevis, breve	*short, brief*
cēlō, cēlāre, cēlāvī	*hide*
hic, haec, hoc	*this, he, she, it*
ille, illa, illud	*that, he, she, it*
imperium, imperiī, *n.*	*empire; power*
legō, legere, lēgī	*read; choose*
lūx, lūcis, *f.*	*light, daylight*
ōrō, ōrāre, ōrāvī	*beg, beg for*
prīnceps, prīncipis, *m.*	*chief; emperor*
quō?	*where to?*
rapiō, rapere, rapuī	*seize, grab*
rēgīna, rēgīnae, *f.*	*queen*
resistō, resistere, restitī + *dat.*	*resist*
reveniō, revenīre, revēnī	*come back, return*
sciō, scīre, scīvī	*know*
sentiō, sentīre, sēnsī	*feel, notice*
sī	*if*
sine + *abl.*	*without*

ORDER OF INFORMATION IN LATIN SENTENCES

1. In a Latin sentence information tends to come in a standard order. Familiarity with that order can help you to read and understand Latin.

2. In general, expect the nominative first, then accusative, and then verb. For example:

    sorōrēs   gladiōs   vēndēbant.
    sisters   swords   they were selling

    The sisters were selling swords.

3. If the nominative does not need to be stated, expect accusative, verb:

    gladiōs   vēndēbant.
    swords   they were selling

    They were selling swords.

4. If there is no accusative, then expect nominative, verb:

    sorōrēs   currēbant.
    sisters   they were running

    The sisters were running.

5. Adverbs, and phrases describing the action, are usually immediately before the verb:

    sorōrēs   gladiōs   in forō   vēndēbant.
    sisters   swords   in the forum   they were selling

    The sisters were selling swords in the forum.

6. A dative noun is usually between the nominative and accusative:

    sorōrēs   cīvibus   gladiōs   in forō   vēndēbant.
    sisters   to the citizens   swords   in the forum   they were selling

    The sisters were selling swords to the citizens in the forum.

7. Adjectives may appear before or after the nouns they describe:

    sorōrēs   cīvibus   gladiōs   pulchrōs   in forō   vēndēbant.
    sisters   to the citizens   swords   beautiful ones   in the forum   they were selling

    The sisters were selling beautiful swords to the citizens in the forum.

    Adjectives of size or number are usually before the noun they describe:

    sorōrēs   cīvibus   multōs   gladiōs   in forō   vēndēbant.
    sisters   to the citizens   many   swords   in the forum   they were selling

    The sisters were selling many swords to the citizens in the forum.

8.   Genitives usually follow the nouns they describe:

sorōrēs	cīvibus	gladiōs	parentum	in forō	vēndēbant.
sisters	*to the citizens*	*swords*	*of their parents*	*in the forum*	*they were selling*

The sisters were selling their parents' swords to the citizens in the forum.

9.   Relative clauses also often follow the nouns they describe:

Sabīna,	quae	paene	rīdēbat,	Alexandrō	appropinquāvit.
Sabina	*who*	*almost*	*was laughing*	*to Alexander*	*drew near*

Sabina, who was almost laughing, drew near to/approached Alexander.

10. Indirect statements use an accusative and infinitive construction. The accusative usually comes immediately after the verb of saying, thinking, or perceiving. The infinitive often comes at the end of the sentence:

servī	dīcunt	hominēs	plaustra	custōdīre.
slaves	*say*	*men*	*carts*	*to guard*

The slaves say that men are guarding the carts.

11. As you become familiar with the usual word order, you may notice when the author departs from that order to emphasize a particular word or point:

Mānium	in viā	invēnimus	mortuum.
Manius	*in the street*	*we found*	*dead*

We found Manius in the street. He was dead.

servum	Rūfīna	videt.
slave	*Rufina*	*sees*

It's the slave that Rufina sees.

Sometimes Latin authors used a symmetrical order of words:

clāmōrēs	hominum	et	equōrum	hinnītus
shouts	*of men*	*and*	*of horses*	*neighing*

the shouts of men and the neighing of horses

Latin authors were also fond of using three parallel examples, as well as removing words such as **et**:

vigilēs,	cīvēs,	servī	servāre	temptābant	virginēs
firemen	*citizens*	*slaves*	*to save*	*were trying*	*young women*

The firemen, citizens, and enslaved people were trying to save the young women.

Latin verbs are sometimes omitted if they can be understood from elsewhere in the sentence:

mīles erat nimium gravis, puella nōn valida, glaciēs nōn firma.

The soldier was too heavy, the girl (was) not strong, the ice (was) not firm.

NOUNS

	First declension	Second declension		
	feminine	*masculine*	*masculine*	*neuter*
SINGULAR				
nominative	puella	amīcus	puer	dōnum
genitive	puellae	amīcī	puerī	dōnī
dative	puellae	amīcō	puerō	dōnō
accusative	puellam	amīcum	puerum	dōnum
ablative	puellā	amīcō	puerō	dōnō
PLURAL				
nominative	puellae	amīcī	puerī	dōna
genitive	puellārum	amīcōrum	puerōrum	dōnōrum
dative	puellīs	amīcīs	puerīs	dōnīs
accusative	puellās	amīcōs	puerōs	dōna
ablative	puellīs	amīcīs	puerīs	dōnīs

	Third declension			
	masculine	*feminine*	*feminine*	*neuter*
SINGULAR				
nominative	fūr	nox	urbs	caput
genitive	fūris	noctis	urbis	capitis
dative	fūrī	noctī	urbī	capitī
accusative	fūrem	noctem	urbem	caput
ablative	fūre	nocte	urbe	capite*
PLURAL				
nominative	fūrēs	noctēs	urbēs	capita
genitive	fūrum	noctium	urbium	capitum
dative	fūribus	noctibus	urbibus	capitibus
accusative	fūrēs	noctēs	urbēs	capita
ablative	fūribus	noctibus	urbibus	capitibus

The vocative case has exactly the same form as the nominative case, except in the singular of the second declension, where -**us** becomes -**e** and -**ius** becomes -**ī**. For examples see page 190.

* The ablative singular of **mare** (*sea*) ends -ī: marī.

USES OF THE CASES

nominative	**amīcus** labōrat.	The **friend** is working.	The noun carrying out the action.
genitive	nōmen **amīcī**	the **friend's** name the name **of the friend**	Possession: of, 's.
dative	puella **amīcō** dōnum dat.	The girl gives a present **to her friend**.	to
	necesse est **amīcō** labōrāre.	It is necessary **for the friend** to work.	for
	puella semper **amīcō** crēdit.	The girl always trusts her **friend**.	Some verbs are used with a noun in the dative case.
accusative	puella **amīcum** laudat.	The girl praises her **friend**.	The noun receiving the action.
	puella ad **amīcum** ambulat.	The girl walks towards her **friend**.	With some prepositions, e.g. **ad** (*towards*) **per** (*through*) **trāns** (*across*) **in** (*into*)
	puella **multās hōrās** dormiēbat.	The girl was sleeping **for many hours**.	How long something lasts for.
ablative	puella cum **amīcō** in **forō** ambulat.	The girl is walking with her **friend** in the **forum**.	in, on, by, with, from, at Often with a preposition, e.g. **in** (*in, on*) **cum** (*with*) **ā/ab** (*from, by*) **ē/ex** (*out of*)
	mediā nocte canis lātrāvit.	**In the middle of the night** the dog barked.	The time when something happens.
	hōrā prīmā puella surgit.	**At the first hour** the girl gets up.	
vocative	salvē, **Fauste**!	Hello, **Faustus**!	Speaking to someone.

ADJECTIVES

	First and second declension			Third declension			
	masculine	*feminine*	*neuter*	*masculine/ feminine*	*neuter*	*masculine/ feminine*	*neuter*
SINGULAR							
nominative	bonus	bona	bonum	trīstis	trīste	ingēns	
genitive	bonī	bonae	bonī	trīstis		ingentis	
dative	bonō	bonae	bonō	trīstī		ingentī	
accusative	bonum	bonam	bonum	trīstem	trīste	ingentem	ingēns
ablative	bonō	bonā	bonō	trīstī		ingentī	
PLURAL							
nominative	bonī	bonae	bona	trīstēs	trīstia	ingentēs	ingentia
genitive	bonōrum	bonārum	bonōrum	trīstium		ingentium	
dative	bonīs			trīstibus		ingentibus	
accusative	bonōs	bonās	bona	trīstēs	trīstia	ingentēs	ingentia
ablative	bonīs			trīstibus		ingentibus	

COMPARATIVE AND SUPERLATIVE ADJECTIVES

Positive		Comparative		Superlative	
laetus	*happy*	laetior	*happier*	laetissimus	*happiest, very happy*
pulcher	*beautiful*	pulchrior	*more beautiful*	pulcherrimus	*most beautiful, very beautiful*
trīstis	*sad*	trīstior	*sadder*	trīstissimus	*saddest, very sad*
dīves	*rich*	dīvitior	*richer*	dīvitissimus	*richest, very rich*
facilis	*easy*	facilior	*easier*	facillimus	*easiest, very easy*

IRREGULAR FORMS

Positive		Comparative		Superlative	
bonus	*good*	melior	*better*	optimus	*best, very good*
magnus	*big*	maior	*bigger*	maximus	*biggest, very big*
malus	*bad*	pēior	*worse*	pessimus	*worst, very bad*
multus	*much*	plūs	*more*	plūrimus	*most, very much*
parvus	*small*	minor	*smaller*	minimus	*smallest, very small*

ADJECTIVES/PRONOUNS

SINGULAR	masculine	feminine	neuter	masculine	feminine	neuter
nominative	hic	haec	hoc	ille	illa	illud
genitive		huius			illius	
dative		huic			illī	
accusative	hunc	hanc	hoc	illum	illam	illud
ablative	hōc	hāc	hōc	illō	illā	illō

PLURAL						
nominative	hī	hae	haec	illī	illae	illa
genitive	hōrum	hārum	hōrum	illōrum	illārum	illōrum
dative		hīs			illīs	
accusative	hōs	hās	haec	illōs	illās	illa
ablative		hīs			illīs	

SINGULAR	masculine	feminine	neuter	masculine	feminine	neuter
nominative	is	ea	id	quī	quae	quod
genitive		eius			cuius	
dative		eī			cui	
accusative	eum	eam	id	quem	quam	quod
ablative	eō	eā	eō	quō	quā	quō

PLURAL						
nominative	eī	eae	ea	quī	quae	quae
genitive	eōrum	eārum	eōrum	quōrum	quārum	quōrum
dative		eīs			quibus	
accusative	eōs	eās	ea	quōs	quās	quae
ablative		eīs			quibus	

	I	we	you (singular)	you (plural)	himself, herself, themselves
nominative	ego	nōs	tū	vōs	
genitive	meī	nostrum	tuī	vestrum	suī
dative	mihi	nōbīs	tibi	vōbīs	sibi
accusative	mē	nōs	tē	vōs	sē
ablative	mē	nōbīs	tē	vōbīs	sē

NUMBERS

1	I	ūnus, ūna, ūnum	1st	prīmus, a, um
2	II	duo, duae, duo	2nd	secundus, a, um
3	III	trēs, trēs, tria	3rd	tertius, a, um
4	IIII or IV	quattuor	4th	quārtus, a, um
5	V	quīnque	5th	quīntus, a, um
6	VI	sex	6th	sextus, a, um
7	VII	septem	7th	septimus, a, um
8	VIII	octo	8th	octāvus, a, um
9	VIIII or IX	novem	9th	nōnus, a, um
10	X	decem	10th	decimus, a, um
50	L	quīnquāgintā		
100	C	centum		
500	D	quīngentī		
1,000	M	mīlle		

The numbers 4–10, 50, and 100 do not change their endings.

The numbers 1–3 change their endings as follows:

	masculine	feminine	neuter	masculine	feminine	neuter	masculine/feminine	neuter
nominative	ūnus	ūna	ūnum	duo	duae	duo	trēs	tria
genitive		ūnīus		duōrum	duārum	duōrum	trium	
dative		ūnī		duōbus	duābus	duōbus	tribus	
accusative	ūnum	ūnam	ūnum	duōs	duās	duo	trēs	tria
ablative	ūnō	ūnā	ūnō	duōbus	duābus	duōbus	tribus	

VERBS

	1st conjugation	2nd conjugation	3rd conjugation	4th conjugation	3rd/4th conjugation
	call	*hold*	*send*	*hear*	*take*
PRESENT (*I call, am calling, etc.*)					
I	vocō	teneō	mittō	audiō	capiō
you (sing.)	vocās	tenēs	mittis	audīs	capis
he, she, it	vocat	tenet	mittit	audit	capit
we	vocāmus	tenēmus	mittimus	audīmus	capimus
you (pl.)	vocātis	tenētis	mittitis	audītis	capitis
they	vocant	tenent	mittunt	audiunt	capiunt
FUTURE (*I shall call, etc.*)					
I	vocābō	tenēbō			
you (sing.)	vocābis	tenēbis			
he, she, it	vocābit	tenēbit			
we	vocābimus	tenēbimus			
you (pl.)	vocābitis	tenēbitis			
they	vocābunt	tenēbunt			
IMPERFECT (*I was calling, used to call, etc.*)					
I	vocābam	tenēbam	mittēbam	audiēbam	capiēbam
you (sing.)	vocābās	tenēbās	mittēbās	audiēbās	capiēbās
he, she, it	vocābat	tenēbat	mittēbat	audiēbat	capiēbat
we	vocābāmus	tenēbāmus	mittēbāmus	audiēbāmus	capiēbāmus
you (pl.)	vocābātis	tenēbātis	mittēbātis	audiēbātis	capiēbātis
they	vocābant	tenēbant	mittēbant	audiēbant	capiēbant
PERFECT (*I called, have called, etc.*)					
I	vocāvī	tenuī	mīsī	audīvī	cēpī
you (sing.)	vocāvistī	tenuistī	mīsistī	audīvistī	cēpistī
he, she, it	vocāvit	tenuit	mīsit	audīvit	cēpit
we	vocāvimus	tenuimus	mīsimus	audīvimus	cēpimus
you (pl.)	vocāvistis	tenuistis	mīsistis	audīvistis	cēpistis
they	vocāvērunt	tenuērunt	mīsērunt	audīvērunt	cēpērunt
PRESENT INFINITIVE (*to call, etc.*)					
	vocāre	tenēre	mittere	audīre	capere
IMPERATIVE (*call!, etc.*)					
singular	vocā	tenē	mitte	audī	cape
plural	vocāte	tenēte	mittite	audīte	capite

IRREGULAR VERBS

PRESENT	I am	I am able	I go	I want	I don't want	I bring
I	sum	possum	eō	volō	nōlō	ferō
you (sing.)	es	potes	īs	vīs	nōn vīs	fers
he, she, it	est	potest	it	vult	nōn vult	fert
we	sumus	possumus	īmus	volumus	nōlumus	ferimus
you (pl.)	estis	potestis	ītis	vultis	nōn vultis	fertis
they	sunt	possunt	eunt	volunt	nōlunt	ferunt

FUTURE	I shall be	I shall be able	I shall go
I	erō	poterō	ībō
you (sing.)	eris	poteris	ībis
he, she, it	erit	poterit	ībit
we	erimus	poterimus	ībimus
you (pl.)	eritis	poteritis	ībitis
they	erunt	poterunt	ībunt

IMPERFECT	I was	I was able	I was going	I used to want	I was unwilling	I was bringing
I	eram	poteram	ībam	volēbam	nōlēbam	ferēbam
you (sing.)	erās	poterās	ībās	volēbās	nōlēbās	ferēbās
he, she, it	erat	poterat	ībat	volēbat	nōlēbat	ferēbat
we	erāmus	poterāmus	ībāmus	volēbāmus	nōlēbāmus	ferēbāmus
you (pl.)	erātis	poterātis	ībātis	volēbātis	nōlēbātis	ferēbātis
they	erant	poterant	ībant	volēbant	nōlēbant	ferēbant

PERFECT	I have been	I have been able	I went	I wanted	I didn't want	I brought
I	fuī	potuī	iī	voluī	nōluī	tulī
you (sing.)	fuistī	potuistī	iistī	voluistī	nōluistī	tulistī
he, she, it	fuit	potuit	iit	voluit	nōluit	tulit
we	fuimus	potuimus	iimus	voluimus	nōluimus	tulimus
you (pl.)	fuistis	potuistis	iistis	voluistis	nōluistis	tulistis
they	fuērunt	potuērunt	iērunt	voluērunt	nōluērunt	tulērunt

PRESENT INFINITIVE	to be	to be able	to go	to want	not to want	to bring
	esse	posse	īre	velle	nōlle	ferre

IMPERATIVE			go!		be unwilling!	bring!
singular			ī		nōlī	fer
plural			īte		nōlīte	ferte

EXPRESSIONS, MOTTOES, AND ABBREVIATIONS

A.D.	annō dominī	in the year of the Lord
a.m.	ante merīdiem	before midday
ad lib	ad libitum	as you desire
c.	circā	about, approximately
cf.	confer	compare (with)
C.V.	curriculum vītae	course of life
e.g.	exemplī grātiā	as an example
et al.	et aliī	and the other people
etc.	et cētera	and the other things
ibid.	ibidem	in the same place (in a book)
i.e.	id est	that is
n.b.	notā bene	note well
p.m.	post merīdiem	after midday
p.s.	post scrīptum	after writing
Q.E.D.	quod erat demonstrandum	(that) which had to be proved
R.I.P.	requiēscat in pāce	rest in peace
S.P.Q.R.	Senātus Populusque Rōmānus	the Senate and the People of Rome
v. or vs.	versus	against, facing

ad hoc	as necessary; temporary
ālea iacta est. (*Julius Caesar*)	The die has been thrown.
alibī	in another place
bonā fidē	genuine; in good faith
carpe diem! (*Horace*)	Seize the day!
cōgitō ergō sum.	I think, therefore I am.
cui bonō?	to whose benefit?
dē factō	in reality
dē iūre	according to the law, in theory
ē plūribus ūnum	out of many, one
fortibus Fortūna favet.	Fortune favors the brave.
in sitū	in (the original) place
mea culpa	my own fault
mēns sāna in corpore sānō. (*Juvenal*)	A healthy mind in a healthy body.
modus operandī	a way of doing something
pecūnia nōn olet.	Money doesn't stink.
per capita	each person
per sē	in/by itself
prīmus inter parēs	a first among equals
prō bonō (pūblicō)	for the public good
quid prō quō	one favor in return for another
quis custōdiet ipsōs custōdēs? (*Juvenal*)	Who will guard the guards?
rēs pūblica	the public situation, the state
status quō	the existing situation
summā cum laude	with great glory
vēnī, vīdī, vīcī. (*Julius Caesar*)	I came, I saw, I conquered.
viā	by way of
vice versā	the other way around
vōx populī	the voice of the people

ENGLISH TO LATIN

able, I am	*possum, posse, potuī*
across	*trāns + acc.*
adopt (a plan), I	*capiō, capere, cēpī*
advice	*cōnsilium, cōnsiliī, n.*
afraid, I am	*timeō, timēre, timuī*
against	*contrā + acc.*
alive	*vīvus, vīva, vīvum*
alone	*sōlus, sōla, sōlum*
along	*per + acc.*
always	*semper*
am, I	*sum, esse, fuī*
among	*inter + acc.*
and	*et; -que*
anger	*īra, īrae, f.*
angry	*īrātus, īrāta, īrātum*
announce, I	*nūntiō, nūntiāre, nūntiāvī*
arms	*arma, armōrum, n. pl.*
arrive, I	*adveniō, advenīre, advēnī*
ask, I	*rogō, rogāre, rogāvī*
ask for, I	*petō, petere, petīvī; rogō, rogāre, rogāvī*
at	*ad + acc.*
at last	*tandem*
at once	*statim*
attack, I	*oppugnō, oppugnāre, oppugnāvī; petō, petere, petīvī*
away from	*ā, ab + abl.*
bad	*malus, mala, malum*
bear (= carry), I	*portō, portāre, portāvī*
beautiful	*pulcher, pulchra, pulchrum*
beg (someone), I	*petō, petere, petīvī*
between	*inter + acc.*
big	*magnus, magna, magnum*
boy	*puer, puerī, m.*
build, I	*aedificō, aedificāre, aedificāvī*
by	*ā, ab + abl.*
call, I	*vocō, vocāre, vocāvī*
can, I	*possum, posse, potuī*
capture, I	*capiō, capere, cēpī*
care for, I	*cūrō, cūrāre, cūrāvī*
carry, I	*portō, portāre, portāvī*
catch, I	*capiō, capere, cēpī*

catch sight of, I	*cōnspiciō, cōnspicere, cōnspexī*
children	*līberī, līberōrum, m. pl.*
come, I	*veniō, venīre, vēnī*
command	*imperium, imperiī, n.*
commander	*lēgātus, lēgātī, m.*
conquer, I	*vincō, vincere, vīcī*
country (= homeland)	*patria, patriae, f.*
country (= land)	*terra, terrae, f.*
country house	*vīlla, vīllae, f.*
crowd	*turba, turbae, f.*
cruel	*saevus, saeva, saevum*
cry, I	*lacrimō, lacrimāre, lacrimāvī*
danger	*perīculum, perīculī, n.*
daughter	*fīlia, fīliae, f.*
dear	*cārus, cāra, cārum*
decide, I	*cōnstituō, cōnstituere, cōnstituī*
deep	*altus, alta, altum*
defend, I	*dēfendō, dēfendere, dēfendī*
demand, I	*postulō, postulāre, postulāvī*
despair, I	*dēspērō, dēspērāre, dēspērāvī*
dinner	*cēna, cēnae, f.*
do, I	*faciō, facere, fēcī*
drag, draw, I	*trahō, trahere, trāxī*
dreadful	*dīrus, dīra, dīrum*
drink, I	*bibō, bibere, bibī*
empire	*imperium, imperiī, n.*
enter, I	*intrō, intrāre, intrāvī*
even	*et*
evil	*malus, mala, malum*
expect, I	*exspectō, exspectāre, exspectāvī*
ex-slave	*lībertus, lībertī, m.*
fall, I	*cadō, cadere, cecidī*
fear, I	*timeō, timēre, timuī*
few, a few	*paucī, paucae, pauca*
field	*ager, agrī, m.*
fight, I	*pugnō, pugnāre, pugnāvī*
finally	*tandem*
find, I	*inveniō, invenīre, invēnī*
first	*prīmus, prīma, prīmum*
flee, I	*fugiō, fugere, fūgī*
food	*cibus, cibī, m.*
for a long time	*diū*

forum	*forum, forī, n.*
freedman	*lībertus, lībertī, m.*
friend	*amīcus, amīcī, m.*
frighten, I	*terreō, terrēre, terruī*
from (= away from)	*ā, ab + abl.*
from (= out of)	*ē, ex + abl.*
garden	*hortus, hortī, m.*
gate	*porta, portae, f.*
generous	*benignus, benigna, benignum*
gift	*dōnum, dōnī, n.*
girl	*puella, puellae, f.*
give, I	*dō, dare, dedī*
god	*deus, deī, m.*
goddess	*dea, deae, f.*
good	*bonus, bona, bonum*
great	*magnus, magna, magnum*
greet, I	*salūtō, salūtāre, salūtāvī*
ground	*terra, terrae, f.*
guard, I	*custōdiō, custōdīre, custōdīvī*
hand over, hand down, I	*trādō, trādere, trādidī*
handsome	*pulcher, pulchra, pulchrum*
happy	*laetus, laeta, laetum*
hard	*dūrus, dūra, dūrum*
have, I	*habeō, habēre, habuī*
hear, I	*audiō, audīre, audīvī*
help	*auxilium, auxiliī, n.*
help, I	*adiuvō, adiuvāre, adiūvī*
hide, I	*cēlō, cēlāre, cēlāvī*
high	*altus, alta, altum*
hold (= have), I	*habeō, habēre, habuī*
hold (= keep), I	*teneō, tenēre, tenuī*
homeland	*patria, patriae, f.*
hour	*hōra, hōrae, f.*
house	*vīlla, vīllae, f.*
hurry, I	*festīnō, festīnāre, festīnāvī*
husband	*marītus, marītī, m.*
idea	*cōnsilium, cōnsiliī, n.*
immediately	*statim*
in	*in + abl.*
inn	*taberna, tabernae, f.*
into	*in + acc.*
invite, I	*invītō, invītāre, invītāvī*
keep (= possess), I	*teneō, tenēre, tenuī*
keep (= protect), I	*servō, servāre, servāvī*
kill, I	*necō, necāre, necāvī*

kind	*benignus, benigna, benignum*
kingdom	*rēgnum, rēgnī, n.*
land	*terra, terrae, f.*
large	*magnus, magna, magnum*
lead, I	*dūcō, dūcere, dūxī*
leave, leave behind, I	*relinquō, relinquere, relīquī*
letter	*epistula, epistulae, f.*
life	*vīta, vītae, f.*
like, I	*amō, amāre, amāvī*
listen to, I	*audiō, audīre, audīvī*
live, I	*habitō, habitāre, habitāvī*
living	*vīvus, vīva, vīvum*
lonely	*sōlus, sōla, sōlum*
long	*longus, longa, longum*
look after, I	*cūrō, cūrāre, cūrāvī; servō, servāre, servāvī*
look at, I	*spectō, spectāre, spectāvī*
love, I	*amō, amāre, amāvī*
maid	*ancilla, ancillae, f.*
make, I	*faciō, facere, fēcī*
make for, I	*petō, petere, petīvī*
man	*vir, virī, m.*
many	*multus, multa, multum*
marketplace	*forum, forī, n.*
master	*dominus, dominī, m.*
meal	*cēna, cēnae, f.*
messenger	*nūntius, nūntiī, m.*
miserable	*miser, misera, miserum*
mistress	*domina, dominae, f.*
money	*pecūnia, pecūniae, f.*
much	*multus, multa, multum*
my	*meus, mea, meum*
near	*prope + acc.*
new	*novus, nova, novum*
news	*nūntius, nūntiī, m.*
no (= not any)	*nūllus, nūlla, nūllum*
not	*nōn*
not any	*nūllus, nūlla, nūllum*
notice, I	*cōnspiciō, cōnspicere, cōnspexī*
often	*saepe*
on	*in + abl.*
only	*sōlus, sōla, sōlum*
onto	*in + acc.*
out of	*ē, ex + abl.*

overcome, overpower, I	*superō, superāre, superāvī*
place, I	*pōnō, pōnere, posuī*
plan	*cōnsilium, cōnsiliī, n.*
possess, I	*teneō, tenēre, tenuī*
power	*imperium, imperiī, n.*
praise, I	*laudō, laudāre, laudāvī*
prepare, I	*parō, parāre, parāvī*
present	*dōnum, dōnī, n.*
prize	*praemium, praemiī, n.*
profit	*praemium, praemiī, n.*
protect, I	*servō, servāre, servāvī*
pull, I	*trahō, trahere, trāxī*
put, put up, I	*pōnō, pōnere, posuī*
queen	*rēgīna, rēgīnae, f.*
quiet, I am	*taceō, tacēre, tacuī*
real	*vērus, vēra, vērum*
relate, I	*nārrō, nārrāre, nārrāvī*
report, I	*nūntiō, nūntiāre, nūntiāvī*
reward	*praemium, praemiī, n.*
road	*via, viae, f.*
Roman	*Rōmānus, Rōmāna, Rōmānum*
rule, I	*regō, regere, rēxī*
run, I	*currō, currere, cucurrī*
run away, I	*fugiō, fugere, fūgī*
sad	*miser, misera, miserum*
safe	*tūtus, tūta, tūtum*
sail, I	*nāvigō, nāvigāre, nāvigāvī*
sailor	*nauta, nautae, m.*
savage	*saevus, saeva, saevum*
save, I	*servō, servāre, servāvī*
say, I	*dīcō, dīcere, dīxī*
seal	*signum, signī, n.*
seek, I	*petō, petere, petīvī*
send, I	*mittō, mittere, mīsī*
shop	*taberna, tabernae, f.*
shout, I	*clāmō, clāmāre, clāmāvī*
sign	*signum, signī, n.*
silent, I am	*taceō, tacēre, tacuī*
slave (female)	*ancilla, ancillae, f.*
slave (male)	*servus, servī, m.*
sleep, I	*dormiō, dormīre, dormīvī*

small	*parvus, parva, parvum*
son	*fīlius, fīliī, m.*
speak, I	*dīcō, dīcere, dīxī*
stand, I	*stō, stāre, stetī*
story	*fābula, fābulae, f.*
street	*via, viae, f.*
stupid	*stultus, stulta, stultum*
suddenly	*subitō*
supervise, I	*cūrō, cūrāre, cūrāvī*
sword	*gladius, gladiī, m.*
take (= capture), I	*capiō, capere, cēpī*
take (= carry), I	*portō, portāre, portāvī*
take (= lead), I	*dūcō, dūcere, dūxī*
tell (= relate), I	*nārrō, nārrāre, nārrāvī*
tell (= speak), I	*dīcō, dīcere, dīxī*
temple	*templum, templī, n.*
terrified	*perterritus, perterrita, perterritum*
through	*per + acc.*
to, towards	*ad + acc.*
true	*vērus, vēra, vērum*
victorious, I am	*vincō, vincere, vīcī*
wait for, I	*exspectō, exspectāre, exspectāvī*
walk, I	*ambulō, ambulāre, ambulāvī*
wall	*mūrus, mūrī, m.*
watch, I	*spectō, spectāre, spectāvī*
water	*aqua, aquae, f.*
way (= street)	*via, viae, f.*
weapons	*arma, armōrum, n. pl.*
weep, I	*lacrimō, lacrimāre, lacrimāvī*
well	*bene*
when?	*quandō?*
why?	*cūr?*
wide	*lātus, lāta, lātum*
win, I	*vincō, vincere, vīcī*
wine	*vīnum, vīnī, n.*
with	*cum + abl.*
woman	*fēmina, fēminae, f.*
wood	*silva, silvae, f.*
word	*verbum, verbī, n.*
work, I	*labōrō, labōrāre, labōrāvī*
wretched	*miser, misera, miserum*
write, I	*scrībō, scrībere, scrīpsī*
year	*annus, annī, m.*
your (singular), yours	*tuus, tua, tuum*

HOW TO USE THE DICTIONARY

Numbers before words

A number before a word means the word appears in the **Vocabulary for learning** list for that chapter.

For example: 11 **dux**, **ducis**, *m.*   *leader*

means that **dux** appears in the Chapter 11 **Vocabulary for learning** list.

Nouns

The information given is: nominative, genitive, gender.

For example: **gēns**, **gentis**, *f.*   *people, race, family, tribe*

- **gēns** is the nominative form (used for the subject of the sentence);
- **gentis** is the genitive form (meaning 'of the people');
- **gēns** is a feminine word.

m. stands for masculine; *f.* stands for feminine; *n.* stands for neuter.

m.f. is used for a word which can sometimes be masculine, sometimes feminine. For example, the word **familiāris** (*relative*) can be either masculine or feminine, depending on the gender of the relative.

Verbs

The forms given are: 1st person present tense, infinitive, 1st person perfect tense.
You might prefer to think of this as: *I do something, to do something, I did (have done) something*.

For example: **laudō**, **laudāre**, **laudāvī**   *praise, admire*

- **laudō** means *I praise*
- **laudāre** means *to praise*
- **laudāvī** means *I (have) praised*

Adjectives

Most adjectives are given with the following forms: masculine, feminine, neuter (all nominative singular).

For example: **plēnus**, **plēna**, **plēnum**   *full*
                    trīstis, **trīstis**, **trīste**   *sad*

Some third declension adjectives, such as **ferōx** and **vetus**, change their stems. For these adjectives, the forms given are: nominative, genitive.

For example: **vetus**, *gen.* **veteris**   *old*

See pages 157 and 160 for more information on adjectives.

LATIN TO ENGLISH DICTIONARY

A

6 ā, ab + *abl.* — *from, away from*
abeō, abīre, abiī — *go away, depart*
abstulī — *see auferō*
11 absum, abesse, āfuī — *am out, am absent, am away*
16 ac — *and*
11 accidō, accidere, accidī — *happen*
10 accipiō, accipere, accēpī — *accept, take in, receive*
āctor, āctōris, *m.* — *actor*
4 ad + *acc.* — *to, towards; at*
adiuvō, adiuvāre, adiūvī — *help*
administrō, administrāre, administrāvī — *manage, administer*
adōrō, adōrāre, adōrāvī — *worship*
4 adsum, adesse, adfuī — *am here, am present*
9 adveniō, advenīre, advēnī — *arrive*
aedificō, aedificāre, aedificāvī — *build*
aeger, aegra, aegrum — *sick, ill*
aestus, aestūs, *m.* — *heat*
aeternus, aeterna, aeternum — *everlasting, eternal*
Āfrica, Āfricae, *f.* — *Africa (Roman province in what is now North Africa)*
ager, agrī, *m.* — *field*
agitō, agitāre, agitāvī — *drive, drive on, chase*
agnōscō, agnōscere, agnōvī — *recognize*
8 agō, agere, ēgī — *do; act; spend (time)*
  grātiās agō — *give thanks*
  age! — *come!*
agricola, agricolae, *m.* — *farmer*
āh! — *ah!*
albus, alba, album — *white; white team*
Alexander, Alexandrī, *m.* — *Alexander*
aliquis, aliquid — *someone, something*
10 alius, alia, aliud — *another, other*
  aliī ... aliī ... — *some ... others ...*
alter, altera, alterum — *the other, another, one of two, the second of two*
11 altus, alta, altum — *high, deep*

3 ambulō, ambulāre, ambulāvī — *walk*
amīca, amīcae, *f.* — *friend (female)*
3 amīcus, amīcī, *m.* — *friend (male)*
āmīsī — *see āmittō*
amita, amitae, *f.* — *aunt*
āmittō, āmittere, āmīsī — *lose*
14 amō, amāre, amāvī — *love, like*
14 amor, amōris, *m.* — *love*
amphitheātrum, amphitheātrī, *n.* — *amphitheater*
amphora, amphorae, *f.* — *amphora, jar*
3 ancilla, ancillae, *f.* — *slave, enslaved person (female)*
angustus, angusta, angustum — *narrow*
animal, animālis, *n.* — *animal*
10 annus, annī, *m.* — *year*
annuus, annua, annuum — *yearly, annual*
ānser, ānseris, *m.f.* — *goose*
ante + *acc.* — *before; in front of*
15 anteā — *before*
Antigonus, Antigonī, *m.* — *Antigonus*
ānulus, ānulī, *m.* — *ring*
ānxiē — *anxiously, worriedly*
ānxius, ānxia, ānxium — *worried, concerned*
aper, aprī, *m.* — *boar*
aperiō, aperīre, aperuī — *open*
apodȳtērium, apodȳtēriī, *n.* — *changing room*
appāreō, appārēre, appāruī — *appear*
7 appropinquō, appropinquāre, appropinquāvī + *dat.* — *approach, come near to*
apud + *acc.* — *at the house of; with; among*
5 aqua, aquae, *f.* — *water*
aquaeductus, aquaeductūs, *m.* — *aqueduct*
āra, ārae, *f.* — *altar*
arca, arcae, *f.* — *crate, strongbox*
arcus, arcūs, *m.* — *arch*
ardenter — *eagerly*
ardeō, ardēre, arsī — *burn, am on fire*
Arelātē, Arelātēs, *f.* — *Arles (town in southern France)*
Arelātēnsis, Arelātēnsis, Arelātēnse — *of Arles*
arma, armōrum, *n. pl.* — *arms, weapons*
artifex, artificis, *m.f.* — *artist*
ascendō, ascendere, ascendī — *climb*

	asinus, asinī, *m.*	*stupid person, fool; donkey*
	aspectus, aspectūs, *m.*	*view*
	ātrium, ātriī, *n.*	*reception room, entrance hall*
	attonitus, attonita, attonitum	*shocked, astonished*
	au!	*wow!*
	Aucissa, Aucissae, *f.*	*Aucissa*
	audeō, audēre	*dare*
5	audiō, audīre, audīvī	*hear, listen to*
16	auferō, auferre, abstulī	*steal, take away, carry off*
	augeō, augēre, auxī	*increase*
	Augustus, Augusta, Augustum	*August*
	aurīga, aurīgae, *m.*	*charioteer*
	auris, auris, *f.*	*ear*
	aurum, aurī, *n.*	*gold*
	aut	*or*
	aut ... aut ...	*either ... or ...*
	autumnus, autumnī, *m.*	*autumn*
	auxiliāris, auxiliāris, *m.*	*auxiliary soldier*
	auxilium, auxiliī, *n.*	*help*
	avis, avis, *f.*	*bird*

B

	bālō, bālāre, bālāvī	*bleat*
	barba, barbae, *f.*	*beard*
	basilica, basilicae, *f.*	*hall*
	Batāvia, Batāviae, *f.*	*Batavia (in Germania Inferior)*
	bau!	*bow!*
15	bellum, bellī, *n.*	*war*
11	bene	*well*
	benignus, benigna, benignum	*kind, generous*
8	bibō, bibere, bibī	*drink*
	blandus, blanda, blandum	*flattering*
	Boārius, Boāria, Boārium	*Boarium, of cattle*
10	bonus, bona, bonum	*good*
	Boudica, Boudicae, *f.*	*Boudica*
	bracchium, bracchiī, *n.*	*arm*
16	brevis, brevis, breve	*short, brief*
	breviter	*briefly*
	Britannī, Britannōrum, *m. pl.*	*Britons*
	Britannia, Britanniae, *f.*	*Britannia, Britain*
	Britannicus, Britannica, Britannicum	*British*

C

	C., *m.*	*Gaius*
2	cadō, cadere, cecidī	*fall*
	caedēs, caedis, *f.*	*killing, slaughter*
12	caelum, caelī, *n.*	*sky, heaven*
	calcitrō, calcitrāre, calcitrāvī	*kick out*
	calidus, calida, calidum	*hot*
	callidus, callida, callidum	*clever*
	Camulodūnum, Camulodūnī, *n.*	*Camulodunum (Colchester)*
	canis, canis, *m.*	*dog*
	Cantaber, Cantabrī, *m.*	*Cantaber*
	cantō, cantāre, cantāvī	*sing*
6	capiō, capere, cēpī	*take, catch, capture; adopt (a plan)*
	cōnsilium capiō	*make a plan, adopt a plan*
	Capitōlium, Capitōliī, *n.*	*the Capitoline Hill*
	captīvus, captīvī, *m.*	*captive, prisoner*
12	caput, capitis, *n.*	*head*
	carcer, carceris, *m.*	*prison*
	carpō, carpere, carpsī	*enjoy, use*
	cārus, cāra, cārum	*expensive; dear*
	casa, casae, *f.*	*hut, cottage*
	cāsus, cāsūs, *m.*	*accident*
	Catia, Catiae, *f.*	*Catia*
	cautērium, cautēriī, *n.*	*branding iron*
	cautus, cauta, cautum	*careful, cautious*
	caveō, cavēre, cāvī	*beware, look out (for), watch out (for)*
	cavē! cavēte!	*look out! watch out!*
	cavō, cavāre, cavāvī	*hollow out*
	cecidī	**see cadō**
	celebrō, celebrāre, celebrāvī	*celebrate*
	Celer, Celeris, *m.*	*Celer*
	celeriter	*quickly*
	celerrimē	*very quickly*
	cella, cellae, *f.*	*room*
16	cēlō, cēlāre, cēlāvī	*hide*
15	cēna, cēnae, *f.*	*dinner, meal*
	centuriō, centuriōnis, *m.*	*centurion (officer in the army)*
	cēpī	**see capiō**
	Cerēs, Cereris, *f.*	*Ceres (goddess of agriculture)*
	certē	*certainly, clearly*
15	cēterī, cēterae, cētera, *pl.*	*the rest, the others*
	Chīlō, Chīlōnis, *m.*	*Chilo*

chorus, chorī, *m.*	chorus, choir
Christiānus, Christiāna, Christiānum	Christian
Christus, Christī, *m.*	Christ
2 cibus, cibī, *m.*	food
cicātrīx, cicātrīcis, *f.*	scar
circumspectō, circumspectāre, circumspectāvī	look around
Circus, Circī, *m.*	*Circus, Circus Maximus*
9 cīvis, cīvis, *m.f.*	*citizen*
3 clāmō, clāmāre, clāmāvī	*shout*
3 clāmor, clāmōris, *m.*	*noise, shouting, shout*
clāmōsus, clāmōsa, clāmōsum	*noisy, rowdy*
clangor, clangōris, *m.*	*noise*
Claudius, Claudiī, *m.*	*Claudius*
cloāca, cloācae, *f.*	*sewer, drain*
13 coepī	*began*
14 cōgitō, cōgitāre, cōgitāvī	*think, consider*
15 cognōscō, cognōscere, cognōvī	*get to know, find out, learn*
cōgō, cōgere, coēgī	*force, compel*
colōnia, colōniae, *f.*	*colony*
columba, columbae, *f.*	*dove*
15 comes, comitis, *m.*	*comrade, companion, friend*
compressus, compressa, compressum	*constipated*
concipiō, concipere, concēpī	*conceive, become pregnant*
14 cōnficiō, cōnficere, cōnfēcī	*finish*
congelātus, congelāta, congelātum	*frozen*
Conimbrīga, Conimbrīgae, *f.*	*Conimbriga (town in Lusitania)*
coniūrātiō, coniūrātiōnis, *f.*	*plot*
conlāpsus, conlāpsa, conlāpsum	*collapsed*
14 cōnsilium, cōnsiliī, *n.*	*plan, idea, advice*
cōnsilium capiō	*make a plan, adopt a plan*
8 cōnspiciō, cōnspicere, cōnspexī	*catch sight of, notice*
14 cōnstituō, cōnstituere, cōnstituī	*decide*
cōnsul, cōnsulis, *m.*	*consul*
13 cōnsūmō, cōnsūmere, cōnsūmpsī	*consume, eat*
10 contrā + *acc.*	*against*
contrōversia, contrōversiae, *f.*	*argument, dispute*

conveniō, convenīre, convēnī	*come together, gather, meet*
cōpiae, cōpiārum, *f. pl.*	*forces, troops*
Cornēlia, Cornēliae, *f.*	*Cornelia*
12 corpus, corporis, *n.*	*body*
Corsica, Corsicae, *f.*	*Corsica (an island)*
cōtīdiē	*every day*
crās	*tomorrow*
crēdō, crēdere, crēdidī + *dat.*	*believe, trust, have faith in*
crocodīlus, crocodīlī, *m.*	*crocodile*
12 crūdēlis, crūdēlis, crūdēle	*cruel*
cubiculum, cubiculī, *n.*	*bedroom*
cucumis, cucumeris, *m.*	*cucumber*
culīna, culīnae, *f.*	*kitchen*
culter, cultrī, *m.*	*knife*
3 cum + *abl.*	*with*
cunīculus, cunīculī, *m.*	*rabbit*
5 cupiō, cupere, cupīvī	*want, desire*
7 cūr?	*why?*
cūrātor, cūrātōris, *m.*	*manager*
cūria, cūriae, *f.*	*Senate House*
cūrō, cūrāre, cūrāvī	*care about, am bothered about, look after, supervise*
Currāx, Currācis, *m.*	*Currax*
3 currō, currere, cucurrī	*run*
cursus, cursūs, *m.*	*race*
custōdiō, custōdīre, custōdīvī	*guard*
5 custōs, custōdis, *m.f.*	*guard*

D

Darius, Dariī, *m.*	*Darius*
8 dē + *abl.*	*from, down from; about*
10 dea, deae, *f.*	*goddess*
5 dēbeō, dēbēre, dēbuī	*owe; ought, should, must*
dēcidō, dēcidere, dēcidī	*fall down*
decōrus, decōra, decōrum	*proper, right*
dedī	*see* dō
dēfendō, dēfendere, dēfendī	*defend*
10 deinde	*then*
dēlectō, dēlectāre, dēlectāvī	*please, delight*
12 dēleō, dēlēre, dēlēvī	*destroy*
delphīnus, delphīnī, *m.*	*dolphin*

dēmōnstrō, dēmōnstrāre, dēmōnstrāvī — *show, point out*

dēnārius, dēnāriī, *m.* — *denarius (silver coin)*

dēnsus, dēnsa, dēnsum — *thick*

dēpōnō, dēpōnere, dēposuī — *take off, put down*

dēscendō, dēscendere, dēscendī — *go down, come down*

dēsiliō, dēsilīre, dēsiluī — *jump, jump down*

dēsistō, dēsistere, dēstitī — *stop*

dēspērō, dēspērāre, dēspērāvī — *despair*

4 deus, deī, *m.* — *god*

dēvoveō, dēvovēre, dēvōvī — *curse*

dexter, dextra, dextrum — *right*

3 dīcō, dīcere, dīxī — *say, speak, tell*

6 diēs, diēī, *m.* — *day*

9 difficilis, difficilis, difficile — *difficult*

difficultās, difficultātis, *f.* — *difficulty*

dīligenter — *carefully*

dīligentissimē — *very carefully, most carefully*

dīmittō, dīmittere, dīmīsī — *release*

14 dīrus, dīra, dīrum — *dreadful*

6 discēdō, discēdere, discessī — *depart, leave*

12 diū — *for a long time*

diūtius — *longer, for a longer time*

dīxī — **see dīcō**

5 dō, dare, dedī — *give*

doceō, docēre, docuī — *teach*

dolor, dolōris, *m.* — *pain*

9 domina, dominae, *f.* — *mistress, lady*

4 dominus, dominī, *m.* — *master*

8 domus, domūs, *f.* — *house, home*

4 dōnum, dōnī, *n.* — *gift, present*

1 dormiō, dormīre, dormīvī — *sleep*

Druidēs, Druidum, *m. pl.* — *Druids*

dubiō — **see sine dubiō**

dubitō, dubitāre, dubitāvī — *hesitate, doubt*

ducentī, ducentae, ducenta — *two hundred*

2 dūcō, dūcere, dūxī — *lead, guide, take*

in mātrimōnium dūcō — *marry*

dulcis, dulcis, dulce — *sweet*

dulcissimus, dulcissima, dulcissimum — *very sweet*

duo, duae, duo — *two*

dūrus, dūra, dūrum — *hard, harsh*

11 dux, ducis, *m.* — *leader*

dūxī — **see dūcō**

E

6 ē, ex + *abl.* — *from, out of*

ea — *they, them, those things*

eā — *by/with/from her, it*

eā nocte — *that night*

eae — *they*

8 eam — *her, it*

eārum — *their, of them*

eās — *them*

ecce! — *look! see!*

effluō, effluere, efflūxī — *flow*

5 effugiō, effugere, effūgī — *flee, escape*

ēgī — **see agō**

1 ego, meī — *I, me*

ēheu! — *ah! oh no!*

ei! — *ai! oh!*

eī — *they; to/for him, her, it*

eīs — *to/for/by/with/from them*

eius — *his, her, its*

elephantus, elephantī, *m.* — *elephant*

emblēma, emblēmatis, *n.* — *mosaic*

emō, emere, ēmī — *buy*

ēn! — *see! look here!*

15 eō, īre, iī — *go*

eō — *by/with/from him, it*

eōrum — *their, of them*

14 eōs — *them*

7 epistula, epistulae, *f.* — *letter*

eques, equitis, *m.* — *horseman, pl. = cavalry*

equitō, equitāre, equitāvī — *ride*

3 equus, equī, *m.* — *horse*

erat — *(he/she/it) was*

erit — *(he/she/it) will be*

erō — *I shall be*

errō, errāre, errāvī — *make a mistake; wander*

ērubēscō, ērubēscere, ērubuī — *blush*

erunt — *(they) will be*

1 es — *you (s.) are*

1 est — *is, there is, he/she/it is*

estis — *you (pl.) are*

2 et — *and*

et … et … — *both … and …*

15 etiam — *even, also*

8 eum — *him, it*

	eunt	*(they) go*
	ēvānēscō, ēvānēscere, ēvānuī	*disappear*
6	ex, ē + *abl.*	*from, out of*
	excitō, excitāre, excitāvī	*wake someone up*
	exclāmō, exclāmāre, exclāmāvī	*exclaim*
	exeō, exīre, exiī	*come out of*
	exercitus, exercitūs, *m.*	*army*
6	exspectō, exspectāre, exspectāvī	*wait for; expect*
	exspīrō, exspīrāre, exspīrāvī	*die*
	exstinguō, exstinguere, exstīnxī	*put out, extinguish*
	exstruō, exstruere, exstrūxī	*build*
	exta, extōrum, *n. pl.*	*entrails*
	extrahō, extrahere, extrāxī	*take out, extract*

F

	faber, fabrī, *m.*	*craftsman*
	fābula, fābulae, *f.*	*story; play; pl. = nonsense!*
6	faciō, facere, fēcī	*do; make*
	familia, familiae, *f.*	*family, household*
	familiāris, familiāris, *m.f.*	*relative*
	fār, farris, *n.*	*grain*
	Faustus, Faustī, *m.*	*Faustus*
	fax, facis, *f.*	*torch*
	febris, febris, *f.*	*fever*
	fēcī	see faciō
	fēlīciter	*luckily, happily; good luck!*
	fēlīx, *gen.* fēlīcis	*lucky, fortunate; happy*
14	fēmina, fēminae, *f.*	*woman*
	fenestra, fenestrae, *f.*	*window*
10	ferō, ferre, tulī	*bring, carry, bear*
	ferōciter	*fiercely*
15	ferōx, *gen.* ferōcis	*fierce, ferocious*
	ferrārius, ferrāriī, *m.*	*blacksmith*
	fervor, fervōris, *m.*	*heat*
	fessus, fessa, fessum	*tired*
3	festīnō, festīnāre, festīnāvī	*hurry, rush*
	fēstus, fēsta, fēstum	*festival*
	fībula, fībulae, *f.*	*brooch, pin*
10	fidēlis, fidēlis, fidēle	*loyal, faithful; trustworthy*
2	fīlia, fīliae, *f.*	*daughter*
2	fīlius, fīliī, *m.*	*son*
	fīnis, fīnis, *m.*	*end*

	firmus, firma, firmum	*firm*
	Flāminius, Flāminia, Flāminium	*of Flaminius, Flaminian*
	flamma, flammae, *f.*	*flame; pl. = fire*
	flammeum, flammeī, *n.*	*bridal veil*
	fluitāns, *gen.* fluitantis	*floating*
11	flūmen, flūminis, *n.*	*river*
	fluō, fluere, flūxī	*flow*
	focus, focī, *m.*	*hearth*
	fōns, fontis, *m.*	*fountain*
	fōrma, fōrmae, *f.*	*creature; shape*
	fornāx, fornācis, *f.*	*furnace*
	fortasse	*perhaps*
11	fortis, fortis, forte	*brave*
	fortiter	*bravely*
	Fortūna, Fortūnae, *f.*	*Fortune (goddess)*
2	forum, forī, *n.*	*forum, market, meeting place*
	fragor, fragōris, *m.*	*crash, noise*
1	frāter, frātris, *m.*	*brother*
	frīgidus, frīgida, frīgidum	*cold*
	frōns, frontis	see scaenae frōns
	frūctus, frūctūs, *m.*	*fruit*
	frūmentum, frūmentī, *n.*	*corn, grain*
11	frūstrā	*in vain, without success*
	frūx, frūgis, *f.*	*crop*
	fuga, fugae, *f.*	*escape*
11	fugiō, fugere, fūgī	*run away, flee*
	fugitīvus, fugitīva, fugitīvum	*runaway*
	fulgeō, fulgēre, fulsī	*flash with lightning*
	fūmōsus, fūmōsa, fūmōsum	*smoky*
	fūmus, fūmī, *m.*	*smoke*
	fundus, fundī, *m.*	*farm*
	fūnis, fūnis, *m.*	*rope*
	fūr, fūris, *m.*	*thief*
	fūrtim	*secretly, like a thief*

G

	Gabrus, Gabrī, *m.*	*Gabrus*
	Gāia, Gāiae, *f.*	*Gaia*
	Gāius, Gāiī, *m.*	*Gaius*
	Gallia, Galliae, *f.*	*Gaul*
	Galliō, Galliōnis, *m.*	*Gallio*
	Gallus, Gallī, *m.*	*a Gaul*
	gaudeō, gaudēre	*am pleased, rejoice*
	gaudium, gaudiī, *n.*	*joy, pleasure*
	gēns, gentis, *f.*	*people, race, family, tribe*

A B C D E F G H I K L M N O P Q R S T V

8 gerō, gerere, gessī — *wear (clothes); wage (war)*

gessī — *see gerō*
Giscō, Giscōnis, *m.* — *Gisco*
glaciēs, glaciēī, *f.* — *ice*
3 gladius, gladiī, *m.* — *sword*
glis, glīris, *m.* — *dormouse, rodent*
gradus, gradūs, *m.* — *step, row*
grātiae, grātiārum, *f. pl.* — *thanks*
   grātiās agō — *give thanks*
9 gravis, gravis, grave — *heavy; serious*
graviter — *heavily; seriously*
grundiō, grundīre, grundīvī — *grunt*
gustō, gustāre, gustāvī — *taste*

H

2 habeō, habēre, habuī — *have, hold*
2 habitō, habitāre, habitāvī — *live*
hae — *these, these women*
haereō, haerēre, haesī — *cling*
hahae! — *ha ha!*
hanc — *this, this woman*
hās — *these, these women*
hasta, hastae, *f.* — *spear*
hercle! — *oh no! oh dear!*
heri — *yesterday*
hērōs, hērōis, *m.* — *hero*
Hettia, Hettiae, *f.* — *Hettia*
heus! — *hey! hey there!*
hī — *these, these men*
hīc — *here*
16 hic, haec, hoc — *this, he, she, it*
hiems, hiemis, *f.* — *winter*
hinnītus, hinnītūs, *m.* — *neighing*
hippopotamus, hippopotamī, *m.* — *hippopotamus*
Hispānus, Hispāna, Hispānum — *Spanish*
historia, historiae, *f.* — *history*
11 hodiē — *today*
7 homō, hominis, *m.* — *man, person, human being*
1 hōra, hōrae, *f.* — *hour*
horreum, horreī, *n.* — *barn, granary, warehouse*
15 hortus, hortī, *m.* — *garden*
hōs — *these, these men*
hospes, hospitis, *m.* — *guest*
9 hostis, hostis, *m.* — *enemy*

hūc — *here, to this place*
   hūc illūc — *here and there*
hunc — *this, this man*

I

8 iaceō, iacēre, iacuī — *lie down*
10 iaciō, iacere, iēcī — *throw*
iactō, iactāre, iactāvī — *throw*
6 iam — *now, already*
12 iānua, iānuae, *f.* — *door, doorway*
ībat — *(he/she/it) was going*
11 ibi — *there*
Icēnī, Icēnōrum, *m. pl.* — *Iceni*
Īdūs, Īduum, *f. pl.* — *Ides (15th day of March, May, July, October, 13th day of other months)*

iēcī — *see iaciō*
igitur — *so, therefore*
ignis, ignis, *m.* — *fire*
ignōscō, ignōscere, ignōvī — *forgive*
ignōtus, ignōta, ignōtum — *unknown*
iit — *(he/she/it) went*
illa — *that, that women, she*
illās — *those, those women, them*
16 ille — *that, that man, he*
16 ille, illa, illud — *that, he, she, it*
illam — *that, that woman, her*
illōs — *those, those men, them*
illūc — *there, to that place*
   hūc illūc — *here and there*
illum — *that, that man, him*
imāgō, imāginis, *f.* — *image, picture*
immortālis, immortālis, immortāle — *immortal*
immōtus, immōta, immōtum — *motionless*
9 imperātor, imperātōris, *m.* — *emperor; general*
16 imperium, imperiī, *n.* — *power; empire*
impleō, implēre, implēvī — *fill*
īmus — *we go*
6 in + *acc.* — *into, onto*
1 in + *abl.* — *in, on*
inānis, inānis, ināne — *empty*
incendium, incendiī, *n.* — *fire*
8 incendō, incendere, incendī — *burn, set on fire*
incertus, incerta, incertum — *uncertain*
incipiō, incipere, incēpī — *begin, start*

incitō, incitāre, incitāvī — *incite, stir up*
inclīnō, inclīnāre, inclīnāvī — *bend, bow*
indicō, indicāre, indicāvī — *point out, show*
Indus, Indī, *m.* — *Indus*
inertia, inertiae, *f.* — *laziness, inaction*
īnfāns, īnfantis, *m.* — *baby*
3 īnfēlīx, *gen.* īnfēlīcis — *unlucky; unhappy*
7 ingēns, *gen.* ingentis — *huge*
6 inquit — *says, said*
īnsānus, īnsāna, īnsānum — *mad, insane*
īnspiciō, īnspicere, īnspexī — *inspect*
īnstitor, īnstitōris, *m.* — *vendor, peddler*
īnstrūmentum, īnstrūmentī, *n.* — *instrument, tool*
1, 7 īnsula, īnsulae, *f.* — *apartment building; island*
13 intellegō, intellegere, intellēxī — *understand, realize*
intentē — *intently, closely, carefully*
13 inter + *acc.* — *among, between*
15 intereā — *meanwhile*
intolerābilis, intolerābilis, intolerābile — *unbearable*
2 intrō, intrāre, intrāvī — *come in, enter*
inūtilis, inūtilis, inūtile — *useless*
11 inveniō, invenīre, invēnī — *find*
invītō, invītāre, invītāvī — *invite*
iō! — *hurray!*
īra, īrae, *f.* — *anger*
9 īrātus, īrāta, īrātum — *angry*
is, ea, id — *he, she, it*
īs — *you (s.) go*
it — *(he/she/it) goes*
ita — *so, in this way*
13 ita vērō — *yes, absolutely*
11 itaque — *and so, therefore*
9 iter, itineris, *n.* — *journey, route, way*
12 iterum — *again*
ītis — *you (pl.) go*
15 iubeō, iubēre, iussī — *order*
Iūlia, Iūliae, *f.* — *Julia*
Iūlius, Iūlia, Iūlium — *July*
Iūnior, Iūniōris, *m.* — *Junior, Younger*
iūnior, iūnior, iūnius — *younger*
Iūnō, Iūnōnis, *f.* — *Juno (queen of the gods)*
Iuppiter, Iovis, *m.* — *Jupiter (king of the gods)*
iūstus, iūsta, iūstum — *right, proper*

5 iuvenis, iuvenis, *m.f.* — *young person*
iuvō, iuvāre, iūvī — *help, assist*

K

Kalendae, Kalendārum, *f. pl.* — *Kalends, first day of the month*

L

13 labor, labōris, *m.* — *work*
1 labōrō, labōrāre, labōrāvī — *work*
lacrima, lacrimae, *f.* — *tear*
9 lacrimō, lacrimāre, lacrimāvī — *cry, weep*
Laecānius, Laecāniī, *m.* — *Laecanius*
laena, laenae, *f.* — *woolen cloak*
laetē — *happily, gladly*
3 laetus, laeta, laetum — *happy*
lambō, lambere, lambī — *lick, lap*
lāna, lānae, *f.* — *wool*
Lar, Laris, *m.* — *household god, Lar*
later, lateris, *m.* — *brick*
lātrīna, lātrīnae, *f.* — *toilet*
lātrō, lātrāre, lātrāvī — *bark*
latrō, latrōnis, *m.* — *bandit, robber*
4 laudō, laudāre, laudāvī — *praise, admire*
lectīca, lectīcae, *f.* — *litter (portable couch)*
lectus, lectī, *m.* — *bed*
lēgātus, lēgātī, *m.* — *governor; commander*
legiō, legiōnis, *f.* — *legion*
1, 16 legō, legere, lēgī — *read; choose*
lentē — *slowly*
lentus, lenta, lentum — *slow*
leō, leōnis, *m.* — *lion*
lepus, leporis, *m.* — *hare*
Letta, Lettae, *f.* — *Letta*
libenter — *willingly, gladly*
liber, librī, *m.* — *book*
9 līberī, līberōrum, *m. pl.* — *children*
līberō, līberāre, līberāvī — *free, set free*
lībertās, lībertātis, *f.* — *freedom*
15 lībertus, lībertī, *m.* — *former slave, freedman*
Licinius, Liciniī, *m.* — *Licinius*
lignum, lignī, *n.* — *log, wood*
littera, litterae, *f.* — *letter*
10 locus, locī, *m.* — *place*
Londīnium, Londīniī, *n.* — *London*
longē — *far off*
13 longus, longa, longum — *long*

A B C D E F G H I K L M N O P Q R S T U V

Luccus, Luccī, *m.*   *Luccus*

lūceō, lūcēre, lūxī   *shine*

lucerna, lucernae, *f.*   *lamp*

Lūcīlius, Lūcīliī, *m.*   *Lucilius*

Lūcriō, Lūcriōnis, *m.*   *Lucrio*

lūdō, lūdere, lūsī   *play, am at leisure*

lūdus, lūdī, *m.*   *game; pl. = races*

lūna, lūnae, *f.*   *moon*

Lūsitānia, Lūsitāniae, *f.*   *Lusitania*

16   lūx, lūcis, *f.*   *light, daylight*

luxuria, luxuriae, *f.*   *luxury*

M

Maelō, Maelōnis, *m.*   *Maelo*

magister, magistrī, *m.*   *employer*

magnificus, magnifica, magnificum   *magnificent, wonderful, amazing*

2   magnus, magna, magnum   *big, large, great*

maior, maior, maius   *bigger, larger, greater*

mālum, mālī, *n.*   *apple*

malus, mala, malum   *bad, evil*

māne   *in the morning*

5   maneō, manēre, mānsī   *remain, stay*

Mānius, Māniī, *m.*   *Manius*

Manlius, Manliī, *m.*   *Manlius*

manus, manūs, *f.*   *hand; group (of people), gang, crew*

mappa, mappae, *f.*   *cloth; flag*

Marcus, Marcī, *m.*   *Marcus*

11   mare, maris, *n.*   *sea*

6   marītus, marītī, *m.*   *husband*

6   māter, mātris, *f.*   *mother*

mātrimōnium, mātrimōniī, *n.*   *marriage*

   in mātrimōnium dūcō   *marry*

mātrōna, mātrōnae, *f.*   *lady, married woman*

maximē   *very much, a lot, very greatly*

maximus, maxima, maximum   *very big, huge; biggest, greatest*

9   medius, media, medium   *middle, middle of*

melior, melior, melius   *better*

meminī   *remember*

mendāx, mendācis, *m.f.*   *liar*

mendīcō, mendīcāre, mendīcāvī   *beg*

mendīcus, mendīcī, *m.*   *beggar*

mēnsa, mēnsae, *f.*   *table*

mēnsis, mēnsis, *m.*   *month*

menta, mentae, *f.*   *mint*

mercātor, mercātōris, *m.*   *merchant*

mēta, mētae, *f.*   *turning post*

metallum, metallī, *n.*   *mine*

1   meus, mea, meum   *my*

7   mīles, mīlitis, *m.*   *soldier*

Minerva, Minervae, *f.*   *Minerva (goddess of wisdom and war)*

mingō, mingere, mīnxī   *urinate*

7   minimē   *no*

ministra, ministrae, *f.*   *employee, assistant*

minor, minor, minus   *smaller; younger; less*

mīrābilis, mīrābilis, mīrābile   *strange, wonderful*

10   miser, misera, miserum   *poor, unfortunate, sad*

mīsī   see mittō

12   mittō, mittere, mīsī   *send*

mōmentum, mōmentī, *n.*   *importance*

moneō, monēre, monuī   *advise, warn*

monēta, monētae, *f.*   *mint, coin factory*

14   mōns, montis, *m.*   *mountain*

mōnstrum, mōnstrī, *n.*   *monster*

morbus, morbī, *m.*   *illness*

14   mors, mortis, *f.*   *death*

mortuus, mortua, mortuum   *dead*

moveō, movēre, mōvī   *move*

8   mox   *soon*

mūgiō, mūgīre, mūgīvī   *moo, bellow*

mulceō, mulcēre, mulsī   *stroke*

multitūdō, multitūdinis, *f.*   *large number, crowd*

multō   *much, by much*

15   multum   *much*

3   multus, multa, multum   *much; pl. = many, a lot of*

murmurō, murmurāre, murmurāvī   *mutter*

13   mūrus, mūrī, *m.*   *wall*

mūs, mūris, *m.*   *mouse; rat*

N

7   nārrō, nārrāre, nārrāvī   *tell, relate*

nāsus, nāsī, *m.*   *nose*

natō, natāre, natāvī   *swim*

naufragium, naufragiī, *n.*   *crash, wreck*

7   nauta, nautae, *m.*   *sailor*

11   nāvigō, nāvigāre, nāvigāvī   *sail*

11   nāvis, nāvis, *f.*   *ship*

-ne   *(marks a question)*

nebula, nebulae, *f.*   *mist*

[14] nec	and not, nor, neither
[14] nec ... nec ...	neither ... nor ...
necesse, *n.*	necessary
[14] necō, necāre, necāvī	kill
neglegenter	carelessly
negōtiātor, negōtiātōris, *m.*	businessman, dealer, trader
negōtium, negōtiī, *n.*	business
[5] nēmō, nēminis, *m.f.*	no one, nobody
Neptūnus, Neptūnī, *m.*	Neptune (god of the sea)
Nerō, Nerōnis, *m.*	Nero
Nerōniānus, Nerōniāna, Nerōniānum	of Nero
[14] nesciō, nescīre, nescīvī	don't know
[8] nihil, *n.*	nothing
nihilōminus	nevertheless
nimium	too (much)
nisi	unless, except
nōbīs	to/for us
noceō, nocēre, nocuī	harm
[5] nōlō, nōlle, nōluī	don't want, refuse
[13] nōmen, nōminis, *n.*	name
[1] nōn	not
nōndum	not yet
[15] nōnne?	surely?
nōnnūllī, nōnnūllae, nōnnūlla	some, several
nōnus, nōna, nōnum	ninth
[4] nōs, nostrum	we, us
nōscō, nōscere, nōvī	get to know
[8] noster, nostra, nostrum	our
notō, notāre, notāvī	mark, brand
nōtus, nōta, nōtum	known, familiar
[10] novus, nova, novum	new
[5] nox, noctis, *f.*	night
[10] nūllus, nūlla, nūllum	no, not any
num?	surely not?
nūmen, nūminis, *n.*	deity; divine power
Numidicus, Numidica, Numidicum	Numidian
[14] numquam	never
[7] nunc	now
[15] nūntiō, nūntiāre, nūntiāvī	announce, report
[9] nūntius, nūntiī, *m.*	messenger; message, news
nūper	recently, not long ago
nūptiae, nūptiārum, *f. pl.*	wedding
nūptiālis, nūptiālis, nūptiāle	nuptial, wedding

O

ō!	o!
obscūrus, obscūra, obscūrum	dark
obstō, obstāre, obstitī + *dat.*	am in the way (of), cause an obstruction (to), block
[10] occīdō, occīdere, occīdī	kill
occupātus, occupāta, occupātum	busy
octāvus, octāva, octāvum	eighth
oculus, oculī, *m.*	eye
[12] offerō, offerre, obtulī	offer
officīna, officīnae, *f.*	workshop
ōh!	oh! oh dear!
ohē!	hey!
[7] ōlim	once, some time ago
ōmen, ōminis, *n.*	omen, sign
[3] omnis, omnis, omne	all, every
operārius, operāriī, *m.*	workman
oppidum, oppidī, *n.*	town
opprimō, opprimere, oppressī	crush, overwhelm
oppugnō, oppugnāre, oppugnāvī	attack
optimē	very well
optimus, optima, optimum	best, very good, excellent
opus, operis, *n.*	work
orbis, orbis, *m.*	globe, sphere
orbis terrārum	world
[16] ōrō, ōrāre, ōrāvī	beg, beg for
ōsculum, ōsculī, *n.*	kiss
[14] ostendō, ostendere, ostendī	show
Ostia, Ostiae, *f.*	Ostia
Othō, Othōnis, *m.*	Otho

P

paene	almost, nearly
palaestra, palaestrae, *f.*	exercise ground
palma, palmae, *f.*	palm; victory
palūs, palūdis, *f.*	marsh
pānis, pānis, *m.*	bread
pantomīmus, pantomīmī, *m.*	mime performer
parātus, parāta, parātum	ready

	parcō, parcere, pepercī + *dat.*	*spare, am sparing of*
	parēns, parentis, *m.f.*	*parent*
13	parō, parāre, parāvī	*prepare*
7	pars, partis, *f.*	*part*
4	parvus, parva, parvum	*small*
1	pater, patris, *m.*	*father*
	patrōnus, patrōnī, *m.*	*patron*
9	paucī, paucae, pauca, *pl.*	*few, a few*
	pauper, *gen.* pauperis	*poor*
	pauper, pauperis, *m.*	*poor person*
	pavīmentum, pavīmentī, *n.*	*floor*
10	pāx, pācis, *f.*	*peace*
	pectus, pectoris, *n.*	*chest, breast*
2	pecūnia, pecūniae, *f.*	*money, sum of money*
	pellō, pellere, pepulī	*drive, push*
	pēnsiō, pēnsiōnis, *f.*	*payment, rent*
3	pepulī	**see pellō**
3	per + *acc.*	*through, along*
	percutiō, percutere, percussī	*strike*
10	pereō, perīre, periī	*die, perish*
	perīculōsus, perīculōsa, perīculōsum	*dangerous*
4	perīculum, perīculī, *n.*	*danger*
	permixtus, permixta, permixtum	*mixed*
	persōna, persōnae, *f.*	*character, part*
	persuādeō, persuādēre, persuāsī + *dat.*	*persuade*
4	perterritus, perterrita, perterritum	*terrified*
	perveniō, pervenīre, pervēnī	*arrive, reach*
9	petō, petere, petīvī	*attack; make for; seek; beg, ask for*
	pff!	*pff!*
	Philētus, Philētī, *m.*	*Philetus*
	philosophia, philosophiae, *f.*	*philosophy*
	pīlum, pīlī, *n.*	*javelin*
	pīrāta, pīrātae, *m.*	*pirate*
	piscīna, piscīnae, *f.*	*swimming pool*
	piscis, piscis, *m.*	*fish*
	pistor, pistōris, *m.*	*baker*
	pistrīnum, pistrīnī, *n.*	*bakery*
	placeō, placēre, placuī + *dat.*	*please*
	plaudō, plaudere, plausī	*clap, applaud*
	plaustrum, plaustrī, *n.*	*wagon, cart*

	plēnus, plēna, plēnum	*full*
	pluō, pluere, plūvī	*rain*
	plūrimī, plūrimae, plūrima	*very many*
	plūs, plūris, *n.*	*more*
	pōculum, pōculī, *n.*	*cup*
	poena, poenae, *f.*	*penalty, punishment*
	poenās dō	*pay the penalty, am punished*
	pompa, pompae, *f.*	*procession*
	pōns, pontis, *m.*	*bridge*
	popīna, popīnae, *f.*	*bar*
	popīnāria, popīnāriae, *f.*	*barkeeper, bar owner*
	Poppillus, Poppillī, *m.*	*Poppillus*
	populus, populī, *m.*	*people*
	porcus, porcī, *m.*	*pig*
8	porta, portae, *f.*	*gate, grate*
5	portō, portāre, portāvī	*carry, bear, take*
	portus, portūs, *m.*	*harbor*
5	possum, posse, potuī	*am able, can*
13	post + *acc.*	*after, behind*
	posteā	*afterwards*
8	postquam	*after, when*
	postrīdiē	*on the following day*
	postulō, postulāre, postulāvī	*demand*
	potuī	**see possum**
	praecipitō, praecipitāre, praecipitāvī	*fall*
	praefectus, praefectī, *m.*	*commander*
13	praemium, praemiī, *n.*	*prize, reward, profit*
	prasinus, prasina, prasinum	*green; green team*
	precēs, precum, *f. pl.*	*prayers*
	prīmō	*at first*
3	prīmus, prīma, prīmum	*first*
16	prīnceps, prīncipis, *m.*	*chief; emperor*
11	prō + *abl.*	*in front of; for*
8	prōcēdō, prōcēdere, prōcessī	*go along, advance, proceed*
	Proclus, Proclī, *m.*	*Proclus*
	procul	*far off*
	prōcūrātor, prōcūrātōris, *m.*	*procurator (province's finance officer)*
	proelium, proeliī, *n.*	*battle*
	prōmittō, prōmittere, prōmīsī	*promise*
6	prope + *acc.*	*near*
	prōtegō, prōtegere, prōtēxī	*protect*
	prōvincia, prōvinciae, *f.*	*province*

	proximus, proxima, proximum	*nearest; next to*
	prūnum, prūnī, *n.*	*plum*
	psittacus, psittacī, *m.*	*parrot*
	pst!	*pst!*
4	puella, puellae, *f.*	*girl*
7	puer, puerī, *m.*	*boy*
	pugiō, pugiōnis, *m.*	*dagger*
7	pugnō, pugnāre, pugnāvī	*fight*
5	pulcher, pulchra, pulchrum	*beautiful, handsome*
	pulsō, pulsāre, pulsāvī	*beat*
	pūniō, pūnīre, pūnīvī	*punish*
15	putō, putāre, putāvī	*think*
	Pȳramus, Pȳramī, *m.*	*Pyramus*

Q

	quadrīga, quadrīgae, *f.*	*chariot*
	quae	*who, which*
2	quaerō, quaerere, quaesīvī	*look for, search for*
	quālis, quālis, quāle?	*what sort of?*
10	quam	*(1) how ... !*
	quam	*(2) than*
	quam + superlative	*(3) as ... as possible*
	quam	*(4) whom, which*
13	quamquam	*although*
	quandō?	*when?*
	quantus, quanta, quantum?	*how big? how much?*
	Quārtilla, Quārtillae, *f.*	*Quartilla*
	quārtus, quārta, quārtum	*fourth*
	quattuor	*four*
	-que	*and*
	quem	*whom, which*
13	quī, quae, quod	*who, which*
	quid?	*what?*
	quiētē	*quietly*
	quiētus, quiēta, quiētum	*quiet*
	quīntus, quīnta, quīntum	*fifth*
12	quis? quid?	*who? what?*
16	quō?	*to where?*
4	quod	*(1) because*
	quod	*(2) which*
13	quōmodo?	*how? in what way?*
2	quoque	*also, too*
	quos	*whom*
	quot?	*how many?*

R

16	rapiō, rapere, rapuī	*seize, grab*
	raucus, rauca, raucum	*hoarse*
	rēctā	*directly, straight*
	recumbō, recumbere, recubuī	*recline, lie down*
12	redeō, redīre, rediī	*go back, come back, return*
	reficiō, reficere, refēcī	*fix, mend, repair*
16	rēgīna, rēgīnae, *f.*	*queen*
	rēgnum, rēgnī, *n.*	*kingdom*
	regō, regere, rēxī	*rule*
	relinquō, relinquere, relīquī	*leave, leave behind*
	repente	*suddenly*
	rēpō, rēpere, rēpsī	*crawl*
7	rēs, reī, *f.*	*story; thing, business, matter, event*
16	resistō, resistere, restitī + *dat.*	*resist*
	resonō, resonāre, resonāvī	*resound*
5	respondeō, respondēre, respondī	*reply*
	retineō, retinēre, retinuī	*hold back, restrain*
16	reveniō, revenīre, revēnī	*come back, return*
4	rēx, rēgis, *m.*	*king*
	rēxī	**see regō**
1	rīdeō, rīdēre, rīsī	*laugh; smile*
	rīma, rīmae, *f.*	*hole, crack*
	rīpa, rīpae, *f.*	*bank (of a river)*
	rīsī	**see rīdeō**
6	rogō, rogāre, rogāvī	*ask, ask for*
12	Rōma, Rōmae, *f.*	*Rome*
	Rōmae	*in/at Rome*
	Rōmānī, Rōmānōrum, *m. pl.*	*Romans*
4	Rōmānus, Rōmāna, Rōmānum	*Roman*
	rotundus, rotunda, rotundum	*round, circular*
	Rūfīna, Rūfīnae, *f.*	*Rufina*
	rūgōsus, rūgōsa, rūgōsum	*wrinkly*
	ruō, ruere, ruī	*rush*
	russeus, russea, russeum	*red; red team*
	rūsticus, rūstica, rūsticum	*in the country*

S

	Sabīna, Sabīnae, *f.*	*Sabina*
	saccus, saccī, *m.*	*sack, bag*
10	sacer, sacra, sacrum	*sacred, holy*

sacerdōs, sacerdōtis, *m.*	*priest*
sacrificium, sacrificiī, *n.*	*sacrifice, offering*
7 saepe	*often*
11 saevus, saeva, saevum	*savage, cruel*
saliō, salīre, saluī	*jump*
saltātrīx, saltātrīcis, *f.*	*dancer*
salūs, salūtis, *f.*	*safety*
2 salūtō, salūtāre, salūtāvī	*greet*
salvē! salvēte!	*hello! hi!*
sanguineus, sanguinea, sanguineum	*bloody*
9 sanguis, sanguinis, *m.*	*blood*
sapiēns, *gen.* sapientis	*wise*
sarcina, sarcinae, *f.*	*large bag*
saxum, saxī, *n.*	*rock*
scaena, scaenae, *f.*	*stage*
scaenae frōns	*stage building*
scapha, scaphae, *f.*	*small boat, rowboat*
scelestus, scelesta, scelestum	*wicked*
16 sciō, scīre, scīvī	*know*
scrībō, scrībere, scrīpsī	*write*
15 sē, suī	*himself, herself, itself, themselves*
secundus, secunda, secundum	*second*
sēcūrus, sēcūra, sēcūrum	*safe*
2 sed	*but*
6 sedeō, sedēre, sēdī	*sit, sit down*
sēdō, sēdāre, sēdāvī	*settle, calm down*
13 semper	*always*
3 senātor, senātōris, *m.*	*senator*
Seneca, Senecae, *m.*	*Seneca*
senectūs, senectūtis, *f.*	*old age*
8 senex, senis, *m.f.*	*old person*
16 sentiō, sentīre, sēnsī	*feel, notice*
Septimus, Septimī, *m.*	*Septimus*
septimus, septima, septimum	*seventh*
sepulcrum, sepulcrī, *n.*	*tomb*
12 servō, servāre, servāvī	*save, protect, keep, look after*
1 servus, servī, *m.*	*slave, enslaved person (male)*
sevēriter	*severely*
16 sī	*if*
sīc	*so, in this way*
Sicilia, Siciliae, *f.*	*Sicily*
sīcut	*just as, like*
signum, signī, *n.*	*sign, signal*

silentium, silentiī, *n.*	*silence*
7 silva, silvae, *f.*	*wood, forest*
simul	*at the same time*
simulācrum, simulācrī, *n.*	*statue, image*
15 simulatque	*as soon as*
16 sine + *abl.*	*without*
sine dubiō	*without doubt*
sīphō, sīphōnis, *m.*	*fire engine, pump*
Sīrēn, Sīrēnis, *f.*	*Siren (mythical creature)*
sōl, sōlis, *m.*	*sun*
soleō, solēre	*am accustomed, used*
sōlum	*only*
11 sōlus, sōla, sōlum	*alone, only, lonely, on one's own*
somnus, somnī, *m.*	*sleep*
sonor, sonōris, *m.*	*shout, sound*
sopōrō, sopōrāre, sopōrāvī	*drug, adminster a drug*
sordidus, sordida, sordidum	*dirty*
soror, sorōris, *f.*	*sister*
spargō, spargere, sparsī	*shower, spray*
spectātor, spectātōris, *m.*	*spectator*
2 spectō, spectāre, spectāvī	*look at, watch*
spēs, speī, *f.*	*hope*
spīrō, spīrāre, spīrāvī	*breathe*
splendidus, splendida, splendidum	*splendid, sumptuous*
spōnsiō, spōnsiōnis, *f.*	*bet*
sporta, sportae, *f.*	*basket*
st!	*hey!*
9 statim	*at once, immediately*
statua, statuae, *f.*	*statue*
stercus, stercoris, *n.*	*dung, muck*
stetī	**see stō**
6 stō, stāre, stetī	*stand*
stola, stolae, *f.*	*dress*
strēnuē	*strenuously, energetically, hard*
12 stultus, stulta, stultum	*stupid, foolish*
10 sub + *acc.* or *abl.*	*under, below, beneath*
4 subitō	*suddenly*
Subūra, Subūrae, *f.*	*the Subura*
Subūrānus, Subūrāna, Subūrānum	*from the Subura*
Subūrānus, Subūrānī, *m.*	*inhabitant of the Subura*
subveniō, subvenīre, subvēnī + *dat.*	*help*

Sūleviae, Sūleviārum, *f. pl.* — Suleviae (Celtic goddesses)

Sūlis, Sūlis, *f.* — Sulis (local Celtic goddess)

1 sum, esse, fuī — I am, to be, I was

13 summus, summa, summum — highest, greatest, top (of)

sumus — we are

sunt — are, they are, there are

super + *acc.* — over

12 superō, superāre, superāvī — overcome, overpower

8 surgō, surgere, surrēxī — get up, stand up, rise

surrēxī — see surgō

sustulī — see tollō

susurrāns, *gen.* susurrantis — whispering

susurrō, susurrāre, susurrāvī — whisper

13 suus, sua, suum — her, his, its, their (own)

T

12 taberna, tabernae, *f.* — shop, inn

tabula, tabulae, *f.* — curse tablet

tabulātum, tabulātī, *n.* — floor, story

5 taceō, tacēre, tacuī — am silent, am quiet

tacitē — quietly, silently

tam — so

13 tamen — however

8 tandem — at last, finally

tantum — only

tantus, tanta, tantum — so great, such a great, so much

Tarracōnēnsis, Tarracōnēnsis, Tarracōnēnse — of Tarraconensis

taurus, taurī, *m.* — bull

tēctum, tēctī, *n.* — roof

tēgula, tēgulae, *f.* — roof tile

tēlum, tēlī, *n.* — missile, weapon, spear

temperō, temperāre, temperāvī — control, restrain

tempestās, tempestātis, *f.* — storm

4 templum, templī, *n.* — temple

temptō, temptāre, temptāvī — try

14 tempus, temporis, *n.* — time

tenebrae, tenebrārum, *f. pl.* — darkness

4 teneō, tenēre, tenuī — hold, keep, possess

12 terra, terrae, *f.* — ground, land, country

orbis terrārum — world

14 terreō, terrēre, terruī — frighten

terribilis, terribilis, terribile — terrible

tertius, tertia, tertium — third

theātrum, theātrī, *n.* — theater

Thellus, Thellī, *m.* — Thellus

thermae, thermārum, *f. pl.* — baths

Thisba, Thisbae, *f.* — Thisbe

tībīcen, tībīcinis, *m.* — pipe-player

5 timeō, timēre, timuī — fear, am afraid

Tīrō, Tīrōnis, *m.* — Tiro

4 tollō, tollere, sustulī — raise, lift up, hold up

tonō, tonāre, tonuī — thunder

torqueō, torquēre, torsī — torture

6 tōtus, tōta, tōtum — whole

trabs, trabis, *f.* — beam, timber

9 trādō, trādere, trādidī — hand over

12 trahō, trahere, trāxī — drag, draw, pull

8 trāns + *acc.* — across

trānseō, trānsīre, trānsiī — go across

trāxī — see trahō

trēs, trēs, tria — three

tribūnus, tribūnī, *m.* — tribune (officer in the army)

trīclīnium, trīclīniī, *n.* — dining room

Trinobantēs, Trinobantum, *m. pl.* — Trinobantes

trīste — sadly

6 trīstis, trīstis, trīste — sad

1 tū, tuī — you (s.)

tuba, tubae, *f.* — trumpet

tulī — see ferō

7 tum — then

tunica, tunicae, *f.* — tunic

1 turba, turbae, *f.* — crowd

tūs, tūris, *n.* — frankincense

tūtus, tūta, tūtum — safe

6 tuus, tua, tuum — your (s.), yours

U

1,11 ubi — where? where; when

ubīque — everywhere

ulterior, ulterior, ulterius — further, more distant

umbra, umbrae, *f.* — shade, ghost

ūnā — together

unda, undae, *f.* — wave

unde — from where

ūnus, ūna, ūnum — one

3 urbs, urbis, *f.* — city

6 uxor, uxōris, *f.* — wife

V

	vae!	woe!
	vah!	ha! huh!
	valdē	very, very much
	valē! valēte!	goodbye! farewell!
	validus, valida, validum	strong
	vallis, vallis, f.	valley
7	vehementer	loudly, powerfully, forcefully
	vēnābulum, vēnābulī, n.	hunting spear
	vēnātiō, vēnātiōnis, f.	hunt
5	vēndō, vēndere, vēndidī	sell
4	veniō, venīre, vēnī	come
	ventus, ventī, m.	wind
	verberō, verberāre, verberāvī	hit, beat
14	verbum, verbī, n.	word
	vērō	indeed, truly, certainly
13	ita vērō	yes, absolutely
	vertō, vertere, vertī	turn
	vērum?	really?
	vērum, vērī, n.	truth
	vesper, vesperī, m.	evening
	Vesta, Vestae, f.	Vesta (goddess of fire and the hearth)
	Vestālia, Vestālium, n. pl.	Vestalia (festival in honor of Vesta)
	Vestālis, Vestālis, Vestāle	Vestal, of Vesta
	vester, vestra, vestrum	your (pl.), yours
	vestīmenta, vestīmentōrum, n. pl.	clothes
	veterānus, veterānī, m.	veteran, retired soldier
	vetus, gen. veteris	old
1	via, viae, f.	street, road, way
	vīcī	see vincō
	victōria, victōriae, f.	victory
	vīcus, vīcī, m.	settlement
2	videō, vidēre, vīdī	see
	vigil, vigilis, m.	fireman
15	vīlla, vīllae, f.	country house, house
	vīmineus, vīminea, vīmineum	made of wicker
3	vincō, vincere, vīcī	win, am victorious; conquer
2	vīnum, vīnī, n.	wine
	violenter	violently
	violentia, violentiae, f.	violence
	violō, violāre, violāvī	dishonor, violate
9	vir, virī, m.	man

	virgō, virginis, f.	virgin, girl, young woman
	viridis, viridis, viride	green
	virtūs, virtūtis, f.	courage; virtue
	vīs, vim, f.	force
	vīs	see volō
	vīsitō, vīsitāre, vīsitāvī	visit
9	vīta, vītae, f.	life
	vītō, vītāre, vītāvī	avoid
	vituperō, vituperāre, vituperāvī	criticize, complain about
13	vīvō, vīvere, vīxī	live, am alive
	vīvus, vīva, vīvum	alive, living
	vix	scarcely, hardly, with difficulty
	vīxī	see vīvō
	vōbīs	to/for you (pl.)
2	vocō, vocāre, vocāvī	call
	volitō, volitāre, volitāvī	fly
5	volō, velle, voluī	want, wish, am willing
4	vōs, vestrum	you (pl.)
	vōtum, vōtī, n.	prayer
12	vōx, vōcis, f.	voice; shout
	vulnerō, vulnerāre, vulnerāvī	wound, injure
	vulnus, vulneris, n.	wound
	vult	see volō
	vultus, vultūs, m.	expression; face

ANCIENT AUTHORS

Apicius: (fourth century AD) is the name traditionally given to the author of a collection of recipes, *de Re Coquinaria* (*On the Art of Cooking*). Marcus Gavius Apicius was a gourmet who lived in the early first century AD and wrote about sauces. Seneca says that he claimed to have created a *scientia popīnae* (snack bar cuisine).

Appian: Appianos (late first century AD–AD 160s) was born in Alexandria, in Egypt, and practiced as a lawyer in Rome. His history of Rome is written in Greek.

Apuleius: Lucius Apuleius (*C.*AD 155) was born in Africa and lived in Carthage. He was the author of the *Metamorphoses*, also known as *The Golden Ass*, a novel about the adventures of a young man who is turned into an ass. He gave lectures on philosophy and a collection of excerpts from these survives, called *Florida* (*Anthology*).

Augustus: Augustus (63 BC–AD 14) was born Gaius Octavius, and became Gaius Iulius Caesar Octavianus when he was adopted by his great-uncle, Julius Caesar. He was known by the title Augustus after 27 BC when he became Rome's first emperor. The *Res Gestae Divi Augusti* (*Deeds of the Divine Augustus*) is an account of the career of Augustus written in the first person. Augustus left the document with his will, with instructions to the Senate to set up the text as an inscription. It was engraved on a pair of bronze pillars in front of Augustus' tomb in the Campus Martius. The original has not survived, but copies were carved in stone on monuments and temples all over the Roman Empire, and parts of these have survived.

Aulus Gellius: Aulus Gellius (*C.*AD 130–180) lived in Rome and Athens, although his birthplace is unknown. His *Attic Nights* is a collection of essays on a variety of topics, based on his reading of Greek and Roman writers and the lectures and conversations he had heard. The title *Attic Nights* refers to Attica, the district in Greece around Athens, where Gellius was living when he wrote the book.

Cassius Dio (also Dio Cassius): Cassius Dio Cocceianus (*C.*AD 150–235) was born in Bithynia. He had a political career as a consul in Rome and governor of the provinces of Africa and Dalmatia. His history of Rome, written in Greek, covers the period from Aeneas' arrival in Italy to AD 229.

Cato: Marcus Porcius Cato (234–139 BC) was born at Tusculum, a town about 16 miles from Rome. He had a distinguished military and political career, reaching the consulship and the office of censor, despite not being born into a senatorial family. He wrote a book on farming, *de Agri Cultura* (*On Agriculture*). Cato was famous for his strictness and his criticism of contemporary morality. He wanted to return to the old Roman values of frugality and simplicity.

Catullus: Gaius Valerius Catullus (*c.*84–54 BC) was born in Verona, in northern Italy, in a wealthy family. Very little is known about his life. He came to Rome as a young man and spent some time in the province of Bithynia on the staff of the governor. He is best known for his love poems.

Cicero: Marcus Tullius Cicero (106–43 BC) was a politician and lawyer, who was a leading figure in events at the end of the Roman Republic. He was born in a town not far from Rome and came to Rome to study. Although not born into the senatorial class, he reached the highest office of state, the consulship. He was executed on the orders of Mark Antony during the unrest following the assassination of Julius Caesar in 44 BC. His surviving writings include speeches for the law courts, political speeches, philosophical essays, and personal letters to friends and family.

Columella: Lucius Iunius Moderatus Columella (wrote *C.*AD 60–65) was born at Gades (modern Cadiz) in Spain and served in the Roman army in Syria. He wrote a treatise on farming, *de Re Rustica* (*On Farming*).

Diodorus Siculus: Diodorus (wrote *c.*60–30 BC) was a Greek from Sicily who wrote a history of the world centered on Rome, from legendary beginnings to 54 BC. Much of the original forty books survives only in fragments. He wrote in Greek.

Dionysius of Halicarnassus: Dionysius (*c.*60 BC–some time after 7 BC) was a Greek historian from Halicarnassus in Asia Minor (modern Bodrum in Turkey). He lived in Rome for many years from about 30 BC. His history of Rome, *Roman Antiquities*, is written in Greek. It started with Rome's legendary beginnings and went up to 264 BC, the First Punic War. Much of it is lost, and the surviving part finishes in 441 BC.

Frontinus: Sextus Iulius Frontinus (*C.*AD 30–104) had a distinguished career as consul and governor of Britain. After becoming supervisor of the water supply (*cūrātor aquārum*) in Rome in AD 97, he wrote an account of the city's aqueducts and water supply, *On the Waters of Rome*, as a handbook for his successors.

Horace: Quintus Horatius Flaccus (65–8 BC) was born in Apulia, in the south of Italy. He was of humble origins, the son of a freedman who worked as a collector of payments at auctions. His father sent him to Rome and Athens to be educated, and he became one of the most celebrated poets of his day. Maecenas, the friend and adviser of Emperor Augustus, was his patron. His most famous works are the *Odes*, short poems on a variety of subjects, but he also wrote *Epodes*, *Satires*, and *Epistles*.

Julius Caesar: Gaius Iulius Caesar (100–44 BC), the general, politician, and dictator, belonged to an aristocratic Roman family. He was assassinated on the Ides (15th) of March 44 BC, by a group of senators who feared that he intended to put an end to the republican system of government and keep supreme power for himself and his family. Caesar wrote an account of his campaigns in Gaul and Britain (58–52 BC), the *Commentaries* (also known as the *Gallic Wars*). They are written in the third person, as if to give an objective account of events.

Juvenal: Decius Iunius Iuvenalis (early second century AD) was born in a town in Italy, but lived in Rome. He was the author of sixteen *Satires*, long poems criticizing and attacking the vices of his fellow Romans. The *Satires* have a bitter humor and pessimistic attitude, and there is much exaggeration. Nevertheless, Juvenal sheds light on contemporary Roman society and provides lots of detail about everyday life.

Livy: Titus Livius (59 BC–AD 17) was born at Patavium (modern Padua) in north-east Italy. Little is known about his life, but he probably came to Rome as an adult. He wrote *A History of Rome*, starting with its foundation and going up to his own lifetime. Originally there were 142 books, of which about twenty-five have survived.

Martial: Marcus Valerius Martialis (C.AD 40–C.AD 96) was born in Spain, and came to live in Rome in about AD 64. He is best known for his short poems, known as *Epigrams*, which often criticize and mock the faults and vices of his fellow Romans.

Minucius: Marcus Minucius Felix (early third century AD) was a Christian who wrote a defense of Christianity, *Octavius*, in the form of a discussion between two Christian converts, Minucius and Octavius, and Caecilius, a pagan. Minucius defends Christianity against the criticisms of Caecilius, and at the end Caecilius is converted.

Ovid: Publius Ovidius Naso (43 BC– AD 17) was born in a town near Rome and educated in the city. He abandoned a public career to become a poet. Emperor Augustus banished him to Tomi on the Black Sea (in modern Romania). According to Ovid, there were two reasons for his exile, ***carmen*** (a poem) and ***error*** (a mistake). The poem was *Ars Amatoria* (*The Art of Love*), advice on how to conduct a love affair, which fell foul of laws introduced by Augustus to improve the morals of contemporary society. The mistake was probably connected to the love affairs of Augustus' granddaughter, Julia. Among his works are love poems such as the *Amores* (*Loves*) and a long epic poem, *The Metamorphoses*, which is a collection of stories from mythology, bound together by the theme of transformation.

Petronius: Petronius Arbiter (died AD 65) was a provincial governor and consul. He then became Emperor Nero's ***arbiter ēlegentiae*** (arbiter of taste), a play on his name; this meant he advised Nero on what was tasteful or elegant. He was falsely accused of being involved in a plot to kill Nero, and committed suicide. Petronius was the author of the *Satyricon*, a novel about the adventures of three young men traveling in southern Italy. The main episode is the ***cēna Trimalchiōnis*** (*Trimalchio's Dinner Party*). Trimalchio is a wealthy freedman to whose dinner party the three main characters are invited. Petronius mocks and grotesquely exaggerates the

vulgar extravagance and bad taste of Trimalchio, and his ostentatious display of wealth.

Plautus: Titus Maccius Plautus (C.250–184 BC) wrote comedies which were based on Greek originals, adapted for a Roman audience, but set in Greece.

Pliny the Elder: Gaius Plinius Secundus (AD 23/24–79) was born at Comum (modern Como) in northern Italy. He is known as Pliny the Elder to distinguish him from his nephew, known as Pliny the Younger. He had a career in military and government service, serving as procurator in several provinces before his final post as commander of the fleet at Misenum in Italy. He dedicated his spare time to research and writing, and among his many learned works is his *Natural History*, an encyclopedic collection of facts and stories about a huge variety of subjects. It is a very useful source of information on many aspects of Roman life. In *Suburani* 'Pliny' refers to Pliny the Younger.

Pliny the Younger: Gaius Caecilius Plinius Secundus (AD 61/62–113) was the nephew of Pliny the Elder. He was born at Comum (Como) in northern Italy. He had a successful career as a lawyer, politician, and administrator, and his final post was as governor of the province of Bithynia. His letters to friends, family, and colleagues include an exchange with Emperor Trajan when he was governor of Bithynia. The letters offer a fascinating glimpse into the lives, attitudes, and politics of the society of his time. Pliny wrote with the intention of publishing his letters, and at regular intervals during his lifetime he published collections of them. Although they are real personal letters, many of them resemble short essays on various themes. In *Suburani* 'Pliny' refers to Pliny the Younger.

Plutarch: Ploutarchos (*C.*AD 46–120) was a Greek biographer, historian, and philosopher. He took the name Lucius Mercius Plutarchus when he became a Roman citizen. Plutarch visited Rome, where he taught and gave lectures, but spent most of his life in his native Greece. Among his many works are biographies of famous Greek and Roman politicians and soldiers, the *Parallel Lives*, so called because they are arranged in pairs of Greek and Roman so that the subjects can be compared. He also wrote biographies of the Roman emperors. His biographies of Galba and Otho survive in full, and there are fragments of his lives of Tiberius and Nero.

Propertius: Sextus Propertius (*c.*50 BC–after 16 BC) was born at Assisium (modern Assisi) in central Italy, and educated at Rome. He wrote poems known as *Elegies*, many of them love poems.

Seneca: Lucius Annaeus Seneca (*c.*4 BC–AD 65) is sometimes known as Seneca the Younger to distinguish him from his father of the same name, who was also a writer. He was born in Cordoba, in Spain, and came to Rome to be educated. He was Nero's tutor and, when Nero became emperor, Seneca became his political adviser. In AD 65, after he had retired from public life, he was implicated in a conspiracy to overthrow Nero and was forced to commit suicide. Seneca was a philosopher, politician, and dramatist. Among his many writings are several works of moral philosophy which contain interesting details about life in Rome in the first century AD. Some of these are in the form of letters to friends and family, including one to his mother, Helvia.

Servius: Marius Servius Honoratus (early fifth century AD) wrote commentaries on Latin literature.

Strabo: Strabo (64 BC–after AD 24) was a Greek from Pontus who came to Rome in 44 BC to finish his education, then visited the city several times afterwards. His *Geography*, written in Greek, is a description of the main countries in the Roman world, including physical geography, history, and economic development. There is also much incidental detail about customs, animals, and plants.

Suetonius: Gaius Suetonius Tranquillus (born *C.*AD 70) was a secretary at the imperial palace. He wrote biographies of Julius Caesar and the first eleven emperors, *Lives of the Caesars*. Although his position gave him access to the state archives, he is not very reliable in his use of sources, and his work relies heavily on uncritical reporting of gossip and anecdote. His other works include lives of teachers of literature and rhetoric, *On the Grammarians* and *On Rhetoricians*; only parts of these have survived.

Tacitus: Publius (or Gaius) Cornelius Tacitus (AD 56/57–after 117) may have been born in Gallia Narbonensis. He had a successful political career in Rome and wrote two major works of history. *Annals* covered the period AD 14–68, from the death of Augustus to the death Nero, and *Histories* continued with the years AD 69–96. Only parts of these works survive. He also wrote a biography of his father-in-law Agricola, the general and governor of Britain. Tacitus used as his sources the writings of earlier historians, official records, and his own experience. Tacitus was a supporter of the republican system of government and a harsh critic of the emperors and the imperial system. He claims to write without prejudice, but his bias is often evident.

Varro: Marcus Terentius Varro (115–27 BC) was born near Rome in Sabine territory. Among his many literary works, only *de Re Rustica* (*On Farming*) survives in complete form. About half of *de Lingua Latina* (*On the Latin Language*) also survives.

Vergil (also Virgil): Publius Vergilius Maro (70–19 BC) was born at Mantua in Cisalpine Gaul and educated at Cremona, Mediolanum (modern Milan), and Rome. Maecenas, the friend and adviser of Emperor Augustus, was his patron, and he became the most celebrated poet of his day. His greatest work is the *Aeneid*, an epic poem which tells the story of the founding of the Roman race by the Trojan hero Aeneas. The poem is a celebration of the origin and growth of the Roman Empire and of the achievements of Augustus. Vergil also wrote the *Eclogues*, pastoral poems about the life of shepherds, and the *Georgics*, a poem about farming.

Vitruvius: Vitruvius Pollio (first century BC), an engineer and architect, wrote *On Architecture*.

TIMELINE

Ruler of Rome

750	
700	Romulus (753–715 BC)
650	King Numa Pompilius (715–673 BC)
600	King Tullus Hostilius (673–642 BC)
550	King Ancus Marcius (642–616 BC)
500	King Lucius Tarquinius Priscus (616–579 BC)
	King Servius Tullius (579–534 BC)
	King Lucius Tarquinius Superbus (534–509 BC)

Romulus (753–715 BC)
King Numa Pompilius (715–673 BC)
King Tullus Hostilius (673–642 BC)
King Ancus Marcius (642–616 BC)
King Lucius Tarquinius Priscus (616–579 BC)
King Servius Tullius (579–534 BC)
King Lucius Tarquinius Superbus (534–509 BC)
Roman Republic (509–27 BC)

Emperor Augustus (27 BC–AD 14)

Emperor Tiberius (AD 14–37)

Emperor Gaius (Caligula) (AD 37–41)
Emperor Claudius (AD 41–54)

Emperor Nero (AD 54–68)

Emperors Galba, Otho, Vitellius, and Vespasian (AD 68–69)

Events in Roman history

753 BC Traditional date of the foundation of Rome. According to legend, Romulus was the first ruler of Rome.
753–509 BC Rome was ruled by seven legendary kings.

c.600 BC Construction of the Cloaca Maxima in Rome.

509 BC King Lucius Tarquinius Superbus (Tarquin the Proud) is expelled and the Roman Republic established.

387 BC Gauls capture Rome.

334–264 BC Rome expands to control Italy.
264–241 BC First Punic War, Rome against Carthage.
218–201 BC Hannibal crosses Alps, invading Italy; Second Punic War.
202 BC Scipio Africanus defeats Hannibal at Battle of Zama.
149–146 BC Third Punic War; Rome defeats Carthage; Africa becomes a province of the Roman Empire.
135–132 BC First Slave War, in Sicily.
104–100 BC Second Slave War, in Sicily.
73–71 BC Third Slave War, in mainland Italy, led by Spartacus.
67 BC Pompey's campaign against the pirates.
55–54 BC Julius Caesar's two expeditions to Britain.
52 BC Vercingetorix leads Gallic revolt against Rome; Battle of Alesia.
44 BC Assassination of Julius Caesar.
31 BC Battle of Actium; Octavian (later Augustus) defeats Mark Antony.

27 BC Augustus becomes sole ruler of the Roman Empire: Rome's first emperor.
25 BC Baths of Agrippa, in Rome, are completed.
19 BC Aqua Virgo completed.

9 BC Consecration of the Ara Pacis.

2 BC Julia, daughter of Augustus, exiled.

AD 14 Pantheon is built on Field of Mars, in Rome.

c.AD 30 Crucifixion of Jesus.

AD 43 Emperor Claudius invades Britain.

AD 52 Aqua Claudia completed.
AD 54 Nero becomes emperor at the age of 16.
AD 58–68 Otho governor of Lusitania.
AD 60 Boudica's revolt in Britannia; Londinium destroyed by fire.
AD 64 Great Fire of Rome.
AD 66–73 The Jewish population of Judaea revolts against Roman rule.
AD 69 Year of the Four Emperors.
AD 70 Destruction of the Temple in Jerusalem.

Events in the rest of the world

776 BC First Olympic Games, in Olympia, Greece.

660 BC According to legend, Jimmu becomes the first emperor of Japan.

563 BC Buddha, the religious leader, is born.
551–479 BC Confucius, Chinese philosopher.
550 BC Foundation of the Achaemenid (First Persian) Empire by Cyrus the Great.
508 BC Democracy is instituted at Athens.
480 BC Persians, led by Xerxes, invade Greece; Persians are defeated at Battle of Salamis.
c.460–370 BC Hippocrates, Greek doctor.

331 BC Alexander the Great founds Alexandria, in Egypt.
323 BC Death of Alexander the Great, at Babylon.
c.300 BC Euclid, Greek mathematician.
c.285–246 BC The Library at Alexandria, in Egypt, is founded.
261 BC Kalinga War between the Mauryan Empire and the state of Kalinga, in India.
221–206 BC King Zheng unifies China as the first emperor of the Qin dynasty.
206 BC–AD 220 Han dynasty in China.
179 BC The earliest evidence for papermaking, in China.
69–30 BC Cleopatra VIII, the last Ptolemaic ruler of Egypt.
c.57 BC Three Kingdoms period begins in Korea.

30 BC Egypt becomes part of the Roman Empire.

c.AD 10–70 Hero of Alexandria, inventor of the fire engine.

c.AD 68 The Dead Sea scrolls are hidden in caves, to save them from the Romans.